THE CLYDESIDERS TRILOGY

MARGARET THOMSON DAVIS left school at the age of
sixteen, working as a children's nurse and having a
variety of other jobs before achieving her ambition
of becoming a writer. She has had over twenty
novels published, many of which have been
bestsellers. Two of her books have also been
adapted for the stage. Over two hundred of her
short stories have appeared in newspapers and
magazines in Britain and overseas, and she has
written an autobiography. Active in a wide range
of literary and other societies, she is in great
demand as an entertaining and informative speaker.
Margaret Thomson Davis lives in Glasgow.

MARGARET THOMSON

DAVIS

THE

CLYDESIDERS

TRILOGY

THE CLYDESIDERS
THE GOURLAY GIRLS
CLYDESIDERS AT WAR

First published 2003
by B&W Publishing Ltd
99 Giles Street, Edinburgh

ISBN 1903265118

British Library Cataloguing in Publication Data:
A catalogue record for this book is available from
the British Library

Cover illustration:
Detail from *Women's Canteen at Phoenix Works, Bradford*
by Flora Lion (1918).
Photograph courtesy of The Imperial War Museum

Printed by WS Bookwell Ltd

ACKNOWLEDGEMENTS

I'm very grateful to the kind friends who helped me with the research for *The Clydesiders*. Farquhar and Cathy McLay for trusting me with their book about John Maclean by his daughter Nan Milton. Molly and Joe Fisher for sharing their knowledge about John Maclean, and Joseph Latham for all the help he found for me on the internet.

The poetry in *The Clydesiders* and *The Gourlay Girls* (with the exception of *Glasgow*, by Albert Goodyear) is by Michael Malone.

VOLUME ONE

The CLYDESIDERS

1914

I

Virginia Watson wasn't allowed to be seen, far less talk to anyone—upstairs, that was. Down in the basement kitchen, talk was permitted to a certain extent. High up under the rafters, in the attic bedroom with Fanny Gordon, the scullery maid, she could talk as long as she could keep awake. Fanny didn't call it their bedroom. To her it was a dark and dismal cell. Fourteen-year-old Fanny, who was two years younger than Virginia and now shared the lumpy iron bedstead with her, had come from a cottage. There she had slept in an attic with her three sisters.

'All right, we were crowded top-to-tail in the one bed, but the attic there was bright and cosy. At night we had two candles. Not like here! Mrs Cartwright must have pots of housekeeping money, and fancy, she's had gas put in all her rooms, but we've to make do with one wee candle.' Fanny pouted. 'Rotten mean, that's what ugly old Mrs Cartwright is. I hate her, so I do.'

Virginia had no love for the Cartwrights either. She too resented the one candle which made it so difficult to read any of her books. But she worried about Fanny's reckless tongue. With a sigh she gave up brushing her long hair. She could barely see her reflection in the pock-marked and chipped mirror.

'You've hardly been here ten minutes, Fanny, and you won't last much longer if anyone hears you talking like that.'

'I'm not daft. I'm not likely to march up to Mrs Cartwright and tell her what a mean old tyrant she is. Ugly as well. Her and her long nose and beady eyes.'

Virginia shook her head. She was seriously concerned for Fanny's

3

job. Mr Gordon's rheumatism, Fanny had confided, was getting worse and the Gordon family were worried in case he lost his job. If he did, it would mean losing his tied cottage. Then where could Fanny go? It was a miracle she'd got the job in the first place, with her cheeky pimply face and wild frizz of mousy hair that looked none too clean.

'Listen,' she told the girl. 'You'd better watch the upstairs servants as well.' The upstairs staff consisted of two house-maids, a parlour-maid, the lady's maid and the butler. 'They're all right but you never know. Better to be safe than sorry.' It wasn't a rule that came easy to Virginia but she had discovered it was necessary for survival.

'Think yourself lucky you've got a job and a decent room to sleep in.'

'What? This horrible cell, you mean?'

'If you saw what I came from, Fanny, you'd think this was a wee palace.'

'Go on,' Fanny scoffed. 'The Gorbals can't be that bad.'

Virginia regretted her words because they could be construed as being disloyal to her parents who were decent, hard-working folk. 'Don't get me wrong,' she said hastily. 'My mum and dad did the best they could. Anything bad about the houses in the Gorbals is the landlords' fault.'

She could understand Fanny's hatred of Mrs Cartwright. She felt the same emotion at the mere thought of the people responsible for the Gorbals slums. Putrid, evil-smelling places that she was sure had been the cause of her sister's death from tuberculosis. She remembered with horror the cramped ground-floor one-room-and-kitchen flat—or 'house' as all tenement dwellings were called in Glasgow. Although it had no bathroom, no inside lavatory, no hot water, her mother worked tirelessly doing her best to keep the place clean. The worst thing to cope with was the common lavatory in the dark tunnel of the close. A damp sickening smell clung everywhere—the room, the kitchen, the close, the lavatory. Her mother tried to ventilate the house by keeping the windows open, even on the coldest days of winter, but nothing made any difference.

'The master seems alright,' Fanny said.

Virginia knew she must mean young Master Cartwright, because Mr Cartwright senior had been away on business since Fanny arrived.

'And how would you know anything about him?'

'I saw him on the stairs when I was taking up the coal this morning.'

'You didn't!' Virginia exclaimed, aghast. It was an iron rule at Hilltop House that downstairs servants must not disturb the family.

'Well, how was I to know he'd be up and about so early?' Fanny's eyes widened with excitement. 'I gave him a smile.'

'You didn't!'

'He smiled back. That's why I thought he seemed alright. Must take after his daddy in looks. He's certainly not ugly like his mammy.'

'All very well for him to smile,' Virginia said. 'He's got plenty to smile about. Not like some folk.'

In actual fact, much the same thing had happened to Virginia only the other day. He had smiled at her but she had not smiled in return. She had lowered her head and bobbed a brief curtsy. 'Easy for him to smile,' she'd thought bitterly, seeing in her mind's eye the difference between his situation and that of her brothers. However, despite her bitterness—or maybe because of it, she couldn't banish his handsome face from her mind. Once, she'd caught a glimpse of him in his smart army uniform. He was training to be an officer. According to the gossip in the kitchen, he had gone into the army rather than into his father's business. However, the parlour-maid insisted that his father wanted him to join the army, and that it was his mother who wanted him to go into the family business.

Nobody was very sure what the family business was, but it meant Mr Cartwright travelling a lot and whatever it was, it certainly made him a lot of money. The lady's maid said that what Mrs Cartwright wanted more than anything was a title, and no amount of money could buy her that. However, she had engineered a friendship with Lady Forbes Linton and encouraged the long-standing friendship between Lady Linton's daughter, Fiona, and her own son, Nicholas. Fiona and Nicholas had been friends since childhood, and the lady's maid said she was sure Mrs Cartwright had set her heart on an eventual marriage between the two young people.

Virginia had once asked Mrs Tompkins, the cook, what Mr Cartwright's business was, but the cook had told her to mind her own business. Virginia had suffered a lot from Mrs Tompkins during the year she had been working in Hilltop House, but it was mostly when Mrs Tompkins was drunk. She was a solid mountain of a woman with the strength of an elephant. Unfortunately she had a weakness for drink and had regular bouts of drunkenness, much to the terror of all the staff, including Mrs Smithers, the housekeeper, and even—

Virginia suspected—Mrs Cartwright. The latter kept well clear of the kitchen area during these lapses, discreetly warned no doubt either by the housekeeper or the lady's maid. Had any other member of staff behaved in such an outrageous manner they would have immediately been dismissed. But thanks to Mrs Tompkins, the mistress was renowned and envied for miles around for her luncheons and dinner parties. If Mrs Cartwright had let Mrs Tompkins go, there would have been plenty of Mrs Cartwright's friends and acquaintances only too ready and willing to snap Mrs Tompkins up. After all, despite her obvious failings, she was a superb cook, even when she was drunk. The other members of staff were not so fortunate, several had been dismissed, and for very minor offences. Mrs Cartwright had a temper, not hot and noisy like cook, but cold and hard as ice.

Virginia kept her head down to avoid any trouble. She had learned how important this was in her last job as a maid of all work in a Glasgow villa. There had been no other staff and, even more than the back-breaking work, it was the isolation and loneliness she experienced there that still haunted her. It had been such a shock after the crowded conditions of her Gorbals home where, day and night, she was never alone. In the villa, she had been expected to do everything, be everything—char-woman, house-maid, nurse, parlour-maid and cook. She never had any help with anything from the daughters of the house, or from the mistress. They were too busy going out shopping, or visiting friends, or playing the piano, or doing cross-stitch or crochet. Virginia had to get up at five o'clock every morning. Every night— usually around midnight—she simply fell into bed aching with exhaustion. All she had to keep her going was looking forward to her one afternoon off a month, although even then she had to be back by ten at night.

Sometimes, by the time she'd cleared the lunch things and washed the dishes, she didn't get away until after two. She suspected the family purposely took longer over their lunch on her afternoon off, just out of spite. She hated them all right. Oh, how glad she'd been to move to Hilltop House. At least she had the company of other servants. She'd hoped to work her way up from kitchen maid to perhaps a parlour-maid, or something in the upstairs staff. But Mrs Tompkins said the mistress would never allow such a thing.

'Why not?' Virginia had asked, 'I'm a hard worker.'

'I know, hen.' Mrs Tompkins replied sympathetically.

She too had dragged herself out of the Gorbals and, when she was sober, their shared background made her feel more kindly towards Virginia than towards the other members of staff. 'But your trouble is you're too nice looking. Mistresses cannae thole a pretty lassie near them. It makes them look bad, you see.'

'I could hide all my hair under my cap.' Virginia had taken it for granted that her hair was the problem. So many people had told her what lovely hair she had, so glossy, such a warm golden colour.

'Och!' Mrs Tompkins shook her head. 'It's no' just your hair, hen. You cannae hide your bonny face. Or these bright blue eyes. And just look at your wee nose compared with the mistress's big beak. No, she'll never let you be seen anywhere near her.'

Virginia wanted to know if all mistresses in big houses were the same about looks. After all, she had no intentions of slaving away in the kitchen and the long dark corridors in the bowels of Hilltop House for the rest of her life if she could avoid it. Perhaps eventually she would be forced to try for a better position in another household.

'Maybe no,' Mrs Tompkins said without conviction. 'It aw depends. If the mistress is young and pretty, she might no' mind sae much, but there's no' likely to be many as bonny as you, hen. You've a real drawback there. Your best bet is to find a decent fella to marry you.'

Most of the female servants, Virginia included, dreamt of escape from drudgery into marriage. Maybe the volatile and gigantic Mrs Tompkins and the prim and petite Mrs Smithers had once nursed such a dream. If they had, their dreams had come to nothing, for although it was the custom to address the cook and the housekeeper as Mrs, neither woman had ever married.

There didn't seem much hope in Hilltop House even for the younger servants. The brief time off once a month didn't give them a chance to meet anyone outside their immediate family. At work the only male employees were the butler who was quite elderly, the chauffeur who was already married, and a gardener who seldom set foot in the big house, except to make sorties into the basement to catch rats.

Fanny hadn't had time to formulate any dreams, at least about marriage. Working in the big house that she'd only glimpsed from a distance through the trees before was still exciting to her. She had no fears for the future. Her only dream was to be rid of her mass of pimples. Her only fear so far was of Mrs Tompkins who, in her last drunken rage, had hurled a ladle at Fanny. Fanny had just managed to dodge it in time, before taking to her heels. Even so, she had giggled about it afterwards.

'She couldn't hit somebody the same size as herself, far less somebody as fast on their feet as me. Her aim's that rotten, ugly old cow!'

Virginia was thinking of this episode while she was walking in the nearby woods later that day, gathering mushrooms for Mrs Tompkins. It was a warm summer's day and she had taken her starched cap off and let her hair tumble loose over her shoulders. There was no danger of Mrs Cartwright seeing her here. Mrs Cartwright was off in her motor car visiting a friend in Glasgow. Anyway, she would never deign to go near such a wild place as the woods. For one thing she might damage her shoes or get the hem of her dress dirtied. As she strolled along, Virginia began to sing to herself, and to the tall trees and tangle of bushes and colourful wild flowers. Sun dappled the ferns and flowers with a shimmering glow. She felt the heat of the sun bathing her face, slowly melting her cares. The insidious buzzing of insects seemed to carry her mind gently out of herself to drift free as the motes of dust suspended in the golden light. It was wonderful to escape for even a short time from the exhausting rigours of her other tasks.

After a time she stopped singing so that she could listen to the birdsong instead. Then softly singing again, she began to gather more mushrooms. Her fingers scrabbled in the musty smelling earth as she plucked the soft cold stems. Then she brushed off the clinging soil and placed the mushrooms carefully into the basket that she carried over one arm. It was almost full but she intended prolonging her freedom as long as possible.

Suddenly she was startled by a loud clapping. She whirled round and struggled to her feet at the unexpected sight of the young master of the house. Nicholas Cartwright smiled with his eyes as well as his mouth.

'You've a voice as lovely as your face. What is your name?'

Virginia lowered her eyes. 'Virginia Watson, sir.'

'May I walk with you, Virginia? I would appreciate your company.'

Virginia thought he must have gone mad. She nodded, unable to think of what else to do, and they began strolling side by side. For a time there was silence, only broken by the faint crunching of their feet on some broken twigs and the melodious song of the birds high among the trees. Virginia took deep breaths of the fragrant air.

At last Cartwright said, 'Have you heard the news? By the looks of things war is going to be inevitable.'

'Are you sure?' Virginia was surprised and confused by this unexpected pronouncement. All the servants had been talking for weeks about the possibility of war, but surely, she thought, it could not really happen?

He sighed. 'Don't you ever read the newspapers?'

She felt a surge of bitterness and anger. Wasn't it just like someone of his class to be so ignorant of the life she and her fellow servants led.

'Well,' she said, forgetting to sound subservient, 'I don't have much time. I get up at five o'clock in the morning and never stop working until nearly midnight. It's a wonderful treat for me to be allowed out like this. And by the way, I couldn't afford to buy any newspapers for myself.' She nearly allowed her bitterness to run completely away with her and add 'on the pittance of a wage your mother pays me', but she controlled herself in time. As it was her heart had begun to thump with fearful apprehension. She knew her outburst had been more than sufficient to result in her losing her job.

Cartwright stopped walking and turned towards her. 'I'm sorry, Virginia. I've obviously no idea what goes on downstairs. That's my mother's province and in any case I've been away from home for most of my life—from boarding school onwards. Do forgive me.'

She gave him a nervous smile. Clearly, he was mad, but quite nice all the same. 'It's all right,' she said. 'I'd heard rumours about the trouble between us and Germany. Mrs Tompkins is always saying we can't trust the Kaiser, even if he is related to the King.' She paused for a moment, then asked, 'If there is to be a war, does that mean you'll have to go away again?'

Now she noticed that he looked terribly sad. His dark, deep-set eyes were clouded with unhappiness. 'I expect so. If it does happen. The Colonel of my regiment is a real fire-eater—he'll be sure to want his men in the thick of things right from the start. After all, it's what we've been training for, and as an officer and a gentleman it's my duty to fight for my country, whenever the need arises.'

She thought then of her two brothers and felt afraid for them, but surely they wouldn't think their country worth fighting for. What had it ever done for them? They'd had to work like slaves when they had work, and starve when they hadn't.

'Since the Austrian Duke and Duchess were killed by that damned Serb,' Cartwright was saying now, 'I've thought war was pretty much inevitable. The Germans have been looking for any excuse to challenge the British Empire. And now they've got it. God alone knows where it will all end.'

Virginia failed to see why her brothers, or even Nicholas Cartwright, should risk their lives over some foreign duke or duchess in some far away land of which she knew nothing. But she refrained from saying so. Instead, seeing the obvious distress in her companion's face, she impulsively touched his arm and told him earnestly,

'I'll remember you in my prayers tonight. I'll ask that you be kept safe.'

'Oh, Virginia,' he said, and stepped close to her. Before she knew what was happening, he had taken her into his arms. She was too shocked to resist as he held her firmly to him and kissed her, long and tenderly.

2

He held her gently for some time, his head resting down on hers. She felt the heat from his body and the beat of his heart. At first she was fearful and horrified at such an unexpected turn of events. If anyone found out this would certainly cost her her job. She would lose a decent roof over her head, enough food in her belly and the few shillings she was able to give to her mother. Good jobs weren't easy to come by, especially for a girl who'd been dismissed.

Then, equally unexpectedly, her fear was swamped by tenderness. Poor young man. She drew back a little to gaze up into his face. In his eyes, she could see as he looked down at her that he was just a sensitive human being. His black hair was rumpled, making him appear very young and vulnerable, although she thought he must be at least twenty. She put up a hand and stroked his hair back. 'Shhh,' she soothed as if he was weeping.

'You're very kind, Virginia,' he said. 'I shouldn't be burdening you with my worries. You'll have more than enough of your own to cope with.'

'No, it's all right. I mean, I'm not really working every minute of the time.' She felt guilty about her exaggeration now. There were quiet spells between meals, especially when it was just family meals. Not luncheons and dinners with lots of guests. At quiet moments, she did manage to slip out like this for a wee while. She seldom had to work until midnight in Hilltop House—usually it was just until ten o'clock, sometimes even a bit earlier. It was different for the lady's maid. She always had to wait until the last minute to help Mrs Cartwright undress in the large, stuffy bedroom. A fire had to be lit and kept burning in Mrs Cartwright's bedroom winter and summer, then the lady's maid had to lay out the clothes that Mrs Cartwright chose to wear next morning. After that, she had to fetch the hot cocoa. Mrs Cartwright always liked a cup of hot cocoa in bed.

'I manage to come here quite often, sometimes just for a few minutes, but it's worth it. It's so beautiful and peaceful.'

'Yes,' Nicholas agreed, and he looked around. 'I used to come here as a boy when I was on holiday from school. Sometimes I brought a book and I would sit under one of the trees and read in peace.'

Virginia could guess what lay behind his words—read in peace. Mrs Cartwright had once caught Nessie, one of the house-maids, dipping into a book in Mr Cartwright's library while she was dusting. Mrs Cartwright had been furious and warned Nessie that if she was caught reading any of the books ever again, she would be instantly dismissed. Her final comment on the matter—'Books are not for reading!'—was the source of great hilarity when Nessie later re-enacted the scene for the benefit of the other below-stairs staff.

'Isn't that jist like that wuman!' Mrs Tompkins said to Mrs Smithers. 'Books are jist for dustin', accordin' tae her. For aw her airs and graces, that wuman's pig ignorant.'

The pinched sallow features of Mrs Smithers had warmed at this. 'Now, now, Mrs Tompkins, I can't allow you to speak of the mistress in those insulting terms, especially in front of the staff.'

It was fortunate that Mrs Tompkins had been sober at the time. Otherwise she wouldn't have allowed Mrs Smithers to remain vertical.

Virginia could quite easily imagine Mrs Cartwright seeing her son's interest in reading as a wicked waste of time. It was a miracle that Nicholas Cartwright had turned out as well as he had. His mother was a cold, domineering woman. Obviously not everyone who was an only child was spoiled and smothered with love. Virginia couldn't imagine Mrs Cartwright ever showing the slightest affection to her son.

Nor could she understand how any mother could banish a young child of seven to the austere regime of a typical English boarding school. Virginia hadn't been at Hilltop House in those days, but Mrs Tompkins had and she told her how Nicholas had been sent away to England.

'To England of all places, and him jist a wee laddie of six or seven. He used to slip down here to the kitchen when his mammy was oot,

I'd give him one of my home-made biscuits and we'd have a wee blether. He came to say goodbye to me, the wee soul, before he was sent away. He was always that polite, a perfect wee gentleman.'

Lucky him, Virginia had thought at the time. Plenty of books and marvellous food and comfortable rooms at a place of learning. One of the best in Britain. How her beloved brothers, self-educated and well-read thanks to books borrowed from the public library, would have relished the chance of such advantages in life.

'Do you mind if we sit down for a few minutes?' Nicholas asked. 'This is such a lovely spot.'

It seemed very odd to have one of the Cartwrights (or anyone) treat her like a lady and ask her permission to do something, instead of ordering her. It made Virginia feel good and secretly grateful to Nicholas Cartwright for the experience.

She sat down on the soft, sweet-smelling grass, laid her basket of mushrooms aside and tidied her dress over her legs and feet. He sat beside her, stretching out his long legs and leaning back against the tree. He remained in thoughtful silence for a few minutes before saying,

'I probably shouldn't have gone into the army, you know. Of course I'll be glad of the opportunity, if it comes, to serve my country. But I've come to the conclusion—rather too late unfortunately—that Sandhurst and an army career was not the right choice for me.'

'What would you rather be doing?'

He hesitated. 'Don't laugh.' He gave a short laugh of embarrassment.

'I won't laugh, I promise.'

'I'd like to be a poet, or at least some sort of writer.'

'But that's wonderful,' Virginia cried out in genuine delight. She'd always had a great admiration for writers. Not that she'd ever known one personally, but oh, how she'd always loved reading. And how she treasured books. Her Auntie Sarah, who had married an office worker and was comparatively well off, had given her a book of poetry on her fifth birthday. On her sixth, she'd presented her with a copy of *Robinson Crusoe*. On her seventh, she'd received *Treasure Island*. Every year until Auntie Sarah died, she'd given Virginia a book on her birthday. Sometimes it was a slim volume of poetry, sometimes a novel. Sometimes even a play. Virginia had been enchanted by writers as varied as Balzac, Jane Austen, Shakespeare, the Brontes, Dickens and Dostoevsky. She'd especially enjoyed reading the biographies of writers. All the books that Auntie Sarah had given her were second hand, and some of them very dog-eared. Probably Auntie Sarah had picked them up from one of the barrows in Clyde Street but what did that matter? They were wonderful books and her most prized possessions. She'd be forever grateful to her Auntie Sarah for opening up such a magic world to her.

In between birthdays, she was a regular visitor to the public library. It was only since she'd left school to go to work at the Glasgow villa that she no longer had time to go to the library or even to read her own books.

'Do you really think it's so wonderful?' Nicholas asked.

'Of course I do. What have you written so far?'

'Oh, only a few poems. I shouldn't think they're very good. But I've started work on a novel. It's not easy finding the time to get on with it. Especially now. Perhaps if things clear up and the war doesn't last long, then I'll resign from the army and really give it a go.' He gave a short laugh again. 'Although my mother and father won't like it.'

'You mustn't listen to them,' Virginia cried out passionately. 'It's your life and it's your duty to make the most of the talent that God gave you.'

'Don't worry, I'm going to write no matter what anyone says.' He smiled. 'Although I'll probably end up starving in a garret—that's if the Kaiser and his Generals ever give me the chance!'

'I'd love to read something you've written.'

'Do you really mean that?'

'Of course I do.'

His eyes immediately lost their sad, resigned look. Virginia's enthusiasm seemed to have raised his spirits and filled him with a new optimism.

'I'll give you a couple of poems as soon as we get home.'

It was then that Virginia realised that for a short but magical interlude, they had been in a world of their own. Now that moment had come to an end.

'Heavens, do you want me to be dismissed? If your mother or anyone else saw us together . . .'

'I'm sorry. I see what you mean. I don't want you to get into any trouble on my account.'

Virginia brightened again. 'Perhaps if you left your poems discreetly somewhere where I could collect them later without anyone seeing.'

He brightened too. 'Good idea. How about under that big Chinese vase in the hall?'

'That would be too difficult for me. I don't often get the chance of going anywhere near the main hallway, but there's a bowl of pot pourri just near the door that leads to the servants' quarters. That would be easier.'

'Splendid. That's what I'll do then. I'll do it right away.'

'I'll run back first.' Virginia struggled to her feet. 'You wait here for a few minutes.'

It didn't seem a bit odd any more to talk to him as an equal. She believed, strange as it might seem to anyone else—either of his class or hers, that they were friends now, no longer master and servant. She turned to wave to him before starting to run, her fair hair streaming out behind her, the basket bobbing on her arm.

'Virginia, wait!' Nicholas called. 'When will I see you again?'

She stopped in her tracks and thought for a minute. 'I'll try to manage tomorrow at the same time. After we get all the lunch things cleared up, cook goes to her room for a rest.'

'Same place?'

'Yes, and I'll tell you what I think of your poems.'

'Oh God!' Nicholas groaned. 'I hope you won't be too hard on me.'

She laughed. 'Don't be silly.' Then off she flew, feeling so happy she could have soared up through the summer's air like a bird. She longed to tell somebody—everybody—all about her exciting experience but at the same time, she wanted to hug it to herself, to cherish it and share it with no-one.

She had also acquired an intense feeling of loyalty to Nicholas Cartwright and that alone would prevent her confiding in anyone.

Just in time as she neared the back of the house, she remembered to pin up her long hair and tuck it under the starched cap that she'd been carrying in the bib of her apron. She tidied her apron and her dress and took a deep breath, and walked sedately the rest of the way.

Soon she was descending into the kitchen via a basement back door. It led down into long, dark and airless corridors. Off the warren of corridors was the larder, cool and dank with a floor of brick and shelves of slate. There were also doors leading to the living quarters of the butler, the housekeeper, and the cook. There were also the still room, the wine cellar and some other store rooms. These dark cellars were infested by beetles, cockroaches and mice. Too often there were rats as well. It was the terror of Virginia's life, as well as Fanny's, to scrub the floors down there. The butler's room, the housekeeper's room and the cook's room were up a few steps at the other end of a passage near the kitchen, and they at least had the benefit of more light, but even those rooms did not escape the occasional infestation of cockroaches. The gardener was called in from time to time to help in the fight against the rats. He was the only one who could boast of some success in the ongoing battle with these relentless vermin.

Virginia helped prepare the vegetables for the evening meal, then she and Fanny washed the pots and pans in the scullery. After that, they tackled the hundred and one other jobs, including washing the dishes that were brought down from the dining room, though knives and silver were cleaned in the butler's pantry. Up to their elbows in soap suds, they were sweating by this time. The hot water and the steam billowing up from the deep wooden sink added to their discomfort.

Despite the irritation of her clothes sticking wetly to her skin and the strands of hair escaping down over her face, Virginia still felt happy and excited. She could hardly wait for an opportunity to slip upstairs and collect the poems.

But every now and again—despite the heat, despite the excitement—she shivered. She was all too well aware of the danger of the situation, and of what would certainly happen to her if she was caught.

3

They met every day, sometimes very early in the morning when the wood was sparkling with dew and the sunlight was just beginning to filter through the high branches overhead. Sometimes they met late at night when they could barely see each other, with only the moon's pale gleam to light their path. If it was early in the morning, Fanny covered for her as best she could, even suffering the terrors of being alone down on her hands and knees scrubbing the warren of dark basement passageways, with scrapings and scurryings threatening her from every shadowy corner.

Virginia had spun a tale to her about secret meetings with a lover, knowing that Fanny would never in a million years guess that it was Nicholas Cartwright she was meeting. Fanny was grateful for any excitement to break the monotony of her working days. Virginia had also promised to read Fanny a story every night from one of her books. Most times, luck was with Virginia and she didn't need Fanny's help. When cook was having her afternoon nap, it was possible to race through any jobs she'd been left to do and then slip out, and away. What made it easier was the lack of lunches and the resulting pile of dishes and pots and pans to be washed. Mr Cartwright was still away on business, although he was expected back very soon. Mrs Cartwright was taking advantage of his absence by dining out with friends in Glasgow and indulging her passion for shopping. The chauffeur kept carrying in piles of boxes containing expensive outfits, hats and furs, all of which caused the lady's maid extra work. Not that Mrs Cartwright would give a thought to that.

Virginia quickly became accustomed to leading a double life. One part—the most important part—was so beautiful she could hardly believe it to be true. Each time she saw Nicholas waiting for her, it was like another miracle. Each time he came towards her, hands outstretched, eyes eager, she ran joyfully towards him. He always brought poems and they earnestly and enthusiastically discussed them. She could see that with each poem he was improving, and told him so. The first poem had been short and clever. He called it a 'haiku', which he said was a Japanese form of poetry. It all sounded very exotic and romantic, and she listened attentively as he read.

Milk's last droplet stains
Forgiven, the past is past
But not forgotten.

Later he began producing more personal poems and she liked them better. She remembered what Coleridge had said: 'What comes from the heart goes to the heart.'

She told Nicholas this too. He said she was his inspiration and his encouragement. He said he owed everything to her. This was despite the fact that she often criticised his work and he hotly defended it. They had many lively, sometimes quite noisy arguments. Then she'd feel guilty and remind him that after all, she'd never written any poetry herself.

'What do I know?' she told him. 'Don't pay any attention to me.'

'Nonsense, you're a wonderful critic. You do know what you're talking about and I value your opinion.'

He wrote,

Cup your hands gently
Keep warm the cradle of skin
Within rests my heart.

Whenever she could she would fly to meet him in their secret place in the woods. He would catch her and joyfully whirl her round and round while she squealed with laughter.

One of his poems was entitled 'You'.

Your laughter tickles
*   my ears*
Your smiles caress
*   my eyes*
Your joy fills
*   my heart*
Your words touch
*   my soul*
You have the essence
*   of an angel*
The touch
*   of a butterfly*
The spirit
*   of a tigress.*

Every moment she could manage, she reread her own treasured books of poetry. She wanted so desperately to be able to help Nicholas, as well as to enjoy informed discussions with him. Once Mrs Tompkins caught her sitting in the kitchen shelling peas but with a book on a chair beside her, on which she was concentrating more than on the job in hand. Mrs Tompkins promptly hit her over the head with the book with such force it caused immediate dizziness and then a throbbing headache for the rest of the day. However she forgot about the pain as soon as she saw Nicholas.

By now she felt as if she'd known him all her life. She knew of his boyhood loneliness as if she'd suffered it herself. She knew about his hated boarding school as if she'd been there with him, hating it too. She saw the military college, heard the shouted commands. Viewed the immaculately uniformed cadets in her mind's eye, thanks to Nicholas's wonderful talent for description. She also knew that the lifelong ambition of his parents was for him to marry Lady Fiona Forbes Linton, the daughter of a wealthy titled friend of Mr Cartwright's. Lady Fiona and her parents had been regular guests at the Cartwrights' luncheons and dinner parties, and the Cartwrights were regular guests at the Forbes Lintons' stately home. But Virginia didn't want to think about that.

'You should be writing your novel,' she told Nicholas. 'You're going to be a famous novelist one day. I feel sure of it.'

'Darling,' he said softly, and she could see the love in his eyes.

It was then for the first time that she realised she loved him too. He kissed her gently—on her brow, on her cheek, in the curve of her neck, on her lips. She responded with a passion she had not realised she was capable of. In bed that night, after Fanny was safely asleep, Virginia wept. She knew that any normal and lasting relationship between the son of such a wealthy family and the kitchen maid was impossible. It would never be countenanced, either by his parents or his class, or indeed by her family or her class. Neither she nor Nicholas voiced this reality. It went without saying. They simply went on being happy in their own secret world where nothing or no-one mattered except each other.

Then war was declared and everything changed. For Virginia, though, the outbreak of war was a dim worry compared with the immediate terror she faced. She had missed a period, something that had never happened before. She had never been even a day late since her periods started when she was twelve years of age. She knew she was pregnant.

At first she didn't say anything to Nicholas. She tried to blot the knowledge out of her mind. It was too dreadful—too disastrous—to contemplate. She was plunged into a nightmare of apprehension and terror. If Mrs Cartwright found out she was pregnant, she would immediately dismiss her. She would think that the father would be some other ne'er-do-well servant. If she knew the truth, she would throw Virginia out without a halfpenny of her wages and make sure she never got a job anywhere else. Virginia had always been a good hard worker, but she could well imagine Mrs Cartwright giving her the reputation of a lazy, immoral slut to all her friends and acquaintances. There would be no limits to Mrs Cartwright's malice.

The workhouse loomed large in Virginia's mind. It was what every person she'd ever known dreaded beyond anything. She vividly remembered how the anxiety of it had haunted her grandmother. It was the reason her mother had struggled to keep Granny with the family in the room and kitchen in the Gorbals until the day she died in the set-in-the-wall bed in the kitchen. Granny had shared the bed with her mother, herself and her sister Rose. Rose used to take bouts of coughing in the middle of the night. One night, Virginia had got up to fetch her a cup of water when she suddenly became aware of how still and cold Granny was. The main thing she felt was relief that the old lady had died safely in bed with her family. They all thanked God that she had escaped the workhouse.

The day before Nicholas left to join his regiment, he gave Virginia a poem to keep. The beauty of it overwhelmed her.

It was entitled 'To my Mentor'.

Here within your bridge of feathers
I bathe in your mind's lambant light.

We soar the skies together
Glide on a cloud of thought,
Ride a current of fascination.

You, sometimes pushing
Always eager
Never harsh.

I feel the warm air
Lift my feathers
And pray that I prove

Deserving
Of the strain
Of your sweat.

'It's beautiful,' she said. 'Thank you, Nicholas. I'll always treasure it.' Then she wept broken-heartedly.

'Please don't,' he pleaded. 'They say the war will be over by Christmas. I'll be back in no time.'

'It's not just that,' she sobbed. She did not want to tell him of her fears for herself—it seemed so selfish when he was marching off perhaps to his death. But she found herself blurting out the truth. 'I'm pregnant, and once it begins to show, your mother will throw me out and I won't know what to do or where to go. I can't go home and be an extra burden to my family. They're nearly starving as it is.'

There was a silence while he held her close and stroked her hair. Then he said, 'I'll tell my mother the truth and say that she must allow you to stay at Hilltop House as long as you wish.'

'Oh no, you mustn't.' Virginia pushed him away in alarm. 'She mustn't know it's you. She'd be furious at me. She'd send me packing immediately.'

'I'll insist on it, Virginia. Then when I return, we'll work something out. I won't allow you to suffer in any way on my account.'

She was collapsing inside as if she was already bereft and alone. She realised that despite everything they had shared, he had no understanding of her life, her world. He had no conception of the harsh and cruel reality that awaited her. They said their goodbyes before returning separately to the house in their usual way.

'It won't be for long,' Nicholas said. 'We'll see each other again soon.'

But she knew that their magic world had gone for ever. She saw his future quite clearly and it wasn't with a kitchen maid from the Gorbals. It would be Fiona Forbes Linton waving him off on the train the next day, and it would be Fiona waiting at the station for him when he returned. Virginia accepted his future life with Fiona and she knew Nicholas did too. It was only right and proper. It certainly did not make her love him any less. She would always wish him every happiness and fulfilment.

That night, her day's work over, she climbed the dark winding stairs to the top of the house. She looked at the attic's grey distempered walls, the bare floor boards, the chipped wash basin, and she knew that this would be the last night she would spend here. Mrs Cartwright would wait until Nicholas was safely away and then she would summon her.

Virginia went down on her knees at the side of her bed and prayed to God for mercy. Fanny arrived while she was still down on her knees.

'Oh sorry,' Fanny whispered, putting an apologetic palm against her mouth. 'I didn't mean to interrupt your prayers.'

'It's all right,' Virginia said, rising. 'I'm finished.' There was an ominous ring to the words. She immediately resented their wider implication. She'd be damned if she'd let somebody like Mrs Cartwright finish her off. She wasn't finished by a long chalk.

Her mouth hardened as she climbed into the high lumpy bed.

'Good night, Fanny,' she said. Then she closed her eyes and began mustering enough courage to face the coming day.

4

The day was not made any easier by the cook getting drunk. Thankfully she had still been reasonably sober when all the staff were lined up in the driveway to curtsy and wave goodbye to Nicholas. In the motor car sat Mr and Mrs Cartwright, Nicholas and Fiona. Mrs Cartwright and Fiona were splendidly attired. Mrs Cartwright wore a huge-brimmed, black velvet hat trimmed with large, curling feathers, a high-necked white blouse and a tailor-made costume in striped suiting. Fiona's black straw hat had a tiny brim but was piled high at the crown with bows of pink ribbon. Her tunic dress was of grey silk but the upper bodice of sheer grey fabric revealed a pink under-bodice. Mr Cartwright was his usual sober self in a dark suit and waistcoat, wing-collared shirt and bowler hat. Nicholas was resplendent in his officer's uniform.

As all the servants waved and called 'Good luck, sir', Nicholas smiled and raised a hand in return. None of the others deigned even to glance in the direction of the servants. The motor car gradually disappeared down the long drive between the avenue of trees. The servants turned back into the house. Protocol was temporarily abandoned because of the stress of the parting with the most popular member of the family. Upstairs and downstairs servants sat together in the kitchen for a comforting cup of tea. All of them, except Virginia, shared their memories of Nicholas. The butler even remembered Nicholas as a baby and toddler. He recalled Miss Kane who had been Nicholas's nanny. The old man shook his head.

'Very severe, she was. Never liked that woman. God alone knows what the poor wee lad suffered, locked up alone with her in that nursery.'

'Sheila knew,' Mrs Tompkins moaned. 'Remember Sheila, the nursery maid. Oh, the tales she used to tell me!' Mrs Tompkins began to weep copiously—the drink often had that effect on her—and wiped at her heavy-jowled face with her apron. 'Aw, the poor laddie. Aw, the poor wee soul.'

Mrs Smithers tutted. 'He's hardly a wee boy any more, Mrs Tompkins. He's a grown man of over six feet tall.'

'Aw, shut up, ya wee nyaff.' Mrs Tompkins growled, as she continued to drown her sorrows with yet another drink. 'He'll always be a wee boy tae me. That's how I'll always remember him.'

Mrs Smithers' small mouth tightened with anger and disapproval, not about Mrs Tompkins drinking—she was well used to that, but at the insulting reference to herself in front of the other servants. It was essential in the disciplined running of any establishment for the staff to have respect for the housekeeper. Being called a wee nyaff did nothing to help Mrs Smithers in her already difficult task. She hesitated, unsure whether to give Mrs Tompkins an immediate repri-mand or wait for a more suitable moment when the cook was sober. She decided on the latter, and instead turned on the upstairs maids.

'Don't just stand there. Get upstairs at once and get on with your duties.'

She followed them smartly from the kitchen and left Fanny and Virginia at the mercy of Mrs Tompkins. The butler, fearing one of Mrs Tompkins' drunken rages, had hastened to his own room as quickly as his tottery legs could carry him. For most of the servants, there wasn't much to do just now as Mr and Mrs Cartwright and Fiona were dining in Glasgow after seeing Nicholas off at the Central Station. Then the Cartwrights were taking Fiona home to Campsie Castle. They were due to return in the late afternoon in time to dress for dinner. Already the lady's maid would be laying out the clothes and jewellery Mrs Cartwright had said she wished to wear that evening.

Mrs Tompkins was singing now, or bawling more like, as she staggered dangerously about the kitchen with a long knife, in prepar-ation for cutting some chops. 'Ae fond kiss and then we sever, Ae fareweel and then for ever, Deep in heart wrung tears I'll pledge thee, Warring sighs and groans I'll wage thee.'

Virginia couldn't bear it. She went through to the scullery where Fanny was shakily peeling potatoes. Fanny whispered to Virginia, 'I don't like the look of her with that knife.'

Too distressed to speak, Virginia nodded agreement and went through to the larder to fetch the milk that cook would need to make the custard. As soon as she arrived back in the kitchen with the big cold jug clutched in her hands, cook bawled,

'What the hell do you think you're doing?'

'You said you wanted it for the custard.'

Keeping a safe distance from the table where cook was hacking at the chops with the knife, Virginia placed the jug on the dresser that stood against the far wall.

'Can you no' see, you idiot, that I'm no' nearly ready to make the custard. That milk'll be sour wi' the heat of this place before I'm ready for it. Can you no' do anything right, you glaikit wee idiot.'

Normally Virginia, like all the other servants, would have kept silent, even agreed with Mrs Tompkins, no matter what she said. Anything to try to placate her and escape a worse fate than just being called names. Today, however, Virginia knew she was going to be dismissed anyway. She had nothing to lose. She didn't care what Mrs Tompkins said or did. Mrs Tompkins couldn't make her suffer any more than she was suffering now.

'Don't you call me an idiot. I've more intelligence than you. I don't drink myself stupid, for a start.'

For a couple of seconds, Mrs Tompkins was stunned into silence. Then with a roar like a stampeding elephant, she lurched enraged towards Virginia, wildly stabbing at the air with her knife, her white cap tipping sideways over one ear. Virginia dodged out of the way, the knife missing her by inches. She felt the cold air of the blade and the smell of the blood from the chops.

'I'll kill you,' the enraged Mrs Tompkins yelled. 'Stand still, you impertinent wee bisom.'

The two house-maids appeared briefly in the kitchen doorway before hastily retreating again. At each lunge, Virginia was too quick for the older and much heavier woman who eventually ran out of puff. Her huge bulk collapsed defeated into a chair, making it give a high pitched squeal of protest. Virginia lifted the jug of milk and took it back to the larder.

In the scullery, a chalk-faced Fanny said, 'Have you gone mad?'

Virginia shrugged and began helping Fanny to prepare the first lot of vegetables. As soon as they were peeled and cut, Fanny nervously carried them through to the kitchen, before retreating back to the scullery again. The icy water in the wooden sink had turned Virginia's hands red with the cold but she wasn't aware of the discomfort. She was thinking once cook either dozed off in her chair, or went to her room for a nap, she would go up the back stairs to the attic and pack her tin trunk. Then all she'd have to do was collect it, put on her coat and slip away. She didn't want to answer questions from any of the servants, or face the ordeal of a tearful goodbye from Fanny. They had become good friends, almost like sisters. They'd miss each other. Virginia had decided she had no choice but to go home to the Gorbals. She'd make some excuse for being dismissed. Then she'd try and find another job, maybe in a factory. Hopefully it would be months before her pregnancy would show and by that time, perhaps she'd manage to save some money.

She didn't dare contemplate ending up in the workhouse hospital. She'd heard dreadful stories about how poor girls had been mistreated there and their babies taken from them. Virginia was determined to keep her baby. She didn't know how she could possibly manage it, but manage it she must. The baby was all she had left of Nicholas. She dreamt it would be a boy with Nicholas's dark eyes and black hair and gentle smile.

Eventually, when she and Fanny ventured back to the kitchen, it was to discover that somehow Mrs Tompkins had managed to prepare a big pot of soup, as well as the chops which lay on a platter waiting to be put under the grill. A steam pudding in a bowl covered with a cloth tied over the top was in a large pot of simmering water on the hob. Mrs Tompkins was nowhere to be seen.

Fanny gave a sigh of relief. 'Thank God. How about a cup of tea? The kettle's on the boil.'

'You go ahead and make it,' Virginia said. 'I've to go upstairs and do something. I'll be back in a few minutes.'

'Oh aye?' Fanny's pimply face broke into a sly grin. 'Meeting that lover of yours again, eh?'

'Upstairs, I said, not outside.'

'All right, all right, there's no need to snap at me.'

'I'm sorry, Fanny. My nerves are a bit shattered. Mrs Tompkins nearly made mincemeat of me. It's lucky I'm so quick on my feet.'

'I know.' Fanny agreed. 'For pity's sake, don't do that to me again. I was afraid you'd had it and I'd be left on my own with her.'

'I'll be back down in a few minutes,' Virginia repeated.

The attic was ice-cold in comparison with the stifling heat of the kitchen, where the 'Black Eagle' cooking range kept the whole room like a furnace. Virginia hastily flung her few possessions into her tin trunk and laid her coat and hat on the bed. The trunk would be awkward to carry but not heavy. It was with a heavy heart, though, that she returned downstairs to join Fanny in the stone-floored kitchen.

Fanny had two cups out on the table and tea already poured. A couple of biscuits balanced on each saucer.

Virginia smiled. 'Good job cook's asleep.'

They weren't allowed biscuits. Biscuits were for the family or for Mrs Tompkins and Mrs Smithers when they were on good terms and having a cup of tea together at the end of the day. Often the butler joined them. Being very elderly (nobody knew his exact age) he sometimes dozed off in the middle of their tea party. Mrs Tompkins and Mrs Smithers would sadly shake their heads. It was a miracle to them how he hadn't been dismissed long ago. Every day they expected him to be made homeless. He had no family and nowhere to go.

Mrs Tompkins said, 'Not that Mrs Cartwright would give a thought to that.'

Mrs Smithers pursed her lips and refused to utter a disloyal word about her mistress, but it was obvious that she agreed. Virginia guessed that the reason the old butler remained was the fact that he knew his job inside out and was still useful to the Cartwrights. No doubt he had been paid the same wage for many years. If he was dismissed, or 'let go' as it was sometimes politely put, Mrs Cartwright would have to pay a younger man much more.

Fanny chattered non-stop in between gulps of tea and mouthfuls of biscuit about how lovely she'd thought the hats and dresses of Mrs Cartwright and Lady Fiona were, and how smart the gentlemen looked, especially Master Nicholas.

Eventually, Virginia warned, 'Shh, I think I hear Mrs Tompkins moving about.' Immediately they both scrambled up to rinse their dishes and sweep away the tell-tale crumbs. They had just finished in time when a bleary-eyed Mrs Tompkins appeared.

'They'll soon be wanting their dinner,' she said. 'Where's Maisie hiding herself now? I hope she's got that table set ready.' Mrs Tompkins had obviously forgotten her rage and the cause of it. Such lapses of memory were quite common with her. They had barely started on their various jobs when a breathless Maisie appeared.

'You'll never guess,' she cried out excitedly to Mrs Tompkins, 'who Madam wants to speak to in the drawing room?'

'Who?'

'Virginia.'

She turned to Virginia. 'What on earth have you done? Madam's in one of her furies. I can always tell.'

Virginia didn't reply but on an impulse she turned to Fanny and gave her an affectionate hug before leaving the kitchen. Going upstairs to the main part of the house, she steeled herself for what was to come.

Virginia entered the lofty-ceilinged drawing room. It had plush buttoned chairs and sofas, the panelled walls were covered with heavy, gold-framed paintings, a variety of tables were scattered around and the tops were cluttered with small ornaments and larger vases. Blinds were half drawn at every window, which had curtains looped and festooned about them. Virginia's feet sank into the richly coloured carpet and made her think bitterly of the bare boards of the attic rooms. She faced Mrs Cartwright with dignity. The older woman's eyes glittered with hatred and disgust. 'You know why you're here.'

'Yes.'

'Yes, Madam.'

Virginia kept silent.

'How dare you!' Mrs Cartwright was even more enraged at this impertinent lack of respect. 'You will leave this house immediately. Immediately, do you hear? And I can assure you that I will see that you are never allowed to work in any other decent household.'

'Yes, you would do that, wouldn't you. Well, I would not want to work for such an ignorant and spiteful woman anyway.'

'You . . . you . . . !' Mrs Cartwright was spluttering with rage now. She looked as if she might have a stroke.

With as much dignity as she could muster, Virginia said 'Goodbye,' and walked unhurriedly from the room.

5

Virginia collected her tin trunk and instead of going down the back stairs to the basement, along the passageways and out the back way, she went through the green baize door and into the main hall. She was still in her reckless, rebellious mood. Awkwardly clutching her trunk, she gazed at the wide carpeted stair and the ornate gas lamps that brightened them every evening. No dark, unlit stairs for the Cartwrights to find their way up and down. These stairs branched out on either side at the top of an oak panelled gallery hung with gloomy paintings of the family and their ancestors.

Virginia now saw all this for what it really was—the Cartwrights trying to ape aristocracy like the Forbes Lintons. The Forbes Lintons *had* illustrious ancestors, the Cartwrights had not. The Cartwrights, however, had money, something that perhaps the Forbes Lintons envied. A surge of hatred engulfed Virginia. What had the Cartwrights, or indeed the Forbes Lintons, done to deserve such a luxurious way of life. It was people like her father and her brothers—who slaved for wealthy people like these—who created their wealth. It was people like herself, slaving in the homes of such people who allowed them to enjoy lives of ease and comfort, and all the time the working class led lives filled with anxiety, poverty, ill-health and constant drudgery. Trembling with the unexpected strength of her emotion, Virginia turned away and left by the front door.

Outside she took one last look at the imposing mansion. She would never see it again. Nor did she want to. Hitching the tin trunk up to balance on her hip, she made her way down the drive and began the long walk to Glasgow. Mrs Cartwright, as she'd expected, had not given her a penny of the wages she was owed and so she had no money to pay for her fare to the city. For miles she tramped along between fields full of butterflies that settled and vanished when the sun went behind a cloud. Every now and again she sat down for a rest and listened to the robins and the wrens until their hectic twitterings encouraged her on once more.

During the night, there had been a nip of frost but now it was a balmy September day. Virginia was thankful for the weather. Had it been in the middle of winter, she might have perished on the journey— or so she imagined. It had been bad enough suffering the winter in the attic. She well remembered rising shivering each morning, then trying to wash in water that had a layer of ice on top of the jug, with the face flannel frozen solid. Then a hurried breakfast of tea and a slice of meat left over from the Cartwrights' dinner from the previous night, and a piece of bread.

Bitterness overcame her again when she thought of the different world Mrs Cartwright awakened to. The house-maids would trudge up and down the stairs with hot water for my lady's bath. The lady's maid would give Mrs Cartwright a cup of tea in bed, and after Mrs Cartwright had had her bath, the maid would help her to dress and do her hair. Mrs Cartwright, and Mr Cartwright if he was at home, and any guests who happened to be staying, would linger over a delicious breakfast—a choice of bacon and eggs, kidneys, cutlets, boiled chicken, omelettes and fish, according to their taste. Plus as much bread, toast, rolls, butter, honey and jam as they desired.

While the family gorged themselves, the maids would be struggling up the stairs with heavy buckets of coal to light the upstairs fires. Rumpled beds had to be made, baths cleaned. Chamber pots had to be covered with a cloth and carried discreetly down the back stairs to be emptied, to avoid offending the sensitivities of the very people who had filled them. Carpets had to be swept, furniture and ornaments dusted, every pane of glass and every mirror polished until they sparkled.

Virginia glanced down at her hands. They were red and roughened by the amount of scrubbing she'd had to do. She thought of the soft white hands of Mrs Cartwright and Fiona and all the pampered women like them, and the hatred in her heart kept her going and saved her from fainting with exhaustion.

She did sit down for a few minutes when she reached Kirkintilloch.

It was a small town that went back to the time of the Romans. She gazed at the old parish church with its crow-stepped gables, and was tempted to go in and pray for help and strength, but she could pray just as well sitting here. She closed her eyes but found prayer impossible in the midst of the bitter turmoil of her emotions. There was nothing for it but to continue on her journey using only her determination and willpower to push forward one foot after another.

It was dark by the time she reached the city of Glasgow. Buildings menaced her on each side with their towering blackness. The gas lamps gave a feeble pool of ghostly light. A man was singing in a drunken moan, 'Keep the home fires burning. . . .'

It reminded Virginia of the war and of Nicholas. Quickly she banished him from her mind. It was too painful to think of him.

At last she reached the Gorbals and Cumberland Street. Almost weeping with relief, she stopped inside the close. All the closes led up to the various flats on each of the three landings and also through to the communal back court, or yard, in which the shared wash houses and middens were situated. Her parents and brothers would be in bed asleep by now, and although she didn't relish the idea of waking the household she had no choice. If the close had been warm and dry, she might have sat down on her trunk, and leaning back against the door, tried to get some sleep until morning. But a cold wind was funnelling through from the street, making her shiver miserably.

She pulled the door bell, then rattled the letterbox for good measure. She listened. There was only the loud snorting and whistling sound of her father snoring. Then a clatter of sound and a cacophony of voices started outside. Virginia knew it must be the bin men but she went to look out the back close. Sure enough there they were in the back yard with candles strapped round their heads and flickering over their brows. String tied round each leg below the knee prevented rats or mice running up their trousers. They were heaving bins onto their backs and trudging out with them to their cart.

Virginia retreated back to pull the door bell again. This time she heard movement inside the house. As expected, it was her mother who came to the door. Her father and her brothers were heavy sleepers but her mother slept fitfully, and sometimes had to get up during the night and make herself a cup of tea in the hope it would settle her. Virginia remembered this from the time she shared the kitchen bed with her mother, and Granny, and sister Rose.

32

Her mother peeped round the door, then gasped at the sight of her. 'Virginia, come away in, hen. What on earth are you doing out at this time of night?' Clutching her grey shawl over her white cotton nightdress, she stood aside to allow Virginia to enter. It only took them a few steps to cross the shoebox of a hall into the kitchen. The hall had a row of hooks on the wall facing the outside door, suspended from which were a shabby collection of men's jackets and dungarees. The kitchen itself wasn't much bigger than the hall. From the edge of the built-in coal bunker and dresser to the fireplace was only a few feet. And from the sink at the window to the edge of the hole-in-the-wall bed measured only a few more feet. In the centre of this small area was crowded a wooden table, four wooden chairs and an armchair on either side of the fireplace. As a result there was hardly any floor space in which to move around.

Janette Watson lit the gas mantle above the fireplace, then turned it down low so that the light wouldn't disturb her sleeping husband. Then just to make doubly sure, she tugged one of the bed curtains further along to shield his face. After giving the fire a poke to bring it to life, she placed the kettle on to it.

'It was boiling just a wee while ago, it won't take a minute,' she whispered to Virginia. 'What happened? Are you all right?'

'Just tired,' Virginia said. 'I was dismissed. She never even gave me my wages and I've had to walk all that way.'

Janette eased the poker in and out of the fire again. 'It won't be long. You'll feel better after a cup of tea.' She fetched the teapot and lifted the tin caddy down from the fireplace.

'Don't you want to know why?'

'In your own time, hen.'

'I was impertinent.'

'Oh dear!' Janette's sigh betrayed her fear that this was bound to happen some day. Virginia had always been a spirited child.

'Well, she was a horrible woman. Nobody liked her.'

Janette nearly added, 'Even so, hen, she was the mistress,' but thought better of it.

Virginia had taken after her father, Tam Watson, as indeed had her brothers. Like most of the country, they used to be good Liberals, but gradually first Tam, then the boys, then Virginia, had developed an angry independent spirit and become socialists. They'd even turned away from God and the church—at least Tam and the boys had.

Janette partly blamed too much reading—and all the meetings and classes Tam went to, run by firebrands like John Maclean. Tam even went to meetings on Sunday afternoons. Now the boys attended them as well.

It wasn't that she didn't believe in education. She'd had a good education herself. She'd left school when she was twelve but her parents had always had books in the house and encouraged her to read. She enjoyed reading, but nice romantic or Christian stories. For one thing, she was far too tired with scrubbing out pubs and halls all day to be able to burden her mind with all this socialist stuff, although Tam kept on pushing high-brow books on her. She had to admit that she did enjoy some of them—but only if they were novels. Not the serious political stuff that he was so fond of. Tam had stuffed the boys' heads with wild ideas he'd got from books like *Merry England* by Robert Blatchford—which he claimed was 'the best introduction to socialism there is'. He'd even got hold of a copy of something called *Das Kapital*—a dreary-looking volume which remained, unread and gathering dust, on the mantleshelf.

Janette never objected, except in a gentle way, about Tam's worrying drift away from the church. It wasn't so much his turning away from church attendance and his criticism of priests and ministers that worried her. It wasn't even his sincerely held views about the unfair distribution of wealth—she knew as well as anyone that it was an unfair world, and when you lived in the Gorbals such an idea hardly came as a great revelation. But she did worry terribly about his hardening atheism. All right, there was a lot wrong with the church and you didn't need to go there every Sunday to be a good Christian, but the actual teachings of Jesus Christ were sacrosanct as far as she was concerned. She had always tried to instill this deep feeling into Virginia, though with how much success she could never be sure. When Virginia had been a child, she had told her stories and shown her picture books about 'gentle Jesus, meek and mild'.

Now, looking at her daughter and seeing the rebellious spark in her eye and bitter twist to her mouth, she doubted that her religious teaching had had much effect.

'I'll start looking for another job right away. Factory work maybe. Anything but service. That's just slavery.'

Janette sighed. 'You think factory work's likely to be any easier? I think you'll soon find, hen, that you didn't know how lucky you were

34

working in that nice big house, getting your bed and board.'

'Och, mammy, you don't understand what it was like, or what that Mrs Cartwright was like.'

'You're forgetting that I had a spell in service myself in my young days.'

'You were lucky. You got a nice unmarried Christian lady who treated you like a daughter. How often do you think that happens?'

'Well, maybe not quite like a daughter, Virginia, but Miss Hamilton was a very good Christian lady, right enough.'

'Well, Mrs Cartwright is anything but a good Christian lady. Although she probably thinks she is because she's a regular church-goer.'

'Och well,' Janette soothed. 'You're here now. Drink up your tea. We'll talk about what you're going to do in the morning.'

'Where'll I sleep?'

'Oh aye.' Janette nibbled worriedly at her lip. It had been over a year since Virginia had slept overnight. She had only ever got a few hours off from Hilltop House. Sometimes she didn't come home on her time off so that she could save her fare and help out with the housekeeping money. She was a good wee soul, really.

'It's all right, mammy. The floor'll do. I'm so tired I could sleep on the edge of a knife. I'll lie down on the rug in front of the fire. It'll be nice and cosy.'

'All right, hen. And here's a cushion for a pillow. And I'll slip one of the blankets off the bed.'

'No, no, you might waken daddy. Your shawl'll do fine.'

'Will you put out the gas?'

'Yes, don't worry. Goodnight, mammy.'

'Goodnight, hen.' Janette gave a faint smile. 'Sleep tight and don't let the bugs bite.' It was something she always used to say when Virginia slept at home. She climbed carefully back into bed and eased herself between the blankets.

Virginia finished her tea, turned off the gas and then settled down in the darkness under the grey woollen shawl. She became aware of the smell of paraffin wax. The wood of the hole-in-the-wall bed had long been infested by bugs but her mother kept them at bay by constantly rubbing every hole and crack with paraffin oil. As Virginia snuggled further down under the shawl, as well as the smell of the wool, she could also detect that of her mother, warm and sweaty from her hard day's toil. The familiar smells comforted Virginia and helped her to relax into a dreamless sleep.

It seemed no time at all until her mother was saying, 'Come on now, hen. You'd best get up before the boys come through.'

'Are they working again?'

'Aye, a lot of folk are being taken on at the munitions factories. Ian's doing that. Duncan's been doing a bit of labouring here and there.'

Her father appeared in the kitchen. He'd been at the lavatory and was in his rolled up sleeves, with a white scarf knotted at his throat.

'I told Ian,' he said, 'that the German workers were his friends. It's the capitalists over there that are the real enemy of the British and the German workers. I told him, but it still hasn't sunk in.'

Virginia thought he looked quite ill. His cheeks were sunken and under his eyes was dark brown crepey skin almost the colour of his bushy moustache.

'It's a good job, Da,' Ian said, following his father into the kitchen. He was a lively eighteen-year-old with laughing blue eyes and curly brown hair. He'd always been popular with the girls. 'And we need the money,' he went on. 'What Ma earns barely gets us a piece and jam for our dinner. Oh, it's you Virginia,' he cried out in surprise and pleasure at the sight of her.

She'd already replaced the cushion on the chair and folded her mother's shawl. She had tidied her clothes and now she was pinning up her hair.

'I've been dismissed.'

Her mother, in an apologetic tone, explained, 'She was cheeky to the mistress.'

Ian laughed. 'Good for you, hen.'

'Will there be any chance of a job in the munitions factory, do you think, Ian?'

'Aye, they're needing as many as they can get now.'

'Not you as well?' her father groaned.

Duncan's big frame filled up all the elbow room that was left in the kitchen. He was a year and a half older than Ian and much more serious.

'You'd be better to stay in service, Virginia,' he said, thumping down at the table.

'That's what you think!'

'Virginia, apart from anything else, service is not dangerous like working with munitions. And you won't like turning yellow either.'

'Yellow?' Virginia laughed. 'You're joking.'

'No, it depends where they put you. In some departments, dust and chemicals fly about and make everyone's skin and clothes turn yellow.'

'Well, I'll just have to hope they don't put me on that.' She shrugged. 'I might not get taken on at all, but I think it's worth a try. Like Ian says, we need the money.'

'It'll be dangerous no matter where they put you.' Duncan had always been the moody, pessimistic one of the family.

'I'm willing to take my chances,' Virginia said cheerfully. 'I believe in equality and if Ian isn't afraid of the work in the munitions factory, then neither am I.'

Her mother cast her eyes heavenwards. That Pankhurst women and her suffragette friends had a lot to answer for. 'Equality,' she said. 'What next!'

6

At first Virginia thought it was great. Starting work at eight o'clock in the morning, instead of five or six. She could hardly believe her luck. It was all very exciting and interesting too. After clocking in to the large, one-storey building, she was given a fireproof overall and a cap that had to completely cover her head. Not one hair must show. Pins, brooches, rings or metal of any kind were strictly forbidden. Rubber shoes had to be worn. She was led down long corridors and into the huge room where she was to begin work.

When she saw the number of girls in the room, she was astounded. She had never in her life seen so many people all together in the one place. Hundreds and hundreds of girls—or so it seemed to Virginia— all dressed the same and standing intent on doing the same thing, or hurrying to and fro. She was given boxes of small brass parts for fuses, to be gauged and checked for rejects. It didn't take her long to learn how to do it and soon her attention began to stray a little. She saw notices stuck up on the dark grey walls. They told the workers where to go in the event of a raid by zeppelins or other aircraft.

Another thing that caught her attention was the fact that so many of the girls had their fingers bandaged. She soon found out the reason. The brass parts with which she worked had sharp edges which cut the fingers and before the day was out, she had to go to the surgery, nursing her hand and trying to catch the drips of blood to prevent them from falling onto her overall.

At the dinner hour, they could all go to a separate room, have a cup of tea and eat their pieces. She was shocked to learn that many of the girls had developed septic poisoning and had to attend the surgery every day to have their fingers dressed. In the light of this discovery, Virginia's euphoria of the morning quickly evaporated. She also soon discovered that the work was repetitious and standing for so many hours exhausted her. By the end of that first day, she was very weary.

'I told you,' Duncan said. 'It's not so great as you thought, is it? And you've already been injured.'

She tried to perk up. 'Oh, stop nagging at me, Duncan. And I'm just a bit tired, that's all. I'll feel all right after I've had something to eat.'

Janette had made soup with some bones, lentils, barley and vegetables. She ladled it out from the big iron pot on the grate. Afterwards, there were sausages and potatoes. Normally they had their dinner, as it was called here (in Hilltop House it was lunch) in the middle of the day but because Virginia, Ian and Duncan were at work all day, Janette had changed things around. She and her husband had their tea together at twelve noon. Tam was a moulder and every morning and afternoon, summer and winter, he went along to hang about outside the iron works in the hope of a job. Usually, if there was any work going it was given to a younger man. But Tam kept trying. Janette always said that it was that heavy work that aged Tam and ruined his health. Their tea was a simple meal of tea and bread and jam, and perhaps a scone or a pancake. Janette, despite working, managed to find the time and enough energy to bake once a week.

'There should be a canteen in that place, not just to serve tea but a decent meal,' Virginia said. 'I'm sure everyone could work better and not have so many accidents if they weren't so tired. A decent hot meal in the middle of the day would keep them going.'

'Aye, you're right,' Ian agreed. 'We've been agitating for that. There's a union meeting tomorrow night about it. Why don't you come along and speak up for the women?'

Virginia was taken aback. 'I couldn't do that.'

'Why not? You spoke up for your rights to Mrs Cartwright, by all accounts.'

'Oh, but that was different. Anyway, it got me dismissed. I don't want to lose this job if I can avoid it.'

'You won't, not if you join the union and get that behind you. Come to the meeting tomorrow and see what you think.'

'I'll see.'

'Good.' Ian grinned and stuck up his thumbs.

Her father nodded. 'Good for you, lass.'

'I never said I'd go. I never said I'd do anything. I'll maybe think about it, that's all I meant.' She continued eating her meal in silence while the men began a heated discussion about the importance of the unions. Ian was all for them, but Duncan and her father argued that the union leaders were too closely associated with the Liberal party. As were the great masses of the workers. But whatever their differences, her father and both her brothers saw socialism as the only way forward.

'If for no other reason,' Duncan told her when the meal was finished and she was helping her mother clear the table, 'you should go and hear John Maclean. He's an inspiration, that man.'

This was something the three men totally agreed on. At the mere mention of John Maclean's name, it was as if a light came on, beamed from their eyes and animated their features. Even Duncan was affected in this way. It made Virginia curious.

'Is he going to be at the meeting?'

'Yes, he'll be one of the speakers.'

'How he gets to so many meetings beats me,' Duncan said. 'He works during the day for five days a week as a teacher. Then every night and at weekends, he's travelling here, there and everywhere—all over Scotland—giving brilliant talks in halls, or at street corners, or at the work gates. And there's the Sunday classes he takes for workers, or anyone who wants to learn. He teaches economics and Marxist principles and industrial history. I'm telling you, his intellect and his energy are superhuman.'

Virginia couldn't help being impressed but Janette was thinking, 'What's his wife and family doing while he's tramping around the country educating the workers?' Although she had to admit that he had done quite a lot of good, if not for his own family, then for other folks. According to Tam, Maclean had once written a pamphlet called *The Greenock Jungle*. It was based on the famous novel by Upton Sinclair called *The Jungle*. The pamphlet exposed the criminal traffic in diseased carcasses by a number of Greenock butchers. It resulted in an enquiry by the local government board and a meat inspector was appointed for the town's slaughterhouses. Maclean had also agitated for, and had been successful in getting, the school boards to feed and clothe and provide free books to children who, because of the unemployment of their parents, would have starved.

So Janette listened patiently and without criticism to her menfolk's

40

passionate enthusiasm for John Maclean. She wondered what Virginia would think of the man. She had no doubt that the girl would go to the meeting. Already she could see a gleam of interest in her daughter's eyes. She sighed to herself. It would only lead to more trouble. Although she loved her family and was proud of them, she wished they could be more contented. They worried her. Sometimes they even embarrassed her. They stirred things up. They not only argued amongst themselves, they argued with friends and neighbours. Sometimes she didn't know where to put her face.

But they seemed to thrive on these arguments and confrontations. She secretly hoped and prayed that Virginia would be different. As she washed the dishes in the black iron sink with its brass swan-necked cold water tap, she murmured to Virginia who was drying the dishes, 'You don't need to go, hen, if you don't want to. Never mind them.'

'Mammy, I'm perfectly capable of making up my own mind.'

'Aye,' Janette sighed, defeated.

Virginia glanced round. Her mother's face was drawn and tired. Her eyes were dull, her hair pinned back in a bun. According to Tam, it had once been 'such a bonny yellow'. It was all faded now and streaked with grey, and she wasn't yet forty.

'Must you go out scrubbing, Mammy? Now that you'll have my wages—I'll give you as much as I can, even though I've got to try to save something. I mean, these days you never know what's going to happen.' Except that she did know. Virginia quaked inside at the thought of the baby. It was just an invisible embryo at the moment but the time would come when it would be obvious and her mother and everyone would know. Her mother would be ashamed of her, and disappointed. She would be branded a fallen woman by everyone else, and regarded as a disgrace and a shame to her family. She could just imagine her father and brothers being ashamed of her. But somehow she would have to survive what everyone would say and think of her.

'Och aye, you're quite right,' Janette said. 'You should save as much as you can, hen.'

'But must you work so hard Mammy?'

'I'm like you. I believe in putting away a few pennies when I can. The boys could be out of work again, and then what would we do? You're a good girl, Virginia. I always appreciated what you gave me. Many a time it saved the day.'

'We're away, Ma,' the boys called out. 'Are you coming, Virginia?'

Virginia grabbed her jacket and the bread and jam her mother had wrapped in a piece of newspaper.

'Cheerio, Mammy.'

'Cheerio, hen, and you be careful in that place. I'm always telling Ian.'

'Yes, yes.'

Duncan soon headed off in a different direction, while Virginia and Ian continued to trudge along side by side. They didn't take a tram to work so that they could save the money for their fare. Coming home, however, Virginia was too tired to face the long walk. On each return journey, she was glad to take the tram. Every night her mother made her the bed in front of the fire with the cushion for a pillow and one of the blankets from her bed. It was cosy enough although it would be a different matter when the colder weather came and icy draughts blew under the doors from the close. The rag rug did nothing to cushion Virginia against the hardness of the floor. She was so stiff and sore each morning, she could hardly struggle to her feet. At night, as she lay trying to sleep, trying to ignore the racket of her father's snoring, she would think of Nicholas. She couldn't help it. She missed him.

During the day, for safety's sake, she had to concentrate on nothing but her work. But never a night passed but she missed him. She missed the sight of him, the sound of him, the touch of him. Over and over again, she relived their meetings. She remembered the joy on his face when he saw her approach. She felt his strong, hard arms around her, his hungry mouth on hers. His hands caressed her breasts, her thighs. He pulled her down beside him onto the sweet smelling earth. They undressed each other and made love. She felt him move inside her now, and she trembled with passion at the vivid memory. Oh, how she longed for him. She remembered how, still naked, they had moved in a dream dance together. She could see the morning mist clinging to the trees, making their white naked figures ghost-like and unreal. Yet it had been so beautiful. And she had loved him. She had believed that he loved her.

It had not been his fault that his mother had got rid of her. He would not know anything about it. Only sometimes she would wonder sadly if indeed he had not, as he'd promised, told his mother to keep her at Hilltop House. He had certainly told her about the pregnancy.

42

Perhaps he'd even done so in order to get rid of her, knowing that his mother would certainly oblige. But it was only in her most exhausted states that such thoughts were able to take hold of her. For the most part, in those quiet times lying in the dark and silent kitchen, she was able to cling to the memories of their love.

On the way to work, she would determine once more to forget all about Nicholas Cartwright. What good did thinking about the past do anybody? She had to get on with her life. She attended several meetings at which John Maclean was one of the speakers. And she discovered that he was indeed a most charismatic man.

It wasn't so much his physical appearance. He was a stockily built man and wore a dark suit, neat collar and tie and a dark homburg hat. It was something about his face with its wide mouth, broad features and prominent cheek-bones. But it was his eyes that were the most compelling thing about him. They were beacons of passion, burning with enthusiasm and sincerity. The whole man was charged with such energy that it was infectious.

He was a masterly speaker, even at—or especially at—rough street meetings in the middle of the clatter of traffic, and with crowds of casual listeners constantly changing and being renewed. At meetings in halls, he could have the audience jumping to their feet and cheering, as he made the air around him spark with the electricity of his presence. Virginia couldn't help being impressed.

He had started to have regular meetings in Bath Street, even in Renfield Street, and not only attracted large numbers of socialists, but also passers-by. The streets became so packed that a child could have walked across the heads of the crowd. People became riveted by John Maclean's passionate speeches. A vast body of men and women would stand for hours in tense silence listening to him. Especially when he talked about the war, the unfolding tragedy that seemed to have cast its dark shadow over all their lives.

At the foot of the street, the tramway office was plastered with poster appeals to men to join the army. And there was John Maclean, standing on a table eloquently exhorting men not to join the army under any circumstances. The war, he told them, was not an accident. Indeed, it was the very nature of capitalism to engender warfare.

'The men you are asked to shoot,' he insisted, his face tense and drawn with earnestness, 'are your brothers. They have the same difficulty as you to find the rent for their miserable dwellings. They have to suffer the same insults from their gaffers and foremen. Do not forget that when the Scottish miners were on strike, they often received financial help from the German miners.' His eyes burned into the crowd. 'The main thing for you to know is that your real enemy is the employers. As long as turning lathes, ploughs, coal cutters, looms, ships—all the tools of wealth production—are possessed by a small class of privileged people, then so long will you be slaves. To get free from this slavery is your main concern. Victory can only be with the assistance of your brothers in other lands. For socialism cannot triumph in one country alone. The victory of socialism must be worldwide. The only war worth waging is the class war.'

Walking home with her brothers after listening to the speech, Virginia felt shattered. She knew that Maclean had affected everyone. Duncan's fists were pushed deep into his jacket pockets. The buttoned jacket was of thin, cheap material and too short and too tight for him. On his head was a cloth cap pulled well down.

'What courage the man has!' Duncan exclaimed, 'To stand up for his beliefs like that. But I reckon he'll pay dearly for those brave words. They'll find some excuse to send him to prison.'

'For goodness sake, Duncan, surely not!' Virginia had protested.

'Right enough,' Ian agreed, 'the greedy bastards that are taking full advantage of the war don't want someone like him stirring up trouble. And there's plenty of folk who'll take his side now they're making us work longer and longer hours and not paying us enough to survive.'

'Aye,' Duncan said. 'It's only too true what Maclean said about industrial slavery under the Munitions Act. I'm with him a hundred per cent. And I'll fight against the capitalist class any day, rather than join their bloody army and murder German workers in the name of King and Country.'

'I'm with you all the way,' Ian fervently agreed.

Virginia had never seen her brothers so fired up. Having listened to John Maclean, she understood how they felt. At the same time, she began to understand her mother's concern and wondered where all this would end.

1915

7

After a few weeks Virginia was moved to a machine shop. There she had to use a heavy industrial press to finish the detonators. It was a task that demanded great care and attention to detail. She had a box of twelve detonators and she had to place one at a time inside a metal cup, put it into the machine and pull a lever. On one occasion a slightly faulty detonator nearly cost her her life, the only thing that saved her was that she had taken the precaution of closing her box of twelve before operating the lever. If the uncut detonators in the box had exploded, she would have gone up with them. As it was, only her hands had been injured.

Later her mother asked anxiously, 'Do you think they've moved you in there out of spite because you've joined the union?'

'No, it's nothing to do with that. Lots of other girls have been moved there in the past. It's what happens. Everybody gets moved from one place to another. I suppose it's so we learn all sides of the job.'

She had been reluctant to join the union at first, and especially to take such an active part in its work. Not because she didn't believe in what it stood for or what she'd argued for. It was just because of her pregnancy. She would have to leave once she began to show. Then, once the baby was born, the chances were, even if her mother looked after it, that they wouldn't take her back. What was the use of getting too involved? Yet, despite these misgivings, she had stood on a soapbox outside the works and rallied all the girls to approach the foreman and demand a canteen. They elected her to speak for them, and gave her their full support. She explained to the foreman and a manager who also appeared on the scene that it would be to everyone's advantage if the girls were able to sit down and have a decent meal. They'd be able to work harder as a result and so produce more. The girls shouted that if they didn't get a proper canteen that sold decent hot food at dinner time, they'd down tools. Whichever argument it was that won the day, one way or another they got what they wanted. Even so, when they got their canteen it was as much as they could do to afford to eat there, but still it was worth it.

Virginia had been four months pregnant when she was moved to the machine shop. Five months into her pregnancy she was moved to the spinning room. It was here that the springs of the fuses were tested. It was the most exacting job of all, requiring good eyesight and constant vigilance to ensure the accuracy of the spring. This procedure caused a fine haze of dust and chemicals to drift about the room, and Virginia soon discovered that it made her skin and her clothes turn yellow. This in turn made her mother's rag rug, her cushion and her blankets turn yellow. Everything Virginia touched took on a yellow hue. Virginia kept apologising but her mother always just said, 'Never mind, hen. As long as you're safe and well.'

She hadn't told her mother—and had warned Ian not to mention it either—of the two most recent accidents in the machine rooms. A man in Ian's room had two of his fingers cut off by an automatic machine. Then a girl who had bent down to pick up some work she had dropped got her cap and her hair caught up in the flywheel of her machine, and was scalped. It was only too true what Duncan had said. The munitions factory was a very dangerous place, and the long hours and exacting work were taking their toll. Virginia began to wonder how much longer she could stand it.

Six months into her pregnancy the chemicals began affecting her skin, not only turning it yellow. Her face, neck and legs began to swell. On being examined by the works doctor, TNT poisoning was diagnosed. The skin broke and fluid escaped. She was bandaged and told to go home and stay there for ten days. For the second time since she went to work there, Virginia was lucky to survive. TNT poisoning often proved fatal and many of those she worked with were not so fortunate. Her mother was in great distress by this time.

'Look hen, that place is killing you. Nothing is worth risking your life for. Certainly not for the pittance they pay you at that place.'

But it wasn't fear for her own life that made Virginia decide not to go back. There was her unborn child to consider—she had no right to risk its life.

'I know. Once I've recovered, I'll look for something else.'

After about a week, she began healing nicely and was beginning to think about going out to search for another job when she was surprised by the sudden appearance of Fanny Gordon in the house. She was in fact more than surprised. She was astounded when her mother, after going to answer a knock on the door, appeared back in the kitchen accompanied by the frizzy-haired scullery maid.

'Fanny!' Virginia gasped. She had never given Fanny or any of the staff her exact address. They knew she came from the Gorbals, that was all. Anyway, why would Fanny want to seek her out, especially during working hours?

'The mistress sent me. She found out that we were pals.'

Virginia gazed at the girl in puzzled bewilderment.

'The mistress sent you?' she echoed incredulously.

Fanny nodded. 'Och it's terrible, so it is. Even I'm feeling sorry for her. She went as white as a sheet and had to lie down. The lady's maid had to give her smelling salts.'

'I don't know what you're talking about, Fanny.'

Janette interrupted, 'The kettle's on the boil. I'll make a nice wee cup of tea.'

Fanny said, 'Oh thanks, Mrs Watson. I feel terrible, so I do. So does everybody in the house.'

'About what?' Virginia cried out in desperation.

Tears welled up in Fanny's eyes. 'It's the young master. A telegram came to say he'd been killed in action. Cook's awful upset. So is Mr Cartwright, but Mrs Cartwright's the worst. In a right state she is. I mean, we couldn't help feeling sorry for her.'

Virginia couldn't talk. Her voice was trapped in the lump that was growing in her throat. Her mother was saying, 'Poor woman. There's nothing worse in the whole world than a mother losing a child. And the poor young man. Och, this war is a terrible thing. All those boys dying out there and for what?' She paused for a moment, lost in thought, before recovering herself and asking, 'Why did she send you here, hen? Was it just to tell Virginia because Virginia used to work there?' Janette looked puzzled.

'No,' Fanny said, 'it was to bring her back with me. Mrs Cartwright's going to their holiday house down the Clyde somewhere for

49

a few months—to see if it'll help her, I suppose. She wants to take Virginia with her. She'll probably take some other servants as well. I hope she takes me.'

The puzzlement still clung to Janette. 'But why Virginia, I wonder?'

'Och, maybe she feels guilty now about sending her packing the way she did, and she's trying to make up for it. The loss of her son has made her see things different maybe. Anyway, she said I was to bring Virginia back.'

'Well, there you are,' Janette addressed her daughter. 'She must have been fond of you after all.'

'Fond of me?' Virginia gasped. 'Mammy, you don't know her like I do. . . .'

'I know the poor woman's lost her only son and must be in need of help and comfort.'

And I've lost my only love, Virginia was thinking broken-heartedly. She wanted to be on her own so that she could weep but she knew no amount of weeping would bring either help or comfort. Fanny was telling Janette he was such a nice fellow. 'Always ready with a smile, so he was. Nice looking as well. It's a shame, so it is. I left Mrs Tompkins—that's the cook—crying her eyes out. Oh, come on Virginia, you can't say no. Anyway, think of the nice long holiday you'll have doon the watter.'

Janette brightened. 'That's right, Virginia. It'll do you a power of good. It's just what you need. Come on now, I'll help you pack your trunk.' Then to Fanny, 'She's been near death's door herself, you know. TNT poisoning. She's been working in that awful munitions factory. It hasn't being doing my Ian's health any good either, I can tell you. I'll be losing him if he doesn't get out of there. I worry myself sick about him.'

'I'd be scared to work in a place like that,' Fanny said. 'You could be blown up at any minute, so you could.'

Janette had hauled Virginia's tin trunk from underneath the hole-in-the-wall bed, had taken Virginia's uniform apron, dress and cap from the dresser drawer and packed them neatly into the trunk.

'Good job we washed and ironed these after you came home.'

'Mammy, you don't understand. I can't bear the thought of going back there.'

'Fanny says Mrs Cartwright's going down the Clyde to her holiday home so you won't be going back to the house for long.'

Virginia was seeing Nicholas in her mind's eye and thinking, 'Please God, don't let him have suffered. I can't bear the thought of him suffering.' She became more and more distraught and less and less able to stop her mother and Fanny forcing her to leave. Fanny picked up the trunk, Janette helped Virginia on with her jacket and buttoned it up as if her daughter was a child again.

'Now on you go, hen. I'll feel so much happier if you're away getting some nice fresh air into your lungs instead of all that poison. I'll miss you, of course, but as long as you're all right, I'll be all right.' Then to Fanny, 'How long did she say?'

'A few months.'

'Och well, you won't be able to come home on your days off, Virginia, but you will write, won't you, and I'll look forward to seeing you when you get back. All right, hen?'

In a daze of distress, Virginia felt herself being hustled out of the kitchen and out of the house. All she could think of was 'Oh Nicholas, Nicholas! Oh my love!'

An anger at God began to fill her heart and mind. How could He destroy such a beautiful, talented young man. It was too cruel, too senseless. Then bitterness rose to the surface. God, if there was a God, had nothing to do with it. It was the men who had started this bloody war who had destroyed Nicholas. She wanted to weep and sob and howl against the generals, the politicians, the capitalists. She hated them all. She felt mad with hatred, hysterical with it. She shivered and shook with it.

'Are you all right?' Fanny asked.

'No,' Virginia said. 'I'm not bloody all right.'

'Och, don't worry. Mrs Smithers gave me money for our fare. So we don't need to walk all the way. We should be in time for our dinner. And Mrs Cartwright'll be all right to you, you'll see. She wouldn't have asked you to come back if she wasn't sorry for throwing you out as she did.'

Fanny half pushed, half lifted Virginia onto a tram car. 'I know there'll be a bit of a walk at the other end. But we can take plenty of rests.'

Virginia stared blindly out of the tram window, lost in a nightmare. It was impossible for her to return to the place that held so many memories of him. She couldn't face it. Yet she sat on in helpless despair, unable to resist whatever fate had in store for her.

8

The meal in the kitchen of Hilltop House was a gloomy one. Hardly anyone spoke. Eventually Mrs Tompkins said, 'It just shows how bad the mistress has taken it when she sent for Virginia. Virginia of all people. The poor woman's gone right off her head.'

This roused Virginia to say sarcastically, 'Oh thanks very much.'

'You know what I mean, hen.'

Virginia wasn't sure that she did.

'She never liked you before.'

That was true enough.

Maisie spoke up then. 'I don't think liking comes into it with her. I don't think she likes any of us. She probably never even thinks of us. Not as human beings anyway.'

'I think she feels guilty about Virginia,' Fanny said. 'Fancy throwing her out like that, without even a minute's notice.'

Maisie shook her head. 'She doesn't normally show signs of guilt. Remember poor Mary. She never showed any guilt or remorse about what she did to her, and Mary with that invalid mother depending on her as well.'

'Aye, but it's different this time.' Mrs Tompkins sighed. 'That's what I'm trying to say. She's been knocked off balance with the terrible news. Her nerves are all to pot. Her feelings are running away with her.'

Maisie looked doubtful. 'She's not taking hysterics or anything. She's just sitting up there as if she's frozen solid. Mr Cartwright's trying to put a brave face on it but you can see he's awful cut up.'

'Poor souls,' Mrs Tompkins said. 'You cannae help feelin' sorry for them.' Then turning to Virginia, 'You'd better away up. It's nearly the time she said.'

Virginia felt more like lying down in bed in a dark room to try to sort things out in her mind. It was urgent to find some way to control her inward hysteria, to find a brave face that she could put on. The last thing she needed was to stand before Mrs Cartwright.

'Away you go,' Mrs Tompkins repeated, this time with an impatient edge to her voice. 'Don't just sit there.'

As if sleepwalking, Virginia made her way upstairs and into the hall. She knocked on the drawing room door.

'Enter!' Mrs Cartwright's voice sounded as cold and as hard as ever. Despite her own sadness, Virginia was shocked at the change in Mrs Cartwright. She seemed to have aged ten years. Although it was only a few days since she had received the fateful telegram, her cheeks were sunken, making her nose look even longer and sharper and her mouth smaller and tighter. Her features reminded Virginia of a picture of a vulture she'd seen in one of her books. But in Mrs Cartwright's small beady eyes there was a look, not just of suffering, but of madness.

Mr Cartwright was sitting in one of the deep buttoned chairs at the opposite side of the fire. He said,

'You have been told about the death of my son?'

'Yes, sir,' Virginia said.

'Naturally we are extremely distressed at the loss of our only child.'

Virginia said, 'All the staff are very distressed as well. He was a very well respected and admirable young man.'

'Thank you, Virginia,' Mr Cartwright said. 'Now my wife and I have a proposition to make to you.' He hesitated. 'This is most difficult and distressing for us both but it's got to be done. You are pregnant with our son's child.'

'Yes.' Virginia's voice turned wary.

'Our grandson.'

Virginia made no comment. It was now occurring to her what they were after, why they had sent for her. She felt faint. Surely they couldn't try to take her baby away from her? Even though they were wealthy and powerful, surely she had the right to keep her baby. They couldn't do this to her. She wouldn't let them.

'If you are suggesting,' she managed in a cold voice, 'that you have any claim to my baby, Mr Cartwright . . .'

'The child is all we have left of our son.' Mrs Cartwright spoke up for the first time.

'That does not alter the fact, Mrs Cartwright, that the baby I give birth to is my child, not yours.'

Mr Cartwright said, 'We could give him every advantage in life. We would deny him nothing. What could you give the child, Virginia? I know where you live. I know the mortality statistics. Do you? What do you imagine the child's chances are of surviving even his first few months?'

'I'll love him and do my very best for him.'

'Oh yes?' Mrs Cartwright spat out the words. 'Like you've been doing already. We know all about how you've been exposing yourself to filthy infections. God alone knows what harm you've done to the child already.'

Virginia felt confused. Had they been having her watched? Had they been asking about her at the factory?

'You talk about love, Virginia,' Mr Cartwright said. 'Did you love my son?'

Before Virginia could answer, Mrs Cartwright cried out in bitter disgust, 'Love? Love? How can you even mention the word in the same breath as that immoral creature's name?'

Virginia was fighting back her tears now. 'Yes, Mr Cartwright,' she managed, 'I loved Nicholas very much indeed. And I believe I knew him better than either of you. Did either of you know he wanted to be a poet?' Her voice cracked. 'That's all he ever wanted to do. He didn't want to go into your business, or to go into the army. He just wanted to be a writer. You didn't know that, did you?'

Virginia's outburst was followed by a long silence before Mr Cartwright sighed and said, 'No, I knew nothing of this.'

'And you wouldn't have understood it even if you had. I was the only one who helped and encouraged him. For a short time at least, he was happy. That's what I have of him, as well as his baby. The memory of his joy at being able to write. It wasn't me that made him happy, it was his writing.'

Another silence.

'You say you knew him,' Mr Cartwright said. 'Do you really believe he would want his child brought up in a slum in the Gorbals. Would he really wish on his child the real dangers of illness and death there. You must try to face the truth of this, Virginia.'

She had been trying for months now not to face the truth of this.

She knew in her heart that to love someone—to truly love them, meant giving them up as she had done with Nicholas. She had loved Nicholas, and still loved him—would always love him—and she had been happy for him to get the best out of life in his work, in his marriage, in his proper place in society.

'Do you realise what you are asking?' she said. 'You are asking a mother to give away her child. How can I do that? It's too cruel.'

'To you perhaps.'

'There's no perhaps about it, Mr Cartwright. I can't do it.'

'But what about the child? Think of the child, Virginia. You're young. You will no doubt get married eventually to someone of your own class. You'll have other children. Think of this child, Virginia. Nicholas's child. If you loved him, if you love the child, you would want him to have a good life. You would want him to claim his birth right. Nicholas's child does not belong in the Gorbals, Virginia. He belongs here.'

Virginia twisted her hands together. She felt ill. The baby was kicking and moving inside her as it had never done before. She imagined that it was urging her to do the right thing, that it was desperately trying to tell her not to deny it this chance.

Mrs Cartwright spoke up. 'You would come with me right away. You would stay in our holiday home in Helensburgh. For the few remaining months until the baby is born, you will live like a lady. I will engage temporary staff there who do not know you. You will enjoy fresh air, good food, every care and attention so that you will be sure to have a successful delivery of a healthy child. This is a once in a lifetime opportunity for you. You must realise that. The chance to live like a lady for a few months. Who else of your class would ever be able to enjoy such good fortune?'

Virginia felt like killing the older woman. It was as much as she could do to keep her hands off her. 'Enjoy such good fortune?' Virginia had never felt so grief-stricken, so distressed, so lacking in good fortune, in her life. 'How can you talk about me enjoying good fortune when you are asking me to give up my child?'

Mr Cartwright rose and stood, hands behind his back, his back to the fire. 'Look, Virginia, we could take this to law. Is that what you want? And do you really believe that any court of law, any judge, would decide that the child's best interests would be served by allowing it to remain with you? Compared with all the advantages we can bestow. I hardly think so, do you?'

And of course, Virginia thought bitterly, the Cartwrights had friends in high places. They had many powerful and influential friends.

Mr Cartwright said, 'Do you really want to endure a long and painful legal dispute over this?'

His wife joined in. 'We'll stop at nothing, you know. We *are* going to have our grandson. He is all we have left of our son.'

Oh, they'd stop at nothing all right. Virginia was certain of that. She said, 'Anyway, what will everyone think if you suddenly appear with a baby? How will you explain it?'

'I have already told Mrs Smithers,' Mrs Cartwright said, 'that the daughter of my late cousin lost her husband in the war and she is expecting his child.'

Virginia could see that would sound believable enough. The telegraph boy was now a dreaded and all too frequent sight. Already he'd been twice to Cumberland Street.

'I have said,' Mrs Cartwright continued, 'that the sea air would do her good and we could help and comfort each other if she came to stay a few months with me there. When I return eventually with the baby, I'll simply say that my relation has died.'

'I see,' Virginia said. 'You have it all thought out.'

'Yes. Mrs Smithers will explain to the staff after I've gone. She will tell them that they have to remain here to look after Mr Cartwright. Also that my relation is bringing her own maid and cook/housekeeper. You are coming to skivvy.'

'I haven't said I'm going anywhere with you for any reason.'

Mrs Cartwright's hollow cheeks flushed with anger. 'The quicker my grandson is away from the pollution of that filthy Gorbals place, the better. Are you wanting to be the death of him before he's even born? Is that what it is, you ignorant malicious girl.'

Mr Cartwright put up a restraining hand. 'Now, now, my dear. Talk like that will not accomplish anything. I'm sure Virginia wants the best for the child. I'm sure she knows what she must do for the best.'

She did, of course, but she could still not imagine how she could, in the end, actually part with her baby. It was unthinkable, and yet . . . She thought of her parents and brothers. Here was her chance to spare them from the shame of her condition.

Summoning her every last drop of courage, she said, 'Very well.

I'll come with you. I'll go and fetch my trunk.'

'No,' Mrs Cartwright said. 'The chauffeur will take it out and put it in the boot of the car. But you will not need anything from it for the next few months. We must, for appearances sake, try at least to make some attempt to make you look like a lady. I will supply you with some of my old clothes. They can be adjusted to fit you where necessary. There will be a dressmaker in Helensburgh if you have not the skill to alter the garments yourself.'

'Very well,' Virginia repeated stiffly. She hated the woman. She had always hated her. How she was going to live in close proximity to her for the next few months without murder being committed, she did not know.

9

Helensburgh was situated at the mouth of the Gairloch on a gently sloping hill. Most of the streets were lined with lush green trees. The houses were handsome villas that sat in large gardens shaded by trees and high bushes. The exception to this was the few central streets where there were shops, with respectable flats above them. There were also a few public buildings like the town hall and the hospital. A wide esplanade from which a pier jutted out ran along the seafront. There was also a public park, a recreation ground and a golf course which stretched across the old Luss road, commanding fine views of the Firth of Clyde. A walk or a drive along the Luss road opened up the wonderful vista of Loch Lomond, Ben Lomond and the grandeur of the mountain scenery beyond.

Virginia would have enjoyed her walks along the Luss road and the esplanade, had it not been for the stiff and silent company of Mrs Cartwright. Mrs Cartwright refused to allow Virginia out of her sight. Virginia had argued about it, lost her temper with frustration about it, all to no avail. She would have run away from the older woman in order to be alone to enjoy the beautiful scenery. Or even just for an hour or two's privacy. However, two facts made this impossible. Firstly Virginia was now swollen and clumsy and not able to run, secondly, Mrs Cartwright was a tall, strong and determined woman who would not have had any problem in physically detaining Virginia.

A strange relationship had been established between them. They were alone together practically every waking moment in the dining room, in the drawing room, in the garden, out walking. Virginia even suspected that Mrs Cartwright spied on her when she was asleep in the bedroom that adjoined the older woman's. Virginia believed that Mrs Cartwright's obsession was driving her close to the point of insanity. She kept anxiously asking Virginia if she felt all right. She had her regularly checked over by a local doctor despite the fact that the doctor kept assuring her that Virginia was a healthy young woman and that everything about the pregnancy was perfectly normal. Mrs Cartwright had given her a wedding ring to wear and had introduced her to the doctor as a poor relation whose husband had been killed in the war.

Mrs Cartwright had even called the doctor out when Virginia had suffered a bout of morning sickness. 'Even I know that morning sickness is normal during pregnancy,' Virginia protested to Mrs Cartwright. The doctor won't thank you for calling him out again, and over something so trivial.'

'I don't need thanks from the doctor. I pay him well and he knows he must come when I wish him to. And I too know about morning sickness. But it normally happens for the first two or three months. That has been my experience and that of all my friends. You could have developed some sort of complication.'

Virginia realised that all Mrs Cartwright's anxieties and concerns were not for her but only for the baby she carried, and her constant questions and anxious looks became almost unbearably irritating. She had no other conversation either with Mrs Cartwright, or with another living soul. Two daily women came in, one to do the cooking, the other to clean, but one way or another, Mrs Cartwright made it impossible for Virginia even to have a few words with them.

One evening, after more than a month of this torment and anxious nagging, Virginia's self-control snapped.

'How do I know that you're not going to give my baby the same unhappy life that you gave Nicholas?'

Mrs Cartwright's gaunt face turned a deathly grey, from which her eyes stared out in naked agony. 'Unhappy? How could he ever have been unhappy? We gave him everything money could buy!'

Virginia began to regret her outburst. There could be no denying the sincerity of Mrs Cartwright's grief, but she had undoubtedly neglected him. 'You never showed him any love or affection. First you shuttled him off to that nanny—a cold-hearted witch she was as well, according to what I've heard. You were always sending him away.'

'But . . . but . . . that's what everyone does. It was the proper thing. Everyone . . . everyone of my class employs a trained nanny. It is for the child's own good. What else could I do?'

Virginia wanted to say, 'Look after him yourself,' but knew without being told that this was not the proper thing in Mrs Cartwright's world, so she kept silent.

Then after a time, Mrs Cartwright cried out, 'The boarding school was the best in the country. We thought we were doing the best for Nicholas. And as for the army—that was his decision . . . his regiment was one of the finest in the land.' She paused in a vain attempt to regain her composure, as the tears began to roll down her face. 'If only he had listened to me, stayed at Hilltop House and gone into his father's business . . .'

Still Virginia kept silent. She had already told the Cartwrights about Nicholas's longing to be a writer. What was the point of repeating it now? Despite everything, she had no desire to distress Mrs Cartwright any further. She still nursed a simmering hatred of the woman, but she couldn't be malicious. She also couldn't help thinking that Nicholas would not want her to hurt his mother.

For the rest of that evening, they had sat opposite each other in the drawing room. Virginia continued as best she could with the baby's jacket she had been knitting. Mrs Cartwright's knitting lay on her lap while her long bony fingers twitched uselessly. The fire was sinking and instead of putting another log on the dying embers, Virginia said, 'I think I'll have an early night.'

'What?' Mrs Cartwright raised a distracted face.

'I'm going upstairs to bed.'

'Oh yes.' Mrs Cartwright rose, allowing her knitting to drop unheeded to the floor. She followed Virginia from the room. Later Virginia could hear her pacing the floor of her bedroom. She doubted that Mrs Cartwright had managed to get even one hour's sleep the whole night. She certainly looked dreadful the next day, so much so that Virginia said, 'You don't look at all well. I think we ought to call the doctor out to *you*.'

'What good can any doctor do me? He can't bring my son back.'

Virginia could not altogether understand the depth of the woman's grief. After all, she had hardly ever been in close contact with her son, far less shown the slightest sign that she loved him and cared about him, while he'd been alive. Unless of course Mrs Cartwright's real problem was guilt. Perhaps now she realised how she had treated her son and was suffering so acutely because she knew that it was too late to do anything about it.

That night Mrs Cartwright broke one of her long silences by saying unexpectedly, 'I did love him you know.'

'Yes,' Virginia soothed, 'I'm sure you did.'

'You don't believe me,' Mrs Cartwright cried out. 'Whatever else you do, don't you dare lie to me or patronise me.'

'All right,' Virginia said in exasperation. 'I can't see how you could have loved him. You didn't show any affection to Nicholas, did you? You never told him you loved him. Not when he was a child, not when he was a man, did you?'

Mrs Cartwright shook her head. 'I'm . . . I'm not that kind of person. I've never . . . my parents never . . .' Her voice tailed off, as she turned her face to the wall.

'She's remembering her own childhood,' Virginia thought, and for the first time she had a glimmer of understanding and sympathy.

Mrs Cartwright didn't know about love. At least she didn't know how to express it. She had probably never been shown love by her parents. Perhaps her life had been more bereft than Nicholas's. At least Nicholas had his dreams.

'Perhaps,' she chose her words carefully, 'Nicholas understood that.'

'What?' The tortured face turned back towards Virginia.

'Perhaps,' Virginia repeated, 'Nicholas understood how you felt and didn't blame you. I know he was a much more understanding and forgiving person than I am. And he loved you,' she added, although she did not in fact know whether Nicholas had loved either of his parents or not.

Mrs Cartwright's eyes filled with pathetic eagerness and hope. 'Did he? Do you really think he did?'

'Yes, I'm positive he did.'

'Did he tell you? Is that what he said?'

'Yes, he did. And he said those exact words.' Virginia felt uncomfortable lying like this but she felt obliged to continue for Mrs Cartwright's sake. The woman was desperate for reassurance.

Mrs Cartwright was visibly trembling now. 'Thank you, Virginia. Thank you for telling me.'

The rest of that evening passed in silence. Next day, however, the questioning began again. Virginia began to feel both their lives were becoming a charade. Mrs Cartwright wanted to know every word Nicholas had ever said about her. Virginia felt pressurised into building endless dialogues in which Nicholas expressed love and admiration for his mother, when in truth Nicholas had said very little—if anything—about her. Eventually, Virginia had to call a halt.

'Mrs Cartwright, I understand how you feel and how you want to know all this about Nicholas, but honestly I've told you all I can. I can tell you no more.'

'Of course, of course, Virginia, I understand, but if you just go over it again. That time he said . . .'

There was no escape. It began to exhaust Virginia and to distress her. She had intended putting the past—at least her memories of Nicholas—behind her. It was too hurtful to think of him and to remember what he had been like, to be with, and all that he had really said to her. Also to be telling so many lies about him, even with the best of intentions, began to seem like a betrayal of him. One day she burst into tears.

'Mrs Cartwright, I can't bear any more of this. Has it never occurred to you that for me to keep talking about Nicholas is upsetting. I loved him too, remember, and I miss him. If you won't—for my sake—stop tormenting me with so many questions, do it for the baby's sake. If you harm me, you'll harm Nicholas's child, remember. Try to think of it that way.'

'Yes, oh yes, of course.' Mrs Cartwright pressed her lips tightly together as if to prevent the escape of another single word. After that, they reverted to their long silences interrupted only by anxious queries about Virginia's health.

Then one night, two weeks earlier than the date the doctor had given them, Virginia went into labour.

10

Virginia let out a high-pitched scream.

'For God's sake, get the doctor.'

Mrs Cartwright's tall figure hovered by the bed.

'I telephoned him. There was no reply. I don't know what to do.'

'Try again,' Virginia gasped. 'Something's going wrong. I know it. It isn't the right date yet.'

'No, no.' Mrs Cartwright's voice was a low tight moan. 'Nothing must go wrong. I'll telephone again.'

She hastened from the bedroom in great agitation. In a matter of minutes she had returned.

'He must be out on another case.'

'Dear Jesus!'

Mrs Cartwright wrung out a face cloth from the basin of water on a nearby table. With a shaking hand, she wiped the sweat from Virginia's brow.

'Don't worry. I'll keep trying until I get him.'

'Don't worry? Don't worry?' Virginia screeched as another agonising pain gripped her. She grabbed at Mrs Cartwright, digging her nails into the older woman's arm. 'Dear Jesus!'

She clutched round Mrs Cartwright's waist and held tightly on to her. Awkwardly Mrs Cartwright patted Virginia's head.

'Everything's going to be all right.'

'How do you bloody know?'

'I've been through this. I know what labour pains are like.'

Another respite from agony came and Virginia relaxed thankfully into it. Mrs Cartwright continued,

63

'What worries me is the pains are coming so quickly. That could mean the baby's about to be born. I had a nurse and a doctor attending me. They saw to the actual delivery. I must try to contact the doctor again. I'll never forgive him if he doesn't arrive in time.'

She disentangled herself from Virginia's rough embrace and hurried from the room yet again. She returned distraught, mumbling half to herself, 'No reply. This is awful. Absolutely awful.'

As she entered the bedroom, she was stunned by the sight that met her eyes. The bedclothes had slipped from the bed and Virginia was lying, legs bent and knees splayed out, screaming and sobbing and panting with pain.

'Good God,' Mrs Cartwright cried out. 'I can see the head! What am I going to do?'

'You'll always be the same,' Virginia sobbed. 'You'll be the same with the baby. You won't know what to bloody do. You never will. You'll be bloody useless, just as you are now.'

Mrs Cartwright took a deep shuddering breath and went over to the bed. 'I was told to push. I remember. That's what you must do.' She spoke calmly now. Calmly and encouragingly.

'It's nearly there. That's right. Good girl. Good girl.'

Sweat was now pouring over Virginia's eyes. Eventually she became aware that the pain had stopped. The sweet relief of it. She was totally exhausted. She was faint and sinking into blackness with exhaustion, but when she heard the infant's cry, she struggled back to consciousness.

'My baby!' She tried to raise herself on one elbow.

The room was empty.

'Mrs Cartwright,' she called out.

Mrs Cartwright, flushed with triumph, appeared in the doorway.

'I telephoned again. The doctor's on his way. But I did everything.'

Virginia nodded. 'Yes, you did very well. Thank you.'

'I helped my grandson to come into the world.' Mrs Cartwright was euphoric. 'I'll have the doctor check him of course but he seems a perfect, healthy little boy. A lovely little boy and he looks exactly like Nicholas when he was a baby. I'm going to call him Nicholas.'

Weak tears streamed down Virginia's face. 'I want to see him.'

'No.' Mrs Cartwright looked alarmed. 'It would be better if you didn't.'

'I want to see him,' Virginia repeated.

'You promised. You gave your word, Virginia. For the child's own good, remember. If you saw him, you'd want to keep him. I can't risk that. I can't risk you taking him to the Gorbals. I care for the child's safety and well being, even if you don't, Virginia.' She flushed slightly and tipped up her chin. 'And I will show him love and affection. I promise you. I will not make the same mistake with my grandson that I did with my son.'

'I won't take him away. I want what's best for him. But I need to see him and hold him just for a few minutes. Please, Mrs Cartwright.'

After a minute's hesitation, Mrs Cartwright said, 'All right. But I'm trusting you Virginia. . . .'

She brought the baby in from the other room. He had been bathed and wrapped in a shawl that had once held Nicholas.

Virginia stretched out her arms. Then gently, tenderly cuddled the warm little body close to hers.

'He is beautiful.'

'Yes.'

'Could you do me one last favour?'

Mrs Cartwright looked wary.

'What?'

'Don't call him Nicholas. He needs to be his own person, loved for his own self.'

'What do you suggest?'

Virginia kissed the downy head. 'I don't know. Richard perhaps.'

'Richard.' Mrs Cartwright savoured the word. 'Richard Cartwright. Yes, it has a good ring to it. Richard it will be then.'

The sudden clang of the doorbell startled them both.

'That'll be the doctor,' Mrs Cartwright said. 'I'll put Richard back in his cot now.'

'Please, let me hold him until the doctor leaves.'

'He'll want to examine you. And the baby. You can't hold him while he's doing that. Quick now, give him to me. I must answer the door.'

She forcibly prised the child from Virginia's arms before hurrying from the room. It was as if she had carved a piece of flesh from Virginia's body. Virginia moaned with the pain of it. To come to terms with her loss she tried to keep visualising the difference between Hilltop House and the room and kitchen in the Gorbals. She had to keep reminding herself of the unsanitary conditions, the stench of the overflowing lavatories. They were always becoming blocked and sending a stinking, germ-laden river down the stairs and through the close. She forced herself to think of the lack of space, the icy cold water, how the little boy would be deprived of every comfort.

Whereas at Hilltop House he would have everything he needed for his health and well being. She had no right to deny him these things. If she loved him she had to let him go. But, oh, the pain of it.

Mrs Cartwright left early next morning. She was standing stiff-backed in the bedroom when Virginia woke up. She was dressed in her outdoor clothes, a wide-brimmed hat decorated with ostrich feathers and ribbons, a long cut-away coat, gloves and button boots.

'I've told the housekeeper to look after you,' she said. 'I have given her another two weeks' wages. I have left an envelope for you on the dressing table. In it you will find enough money for your return journey and a little extra to tide you over until you can find work.'

'You're leaving now?' Virginia could not believe it. 'Right now?'

'There's no reason for me to stay any longer.'

There was an awkward silence. Virginia felt shocked. Mrs Cartwright's face was an expressionless mask.

'The housekeeper will take good care of you. There is no longer any reason for me to remain. And I see no reason why our acquaintance should be further prolonged. Richard is mine now, and I do not expect ever to see or hear from you again.' Mrs Cartwright's expression softened slightly. 'You have made the right decision, Virginia. Now get on with the rest of your life.'

Now, on top of Virginia's anguish about giving up her baby, she felt another layer of hurt. She chastised herself about it. Why should she feel hurt at Mrs Cartwright's sudden departure. How had she been expecting Mrs Cartwright to behave? What had she been expecting her to do? Nevertheless she did feel hurt. Hurt and used, disappointed and depressed.

For a few days, she couldn't even be bothered eating. She just turned her face to the wall and lay under a black cloud that was too heavy to fight against, even if she'd wanted to. Then she'd overheard a conversation between the housekeeper and the other servant.

The housekeeper was saying, 'I know, and the poor lady had to take the baby away to look after it. Of course, the girl has lost her husband.'

'So have thousands of other folk.' The other servant sounded indignant. 'I know five women in our street who've lost their men and they didn't lie about like her feeling sorry for themselves. They've had to get on with life.'

'Aye,' the housekeeper sighed. 'It's an awful business. I know a few poor souls like that myself. One woman, Mrs Spencer, has lost her husband and her two sons.'

'My God. Is that not terrible?'

'Aye. I saw her just the other day. There she was with the dignity of a queen and a smile and a brave nod for everybody. Wonderful woman. Her men would have been proud of her.'

Virginia felt ashamed. She struggled up right away, washed and dressed and rang the bell for a cup of tea and something to eat. Her anguish and depression did not go away but she began to fight against them. She had done the right thing for her son. Now she must, as Mrs Cartwright said, get on with the rest of her life. She could not force herself to have any conversation with the two women who continued to come in daily but at least she made herself get up every day, eat properly and go out for walks in the fresh air. By the time the house was due to be locked up and she had to leave, she at least felt physically recovered.

Returning on the train bound for Glasgow's Central Station, she began to think of what she could do to start earning some money. Mrs Cartwright had added a few pounds extra to the rail fare. The money meant nothing to her—all she cared about was that they would give a good home and a good upbringing to Richard. She had every confidence that they would do so, and that they would spare no expense, no trouble, to give their grandson every advantage in life. Hopefully they would show him plenty of love and affection too. He was a lucky little boy. She must cling to this thought for now and be glad for him.

Virginia realised that she could go back to the munitions factory. She did say this to her mother after she had been welcomed back into the family home. But her mother had become so distressed, she was forced to give up the idea. Although she secretly knew that if she couldn't find any other employment, she'd have no choice but to return there.

'I'm nearly distracted with worry as it is with Ian being in that place day and night.' Her mother said, 'He does as many night shifts as day shifts and it means I can't sleep for worrying about him now. There's been so many accidents in that place.'

'Ian's all right,' Virginia said, trying to cheer her up. But she knew that Ian was Janette's favourite and if anything happened to him it would destroy her. She looked like death as it was. She'd lost weight, and her face had a sunken look.

'Mammy,' Virginia said eventually, 'I think you should go and see the doctor. You don't look well. I'm worried about you.'

'Do you know how much it is to see a doctor?' Janette asked. 'You surely think I'm made of money.'

'I've got a wee bit extra with working in Mrs Cartwright's holiday home. I'll pay for the doctor. Please go, Mammy. I'll come with you.'

'Well, all right, hen. Just to please you.'

Virginia braced herself for the bad news that she feared the doctor would give them. But before they even reached the surgery, they heard other news that shocked not only them but the whole of Glasgow.

II

They heard the explosion. It was muted, far off, but they felt the tremor under their feet. As the tremor subsided, a pall of black smoke was rising in the distance. Instinctively, they knew what it meant.

'Oh no,' Janette's shoulders hunched and she tightened her shawl under her chin. 'Please God!'

'It might not be the works,' Virginia said but not very convincingly. It was the munitions works all right. She frantically prayed that Ian was not one of the casualties. Please God, no, she was thinking along with her mother. Please God, no!

They had been on their way to the doctor's surgery but were stopped in their tracks. Janette leaned heavily on Virginia's arm. She said, 'We'd better go back.'

Virginia didn't argue but just held tightly to her mother's arm and turned her back towards Cumberland Street. In the house she led the dazed Janette to a chair and then put the kettle on. It was always on the hob and didn't take long to come to the boil.

'It might not be the works, mammy,' Virginia repeated.

Janette didn't answer. She was just staring sightlessly ahead. Outside a back court entertainer had begun singing 'The Old Rugged Cross'. Virginia jerked open the kitchen window and flung out a coin, at the same time shouting, 'For God's sake, away you go. My mammy's not well.' Then she retreated back into the kitchen and shut the window. She put out a couple of cups. The milk and sugar were already on the table.

'Come on, mammy, drink this. I'll go and see if I can find out what's happened.'

She had to hold the cup to her mother's lips. 'Come on, mammy. Please. It'll make you feel better.'

Janette made an attempt to rally. She accepted the cup and held it between her palms.

'Thanks, hen. On you go.'

Outside in the close, Virginia stood for a moment to gather her courage. She was hardly aware of the briquette man as he passed by, whirling his wooden rattle and bawling, 'Coal briquettes, coal briquettes, ye'll all be cauld if ye forget, yer coal briquettes.'

Ian might be safe. And in any case, it wouldn't do any good if she went to pieces now. If anything had happened to Ian, her mother would need her. She had to be strong for her mother and father's sake. Duncan's too. He and their father would have been waiting as usual outside the wall of Dixons in the hope of getting work. They would have heard the explosion. Virginia's feet quickened through the narrow cobbled streets that were crowded with barefoot children and women standing in close mouths gossiping. Some had babies wrapped in their shawls.

Reaching Dixons Blazes, as the blast furnace was nicknamed, Virginia gazed anxiously at the crowd of men, some shuffling around the gates, some trudging back and forth alongside the high brick wall. Others were huddled together against the wall. All were dressed like Virginia's father in thin trousers tied with string beneath the knees, shabby jackets, white fringed mufflers and cloth caps pulled well down over their brows as if to hide the misery in their eyes.

Virginia spotted Duncan first because he was taller and heavier-built than the rest. Tougher looking too with his broken nose and dour aggressive look. Most of the younger men, like the older ones, were thin and emaciated, with lacklustre eyes.

'Duncan,' she called out. 'Have you heard anything about that explosion? Mammy's worried in case it's where Ian works.'

'Aye, it's in the factory, they say. Da's away there to see what he can find out. He told me to stay here in case I missed a job. But there's nothing doing. Even if I did get offered work I wouldn't be able to concentrate. I told Da. He shouldn't be long if you want to wait.'

They stood in silence among the shuffling crowd of men for a few minutes. Then Duncan said, 'Here he comes.'

They knew as soon as they saw his tear-stained face that the worst had happened.

70

'Oh Christ,' Duncan said.

Virginia ran towards her father. He shook his head.

'It was his department. All killed. All killed. . . .' He shook his head again as the tears streamed down his cheeks and gathered wetly on the edges of his moustache. 'He was such a cheery soul. Everybody liked him.'

Duncan reached him and grabbed hold of his arm. Virginia linked into Tam's other arm.

'Come on home, daddy,' she said.

'Had you no' better stay, son?' Tam's tragic gaze turned on Duncan. 'What if a job comes up?'

'Da,' Duncan said firmly, 'I'm coming home with you. We need to stick together at a time like this.' Then, 'Who's going to tell Ma?'

Virginia said, 'She'll know as soon as she sees us. I think she knows already. When we heard the explosion . . .' She couldn't continue. She was thinking 'Why couldn't it have been me instead of Ian. What have I got to live for?'

They made the journey home slowly, reluctantly, each dreading Janette's reaction to the dreadful news.

She was sitting exactly where Virginia had left her, still clutching at the tea cup. Virginia gently took the cup from her.

'I'll make some fresh, mammy.'

'It won't make me feel any better, hen. Nothing will. Not ever again.'

'Ma, Ian thought the world of you,' Duncan said. 'He wouldn't want you to be sad.'

'Aye,' Tam said. 'He was a good lad.'

'Did you go?' Janette asked Tam.

'Aye. They told me the whole department went up. Aw those good men. And for what? To line the bosses' pockets. Ian never complained, but he knew what the bosses were like. They were aw working longer and longer hours for less and less money. And this is their reward. . . .'

'Daddy,' Virginia protested. 'This isn't the time for politics.'

'It's exactly the time,' her father said angrily. 'By God, it is. This bloody war that our Ian died for is a war for trade. Never mind all that King and Country nonsense!'

'All right, all right, Daddy.'

'No, it is not all right. I've just lost my son because of them. The rumour is that some of these firms are selling war material to neutrals.

Knowing full well they're being resold to Germany. They don't care who they sell them to. As long as they make their bloody profits.'

Duncan touched his father's arm. 'I know you're angry, Da—'

'Of course I'm bloody angry. I've a right to be bloody angry.'

'I know. And so am I. But you're upsetting Ma.'

Tam sat down on the nearest chair.

'I'm sorry, hen. It's just . . .'

'I know, Tam,' Janette said.

Virginia poured out the tea.

'Have we any whisky?' she asked Duncan. 'A wee drop of whisky in the tea might help to steady us.'

Janette said, 'In the press.' She nodded towards the cupboard on the wall at right angles to the kitchen sink. Virginia found a half bottle that her mother kept for medical emergencies. She poured some into each cup.

They sipped from their cups in stunned silence. Soon there was a knock at the door. Virginia opened it and ushered in two of the upstairs neighbours—Mrs MacDougal and Mrs Friel.

'We've just heard.' Mrs Friel was a plump little woman with loose pouches of cheeks and a pink scalp shining through wispy grey hair. 'We're that sorry, hen. Is there anything we can do fur ye?'

'Aye, anything at aw, Mrs Watson.' Mrs MacDougal was thin and bent, with an unhealthily flushed face. Recently Janette had remarked, 'I think poor Mrs McDougal's got the consumption. She's just wasting away.'

'That's kind of you. Sit down and have a cup of tea. I'm sorry I haven't any scones or anything to offer you.'

'Don't be daft,' both the neighbours cried out. 'A cup of tea'll do us fine.'

Later in the day, they were both back, Mrs Friel with a plate of scones she had baked specially and Mrs McDougal with some home-made pancakes. A continuous stream of neighbours came and went during the next few days, all offering support and comfort.

Ian's body was brought home. The closed coffin was propped between two chairs in front of the room bed. Tam and Duncan slept in the bed, and Virginia shared the kitchen bed with Janette. The minister came the next day and gave the service and the coffin was carried out of the close and on to the hearse. Outside, strangers and neighbours alike took off their caps as a mark of respect, and stood silently as the hearse passed slowly along the street. And along the whole street every blind was drawn.

The women stayed behind in the house and prepared the formal tea for the men's return from the graveside. All the neighbours had contributed to the meal so that it could be the usual steak pie and peas, home-made scones and cakes. There were big pots of piping hot tea, as well as whisky, to warm the men up. It was a cold rainy day more like January than July.

The kitchen was packed with women all bustling and bumping into one another in the small space. They wouldn't allow Janette to do anything. One of them took the pulley down, removed all the washing that had been hanging from it and dangling over the table. She folded it, then stuffed it out of sight behind one of the bed curtains.

'Just you sit there and relax, hen,' they told Janette. 'We'll see to everything.' Janette allowed herself to be pushed into a chair. She sat with dull eyes and hands lying limp on her black-clad lap.

Virginia said, 'I'll see to the room.' She needed to be on her own for a few minutes. There she busied herself putting back the chairs that had held her brother's coffin. She rubbed the duster over them and the high chest of drawers and the window ledge. The room was in shadow because of the drawn blinds. It had an almost greenish tinge as if it was under water. There was the silent aura of death about it. Only then did the loss of her brother seem real. Before, it had been like a waking nightmare, now it was cold, dismal reality. She felt broken-hearted. Standing by herself in the centre of the gloom, she wept and sobbed until she was exhausted. Later, Mrs Friel came looking for her.

'Och, come on, hen. Here, use ma hanky. You've got to be brave for your mammy. That's the men back. Come through and help dish their tea. Or just sit and keep your mammy company. We can manage fine, don't worry.'

Virginia nodded, then dried her face.

'You've all been awful kind.'

'Och, what are neighbours for? You'd have done the same for us. Your mammy's helped us many a time. Are you going tae be all right now, hen?'

Virginia nodded.

'Come on through then.'

The men had the first sitting but even then it was a terrible crush at the table. There was much talk, even laughter now. Eventually the men went through to the room for a glass of whisky and a smoke. Some sucked at clay pipes. Others enjoyed a comforting puff at a Woodbine. The women gathered round the table for their meal. They too chatted away in an attempt to be normal and cheerful. Even Janette made a brave effort. So did Virginia.

It wasn't until much later, when the last guest had said their goodbyes and Virginia, Janette, Tam and Duncan were in the house alone, that silence descended once more. There was no longer any excuse or even energy left to put on a brave face, to pretend to be cheerful.

Tam said, 'I'll just go on sharing the bed with Duncan. It's not right that you sleep on the floor, Virginia.'

'Are you sure, daddy? I don't mind.'

'No, no, hen. You cuddle in with your mammy.'

None of them kissed each other goodnight. They'd never been a demonstrative family. Except Ian. He had always been easy going, open and affectionate.

Virginia put out the gas, climbed into bed and lay stiffly beside the equally stiff form of her mother. They didn't speak. There was nothing left to say.

12

Virginia had to find work as quickly as possible. Her mother was no longer able to go out scrubbing, and nowadays she was barely able to creep about the house. Her skin had gone an unhealthy putty colour and she had begun to suffer from breathlessness. It was as much as she could do to make a pot of tea or peel a few potatoes. Neither Tam nor Duncan could find a job. They might have been able to find work at the munitions factory, but their socialist, anti-war principles made that an impossibility. Virginia didn't blame them, especially after what had happened to Ian. She couldn't face going back there herself, and the thought of any of them working there now would have been more than her mother could bear. But something had to be done as there was now absolutely no money coming into the house.

The money Mrs Cartwright had given her had been used up. For a time she managed to get a few hours work each week at what her mother had been doing—scrubbing out pubs. It sickened her beyond measure each time she went into the stale, stinking places. The air was thick with the previous night's tobacco smoke. The floors were covered with vomit, and stained with dried-up beer. Added to this was the never-ending struggle to keep their close in Cumberland Street clean. Sometimes Virginia would just stand and stare helplessly at the narrow entrance to the tenement, with its paved corridor and stone stairs leading up to one of the communal lavatories and think, 'Why bother trying to keep this place decent? What's the use?' Her only comfort was that she hadn't brought her baby to this stinking hell hole. At least her son wouldn't have to suffer the deprivation of living like this.

Over and over again, she'd scrub the few yards of the close out through to the back, hardly able to see what she was doing because during the day only a dim light managed to penetrate the close. At night there was a feeble yellow flicker from the tiny gas mantle on the wall above the stair foot. All the stone steps were broken with jagged edges where bits of tread had fallen away. Care had to be taken going up to the lavatory, and most people at some time or other had fallen and injured themselves. The lavatory in the back close had long since become totally unusable. The whole place deeply depressed Virginia. She was depressed enough as it was with missing her baby, without having to look at walls with plaster coming away from ceiling to floor every miserable day. In the yard, stray cats and rats furiously scavenged and scattered the rubbish all over the broken flagstones. At first she had tried to sweep the yard and keep it tidy, but it was a hopeless task. Just as it was hopeless to try to keep the close, the stairs and the landing decent. They all kept trying, all of the neighbours, but the landlord now refused to have the lavatory fixed and so it went on overflowing. The mixture of urine and faeces kept cascading down the stairs, sickening everyone with the stench of it. No repairs or maintenance of any kind was ever done to the building. Yet the tenants were forced to pay ever-increasing rents.

Yet despite her depression, there was emerging in Virginia a sense of outrage. Her stay in Helensburgh had shown her how people with money lived, and she was angered that decent working-class folk should have to put up with such conditions as these. She and her father and brother fuelled each other's anger, and she began going with them to John Maclean's meetings. At one meeting in Bath Street, he told the audience that four hundred shipwrights at Fairfields had stopped work in protest against the Munitions Act—better known as the Industrial Slavery Act. Maclean said it was meant to tighten the chains of economic slavery on the workers. Virginia stood with the huge crowd, transfixed by the man's passionate address.

'You have lost,' he declared, his arms stretched out as if longing to encompass every soul there, 'the right to organise, the right to strike and the right to move from workshop to workshop. In ordinary times, the capitalists would find themselves faced with the unanimous opposition of the working class if they attempted to interfere with workers' liberty to move from one firm to another. In fact they did not make the attempt.' His lips tightened with contempt. 'But the war, the glorious war, gives them the opportunity, the excuse, they desire. . . . Comrades, capitalism is the right to rob you—you, the real creators of wealth. Capitalism must be killed, and it can be done in twelve solid months, starting any time, if the workers are ready. Emancipation of the working classes must be achieved by the working classes themselves.'

Soon after this, seventeen men from Fairfields were hauled before a Munitions Tribunal and each was fined £10 with an alternative of thirty days in prison.

Maclean exhorted the men not to pay the fine, promising that if they were sent to prison there would be an uproar and they'd have the support of all workers. Only three men followed his advice, but there was indeed an uproar and the Fairfields & Govan workers prepared for a strike. The union officials quickly took the matter into their own hands. The workers thought they were going to call a strike but instead they called for a government enquiry. That dragged on for so long that the union officials were discredited and lost their influence over the workforce. The real leaders, as Maclean always said, were to be found in the workshops.

By the end of October, Maclean was summonsed under the Defence of the Realm Act and his trial was fixed to take place a few weeks later. Both Tam and Duncan had now become active agitators and when yet another crippling rent rise was demanded they, and a great many others, refused to pay. This added worry was too much for Janette. She seemed to be shrinking before Virginia's eyes, bent like an old woman, her eyes staring and haunted.

'It's all right, mammy,' Virginia tried to reassure her. 'They can't evict you. We're all standing together and refusing to allow the factor even to get near any of the closes.'

'I'm not worried about that. I'm not worried about myself,' Janette said. 'It's Tam and Duncan. They're getting deeper and deeper into trouble. I'm worried about you as well, Virginia. I thought you were all pacifists, but there's nothing but anger and fighting all over Glasgow now and you're in the thick of it with the rest of them. Now we're all being sued at the Small Debt Court. I'm ashamed, Virginia. Me and all my good respectable neighbours getting sued for debt. I'd rather have paid the extra rent.'

'Mammy, you couldn't pay it. You haven't got the money. Anyway, nobody's going to pay it. We're going to collect John Maclean at his school and then gather in front of the court. The sheriff will have to back down.'

'I thought Maclean had been dismissed long since.'

'Oh, they're trying to dismiss him. It's a disgrace. It's because he's an atheist. He's refusing to fill all his pupils' heads with superstitious nonsense.'

'Virginia!' Janette trembled with distress. 'I don't want you to have anything to do with any atheists. You were brought up to be a good Christian girl.'

'Oh mammy!'

'He causes nothing but trouble, that John Maclean.'

'Yes, trouble for the capitalists and the bosses. Anyway, I've got to go now, mammy.'

Virginia rushed away to meet up with her father and Duncan at Lorne Street School in Govan. When she arrived there, they were talking to someone she hadn't met before. He was a sturdily built young man with short, tufty, brown hair, bushy brows and piercing eyes. He was introduced as James Mathieson, a teacher who worked with John Maclean and knew him well. When he shook hands with Virginia, she nearly cried out—he had such a strong grip her hand felt crushed. The mass of people who were now milling all around the school were shouting for Maclean. Virginia could see, in the way that he was lustily joining in the shouting with the others, that Mathieson shared much of Maclean's fervour.

Eventually the great man emerged from the school and Mathieson was one of those who rushed forward to carry him shoulder high through the streets until they reached the Sheriff Court. There, a crowd of over ten thousand people had gathered. Every street was packed and all traffic had been brought to a halt. Poster boards, picked up from newspaper shops, were improvised, placed on willing shoulders, and the speakers lifted onto them. Maclean was speaking directly in front of the court. Roars of rage kept erupting from the mass of listeners as they heard about the robbery and injustice of the factors. Inside the court, which was packed with a deputation from factories and yards, the Sheriff and his clerks sat ashen faced with anxiety. Eventually realising the situation was becoming dangerous, the panic-stricken Sheriff telephoned Lloyd George, who was then the Minister of Munitions. Lloyd George, looking to calm the situation, and no doubt influenced by the Sheriff's anxiety, told him to stop the case immediately and instructed him to announce that a Rent Restriction Act would be introduced as soon as possible.

When they heard this news, the crowd was elated and there was spontaneous dancing in the streets. Virginia found herself whisked off her feet by James Mathieson. Eventually everyone calmed down, and by the time the crowds dispersed Virginia was laughing and breathless.

'You don't know your own strength,' she told Mathieson. 'I'm so exhausted I can hardly stand.'

He locked her arm in his. 'Hang on to me and you'll be all right. Come on, we'll have a seat in the park for a wee while. Then I'll take you home.'

They found a seat in the park and although it was a cold November day, Virginia still felt flushed and hot.

Mathieson had begun talking about Maclean. 'His background is similar to mine, you know. His parents, like mine, were victims of the Highland Clearances. Like him, I've been brought up with tales of the suffering the landlords inflicted on our people. They forced our families—decent, hard-working folk—from their homes and farms and left them with nowhere to sleep, nothing to eat and no means of earning an honest living. Many of their friends had to take ships to America, husbands were parted forever from their wives, and parents never saw their children again.'

Mathieson's face darkened as he spoke, as if a heavy thundercloud was passing over it. 'My grandmother had to walk most of the way to Glasgow with my mother in tow and carrying her baby brother. My grandfather had walked the journey before her to find work and a roof over their heads. Much the same happened to John's parents and he hates the landowners as much as I do. The landowners and all the bloody capitalists.'

Virginia put her hand on his arm to comfort him, much as she'd once done with Nicholas. She felt the tremor of his distress and passion.

'I understand. Really I do. But it doesn't do any good to get so upset,' she told him gently. But he answered in a fury,

'Yes it does. It does! That has been the trouble. Nothing will ever change unless people have the will to stand up and be counted. I suppose that makes me a revolutionary.'

'Are you not a pacifist?'

'I will not fight and kill any working class man—in France, Flanders or anywhere else. Like Maclean says, the only war worth waging is the class war. The rich are nothing more than murderers. You only have to look around you at the misery we endure every day, while they live in pampered luxury.'

Virginia shivered and Mathieson immediately looked concerned.

'Are you cold? Do you want to go home now?'

'Yes. I didn't realise how cold it was before,' she said. 'Thanks to all that dancing.'

They began making their way out of the park, their feet crackling the frosty grass. Once more she was surprised at the natural way Mathieson tucked her arm through his. To anyone else it must have looked as if they were sweethearts and had known each other for years, instead of barely a few hours. He did not seem in the least conscious of anything unusual in his behaviour. As they walked, he talked of Maclean again and the beliefs that he shared with him.

Virginia couldn't help thinking of Nicholas and remembering him in his khaki uniform, remembering his gallantry and patriotism. He had gone to war with a heavy heart, yet believing that it was his duty to do so. She could not think of Nicholas as her enemy, just because he happened to belong to the class that Maclean and Mathieson so despised. Her depression returned. Thinking of Nicholas, her heart ached for him, and she suddenly felt utterly exhausted, not only by the events of the day but by James Mathieson's unrelenting bitterness.

'I'd better go in.' She said as they reached her close. 'I didn't realise how late it was. Mammy'll be worried.'

At last she managed to escape into the house. Janette, her shawl clutched tightly around her, was anxiously waiting.

'Where on earth have you been? Tam and Duncan are in their beds.'

Virginia flopped down onto a chair.

'With James Mathieson. What a talker that man is. I just couldn't get away from him. Did daddy tell you about what's happened with the rents?'

'Aye, but what's next? There's nothing but trouble nowadays. One thing after another.'

'That's not daddy's fault, mammy. It's the fault of the landlords.'

'Och, don't you start, I've had enough of that already the day. Fine words never fed anyone and all this talk isn't getting any food on the table is it? There isn't even a spoonful of tea left in the house.'

'I'll go out first thing tomorrow and look for a job.'

'Where? Surely not at the munitions works?'

'No. Not there. I'll find something else. I promise.'

Once she had undressed and climbed into bed, Virginia tried to think of some way, any way, to make money. Eventually she did think of something. There were the so-called 'old clothes' that Mrs Cartwright had given her. In fact they were good quality garments that might be worth quite a decent sum of money. If she could hire a wee barrow she could try to sell them. Barrows could be hired by the day, and there was always a whole line of them in Clyde Street alongside the river with traders selling everything from pins and needles to stags' heads. Although she was thankful she'd thought of a solution, albeit a temporary one, for her family's problems, at the same time she felt sad. The clothes, belonging to Nicholas's mother and the world he had belonged to, were her last link with him.

Then she remembered a few lines from one of the poems he had given her. It was called 'The Rocking Horse'.

I touch my ear to the soft stretch of skin
and hear the music of a new pulse.

Impending joy until
sharp fragments of memory
tear the gauze curtains of my past.

Runners dusty and cracked
supported hooves
that sparked on the golden trail
of my childhood.
Handles and stirrups
offered safe grip.

My father scolded,
thrust a tin soldier with gun
and hard eyes into my small
unwilling hands.

I touch my ear to the soft stretch of skin
And hear the music of a new pulse.

Its beat a balm to my past.

As she sobbed in silent grief, Virginia remembered also the words of James Mathieson—aggressive and filled with fury.

'I loathe and detest them. Every last one of the so-called upper classes. Come the revolution, you and I will see them stripped of everything they possess, ground into the dust by the righteous anger of the working class.'

Virginia could only be grateful that in his short life Nicholas had never been exposed to such hatred.

1916-17

13

'Squeeze yer barra in here, hen.' The woman grinned invitingly at Virginia before introducing herself. 'Ma name's Aggie—Aggie MacAllister.' She was a long, loose-bosomed woman in rolled-up shirt sleeves with a brown sacking apron tied round her waist.

'Mine's Virginia. Virginia Watson.'

'Virginia—sounds posh.'

'I come from Cumberland Street.'

'Ye even talk posh.'

Virginia laughed. 'Do I? I suppose that's with hearing folks talk in the big house. I used to be in service up there.'

'Fancy!' Aggie said. 'Is that where you pinched aw them fancy claes?'

'Oh no, I didn't steal them. The lady gave them to me.'

'Aye, like the King gave me aw them braces an' boots. Them are aw His Majesty's hats as well.'

'Honestly,' Virginia said. 'She told me they were her old clothes. She'd bought loads of new ones and didn't want these old ones any more.'

'They're bloody perfect.'

'I know. But that's how rich folk are. They get fed up with things and just buy more. Money's no object for them.'

'Well, yer best bet, hen, is a shopkeeper. Or any kinda better-off folk. Some o' them wander alang here lookin' fur a bargain. They'll huv mair cash tae gie ye a decent price. Anyway, best o' luck.'

'Thanks.'

People had begun to crowd round all the barrows in Clyde Street facing the expansive River Clyde. Most women in the crowd wore shawls over their heads and shoulders but there were some potential customers in wide brimmed or high crowned hats and long coats. Likewise, most men were in cheap, tightly buttoned jackets, with the usual white mufflers at their throats and cloth caps sitting squarely on their heads. But quite a few men were to be seen in collars and ties, and bowler hats, and homburgs. Virginia noticed that many of them were most interested in a nearby book barrow. The thought flickered through her mind that she could also sell her books, but she immediately shrank from the idea. Her books were like much-loved friends. Some of the barrow renters were shouting out encouragement to shoppers.

A fruit barrow man with his broad Glasgow bawl of, 'Honey Perrs. Honey Perrs. Mooth watterin' honey perrs.'

A frowsy fish woman wearing a long black skirt, a sackcloth apron and her man's cloth cap was crying out, 'Fresh finnan haddies—Gie yer man a treat. Gie him wan fur his tea. Go on, hen, he'll luv ye fur it.'

One of the book men was small and bandy legged, and had to stand on a stool to reach the books. Stiff-faced with cold, he kept stomping around his barrow and rubbing his hands in an effort to keep his circulation going. The icy breeze from the river was obviously cutting through his thin jacket. Virginia felt chilled to the bone herself, but at least she was healthy and strong. There were too many under-sized, bandy-legged folk in the poorer areas of Glasgow. This was usually the result of rickets, a disease which stunted childrens normal development. Rickets was caused, so Virginia had heard, by lack of proper nourishment. She was thankful that, despite her family's poverty, her mother had always managed to keep her family well fed— making nourishing pots of lentil or mutton broth, shepherd's pies and rice puddings. They seldom went hungry, especially when her father was working. She had happy memories of slices of fresh new bread liberally spread with pink-coloured Co-operative apple jelly. It was a long time since there had been such a mouth watering luxury in the Watson house. Virginia resolved that if she sold any of the clothes she'd buy a jar of apple jelly in the Co-op on her way home. It would be a treat and a nice surprise for her mother.

Before long, she had quite a crowd round her barrow, admiring the dresses, capes and coats. But most people could not afford to pay what Virginia was asking for each garment. Although they realised she was not overcharging, being well aware of what such clothes would have originally cost in the shops in Sauchiehall Street.

Virginia was just about to drop the prices when a respectably dressed woman bought a black velvet shoulder cape and a pair of long black gloves. Then her companion purchased a loose-fitting tailored day costume. Virginia was delighted—she now had enough money for a lot more than just a jar of Co-op apple jelly. Enough in fact to feed the family for several days.

She didn't manage to sell anything else that first day, and she was glad to give up eventually, trundle the barrow back to its owner, then make her way home, carrying the bundle of left-over clothes slung over her shoulder. Her feet were like blocks of ice, but she knew that her mother would have the fire on and she'd soon thaw out. There was still some coal in the bunker and now she'd be able to give her mother enough money to get another bag put in. Geordie the coalman was a regular sight in the street, ambling along beside his Clydesdale bawling out,

'Coo-ee! Coo-ee!'

There was no mistaking him—a muscly, moustached man with a voice like all the foghorns on the Clyde put together.

His ringing call drowned out all the other noises of the street for a moment, even the rag man who passed by blasting energetically on his horn.

Janette was pleased with the apple jelly and the fish and chip suppers Virginia had brought. Tam and Duncan immediately dived into the food, not even waiting for Janette to bring out plates or to get cutlery on to the table. They ate with their fingers, relishing each morsel of fish, each chip, straight from the newspaper wrapping.

Afterwards, they smacked their lips and Tam said,

'God, that was good, hen. You're a wee miracle worker. It must be a year or more since we've had a fish supper.'

'Aye,' Duncan agreed, leaning his big frame back in this chair and patting his stomach. 'I enjoyed that.'

The small kitchen was warm and redolent with the aroma of fish and chips and the mouth-watering tang of vinegar which the chip-shop man had liberally sprinkled over each supper. The food had created a happiness and contentment which, although temporary, was nonetheless real and keenly appreciated. They all sensed it, and clung to the intense pleasure of it for as long as possible.

Tam took out an old Woodbine packet in which he used to collect tobacco from 'douts', cigarettes smoked down until they were too short to hold between the finger tips. He had picked away the bits of cigarette paper and teased out what was left of the tobacco. Now he had enough to rub between his palms and, using a piece of newspaper for wrapping and a bit of gummed paper from the flap of an old envelope, he made a new cigarette. It was bulky and lumpy in shape but he enjoyed taking a long slow draw on it, expanding his chest and holding in the smoke, until eventually blowing it out between narrowed lips.

'Aye,' he said. 'You did well, hen.'

'And no bosses either,' Duncan added. 'Good for you. By the way, James is coming round tonight.' He grinned. 'You made a big impression there, Virginia. It looks as if he wants to start courting you.'

'He never said anything to me. About coming round, I mean.'

'Maybe so. But what do you bet when he arrives, it won't be me or da he'll ask to go out with him?'

Virginia felt disturbed and slightly annoyed. She didn't want to start walking out with anyone, especially someone as sure of himself as James Mathieson. It wasn't that she didn't like, even admire, the man. She had always admired anyone with brains and an education. She even agreed with most of his political beliefs. The simple fact was that she could not forget her feelings for Nicholas Cartwright. But what was the use of that?

When Mathieson arrived, he had to squeeze into the kitchen. He stood against the coal bunker and refused Janette's offer of a chair at the table.

'I was hoping,' he addressed Virginia, 'that you'd accompany me to a show at the Pavilion. I've heard it's very good. And we should support that theatre as much as we can. They've allowed us to hold many a good meeting there.'

Virginia was embarrassed by the barely suppressed hilarity of her father and brother. To escape it she rose and said, 'Yes, all right. I'll fetch my coat.'

Then she felt embarrassed at appearing so eager when she wasn't eager at all. Later, however, as she walked arm in arm with James and felt the warmth of his body so near to hers, her pulse quickened.

Nicholas had awakened her to the pleasures of the body and despite herself, she was awakening again.

They both enjoyed the show in the Pavilion, although Mathieson's laughter at some of the turns surprised her. It was loud and robust and up until that point, she had regarded him as far too serious and intense. She hadn't been able to imagine him relaxing and laughing so heartily. Later, as they chatted about the show and laughed over it again in the tramcar on the way back to the Gorbals, she was more relaxed herself than she'd been for a long time. Once in her close, Virginia was able to say truthfully,

'I've really enjoyed myself tonight. Thanks, James.'

'My pleasure. I hope this will be the first of many enjoyable evenings.'

She smiled. 'We'll see. I'd better go in now.'

'Am I not even going to get one wee kiss?'

She hesitated for one shy moment before giving him a peck on the cheek. But his arms went immediately around her and gripped her close. He gazed down at her and said softly,

'Is that what you call a kiss? Here, let me show you.'

His mouth fastened down over hers, hard and demanding. He held her body so tightly, her breasts were crushed against him and she felt the hardening of his penis against her groin. Panic mixed with arousal. She struggled and pushed at him in an effort to break free.

'For goodness' sake,' she gasped breathlessly. 'What do you think you're playing at? We're right outside mammy's door. She could open it at any minute.'

'Come on through to the back close then.'

A dark corner of the back close was the only place that Gorbals lovers, or lovers in any poor district, could expect to be left undisturbed. Most tenement flats were overcrowded and there was never any chance of privacy.

'No, I want to go in. Let go of me.'

'You're a bonny fechter as they say, and I admire you for it, Virginia. But you'll soon find out that I never take no for an answer.'

'Let me go at once.' Her voice was rising in panic.

He immediately lifted both hands in a gesture of capitulation.

'All right, all right. I only meant that I'm determined to see you again. You're the girl for me, Virginia. I knew it the moment I saw that beautiful blonde head of yours.'

'Goodnight, James.'

'Goodnight, sweetheart.'

Hastily she slammed the door behind her before he could touch her again. She felt angry and shaken but aroused nevertheless. That night, lying in the bed recess beside the quiet form of her mother, she imagined what it would be like to have sex with James Mathieson. Her imaginings made her body pulsate almost to the point of orgasm. She had to turn away and lie curled up on her side in case her mother would suspect anything. She felt ashamed of the desire that was taking possession of her. Yet in the cold light of day, she told herself that it was perfectly natural and nothing to be ashamed of. She was a healthy young woman and there was now no other man in her life. She had already decided to accept another invitation to go out with Mathieson before he'd even asked her.

On their second 'walking out' a week later, he made no attempt to get her into the back close, or even kiss her. This disturbed her even more. The next time his kiss was gentle, almost absent-minded. She discovered later that his widowed mother had taken ill. On subsequent meetings they attended John Maclean's classes together and his talks in Bath Street. On each occasion, Mathieson showed passion in his agreement with Maclean but with her he behaved with admirable restraint. She was beginning to wish that he would sweep her off her feet and into the back close. Or anywhere at all to have sex. She felt ashamed of lusting after him. Especially while he was so worried about his mother. For a time he didn't come to see her or meet her. When his mother eventually died of TB, it took him some time to get over her death. Yet although Virginia missed him, she knew she didn't love James Mathieson. At least, not in the way she'd loved Nicholas. Despite trying to erase the memories of Nicholas from her mind, his face would still return at unexpected moments to sadden her. She'd see his dark eyes, his blue-black hair, his tall, elegant figure. Then into her mind would come the memory of the baby he'd never seen and pain would tear at her heart. Her only escape from this pain was to keep as busy as possible. She did this not only by working at the market, but by going out scrubbing again after she'd sold all the clothes and some of her books. She also began helping James by distributing political pamphlets. Sometimes, she would even speak at meetings he'd organised. Like Maclean, James was a fervent champion of women's rights, arguing in favour of equal pay for equal work. Virginia was more than happy to support him in his work for this cause.

Virginia sometimes wondered how Mrs Cartwright was coping. She thought of her now without any bitterness. Mrs Cartwright was simply a product of her class, just as Virginia was a product of hers. Now she only remembered the older woman's human side, and the way she'd eventually succeeded in being a practical help at the birth, her excitement and her pride in having helped bring her grandson into the world. Virginia could imagine Mr Cartwright being proud too. Baby Richard was no doubt a comfort to them both, and Virginia tried to find solace in that thought.

'Get on with the rest of your life,' Mrs Cartwright had told her.

'All right,' Virginia thought. 'I will.'

14

On Sunday 6th February 1916, Maclean was speaking at the usual
Bath Street meeting when he was suddenly seized by the police and
taken to Edinburgh Castle as a prisoner of war. James Mathieson
nearly got arrested for trying to stop the police arresting Maclean.
Virginia had to drag him off before he made things worse than they
already were. It was only because of widespread protests that the
authorities agreed to release Maclean on bail. His trial was set for the
11th of April.

Mathieson became more and more incensed as socialist newspapers
like *Forward* and *Vanguard* were banned. Late one night police raided
the Socialist Labour Press in Renfield Street, seized the type and
manuscripts of *The Worker* and closed the premises. The editor was
arrested along with other socialist leaders.

With Maclean out of the way, Mathieson took the lead in speaking
at Bath Street, at street corners and at factory gates. By this time, he
and Virginia had been walking out regularly and he was a frequent
visitor to her home in the Gorbals. Janette had come to regard him
almost as one of the family and she was now worrying about him as
well as Tam and Duncan.

'James, son,' she told him, 'can you not take a lesson from John
Maclean and the rest of his crowd. They've all ended up in jail and
so will you if you're not careful. You could lose your job.'

'One thing I've learned from John Maclean is to be honest and
stand up for my socialist beliefs, Mrs Watson.' His eyes strained with
sincerity. 'And I'll do that till the day I die—no matter what the cost.
You see, it's not the individual that matters, it's the success of our

collective struggle against the oppressors.'

Janette did not look convinced by James' bravado. Part of her concern was that Virginia was spending more and more time helping him. She now attended all his meetings, not only distributing pamphlets but helping to write them.

Virginia herself admired Mathieson's courage, his idealism and his talent as a public speaker. Maclean had taught him well, and in his public speaking he was showing much of Maclean's fire, dedication and ability to grip and hold an audience. He was also, with other comrades, trying to continue Maclean's work for the Scottish Labour College. Virginia could see, however, that he did not have Maclean's superhuman energy. Nor Maclean's calmness under pressure. James could lose his temper with hecklers. Especially if one of them shouted, as they often did, 'You're no' even a bloody worker!'

She had often seen him almost collapsing with exhaustion after a difficult and rowdy meeting. Sometimes, in this over-tired state, he would snap at her. Afterwards he would nurse his head in his hands and say, 'I've had one hell of a day. It wasn't the easiest of days at the school and then there was all that aggravation at the meeting. It's those damned police infiltrators—they come in plain clothes and mix with the crowd and try to stir up as much trouble as they can.' He sighed. 'But I shouldn't take it out on you. I'm sorry, Virginia.'

Now, looking at his earnest face topped with hair that was sticking up in untidy tufts, she felt a tenderness towards him.

'It's all right, James. You're just doing too much. Mammy's quite right.'

'I thought you understood. I thought you believed in what we're fighting for.'

'I do. I do. But what good are you to the cause if you're in jail?' She hesitated, then added in a whisper because they were in the kitchen at the time and her mother was washing the dishes over at the sink, 'I'm fond of you, James. I care about you. I don't want anything bad to happen to you.'

He squeezed her hand and the passion glowing in his eyes told her he longed to do much more. Later that evening, after they'd been to a meeting in the Pavilion Theatre, he tried to pull her into the back close but she refused to budge from her mother's doorstep.

'It's just . . .' She tried to think of a way to explain. 'It's not that I don't want to . . . you know. But it's such a terrible place.' Her voice shook. 'Terrible. I hate it. I hate the whole stinking place. It's not even fit for animals.'

He nodded. 'You're quite right. I wish I was still living at home. We could have gone there. But after mother died, the bastard of a landlord put me out. The rent book was in her name although I always paid the rent.' His mouth twisted with bitterness. 'He would never allow my name to go on the rent book. The factor said it was because I was too much of a troublemaker. Now, in my digs, there's no privacy at all.' He gazed down at her very seriously.

'Virginia, it's time we were married. We should be looking for a place of our own. We can't go on like this.'

What he said made sense. He was a good man and she thought he loved her, although he'd never actually said the words. There was nothing unusual in that. Scotsmen were notoriously reticent in appearing to be what was regarded as 'soft' or 'soppy'. She'd certainly could not imagine her father ever being romantic towards her mother. Although she didn't doubt that he had always loved her.

Nicholas had been romantic. He had not been afraid to show tenderness and to speak the soft words of love. Thinking of him made the usual weight of sadness descend on her.

'Virginia,' Mathieson repeated with some aggression. 'Didn't you hear what I said?'

She knew it wasn't fair to go on as they had been.

'All right,' she told him. 'I'll start looking for a place.'

Immediately he grabbed her and held her tightly against him as he kissed her deeply, his tongue prising open her mouth and searching inside. She experience such a surge of lust, she could have allowed him to take her right there and then. However, the neighbour in the close opened her door to let her cat out.

'Hello therr,' she laughed. 'Sorry fur interruptin' yer winchin', but yer askin' fur it standin' therr. That's whit the back close's fur.'

Virginia pulled the door bell.

'It's all right, Mrs MacKechnie, I was just going in. Goodnight, James.'

She could see the anger and frustration in his face but her mother arrived at the door and he had no opportunity to say anything more than a brief goodnight.

She had long since realised that James Mathieson had a volatile and fiery temper and she suspected that one day it would get him into serious trouble. And it did. It was what happened to John Maclean at his trial that was the catalyst.

At the trial, the six counts of the indictment against Maclean were read out with all due solemnity. Each was connected with statements he was alleged to have made at different meetings.

1) That conscription was unnecessary, as the government had plenty of soldiers and munitions; that after the war, conscription would be used to secure cheap labour; that should the government enforce the Military Service Act and the Munitions Act, the workers should 'down tools'; that if the British soldiers laid down their arms, the Germans would do that same, as all were tired of the war.

2) That the workers should strike in order to attend a meeting.

3) That the workers 'down tools' and resist conscription.

4) That if conscription became law, the workers would become conscripts to industrial labour—the real aim of the government.

5) That the workers should strike and those who had guns should use them.

6) That the workers should sell or pawn their alarm clocks, sleep in in the mornings and not go to work.

Maclean pleaded not guilty and put up a very good defence. He dealt with every charge and especially ridiculed the charge that he'd asked the workers to use guns. 'That type of thing might be good enough for men in Dublin,' he pointed out, 'but it is no good whatever for the Clyde workers. Even if they had the inclination to use guns, they have not got them.'

In the end, he was found guilty on the first four charges. Not proven on the fifth and not guilty on the sixth. The packed court was stunned not so much by the guilty verdicts as by the judge delivering a sentence of three years penal servitude. That meant imprisonment with hard labour. Maclean however was unperturbed. As he was led away, he turned and waved his hat to his wife and friends. They in turn promptly stood up and sang 'The Red Flag' as they'd never sung it before.

Mathieson was consumed with fury at the sentence. Maclean had been branded a traitor to his country and an enemy of the people. James couldn't bear this slur and he immediately called a meeting outside the court. He actually stood in the entrance and addressed the crowd. Virginia tried to calm him and pull him away but it was no use. He told his audience that Maclean was absolutely right.

'Conscription means bringing all young men under the control of the military authorities. That includes men in the factories and workshops, as well as in the field of battle. All the workers would come under military discipline. Men, as a result, would be bound hand and foot to the bosses, to the factory owners. The only weapon we can use is to strike. That's the only weapon we have!'

By now a crowd of policemen had appeared, batons drawn.

'For God's sake, James,' Virginia shouted at him. 'Stop this.'

But ignoring her, he carried on, 'John Maclean is a revolutionary socialist and so am I, comrades! And we are Internationalists. We will not do anything to help the capitalists in their war against our fellow workers in Germany or anywhere else in the world!'

The police pushed through the crowd, jerked Virginia roughly aside and grabbed Mathieson. He struggled wildly and one policeman lashed out with his baton. Despite his powerful build, the force of the blow, quickly followed by a second and then a third from another policeman, felled Mathieson. As he lay there in a crumpled heap, there was a roar of rage from the crowd who stampeded forward, fists flying. The police lashed out viciously with their batons, and when further reinforcements arrived on the scene the unequal struggle came to an abrupt end and order was restored.

Virginia was shocked at what had happened to Mathieson. He was in a dreadful state, with blood pouring down his face from a wound on his head. She tried in vain to stem the flow with a ripped-off piece of her white petticoat.

'Don't worry,' he told her. 'It's not serious. I'll live.'

'Aye,' one of the policemen said, 'and it'll be in Calton Jail for a while, my lad.'

Sure enough, James wasn't even allowed bail, and he soon joined Maclean in Calton Jail in Edinburgh, a gloomy tomb-like building which was notorious as the worst prison in the country. No books, writing materials or cigarettes were allowed. The prisoners were not allowed their own food or clothes. Sanitary conditions were terrible and bunks were as hard as concrete. But worst of all was the 'separate and silence' system, where each prisoner was confined alone in a cell so tiny there was scarcely room to move about. Only half an hour of exercise in the sunless courtyard was allowed and even then, the silence was rigidly enforced. All of these things were torment enough for anyone, but for men like Maclean and Mathieson, it was torture to be without literature and newspapers and to suffer the terrible isolation and nerve-racking silence. But at least Mathieson caught glimpses of Maclean and other socialist friends who had also been incarcerated.

The prisoners were moved, and Mathieson was sent north to Peterhead prison, where he had to work outside in gangs in all sorts of weather. Even there the regime of silence was strictly observed, with severe punishments meted out to anyone who dared utter a word. And the warders were well qualified to enforce these punishments, having been specially chosen from the army, the police force and mental asylums for their harshness and brutality.

It was hell for James Mathieson, but it was also terrible for Virginia. Once more the war had torn her life apart. Still, at least James was alive. . . .

It was not until June 1917—a little more than a year after he had been locked up—that Mathieson was finally released.

Virginia was shocked at the change in him. He had lost a lot of weight. This, he told her, was inevitable because the food was so inadequate. He said no more about his time in prison, but Virginia guessed that he'd suffered much more than hunger. She had only been allowed to make a couple of visits while James had been in prison and she had seen that he didn't look well. But he had always put a brave face on things. He never wanted to talk about himself but was always anxious to know what was happening outside. Were the workers' economics classes still being held and were they still well attended? Were their comrades speaking regularly in the Pavilion and in Bath Street and at factory gates? He seemed to have lost interest in anything other than politics.

It wasn't until he had been released from prison that Virginia was able to tell him all her news. Duncan had got married—a shotgun affair—to a girl called Celia. He'd also been conscripted. Celia wouldn't hear of what she called the disgrace of him becoming a Conscientious Objector.

Tam said, 'That girl has got Duncan so much under her thumb he's gone like a lamb into the army. Proud as punch she was to see him in uniform. Stupid bitch. A good thrashing's what she needs to bring her to her senses.'

Tam was refusing to allow Celia over his doorstep.

'I'll never forgive that girl for ruining Duncan,' he told James angrily, 'He was always such a sensible boy before he met her.'

James had been dismissed from his teaching post and had been thrown out of his digs. Even if he had not lost his job, he would not have been fit to do any kind of work for a while yet. He needed plenty of rest and good food to build up his strength. Almost before Virginia realised what was happening, and certainly before she had time to think whether or not it was the right thing to do, it was agreed that she and James would have a quiet wedding. Then they would live with the Watsons until they could get a place of their own. Tam had already gone back to sharing the kitchen bed with Janette, and Virginia now had the room bed to herself.

Until the young couple were married, however, there was no question of them sharing the room bed. Neither Janette nor Tam would have countenanced such an impropriety. Indeed it was going to be embarrassing enough for all of them even after they were married. Meantime Mathieson had to share the room bed with Tam and Virginia moved back to the kitchen bed with her mother.

They wasted no time in arranging the registry office ceremony. Most wartime marriages took place at the registry office. There was seldom time to arrange a big church wedding, and weddings were often hurried affairs arranged during a soldier's brief leave. Janette was sad that James and Virginia weren't going to be blessed in the church, but she had long since resigned herself to the fact that they were both atheists.

Virginia had carried on with her job scrubbing, and now cleaned out halls as well as pubs. It was hard work and she hated it but at least it put food on the table and coal on the fire. Despite his frailty, James was desperate to find work.

He said, 'I'm no' going to allow my wife to keep me. It's not right.'

Tam overheard him and asked sarcastically, 'Oh aye? You're going into the munitions, are you? You're going to make guns to kill your fellow workers, are you?'

'I'm sorry, Tam,' James said. 'I wasn't sniping at you. I respect the way you've stuck to your principles. And I will too. I was thinking more of something in the teaching line. The Labour College pay a few of the tutors. I might have some luck there.'

'That's all very well,' Virginia told him, 'but in the meantime, I'm going to see that you get your health and strength back. You'll rest here and eat decent meals for another few days before you even think about working.'

Tam laughed.

'Here, you'd better be careful, son. Or you'll be under her thumb before you know it.'

'No chance,' Mathieson said without laughing. It occurred to Virginia then that he hadn't really much of a sense of humour. He was a very serious minded man. She sighed to herself. At the moment she not only didn't feel in love with him, she didn't even lust after him. It was true, however, what her mother said. He was a good, decent man. She should think herself lucky.

She tried to.

15

For the wedding James wore his homburg hat, a dark suit and stiff-collared shirt. Virginia perched a flowerpot hat over her long silky blonde hair which she'd wound into a chignon at the nape of her neck. White gloves matched the flowers on her hat. A blue coat, hobble skirt and long button boots with Louis heels completed the outfit. Duncan was home on leave before being sent to France and he looked enormous in his khaki uniform and Army boots. He and Celia were witnesses. Celia was a tiny girl with mousy, finger-waved hair peeping out from under a wide brimmed hat. She giggled all the time, even during the wedding ceremony itself, and kept fluttering her eyelashes at Duncan as she clung to his arm. Duncan seemed to enjoy all Celia's infantile attention, but James was distinctly unimpressed. Afterwards, he told Virginia 'That girl's a right pain in the arse. She'd drive me mad.'

Virginia agreed. 'I don't know what Duncan sees in her. She's not even all that pretty.'

'She must have something.'

They both silently wondered if Celia was good in bed. That was the only thing they could think of that could explain Duncan's obvious infatuation. Virginia was anticipating her own coupling with James with mixed feelings. Despite the fact that it was nearly three years since her time with Nicholas, she had never been completely able to banish the memory of his love-making. Weeks, months would pass and it was as if he'd never existed. Then suddenly, without warning, she would be dancing naked with him in the misty beauty of the woods. Their bodies warm against each other, yet fresh and tingling with dew. She could feel his lips nuzzling her neck. She could hear his cultured voice intoning beautiful lines of poetry to her. His voice was a joy to listen to. It was so different from the broad Glasgow voices she was now used to, with their glottal stop and hard, often coarse, edge.

Thoughts of Nicholas would bring thoughts of her baby and she'd long for them both. The longing came to her on her wedding day and she felt ashamed to be standing beside James, taking solemn vows to love, cherish and obey him until death parted them, when she was thinking of how death had parted her from her love. Gazing up at James's serious face, she determined to put everything else out of her mind once and for all and to concentrate only on being a good and faithful wife to him.

After the ceremony they went to Miss Cranston's for high tea. Then they went to the Central Station to see Duncan off as he was due back with his unit that night. As usual, Central Station was crowded with folk seeing off their friends and relations in the forces. Duncan's train was packed solid with the boys and as many as possible were hanging out of doors and windows to wave a last goodbye. Wives and mothers were standing with tears streaming down their faces and singing 'Will ye no' come back again', and the station echoed to the mournful refrain.

After seeing Duncan off and saying goodnight to Celia, James and Virginia made their way back to the Gorbals and to the Watsons' room and kitchen. They had not yet found a place of their own and so would have to start their married life in Janette's front room.

Janette had said her goodbyes to Duncan earlier in the day. Her first words now as soon as Virginia and James showed their faces in the kitchen were,

'Did he get away all right then?'

'Yes, mammy,' Virginia said. 'Will I make a cup of tea?'

Her mother nodded.

'He didn't need to go. I wouldn't have minded him being a C.O.'

'It's that stupid lassie.' Tam had been sitting by the fire drawing on a Woodbine. 'She'll be the death of that lad yet.'

'Daddy!' Virginia cried out reprovingly. 'Be quiet. You're just upsetting mammy.'

Janette said, 'The telegram boy's never away from here.'

James took off his hat and coat and hung them on the peg in the lobby. Then he settled himself at the table. 'That doesn't mean anything's going to happen to Duncan, Mrs Watson. Thousands and thousands of men are out there and surviving. They've made it through Ypres and The Somme, so maybe the worst's behind them. Let's just hope sanity will prevail and the whole damned thing will soon be over.'

'Aye, I hope ye're right son,' nodded Tam in agreement.

'Celia's just a silly young girl,' Janette said. 'But if anything happens to Duncan, she'll feel as bad as any of us.'

'Huh!' Tam shouted derisively and tossed his cigarette dout into the fire. Immediately regretting this angry and thoughtless act, he shouted, 'Now look what she's made me do!'

Virginia shook her head at him, and in an obvious attempt to change the subject said to her mother, 'I thought it all went very well today. It was over a bit quick, right enough, but that's because there was a queue waiting. And the haddock and chips we had at Miss Cranston's was nice, wasn't it, James?'

'Very tasty,' James agreed. 'We all enjoyed it. Then we went to see Duncan off at the Central. The place was absolutely mobbed. We would hardly move along the platform.'

'Was he upset?' Janette asked.

'No, not a bit. He waved to us very cheerily.'

Janette sighed. 'He was never one to show his feelings.'

'Here, drink your tea, mammy.' Virginia poured everyone a cup and then took the tin biscuit barrel down from the mantelpiece. With her last wage packet she'd bought some digestives, her mother's favourite. 'And have a biscuit.'

'Thanks, hen. You're lucky you're a bit older than Duncan, son. You'll not be bothered with this terrible conscription.'

'Oh, it'll probably come to me yet. But I'll go to prison rather than have anything to do with this capitalist war.'

Virginia lingered over her tea. She suddenly had the feeling that James was a stranger. But, for now, embarrassment was the thing uppermost in her mind. It somehow didn't feel decent to go and share the room bed with a man. They would just be through the wall from her mother and father.

Eventually Tam said, 'Are you two going to sit there all night. I want to get to my bed.'

James immediately rose and bade Tam and Janette goodnight.

Virginia said, 'I'll just wash up these cups.'

Janette got up. 'No, no. I'll do that. Away you go, hen.'

Through in the room, Virginia whispered, 'The quicker we find a wee place of our own, the better. I feel embarrassed, don't you?'

James had begun to undress. He shrugged. 'A bit. But don't worry, we'll find somewhere.' Once naked, he folded his clothes neatly on to a chair. Then he climbed up on to the high set-in-the-wall bed. 'Hurry up,' he told Virginia. 'This room's like the North Pole.'

Virginia had been staring at his stocky frame. His muscly upper back made his shoulders look rounded. His chest was covered with a mat of hair that thinned to a line travelling down over his abdomen. Then it tufted out over his bulging genitals. It was gingery brown, not light brown like the hair on his head. She experienced a surge of distaste bordering on revulsion, yet at the same time lust came throbbing to life in her. As quickly as possible, she undressed and climbed into bed beside him. He immediately grabbed her against him and fastened his mouth over hers. In a few minutes he had mounted her and the bedsprings began to creak loudly.

'Shh, shh,' Virginia hissed jerkily. 'They'll hear us.'

But he just went on grunting with pleasure, the sounds filling the room and, Virginia feared, passing through the wall of the kitchen, right into her mother and father's bed. Her body and mind split. She was physically excited. Her body opened to James, indulged him, indulged herself. Her mind squeezed shut, in an effort not to think of her father and mother listening. Afterwards she wished the immediate peace of sleep could black her out as it had with James. For hours she lay staring into the darkness feeling acutely embarrassed and ashamed. She knew that being married made love-making between husband and wife a perfectly natural and acceptable fact of life that neither her mother or father would object to. But it was embarrassing nevertheless. She determined to waste no time in finding a place where she and James could live in decent privacy. She must have dozed off eventually because she woke with James shaking her shoulders.

'Come on, Virginia. Time you were up. We've a lot to do.'

'Have we?' Virginia murmured sleepily while at the same time beginning to struggle out of bed.

'Lloyd George is coming to Glasgow today. They're giving him the 'Freedom of the City', would you believe? There's going to be thousands on the streets, all demanding Maclean's release.'

'Oh yes, I forgot.' She pulled on some clothes, tugged a brush through her long hair and started plaiting it as she followed James through to the kitchen.

'Hello, hen.' Her mother was standing at the fire, stirring a black iron pot filled with porridge. 'Did you have a good night?'

Tam chuckled. 'I don't think there's any doubt about that. It was her wedding night, Janette.'

Both Janette and Virginia flushed and Janette said, 'You know what I mean.'

It was what she usually asked first thing in the morning, and simply meant—did you sleep well.

James said to Tam, 'You'll be going out to welcome Lloyd George, Tam?'

Tam sat down at the table as Janette began dishing out the porridge.

'He'll get a welcome here that he'll not forget in a hurry!'

'We'd better get out early. I was just saying to Virginia, there'll be thousands. And all demanding John's release.'

'Aye, don't worry, I'll be there all right.'

Janette sighed. 'For goodness' sake, try not to get yourself arrested. You especially, James. Remember you're a married man now with Virginia to think about.'

'Virginia's coming as well.'

Virginia would have preferred it if he'd asked her first, but she'd always gone to the demonstrations before so it was natural for James to take it for granted she'd be at this one as well.

'I thought,' she said, 'you were going to ask about work at the Labour College first.'

James nodded. 'Yes, there's time to do that. I'll go as soon as I've finished this. You wait here. I'll come back for you.'

He washed his face and neck at the jawbox—as the sink in Glasgow tenements was called. He plastered Brylcreem on his hair, but it was too short to smooth down, and always stood up in tufts. He put on his homburg, gave it a pat and said, 'Right, I'll see you later. Wish me luck.'

'Good luck, son,' Janette said.

Virginia was still drinking her tea but she raised a hand in goodbye to him as he strode purposefully out of the house. Virginia prayed that he would get a teaching job. She couldn't imagine him hanging about the house doing nothing. She could imagine how restless, angry and frustrated he would become. He would be very hard to live with.

She washed up the breakfast dishes and replaced them in the press beside the sink. Then she went through to the room and made the bed. After that she went back to the kitchen and asked her father to go through to the room while she had a wash.

While she was at the sink there was a knock on the outside door. Virginia hurried to finish her ablutions. She could hear her father going to the door and saying,

'Oh, it's you, Mrs McKechnie. Come away in, hen.'

Virginia just managed to throw on her clothes in time before the kitchen door opened and her father and the neighbour came in.

'Hello hen,' Mrs McKechnie greeted Virginia. 'Ah jist brought ye this wee mindin'.' She produced a teapot and a teapot cover. 'Ah know ye said it was jist a quiet affair wi' yer brother goin' away tae the army and aw that, but here's a wee teapot anyway.'

'Oh thanks, Mrs McKechnie. It's lovely and I'll need one when we get a place of our own. I'm going to start looking tomorrow. Today there's a big demonstration. . . .'

'Aye, they're gatherin' in the streets already. I'll be there masel. Ah'd better away back in and get ready. Ah'm takin' the weans as well.' She laughed. 'Ah've telt them they've tae shout as loud as they can—Free John Maclean. They're aw excited already.' She gave a wave to Virginia. 'Aw the best, hen.'

'Thanks, Mrs McKechnie.'

Janette saw her neighbour to the door. When she came back she said to Virginia, 'Fancy her taking her weans. They could get hurt in all that crowd. I'm worried enough about you and James and Tam.'

'It's a friendly crowd, mammy.'

'Friendly? With all that shouting?'

'We'll all be shouting at Lloyd George, not at each other. Do you want me to give this floor a wee scrub while I'm waiting for James?'

'No, just leave it for today, hen. It's more the floorboards to scrub than the lino now with all these holes.'

'If I make enough in the next week or two, mammy, I'll buy you some new lino. There's a man down at Clyde Street sells it really cheap.'

'You'll do no such thing,' Janette said. 'You're a married woman, don't forget. You'll need all you have for your own wee place when you get it. And if James gets work, he won't let you go out scrubbing.'

Virginia couldn't deny this but she insisted on black-leading the range and energetically rubbed all the steel bits at the front with emery paper. She was barely finished when there was a loud rapping at the door.

'That'll be James,' said Virginia, washing her hands at the sink. She took the towel from the hook inside the press door and went to answer the knock as she rubbed her hands dry. Already she could recognise James's impatient, aggressive knock. As soon as she opened the door, James pushed past her into the kitchen. He was rubbing his hands with glee.

'I got it,' he said. 'The teaching job. It's not much money but still it's better than nothing and I can feel I'm doing something useful.'

'Aye, you're right, son,' Tam agreed. 'If there's one thing the working class need it's education. Good for you, son. Congratulations.'

'Thanks, Tam. Come on, Virginia, get your coat on and we'll be away. Are you coming, Tam?'

'I've some pals coming for me. They'll be here in a few minutes. On you go with Virginia, son.'

'Cheerio, mammy,' Virginia called once she'd grabbed her coat and struggled into it.

'For pity's sake, be careful,' Janette pleaded.

'Yes, yes.'

And off they went into the streets that were already heaving and seething with people. All over Glasgow, there was a buzz of excitement—but anger and hatred were also in the air. It was the calm before the storm.

16

'I can't help worrying about the McKechnie children,' Virginia said. 'They could be trampled to death in a crowd like this.'

The workers had come out on to the streets in their thousands, and everywhere yells of 'Release Maclean' tore through the air. Everyone surged in the direction of St Andrew's Hall where Lloyd George was to be speaking. All along the route onlookers struggled to get near his car—which had been slowed to a snail's pace—but he was surrounded all the way by soldiers and policemen. When he finally appeared at St Andrew's Hall, he was met by a huge, threatening mass of men and women, many waving the red flag. An enormous red flag was flying from an adjacent building.

'Release John Maclean!' The chant grew to thunderous, ear-splitting proportions. Then word was given that Maclean would be released next day and the chants gave way to riotous cheering. The whole crowd immediately made for Duke Street prison where they raised lusty cheers in the hope that Maclean—who was inside—would hear them.

Next day, James and Virginia were in the crowd who welcomed Maclean on his release and went to hear him speak at what they both agreed was the most inspiring meeting they'd ever been to. Many had feared that Maclean would have lost much of his intensity after his suffering in prison. But all the old passion, enthusiasm and devotion to the socialist cause was still there.

'Comrades!' he had greeted them as the cheering subsided 'Glad as I am to be back with you once more, let us not forget those I have left behind. Those brave souls still suffering, whose only crime is to stand up and speak out for what they believe!' He ended on a rousing note by declaring that the workers' movement must stand firm in both its opposition to the war and the continuing struggle to overthrow capitalism. Fists were then raised in salute as a stirring rendition of 'The Red Flag' rocked the hall.

'Wasn't that bloody marvellous?' James said to Virginia on the way home in the tram car. He had to raise his voice to be heard over the rattling and clattering of the tram.

She knew what he meant. The audience had been euphoric and this feeling still clung to her.

'Marvellous,' she agreed.

James continued, 'He's the catalyst that makes everything happen. He rouses indignation, sweeps aside doubts and hesitations, inspires courage and confidence.' He folded his arms at the back of his head and relaxed against them. 'He's such a brilliant educator as well—there's already hundreds enrolling in his new classes—he's so clear-headed about society and about the war. The energy of the man!' James heaved a sigh of admiration. Virginia hugged his arm in enthusiastic agreement.

When they arrived home it was getting late, but the house was empty. Tam was still out on the streets and Janette had left a note to say that she was visiting one of the upstairs neighbours. Their euphoric excitement was immediately channelled into sex and they couldn't get into the room and on top of the bed quickly enough. Rejoicing in the fact that they didn't need to care about making a noise, even Virginia let herself go and her moans and squeals rivalled Mathieson's groans and shouts in loudness and abandon. Afterwards they were both exhausted. Mathieson collapsed back off her.

Virginia suddenly felt depressed.

'We'd better get up before mammy and daddy come back.'

'Right.' Mathieson jerked into a sitting position then swung his feet out of the bed. 'I'll away upstairs to the lavatory.'

Virginia went through to the kitchen and hastily, furtively, washed between her legs. She hoped Mathieson would wash himself before her parents returned. She didn't want them to smell sex on him. However, he actually arrived back at the same time as her mother and father and so didn't get the opportunity.

Tam had barely set foot in the kitchen when he announced in an absolute fury, 'Do you know what I've just found out?' His face was flushed and his moustache looked wildly untidy as if he'd been tugging and rubbing at it.

'What?' Mathieson asked.

'Who do you think owns that death-trap where our Ian worked?'

'I've no idea, Tam.'

'That bastard that Virginia worked for.'

Virginia's legs gave way and she groped for the nearest chair.

'Mr Cartwright?'

'Aye, George murdering Cartwright!'

'Are you sure, daddy?'

'Of course I'm sure. It's all round the place. I got it from a union man. The union's been fighting for better and safer conditions and this bastard appeared and talked them down. Spouting all about patriotism and the war effort and how his son had been killed doing his duty without a word of complaint. Holding up his son as an example to the men. Trying to shame them back to work to pile up more profit for him and to hell with how many of them get killed.'

Now James was flushed with rage. 'Bastard! For him to be blown up in his own bloody factory would be too good, too easy for him. He needs to suffer something much worse! Something—'

'James, for pity's sake!' Virginia interrupted, distressed by the mad gleam in his eyes, the tightness of his mouth and the scarlet blotches of colour firing his cheeks. 'Control yourself, or you'll be taking a fit or a heart attack.'

'I've no pity for the likes of him and neither should you. He's responsible for what happened to your brother—and many other women's brothers as well. Many other women's sons. He deserves no pity and no working man will give him any. We'll organise a march to his house, drag him out if necessary and—'

'No, James, you mustn't,' Virginia cried out in panic. 'You'll only be flung back in prison again. For goodness' sake, have a bit of common sense and self control for once. For my sake if not for your own.'

Janette spoke up then. 'Virginia's right, son. I don't want you to go either. It won't bring our Ian back. It'll only mean we'll lose you as well. So sit down and try and calm yourself. Have a wee drop of whisky in your tea.'

He sat down at the table but Virginia could see a pulse beating furiously in his neck.

'I know how you feel, son,' Tam said. 'I feel the same. But we'd better think what we're doing here. Let's try to simmer down and have a think about a better way to deal with this.'

James nodded. Then, 'To think my wife slaved after him.'

'Not him,' Virginia said. 'I mean, I just worked in the kitchen. He was hardly ever in the house. I didn't even see much of Mrs Cartwright until that time at her holiday house.'

'It's the same thing. You were helping to keep the wheels of capitalism running smoothly. I'll make sure you never have to do anything like that again.'

Virginia was becoming irritated. 'What do you mean? Anything like what?'

'Working for any other rich bastards like the Cartwrights.'

'Don't worry. I've no intention of ever going back into service. I didn't enjoy it, you know. I was just trying to make a living and help mammy with the rent. And none of us knew what business he was in.'

Janette patted her hand. 'It's all right, hen. You did your best. You didn't mean any harm.'

'What do you bet,' James said, 'we'll find out he owns not only his bloody factories and hundreds of acres around his house, but half the Highlands as well!'

'Not all that again!' Virginia said. 'You and your obsession with the Clearances. It happened long ago, James, and whatever you may think, it had nothing to do with Mr Cartwright.'

James ignored her and carried on 'I'm telling you. It's people like him who own half of Scotland. People like him who made my family suffer. Homelessness, humiliation and death.'

'You don't know that he or any of his ancestors or his friends ever had anything to do with land in the Highlands.'

'Who's side are you on?' James demanded. 'I thought you were supposed to be a socialist.'

'I am. You know perfectly well I am. But you're just being ridiculous.'

James's eyes bulged with fury. 'Ridiculous, am I? Ridiculous to remember what happened to my mother and father and grandmother and grandfather? Ridiculous to care, is it?'

Janette leaned over the table and patted James's hand. 'Now, now, son. Drink up your tea. She didn't mean that. You're a good loyal son to your folks. I can see you care about them and their memory. But I'm sure they wouldn't want you to get into serious trouble because of them, son.'

Tam was carefully rolling a Woodbine. 'Anyway, no harm in organising a wee protest.'

'Have you no sense either? Virginia said impatiently. 'Can you not see the state James is in. You've done enough to stir him up already.'

'Huh?' her father gasped indignantly. 'Do you hear that, James? What did she expect me to do? Not tell you about who owned the factory where my son was killed?'

'Now *you're* being ridiculous,' Virginia said.

'That's enough,' James growled. 'Don't speak to your father like that. Go through to the room.'

'What?' Virginia gasped, half laughing.

'Go through to the room. I'll be there in a minute.'

'You've a nerve. I'm not your servant to order about. Some socialist! And after all I've heard you saying about women's rights!'

Janette was becoming agitated. 'Now, Virginia, James's your man and he's upset. We all are. Away you go through, the pair of you. Tam and me want to get to our bed.'

Without another word Virginia got up and walked out of the kitchen. She was furious and had developed a thumping headache. As James followed her she turned on him, 'Don't you ever order me about like that again, do you hear?'

James sat down and nursed his head in his hands. 'I'm sorry. I got carried away. It's just that bastards like Cartwright shouldn't be allowed to get away with it. All the misery and suffering they cause.'

Virginia's anger melted away at this. She put an arm around Mathieson's shoulders. 'Come on to bed.'

He nodded and began tugging at his tie. Once in bed, he lay stiff and tense.

'I remember my grandmother, you know. A lovely old lady she was. She didn't deserve to suffer as she did. And my grandfather was a real gentleman. When I think of what they were made to go through. Thrown out of their home in the middle of the night, left to walk about cold and hungry, and with young children. Can you imagine it? And despite it all, they retained their decency and their integrity to the last.'

'Shh, shh,' she soothed. 'Try to get some sleep, James. You've your job to think about, remember. You'll be doing something really worthwhile at the college.'

'Yes, you're right. It's important that workers are educated and ready for the revolution. Then the Cartwrights of this world won't know what's hit them. When I think of young men, like your brother, with everything to live for, ending their days in that factory, while Cartwright in that grand house of his hasn't a care in the world.'

'Shh, shh.'

'I want to kill the bastard. . . .'

17

Since October 1917, when the first shattering news of the Russian Revolution reached the west, the British government had been acutely concerned about the worsening situation on the Clyde. The authorities began to refuse permission for any socialist or workers' meetings to be held in any of their halls. Only the Pavilion Theatre continued to allow meetings and workers congregated there whenever possible. However, this did not affect the hastily-arranged protest meeting in connection with Cartwright's factory, as it was to be held in the open outside the factory gates.

Despite Virginia's pleadings and angry remonstrations, the meeting had hardly begun before James jumped on to the soap-box and tried to rouse the workers to march to Cartwright's home. Fortunately, other speakers argued against this rash action. James, however, persevered, and there was a point when the crowd seemed to be swayed by his arguments. In desperation, Virginia got up on the soap box and told the crowd that she had lost a brother in one of the accidents in this factory, but she didn't believe that any safety regulations or improvements would be won by attacking Cartwright's home. Quite the reverse. 'We have to make our situation and our protests known in calm and logical arguments by letter, and by organised, lawful representations to the police and to the government.' Many nodded their approval of Virginia's arguments, she received a round of applause and her recommendations were adopted. James was furious.

'Why do you keep sticking up for the Cartwrights?'

Virginia rolled her eyes heavenwards.

'I wasn't "sticking up for the Cartwrights", as you put it. You've missed the point of what I said. It would have done nothing but harm to the cause if they'd followed you. It wouldn't have been a peaceful demonstration, James, and you know it. You're no John Maclean. You can't keep your temper. He can.'

However, once the meeting was over, James' anger was soon diffused. He was hard put to it to keep up with his work—all his time was taken up with tutorial duties at the college and travelling around teaching classes of workers all over the country. Meanwhile, Maclean had gone down to England where he'd been invited to address a variety of meetings. As James told Virginia, after he'd arrived home utterly exhausted one night, 'The work Maclean's doing this winter has never been and never could be equalled by anyone. I just don't know where he gets the energy.'

Apart from his educational work, Maclean was carrying on terrific propaganda and agitational campaigns, devoting every waking moment to the revolutionary struggle. Above all else, his message was that the workers should have faith only in themselves. They must, with boldness and confidence, take matters into their own hands and seize both the land and the means of production.

Virginia and James normally went together to Maclean's meetings, but her mother took a dose of 'flu, and so Virginia was kept busy nursing her back to health.

No-one cheered on Maclean or supported him more eagerly and enthusiastically than James Mathieson. He agreed with Maclean on everything, including his prophecy that the war, far from being the war to end all wars, would be followed by another war within twenty years. And one day there would be a war with America.

Virginia ridiculed this idea. 'A war between Britain and America? That's crazy, James. I don't believe for one moment that will ever happen.'

'It'll be an economic war with them,' James said. 'You should have heard John explain how he believes it will happen. I wish you'd been there, Virginia. It always comes down to money, you know—the ruthless pursuit of profit regardless of human suffering.'

Virginia had also been looking for a place of their own, and went with James to see a 'single end', a one apartment house in the Calton district. The district was on the opposite side of the river from the

Gorbals. It was bounded by the Saltmarket on the west and the River Clyde between Albert and Rutherglen bridges in the south. Main Street, Bridgeton was part of the eastern boundary, and Gallowgate the northern. Of the five streets which converged on Glasgow Cross, three were associated with the Calton ward—Gallowgate, Saltmarket and London Road.

On their way to view the single end in Bankier Street, James and Virginia walked through Glasgow Green.

'There used to be fairs here in the last century,' James said. 'Opposite the court house. But there was so much trouble it was decreed that boothkeepers must keep beside them a halbert, jack and steel bonnet. They must have been turbulent times.'

Virginia couldn't resist remarking with a touch of sarcasm, 'Not like now.'

James didn't seem to notice the sarcasm and continued with his lecture. 'Calton used to be famous for its weaving industry. All the weavers lived here in Bankier Street.'

'I've heard of the Calton weavers, right enough, but I didn't realise they came from Bankier Street.'

'Yes, it was called Thomson's Lane then. They were paid such a wretched pittance that they went on strike for a decent wage. The employers refused to give them a penny. They demonstrated and the military were called out, the Riot Act was read and then the guns were turned on the weavers. There's a tombstone in the local grave-yard. It says on it, "They were martyred by the military".'

They had reached the close of one of the gloomy four storey tenements. Mathieson looked around.

'What a dump!'

Before coming to live in the Gorbals, James had lived in his mother's more respectable room and kitchen in Shawlands. His digs had also been in a comparatively comfortable and respectable area.

'There's nothing else. At least at a rent we can afford,' Virginia told him. 'There's no use in turning up your nose at it.'

'I wasn't turning up my nose at it. Not in the way you mean. I was just thinking what a disgrace it is that landlords expect human beings to live in overcrowded conditions in places like this.'

'Right enough. But it won't do any harm to have a look anyway.' Virginia linked arms with him. 'It's upstairs. One up.'

They passed the lavatory on the first landing. The usual smell followed them as James put the key in the door and pushed it open. A dingy shoe box of a lobby led directly into the kitchen which was also to act as living room, dining room and bedroom. There was the usual hole-in-the-wall bed with space underneath to store belongings, including the zinc bath. A black range and a press took up most of the wall. Opposite was the built-in bunker and dresser, high above which were two long shelves. Lastly, over at the window, was the black sink and swan tap.

They surveyed it all in silence. Then Virginia said, 'At least it faces the front.' From the window the only view was of the equally gloomy tenements across the narrow road.

Then Virginia rallied. 'Don't worry, I'll soon have it cleaned up and cosy looking. There's our wedding presents, and I'll get a few things cheap from my friends at the Clyde Street barrows.'

James said, 'I know an unemployed cabinet-maker. He'll make me a table and chairs.'

'Great. That's all we need really. Mammy's knitted a blanket with all the odd bits of wool she's collected.'

'Like Joseph's coat of many colours.' James smiled.

'She knitted squares and then sewed them all together. She crocheted the squares for the blanket on her own bed. It's nicer than any ordinary blanket you could buy in the shops.'

'I'm sure. It's very kind of your mother to go to all that trouble.'

'And there's the teapot from Mrs McKechnie, and a big iron soup pot from Mrs Friel, and a kettle from Mrs MacDougal—'

'All right, all right. You don't have to go through the lot. I suppose we've no choice but to take it.'

'Come on, let's go to the factor's office,' Virginia said, 'We can get the rent book. Then I can start getting this place cleaned up.'

They couldn't afford linoleum to begin with, so after Virginia scrubbed the floorboards, she polished them. She scrubbed the space under the bed very thoroughly before packing it with as many of their belongings as possible, including James' books and her own. The shelves above the coal bunker and dresser had to hold dishes and a couple of 'wally' or china dogs they'd been given by one of Virginia's barrow friends. Another friend who sold odd dishes and pieces of cutlery from her barrow had given her five big dinner plates and a tureen. Virginia had also bought a piece of red and cream checked oilcloth to cover the table. She was pleased with that as it made the tiny room look more cheerful and homely. A glass cover for the gas mantle was decorated with red poppies and the bright, multi-coloured blanket brightened the bed recess area. Although she hadn't been able to afford bed curtains or a valance to hide all the articles stuffed under the bed, she looked forward to getting some nice cream-coloured material eventually and making her own curtains. Once that was done, the place would look very nice, she told herself proudly. With the range sparkling and the fire glowing and everything spotlessly clean, it would be a cosy little place with all anyone could need for their comfort. James, however, simply reminded her of the lack of hot water and the lavatory out on the downstairs landing.

'But all the same,' he conceded, 'you've done a grand job.'

She was sweating and exhausted with all her hard work and would have loved a luxurious hot bath. But by this time she hadn't enough energy left to pull out the zinc bath and start filling kettles of water. She just fell into bed. Mathieson immediately got on top of her.

'No, James. Not tonight.'

'I've been looking forward to this all day. It's all that's kept me going. Coming home to you.'

She was barely able to whisper, 'All right.'

She felt sore now as a result of his desperate passion. And he was a heavy man. At times unable to lift her chest to breathe, she thought she was going to die. Then it was over, his passion spent, and he rolled off her and within minutes he was sound asleep. She felt exhausted but lay wide awake and feeling sad. She told herself that she was lucky to have a good man who would work for her and give her housekeeping money and never abuse her. Yet the sadness remained. She reminded herself how many women she knew were beaten by their men. Others never received a penny from theirs. Most of the men were unemployed but often they gambled or drank what little money there was. James neither drank nor smoked. He was totally devoted to the betterment of his fellow beings. She admired and respected him for that. But still the sadness weighed heavy on her soul.

Next day she was up early seeing to her husband's breakfast. Then after he left for one of his classes, she washed the dishes and tidied up and went out for something for his dinner. Bankier Street had shops underneath all of its bleak tenements and she first went to the grocer's and bought bread and potatoes. She could make a lot of economical dishes with potatoes. She was just passing the paper shop clutching her messages in one hand and her purse in the other when her eyes caught sight of something in bold, black type on one of the billboards outside the shop.

It was the name 'Cartwright.'

She stopped and read, hardly daring to believe her own eyes— 'Nicholas Cartwright found alive.'

Her legs gave way. She dropped on to her knees. Her purse and her message bag tumbled on to the ground. She crumpled forward. The last thing she remembered was seeing potatoes rolling away down the street.

18

When she came to, she was being propped up on a chair inside the paper shop.

'Are ye aw right, hen?' A small woman with bandy legs and a frizz of uncombed hair was bending close to her face. She reeked of whisky. 'Ye gi'ed us a hell o' a fright. Here's yer purse and yer message bag. Ah gathered up aw yer tatties.'

'Thanks very much.' Virginia took a determined grip of the purse and the bag. 'I'm fine now. I'll just buy a paper and then I'll get off home.'

'Wid ye like me tae come wi' ye, hen?' The woman looked none too steady on her feet.

'No, no,' Virginia hastily assured her. 'I'll be perfectly all right. But thanks all the same.'

'Ta, ta, then.'

'Cheerio and thanks again.'

As soon as the woman had disappeared outside and the shop assistant had finished serving a customer, Virginia struggled up and with shaking hands took a copper from her purse and asked for a newspaper. As soon as she got back to the single end, she collapsed into a chair and started reading the article about the Cartwrights. Mr and Mrs Cartwright had been contacted by the War Office and told that their son, Lieutenant Nicholas Cartwright, had been found in a military hospital in the South of England. He had been suffering from shell-shock and loss of memory as a result of a head wound. The confusion over Lieutenant Cartwright's fate had arisen because his watch and other personal effects had been found near another, otherwise unrecognisable corpse in the same area of the front-line where he had been posted as 'missing in action'. Naturally enough, this corpse had been presumed to be that of Cartwright and his family had been duly informed of their son's tragic death. Lieutenant Cartwright was not yet fit enough to travel but in a few weeks time, his parents would be allowed to take him home for a further period of convalescence. Needless to say, the article concluded, Mr and Mrs Cartwright were overjoyed at the wonderful news.

Virginia felt absolutely shattered. For a few minutes she became hysterical, laughing and weeping at the same time. After she managed to control the mad sounds she was making, she still went on trembling. She hadn't the strength to get up from her chair. She didn't know what to think, or what to do. A loud knocking forced her to try and control herself, and like a drunk woman she staggered towards the door.

'Hello therr, hen,' Standing on the doorstep was a long leek of a woman in a fusty black dress. She had a red nose on a face like a sad bloodhound. Her grey hair was pinned severely back. 'Ah'm Mrs Finniston, wan o' yer neighbours.' With a sniff, she jerked her head to indicate across the landing. 'Ah wis speakin' tae Mrs McGann and she telt me ye wisnae well.'

'Come in.' Virginia stood back to allow Mrs Finniston to sail into the kitchen. 'How did she know where . . .'

'Och, she saw ye goin' up the close and knew ye must be the wan that's jist moved in tae this hoose. Ah meant tae come and see ye anyroads. Here's a wee mindin' for ye.' She handed Virginia a glass butter dish with 'Welcome to Scarborough' emblazoned on it.

'Thanks very much,' Virginia said. 'I haven't got a butter dish.'

'There ye go then.'

'A cup of tea?'

'Aye, ah might as weel.' Mrs Finniston sniffed again. She obviously had a problem with her nose. She sniffed quite a lot. 'Ye've done a lot o' work on this place. Ye'll no' get any thanks fur it.'

'From the landlord, you mean?'

'The rents keep goin' up. Ma Jeannie's gettin' merrit on Saturday an' the other day she an' Danny got a single end across the road. The very same as oors but that crook o' a landlord's askin' mair rent fur it. The exact same as oors.'

'Fancy!' Virginia tried to sound sympathetic but her mind and her emotions were still bound up with what she'd just read in the newspaper. The kettle had been simmering on the hob and she made a pot of tea while Mrs Finniston went into some detail about her daughter's forthcoming wedding. It was to be in the registry office, and then a sit-down tea of steak pie, peas and potatoes, followed by Scotch trifle, was to be served in The Coffin.

'The Coffin,' Virginia echoed in horror.

'It's shaped like wan. The hall.'

Afterwards there was to be dancing to Jocky Scott's band which consisted of a piano accordion and a set of drums. The whole thing, according to Mrs Finniston, was costing her 'a fortune'.

'You an' yer man huv tae come alang.'

'Oh, I don't think . . . I mean, I don't know your daughter. I don't know anybody yet.'

'A good chance tae get tae know everybody at wance. Aye, you an' yer man come alang tae The Coffin. Ah might as well be killed fur a sheep as a lamb. It's the Co-op caterin'.'

'Oh, very nice.'

'That's settled, then.'

'Well . . .'

'If ye huvnae any biscuits, ah'll bring some in frae next door.'

'Oh, no. I mean, yes.'

Virginia hurried over to the press and brought out a packet of tea biscuits.

'Nae biscuit barrel, hen?' Mrs Finniston helped herself to a biscuit. 'Ma Jeannie's got three fur presents. Ah'll ask her tae gie ye wan.'

'Oh no, please. My mother's got one for me,' Virginia lied.

'She goat two fireside sets.' She glanced at the range. 'Ah see ye've got a set. It's no' as nice as the wans Jeannie's got though. So whit's up wi' ye? Are ye gonnae huv a wean? There's twenty up this close.'

'Oh no. No. I just felt a bit faint. I had forgotten to eat anything. I've been so busy with the house.'

'Ye'll no' get any thanks fur it. Mrs Taylor in the close killed hersel' trying to keep the place clean. Fightin' wi' the rats when wan o' them killed her.'

'A rat killed her?' Virginia was momentarily distracted from her thoughts of the Cartwrights.

'The bite went septic. She died in agony.'

'That's awful!'

'Dinnae think ye'll be safe wan up. They can climb like nae-buddy's business. Up the stairs, up the walls. In the doors, in the windies—'

'Yes, well,' Virginia interrupted in desperation. 'It's time I was getting on with my husband's dinner.'

Mrs Finniston heaved a deep sigh. 'Aye, right.' She rose. 'Ah ken when Ah'm no' wanted.'

'Oh, I didn't mean . . . You're very welcome. But I've not been married very long and I worry about cooking. I'm not used to it yet. It takes me ages.' She followed Mrs Finniston's tall straight figure to the door. 'Thanks for coming.'

'Aye, right,' Mrs Finniston sniffed. 'On ye go, then. Ah'll see ye an' yer man at The Coffin the back o' six.'

'Lovely.' Virginia managed a grateful smile. 'Thanks very much, Mrs Finniston. I'll look forward to it.'

She shut the door and leaned against it for a minute before returning to the kitchen. There, she picked up the paper again. She couldn't believe it. Her mind couldn't take it in. She forced herself to begin peeling potatoes at the sink. Down in the back yard a man in the usual shabby uniform of the unemployed was singing a Catholic song. Most of the Calton area was populated by Catholics, a fact which livened up the annual Orange walk. They made a point of marching down every Catholic road and banging their drums as loudly and provocatively as possible, especially when they passed a chapel. James was very much against this. It was another thing they had in common. He was always going on about how the working class would never make any worthwhile progress if they fostered differences and fought among themselves. She put sausages into the frying pan and watched them sizzle. She added chopped onion, and the pungent smell quickly filled the small room.

The paper was lying open on the chair and she kept glancing over at it as if she might have dreamed the whole incident. But it was always there.

James didn't notice it at first when he came in. He went straight over to the sink, washed his hands, then stood drying them on the towel hanging inside the press door.

'You'll have to remember to buy candles for when we go to the lavatory. Even during the day, once you shut the door, it's pitch black in there.'

'I'll get some this afternoon.' She dished his meal. 'Sit in at the table and take this while it's hot.'

He sat at the table with his back to the chair and the paper. Virginia wondered if she could surreptitiously remove it, hide it under the pillow in the bed perhaps. Anything to do with the Cartwrights—even the mere mention of their name—could ignite one of James' dreadful rages.

'Aren't you having anything?' he asked as he cut up the sausages.

'Yes, I'm just dishing it.'

She put her plate on to the table but hesitated about sitting down.

'Is something wrong?' Mathieson asked. How could she hide it from him? If he didn't see it on the billboards, somebody was bound to tell him.

'It's just something in the paper.'

'What was it? Have you got it there?'

He turned and saw the paper. He stretched out and picked it up.

'Good God,' he shouted. 'Could you beat that? So much for his patriotic sacrifice speeches to the workers. Thousands of ordinary men are dying in the trenches and this rich bastard, this bastard who's always enjoyed a privileged life, he survives. Can you beat it?' he repeated. 'How lucky can you get?'

Virginia didn't say anything.

'I hope he dies before the Cartwrights see him.'

'James!' Virginia cried out. 'What a thing to say. You don't even know him.'

'He's had more than his fair share of the good life. Why should I care about him?'

'He's a human being who must have suffered in the trenches. He's been seriously injured.'

'He'll get the best of attention. Once he's home he'll be spoiled and cossetted and have everything that money can buy. While thousands of other men will face nothing but misery, unemployment and homelessness when they get home. I don't understand why you keep sympathising with the Cartwrights.'

'I don't keep sympathising with them. I just don't like to see you getting so angry and bitter. I worry about you making yourself ill.'

'He'll come home and after he's been petted and pampered he'll marry into some other rich family and so capitalism will be strengthened and perpetuated. Just you wait and see. And George Cartwright will no doubt get a knighthood for his services to the war effort. It makes me sick, just thinking about it.'

Virginia pushed her food absently around her plate. Maybe James was right. That's exactly what would happen. In sudden panic she realised she was in imminent danger of weeping. She got up and went over to the range.

'I forgot to make the tea.' She kept her back to the table, her chest heaving jerkily, her lips desperately pressed together in an effort to suppress her sobs.

James took no notice and continued reading the article. 'It is wonderful news, Cartwright is quoted as saying. The injustice of it! Here's a man who wouldn't even spend one penny on safety measures in his factory to save good working men from being blown to pieces! So why should his son be spared?'

But Virginia didn't hear a word James said. All she could do was think of Nicholas and thank God he was safe.

19

'Where's yer man, hen?' Wee Mrs McGann staggered towards Virginia not because she was drunk but because her legs were so badly deformed with the rickets.

'He had a class to go to.'

'A class? Hiv ye merrit a wean or whit?'

'He's a teacher.'

'Aw, a shame. He'll miss a good feed.'

Long wooden tables covered with white sheets stretched the full length of The Coffin and were set with cutlery, salt and pepper pots, bottles of HP sauce and saucers of butter. There were also plates heaped with slices of the Co-op's 'plain bread', as opposed to 'pan bread' which was more expensive and not nearly so popular.

They were joined by a fat Buddha of a woman with a fluff of dark facial hair around her mouth and chin.

'We're jist waitin' fur the bride.'

Mrs McGann confided in Virginia, 'Her Aunty Lizzie made the dress. She's a wizard wi' a needle is Lizzie. Lives across the road frae us. She's here somewhere.' She tried to stand on tiptoe to gaze around but failed and staggered back. 'Anyway, ye're sure tae meet her. An' if ye want anything made up, she's yer man.'

'Aye,' the Buddha agreed. 'Lizzie's a great wee seamstress. She made a rerr shirt fur ma man tae wear at his funeral.'

'Oh, you're a widow?' Virginia murmured sympathetically.

'Naw, Ah like tae be prepared but.'

Mrs McGann gave a screech of laughter. 'Be prepared! Ye should be in the Boy Scouts, Annie.'

The band suddenly burst into a rendition of 'Here Comes the Bride', and The Coffin was soon filled with heartfelt cries of 'Och she's lovely, so she is,' and 'She looks a real treat, so she does.'

Jeannie Finniston had obviously become Mrs Chapman in the nick of time. Despite the crafty width of her white crinoline wedding dress, Virginia recognised the wide-legged, leaning back, carrying everything before her walk of a heavily pregnant woman. Danny Chapman, a cocky youth with a Glasgow swagger and a wide grin, followed his waddling wife up to the top table. Then there was a loud scraping of chairs as everyone got seated. No sooner, however, had the Co-op waitresses bustled in with the first plates of steaming steak pie than the bride gave a sudden howl of anguish.

'Mammy, daddy!' she bawled at Mr and Mrs Finniston, 'Get me tae Rottenrow.' Rottenrow was the maternity hospital.

Her new husband looked pained. 'For Christ's sake, Jeannie, can ye no' wait till after oor tea.'

'Naw Ah cannae, ye stupit wee bastard!'

Jeannie was being helped up by her mother who was saying to Mr Finniston, 'Are ye gonnae sit there an' listen tae that selfish wee nyaff tryin' tae stoap oor Jeannie gettin' tae the hospital?'

Mr Finniston rose and pointed a finger at Danny. 'See you, if ye dinnae shut yer stupit mooth, ah'll shut it fur ye. Ye think mair aboot yer tea than ma lassie.'

'She's actin' the goat,' Danny said. 'Ah never came up the Clyde in a banana boat. She's been hunky dory aw day. Things cannae happen aw of a sudden like that.' He turned to his wife who was now on her feet and clinging to her mother. 'Sit doon an' stop yer carryin' on. Ye're gi'en us a showin' up.'

'Mammy, daddy!' the bride screeched.

Her daddy pushed his wife and daughter aside, grabbed the groom by the lapels and hoisted him up. Then he gave him what was commonly known as a 'Glasgow kiss'—he head-butted him, and blood immediately spurted from the young man's nose. The best man jumped to the rescue.

'Here, hang on therr! Ah'm no' huvin' this.' And he landed such a punch, it knocked the older man on to his back. In a matter of seconds, all was in uproar, with the bride's guests versus the groom's guests. Even the women laid about each other with their handbags. In the midst of the chaos, a hysterical Jeannie was bustled out of the hall. Virginia later learned that the baby had arrived within minutes of Jeannie's arrival at the hospital. Meantime, Virginia slipped away unnoticed and thankfully returned home.

Thoughts of Jeannie's baby brought back thoughts of her own. Richard must be nearly three by now. He'd be talking and running around. She tried to imagine him with black glossy hair and deep dark eyes and a beautiful cultured voice like Nicholas's. She longed to catch a glimpse of him. She longed for a glimpse of Nicholas too. Once Nicholas had returned to Hilltop House, maybe she might somehow find a way to see him.

The thought only lasted a moment. She knew it was neither possible nor wise for her to venture anywhere near Hilltop House. Nicholas had his own life to lead and she had hers. They had both known right from the beginning that it was impossible for them to have any lasting relationship. A chasm of class and background separated them and always would. And now she was a married woman. She determined to be glad for Nicholas, to be thankful that he was alive and to wish with all her heart that he would have a happy, fulfilling and peaceful life from now on.

She went over to sit at the window to watch for James. Several women on both sides of the street were having what was called a 'hing'. The window would be opened, a cushion placed on the window sill, and then the woman of the house would rest her folded arms on the cushion and gaze out at the panorama of life going on outside. She could also call out to others having a hing and exchange a bit of gossip.

Virginia couldn't bring herself to have a hing at the window. She felt the need of a certain amount of privacy. Although she did open the window a little so she could get a breath of air. She sat in the shadows of the room and gazed out. The street was packed even though it was becoming dark and the lamplighter was tramping along with his pole. She could hear the clatter when the gas flap went up and let the end of the pole through. Then there was the plop when the light came up and the tinkle of the flap when it went down again. It reminded her of a poem she'd learned at school.

> *My tea is nearly ready,*
> *And the sun has left the sky.*

It's time to take the windie,
To see the Leerie going by.

She watched as the yellowish pools of light surrounded each lamp post, and the eerie glimmer came to each dark close. Groups of women stood laughing and talking in the road. Some were wrapped in tartan plaids, some had babies slung securely in the inner fold and held close like a papoose. Barefoot boys were running about kicking a home-made ball. Girls played peevers with boot polish tins. Others were skipping with bits of clothes rope and singing in time.

Eventually Virginia saw the stocky figure of James coming along. He looked tired. There was a droop to his shoulders and he was walking slowly. He smiled at some children who dribbled a ball past him. Virginia went to the door to give him an affectionate hug of welcome.

'What did I do to deserve that?' he said, peeling off his coat and hanging it on one of the hooks in the lobby.

'Just being you,' Virginia said. 'Are you ready for a cup of tea.'

He nodded. 'I'm surprised you're home. Weddings usually go on later than this.'

'I know but it turned out a right shambles. Everybody started fighting one another.'

'No!' He went over to hold his palms in front of the fire, then rub them together. 'What went wrong?'

'It's a long story and you look tired. I'll tell you all about it later. Drink your tea and then get some sleep. You've been on the go all day.'

'John's been invited down to England for a lecture tour. He'll be a lot more tired than me before he's done.'

'You know what he's like. You said yourself he's got superhuman energy.'

'Aye,' he sighed, 'right enough. I wish I could match it.'

'You do more than your fair share, James. I'm proud of you.'

He looked up in surprise. 'Are you?'

'Of course I am. You're a marvellous worker for the cause. Everybody knows that.'

Pleasure brightened his face. 'Aye well, I do my best.'

Virginia poked the fire into crackling life. The warm light from it and from the gas mantle which hissed above it gave the small room a cosiness which prompted Virginia to remark,

'This isn't so bad, is it? It'll do us for a while anyway. And the neighbours are all very nice and friendly.'

'I suppose,' Mathieson said. 'As long as you can stand it.'

'I'm all right.'

'It's not all right that you should have to live in a place like this, Virginia. Not you, not anyone.'

'You know what I mean. It'll do us just now.'

'It'll have to, won't it?'

Thumping and banging sounds started to come from upstairs, accompanied by screams and oaths. James added ruefully, 'Sounds as if your wedding fight is continuing above us. We'll be lucky if we get any sleep at all.'

He undressed and heaved himself into the bed. Virginia followed him after giving the fire some more attention, and turning out the gas. Once in bed, she put her arms around him. She wanted to be held and loved and reassured.

But James said, 'Sorry, I'm absolutely all in.'

'That's all right,' she said, giving him a peck on the cheek before turning away. As she lay, as usual, listening to his heavy breathing punctuated by the occasional jerking snore, tears filled her eyes and spilled down her cheeks. She had never felt so isolated, so alone.

'I'm going to have to work extra hard while John's down in England,' James said the next day. 'There's nearly two thousand enrolled in the classes already.'

'Well, just try not to overdo it. Nobody can be expected to go on working night and day.'

He shook his head. 'You're an awful worrier.'

After he had left the house, Virginia went to the library to read the newspaper there and see if there was anything else about Nicholas. There was the usual propaganda about the war, and the usual attacks on C.O.s and on John Maclean and what were referred to as the 'Red Clydesiders'. Never before in living memory had there been such vitriolic attacks by the newspaper writers on their fellow citizens. There were several sensational features about 'The man who came back from the dead', as they were now calling Nicholas. Eventually, she found an article, a well-written piece, about him. It spoke of his courage, his leadership as a young officer, and even his talent as a writer.

Virginia wished she could show the article to James.

'See,' she wanted to say. 'How can you hate such a man. Especially after what he has suffered.'

But she knew she could not do it. She would have to make sure she never mentioned Nicholas Cartwright ever again. To James, Nicholas must remain no more than a forgotten story in a yellowing, discarded newspaper.

1918

20

'The thing is,' James explained, 'there's a large body of people in the country now who want the war to stop immediately. But the powers that be are determined to crush Germany completely so that she'll never rise again to threaten the British Empire. They know,' he continued grimly, 'that this rising anti-war tide must be stemmed. They also know that the Clyde is the danger spot and John Maclean's the centre of the movement. So he must be silenced.' James had just told Virginia of Maclean's arrest.

'When did it happen?' she asked.

'As soon as he returned from England. He's been charged with sedition and refused bail. We're organising a demonstration on May Day to show our solidarity. The press is trying every trick in the book to stop us, but they won't succeed.'

And they did not. Over a hundred thousand workers took the day off to march in the procession, and thousands more, Virginia included, lined the streets as they passed by. Glasgow was afire with red banners, red ribbons and red rosettes. The air was alive with revolutionary songs and with the stirring sound of massed bands. Virginia felt excited, uplifted and proud. She hurried along to Glasgow Green where orators spoke from twenty-two different platforms, and every platform commanded a crowd. Virginia pushed her way to the front of the crowd who were listening to Mathieson speak and at the end of his oration, she cheered him along with the rest.

The extraordinary events of the day ended with the enormous crowd marching to Duke Street prison where three times a tremendous shout arose from thousands of lusty throats,

'John Maclean! John Maclean! John Maclean!'

Eventually Maclean was taken to Edinburgh to face trial in the High Court. Virginia and James were there to support him. In an impassioned speech to the jury lasting seventy-five minutes, he stripped the war of all its glamour, and made clear its real meaning. He also made plain his darkest forebodings of another war to come. The newspapers called this the ravings of an unbalanced fanatic. But Maclean had been called insane before. As he said to the court, 'No human being on the face of the earth, no government, is going to take from me my right to speak, my right to protest against wrong, my right to do everything that is for the benefit of mankind. I am not here then,' he continued, 'as the accused. I am here as the accuser of capitalism dripping with blood from head to foot.'

Despite Maclean's powerful oratory, the sentence of the court was penal servitude for a period of five years. Maclean looked taken aback by the severity of the sentence but as he was being led to the cells, he turned to the gallery where Mathieson and the rest of his comrades were sitting and cried out,

'Keep it going, boys. Keep it going!'

At first James was deeply shocked, then shock was swiftly replaced by righteous anger.

'Bastards! Bastards, the lot of them! Cartwright and his capitalist cronies will be rubbing their hands in glee at this. They'll think that getting rid of John Maclean will finish us off, but it won't. I'll see that it won't.'

Virginia was angry too. There was no justice in such an outrageously severe sentence. Five years! For simply expressing the views he'd held all his life. She caught a glimpse of Mrs Maclean's distressed face and felt keenly sorry for her. How on earth were she and her daughters going to survive while John was locked away for so long?

Virginia and James discussed the trial and the sentence all the way home. They had never before been so much in agreement with one another. On reflection though, Virginia worried about how much and how deeply it seemed to have affected James. He would be going insane if he wasn't careful.

He couldn't stop talking about it. He couldn't make love for brooding about it. He only ate absent-mindedly. His talks to his classes and his street corner oratory became more and more wild, as he put himself at the forefront of the many mass demonstrations to free

Maclean. The whole movement was involved in the fight on Maclean's behalf.

'The authorities are beginning to think John's about as dangerous in jail as at liberty. They're dead against the July demonstration we've got planned. But it's going ahead all right.'

When the time came for the demonstration, Virginia went with James to George Square. The police were out in full force and she couldn't help but feel apprehensive. However, nothing happened there and the crowd, led by a band playing 'The Red Flag', set off in the direction of Jail Square. The police followed. Once Jail Square had been reached, Virginia's anxiety increased when she now saw that the crowd of demonstrators were surrounded by a force of hundreds of policemen. Suddenly, without any provocation whatsoever, the policemen drew their batons and the wildest scene ever witnessed in Glasgow began. Hundreds of unarmed men and women were struck down with sickening violence. Almost immediately, James was felled at Virginia's feet and she knelt beside him, trying desperately to stem the blood pouring from a wound above his eye.

Somehow she managed to drag him away from the crowd and get him to safety. Later, as his wound was being dressed, he was white-faced but still defiant.

'We'll have our revenge yet,' he told her. 'And what a revenge it'll be!'

'I wish you wouldn't talk like that, James,' Virginia said wearily.

'Why not? It's the truth.'

'It won't do us any good. It won't do John Maclean or his poor wife and family any good either.'

'Don't be so selfish and small minded.'

She sighed but didn't say any more. She supposed leaders like Maclean and Mathieson always suffered for their causes. As their families always suffered as well. She supposed it was inevitable and she didn't know what the rights and wrongs were in such a situation. Good men like Maclean had to devote themselves totally to great causes, and he had accomplished a great deal for the working man. Perhaps it was too much to expect that he should accomplish any more than he did for his wife and daughters. They obviously loved him and were totally loyal to him. That surely said something.

James was out as usual at his classes and meetings the next day as if nothing had happened. Yet he was obviously in pain from his head-wound, and she could see the strain in his face and the haunted look in his eyes. Virginia had arranged to visit her mother and so after breakfast, she set off for the Gorbals.

'There's a letter for you,' her mother greeted her and took down an envelope that was propped up against the tea caddy on the mantelpiece.

'Thanks, mammy.'

'It must be somebody that doesn't know your new address.'

Virginia opened the envelope. Inside was one sheet of paper with the Hilltop House address at the top. The letter couldn't have been briefer, yet she could hardly believe what it contained. It just said to meet at their usual place the next afternoon and it was signed 'Nicholas'.

Virginia hastily stuffed the letter into her pocket and sat down on the nearest chair. For now, she would just have to stay calm and try not to think about what this could mean. Her mother had her back to her and didn't notice her distress.

'I won't be a minute, hen. The kettle's on the boil.'

'I've brought a packet of biscuits.'

'Och, you didn't need to, hen. But I'll enjoy them just the same.'

'Have you heard anything from Duncan recently?'

'I had a wee letter not long ago. He's fine, he says, but he wouldn't tell me if he wasn't fine. He wouldn't want to worry me so I don't really know. He asked me to look after Celia until he gets back.' She smiled. 'You can imagine what your daddy said about that.'

'You can't blame him.'

'Och, I know. But she's just a silly wee lassie.'

Virginia stayed for an hour or two chatting until her mother said, 'You'd better away home and make your man's tea now, hen.'

'Yes.' Virginia rose. 'Take care of yourself now, mammy.'

'I'm all right. Your daddy's got a few days' work and it's fair cheered us up.'

Out in the street, Virginia gave her mother a wave. As the older woman turned away from the window and Virginia began walking down the street, she noticed the now familiar figure of the telegram boy on his red-painted cycle. As usual he looked bursting with importance in his fitted blue jacket and high, round collar. There was a red stripe down the side of his blue trousers and around the band of his hat. As Virginia crossed the road, she was horrified to see the boy stop at her mother's close. Virginia, in sudden panic, raced back and got to her mother's door while the telegram boy was still standing waiting for her mother to open it.

'Telegram for Mrs Watson,' he called. Her mother opened the door. Virginia said to the telegram boy, 'I'll take it.'

'It's addressed to—'

'I know.' She snatched it from the boy, got inside the house and closed the door.

'Oh, mammy,' she said to the stricken figure of her mother. 'Come on into the kitchen and sit down. I'll open it.'

'We regret to inform you,' she read out loud, 'that Duncan Watson has been reported missing in action, believed killed. . . .' Her mother groaned and slumped to one side. Virginia threw down the telegram and rushed to support her.

'Oh mammy, mammy,' was all she could say. What use were words at a time like this?

Slowly her mother recovered herself and the first words she said were, 'That poor wee lassie will have had one as well. I'll have to go and see her. Will you come with me, Virginia?'

'Of course but you're not really fit enough, mammy. I can go on my own.'

'No, it's my boy and her man. We need to be together, Celia and me. You help me to get there. And then come back and tell your daddy. He'll be home from work in about an hour.'

As an afterthought, her mother said, 'What about your man?'

'Oh, never mind about him just now.'

Janette gazed at her.

'You shouldn't talk like that about your James. You must treasure him.'

Virginia stared at her mother's tragic face and marvelled at her courage as she rose with dignity from the chair.

'Treasure him, Virginia.'

21

Celia was a pathetic, dazed creature. They had found her wandering about the street in her slippers and without a coat or hat or even a shawl around her. She hadn't recognised them at first.

'Come on back to your house.' Janette had put a comforting arm around the girl's shoulders. 'I'll stay with you.'

In a way it was a good thing that Celia was so helpless. It gave Janette something positive to do and kept her own mind from being overcome with grief. Tam had taken refuge in rage.

'What did he die for? What did my son die for? Cannon fodder. That's all he was to these bastards pushing pins about on a map. Thousands are being slaughtered for a few yards of mud. Why did he have to go? It was against all he believed in to fight against his fellow workers. It was that bloody girl. He did it to please her. And now he's dead.'

'Och daddy, don't blame Celia.'

'You've changed your tune. Well, I never will. That girl is as responsible for my son's death as the bastards that pulled the trigger.'

'I've seen her. She's distraught. He was her man.'

'Guilt,' Tam said bitterly. 'Don't you ever let that girl come near me again or I won't be responsible for my actions.'

'She was barely seventeen when she married Duncan. Lots of girls haven't any sense at that age. They've all sorts of romantic, silly ideas. They don't think. . . .'

'Aye, well, she'll have plenty to think about now. Where's your mammy?'

'She's staying at Celia's place tonight. She's had to get the doctor for her.'

'Janette's far too soft for her own good. You tell her from me that she'd better not stay there for much longer or I'll go over there and haul her out.'

'No you won't, daddy.'

Tam never had been violent to Janette or any woman in his life.

'Have a wee dram.' Virginia put what little money she had on the table. 'Go to the pub and talk to your pals for a while. Will I ask James to come over? Mammy might have to stay a few days. Celia hasn't got anybody else.'

He suddenly looked deflated. Clearly he was devastated by the death of his one remaining son. She was worried about him.

'Aye, if you like, hen.'

James was even more enraged than Tam at the news, when Virginia got back to Bankier Street and told him. But his anger was not aimed at Celia. It was directed at the government, the generals, the munitions makers. 'Men of wealth and influence,' he said bitterly, 'who continue making huge profits at the expense of men's lives—good men like Duncan.'

'Could you go over and stay with daddy for a couple of days, James? Mammy's with Celia and I don't think he should be alone. I could go but I think he'd appreciate your company better.'

'Yes, of course,' James agreed. 'I'll have to keep going to my classes but I'll arrange it so that if I'm not with him, someone else will be there. Is he on his own just now?'

'I told him to go out and have a dram with his friends. He'll be in the pub.'

'I'll go and meet him there so that he doesn't need to go home to an empty house.'

'That's kind of you, James. I know he'll appreciate it.'

She packed a clean shirt and a few other things he'd need into a small case while he put on his coat and hat. He looked tired and more in need of going to his bed than trailing away across the river to the Gorbals and then having to cope with her father who was probably drunk by now.

'I really appreciate what you're doing,' she repeated. 'You're a good man, James.'

'Give me the case,' he said impatiently, 'and stop blethering or I'll miss the last tram.'

This was an exaggeration. There would be plenty of trams rattling and clattering about for a while yet. But she could see he was embarrassed. He didn't know how to cope with compliments.

'I'll see you in a couple of days or so,' he told her. 'And don't worry. Tam'll be all right. He comes from good tough working-class stock. Like the rest of his class he's had to weather many a bad storm.'

The door banged shut and left Virginia standing in the tiny windowless lobby. A couple of steps took her into the kitchen. She looked out the window and watched James make his way along the street. He didn't look up to wave to her.

Her own mind and her emotions were in turmoil. She grieved for her brother. But she couldn't put Nicholas out of her mind. She felt ashamed and guilty to be thinking of her lover at a time like this. There was no way that she could have a secret tryst with him. It would be wicked at any time to deceive her husband—even if it was only an innocent meeting. But to take advantage of the tragedy of her brother's death and James' absence because of his kindness would be totally unforgivable. Especially when the meeting was with one of the hated Cartwrights. She dreaded to think what James might do if he found out.

Yet, how she longed to see Nicholas, to be held by him, to comfort him and be comforted by him. She visualised him going to their secret place in the woods and waiting for her. Waiting and waiting. He obviously didn't know that she was married. He wouldn't understand when she didn't appear. He would be hurt and disappointed and sad. He would think she no longer loved him.

But then another thought came to her. He must have come through a great deal of pain and suffering—how could she add to that pain now? The more she thought about it, the more she became convinced that she had to go. She *would* go.

By the next day, she was collapsing inside with fear and apprehension thinking of the dangers of what she was about to do, and the amount of nerve it would take. But then, there had always been danger in her relationship with Nicholas. She thanked God that she hadn't given her father her last penny. She still had some money in her purse to pay for the bus that would take her to the nearest point to Hilltop House and the woods. She would have to walk the rest of the way, but she'd walked further than that before.

The woods were just as she remembered them. Greenery dappled by shafts of light and the heady, sweet, pine-scented air. Despite her trembling excitement, she noticed the new autumn tints on birch and bracken. She remembered dancing with Nicholas on this soft, mossy earth. Oh, how they'd danced. His tall, lean, broad-shouldered figure came to vivid life in her mind, his smooth black hair, his dark deep-set eyes, and how they'd fixed on her. He'd looked long and seriously as if imprinting her every feature forever in his mind.

Then suddenly he was there before her. Her first reaction was one of shock. He looked haggard. His handsome face seemed as if it had been hollowed out, flesh had been pared away and only the bone structure remained—a skull covered with skin from which haunted dark eyes stared out.

'Oh Nicholas, my love.' She ran to him, her arms outstretched, to pull him close to her. His arms caught and held her. He kissed her hair, her brow, her eyes, her throat, her lips.

'Virginia, how I've longed for this moment. Ever since I regained my memory.'

He told her how things had slowly come back to him. Scenes from his childhood. The trenches. . . . He paused for a moment. Then continued, 'I suffered everything all over again. But then gradually, another memory kept recurring. I kept seeing these woods and feeling the peace of them. I saw you. I heard your voice. That's when I knew I was going to get better. I had a reason to recover. I wanted to get well. I had to get well enough to get back here and to you. Oh Virginia, I love you. I've never stopped loving you.'

She kissed him and stroked his hair. 'And I love you, Nicholas. Nothing has changed as far as our love is concerned. But so many other things have happened.'

His eyes suddenly shone with happiness.

'Yes, our son. What a beautiful child. Virginia, you have made me the happiest man on earth. My only sadness and regret is that my mother did not keep her promise to me.'

'She did look after me and helped me at the birth.'

'Yes, but she'd already put you out of the house. And she abandoned you again after the birth.'

'We agreed it would be best for your son.'

'*Our* son. If you had been from Campsie Castle, or any other upper-class home, would she have taken your baby and sent you away, Virginia?'

'Of course not. But I was a kitchen maid from the Gorbals.'

'Virginia,' Nicholas said, 'listen to me. This war has changed many things and one of them is this rigid adherence to class. You are a beautiful, intelligent, loving person and I love you. I don't care about you being a kitchen maid. I never did. I don't care where you come from. I want you to be my wife.'

He put up a palm in a gesture to stop her astonished protests. 'And I don't care what my father or mother, or your father or mother, or anyone else in the whole universe says or thinks.'

She knew she should tell him that she was now a married woman. But the sight of him, his closeness, brought up such strong feelings of desire that all other thoughts were driven from her mind. 'Oh Nicholas, make love to me, please. Just the way you used to.'

They undressed each other and he kissed every part of her, gently reaching down to each foot and each toe. Gradually his passion increased and she began to moan with pleasure and love. They came to a wonderful climax and he held her afterwards and whispered how much he loved her and would always love her. At last they dressed and Nicholas said,

'You must come back to the house with me now and we'll tell my parents that we are going to be married.'

'No, Nicholas,' Virginia told him sadly. 'I can't do that.'

'Darling, have faith in yourself. I know it will be an ordeal, but they'll come round in the end.'

'It's not that, Nicholas. I wish that was all it was. I wouldn't think twice about facing your parents now as long as you were by my side.'

'Well then . . .'

'I told you so much had happened. I didn't just mean the birth of Richard. Afterwards I became involved in politics. And there was this man who used to come to meetings with my father and brothers. We all went together and then gradually . . . eventually he asked me to marry him. I thought you were dead, Nicholas. I never forgot you. Never stopped loving you. But I thought . . .'

Nicholas looked stunned. Then he took a deep breath and said, 'I understand, darling. It was foolish and self-centred of me not to think of that possibility.'

'Oh Nicholas, I'm so sorry. I feel I could die of sadness. I don't know how I'll go on living without you.'

Nicholas put his arm around her.

'Now that I have found you again, do you actually think I'm going to let you go?'

22

'It's impossible,' Virginia kept insisting.

Nicholas shook his head. 'I keep telling you, Virginia, I don't care about class. I don't even want to talk about it.'

'Nicholas, you don't understand. My husband and all the people I know talk of nothing else. They've suffered because of it, you see. It's not so easy for them just to forget. Especially James. Nicholas, he's so full of hate, he frightens me sometimes. I daren't think what he'd do if he found out about us.'

'Nevertheless, he'll have to know, Virginia. You'll have to get a divorce. I'll talk to him. I'll explain that we knew each other and loved each other long before you met him.'

'Oh no, Nicholas, please. He'd kill you, I know him. Oh please, promise you won't go near him.'

'Virginia,' Nicholas said gently. 'You're obviously afraid of him. All the more reason to end the marriage.'

'I'm afraid for you because I love you. I can't bear anything to happen to you. I couldn't go through all that suffering again.'

'I'm not afraid of him, Virginia.'

'That might be so but it wouldn't make any difference. He not only hates your class, he hates your family. My brother Ian was killed in an accident at your father's munitions factory.'

'Oh God!' Nicholas closed his eyes. 'I'm so sorry.'

'It wasn't your fault. It had nothing to do with you, Nicholas. But you're a Cartwright. That's more than enough reason for James to hate you—without knowing anything about us.'

'But he'll have to know sooner or later.'

'Leave things as they are just now. Until I've had time to think. Until I can work something out. Please, Nicholas. Let's just go on meeting here as we used to.'

He hesitated. 'All right, we'll do as you say for now. But whether you agree or not, Virginia, the time must come when all this will have to come out in the open.'

'Yes, I know. But not right now. It's too soon. Especially after Duncan's death. My family have enough to cope with at the moment.'

'Of course.' He shook his head. 'What am I thinking of? Of course you must have time, darling. Take all the time you need. But promise you'll meet me here as often as you can. Until we can be together for good.'

They arranged when she would come again before reluctantly parting. Her whole body still throbbed with the passion of his love-making. Her skin tingled. Her mind was racing in confusion and fear. Her love affair must never be brought out into the open. Never. But how to prevent it? She had a temporary reprieve but that wouldn't last for ever. If she did not keep meeting Nicholas in secret, he would come after her. Then James would find out and all hell would break loose. If it had been anybody else but Nicholas Cartwright. If it had been anybody else but James Mathieson. . . .

When she arrived back home she flopped into a chair, mentally, emotionally and physically exhausted. She hadn't even the energy to make herself a cup of tea. But a few moments later she was roused by a knocking at the door. With a supreme effort she dragged herself up and went to open it.

There on the doorstep stood two women—wee bandy-legged Mrs McGann and big Annie. Virginia had not yet learned Annie's second name. Everyone just referred to her as big Annie.

'We heard about yer brother, hen,' Annie said in a low, suitably sympathetic voice. 'We're that sorry, but.'

'Aye,' Mrs McGann echoed. 'That sorry, so we are.'

'Come in,' Virginia said listlessly. They followed her into the kitchen.

'Ye look fair done in, hen. Sit there and Ah'll make us aw a cup o' tea.'

Virginia obediently sat down. Her mind was still gripped by the awful dilemma she was in, while at the same time she was suddenly overwhelmed with grief for her brother. It was all too much.

'It's yer poor mammy who'll be the worst but,' Annie said.

'Aye,' Mrs McGann echoed, 'the poor soul.'

In a daze, Virginia offered them biscuits from the box on the mantelpiece.

'Och, we aw need tae stick thegither when there's trouble, sure we do, Annie.'

'Och aye, aw the time. Here, gypsy creams. You're well off, hen.' Then suddenly realising her good cheer was tactless in the tragic circumstances, her face quivered with regret. 'Eh, Ah meant . . . Ah didnae mean . . .'

'It's all right.' Virginia forced a smile. 'Enjoy them. You're very welcome. No, I won't have one just now. But thank goodness for a cup of tea. It's putting some life back into me already.'

'Where's yer man. Is he hiding frae me, or somethin'?' Mrs McGann gave a whoop of laughter, then smothered it behind a hasty palm. 'It's just Ah seem tae always be askin' ye that,' she said in a small voice.

'I don't blame you. He's out first thing in the morning and sometimes doesn't get back until late. But he's with my daddy just now. My mammy's helping my sister-in-law. My husband and my daddy have been good friends for a long time. We thought he'd be better comfort for daddy than me.'

'Aye, well, don't you worry, hen, we'll see tae you, so we will.' Mrs McGann staggered over to refill Virginia's cup.

'I'll be all right.' Virginia smiled. 'I'm a lot tougher than I look.'

Annie shook her head. 'There's no' a pick o' flesh on ye, but.'

'I've always been like this. I'm really very strong and healthy.'

'Fancy. An' you wi' such fair hair an' such a peely-wally face,' Mrs McGann said. 'Mair like a candidate for TB.'

'No, honestly. I worked for a while out in the country. I suppose the country air helped. My sister never saw outside the Gorbals. She died of TB.'

'There ye go, then.' Annie's voice had become doom laden. But she perked up a bit at the sound of the door bell ringing. 'That'll be Mrs Dolan. She said she might call round.'

'Ah'll go, hen.' Mrs McGann tottered towards the door and returned almost immediately with three women wrapped in tartan plaids. Virginia had seen them in the street but had never actually spoken to any of them. The kitchen was now packed.

'We're awfu' sorry, hen,' they said in unison.

'Thank you,' Virginia said. 'There's a cup of tea, I think. Is there enough left, Mrs McGann?'

'Dinnae worry, hen. I'll soon fill the pot up again.'

'There's gypsy creams,' Annie confided in a respectfully serious voice. After a while, Virginia was surprised but relieved to hear James' key in the door. He looked taken aback at the sight of the crowded kitchen. The ladies immediately rose.

'We're just goin', Mr Mathieson,' Mrs McGann informed him. 'We've jist come in tae give ye our condolences.'

'Oh, thank you very much.' He squeezed back against the coal bunker to allow the ladies to pass. After they'd gone, Virginia said,

'I thought you were staying at daddy's tonight.'

'I am. I'm on my way there. I just came to collect some papers I'll need for tomorrow. Have you heard the latest?'

'No. What?'

'They're force-feeding John. Twice a day, they shove an india rubber tube down his gullet or up his nose. He's being tortured. It's a bloody disgrace. I've called a special meeting about it.' He flopped into a chair. 'I tried to get permission to visit him but they wouldn't hear of it.'

'How did you find out?'

'From Mrs Maclean. She's taking it very badly. John suspected that his food was drugged last time he was in prison and this time he was sure of it. He tried to refuse the food. Then he did his best to fight them off when they tried to force-feed him. But he was outnumbered and it was hopeless.'

James shook his head. 'Those bloody maniacs of guards. They hate him at the best of times. You can imagine how they made him suffer!'

'You look tired, James. Maybe I'd better go over to daddy's and let you get to your bed.'

Mathieson pulled himself to his feet and went over to drag a case from under the bed.

'No, your father's expecting me. I can tell him all the latest about John. It'll take his mind off things.'

He selected some papers and notebooks from the case and stuffed them into his coat pocket. 'I'll away. I'll stay with him until your mother gets back.'

Virginia nodded.

He turned at the door. 'There's going to be demonstrations all over Scotland and England. They won't get away with this. They'll have to release him.'

'I hope you're right,' Virginia said.

Then he was gone.

She looked bleakly round the small room. For a short time she'd been proud of what she'd accomplished here. The way she'd white-washed the walls and polished the floor and displayed her dishes up on the shelf and spread out her pretty knitted blanket over the bed.

Now she gazed at it in the knowledge that it was just the same as thousands of other tenement kitchens with its ugly black sink and range and the coal bunker from which black dust billowed over everything every time the coalman called. And in every tenement was the same suffocating six-by-four hole-in-the-wall bed.

The room pressed in on her. Panic swelled up to her throat. Her breath quickened. She had to grip the arms of her chair and force herself not to get up. Not to try to escape.

23

The newspapers kept up their vitriolic attacks on John Maclean. The *Glasgow Herald* produced a special two-column article on the menace of Bolshevism in Scotland, arguing that in any other country Maclean would have been put to death.

'Bolshevism, or to call it by its old familiar name, anarchy, is not only a disease, it is a crime which, like any other form of morbid and unnatural offences, immediately brings a host of weak-minded and degenerate imitators in its train.'

But by this time the working men and women of Glasgow had learned to think for themselves. Even if some didn't understand or believe in all of Maclean's ideas, he remained their friend and their hero. They continued to fight for him and were united in the battle to get him out of prison.

Meanwhile, events were taking place in Germany that were striking terror into the hearts of the British government. The German fleet had mutinied. Its bases were in the hands of the elected workers. By 8th November 1918, revolution had triumphed all over Germany and a German Republic was proclaimed.

'Now,' James told Virginia jubilantly, 'Remember what John Maclean said at the trial—the working class, when they rise, are more dangerous to capitalism than even the German enemies at your gates.'

All the Cabinet agreed that the real danger now was not the Boches, but Bolshevism.

The Armistice was signed on 11th November. James did not share the country's wild jubilation at this news. He refused to join the street party and the neighbours—adults and children—as they danced for joy and relief in the streets.

'Maclean is still lying in Peterhead prison being force-fed twice a day. It's a disgrace. He'll be lucky to survive all that he's suffered.'

Virginia had no heart for celebration either. She kept thinking of her brother—buried in an unmarked grave, somewhere in a foreign land.

'They'll surely release him now that the war's over,' Virginia said. 'And especially after all the demonstrations in London. It must be obvious to the government that it's not just Glasgow people who are outraged at his treatment.'

James nodded. She could see that his mind was far away from her. He was already planning his next letter to the government, his next street corner meeting, his next demonstration.

She felt both guilty and glad of all his many distractions. It made it so easy for her to be with Nicholas without James knowing anything, suspecting anything, or even noticing that she had been away. He had come back unexpectedly one afternoon to an empty house, but when she returned, still floating on a wave of love and passion, he hadn't even asked her where she'd been. His lack of interest, his blindness, made her more and more daring. She was meeting Nicholas twice, sometimes three times a week now. A couple of times he'd taken her for a run in his open-topped car. She thought he looked wonderful in his long leather coat, leather cap and goggles. It was only afterwards that she experienced a pang of fear. What if someone had seen her? But she knew no-one from the Calton or the Gorbals would be anywhere near country roads on a cold November day.

The only trouble was, Nicholas had begun to say, 'Don't you think it's time now for us to speak to your husband and parents? And to my parents. I'll see my lawyers as well. I want us to be together, Virginia.'

He had wanted to bring Richard with him on one of their secret meetings but she had panicked and said no, not yet. She'd made all sorts of excuses. The truth was that she knew once she'd seen the little boy, once she'd held him in her arms, she wouldn't be able to let him go. Then of course all hell would break loose. Mathieson must never find out. Nicholas had no idea what he was like. There was no way that she and Nicholas could be together as a family. No way that they could get married. She couldn't risk what would happen.

But Nicholas was showing a determination that she hadn't realised he was capable of. He had begun insisting that she must make up her mind. She must settle a date. Next week, next month, but no later. They had to decide on an exact date now, and keep to it. . . . She opted for the end of the following month to give her time to think and gather enough courage to tell Nicholas, not James, that they would have to part. It was the only way.

She didn't know how she was going to do it. She loved him so much, so tenderly, so passionately. They were like one flesh together. Sometimes it felt like a dream being with him. She wanted it to go on forever. She dreaded having to hurt him by saying goodbye. Her life and happiness would end that day. But if she didn't go through with it the consequences for all of them would be too terrible to contemplate.

Meanwhile, James and his comrades were planning a welcome for John Maclean, whose release was imminent. Maclean had told his wife to keep the exact date a secret. He wanted her alone to meet him at the station, because he did not feel fit to cope with a crowd. The good news, however, could not be kept a secret, and all Glasgow knew and was ready.

On 3rd December, thousands of Glasgow men downed tools, left their places of work and came out onto the streets to welcome Maclean. He was to arrive at Buchanan Street Station and by the time his train was due, the crowd had swelled so much that the traffic was brought to a standstill. The whole city was agog with excitement and joy. When Maclean eventually appeared, cheers roared up from thousands of fervent throats, immediately followed by a vigorous rendition of 'The Red Flag'.

'I'll never forget this day as long as I live,' James told Virginia afterwards. She too had found it unforgettably impressive, the sight of Maclean's carriage being dragged through the thronged streets by a score of men who had willingly taken the place of horses was a remarkable sight. The exultant mass of people, the incessant cheering and joyful singing were amazing. But most moving of all was the sight of John Maclean, standing upright in the carriage, supported by friends and waving a huge red banner with an air of triumph and defiance. Yet it was obvious that the man had suffered. Despite his defiance, he looked haggard and ill. The procession halted at Calton Place and short speeches were made, although Maclean himself did not speak. It was said that his throat was so badly affected by the brutal force feeding he'd suffered that it was likely to give him trouble for the rest of his life.

After it was all over, Virginia and James left arm in arm. We must seem, Virginia thought ruefully, an ideal, happily married couple. For all she knew, James was happily married. He certainly never complained. Perhaps if she had never known Nicholas, she might have felt happily married too. As it was, she felt more and more alone when she was with James. In her mind and in her heart, she was always with Nicholas.

On the way home, they decided to call in to see her mother and father. Virginia had been worried about her mother's heath for a long time, but especially since Duncan's death.

'The only thing that keeps me going,' Janette would say, 'is the thought that I might have a wee grandson yet. I want to live to see him. It's such a comfort to me,' she always added, 'that you're comfortably settled with a good man, Virginia.'

This was another reason why she couldn't break up her marriage. It would kill her mother.

'Oh, come away in.' Her mother's face lit up with pleasure. 'Hello, James. Nice to see you, son.'

She led them into the kitchen and went straight to the range to make a pot of tea. 'Sit ye down.'

'I'll make the tea, mammy,' Virginia said.

'No, no, hen. I'm fine.'

She didn't look fine with her thin face and dark skin hanging loose under her eyes.

'Is daddy not back yet from the welcome?'

'No, but he shouldn't be long. How was it?'

'Marvellous. Wasn't it, James?'

James had taken to smoking a pipe and he was intent on filling it. 'Indeed it was, Mrs Watson. I wish you'd seen it. I don't think Glasgow will ever witness the likes again.'

'They took the horses from the carriage and a crowd of men pulled it instead.'

'Goodness me, that must have been a sight worth seeing, right enough. You can fetch the cups out the press, hen.'

'Right. He didn't look well though. And he couldn't speak.'

Mathieson paused in his efforts to light the pipe. 'Is it any wonder? After all he's been through. He's always had such a powerful voice. They found a way of silencing it. But give him time. He'll be speaking again. He won't allow them to defeat him.'

Just then Tam burst into the kitchen. 'What did you think of that then?' He addressed Virginia and James.

'We were just telling mammy.'

'The workers,' James said in between puffs, 'recognise a great man who's totally sincere and devoted to them. That's what today was all about.'

'Aye,' Tam said, 'and what a turn-out! I've got a half bottle here. Would you like a wee drop in your tea, Janette? You too Virginia? James and me can have ours neat.'

Janette passed over her cup. 'It'll maybe put a wee bit strength into me.'

James lifted his glass. 'Here's to John Maclean and the revolution!'

Tam echoed grandly, 'John Maclean and the revolution!'

Janette shook her head. 'All this talk about revolution. As if there wasn't enough trouble in the world. I'm just thankful the war's over. So many good lads killed.' Helplessly, she shook her head again. 'Our Duncan . . .'

'Drink up your tea, mammy. It won't do any good getting upset.'

'No, you're right, hen. I was always that proud of him. He was such a fine looking lad, wasn't he?'

'Yes, he was, mammy. And he thought the world of you.'

Janette nodded and began sipping at her tea. 'War is such a waste,' she said eventually.

'Indeed it is, Mrs Watson,' James said. 'As I've said many a time, the only war worth fighting is the class war.'

'Which reminds me,' said Tam, 'have you seen today's paper?'

'No,' James replied. 'Why?'

'There's an article about the Cartwrights. They're going to buy a whole lot of land up north. It says George Cartwright thinks it'll be the best kind of life for his son and that wee boy they're bringing up. Easy for some, eh?'

Mathieson's fist clenched round the stem of his pipe until his knuckle whitened.

'Next thing they'll be flinging out the crofters and everyone else who's trying to make a living on the land. That's what people like them always do—get rid of anyone who gets in the way of their hunting, shooting and fishing. If I had my way, it'd be the Cartwrights who'd be shot, not a load of defenceless animals.'

Janette and Virginia exchanged worried glances but neither of them spoke.

24

A wee unshaven man in a flat cap was singing drunkenly in Bankier Street and doing a soft shoe shuffle on the cobbles.

> *If you were the only girl in the world,*
> *And Ah wis the only boy,*
> *Nothin' else wid ma-er in the wurld the day,*
> *Ah wid go on lovin' in the same auld way. . . .*

Virginia hurried past, forcing a path through the crowd of giggling barefoot children who surrounded the man. She caught a tram and then a bus and then ran almost all the rest of the way. She was breathless by the time she reached their meeting place. Nicholas was waiting and immediately caught her up in his arms and whirled her around as he'd so often done before. This time she didn't throw back her head and laugh with joy.

'Darling, what's wrong?' Nicholas was concerned.

'Why didn't you tell me, Nicholas?'

His deep set eyes creased with puzzlement. 'Tell you what?'

'About your father buying an estate up north and all of you going to move there. It's in the papers.'

'Oh that! Nothing's settled yet. I only found out myself the other day and I was going to tell you. My father is a strong-willed man used to getting his own way. He isn't in the habit of consulting anyone. If he wants to do something, he just goes ahead and does it.'

'But will you all be going up to the Highlands?'

'My father has decided to retire and live up there. And he expects me to go with him. But I wanted to discuss it with you. It might be a good idea—not to live with my parents but perhaps for us to have a cottage on the estate.' He sighed. 'I've come to realise I'm never going to be much of a poet, Virginia, but I do feel I've something worth saying—perhaps in a novel. But to write a novel I need time to concentrate. A cottage away from it all in the Highlands might—'

'I think your poetry is wonderful,' Virginia interrupted in protest.

He smiled and kissed the tip of her nose. 'I think you're prejudiced, darling. But I know my limitations. Anyway, I've been scribbling away, and I mentioned it to a friend who's a literary critic. He persuaded me to show him what I'd done, and the other day he came to see me. I must say, I was actually rather embarrassed at the strength of his enthusiasm. He seemed very impressed, to put it mildly. Far more impressed than he's ever been about my poetry.'

'Well, I don't care what he thinks about your poetry. I think—'

'Never mind that. What do you think about us going to live up north, that's the important question at the moment. One of the alternatives is going through to Edinburgh. Or, we could always go down to London. What do you think? We'd have to consider what would be best for Richard as well.'

She wouldn't have cared where they lived as long as they could be together as a family.

'I'll think about it, Nicholas, and let you know.'

'Virginia, you really must make up your mind soon. About everything. What good can it do to keep postponing the decisions we have to make? It doesn't make them become any easier.'

'I know.' Worriedly she bit her lip.

'I've told you,' he said, 'I'll come with you to tell your parents and your husband. I'll be there by your side to support you. You don't need to say anything if you don't want to. I can do all the talking. But this is something that has to be done, Virginia.'

'I know.'

'Well then?'

'We agreed the end of January.'

He sighed. 'Very well. But not one day after that, Virginia. By then we must decide how we tell everyone and where we go. But whatever we do and wherever we go, we'll be together as a family. That's the important thing.'

She nodded and he continued, 'You must know that apart from

anything else you can't keep trailing away out here like this in all weathers. It's ridiculous. If you'd even allow me to meet you in town nearer where you live . . .'

'No, no. Someone would be bound to see us.'

'Anyway, enough's enough. A few more weeks, Virginia. Then, whether you like it or not, I'll turn up on your doorstep and insist on speaking to your husband.'

'I promise, Nicholas. We'll discuss everything and settle everything at the end of January. The armistice and all the celebrations have stirred everything up for my mother. It's made me think of Duncan too and wish . . .' Her voice broke.

'I know, darling.' He took her in his arms and stroked her hair. 'But try to think of the future, for our son's sake. Think of us being together. Think how wonderful it will be. Hopefully, we'll have time to organise a place to live before then. I have some money of my own. Enough to buy a small place in Edinburgh, or London.'

She clung to him, her eyes closed, imagining how wonderful it would be. For the first time she began to consider the possibility of running away with Nicholas and Richard. Not telling anyone. Just disappearing. The thought of such an action raised her spirits and gave her an immediate surge of passion. She began to passionately caress Nicholas until they were both breathless and urgent to come together and reach a climax.

Afterwards Nicholas laughed. 'Do you think we'll be able to enjoy this as much indoors on a soft bed with no danger to excite us? I know there's not all that much chance of being discovered. This is private land. Nevertheless there is the possibility of a gamekeeper, or poachers, or ramblers or trespassers—'

'Stop it!' Virginia scolded. 'Thinking like that is more liable to put me off than excite me.'

'That's your story,' he said. 'You know you revel in a bit of danger.'

'I do not!'

Suddenly he burst from their shady hideaway and stretched out his arms, shouting, 'Here we are. Two lovers. Nicholas Cartwright and Virginia Mathieson and we don't care a damn who knows it.'

'Nicholas!' Virginia clawed at his arm. 'Have you gone mad?' She was trembling with shock.

'Mad with happiness. Happy that the terrible carnage of war is over. Happy to be alive, to be in love, and to have lived to see my beautiful son. I can't bear any more of this secrecy, Virginia.'

'You promised. Please, try to be patient for just a little while longer.' She hesitated. 'A thought has just occurred to me, Nicholas. There is another option.'

'What do you mean?'

'We could just go. Disappear. That way we would avoid all the trouble this will cause. James has such a violent temper and I'm scared of what he might do.'

'That might be easier perhaps. Cowardly definitely. I have no intention of taking that option, Virginia, and neither should you. Is this what it's really all about? Not consideration of your mother or anybody else? Just fear of your husband?'

'It was only a passing thought.'

'Well, let it pass right out of your head. We're going to face everyone together. We're going to tell them the truth.' He looked thoughtful. Then he burst out, 'For goodness sake, Virginia, think what that would do to your mother. Not knowing what's happened to you. And what it would do to my mother not knowing what's happened to Richard.'

'Forget what I said. I'm sorry. Just forget it.'

He didn't say any more but the atmosphere between them had changed. When the time came to say goodbye she tried to recapture their closeness and warmth. She twined her arms around his neck and kissed him and told him she loved him. He melted at that and smiled down at her.

'I love you, darling. I've always loved you and I always will. You know that.'

'Yes.' She kissed him again. 'I can't come here at Christmas, remember. James will be on holiday from the College. But I'll write to you.'

Always when they didn't manage to meet, she sent him a love letter, but warned him never to write to her. James received a great deal of mail and was always first to greet the postman each morning.

Nicholas sighed. 'You don't know how glad I'll be when all this secrecy is over, Virginia. I really hate it.'

'You don't hate seeing me, I hope.'

'I hate seeing you for such brief, furtive moments. It's got to stop.'

'I know.' Hastily she kissed him again. 'Soon, I promise. Now I'll have to run.'

He was right, she knew. It was cruel of her to keep him waiting like this. She tried to summon the courage to speak to James. Perhaps she could speak to her mother and father on her own. And then she could protect Nicholas by speaking to James herself. But first she had to make up her mind what was possible as far as the future was concerned. How would her mother react if she decided to go ahead and end her marriage? How would her father feel and what would he think of her for becoming part of the Cartwright family? He'd probably disown her. . . . She could live with that. But could she destroy James? He trusted her completely. If she decided to leave him, she daren't think what the knowledge of her betrayal would do to him.

Most of all though, she worried about what he would do to Nicholas. Nicholas had fought in the trenches. If it came to blows, as Virginia feared it might, Nicholas would stand his ground. But Nicholas was a gentleman. He would not be prepared for the sort of violence James was capable of. Her stomach caved in with fear and horror every time she imagined Nicholas's tall, slim, elegant figure standing before James' stocky, pugnacious build. She heard Nicholas's quiet cultured voice explaining to James that he and James' wife had been lovers for years and that they had a child. She imagined James' rage. He had always been aggressive and with such provocation he would be more than capable of murder.

But perhaps if she told him herself? She couldn't imagine him being violent to her. He had always condemned men who physically abused women. He might still rush to seek Nicholas out but at least she could get a message to Hilltop House to warn Nicholas. And she could call the police.

Even while these thoughts raced through her mind, she felt a great sadness for James. She had always admired his many good qualities and still did. She was fond of him. Their marriage was better than most she'd seen or heard about. If he asked her 'What have I done to deserve this?', she would have to say 'Nothing.'

It was a dreadful thought to have to face him with the truth about her and Nicholas. She couldn't sleep for going over and over it in her mind. Sometimes she even felt like running away on her own. Too easy and too cowardly, Nicholas has said, and he was right.

She began rehearsing what she would say to James, and to her mother and father. It might soften the blow to her mother if she learned the truth about the grandson she had always longed for.

How to begin?

'James, there's something I must tell you . . .'

'Mammy, sit down and try to keep calm, please. A long time ago . . .'

Once upon a time. Sometimes it felt like that, just a story. A story that could never come true. A story that would end tragically.

1919

25

Virginia planned to speak out as soon as Christmas was over. But before she got the chance, James became involved in yet another crisis.

The Clyde Workers Committee had held a conference of shop stewards in the shipbuilding and engineering industries, and decided to support the miners and strike for a forty-hour week.

'You see,' James explained to Virginia, 'demobilisation has created terrible unemployment and this way, if the employed work less hours, ex-soldiers will be able to find work and make a decent living.'

James helped draw up a manifesto and copies of it were sent out to all the industrial centres throughout Britain. A general strike was to take place on Monday 27th January. James had never been more intense. He was working and speaking as he'd never done before. Virginia simply didn't have the heart to undermine him at this important time.

On the 27th, he told her triumphantly, 'The shipbuilding yards and engineering shops are empty and the strike's spreading rapidly all over the country. There's a huge rally being held in St Andrew's Hall in a couple of days. We're going to march from there to the City Chambers. A deputation is going to speak with the Lord Provost. We're going to tell the Council to force employers to agree to the forty-hour week.'

James and his comrades saw the Provost and put their case, and he asked them to return on the 31st for his answer.

'I think it's going to be all right, Virginia. It means that all those unemployed ex-soldiers will get work—and all thanks to their fellow working men.'

Virginia asked what was going to happen at the rally on the 31st.

'It'll be a huge celebration of the power of the working class. Everybody will be there. It'll be a great day. You must come along and share it with us, Virginia.'

'Of course I'll be there.'

The truth was she was sick of mass demonstrations and rallies. She was sick of politics altogether, but she recognised that the action taken in this case was needed. She knew she was being selfish in just wanting to get on with her own life. She had never felt like this before. She still believed in the rightness of the socialist cause, but now all she longed for was to be able to go away with Nicholas and Richard and live a happy, peaceful and secure life. Now she wanted something for herself more, far more, than for other people, fellow socialists or not. She realised, not for the first time, that she did not have James' passionate dedication. Despite all this, to please him, she agreed to join the huge gathering in George Square.

When the day finally came, thousands of strikers poured in to the square from all directions. Virginia had arrived early with James, who had left her at the front of the City Chambers while he went in with the deputation to hear the Council's decision. The deputation were confident and expected no trouble—although they were somewhat taken aback to see the square lined with hundreds of policemen, both mounted and on foot. After the deputation went inside the building, the crowd waited peacefully and listened to speeches from William Gallacher and others.

The frost was still sharp in the air, causing breath to steam in gentle waves above the demonstrators. There was a palpable air of excitement and anticipation as the buzz of animated talk rose and fell in the square.

The police horses, skittish because of the ice under foot, snorted and stamped, making occasional sparks as hoof struck cobbles. One huge black horse lunged and pranced, its eyes rolling nervously, its nostrils flaring. As it champed and chewed at its heavy steel bit, flecks of saliva sprayed steaming on to its powerful neck. The constable tugged and strained on both reins and stirrups to control the nervous beast as it surged forward. The arrogant head was pulled back and the animal retreated, high stepping, to its line. But suddenly its back legs slid from under it and it clattered and collapsed onto the cobbles, causing horses on either side to whinny and spring sideways in panic.

Across the square, other mounted officers and constables on foot saw a surge in the crowd, heard a roar of voices and the sound of a horse in distress. They witnessed the sudden swirling and circling of horses and, nerves already stretched to breaking point by fear and apprehension, they broke ranks, drew their batons and charged. Horses pressed forward, constables ran swinging their batons, lashing out wildly in all directions. Virginia found herself screaming along with other women and children in the crowd.

Blows fell indiscriminately on strikers, bystanders and those who had simply been drawn to the scene through curiosity. Men and women, surprised and unarmed, went down like ninepins. In a few minutes, the whole square was in uproar. The strikers quickly recovered their wits and began fighting back with their fists. The deputation inside the City Chambers, hearing the noise, came rushing out to restore order. One of them, David Kirkwood, was immediately felled by a policeman and carried away unconscious. James was yelling frantically for everyone to leave the square and go to Glasgow Green until a mounted policeman struck him a glancing blow that knocked him to his knees.

Virginia ran to him. But before she could get him to the shelter of the City Chambers entrance, they were engulfed by a sea of violence. Outraged strikers had now ripped up iron railings and engaged in brutal hand to hand combat with the police. A lorry full of lemonade bottles parked in a nearby street was commandeered and the bottles used as weapons. In the face of such stubborn resistance, the police were forced out of the square.

But eventually the Riot Act was read by the Sheriff of Lanarkshire. In a loud voice he commanded silence before bawling out, 'Our sovereign lord the King chargeth and commandeth all persons, being assembled, immediately to disperse themselves, and peaceably to depart to their habitations or to their lawful business, upon the pains contained in the Act made in the first year of King George for preventing tumults and riotous assemblies. God save the King!'

The strikers knew only too well that to remain assembled for an hour after the Riot Act was read constituted a felony. At one time the penalty was death. Now it could mean penal servitude for life. However, the strike leaders, including James, were quickly rounded up and arrested and soon after the Act was read, the crowd began to disperse.

Virginia could do nothing more for James that day, so she went to the Gorbals in case her father had been involved and her mother was alone. But her father had arrived in the house before her.

'Wasn't that a bloody disgrace?' he said. 'It was a perfectly peaceful crowd waiting for the Council's answer. Well, they got the answer all right. Bloody violence.'

'James has been arrested.'

'Oh no,' Janette groaned. 'He wasn't hurt again was he?'

'No, they just dragged him off with the others.'

'What'll happen to him, hen?'

'I don't know. I just hope they don't put him in prison again.'

'Most of them will be charged with incitement to riot,' Tam said. 'But not James. He was inside the Chambers, wasn't he? He didn't do any inciting either that day or before it. No, don't worry, hen. He'll get off. You'll see.'

'Will they let him out on bail, do you think?'

Tam shrugged. 'Couldn't say. They might do but I doubt it. Not tonight anyway.'

'I was wondering about staying here tonight but maybe I'd better go home just in case.'

'Well, hen,' her mother said, 'you know you're always welcome here but your place is with your man, especially at a time like this.'

'Anyway, I'd better go,' Virginia said.

'Are you not going to have a wee cup of tea first?' Janette rose to fetch the teapot.

'No, mammy. I'll have a cup of tea when I get home. I'll maybe see you tomorrow or the next day—as soon as I find out what's happening to James.'

'Aye, all right, hen.' Janette saw her daughter to the door.

'Cheerio, daddy,' Virginia called before leaving. Her mother gave her a wave from the window and Virginia smiled and waved back. She didn't feel like smiling. She was concerned about James but angry at him too. She felt as if he was purposely doing everything he could to prevent her from speaking to him about ending their marriage. She wanted to discuss things calmly and logically, to tell him that her original association with Nicholas had nothing to do with him. And it was only because she'd thought Nicholas was dead that she had turned to someone else. She'd tried to be a good wife, but when Nicholas came back . . . That was going to be the really difficult part.

There was no escaping the fact that she had been unfaithful and betrayed James. But it was so difficult to talk to him about anything except politics. It was his only interest, the be all and end all of his life.

He'd taken her for granted. She felt angry at that too, remembering times he had been insensitive to her needs, or never really listened to her. By the time she got back to the Calton and Bankier Street, she had worked herself up to a fury of resentment against him. He cared more for all his so-called comrades than he'd ever done for her. She was ready to blurt out the whole story about herself and Nicholas as soon as she entered the house. But James wasn't there. He couldn't have got bail after all.

The place was silent and empty.

Once again she felt oppressed by the small, one-roomed house. It was becoming unbearably claustrophobic. She couldn't stand it. On an impulse, she ran out of the house, down the street and away to the nearest telephone box. The operator put her through to Hilltop House. If Mr or Mrs Cartwright answered, she would just hang up. But it would likely be the butler or the housekeeper. She put a handkerchief over the receiver when Mrs Smithers answered.

'I'd like to speak to Mr Nicholas Cartwright.'

'One moment, please.'

Then there was Nicholas's voice. 'Yes?'

'Nicholas, it's me. Can I see you. Can you meet me at Kirkintilloch at the bus stop?'

'Of course. When?'

'I'm on my way to catch the bus now.'

'I'll wait across the road in the car.'

'All right.' She hung up.

She couldn't bear to lie alone in the poky little room just longing for Nicholas. She had to be with him. Her mind and her body were desperately crying out for him. As promised, he was sitting in his open-topped car waiting for her. Not caring who saw her, she ran across the road, got in beside him and, for a few seconds, clung round his neck.

'Darling, what on earth's happened?'

'Can we go somewhere we can be alone?'

'Yes, of course.'

He started the car and they headed out of the city. Soon they found a small inn beside the canal. Before they entered, Nicholas said, 'Can you stay the night?'

'Yes.'

So he booked them in as man and wife. She didn't hear nor care what name he used. He got his room key and put an arm around her.

'Come on, we can talk upstairs. It'll be more private.' They could see the bar from where they stood in the small dark oak-beamed foyer. The bar was also low ceilinged, with ancient-looking beams and panelled walls. It was crowded with men and hazy with tobacco smoke. They passed it and climbed the narrow stairs in silence. Once in their room, Nicholas took her in his arms and said,

'Now, what's all this about? Why the sudden panic?'

'You know, Nicholas, I get just as frustrated as you. I long to be with you and Richard. . . .'

'Well then, why don't we talk to my parents tomorrow and then we can drive into Glasgow and talk to your husband. Or talk to him first if you like.'

'I want to. I want to. Believe me.'

'All right, we'll do it.'

'You don't understand. It's not as easy as that.'

'I've never said it would be easy, Virginia.'

She went over and sat on a basket chair near the window. From there she could see the gleam of the canal through the trees.

'I'm not thinking of how it will be for us. It's James. He's in trouble again. We were both in George Square for the demonstration. And when it all went wrong and turned violent. . . . It wasn't his fault, but he's been arrested. Daddy thinks he'll get off all right. But would it really be right for me to tell him at a time like this. I mean, honestly, Nicholas?'

Nicholas flopped down on to the bed.

'Damn!'

'Exactly.'

'I suppose we'll have to wait until his trial's over and hope he does get off. But on one condition, Virginia.'

'What?'

'Now that at least we've finally taken the plunge and come to a hotel, promise me we'll continue meeting here. Let's face it, darling—in the woods, in the winter . . .' He grinned. 'It's enough to cool anyone's ardour.'

'I haven't noticed it cooling yours.'

'But this is much more civilised, don't you think?'

She gazed appreciatively around the cosy half-panelled room with its Axminster carpet and comfortable bed.

'Yes.' She smiled back at him.

26

Lying in the steaming hot bath in the hotel bathroom the following morning, Virginia savoured the wonderful luxury of it. She felt totally removed from the difficulties and discomforts of a lifetime of bathing in a zinc bath, or trying to keep clean by washing at the kitchen sink. Or, as a very young child, being taken down to the back-yard wash-house to be bathed in the left-over water of somebody else's washing.

But she still felt bitter. So many people like herself, like her mother and father and brothers, like everyone they knew and had ever known, had to suffer a thousand indignities like that every day. Why should that be? It was intolerable. Suddenly she thanked God for men like her husband and John Maclean. They were the ones who were devoting their lives to changing the system that kept the vast majority of people living in desperate and dreadful conditions. What would happen without men who fought tirelessly to improve the conditions of the poor, the helpless and the unemployed? She supposed the rich would go on getting richer and the poor poorer, just as they always had done. Children would go on dying unnecessarily in the slums. Or if by some miracle they survived, they'd suffer all the ills that poverty, bad housing and under-nourishment so often led to—tuberculosis, rickets, whooping cough, measles, diphtheria, scarlet fever and meningitis. The fever van was never away from the streets, and the sanitary men were always coming round to disinfect the houses.

Virginia remembered how the men had come to the house when her sister Rose took ill. Everybody had to get out while the men burned rock sulphur on a shovel heated over the fire, and walked around wafting the acrid fumes about the place. She thought of the overflowing lavatory and bins, and rats, and bed bugs, and beetles. Long ago they should have knocked the whole building down and built something fit for human beings to live in.

Never before had she realised so clearly and strongly how right James was. Never before had she so admired what he was trying to do. Lying in the hotel bathroom, every pore of her body greedily appreciating the warm soapy water, she forgave James all his faults. He could get angry, he could fly into rages, but his anger was justified. He was entitled to be angry.

But she couldn't feel angry at Nicholas—even though he was a part of the system James was trying to overthrow. She had been awakened during the night by his sudden shout, as he jerked up in bed, eyes staring, sweat pouring off him. She had put her arms around him and tried to soothe and comfort him. He had told her about the nightmares he still suffered—terrible visions of horrors he had witnessed in the trenches.

A knock at the bathroom door brought her back to reality. She'd locked it because she treasured these brief moments of private luxury. Bath time would have no special meaning to Nicholas. It was something he would always have taken for granted.

'It's quite a nice day,' Nicholas called through the door. 'Would you like to go for a spin?'

'Yes, I won't be long.'

A drive in an expensive motor car, yes. Why not savour the comfort and luxury of it all, savour the sweet side of life for as long as possible. It couldn't last. But she would remember all this. Every single moment of it.

She laughed as they raced through the countryside, her scarf flying out behind her in the wind. Her normally pale cheeks became rosy, her eyes sparkled with excitement. Eventually Nicholas stopped the car and turned to her. 'I've never seen you look happier or more beautiful, Virginia. This is how it's going to be all the time. We'll be so happy together. When will I see you again?'

She felt suddenly deflated.

'It depends.' She shrugged. 'I just don't know what's going to happen. And what if you go up to the Highlands . . . ?'

'Don't be silly. I'm not going anywhere without you. Do you know, I don't know which is worse—the way my mother and father never seemed to have the slightest interest in me when I was a child, or now

169

when they both seem to have gone to the opposite extreme.' He shook his head. 'One of the things they can't understand is how I've no interest in Fiona. They've done everything possible since I've come back to encourage me to take up with her again. But now I think they've come to the conclusion that I haven't sufficiently recovered my wits yet, and a change of scene will do the trick.' He laughed. 'I bet they're hoping to get the Forbes-Lintons up there as long-term guests. I've no doubt that right now they'll be planning a really jolly summer for Fiona and me.'

'Maybe that would be for the best.'

Nicholas suddenly grabbed her shoulders and shook her. His eyes suddenly seemed like dark pools that frightened her. For a moment he seemed unhinged, out of control.

'Don't you dare talk like that. Don't even think like that. You belong with me and if I go away you'll be the one who will spend the summer with me. The one who will be with me for the rest of my life, do you hear?'

'Yes, darling,' she said helplessly. 'It's just there are so many things against it. So many difficulties to overcome.'

'We'll overcome them together. We have a child to think of, remember. He deserves to be brought up in a proper family with his mother as well as his father.'

She nodded. 'I'll have to go now. It's time I was catching the bus at Kirkintilloch.'

Once in the small town, as she was getting out of the car, Nicholas said, 'Promise you'll telephone me as soon as possible.'

'I promise.'

He looked so strained at times despite his cheerful bravado. She worried about him. Once she'd given him her promise, however, his expression changed and he gave her one of his beautiful smiles. Beautiful was the only appropriate word she could think of to describe him to herself. He would have been embarrassed and laughed at her if she'd told him. But he'd always been beautiful to her.

She waved him off and in a matter of minutes she was sitting in the bus en route for Glasgow. Soon she was walking reluctantly along the crowded Bankier Street. One of the group of shawl-wrapped women called to her.

'Hello therr, hen. Been stayin' wi' yer mammy?' It was the ample bosomed Mrs Gilhooly from the top flat.

'Yes.' Virginia smiled. 'How's your husband?' Mr Gilhooly suffered a lot with his chest.

'Och, hawkin' an' spittin' wi' the best o' them. Ah hud tae get out though. I wis beginnin' tae boak.'

Virginia tried to look suitably sympathetic.

'I'd better go and get something ready for the dinner.'

'Aye, they're sayin' most o' the boys will be oot the day—yer man'll be hame fur his tea Ah'm sure. Och well, make the most o' yer wee bit peace, hen. Ah wish they'd lock ma Charlie up and gie me a bit o' peace.'

Once in the house she realised there was no food in the cupboard and only half a loaf in the bread bin. She didn't feel like going out to the shops. It meant running the gauntlet of the crowd of women in the street. She didn't mind stopping to chat to them. It wasn't usually a problem. Today, however, she needed time to think. Not that thinking did much good. It never resolved anything. Conflicting thoughts kept chasing one another round and round in her head. One minute she'd be thinking she couldn't leave James. The next minute she was thinking she couldn't finish with Nicholas. That would be too cruel. He needed her. Sometimes she detected such a haunted look about his eyes, and she knew that dark horrors still clung to him, things he'd seen that could never be spoken of and never forgotten.

She was sitting beside the unlit fire staring into space when James opened the front door and came into the room. Virginia got up.

'James, what happened? I'm so glad they've let you out.'

He rubbed his broad hands together. Nicholas had slim hands. His fingers were long compared with James' short stubby ones.

'The Workers Committee kept their word and came up with the bail money. Any tea on the go?'

'Oh, I'm sorry. I just couldn't get going today. I've been so worried. I haven't even lit the fire.'

She hastily began raking it out. 'It won't take long to get started.'

James took the empty coal scuttle over to the bunker and energetically shovelled coal into it.

'They've still got Shinwell, Murray, Gallacher, Kirkwood, MacArtney and Bremner. You should just see what it's like out there today, Virginia. Glasgow's been turned into an armed camp. They've sent soldiers from England overnight—the city's full of them. There's even tanks on the streets. Tanks and machine guns everywhere! Can you believe it? And all we did was have a peaceful gathering in the square. I mean . . .' He shook his head in disbelief. 'It was like a gala day outing, wasn't it? So what on earth are they going to do with all these soldiers? It's probably just to intimidate us. They know we can't take on the army, even if we wanted to.'

The fire crackled and sparked into life. The heat took the chill off the room. She put the kettle on.

'I haven't even been for any messages. After I make a pot of tea, I'll run down to the shops.'

'Get me a paper, will you?'

'Would you like a bit of bacon and maybe an egg and some fried potato scones?' She knew he enjoyed that.

'Have you enough?'

She went for her purse and studied its contents. 'Yes, I'll manage.' It occurred to her though that if James ended up in prison, she'd be forced to go out scrubbing again. Remembering the stinking pub lavatories made her shudder.

'What's up?' James asked.

'Somebody walked over my grave.' It was a common enough saying but today it somehow had an ominous ring. She struggled into her coat and clutching her purse and her message bag, she left the house.

'I won't be long,' she called back over her shoulder. She could hear James jabbing at the fire. Already his thoughts would be far away from her. They'd be with his comrades in cold police cells.

'Ah saw yer man goin' in.' Mrs Gilhooly was leaning against the wall talking to Mrs McGann in the close. Her bosom, supported by her folded arms, heaved with laughter. 'Ye didnae get much peace after aw, did ye hen?'

Virginia squeezed between the women in order to get past.

'I'm just glad he's all right.'

Mrs Gilhooly gave another roar of laughter. 'Aye, ye can say that again. A nice lookin' wee fella. Ah'd be glad he wis aw right if he wis mine as well.'

Virginia supposed that he was a nice looking man—compared with other grey-faced undernourished men in the neighbourhood. He looked fit, tough even, with his broad face, deep cleft chin and cropped hair that stuck up like a wire mat. He was different in the way he dressed too. He always wore a respectable shirt and tie and a homburg hat.

If only she loved him as he deserved to be loved. But she couldn't. No amount of thinking about it was ever going to make that happen. When she returned to the house, he was sitting at the table writing in a notebook. He had taken to wearing glasses when writing or reading—cheap-looking, steel-framed things. He cleared his papers away when she dished his meal. Then she sat pretending to eat a piece of bread and jam and watched him wolf down his fry-up. Eventually he noticed.

'Aren't you having any?'

'I'm not hungry. I had something not long before you came in.'

'How's your mammy?'

Virginia felt suddenly wary. 'Oh, struggling along the same as usual.'

'Mrs Gilhooly was saying you'd just got back from there.'

'Yes, I thought I might as well stay the night. It didn't look as if you would be getting home.'

'Quite right. You were best with your mammy. She's had a hard time of it with one thing and another.'

'I know. I worry about her.'

'I'm glad Tam didn't get hurt or pulled in by the police. It was terrible, wasn't it, the way the police laid into innocent people. Glasgow folk won't forget or forgive them for it in a hurry.'

'I suppose they were acting under orders,' Virginia said.

'Oh, I've no doubt about that. There's a rumour going around that most of them had to get drunk first. They couldn't bring themselves to do it otherwise. But I don't know how much truth there is in that.'

'Oh well,' Virginia sighed. 'Thank goodness it's all over.'

'Over?' James gave a mirthless laugh. 'Don't fool yourself. The trouble's just started.' His words made Virginia think about the trouble that would arise if he found out she hadn't been sleeping at her mother's. The only way to avoid this that she could think of was to get to her mother before James did.

But what could she say? Unless, of course, she admitted the truth.

27

She decided not to say anything. James was going to be busy every minute of most days and nights helping Maclean and others to raise money for the defence of those who had been arrested. Maclean had been away speaking in England and so had not been in George Square on what was becoming known as 'Bloody Friday'. The chances were that James would not be visiting her mother during the couple of months before the trial and by that time the night she was supposed to stay at her mother's place would have been forgotten.

During the next two months, more and more often, she met Nicholas at the small hotel, sometimes during the day. Sometimes during the evenings when James had a class to teach, and she made sure that she was always in just before he arrived home. She would bank up the fire with dross and briquettes before she left so that all she needed to do when she returned was poke it into life and put a few pieces of coal on top. She also left the kettle on the hob and set cups and plates out on the table and a sandwich ready for Mathieson's late snack. She was becoming very well organised. More daring too.

Nicholas had begun meeting her in town. She had been adamant that he mustn't do this. It was too risky. In Glasgow she was well known as James Mathieson's wife. Nobody knew her in Kirkintilloch where Nicholas normally picked her up. But one day she had been standing in the bus station at her usual time when suddenly Nicholas's tall figure appeared in front of her.

'Come on,' he said, 'the car's round the corner.'

She went with him to avoid creating any fuss and even more attention than his handsome, expensively-dressed figure had already caused. But she hissed at him,

'Why have you done this?'

'Because I can't put up with this one moment longer. I'm not going to allow you to wait about in the cold and travel in buses when I'm sitting comfortably in a car. I'm going to drive you back as well.'

'Oh, Nicholas, I don't mind.'

'But I do. I mind very much.'

'What if someone sees me and recognises me?'

'We'll just have to cope with that the best we can if it happens.'

Her heart was racing with fear as she sat in the car and they set off down the road, and not because of Nicholas's slightly reckless, over-confident driving. All she feared was that she would be found out. But she soon began to feel exhilarated as they left the city and began to race along country roads.

'We could always book into a hotel in town,' Nicholas said.

'No!' she shouted at him in panic. 'Definitely not, Nicholas.'

He laughed. 'We only live once. Why not live dangerously?'

'Because I hate living dangerously.'

'What do you think you've been doing all this time?'

She leaned back and closed her eyes in despair. 'I suppose you're right.'

They had become well known to the innkeeper by now, but he was a discreet man and never questioned their regular bookings. Not even when they spent only an afternoon in their room. During the winter, the only trade that kept his business going was the small bar—and even that was only full at weekends—so he was glad of their regular custom. He became quite an ally, often slipping them the key of their usual room with a conspiratorial lowering of his voice and a promise of afternoon tea brought up to them before they left. Virginia suspected that what helped to oil the wheels was Nicholas's generous tipping.

The afternoon tea always added to Virginia's enjoyment. On a silver cake-stand, there were sandwiches and home-baked scones, and an apple tart or a Victoria sponge. A maid, dressed much the same as the maids at Hilltop House, brought in the trolley. Virginia loved acting the lady. She'd once said this to Nicholas and he'd impatiently replied,

'You *are* a lady.'

She loved him for that. And for the way he had gone on to unfasten her fair hair and stroke it and kiss it and say, 'And a very beautiful lady. I'm a very lucky man.' She felt lucky too as she lay naked in his arms, flesh against familiar flesh, feeling so much a part of him it was as if they were one person. Often they'd suddenly say the same thing at the same time. Then they'd laugh at the wonder and the surprise of it.

Then one day, Nicholas said, 'My father's pleading with me now to at least go up and look at this estate he's buying. He says he wants my advice. He wants to know what I think of it and what I feel needs to be done with it. It's all a ploy. My mother and father will stop at nothing to get me to settle on the estate.'

'There wouldn't be any harm in going and having a look.'

He shrugged. 'I suppose not. I could use the visit to look around and see what property there is on the land. If I saw a really nice cottage that I thought you'd like . . .'

'It's what you'd like and what you'd want to do that matters, Nicholas.'

'No, it is not. All that matters to me is your well-being and happiness. But I'll go and have a look at the place. At least it'll placate my parents for a while. It'll mean I'll be away for a few days. A week perhaps.'

She gazed at him wistfully. 'I'll miss you.'

'And I'll miss you, darling. I won't go if you don't want me to.'

'No, it's all right. Honestly, you go. I'll look forward to hearing all about it when you get back.'

They made tender love. He licked every inch of her skin, even between her toes, until suddenly she felt unbearably passionate. She wanted to clutch him tightly inside her and never let go.

Afterwards Nicholas sighed, 'Oh Virginia, if only you'd stay in my arms the whole night through. Remember that night you did stay—how wonderful it was?'

She remembered. 'No, I'll have to go. James will be home tonight.'

'If you must, you must, but I'm driving you back to Glasgow.'

'I wish you wouldn't. I'd be perfectly all right on the bus.'

'I'm not going to argue. I'm driving you back to Glasgow.'

To add to her anxiety, he did not stop at the bus station but carried on towards the Calton. 'Nicholas, for God's sake, you're surely not going to go right to Bankier Street?'

'I'll drop you a few streets away.'

'No nearer then. Any cars draw attention round here.'

'Are you sure you'll be all right. It looks a very rough area.'

'Nicholas, I've been brought up in a much rougher area than this.

Just let me out of the car. Please,' she added, struggling not to spoil their time together by being impatient with him.

He stopped the car and she hastily got out. He raised a hand in goodbye, before speeding away. She felt sick with apprehension. There were people jostling out of nearby pubs. Some were arguing noisily. Others were swaying about and singing.

> *Swanee,*
> *How ah love ya, how ah love ya,*
> *My dear auld Swanee. . . .*

Two men, arms around each others' shoulders, were giving a rousing rendition of

> *Ye'll tak the high road*
> *An' Ah'll tak the low road,*
> *An' Ah'll be in Scotland afore ye. . . .*

Knots of women were gossiping in closes but Virginia didn't recognise any of them. As she hurried past, a man shouted after her, 'Hello therr, hen!'

She realised he was just trying to pick her up. He didn't know who she was. Still, she felt agitated and on edge, even when she was safely in the house and had lit the gas mantle and poked the fire into a good blaze. Undressing quickly, she put on her white cotton nightie and the blue cardigan her mother had knitted for her. It had to seem as if she'd been relaxing at the fireside for hours. Looking around the room, she thought, 'This is the full extent of my home in which James and I sleep and eat and try to keep ourselves clean. One poky room only half the size of the hotel bedroom I've just left. The kitchen alone at Hilltop House is three or four times the size of this place.'

She hated it.

Suddenly she was startled by a knock at the door. James had his key so it wasn't him. For a dreadful moment, a crazy idea came into her head that it was Nicholas. She could hardly gather enough strength to get to the door. Clutching her cardigan around her with one hand, she opened the door a crack.

'Ur ye aw right, hen?' It was Mrs McGann.

'Yes, fine. Come in.' It wasn't the done thing to keep a neighbour standing on the doorstep.

Mrs McGann stumped from one bandy leg to the other into the kitchen.

'Oh my, ye're rerr an' cosy in here. Ye've goat it like a wee palace, so ye have.'

'Sit down, Mrs McGann. A cup of tea? I've just made a pot.'

'Is yer man at wan o' his classes, hen?'

'Yes, but he'll be in any minute.'

Mrs McGann pulled herself to her feet. 'Oh, Ah'd better make masel' scarce then. Ah jist came to check ye wisnae ill in bed or lyin' deed on the flair. Ah hidnae seen hint nor hair o' ye fur a while an' Ah've been chappin' at yer door mair than wance.'

'Oh, no, I'm fine. It's just I've to go out a lot too. I help my husband when I can. He's trying to raise money for the defence just now as well as attending to his other work.'

'Aw, the soul! He's a good lad, isn't he? He's in the same mould as oor Johnnie.'

'Johnnie? Oh, you mean John Maclean?'

'Aye. Know whit he did the ither day? A poor widow buddy in his street whose wean wis ill hudnae a penny tae pay the doctor. He went tae her hoose, and gave her aw he had tae pay the doctor and get the wean an' hersel' some nourishment. An' she'd never even asked. There's many a buddy begs for charity though an' if John has it, he gies it.'

Mrs McGann was making for the door as she spoke. 'That's the kind o' man oor Johnny is. He looks as if he needs aw the nourishment he can get hissel' at the minute. The poor man disnae look right.'

'I know,' Virginia agreed. 'James was just saying that the other day.'

'Well, cheerio the noo, hen.'

'Cheerio, Mrs McGann.'

Mrs McGann was only away a few minutes when James arrived. He went straight over to the fire, bent forward and rubbed his hands near to the warmth. He did this every time he came in and it had begun to irritate Virginia, although she knew it was unfair of her to feel as she did. Why shouldn't her husband seek warmth as soon as he entered his own house? He'd probably been standing talking at street corners for hours. Even the rooms in which he taught his evening classes were pretty cold and comfortless.

'The tea's made,' she told him. 'And there's a nice sandwich.'

'Thanks, Virginia.' He took off his coat and hat and hung them on one of the hooks in the lobby. He came back in, rubbing his hands together again. 'You'll be glad to hear we've managed to raise quite a sum. If it goes on like this, it looks as if there's going to be plenty to cover everybody's defence.'

'That's good news.'

She poured out the tea.

'I bumped into Mrs McGann there.'

'She was in here having a chat for a wee while.'

'She told me she'd been worried about you.'

'I don't know why.'

'She thought you'd been ill, apparently.'

'I don't know why,' Virginia repeated.

'She'd knocked on your door a few times and got no answer.'

Virginia rolled her eyes. 'It's worse than the Gorbals here. You can't move without somebody checking up on you.'

He gave her an odd look. 'Don't you think that's a good thing? It's a sign of caring. Of good neighbours.'

'Yes, I suppose it is. It's just . . . I've been trying to have a peaceful read and there's always someone coming to the door. And sometimes I go for a walk in Glasgow Green. Just to think in peace.'

There was some truth in this. Nicholas had given her several books and she'd been trying to read them in secret. She had also gone for the occasional walk in Glasgow Green to try to think things out.

In between bites of his sandwich, James laughed. 'Like James Watt.'

'What?'

'James Watt was walking in Glasgow Green having a quiet think when he invented the steam engine.'

'Oh yes.' She managed to laugh as well. 'I'd forgotten about that. Mrs McGann was telling me about John giving his last penny to that widow woman.'

James was immediately filled with interest and enthusiasm, and the conversation was safely deflected into more normal channels. It occurred to Virginia, however, that she was skating on ice that was becoming dangerously thin.

28

It was fortunate that Nicholas was away and she didn't need to disappear from the street for at least a week. That gave Mrs McGann and anyone else time to forget her disappearances.

The week also taught her that she couldn't live without Nicholas. She had made up her mind. She needed to be with him and their child. If James was found not guilty and avoided a prison sentence, then she'd tell him the truth. She might speak to her mother and father first and then to James. But one way or the other, she'd tell him. It would be better to face him on her own, rather than have Nicholas suddenly appear. The more she thought about being with Nicholas and Richard, the more enchanted she became with the idea. She had never stopped longing to be with her baby. Yet there was always an underlying sadness at having to hurt James. But it had to be done.

If he was found guilty and sent to prison, that would complicate things. She wasn't sure what she would do then. Wait until he came out? But that might take years. She would just have to wait and see what happened at the trial. Meantime she could only hope and pray that he would be acquitted. Occasionally the thought struck her that it would be better if he were jailed. Then she could tell him without worrying about the consequences. That way Nicholas would be safe too. But she chided herself for even contemplating such a cowardly course of action. If James was flung in prison again, that would be more than enough for him to suffer.

Sometimes she even persuaded herself that perhaps James wouldn't be all that upset at losing her. After all, he spent so little time in her company. Even at mealtimes or in bed before an energetic but brief coupling, he'd seldom talked of anything to do with their personal lives. At the moment his main interest, apart from raising funds, was the fate of the Scottish Labour College. This was something that Maclean was particularly keen on and, as usual, James followed suit.

Virginia realised that it wouldn't be losing her that would enrage James. It would be her relationship with Nicholas. In his eyes, her greatest sin would not be the betrayal of her husband, but of her class.

As soon as Nicholas returned, Virginia was able to tell him about the latest conferences James would be attending and how that would mean they would have plenty of opportunity to see each other before the trial. After the trial, if all went well, they could be together for good. Now that her decision had been made, a general mood of recklessness took possession of Virginia. No longer did she object to Nicholas meeting her in the Calton and bringing her back there afterwards. No longer did she worry about staying out overnight. If James was away overnight, then she stayed with Nicholas at the hotel. Let the neighbours think what they liked.

Then one day, one beautiful, never-to-be-forgotten day, Nicholas said he had a surprise for her. They weren't going to the hotel because he had something even better planned. He drove her to a large mansion house surrounded by a garden and trees. He stopped and got out of the car but told her to wait where she was, he would only be a few minutes. He returned holding the hand of a small boy in a school uniform. He was a slim, finely featured child with dark hair and brown eyes. There was a look of Nicholas about him but she also saw a resemblance to herself as well. She could have fainted with joy, she felt so ecstatic.

'Virginia,' Nicholas said. 'I'd like you to meet Richard.'

The little boy politely put out a hand. 'How do you do?'

Virginia held the small hand in hers. Eventually she managed, 'I'm very pleased to meet you, Richard.'

'I thought we'd take Richard for a spin today. How about the seaside, Richard?'

Richard instantly abandoned his concentrated politeness. He jumped up and down, and with a huge grin on his face he clambered into the car.

'That's right. You sit in the back seat. And you, Virginia, sit in beside Richard. All right?'

Virginia was too happy to speak. She wanted to hug the wee boy. She wanted to keep touching him and hugging him but she knew that young children, boys especially, didn't like being overwhelmed and babied. She sat beside him. They smiled at each other. As the car started off, she said, 'I wonder if daddy will buy us ice cream at the seaside. Do you like ice cream?'

'Oh yes.' He bounced up and down on the seat. 'Very much indeed!'

Soon they were all laughing together. And by the time they'd reached Helensburgh, Virginia and Richard were firm friends. It was lunch time and they were hungry so they made straight for a restaurant.

'You've made quite an impression,' Nicholas said while Richard was skipping ahead. 'I thought it best to introduce you as Virginia, not mummy at the moment. That can come later. Was that all right?'

'Yes, yes. Everything's just perfect, Nicholas. Thank you for bringing him. I know I wouldn't allow you to bring him before, but now that I know that we're going to be together it seems like the time is right.'

'That's what I thought. And I thought it would be a good idea for him to get to know you by stages.'

She was completely enchanted by Richard and enjoyed making him laugh at the beach after the meal. They bought a beach ball and the three of them played a riotous game of football. Richard laughed so much at her efforts to kick the ball that at one stage he collapsed on to the sand and rolled about in helpless hilarity.

Later she showed him how to build a sand castle, while Nicholas went to buy ice cream. When he returned with the cones, Virginia said, 'Do you know what we called these when I was your age? What they are still called where I live?'

Richard shook his head. His mouth and cheeks were white with ice cream. There was even a blob on the end of his nose. Virginia thought she'd never seen such a lovable looking child.

'What?' he asked with interest.

'Pokey hats.'

'Pokey hats?' he echoed, nearly choking with laughter. Nicholas laughed too.

'Honestly,' Virginia said. 'Pokey hats.'

Eventually they'd made their way back to Glasgow, this time with

Richard asleep in her arms. While he slept, the tears ran down her cheeks. Nicholas caught sight of her.

'Darling,' he said, 'everything's going to be all right.'

'I know,' she told him. 'I'm so happy.'

Nicholas dropped her off at the hotel. But first she had to release herself from Richard's embrace. It was then he woke up. 'Where are you going, Virginia?' he asked sleepily.

Nicholas said, 'This is where Virginia's living just now.'

Richard gazed up at the hotel's sign creaking in the wind and read, 'The Canal Inn. Where's the canal?'

Nicholas said, 'Come on, we'll show you and then we'll have to get back to Hilltop House.'

Nicholas and Richard returned to the car and she waved them off. When Nicholas came back to the hotel, they lay in each other's arms and spoke about Richard and their plans for him and their plans for each other. She would have to try to get a divorce from Mathieson as soon as possible. But the law usually moved at a snail's pace in these matters and so they would just set up house together right away and get married as soon as Virginia was free.

They had decided not to live on Nicholas's father's Highland estate. 'I think it will be best if I'm completely independent,' Nicholas said. 'How about if we make a fresh start in Edinburgh? There are good schools there for Richard and I could start looking for a flat. There are some lovely New Town properties I think you'd like.'

'That would be wonderful, Nicholas.'

'We could drive through to Edinburgh soon and look at a few places together.'

And so it was arranged. Virginia could hardly wait. She cleaned the single end automatically. She took her turn at washing the stairs. She made James' meals. She allowed him to have sex with her. But all the time, day and night, only an empty shell of herself was functioning in the Calton. Her real living vibrant self was with Nicholas and Richard.

Then one day James announced he was going to the last of the conferences before the now imminent trial. It was to be held in Aberdeen and he would be staying overnight.

Impatiently she watched his stocky figure topped by his shabby homburg stride purposefully away down Bankier Street and disappear.

As soon as he was gone, she flung on her coat and rushed to the telephone box. As usual, Mrs Smithers answered.

'Master Nicholas is not at home, madam,' she said.

'When will he be back?'

'He is expected shortly.'

'Could you give him a message?'

'Certainly, madam.'

'Just say usual time, usual place today.'

The housekeeper repeated the words, 'Usual time, usual place, today. And who shall I say called?'

'He'll know who it is.'

Abruptly she hung up and hurried away to catch the bus. It was a bright April day. There had been an early morning shower but now the sun was shining and glistening on the bushes and trees beside the road that led to the hotel. From the bus stop she headed down a side road to the hotel. Through the trees the canal glimmered and she could smell the brown earthy towpath. From the room she always shared with Richard, they would be able to see the canal snaking along, smooth and dark and quiet. Her feet quickened as she thought of Nicholas waiting for her. Into the small cool foyer now, with its floor ambered by the light filtering through the glass panels in the door. Up the narrow staircase, dark oak bannister, red turkey carpet. Bursting into the room, her face alight with love. She froze. Sitting over on the basket chair was Mrs Cartwright.

'How did you . . . ?' Virginia began.

'I overheard the housekeeper.'

'But . . .'

'And the rest I already knew from Richard.' Mrs Cartwright's face was contorted with disgust. 'You had an innocent child brought to this hotel where you were having your illicit rendezvous. You involved my grandson in your sordid—'

'My son. And there is nothing sordid about my feelings for Nicholas. He is the father of my child and we love each other. I—'

'You are a married woman. And you must know that it is quite common for women of your class working in domestic service to tempt the man of the house. In your case, you were fortunate. Instead of having some back street abortion, as most of these women do, your child was given a wonderful chance in life.' Mrs Cartwright was sitting straight-backed, her gloved hands clutching tightly at the purse in her lap. 'I have kept my side of the bargain. I have given Richard everything including my love and attention. You have betrayed your promise. You have gone back on your word.'

'I'm sorry. But that promise was made when we both believed Nicholas was dead. Everything changed when he returned.'

'You have taken advantage of Nicholas's situation. I will never forgive you for that.'

'I don't know what you mean.'

'My son has not recovered from all that he suffered in the war. He puts on a brave face but I have heard him cry out in the night. I have seen the distress, the haunted look, in his eyes.'

'I know. And I want to help him. He needs me.'

'No, he does not need you, Virginia. He is still in a vulnerable and confused state. What he needs is quiet and stability so that he can get back to normality. He cannot be exposed to the scandal of a liaison with a married woman—especially one who's husband and friends are all Bolsheviks and revolutionaries.' She heaved a shuddering sigh. 'How can you say that you love my son when you obviously think nothing about putting him in such a dangerous position?'

'My husband's a teacher. He's not a Bolshevik, or a violent man.'

Mrs Cartwright flicked a withering glance in Virginia's direction. 'Don't lie to me. I can see that you are lying. And I read the newspapers. Your husband has been in prison and he's likely to be in prison again. The last time he was arrested, he and his friends were causing a riot—attacking the police with iron bars and bottles—and you say he's not a violent man!'

'He was trying to stop the violence. But all this has nothing to do with you, Mrs Cartwright. Nicholas and I are going to work everything out together.'

Mrs Cartwright shook her head in disbelief. 'It has always been Nicholas's destiny to marry Fiona Forbes-Linton, to unite our two families. This was what we all wanted, the fulfilment of everything our family has worked for.'

Her face darkened as she went on. 'How dare you try to ruin his life, destroy his future, by plunging him into your disgusting, immoral world, your world of instability and violence. You say you love him, but how can you, when you are so willing and eager to drag him down to your level?'

'For goodness' sake,' Virginia tried to sound angry even though she was beginning to see a grain of truth in some of what Mrs Cartwright was saying. 'You're being ridiculous, suggesting that I would do anything to harm your son, that in some way I'm going to ruin his life.'

'But you are, you and the whole sordid world that you are part of. What do you think your husband will do when he finds out about Nicholas?'

Virginia could not answer. Although she knew the answer only too well.

'You know in your heart that I am right, Virginia,' the older woman said. 'I love my son and I love my grandson. I want to see them live happy, peaceful and secure lives. As I've already reminded you, I have kept my promise.' She flushed and turned her head as if she was gazing in a dignified manner at the view from the window. 'I am imploring you, Virginia, to keep yours. It's not too late. Please think this through. Think of the future and what it would mean for Nicholas and Richard. If you really, truly love them as I do, please think of what is best for them.' Her voice broke and she pressed her lips tightly together.

There was a long drawn-out silence. Then Virginia whispered miserably, 'I'll try.'

29

If she could find some way of avoiding the inevitable conflict, if she could get away from James before he knew anything about Nicholas. That was what she kept trying to think of. She could not risk Nicholas turning up on her doorstep. Not for any reason.

But if only they could be left in peace to bring up their son and be happy. They loved each other and that was all that mattered. Mrs Cartwright didn't understand, but she did have a point concerning the trouble James could cause. Something had to be done about that. She telephoned Nicholas and said she couldn't get away until after the trial, which was now due to start in a couple of days.

Virginia was in the public gallery of the High Court for the duration of the trial. The jury eventually returned a fourteen-to-one majority verdict that Gallacher and Shinwell were guilty of incitement to riot, and Gallacher, Murray and MacArtney were guilty of rioting. All the others defendants, including James, were acquitted. As he left the court, James talked heatedly about the unfairness of the verdicts.

'Even the Lord Justice Clerk thought it was a farce! Did you see his face?'

The newspapers were full of accounts of how the jury had reached their decision.

'Can you imagine it?' Mathieson said. 'Bremner only got off because some of the jury men thought he had a nice open face—and because they thought he had saved a policeman from being thrown into the Clyde.'

'Was that not Kirkwood?'

'Of course it was Kirkwood who saved the policeman. They didn't know what they were about, that bunch of idiots!' James' anger was fuelled by the fact that Shinwell was sentenced to five months' imprisonment and Gallacher to three.

'But surely that was quite lenient?' Virginia interrupted, 'considering some previous sentences. If John Maclean had been there, he would probably have got five years.'

'Oh, I know, but it still makes me mad,' he added bitterly.

'It's obvious they're afraid of a Bolshevik revolution, like the one in Russia, happening here,' Virginia said, 'and because of that I think it was a mistake to raise the Red Flag in the square. Especially such a huge one.'

'Och, that wasn't official. It was just one of the strikers letting his good spirits and enthusiasm run away with him. He didn't mean any harm. He just climbed on to the plinth to wave the flag.'

It was while they were discussing the sentences that Tam came to the door.

'Come in, daddy. We were just going to have our tea. Sit down and have something to eat with us.'

'No hen,' he said, 'I just came to tell you that your mammy's not at all well. She hasn't been able to get up these past two or three days and she takes awful breathless turns. She'll not admit she's in pain. You know what she's like, but I think you'd better come and see her.'

Virginia felt a rush of panic.

'I'll get my coat.' She snatched it from the peg and struggled into it.

James said, 'I'll come over as soon as I've finished at the college.'

She didn't care what James did. All she cared about at that moment was her mother. She was shocked at the sight that greeted her when she arrived in the Gorbals kitchen. Janette was lying on her back on the high bed. Her sunken eyes were closed, her hollow cheeks sagged allowing her mouth to hang open. Virginia thought she was already dead.

'Mammy,' she screamed and ran to her.

Janette's eyes opened and she made an attempt to smile.

'Oh, it's you, hen. You gave me a fright there.'

'I'm sorry, mammy. I'm just upset to see you like this. Have you sent for the doctor?'

'Och, what can they do, hen? It's a waste of Tam's hard-earned money. Anyway, he's spent all he has buying me tasty wee bites to try

188

and tempt me to eat. He's been that good to me. He brought me a nice wee bit of haddock the other day, didn't you Tam?' Her voice had faded to barely a whisper.

Tam looked anxious.

'Maybe I shouldn't have got that haddock. Now I haven't enough for the doctor. But she wasn't eating anything and I thought . . .'

'You did your best, daddy,' Virginia said. 'Come on, we'll see how much we have between us.' She went over to the table and emptied her purse onto it. Her father dug deep into his pockets but could only find a few coppers.

'We need at least two and six for a visit,' Tam said.

Virginia was carefully counting out the coins that she had. 'We've just enough,' she said. It would leave her without even her tram fare back home. But that didn't matter, the priority at the moment was to get a doctor to her mother.

They carefully put the coins into an old envelope and Tam hurried off to the nearest doctor's surgery. Virginia turned back to the bed to gently smooth back her mother's hair.

'You're going to be all right, mammy.'

Her mother opened her eyes and gazed sadly at Virginia. 'Och, hen, you know that's not true. I didn't want to worry your daddy but I've an awful pain in my chest. It'll be my heart. It's what killed my mother. But I'm not worried. I'm just glad to be united with my boys. Oh, it'll be that good to see them again.'

'Please mammy, you mustn't talk like that. What about daddy and me?'

'You've got your good man and Tam's got all his pals and his politics.'

'Politics!' Virginia scoffed. 'What are they to him compared with you?'

Her mother smiled faintly. 'Oh, I've never pretended that I could compete with the cause, hen. It's that strong, you see. My life's always been him and my weans. His life has always been his socialism.'

It occurred to Virginia that this was also true of James. And of John Maclean as well. Maclean was seldom at home with his wife and daughters. He was so often touring around England and Ireland now, as well as Scotland, speaking, sometimes two or three times a day. He'd be killing himself if he didn't slow down. He was still dressed like James in a suit and collar and tie and homburg, but his collar was frayed and his suit was paper thin. He'd saved up five pounds to buy a new and much needed suit, but James had told her he'd ended up giving the money to the striking miners.

'I'll make you a nice cup of tea,' Virginia told Janette.

'I don't think I've the strength to sit up to drink it, hen. I'll tell you what I'd rather you did.'

'What?'

'Hurry and clean up the kitchen as much as you can before the doctor comes. I'm that ashamed for anybody to see it like this. I've not been able to keep it tidy these last few days.'

'Don't worry. I'll soon have it like you used to.'

Virginia rolled up her sleeves and grabbed her mother's apron that was hanging behind the press door. She filled a pail of hot water from the kettle, filled the kettle again and put it on the fire. As rapidly as she could, she washed all the surfaces, the mantelpiece, the fender, the coal bunker, the dresser. Then she got down on her hands and knees and began energetically scrubbing the floor. She was nearly finished doing this, her face wet with perspiration, when she heard her mother gasp for breath.

Virginia struggled to her feet and rushed across to the bed. Janette was clawing the air, fighting to get up, frantic to draw breath.

'Mammy!' Virginia wailed, not knowing what to do. 'Oh, mammy!' She ran over to the sink and jerked open the window. The stinking air from the rubbish-strewn, rat-infested back yard wafted in. She stumbled back to the bed, completely caught up in her mother's panic. She tried to hold on to her. Tried to calm her, comfort her, but her mother kept thrashing about, and now, crying out pitifully with the pain.

Just then Tam returned with the doctor. Virginia had never been so glad to see anyone in her life. The doctor took one look at Janette and immediately opened his case and began preparing an injection. Within a few short moments, he had administered it, and Janette began to subside, to calm down.

'Oh, thank you, doctor,' Virginia said. 'She looks so peaceful already. That was dreadful. My poor mother.'

Tam said, 'Aye, I've never seen her in as good a sleep as that for a long time. Her nights have been awful bad. Sometimes she hasn't been able to close her eyes at all.'

The doctor snapped his case shut. 'I've given her some morphine, but I'm afraid her heart's giving out. There's nothing more I can do for her now. The chances are she'll just slip away in her sleep. And if she does, I think it'll be a blessed release.'

Virginia was too shocked to say anything. Vaguely she heard Tam and the doctor talking together before he eventually saw the doctor out.

'Thank God he managed to come and stop her pain,' Tam said when he returned to the kitchen. 'I couldn't watch your mammy suffer like that any more. It's more than human flesh can stand. Poor old Janette.'

'But mammy isn't old,' Virginia said. 'She should be enjoying the prime of her life. It isn't fair.'

Tam sank miserably into a chair and started rolling a Woodbine with shaking hands.

'Fair? What's fair around here? Your Mrs Cartwright has a holiday home. She got all the rest and good food and fresh air she wanted and with you to pander to her every need. What has your mammy ever had?' Tears were welling up in his eyes and he angrily raised his voice. 'I can't even get a decent bloody cigarette!'

Virginia went over to the bed to check that her mother had not moved and was still sleeping peacefully. Then she said to Tam, 'I'll make us a cup of tea.'

'Aye, all right, hen. Sorry for the language.'

'It's all right. I feel like swearing myself at the unfairness of it all.'

She made the tea and they sat opposite each other drinking it in silence until Virginia said,

'That's the door.'

She went to answer it and then ushered in plump little Mrs Friel.

'How's your mammy, hen?' Then, catching sight of the still figure of Janette in the bed, she lowered her voice to a whisper. 'Aw, she's huvin' a wee sleep. Ah'll no' bother ye, then. You know where Ah am if she needs me.' She backed carefully, quietly, towards the door. 'Anythin' ye need, mind. Jist ask.'

Virginia nodded her thanks. Afterwards she said, 'When James comes, I'll tell him I'd better stay the night.'

'The bed through there'll take the two of you.'

'Yes, I expect he'll stay too. If that's all right with you.'

'Of course hen. I'll be glad of your company. I hope Janette'll not take another turn, though. What can any of us do? It's just terrible.'

'Try not to think about it, daddy.'

'It doesn't bear thinking about.'

'I've got a couple of coppers left. Do you want me to go out and get you a paper?'

'No, hen,' he replied quickly, a note of panic in his voice, 'No, you just stay here. When did James say he'd be?'

'He should be here any time now, daddy.'

They had another cup of tea and before they'd finished it there was a knock on the door. Virginia went to answer it and came back followed by James's stocky figure. He took off his shabby homburg and unbuttoned his coat.

'How is she?'

'The doctor's given her something to ease the pain. She's sleeping now. There's tea in the pot.'

'Thanks.' He went over to the bed to stand looking at Janette. Then he bent closer. When he turned round again, the look on his face told them what he was going to say before he said it. 'Virginia, Tam, I'm sorry. . . . She's gone.'

Both Tam and Virginia stared uncomprehendingly at him until he repeated, 'She's gone. She's died in her sleep.'

'Oh no.' Virginia began to weep and rushed over to the bed. 'Oh no, mammy!'

Tam sat on like a statue.

After a time, James took hold of Virginia and forced her back down on to the chair.

'There's things to be done. Arrangements to be made. It's a good job we're here. Control yourself, Virginia, for your daddy's sake.'

Virginia nodded and rubbed at her face with the apron she was still wearing. Suddenly Tam said, 'I'm not having any ministers or any of that damned religious mumbo-jumbo.'

'I know how you feel, Tam,' James said. 'But I think we should respect Janette's beliefs—mistaken though they might have been.'

'Yes,' Virginia said. 'Mammy was a true believer. She must have a decent Christian funeral.

Tam said brokenly, 'I can't even afford to pay the minister.'

'Don't worry about that,' James said. 'I'll sort that out.'

Tam nodded, 'You're a good man, James.'

1920

30

'I'm so sorry about your mother,' Nicholas said. They were walking together alongside the canal. Earlier they'd made love and he'd agreed that it wasn't yet the right time for her to make the break and to start the new life they planned. They had waited for a number of weeks after the funeral before they even met. In a sense, Virginia knew that they should not be meeting at all—the memory of her encounter with Mrs Cartwright was still painfully fresh in her mind.

After a few minutes he said, 'I don't even know if this is the right time yet to tell you my good news. I don't want to appear insensitive.'

'Och, tell me, please. It'll maybe help to cheer me up.'

'My book has been accepted for publication. I didn't tell you before. I could hardly believe it myself. You had so many other things on your mind. The trial, and then your mother's death.'

'You mean you've been keeping this from me all this time? How on earth did you manage to contain yourself? Darling, congratulations, it's wonderful.'

'As I say, I can hardly believe it. It still hasn't sunk in but the publishers are rushing it out. They think it's going to be a great success.' He laughed. 'Fame and fortune. It looks like I'll have no money worries from now on, according to them. And it means I won't have to rely on my parents' support any longer. Perhaps we can buy that house in Edinburgh after all.'

'When's it coming out? You've been so secretive about this. I don't even know what it's called or what it's about.'

'It's called *Scenes from the Inferno*, and it's based on the experiences of myself and my comrades in the trenches. My editor has been saying such embarrassingly kind things about it—he reckons it's just about the best book to have come out of the war so far. He says he's never read anything so powerful and moving. I'm sorry I couldn't talk to you about it, as I did with my poetry. It's just . . . I felt if I discussed it with anyone I would talk it out instead of writing it.'

'I'm so happy and excited for you, Nicholas.'

'They want me to do all sorts of lecture tours and personal appearances—all over Britain. There's even talk of America, but I won't have anything to do with that. I'll put them off until you're free and we can get married. Or at least until we are able to go together.'

'No, you mustn't, darling. Please. Maybe this is the answer to all our problems. While you're away, it'll give me time to get everything sorted out with James without a confrontation. With you, I mean. And it'll also be a test of your love.'

'Virginia, I don't need any test. I've had enough tests and for far too long.'

'What I meant was, you'll be meeting all sorts of interesting new people. . . .'

'Virginia.' It was the first time she'd seen anger getting the better of him. 'Stop talking nonsense. I understand how you must be feeling at the loss of your mother. I understand all the problems you've had to cope with, but now you're beginning to make stupid excuses. You must take me for a fool.'

She was shocked. 'No, Nicholas. I was just trying to be fair. You deserve this success. I don't want anything to spoil it for you.'

'That's not what it sounded like.'

'Oh, darling, I'm sorry.' She wound her arm around his neck. 'I hardly know what I'm saying just now. All I know is that one day, I'll be free and we'll be married. The time will fly past if you just relax and enjoy your success. Go ahead and do whatever your publisher suggests. You can write to me while you're away and keep me up to date with everything. But you'll soon be home. The time will fly past.'

He sighed and shook his head. 'Has there ever been anyone, I wonder, who has had a love affair lasting as long as ours?'

'Of course, hundreds. Some people have had affairs that went on for a lifetime.'

'Well, I've no intention of going on like this for a lifetime.'

'Nor have I.' She stood on tiptoe and kissed him. 'But all the time we've waited will be worth it in the end.'

'Are you sure you want me to go ahead with promoting this book?'

'Definitely. It'll give me a better chance to sort things out with James.'

'But we always said we'd talk to him together, Virginia.'

'No darling, *you* said we'd talk to him together. I know James, and that is what has been worrying me all along. I need to do this on my own, Nicholas, and in my own way. Trust me, please.'

Reluctantly he agreed. 'If you're absolutely sure that's what you want and that it's the best way.'

'Yes, I am.'

She felt elated afterwards. Here, at last, was the solution. It didn't make what she had to do any easier, for herself at least. But she didn't care about herself. As long as Nicholas and Richard were safe.

It wouldn't be any easier either to leave James. But she would try to make him understand that she didn't want to hurt him and had never intended to cause him any unhappiness. He would be angry at her. He would probably rage at her. He would threaten to confront Nicholas. But she would tell him that Nicholas had gone. Hopefully, by the time Nicholas returned from America, James would have calmed down and accepted the inevitable.

Meantime she would choose her moment carefully. And afterwards, her bolt hole would be in the Gorbals with her father until she and Nicholas could find a suitable home. Her father would not disown her now, she felt sure. She was the only family he had left. . . .

She felt happy and relieved, just to be making a final decision. She wished now that she'd been able to make it long ago. John Maclean's wife had left him in the autumn of 1919 and one of his daughters had been put into the care of Maclean's younger sister. The other girl had gone to live with his wife's brother in Maryhill. According to James, there had been no ill feeling about the separation. It was simply a case of Maclean having no money with which to feed and clothe them. But he kept in contact with them by letter. He wrote especially to the girls. James said, 'He tells them to sing 'The Red Flag' every day and never forget it. He tells them to remember every day that the masters rob the workers and that socialism is the only thing to stop the robbery.'

'That's a bit serious for such young children.' Virginia had said, 'I don't think I'd want my children to be singing 'The Red Flag' every day and worrying about the masters robbing the workers.'

'That's the trouble with you,' James said angrily, 'you're not committed enough. You've allowed yourself to be corrupted by your contact with wealth and comfort.'

'What nonsense, James. Honestly, sometimes you talk complete rubbish. All I'm saying is that they should be enjoying children's songs and stories—daft rhymes and fairy tales and things like that. Things to stimulate their imaginations or make them laugh. They'll have to face the bad things in life soon enough.'

'Oh well, I'm sure he does that too. He's good with children. He's a teacher, remember. But he wants to bring his children up with the right beliefs and values. I remember asking him what he did about the religious instruction all the children got at school. He told me his daughters stood outside the class, along with the Jewish children. He warned them never to worry about the silly ghost stories in the Bible and the silly stories about a good God who lets soldiers kill other men to please the rich. I thought, "Good for him, and if I have any children, that's how I'll bring mine up." '

Talk like this confirmed Virginia in the rightness of her decision to leave James. She regarded herself as a socialist, but she would never expect her children to be exposed to so much politics so young. She wasn't even sure if she'd want to deny them religious instruction. Above all she would want them to think for themselves and to make up their own minds.

Mathieson was becoming more and more involved in the formation of a Scottish Communist Party, as well as helping Maclean and his ragged army of unemployed men in their campaign to force the Parish Councils to grant larger amounts of relief. Men who couldn't find work could be refused 'outdoor relief', which meant they had to live in the poorhouse in Barnhill, separated from their wives and families. Even when they got relief, it was barely enough to live on. He had been going on and on about the unfairness of it for weeks. So much so that something finally snapped inside Virginia and she knew she couldn't wait another day.

The crisis came as he was lecturing her about a down-and-out from Bridgetown called Matthew Fry, who'd been refused assistance and only offered the poorhouse. He was so distressed at the prospect of being separated from his wife and family, he'd gone to Maclean's house to ask for his help.

'Right away, John took Matthew in the tram-car to the City

Chambers, marched in and demanded that the Chief Officer of the Parish Council be sent to speak to him. And when the officer came, John demanded that Matthew be given outdoor relief and if he didn't get it, there would be a gigantic demonstration in the square the next day.'

James laughed uproariously. 'Matthew Fry was sent at once to the cashier with an authorisation from the officer for a cash payment. They knew John would be able to do it, you see. They knew he was a man of his word.' He suddenly glanced at Virginia. 'Are you listening to me?'

'I've been listening to you for years!' she burst out. 'Politics, politics, politics. Nothing but politics! If only, James, you could have left them on the doorstep every time before you stepped into this house, we might have got on better.'

James stared at her in astonishment. 'We get on perfectly well. . . . We're both interested in politics. It's something we've always shared. I don't understand what you're complaining about. What's got into you all of a sudden?'

'It's not all of a sudden, James. Talk about listening? You've never listened to me. Never thought about what my real interests are, what I really feel, what I really want. Never thought about me at all.'

'But . . . but . . . this is preposterous. Have you taken leave of your senses?'

'The only mad thing I've done is to talk myself into staying with you for so long.'

'What do you mean? What on earth have I done? I've always tried to be a good husband. I've always been faithful to you. And I don't drink. I don't smoke. Any money I earn I give to you. What more can I do?'

He was so genuinely uncomprehending that her anger fizzled out. 'You don't understand, James.'

'No, I don't.'

'It's not really that you've been a bad husband. Just not the right one for me.'

'But we've been happily married for years. We've never even had one argument.'

'As far as arguments are concerned, I've never had much of a chance to say anything except just agree with everything you've said about politics.'

'But you've always been a socialist—just like the rest of us.'

'I'm a socialist but not a revolutionary, James. I don't want a socialist revolution or any other kind of revolution.'

'But Virginia, John says—'

'I know what John says. And I know that most of what he says is right. I know he's an exceptional man, James, and a good man. I know he's everyone's hero, especially yours. So much so that you never stop going on and on about him. I've got to the point where I can't stand to hear his name.'

'Oh well.' James looked deeply hurt. 'If that's the way of it, I'll never mention him in this house again.'

'Damn it,' she said, frustrated. 'Here we go again! This isn't about politics. But it's where we always seem to end up.'

'Is that so. Well, what did you want to talk about then?' James was angry now. 'Go on then, I'm listening.'

31

'You know that I used to work for the Cartwrights at Hilltop House before the war?'

'Yes, why?'

'While I was there I got to know their son, Nicholas.'

James' mouth twisted sarcastically. 'Oh yes, the big war hero. I know all about him.'

'No, you don't, James. You know nothing about him.'

'I know he's the product of a family that represents the worst elements of capitalism.'

'There you go again. You can't see past politics.'

'I'm just stating a fact.'

'Well, here's a fact for you. Nicholas and I were lovers and I became pregnant.'

The colour drained from her husband's face. There was a kind of pleading in his eyes. She turned away to avoid his desperate stare.

'It was long before I knew you, James, and so it had nothing to do with you.'

'The usual story,' James said, through gritted teeth. 'A rich bastard taking whatever he wants from life. That's why you were flung out, of course. It's been the same for centuries. They use girls like you and then toss them out onto the streets. And you wonder why I'm such an ardent socialist. Why I'm all for a revolution. And a bloody one at that!'

'It's true that Mrs Cartwright dismissed me when she found out. But it wasn't Nicholas's fault.'

'How can you say that?'

'Because I know he pleaded with her to look after me until he returned from the war. He was sent to the front before he could do anything else to help me. I only told him about the pregnancy the night before he left.'

'And you believed that story? More fool you.'

'I had his child, James, and Mrs Cartwright took him and has looked after him ever since.'

'You mean, there's . . . his . . . bastard!'

'His name is Richard and he's a lovely little boy. You must keep this in your mind, James. All this happened long before you and I even knew each other. Then when I did meet you, as far as I knew Nicholas was dead. That part of my life was past. I was fond of you and I admired you and yes, we had our political beliefs in common. I married you in good faith, James, and I had every intention of staying faithful to you.' She forced herself to meet his shocked stare. 'But then when Nicholas came back . . . you see, I've never stopped loving him. I tried to forget. I tried not to think of him. But when he came back, when I saw him again . . .' She hesitated then went determinedly on. 'We became lovers again, James. I love him and I want to be with him and my son. That's why I'm leaving you.'

James' mouth worked soundlessly for a few seconds. Finally he uttered, 'Leaving me . . . for that Cartwright bastard!'

'James, please. He's not to blame for anything his father's done. Nicholas is as good and honest a man as yourself.'

'Don't you dare compare that capitalist bastard with me! All my life I've fought against . . . fought against . . .' He staggered and fell against the fireside chair.

'James,' Virginia cried out. 'Please, I can't bear to see you in such a state. You'll make yourself ill.'

But it was already too late. His face, his whole body, had become contorted. His eyes were staring out of his head. He tumbled helplessly from the chair onto the floor.

'Oh James!' She wept as she tried in vain to lift him back on to the chair. 'I'll call the doctor. I'll run all the way there and back.' She struggled to her feet. 'I'll fetch the doctor. You'll be all right.'

Weeping in distress she flew from the house. In the streets clusters of women turned to stare at her and call after her, 'What's up, hen?'

After she'd called the doctor and was running back, they called to her again and she gasped out, 'I think my husband has taken a stroke.

I was getting the doctor.'

'Oh my!' There were gasps of horror and sympathy. 'Is there anythin' we can dae, hen?' they asked as they followed her back to the house.

When she got there, she found two of the neighbours, Mrs McGann and Mrs Finniston, were dragging James across the floor towards the bed.

'Oh, there you are, hen,' Mrs McGann puffed out. 'We saw yer door open. Were ye getting the doctor?' They were both breathless with their exertion. Now they were attempting to hoist James up to the high bed and finding it doubly difficult because of their difference in height. Mrs Finniston was very tall, and Mrs McGann was very small. Virginia rushed to help them.

'Yes, he'll be here as soon as he can.'

It was a terrible struggle because James was sturdily built, but eventually the three of them managed to get him on to the bed.

'We'll help ye get his claes aff,' Mrs Finniston said.

'No, no, thanks all the same but I'll manage that. I'll see you later and let you know what the doctor says.' Virginia replied as she eased them towards the door.

'I reckon it's a stroke, hen.' Mrs Finniston shook her head. 'That's what the doctor'll say. The same thing happened tae ma sister's man. The very same. He didnae last long. The doctor gave him a month but Charlie didnae last three weeks—'

'Well, anyway, thanks again,' Virginia interrupted and shut the door. She hurried back to gaze helplessly at Mathieson's grotesquely twisted face. All she could think to do was loosen his collar and tie.

'The doctor'll be here in a minute, James. You're going to be all right,' she added, as much to reassure herself as him.

She felt as though she was going to collapse. Her mind was reeling with guilt and regret. Never for one moment had she thought that this could happen. It was just terrible. 'If he dies,' she repeated over and over again to herself, 'I'll have killed him. God, don't let him die. I'll never forgive myself.' She was in such a panic-stricken state that she didn't hear the knock at the door at first. Then Mrs McGann's voice squeezed through the letter box, 'It's the doctor, hen. Come on, open the door.'

Virginia ran to let the doctor in. It only took him a matter of minutes to look at James and announce he'd arrange for the ambulance to remove him to hospital. The doctor left again and Virginia sat by the bed until the ambulance arrived and then she followed them as they carried James downstairs on a stretcher.

A crowd of men, women and children had gathered out-side the close. Women were also leaning on windowsills gazing out at the scene. Men took off their caps as the stretcher passed as if James was already dead. Women murmured, 'Poor Mr Mathieson. Such a guid wee soul.'

'Aye, like oor Johnny, wearin' hissel oot helpin' folk.'

'A guid soul. Aye. He disnae deserve this.'

It took all Virginia's strength to climb into the ambulance. She was beyond tears now. All she could do was pray. In the hospital, they took him away and she sat on her own for what seemed like an eternity before a doctor came to speak to her.

He explained that James had suffered a very serious stroke. Her husband was partly paralysed and had lost the power of speech. The doctor expressed his sympathy. They would do what they could but. . . . She hardly heard anything else. She didn't need to. She could tell just by looking at the sympathetic young doctor's eyes that he wasn't optimistic about James' chances of recovery.

In a daze, Virginia allowed herself to be led by a nurse into a long ward and shown James' bed. A chair was brought and put beside the bed. She collapsed into it and stared at James. A trickle of saliva began to dribble out of his mouth and down his chin. She quickly fished out her handkerchief and dabbed his face dry. She didn't know what to say to him or even if he could hear her. She couldn't even meet his eyes.

For days after that she would sit beside the bed every afternoon in a strained silence. Sometimes she'd get up and dab at his face or arrange his pillow more comfortably or straighten the bed clothes. Then she'd sit down again. But as the days went by, there was no visible improve-ment in his condition.

Guilt consumed her. It wasn't only that she felt she'd caused his stroke. It was the fact that she had never really loved him and could not feel love for him even now.

She'd come back again every evening and sit in silence once more. It was truly terrible. She wanted to be miles away, anywhere but in the bleak hospital that smelled of sickness and death. She'd written to Nicholas several times—in England and then in America. At her request, he'd sent letters to her care of her father's address. At first her letters had been normal, full of all her news. But after James' stroke, they became short and strained. She'd stopped mentioning James, and had never told Nicholas about his stroke. She couldn't face putting her guilt into words. Nor could she risk Nicholas suffering the same guilt. He had suffered enough in his life.

Eventually, Nicholas asked in one of his letters if she'd told James yet. She replied that she'd told him long ago. She even lied about the way he had taken it. How he'd surprised her by being reasonable and understanding. He had been sad of course, and upset that of all people it had been a Cartwright but he'd come to terms with that. The separation had been perfectly amicable. Finally she wrote and told Nicholas that James was now ill and in hospital, as if it had just happened. She had to avoid the slightest hint of any connection with the real cause. For his sake, as well as her own. She said that she was now visiting James several times a week and she'd gone out to work to make some money to keep herself.

Nicholas immediately wired her a large sum of money and told her to stop working at once. He insisted there was absolutely no need for her to go out to work. He went on to argue that she could have no reason to refuse his money, since her separation from James was out in the open, and amicable. . . . She could have replied that, just then, she welcomed doing jobs she loathed and detested, regarding them as some sort of penance, something that she deserved. But she didn't tell him.

She did confess, however, that she felt totally alienated from James. She couldn't even bring herself to speak to him. She knew it wasn't fair. He couldn't help looking so dreadful but she was repulsed by him. He wasn't the James she had known any more. The stroke had turned him into something grotesque, no longer even a man.

Nicholas was obviously shocked by her confession. She received a letter by return of post telling her she must try to imagine what it would be like to lie in that hospital bed unable to communicate. Especially for a man like James whose whole life had been spent communicating his ideas to others. She could understand where this depth of sympathy was coming from. Nicholas had once been in hospital and unable to communicate. He had been unable to remember even who he was. For months he had lain in a terrible no-man's-land of silent isolation. In a strange way this not only drew

Nicholas closer to James, but distanced her from both men.

She began making excuses to herself for not going to the hospital every visiting time. What was the use, what good was it doing? Perhaps she could even be doing him harm. Her visits might be making him as uncomfortable as she, as they sat together through the long, terrible silences. He was probably relieved when she didn't turn up. And she was turning up less and less often. She tried to explain this to Nicholas, knowing at the same time that he would only grow more shocked at her. He didn't understand. But she had reached the point where she no longer cared. She wrote and told him that she couldn't cope any more. She simply could not force herself back to the hospital again. She had stopped going to see James because she felt he really was no longer there.

Nicholas by this time was on his way home from America. She couldn't even feel excited by this fact. She had lost her way completely, and felt she had made a complete mess of her life. Even worse, she had made a mess of everyone else's life. She should never have married James knowing that she didn't love him. Having done so, she should never have been unfaithful to him. Nor should she have kept Nicholas hanging on for all this time. He should have been free to turn to someone else who would have been willing to marry him and give him the happiness he deserved.

Day after day, she locked herself in the single end in the Calton and sat nursing her head in her hands. She felt the walls and ceiling pressing further and further in on her. Neighbours knocked on the door and she ignored them. Let them think she'd gone to the hospital. Let them think she'd gone back to live in the Gorbals. Let them think whatever they liked.

32

'Could I speak to Virginia, please,' Nicholas said.

Tam stared at him.

'And who might you be?'

'Hasn't she told you about me?'

'No.'

'Well.' Nicholas hesitated uncertainly. 'I'm a friend of Virginia's. I take it she's not in at the moment.'

'She'll be where she usually is—at the hospital visiting her husband.'

'Right.' Nicholas had not been asked in. He turned away from the door, then turned back again for a moment to ask, 'Have you been in to see him?'

'Just the once. That was enough. I don't think he even knew me. Didn't make any sign. Couldn't speak or anything. There was no point in being there.' He shook his head. 'A terrible tragedy.'

'Yes indeed,' Nicholas thought in sudden anger. But he just said in a calm voice. 'Just tell Virginia that Nicholas called. She knows where to contact me.'

Nicholas went out of the close and found a crowd of children milling around his car. A few hunched-shouldered men, fists plunged deep into the pockets of their trousers, were viewing it as well. Nicholas bid them a polite good afternoon and managed a smile at the children as they cleared a path for him. He felt appalled at the place, at the close, at the buildings, at the street. No human being should be expected to live in such conditions. His heart went out to Virginia. How on earth had she managed to survive in such a place. The Calton wasn't much better. He remembered the area from when he'd given her a lift home. She had written to say that when she'd left Mathieson, she had gone to stay with her father in the Gorbals. He had been glad that at least she'd made the break but he could see that the Gorbals was even worse than the Calton and he felt he must do his best as soon as possible and get her out of here and into a decent house. There were nice areas in Glasgow, but it would probably be best to make a fresh start away from the city.

He was appalled at the slums but he was even more appalled at James Mathieson's situation. The poor man was lying alone and helpless, cut off from the world, out of touch with everything, not knowing what was going on. Despite what Mr Watson had said, he doubted that Virginia would be anywhere near the hospital. The thought of Mathieson's predicament haunted him because it inevitably reminded him of his own nightmarish experiences in hospital, lying there unable to communicate with his family or anyone else. He couldn't get it out of his mind. He couldn't get James Mathieson out of his mind. But Virginia might have come to her senses, and started visiting him again. He appreciated it was an awkward situation for Virginia, to say the least. But still the man needed to know that somebody cared about him. It was a case of common humanity. On an impulse, he turned the car towards the hospital, stopping en route to buy a few newspapers—the *Glasgow Herald* and a couple of socialist papers. Once in the hospital, he asked what ward James Mathieson was in and was given directions.

He had never seen such a depressing place. It was even worse than the military hospital where he'd spent his lost time. A nurse pointed out Mathieson's bed.

Nicholas fetched a chair and sat down at the side of the pathetic, propped-up figure. He touched the withered arm. 'I hope you'll forgive me if I've done the wrong thing by coming here, James. I've had a similar experience in hospital, you see, and I know what you must be feeling. And when Virginia wrote to me and said that she had stopped visiting you, I felt I had to do something. She's just upset to see you suffering. It's not that she doesn't care about you. Even though you and she are separated, I'm sure she still cares about you. And I would like to say how glad and grateful I am that you have behaved so reasonably regarding the separation. I know it must have come as something of a shock that she and I have a child, but it's wonderful that you've been so understanding. I've always admired anyone who stands up for their principles as you do, but I must say my respect for you has increased greatly on account of the way you have behaved in this matter.'

He spread the newspaper on the bed. 'Anyway, I thought you'd feel out of touch with what's been going on. So how about if I read all the news to you?'

He read through every word in the *Herald*—even the sports pages. Then he ploughed through the socialist papers. There was still a few minutes left of the afternoon visiting time so he simply talked to Mathieson about all sorts of things, his own beliefs and opinions. He told Mathieson that since being away at the war, his views on a lot of things had changed dramatically and he now considered himself something of a socialist. He was also now very much anti-war.

'I've written a poem that goes some way to expressing my feelings about the war. I'll come back this evening and read it to you. You might find it interesting.' He rose and touched James' arm again. 'Try to keep your spirits up. You'll come through this. From what I've heard about you, you're a fighter. Keep fighting, James.'

He drove back to Hilltop House to an enthusiastic welcome from Richard, as well as a warm one from his mother and father. They were making a real effort to be more affectionate towards him than they'd ever been before in his life. It was almost pathetic. He wasn't used to seeing them like this. But he did appreciate that they were giving Richard a far better childhood then they'd given him. They doted on Richard. They would miss him when he and Virginia took the little boy away.

He and Richard had a game of football and then they all enjoyed tea together. Nicholas was constantly amazed at how different his parents were with Richard. He vividly remembered when he was a child, before he was banished to boarding school, how he had been given a frugal tea in the nursery by his ghastly nanny. She had missed her vocation, she would have been more suited to being a prison warder. A very strict, severe and unloving creature she'd been. He'd never allow anyone like that near Richard. Now, there was a plump, jolly girl in the nursery, and Richard had the freedom of the house for most of the day when he wasn't at school, skipping happily through whatever room took his fancy.

Nicholas decided that it would be better to look for a house with a garden so that Richard could have somewhere to play outside. Either that or a house near a park. As yet he hadn't told his parents of his plans. He wished that they would stop trying to persuade him to go with them to the Highlands. He'd told them that he would be happy to visit them, to spend holidays with them, but that he was not going to take up permanent residence there.

Yes, it was a lovely estate, he agreed. Yes, the castle they'd bought had an interesting history and was most impressive. Yes, it could make an ideal background for a novel. But he was not going to live there.

They insisted that the peace and quiet of such a remote and beautiful place would be much more conducive to his writing than life in a busy city like Glasgow. They had gone from one extreme to the other, becoming suffocatingly, irritatingly possessive towards him. He supposed it was understandable to a certain degree, after thinking he was dead and then suddenly finding him again. He tried to understand and be patient, but he knew he would be very glad to get away—to feel free to live his own life.

After dinner, avoiding their questions about where he was off to, he drove back to Glasgow and the hospital. He took his poem and his novel. He would not normally have imposed his work on a captive audience, but the circumstances weren't normal. He thought it might help James to understand that everything in life wasn't either black or white, that there was more to Nicholas Cartwright than just his name or his background. From what Virginia had told him about Mathieson, he was very bitter and full of hate towards anyone who wasn't of his class.

'My poetry, and particularly my novel,' he thought, 'should at least show James that I'm just an ordinary human being like himself.'

He also took some lemonade and a few bottles of beer. He didn't know whether James would be allowed the latter but he could always check with the nurse. He didn't see a nurse in the ward at first and so after greeting James, he put the bottles on the bedside locker.

'I'll check with the nurse before I leave. To see if you're allowed any of this,' he explained. 'I hope they will allow it.' It suddenly occurred to him then that Mathieson might not drink. Many fervent socialists were also strong temperance men. 'On the other hand,' he added, settling himself down on the chair, 'you might be TT. If you are, the nurse can always give it to someone else.' He brought out his poem, *Tagged*.

'I hope this might interest you as an expression of what war means from the point of view of an ordinary soldier. My novel gives a more detailed vision of the effect war can have on people. I know you were strongly anti-war and I thought it might at least pass the time if I read a bit to you on each visit. For a week anyway. I'm thinking of looking for a place in Edinburgh—but I could still come and see you from time to time. I'd have to come through to see my parents anyway.' He smiled. 'They dote on my little boy. They'll want me to bring him as often as possible. In a couple of months, their place up north will be ready and they'll be selling Hilltop House and moving up there.'

He sighed. 'They want me to go with them but Virginia and I have already talked about the possibility of settling in Edinburgh. I haven't seen her yet since I've been back from America. I understood when you and she separated she went to live with her father in the Gorbals. I went to see her there but she wasn't in.' He sadly shook his head. 'That was an eye-opener to me—seeing that place. It's a disgrace that decent people are forced to live in such terrible conditions. When I think of the men coming back from the war to places like that . . .' He shook his head again. 'It's absolutely disgraceful. Do you know, something has just occurred to me, James. Perhaps I should stay here in Glasgow, and write a novel about things like that—about the terrible gulf between the rich and the poor.'

He was suddenly beginning to feel quite excited. 'The good and the bad in both—but exploring the effects that environment has on people. The unfair advantage in life that money gives . . . I wish you could tell me what you think of the idea. I'll have to discuss it with Virginia. She could be of help to me, couldn't she? When you think of it, she's had experience of both kinds of life. Or at least she's seen what life is like in a big house. And she knows all about life in the slums. I must speak to her about this right away.'

He looked puzzled for a moment. 'I wonder where she is. I only had a few words with her father but I gathered she hadn't told him anything about me. I expected with her having left you to live with him, she would have had to explain. Anyway, I hope you don't mind me inflicting my writing on you. This poem simply illustrates how the war changed me from the man that I was when I went off to war thinking of it as patriotic duty. The poem is called 'Tagged'.

The tag tied
To the bloodless toe

Bears only his name
and number.

And registers nothing
Of youth consumed by the bullet's bite
Or sorrow and forced loathing
As another's gun stormed
At the brief candle of his light.

It should read
In carnage red
Of war's pity and waste
But would be delivered
By those who would ignore

To those who cradle
A corpse's smile
Dessicated heart
Fruitless seed

Like diamonds drained
Of light and clarity
Diamonds that bear razor edges.

Hastings, Crimea,
Passchendale . . .

'Now . . .' he said after a few moments of silence, I don't know what you'll think of that as a piece of poetry. You were a teacher and I expect you'll have good critical judgement in these matters. All I can claim is that it expressed my true feelings when I wrote it. But as I told you earlier, I think I've explored my feelings in more depth and with more success in the novel.'

He cleared his throat. 'Well here goes, my friend. Chapter One . . .'

33

'You did what?' Virginia cried out incredulously.

'I went to see him. And I'm glad I did, Virginia. He's a poor soul lying there alone. I don't know how you can bear *not* to go and visit him. After all, he has been so understanding about your love for me. His generosity of spirit is an example to us all.'

They were in the hotel, and at first everything had been wonderful. For a few brief moments she had been able to forget the overwhelming sense of guilt she felt about what had happened to James. And the way she had kept the truth from Nicholas. It had been so good to see Nicholas again. He had grabbed her and whirled her around in his usual joyous way and then covered her mouth with kisses before she could utter a word. Passion had overcome her. She forgot about everything else except his passionate love-making. He'd never been so wildly passionate. Afterwards she laughed and said,

'Talk about absence making the heart grow fonder!'

'I'm so happy to see you again and to know that at last our lives are coming together as they should—as I've always wanted them to. All I've to do now is confront my parents and tell them of my plans. I've already told James.'

She was horrified but Nicholas went on to say, 'He couldn't tell me what he thought, of course, although he was fighting to try. Happily his voice will come back in time. I told the doctors to give James any specialist treatment available—at my expense. Not to let on to him though that I am paying for it. I thought it was the least we could do, Virginia.'

'It's one thing to pay his expenses but how on earth do you think you're helping him by going into the hospital, Nicholas. I don't understand.'

'I can see you don't. But try to think of the situation from his point of view. He's a man of action. Despite his terrible state, I'm sure he's still committed to everything he believed in before. How do you think he feels lying there deserted by everybody who thinks of him as written off, as already dead?'

'But . . .' Tears welled up in her eyes. 'He might as well be dead. He can't talk or move. He doesn't know what you're saying or even if you're there at all.'

'You're wrong, Virginia. His eyes are full of expression and he is beginning to regain some movement. I think one of the most important things is to channel his strong spirit, give him a reason to live, a reason to fight to get back the kind of life he was so passionate about.

'His politics, you mean.' Virginia could not hide the bitterness in her voice. James' passion had never been for her. 'Why are you doing this, Nicholas?'

Nicholas stared at her. 'I've told you, it's the least I can do, the least *we* should do, to help the man. It's just common humanity. I'd do it for anybody. But I think we especially owe it to him. You should visit him, Virginia. You could go every afternoon and I could go every evening. It's only for an hour at a time.'

She felt a tremor of horror again. She desperately wanted to tell him that she'd lied about being separated and living apart from James. That James had not known about her affair until the last moment, and it had been the shock of that which had caused his present condition. The doctor had said that overwork—and his previous head injuries—could also have been factors. He'd certainly been pushing himself too hard, and he'd suffered severe blows to the head on more than one occasion, but deep down she knew that finding out about Nicholas Cartwright was what had finally broken him. The mere mention of the name Cartwright in connection with her had almost killed him. Now she had the added guilt about how James would be feeling at having Nicholas visit him. It was all her fault for lying to Nicholas. She had only meant to protect him, but now she would never be able to make him understand that. Nor would he ever be able to forgive her. He thought he was helping James when in actual fact, because of her, he was making him suffer all the more.

She could only hope that James was not able to understand or feel anything. Then she immediately felt ashamed and even more guilty for thinking that. Nicholas was right. It was the least she could do to conquer her feelings and visit James, and try in whatever way she could to help him.

'All right,' she said. 'I'll go in the afternoons.'

'Good.' He kissed her. 'There's no reason why we can't all be civilised about this. I've been telling him my views on the war. And I was saying that I hoped that perhaps, one day, we could be friends. After all, there's enough hatred in the world without us adding to it.'

They were staying overnight and had ordered dinner in the small dining room downstairs. As they went in and sat down to have their meal, Nicholas said, 'It feels good, doesn't it, that we no longer need to hide away and be so secretive?'

Virginia smiled ruefully. 'We wouldn't feel so good if your mother and father walked in and found us sitting here. At least I wouldn't.'

He shrugged. 'Perhaps. But in any case I think it's time I told them that I'll be leaving soon. Well, they know already. They just don't want to accept it. I don't mean they know about our plans, but I have told them I'm definitely not going with them to their Highland estate. I'm going to be living my own life. By the way, I've been telling James that I'm thinking of setting my next novel in Glasgow and—'

'Why have you chosen Glasgow,' Virginia interrupted.

'Well, I was thinking that I might explore how social conditions have changed since the war. I'd also like to show what life is really like—for both rich and poor. Maybe, in some small way, I can help to heal the divisions in society that ruin so many people's lives. If I'm going to do this, it would help if we looked for a house in Glasgow—perhaps in the West End near the Botanic Gardens. It would be good for Richard, and convenient for the Mitchell Reference Library whenever I needed to do research there.'

'Yes, I'd like that. There are some lovely flats in the West End.'

'And terraced houses and villas.'

'I'd be quite happy in one of those big roomy flats.'

'Well, we can begin to look and see what's available. Tomorrow I'll clear things up with my parents and I'll meet you here in time for dinner in the evening, after I've been to see James. All right?'

'Yes, all right.'

'And don't forget you said you'd go to see him in the afternoon.'

'Don't worry, I'll go.'

To change the subject she steered the conversation back to his new novel and soon they were both enthusiastically discussing the project. Virginia could see how she would be able to help Nicholas with his research and she was looking forward to working with him. Yet all the time, at the back of her mind, the ordeal of the next day's hospital visit remained to haunt her.

Nicholas left the hotel after breakfast to return to Hilltop House. She took her time, pottering about the bedroom, going down to the dining room for coffee, going for a walk along the canal, having a leisurely lunch. Eventually she could delay the evil hour no longer and she went to catch a bus to Glasgow and then a tram to the hospital.

Once there she braced herself to walk into the ward and face James. But she could only briefly allow her eyes to meet his before sitting down beside the bed. Eventually she broke the silence to say,

'Nicholas persuaded me to come, James. I was terribly shocked to hear he'd been visiting you. You see, he's under the impression that we've been separated from some time. I even let him think that it was an amicable separation. He has no idea that your illness had anything to do with . . .'

Her voice faded into silence. At last she managed to continue, 'I know what's happened to you has been my fault. The shock of me telling you. I didn't tell Nicholas the truth because I felt he had suffered enough without knowing what really caused your stroke. He looks all right, James, but he still hasn't fully recovered from the war. He has nightmares and . . . and . . . I just felt I couldn't add to them by burdening him with the same terrible guilt that I feel about you. I'm so sorry about everything. I didn't mean to hurt you. But I had to tell you. I can't help loving Nicholas. And I've never stopped longing for my baby.'

Tears escaped and ran down her face. 'I've been too ashamed and guilty to come in and see you like this, knowing all the time that it was my fault. And now for you to suffer Nicholas coming here. I know how you must hate him but I don't know what to do. He thinks he's helping you.'

After a long silence, Virginia rose. 'I'll go now. But I'll be back tomorrow. Nicholas made me promise to come in every afternoon and he's coming every evening. I'm so sorry, James,' she repeated.

She could see James's mouth moving but only strangled, incomprehensible grunts emerged. She couldn't bear to listen, and she turned and walked away.

Nicholas took in the day's newspapers and read them to James. He detected a twitching of James' eyelids and one of his hands, and felt cheered about this. After the newspaper reading, he told him how he'd now seen Virginia and they'd arranged to take turns visiting him. They were also going to start looking for a place in the West End. A flat probably. He said how he thought Richard would enjoy playing in the Botanic Gardens. Nicholas said he hoped that they could become friends after he got out of hospital and he'd always be welcome to visit them.

'Now, I'm going to be selfish again and read you another few chapters of my novel. By the time I've gone through the whole book, hopefully you'll be fully recovered and you can discuss it with me— or you can at least tell me what you think of it! And any criticism and comments would certainly be of value to me when I'm writing my next novel. I've been talking to Virginia about my ideas and I can see she's going to be a great help. But then she's always inspired me and encouraged me with my writing. Long ago, before the war when she worked at Hilltop House, we used to meet secretly in the woods and I'd give her my poetry to read. She was the first person who knew I'd written anything. My mother and father have always had their own plans for my life and they certainly never included being a writer. A soldier, yes. The heir to my father's business empire, yes. But a writer?'

Nicholas laughed. 'I knew they'd squash that idea right away. But Virginia changed my whole life. She was such an inspiration and a help to me. She gave me the self-confidence to believe that I could be and should be a writer. I'll always love her and be grateful to her for that. But I'd better get on with our reading or it'll be the end of visiting time before I've even started.'

However, he did manage to finish the reading in time. There were even a few minutes to spare.

'I had the most dreadful time this morning,' he said. 'I told my mother and father about my plans for setting up home with Virginia. They were absolutely furious. Then when they saw that I wasn't going to budge, my mother became tearful. It was awful. Before Richard, she used to be a cold and unfeeling woman. All my life that's how she seemed to me. My God, James, I thought even my father was going to weep. It was terrible. I can only hope that in time they'll get used to the idea. But they're going to live up north—I think I told you—and then they'll be far away from Richard. That's what really matters to them—I don't think they really care all that much about me.'

He sighed. 'But it's their own fault. All those grandiose ideas about a castle and an estate in the Highlands. It's like a whole different world—but it's their world, not mine, I'm afraid, and they'll have to inhabit it without me and without Richard. Oh, if they come to think of Virginia differently and accept her for who she is, then maybe things will improve between us. But I doubt they'll ever change.' He laughed. 'I'm afraid we'll never convert them to socialism, James.'

He rose. 'It's time to go now. See you tomorrow night.'

Again he felt sure there was a response from James. 'Progress at last!' he thought, as he made his way cheerfully to the stairs and out to his car.

34

Each day, Nicholas read the newspapers to James. Then after chatting to him for a time, he would work his way through whatever socialist papers he was able to find. One day, he came in with a copy of *The Vanguard*. In it there was an article by Maclean, entitled 'The Irish Fight for Freedom'. Nicholas marvelled at men like Maclean and Mathieson who could have such passionate belief in a cause that they devoted their whole lives—practically every waking moment—to it. Speaking all over the country, writing so many articles and pamphlets, teaching the thousands of working men who filled their classes. He confessed to James that, although he had become more politically aware than he used to be, his overriding interest was in people. That was what he wanted to write about. People were his passion, not causes.

'It takes all kinds, I suppose,' he told James. 'It would be a dull world if we were all the same. But although I could never be like you or Maclean, I can admire your dedication. And the energy you put into it.'

He glanced at his watch. 'Anyway, here's Maclean's latest pamphlet. I haven't time to read it all now but I'll give you a summary instead.' He began, 'He points out that the recent war was supposed to be fought to defend the rights of small nations. But in the General Election of 1918, and at the municipal elections and county elections of 1920, Ireland voted with a huge majority for an independent republic. Instead of that Ireland got an army of occupation with aeroplanes, tanks, etc. He compares what the British are doing in Ireland with what Churchill did in Russia.'

Nicholas shook his head. 'Apparently Churchill spent two hundred million pounds in direct and indirect attempts to overthrow the Russian Republic because he said it was "a dictatorship by terrorists". Two hundred million pounds!' Nicholas repeated. 'That would have been enough to clear away all the slums in Glasgow and build decent houses for everyone. Anyway, Maclean goes on to describe some of the repressive measures taken against the Irish and claims that it's impossible to expect the Irish to suffer this kind of terrorism without some kind of retaliation. He wants Scotland to protest about it.'

Nicholas and Virginia continued with their house-hunting. They had looked at quite a few flats and had recently fallen in love with a beautiful house in Kirklee Terrace, just next to the Botanic Gardens. It would cost more than he'd originally planned to spend, but his book was doing well, and after he and Virginia had discussed it, they had decided they could afford it.

Once they'd put in an offer for the Kirklee Terrace house and it had been accepted, Nicholas felt it was time to take Virginia to visit his parents. He said to her,

'I want to introduce you to my father and I want to show both my parents how proud of you I am.'

'Darling, your father has met me. It was both he and your mother who persuaded me to allow them to bring up Richard.'

'Nevertheless, I want them to see how much we love each other and want to be a family together with Richard.'

She agreed to accompany him but when she looked so worried and unhappy, he said, 'There's nothing to worry about, darling. It doesn't matter what they say. They can't come between us.'

'It won't be just class differences they'll find a problem with, Nicholas. It'll be the morality. Or immorality, as they'll see it, of us living together without being married.'

'Well, they'll just have to put up with it until you and James are divorced. They'll not be the only ones to say we're living in sin. But I don't care what anyone thinks or says. Do you?'

'Then there's the fact that I've nothing decent to wear.'

Nicholas tossed back his dark head and laughed.

'Ah, that's what's really worrying you, is it? Well, we'll soon fix that. You'll go to the best shop in Sauchiehall Street and buy the most fashionable outfit you can find.'

Later he told James about all this, describing the smart outfit she'd bought and how it had helped her self-confidence when they set off to visit Hilltop House.

'She looked really lovely, James. It was a pale blue outfit with a wide-brimmed hat. The colour matched her eyes. And oh, that beautiful golden hair of hers. I'd never seen her look so beautiful. Or so dignified. I was really proud of her.'

It hadn't been an easy visit. His parents had been stiff and cold. Polite of course, but they'd tried to freeze Virginia out at first by addressing any remarks to Nicholas and ignoring her. Virginia had put a stop to that herself.

'Mr and Mrs Cartwright,' she said firmly, 'I know how you must feel and you have my sympathy. You have been wonderful with Richard and I thank you for that. But you're not getting any younger and, apart from anything else, it wouldn't be easy to continue what you've been doing.'

'We neither need nor want your thanks.' Mrs Cartwright looked down her long nose at Virginia. 'And we are perfectly capable of continuing to see to our grandson's welfare.'

'Mother,' Nicholas said. 'Neither you nor father have thought this through. You're going to live in the Highlands. If we left Richard with you, what about a school for him out in the wilds? What about friends of his own age? But anyway, the fact is, Richard is our son and he's coming to live with us.'

Virginia said, 'You will be welcome to visit him as often as you like. There's plenty of room in our house in Kirklee Terrace for you both to stay. And if you wish we can bring Richard to visit you during the summer holidays. It would be so much better for Richard if there was no unpleasantness or ill feeling between us.'

Mrs Cartwright didn't reply but she rang the bell for tea. To Virginia's surprise, it was Mrs Smithers, the housekeeper, who pushed in the tea trolley. Virginia greeted her with a smile.

'Hello, Mrs Smithers. It's nice to see you again. I hope you're well.'

Mrs Smithers fussed with the tea cups and made no reply. Plainly, she was deeply embarrassed.

'That will be all, thank you.' Mrs Cartwright dismissed the housekeeper from the room.

Virginia knew that in Mrs Cartwright's eyes she had committed a social faux pas, but she didn't care. It was Mrs Cartwright who was at fault by not moving with the times. No wonder girls were refusing to go into service nowadays.

They drank their tea in silence except for the heavy tick tock of the grandfather clock in the corner. Eventually Nicholas said, 'Virginia has told me, mother, how well you looked after her when you were both in Helensburgh and how wonderful you were at the birth.'

Virginia could see that he'd found a soft spot.

'I did my best. And it's good to know I helped my grandson into the world.'

'Yes, you really were wonderful,' Virginia said. 'I don't know what I would have done without you.'

Mr Cartwright cleared his throat. 'My wife has always been a very capable woman.'

'You seemed to get on together then, mother,' Nicholas said. 'And I'm sure you and Virginia can get on well together again. If you'll just give her a chance.'

'You talk about living as a normal family, Nicholas,' Mr Cartwright said. 'But Virginia already has a husband.'

'They have been separated for some time now, father. And it has been very amicable. He's ill in hospital at the moment. The poor fellow has taken a stroke, but both Virginia and I are visiting him regularly. There will be a divorce as soon as it's possible. Then Virginia and I will just have a quiet wedding.'

'Why don't you wait until Virginia is free,' his father said. 'And see how you feel then.'

'Father, have you not been listening to what I've been saying. We love each other. We've already set up home together. All we need to complete our happiness is our son.' He replaced his cup on the tea trolley. 'I've already spoken to Richard and told him he'll be coming to live with us. He's quite excited about the prospect. He's looking forward to it.'

'We have a lovely room all prepared for him,' Virginia told them eagerly. 'Do come and see it. Please come and visit him.'

Despite sitting rigidly straight-backed in her chair, Mrs Cartwright was now visibly trembling. 'How can you do this to us? We've loved and looked after the child for all these years. I'll never forgive either of you.'

'Oh mother,' Nicholas groaned. 'What's the good of talking like that. It was your choice to take Richard. Virginia didn't want to part with him. You should be glad that he'll be reunited with his mother now in a good home.'

Mr Cartwright said, 'You must appreciate that this isn't easy for your mother, Nicholas. I think it really would be better if you gave us more time to—'

Nicholas rose. 'I can see that there's no point in continuing this conversation. Please tell the nurse to have all Richard's clothes and belongings ready. We'll call for him on Friday after Virginia's hospital visit.'

Virginia followed Nicholas to the door, turning for a moment to say before leaving, 'Please remember that it's not a case of you never seeing Richard again. I meant it when I said you'd always be welcome.'

On the way back to Glasgow, Nicholas said, 'You were very generous, darling. After all you've suffered. I haven't forgotten that my mother dismissed you the moment my back was turned.'

'Oh, I don't believe in harbouring resentments. I saw enough of that when I lived with James.' She sighed. 'He was so full of bitterness and hatred. He absolutely seethed with it at times.'

'That's what could have made him a candidate for a stroke. It's not healthy to be like that.'

'No, I suppose it isn't. I used to warn him about getting so worked up about everything.'

Before going to visit the Cartwrights, she'd made her usual visit to the hospital. She still found it difficult to talk to James or even to look at him. Unlike Nicholas—who seemed to treat James as if he was perfectly normal. Even more than that, he treated him like a close friend. When she did look at Mathieson, she wondered what was going on in his mind. She was beginning to think Nicholas was right, that James was able to understand everything. His eyes were those of a thinking, feeling person trapped in a useless body. Yet she was never sure what the expression in those eyes meant. Or how to interpret the twitchy movements he could now make.

Nicholas believed Mathieson's eyes were expressing interest and enthusiasm when he read to him. He could see fire and anger too, but Nicholas said that was in response to some of the terrible things that were happening in the world.

She couldn't help feeling uncertain and worried though. Especially on the Friday afternoon when Nicholas came for her at the hospital. He arrived early and marched right into the ward—he was so eager and excited about going to collect Richard.

'Hello, old chap,' he greeted the twitching figure in the bed. 'This is the happiest day of our lives, the day Virginia and Richard and I start a proper family life. Maybe you'd like to meet Richard? We could bring him in one day. Anyway, I'm sorry I can't stay longer. Come on, darling,' He grabbed Virginia's hand and hauled her away, calling out to James, 'See you later, old son.'

On the way outside, Virginia said, 'Do you think it was wise letting James see us together like that, Nicholas?'

Nicholas looked surprised. 'Why on earth should you feel that? He knows all about us.'

Perhaps it was because she'd felt like that about James so often before. Suddenly Nicholas shouted, 'Good God, look at this!'

The streets were seething with hordes of cloth-capped men. It was the biggest crowd Virginia had ever seen.

'It must be some sort of demonstration.'

In the middle of the mob a man had been hoisted far above all the others. A sturdily-built man in a shabby homburg. As he spoke, he was waving one fist high in the air. In the other he was clutching a huge red flag which was snapping violently in the wind.

Virginia felt faint. 'For a moment,' she said shakily, 'I thought it was James.'

Above the noise of the crowd that surged all around them, Nicholas shouted back joyfully,

'One day it will be James,' he said. 'Just you wait and see.'

The GOURLAY GIRLS

1932

I

Wincey stood very still and watched her grandfather. He was choking, gasping for breath. She had seen him taking seizures before. He had a heart condition and on the few occasions when she had been present, her grandmother had ordered her to run upstairs and fetch the old man's tablets from the bathroom cabinet. Upstairs and downstairs she'd flown, so that Grandmother could take a tablet from the bottle and press it into Grandfather's mouth. It only took a few seconds after that for the seizure to calm and for Grandfather to seem perfectly all right. A bit tired looking perhaps. Otherwise he was to all appearances her big, good natured, kindly, smiling, loving Grandfather Cartwright. George, to his wife Penelope.

Wincey wasn't sure now which one she hated more—so called loving and devoted Grandfather or unloving, uncaring Grandmother.

Grandmother was different with her brother Richard. Richard, five years older than Wincey, was the clever one and the favourite of the family. How Grandmother's beady-eyed, long-nosed face would soften at the sight of 'her handsome boy', as she called him.

Wincey didn't mind. That was something she could understand. Richard was easy to love and admire—he was tall and slim, dark-eyed and dark-haired like her daddy, and just as handsome. Quite unlike Wincey with her fringed red hair and freckles, or their mother who had fair, golden hair.

Sometimes her mother and father would laugh and say, 'I don't know where Wincey came from.'

She came from them, the same as Richard. But her mother and father seemed to think that she was different. Most of the time they completely ignored her, lavishing all their attention on the literary and political friends who were so often in the house.

Her mother and her first husband, James Mathieson, had never had any children. Mathieson was one of her mother's set. He had divorced her for adultery not long after the Great War. Her mother had no shame. She and her father had been lovers for years. Wincey had overheard her grandmother and grandfather talking about it. Grandmother never tired of saying that it wasn't decent the way the two men had become friends, and 'that dreadful communist revolutionary', as she called Mathieson, visited Nicholas's house.

Richard was at boarding school in Edinburgh, but he returned home to Glasgow most weekends and saw a lot of their grandparents. They both loved Richard, especially Grandmother. When she came to visit them, Wincey was usually sent to keep her grandfather company. His heart condition often prevented him from getting out and about. She saw this as yet another example of her parents trying to get rid of her one way or another.

She was supposed to be her grandfather's favourite. Grandfather was supposed to love her best.

For most of her twelve years, she had believed this. Now she knew better. Yet the truth was so terrible, so painful, so confusing, she couldn't cope with it. Her mind, as well as her heart, ached with it. It paralysed her.

Earlier, when she'd cringed away from him, he'd pushed money into her pocket. 'A wee present,' he'd said, 'for being Grandfather's good girl. You buy yourself something nice, eh?'

Now all she could feel as she stood staring at the old man was bitterness and hatred. He was trying to mouth the word 'tablets'. His eyes bulged with pleading. He clawed the air. She didn't move. The expression in his eyes changed to disbelief, then to terror. Eventually his gasping stopped. His body slumped. His mouth sagged.

The room weighed heavy with stillness, then gradually—in the far distance, as if coming from another world—she heard the faint rumble and clang of tram cars. The sound frightened her. It brought an air of reality back into the room. Her grandfather was still slumped in his chair, his head twisted to one side, his mouth hanging open. His eyes were open too. It was his eyes that brought the full realisation of what had happened crashing in on her. She began to tremble and moan with the acuteness of her distress.

The emotional confusion that had been plaguing her became stronger. To it was now added terror, and the need to escape became overwhelming.

She raced from the room and out of the house onto Great Western Road. She was oblivious of the rain gusting along the wide street, with its large stone villas set well back on either side and partly hidden by trees. She was panic-stricken, especially when she realised that she'd reached the part of the road that reared up to form Kirklee Terrace, where she lived with her mother and father. One of them could be looking out over the grassy bank, down onto Great Western Road.

At the end of the terrace was the private entrance to the park known as the Botanic Gardens. Further on, level with the street, was the main entrance. Wincey ran through it and along the nearest path, knowing that now she'd be well hidden by trees. Even if anyone in the family looked out of one of the windows that faced onto the park, it would be impossible to see her.

Yet she felt no satisfaction at this thought. She desperately longed to be able to run to her parents and be comforted by them, to be told that everything would be all right. She ached to be made to feel loved and secure. But they'd never made her feel that. She didn't dare think how they would be towards her now. Yet she wept with her need of them.

Tears mixed with the rain, blurring her vision and she began to shiver as she became aware of her white blouse, navy cardigan and pleated skirt clinging wetly against her. The path had disappeared under angry puddles that were being whipped by rain and wind. Everywhere was fast becoming a quagmire. Her stockings were spattered with mud, her shoes sodden and squelchy with water.

She tried to get onto the grass to escape from the puddles but slipped and fell. Now everything was covered with mud. Her fringe stuck wetly to her forehead; her white blouse, her cardigan, her skirt, her shoes—everything was ruined.

Trying to scramble to her feet, her skirt caught on a bush and, desperately tugging at it to free it, she caused a ragged tear. Almost mad with panic now, she ran, stumbled, fell, ran again.

Eventually she reached another gate, ran through it, and found herself on an empty, windswept street. She kept running this way and that until she was exhausted. Then she remembered the money her grandfather had pushed into her pocket. She boarded a tram car and sat shivering on the nearest seat. The conductor looked at her suspiciously. 'Where are ye goin'?'

Wincey just held out some coppers without saying anything.

The man shrugged and handed her a ticket. Her mind was in such a turmoil, she just wanted to be safely home in bed, with the events of the last hour never having happened.

But they had happened, and she shivered all the more at the thought of her parents' coldness. Now they'd have very good reason to hate her. She couldn't bear the thought of their cold, shocked faces, so she blanked them out of her mind.

It was early evening but it was already getting dark and the rain was beating relentlessly against the tram windows. The tram was lurching to a halt now as the conductor approached her and said, 'Ye'll huv tae get aff noo, hen. Either that or buy another ticket.'

Dazed and without a word, she left the tram and started wandering about the dark, mean looking streets between the high tenements. She had no idea where she was. After what seemed like hours, she could walk no further and sank down on to the pavement. With her back propped against a tenement wall, she wept broken-heartedly.

'What's up, hen?'

Wincey wiped at her eyes and saw a young girl crouching down in front of her.

'I don't know where to go,' Wincey managed.

'How? Huv ye no' got a mammy an' a daddy an' a home tae go tae?'

Wincey shook her head. The girl, Wincey later discovered, was fourteen-year-old Florence Gourlay, two years older than herself. Florence had a highly dramatic turn of mind and thrived on crises, real or imaginary.

'So ye're an orphan?'

Wincey nodded.

'So ye've run away so they won't put you into an orphanage—or into the workhouse?'

Forgetting her tears, Wincey stared curiously at the girl. She managed to nod again.

'Och, never mind,' Florence said. 'Ma mammy'll take ye in. She's always takin' folk in.'

'Is she?' Wincey said in surprise.

'Och aye, our place is like a doss house sometimes. Girls come down from the Highlands an' stay for a few days at our place until they get fixed up wi' a nurse's job at wan o' the hospitals. Ma mammy used tae come from the Highlands. Come on.' Florence got to her feet. 'I'm soaked an' freezin' tae death. An' starvin' intae the bargain.'

Wincey struggled to her feet. The streets glistened darkly with rain. Greenish pools of light wavered under gas lamps. The high black tenements dwarfed the two bedraggled figures as they began trudging along.

'Whit's yer name, by the way? I'm Florence.'

'Wincey.'

'Wincey! Where did a funny name like that come from?'

'I was christened Winsome.'

'That's even worse,' Florence laughed.

'Then when I went to school we learned that rhyme about Incey Wincey Spider and everybody started calling me Wincey—even at home.'

'Ah hardly ever went tae school so ah dinnae know any rhymes. Is that like a poem?'

'Sort of, I suppose.'

'Didn't ye mind?'

'What?'

'Bein' called after a spider?'

'I never thought of it like that. It just sounded better than Winsome. More friendly, somehow.'

'Aye, right enough.'

Wincey managed to find out from Florence as they went along that she lived in Springburn, in one of the tenements in Springburn Road. Wincey had heard about Springburn at school. Most people in the area had worked in the building and maintenance of the railways, in the workshops and repair yards of the North British Railway Company at Cowlairs, of the Caledonian Railway Company at St Rollox, and the North British Locomotive Company, the largest of its kind in Europe.

She remembered her teacher saying that no-one knew for certain how Springburn had originally got its name, but that among the nearby hills there were many springs and burns and wells. With the coming of the railways and new housing, however, there was certainly nothing rural about the place now. The teacher had shown the class pictures of the streets black with workers pouring out of all the railway works, but now there was a depression and many men were unemployed, hanging about aimlessly on street corners.

'Have you any brothers or sisters?'

'No brothers, but ah've an older sister, Charlotte, an' two younger ones. They're twins—Euphemia and Bridget. We tried tae call Euphemia Phemie but ma mammy wouldnae let us. She likes tae be proper.'

'Are they all living at home?'

'Aye, ma granny as well. Here we are.'

They stopped at a dark close-mouth, one of the many tunnel-like entrances to the tenements. Wincey groped her way nervously along.

'Isn't there a light?'

'Naw, the leerie's supposed tae come but he hisnae done anythin' wi' this close for ages. Maybe it's run out o' gas. I don't know. Just hang on tae me goin' up the stairs, ye'll be all right.'

Three flights of stairs up, Florence thumped loudly on one of the top flat doors. It was opened by a tall, delicate looking girl with a pale face and fair hair pinned back with kirby-grips. As they all walked through the small box of a lobby, and then into a gas-lit kitchen, Florence nodded towards the tall girl.

'That's Charlotte.' Then, once in the kitchen, she announced, 'This is Wincey. Her mammy an' daddy died o' the flu an' she wis goin' tae be locked away in an orphanage an' she didnae want tae go. So ah brought her home wi' me. She can stay here, can't she, Mammy?'

'Would ye listen tae the cheek o' that?' This came from an elderly woman of ample proportions, who filled to overflowing a rocking chair by the fire. She had floppy cheeks and no teeth. 'As if we huvnae enough tae contend wi' here!' Red rimmed eyes glared at Wincey. 'Away ye go back where ye belong—ah dinnae care if it's the orphanage or the workhouse, ye cannae stay here.'

Tears of disappointment and fatigue overflowed and spilled down Wincey's cheeks. A thin, bent woman with wispy salt and pepper hair knotted back into a bun was standing over at the sink. She said in a soft Highland voice,

'Now, now, Granny. We can't turn a poor bairn out on a night like this.'

She smiled at Wincey. 'It's all right, dear. Come over here and wash your face and hands. I'll make a cup of tea and you'll soon feel better.'

'Florence Gourlay,' the old woman raged, 'will get us aw intae serious trouble yet wi' that imagination o' hers, an' aw the downright lies she tells. You mark ma words!'

She turned to the man wearing a cap—or bunnet—with the skip pulled well down over his eyes who was sitting on one of the chairs jammed close together around the cluttered table.

'Are ye a man or a mouse, Erchie Gourlay? Are ye just gonnae sit there an' allow this? We'll aw end up in the workhouse at this rate. How many mair mouths can we feed? We cannae feed oursels.' She cocked a thumb towards her daughter-in-law. 'Thanks tae her extravagance.'

Erchie appealed to his wife. 'We'll manage, sure we will, hen.'

Teresa smiled and Wincey wasn't sure then what age she might be. Her smile made her look younger than the scant faded hair suggested. She was a patient, good natured woman but there was a thrawn bit— even a slyness—about her at times. She secretly enjoyed getting any small victory over her mother-in-law.

'Yes, of course we'll manage,' Teresa said calmly. 'With God's help.'

Florence led Wincey over to the black sink. She winked at her and whispered, 'Ah told ye.'

'You give your feet a wipe,' Teresa instructed Florence. 'You're getting mud all over the floor.'

'What God'll help you?' Granny asked.

'We all worship the same god, Granny,' Teresa said gently as she settled the kettle on top of the glowing embers of the fire.

'You're a Pape,' Granny accused. 'You worship that picture.' She pointed to the painting of Jesus that hung on the far wall of the recessed bed. 'Wearin' a gownie! Ye worship beads an' idols an' graven images. Ah'll never know what possessed ma Erchie tae marry a Pape. An' us a respectable Orange family an aw.'

'Ma,' Erchie protested, 'ye're no' tae upset Teresa.'

'Upset her?' Granny scoffed. 'Upset *her*! Nothing ruffles that one's feathers. It's well seen who that lyin' wee trouble-maker takes efter.'

She glanced over at Florence who was going into contortions in her efforts to wipe the mud off her bare feet. Charlotte spoke then.

'Mammy, I'd better away through and finish that dress.'

'Charlotte is a lovely sewer and dress maker,' Teresa told Wincey. 'Between us we make a decent living.'

'Decent? Decent?' Granny bawled out. 'Whit's decent aboot livin' here?'

Wincey couldn't help thinking the same thing. The gas mantle over the mantelpiece barely lit the kitchen. Even with the bright flames of the small, barred fire, most of the room was shadowy. Wincey couldn't imagine where everybody slept—there was only one recessed bed and hardly an inch of floor space.

As if reading her mind, Florence said, 'Come on through and ah'll show ye where we'll sleep.'

Teresa called after them, 'Take your wet clothes off and I'll get them dried.'

As they were crossing the lobby, there was knock at the front door and Florence opened it to reveal two small girls, both with mops of curly brown hair.

'This is Wincey. She's an orphan an' ah found her lying half dead in the street an' Mammy said she could stay here. Wincey, they're ma twin sisters—Euphemia an' Bridget.'

'Hello,' the two girls murmured. They looked tired and cold and their clothes clung wetly to their bodies. Each was carrying a shopping bag from which issued the tantalising aroma of fish and chips. Suddenly Wincey realised how hungry she was. She couldn't remember when she'd last eaten.

'You couldn't have timed it better,' she heard Teresa tell the girls. 'I've just this minute masked the tea. Och, poor wee things, you're soaked. Never mind, you'll soon dry out and once we've had a nice cup of tea and a fish supper, we'll all feel fine and happy.'

Wincey couldn't believe she'd ever feel happy again. At the same time, she was grateful to have found shelter. The front room, as Florence called it, was not much bigger than the kitchen. It too had a curtained recessed bed with a high mattress. Opposite there was a fireplace, in front of which sat an ancient looking sewing machine and a stool. The fireplace had a surround of dark maroon tiles but the grate was empty and the room gripped with an icy chill.

A settee covered in cheap leather substitute and two matching easy chairs were crowded into the room. The back of the settee had a row of tiny wooden pillars topped with a padded rail. The floor was covered with linoleum which was referred to as wax cloth. On the walls, a dark brown varnished dado was topped with heavily patterned wallpaper.

'Where does everybody sleep?' Wincey asked.

'Mammy an' Daddy are through in the kitchen bed. Granny sleeps on a hurly bed in front o' the fire. She couldnae climb up to the bed.'

'What's a hurly?'

'Ye don't even know what a hurly bed is!' Florence shook her head in disbelief. 'It's a wee bed that hurls out from under a big bed. You an' me'll have a hurly bed from under this room bed. Charlotte sleeps in the big bed—she's sixteen. The twins—they're just twelve—and they sleep wi' her.'

'Goodness!'

'What's wrong wi' that?'

'Nothing,' Wincey assured Florence hastily. 'Nothing at all.' But she'd never heard the like of it in all her thirteen years. At home she'd always had a room of her own and a much bigger room than this.

'Right,' Florence said, struggling out of her thin dress, 'get yer clothes aff an' we'll go through an' get somethin' tae eat.'

Wincey was both shocked and frightened.

'I couldn't do that.'

'Why no'. They're soaked.'

'But . . . but . . . Your father's through there.'

'What's wrong wi' that?'

Florence looked perplexed and annoyed, as if Wincey was implying some sort of criticism of her father.

'It's just . . . I'm a bit shy, I suppose.'

Florence laughed. 'Don't be daft. We keep our knickers an' simmets on. So there's no need. It's not as if we're grown up, like Charlotte.'

Wincey was afraid not to go along with Florence, in case she caused offence and was ordered to leave. But she was more than afraid. She was feeling so vulnerable, she was almost in a state of collapse, as she eventually—dressed only in her knickers and vest—followed Florence through to the stuffy, gas-lit kitchen.

2

Teresa manoeuvred the steel poker through the ribs of the knee high fire and made the flames spark brighter. The fire was part of a black, cast iron range that had a high, overhanging mantle shelf. Along the mantle shelf, Wincey could see by the light of the softly hissing gas mantle a tin tea caddy, a box of matches, candles, a spare mantle for the gas, a pile of pennies for the gas meter, a pair of china wally dugs, a pair of brass candlesticks, a green packet of Woodbine cigarettes and a brass ashtray. Hanging on one side of the mantle shelf was a triangular box of stiff card holding spills.

From the other side hung a ladle and partly along the front, a potato masher, a toasting fork, a cheese grater, and a frying pan. Also along the front was fastened an expanding rod. Draped over it were a tea towel and several pairs of socks. A stone hearth was bordered by a brass fender with a padded box on either side.

Euphemia and Bridget were each sitting on one of the boxes. They had stripped off their dresses and steam was rising from their vests as they crouched as near as possible to the fire.

Teresa went to a hook that was on the wall beside the curtained bed and undid the rope that was twined around it. A four barred pulley came trundling and squeaking down from the ceiling and hung over the table.

'Give me all your wet things,' she said. 'They'll soon dry on the pulley.'

Wincey's hands trembled as she handed over her skirt, cardigan, blouse and stockings. She felt naked and painfully vulnerable without her clothes. The strange place and so many strange people confused her. She wondered hopefully if it was just a dream, one of the too-frequent nightmares she'd been having recently. She tensed her body, willing herself to wake up, willing everything and everybody to disappear. But they didn't.

Teresa said, 'Sit down at the table, Wincey, and drink your tea. It'll heat you up. Wincey? That's an unusual name. How did you get that, dear?'

Before Wincey could reply, Florence announced breathlessly, 'The minute she was born, a spider dropped from the ceiling on tae her, so it did. That's why they called her Wincey—because there's a rhyme, *Incey Wincey Spider*. They called her after the spider, so they did.'

'Ooh!' All the females in the room made a face.

'That's horrible,' Bridget said.

Erchie laid down the *Daily Worker* newspaper he'd been reading and gave Bridget a warning look. 'Watch your tongue. You'll upset the wee lassie.'

He was sitting next to Wincey and he put an arm around her shoulders. 'Never you mind them, hen. I think Wincey's a lovely name, and you're a lovely wee lassie.'

The sleeves of his striped shirt were rolled up and Wincey could feel the heat of his skin and the hairs on his arm. She shrank back trembling with agitation, but he didn't seem to notice. Nobody did. They were now all enjoying their tea, especially old Granny. She was making noisy slurping sounds and stuffing chips and bits of fish in between her gums. Her rocking chair squeaked backwards and forwards.

'Wire in, hen,' Erchie said. 'There's no standin' on ceremony here, it's every man for himsel'.'

The keenness of Wincey's hunger stoked by the hot smell filling the small room overcame every other feeling. She picked up a chip and began to eat. The fish supper was delicious—hot, salty and vinegary. She'd never tasted such delicious fish and chips. Nor had she ever eaten fish and chips with her fingers—especially out of a newspaper. Teresa was right, the hot tea and the food did make her feel better. Only she wished Erchie wasn't sitting so close to her. She kept trying to shrink further away. She kept giving him sidelong, apprehensive glances. He seemed harmless enough.

But then, so had her grandfather.

Teresa said to Bridget, 'Away through and tell Charlotte to come and get her supper.'

Wincey became aware of the rattle and whirr of the sewing machine. It didn't stop and when Bridget came back into the kitchen, she said, 'She's no' hungry and she has tae get that dress finished for Mrs Tompkinson.'

Teresa shook her head. 'No wonder she's so thin. I'm really worried about her.'

Granny's gums stopped their munching. 'It wid fit you better tae be through there workin' instead o' sittin' here talkin'. That girl's aye gettin' the heaviest end o' the load.'

'Now, Granny,' Teresa said calmly, 'you know fine I do my share. But I have to see to the cooking and cleaning and other things as well.'

'Cookin'?' Granny scoffed. 'When did ye cook this?'

'I'm going to make a nice pot of broth for tomorrow.' She turned her smiling attention on Wincey. 'Eat up, dear. Mr Nardini always gives us extra pieces of fish so there's plenty. He's a good soul, and nobody can make a fish supper like the Italians.'

'Same wi' the ice cream,' Erchie said, smacking his lips. 'An ice cream wafer,' he added wistfully. 'Oh, ah could murder wan o' them right now.'

'I hadn't enough left for that,' Teresa said apologetically. 'But never mind, Erchie, you'll be able to get a job soon and we'll be all right.'

Erchie sighed. 'Ah wish ah could believe that, hen.'

Teresa turned to Wincey and said proudly, 'Erchie was in the navy. Everything was fine until they cut his money. A right disgrace it was, wasn't it, Erchie?'

'Aye, ten per cent. An' it wisnae as if we were well paid in the first place. It wisnae sae bad for the officers. It wis just a drop in the bucket tae them. But tae us matelots, it wis terrible. A real disaster, especially for men like mysel' wi' a wife an' family tae support. We were at Inver G when we heard about it.'

'That's Invergordon,' Florence interrupted for Wincey's benefit. Florence had obviously heard the story many times before.

'Aye,' her father sighed, 'ah must admit there wis a right panic at first. Before anyone wis briefed right, the newspapers got hold o' the story, ye see, an' got it aw wrong. They were sayin' it wis twenty-five per cent so ye can imagine how we aw felt.'

Florence cut in again. 'Ye mutinied, didn't ye, Dad? There wis a big mutiny an' aw the men stopped the ship frae sailin'. An' aw the captains were furious an' threatened aw the men—'

'Hang on,' Erchie laughed. 'Ye're an awful wee lassie for gettin' carried away. We had meetin's in the canteen an' on the fo'c'sle an' there wis a lot o' speech makin' and cheerin' and singin', an' some o' the ships couldnae sail, right enough.' He became serious again. 'Ah wis lucky, ah suppose. Ah wisnae wan o' the men who were jailed. Ah wis just wan o' the crowd o' matelots who were discharged from service.'

'An' now,' Florence said, 'he cannae get a job anywhere. Poor Daddy has tae sit here aw day long just twirlin' his thumbs, so he has.'

'Will you be quiet, Florence,' Teresa scolded. 'Your daddy does *not* sit here all the time. He keeps trying his best to get a job. It's not his fault there's no jobs going.'

'Ah never said it was.'

'Just be quiet, I said.'

'Aye,' Granny agreed. 'She blethers on far too much, that yin. If ah've said it once, ah've said it a hundred times—that girl'll get us aw intae trouble yet.'

Teresa was gathering up a few chips and a bit of fish onto a plate. She placed a fork beside it. 'Nobody touch this. I'll go through and take over the machine and make Charlotte come for a bite. She's very finnicky,' Teresa explained the plate and fork to Wincey. 'I'm usually the same myself but a fish supper out of a newspaper has a special taste, don't you think?'

Wincey nodded her agreement.

'And you pair,' Teresa addressed Euphemia and Bridget, 'get rid of all the paper and give the table a wipe over. I'll put this plate in the oven for a minute to heat it up again.'

The oven was part of the range and situated on the left side of the fire. Teresa had to squeeze sideways from her side of the table to go over to the oven. Everybody had to squeeze sideways to go anywhere in the kitchen—it was so small and packed—although it only contained a table, four wooden chairs, four stools, a rocking chair and a basket chair. The bed recessed into the wall opposite the sink was draped with fawn curtains and valance, and was a permanent fitment. Now it was in deep shadow. The gas light was not strong enough to brighten any corner of the room. The coal bunker was opposite the fireplace and had a long shelf above it. The kitchen was not even as big as the pantry at Wincey's Grandmother Cartwright's house. That kitchen was like a ballroom in comparison with this one.

In a minute or two, Charlotte entered and sat down at the table. Erchie said, 'Is it nearly done, hen?'

'Mammy's just finishing it off. I'll be able to deliver it first thing in the morning. It'll just need a wee press.'

'Great! That's great, hen. Come on, eat up. Ye deserve it.'

The younger girls cleared away the debris the others had left, and gave the table a wipe before taking the plate out of the oven. Charlotte smiled her thanks at them and began daintily forking bits of food into her mouth. She was poorly but cleanly dressed and with her straight brown hair held back behind each ear with a kirby-grip.

'I hope she likes it,' she said, 'and gives me another order.'

'It's terrible,' Granny shook her head, 'that we've tae be dependent on rubbish like that.'

Charlotte flushed. 'It is not rubbish. I do a good job. It's a beautiful dress.'

'Och, ah dinnae mean the dress, ye silly bissom. Ah mean that woman ye've got tae slave for, an' aw the rest o' the toffee nosed bitches over in that West End.'

'Mrs Tompkinson is not rubbish. She's a nice woman in her own way. She just doesn't know—doesn't understand—anything about how other people have to live. People in places like the West End and Bearsden and Giffnock and Newton Mearns live in a different world from us.'

Wincey wanted to say a heartfelt 'How right you are!' but didn't want to risk giving anything away about herself.

Erchie said, 'Her in the West End—Tompkinson, did ye say her name was, Charlotte?'

'Yes.'

'That wis the name o' our rear admiral. He wis senior officer o' the Atlantic fleet. Ah wonder if she's any relation.'

'Oh, I shouldn't think so, Daddy.'

'Ask her when ye deliver the dress tomorrow.'

Charlotte laughed. 'I'll just be checking on the fitting and collecting my money. I'm not likely to be chatting to her. People like that don't chat to servants, Daddy.'

'Bad bitches,' Granny growled. 'Aw tarred wi' the same brush. Think they're better than us but they're no'.'

Erchie laughed and said to Wincey, 'Ma's a bit of a commie. She used tae march behind Maclean. An' she'd be out there supportin' Jimmy Maxton if she wis able.'

Wincey wondered what everyone's reaction would be if she told them that her mother and father had known Maclean and now knew the equally charismatic but more eccentric looking Maxton. She had been brought up on stories about Maclean, and even had a vague recollection of being carried on her father's shoulders at his funeral nine years ago in 1923 and feeling frightened at the size of the vast crowd. Maclean had been a hero—a pacifist who had been sent to prison on several occasions for upholding his beliefs. He had also formed what was called the Tramps Trust Unlimited and campaigned for a miner's wage and a six-hour day, and full wages for the unemployed. He also established the Scottish Workers' Republican party. Oh, she knew all about politics and politicians, all right.

Her mother was always out with them, or working on their behalf, or entertaining them in the house. Her father would join them if they came in the evening. There was always much serious talk and discussion then. During the day, he'd stay shut away in his writing room.

Grandmother Cartwright disapproved of all of this, particularly their involvement with James Mathieson. 'What's going on, that's what I would like to know?' she never tired of asking her husband, her son and anybody else in her circle. 'A *ménage à trois?*'

Grandfather usually shook his head at this. 'Shouldn't think so. It's just they've got all that socialist nonsense in common.'

'And who's fault is that?'

Few things made Grandmother more furious than the mention of socialism. 'Our Nicholas had no interest whatsoever in anything like that. To think we sent him to the best boarding school in the land! Then Sandhurst! To think he got his commission in the army—he was a good loyal subject of the king. It's been that girl who's corrupted him.'

'I know,' Grandfather would agree. 'But unfortunately there's nothing we can do about that now. The damage has been done.'

'That's what happens when somebody moves out of their class.' Grandmother liked to think she resembled a thin version of the old Queen Victoria, and judging by some of the late queen's photographs, Mrs Cartwright did have the similar beady eyes and small tight mouth. 'Virginia is—and always will be—nothing more than a common scullery maid. I don't know what my son ever saw in her. Or rather,' she paused and sniffed her distaste, 'I do know but it's something too disgraceful to talk about.'

Everybody knew, including Wincey. While Virginia had worked as a scullery maid for Mrs Cartwright, she'd had a love affair with the only son of the house, and while he'd been away in the War, Virginia had his child. That was Richard.

After Nicholas had been reported killed in action, Mrs Cartwright had taken the child from Virginia. Some time later, Virginia had married Mathieson. Then Nicholas had turned up in a hospital in England. Nicholas had been badly injured and suffered loss of memory, and the trauma of shell shock. He had lain in the military hospital for a considerable time before his identity was discovered. It had been this hospital experience that had given him sympathy for and understanding of Mathieson—who had later suffered a stroke and had also spent a traumatic time in hospital. As a result the two men had become firm friends.

But Mrs Cartwright could never understand their relationship. The whole set-up of her son's house in Kirklee Terrace—indeed his whole life—was beyond her. He had become a writer and she had no time for any of his literary and artistic friends. Every one of them horrified her with their loose, bohemian ways. As she often said, it was that awful girl who encouraged him with this writing business in the first place. She still referred to Virginia as a girl, although Virginia was now thirty-three. She still thought of Nicholas as a boy although he was now thirty-seven.

'That's why,' she told her husband, 'we must encourage Richard to spend as much time as possible with us when he's on holiday from boarding school. We don't want him corrupted by that awful girl as well.'

As usual, her husband agreed wholeheartedly. He shared her horror of all things socialist. 'Communist revolutionaries and trouble makers, the lot of them,' he said bitterly. As well as owning munitions factories before he retired, he had also owned tenement property in Glasgow and still remembered the trouble the rent strikes had caused him. Wincey had heard the other side of the same story from her mother, from Mathieson and even from her father. For a long time she'd been confused by the conflicting versions she'd heard in her mother's house and her grandparents' house, but now seeing for herself the conditions people had to live in, she could well understand why people went on strike and refused to pay increased rents. Especially when, during the war, most of the men were away fighting for king and country. It was a disgrace, her mother had said, and now Wincey agreed with her.

She became aware of Charlotte speaking to her.

'Can you sew, Wincey?'

'I've done a little embroidery but I've never used a sewing machine.'

'Embroidery?' The others laughed uproariously, and Wincey suddenly realised that, to them, embroidery was a luxury, a pastime for those who didn't have to spend every waking moment trying to earn a living.

'Just at school,' Wincey hastily explained. 'The sewing teacher was only showing us what it was.'

She felt shaken. The realisation suddenly came to her that she could never go home. No-one must find out what she'd done. No-one must know who she was. She was isolated in this awful place for ever. But then, she'd always been isolated. And at least here, people seemed to care about her.

3

Nicholas was at a crucial stage in the creation of his new novel. He had never found novel-writing easy. People often said that poetry must be easier to write because it was so much shorter, but as far as he was concerned, all writing was hard work. Not that he was complaining. He loved his work and felt very fortunate that he was now able to make a living from his novels. There might be praise for poetry, but, he had long since discovered, little financial benefit.

Some verses written in a few snatched moments of privacy while he'd been at school and then in the army had been all he could manage at first. For a long time, they had to be kept secret. He knew only too well how disapproving his mother and father would be if they found out. Only Virginia knew and understood. And she was encouraging—he could never thank her enough for that.

He had thanked her many times, through his poetry. In his first novel, too, he'd managed to express his love for her. Now, it pained him to see her so unhappy. He was equally distressed at the disappearance of their daughter, but he was also secretly ashamed of the recurring feeling he had that his father's sudden death and Wincey's inexplicable disappearance were having an adverse effect on his novel. Even at normal times he resented anything that disturbed his writing.

Virginia had long since learned not to enter his writing room while he was working, and the children had quickly realised that the good-natured, smiling father they knew outside the writing room was very different from the impatient, angry character inside that room, if they interrupted him.

Very few things made him lose his temper, but having his work interrupted was certainly one of them. He had been suppressing these feelings since Wincey's disappearance. At first, he had gone out to look for her. He had co-operated with the police search, his mind aching with trying to think of where she might have gone and what could have happened to her. He and Virginia had talked endlessly about every possibility. Friends kept dropping in or telephoning to ask for news or to offer any help they could. In the end, everyone feared that when she had found her grandfather dead, she had run from the house in a blind panic and fallen into the river.

But the River Kelvin had been dragged and nothing was found. Even his mother, who had never shown all that much interest in or concern for Wincey before, was now looking pale and withdrawn. Naturally, she had been shocked and distressed at the death of her husband, although even then she had succeeded in hiding her emotions. That was her way. She became stiff and dignified, her face closed, her eyes hardened. But she had asked about Wincey.

As the days and weeks dragged past without any news of Wincey, they all tried to carry on as normal. But even when Richard came home at weekends, the underlying tension and strain was always there. Nothing was quite the same. Nicholas went out drinking with his literary friends—which was something of temporary help—and at least they understood about his novel. People like Mathieson and their more politically active friends, good and sympathetic though they were, had not the same understanding. His life was in chaos. He felt everything was slipping away from him, never to return.

Eventually, sitting listlessly with Virginia over a cup of coffee in the kitchen, he suddenly burst out,

'We can't go on like this, Virginia. We have to get our lives back to normal. I'm going to start writing again.'

'Normal?' She gazed at him with sad eyes and a bitter twist to her mouth. 'What can be normal now?'

'We can't go on like this,' he repeated.

'How can you even think of writing at a time like this?'

'I'm not doing any good sitting here like this, am I? Nor are you. We've done all we can. We'll just have to leave it to the police now.'

'They haven't done any good either.'

'I'm sure they've done their best and will continue to do their best, Virginia. It's not helping the situation allowing ourselves to be overcome by depression. Look at you. You don't look well. I'm worried about you.'

'Worried about me,' she scoffed. 'Don't give me that, Nicholas. I know you. All you're worried about is your precious writing.'

'Are you accusing me of not caring about my own daughter?' he suddenly shouted at her, as he half rose, sending his chair crashing back. He knew he was over-reacting because of guilt. He was angry at himself more than her. All the same, he did care about Wincey. Virginia had no right to imply that he didn't. She was nursing her head in her hands now.

'Oh, shut up, Nicholas. Run away to your damned writing room, for pity's sake, and give me some peace.'

'I've done everything I possibly could. No-one could have done more,' he insisted. 'I've walked the streets for days. I've—'

'Yes, all right, all right. I wasn't accusing you of anything.'

'And after all, I've a living to earn, and Richard's school fees and God knows what else to keep paying.'

'I said all right, Nicholas. Just leave me alone.'

He left the kitchen and once in his room, he still felt angry. Yet there was relief too. He did care about his daughter. He cared about her acutely, painfully, but here—in his sanctuary—he could escape the pain. He could enter another, different world. Here he could change things, create problems and then solve them. He could make people sad, and then happy. Danger could turn to safety. Here he was all powerful. Here he *could* do more.

Virginia's emotions were in turmoil. She felt absolute anguish every time she thought of Wincey. It was everyone's unspoken opinion that she must be dead. She had drowned and been washed away, either in the River Kelvin or the River Clyde. There could be no other reason why she had not been found alive and well. Her disappearance had been reported in the *Glasgow Herald*. There had been pictures of her. Her auburn hair, her face, with its dusting of freckles, were unusual in a way, but she had a sultry beauty despite the fact that she was obviously just a child in school uniform.

A reward had been offered for any information. The size of that reward, the police assured Virginia, would encourage someone to come forward. But no-one had. A thousand times in her imagination Virginia had suffered the agonies of drowning with Wincey. It was unbearable to think of the child suffering alone. Yet, at the same time, she clung to the hope that somehow, somewhere, Wincey might still be alive. It was true what Nicholas had said—they had done everything they could.

Yet the many unanswered questions about the dreadful day Wincey disappeared continued to haunt Virginia. Mrs Cartwright had been worried about the state of old Mr Cartwright's health before she had left for her bridge afternoon. As a result she had returned much earlier than usual, only to find that her husband was dead and Wincey had vanished into thin air. The child had no money. She wasn't wearing her coat or hat or gloves. They had all been lying in the Cartwright hall where she had left them when she arrived. It had been a wild afternoon with wind gusting furiously along Great Western Road. Rain had been streaking down, hardening into hailstones to drum against windows and doors. What could have made Wincey rush out unprotected on a day like that?

Virginia wept. Then she dried her eyes, overcome with bitterness. It was all right for Nicholas. He could escape into his fictional world. That was where he really belonged—where he was truly happy. He could shut Wincey out. He could shut everybody and everything out. That's what he always did. It had never bothered her before, she had simply accepted it, but now she almost hated him for it. She wondered if he cared at all about Wincey.

She tried to tell herself that she was being unfair. Of course he cared about his daughter. His love for the child had been expressed in his poetry. She remembered a poem he had written about Wincey:

> Minutes rush
> A tiny yawn holds parents
> Captive in a cocoon of wonder.
> What dreams visit her
> As perfect hands stretch
> To grab at the hope charged air.
>
> Minutes rush
> While lashes, long and dark,
> Lie pillowed by cheeks
> Of impossible softness.
> Milk sated lips pout
> With contented sighs.

Minutes rush
As varied and fleeting emotions
Vie for attention.
But mother and father dare not blink
As they attend the next murmur,
The next tiny movement,
The next breath,
And still, the minutes rush.

She remembered him gazing in wonder at the baby, tenderly nursing Wincey in his arms. Of course he loved the child. Of course he'd done his best for her. But still the irritation, the resentment against him, lingered, refusing to be completely banished.

Unable to sit alone with her thoughts for a minute longer, she rose and went for her coat and hat. She decided to go and see Mathieson. At least he would be able to take her mind off all her troubles, even just for a short while. He was not long back from London where he had been supporting the Hunger Marchers. The marches had been flash points for violent anti-government protests across Britain in the past two weeks. The last time she had seen him was when he came for lunch and he had given her and Nicholas a vivid description of the fifteen-thousand-strong rally in Trafalgar Square and the scene when two thousand marchers from the provinces joined thousands of supporters in Hyde Park. Nearly five thousand police fought with them for two hours. Fifty people were injured and fourteen arrested. During an East End visit, Prince George had been met with shouts of 'Down with the means test, we want bread'. Mathieson had hardly changed since she first knew him as a zealous young socialist during the war. Despite the disabilities he'd suffered since his stroke, he was still able to give lectures on politics and economics at the Scottish Labour College. One side of his face still bore the unmistakable signs of his stroke, and he had to walk with the help of a stick, but despite all this it seemed as though nothing could slow him down or deflect him from his devotion to the 'Cause'.

Mathieson now lived in a one-bedroomed flat above the shops in Byers Road, within easy walking distance of Kirklee Terrace. Virginia was glad of her long coat with its high fur collar and her tight fitting cloche hat as she braved the bitter November wind outside. It had been a cold day like this when Wincey disappeared, and her thoughts returned once more to her lost daughter as she hurried along Great Western Road, then turned down into Byers Road.

She felt as if she was going mad. It was the not knowing, not understanding what had happened. The growing possibility that she would never know. At the same time she couldn't imagine herself ever giving up hope. One day, she would uncover the truth.

4

'How about this, Daddy?' Charlotte said. 'When I was delivering Mrs Tompkinson's latest outfit, I saw a broken down sewing machine left out at the back of the house for the bin men to collect. How about if you collect it instead, bring it back here and see if you can mend it? If you could fix it up, I could teach Wincey and Florence to use it. They could work shifts on that machine. Then with Mammy and me on the one we've already got, we'd be able to take on more work.'

Erchie's face brightened. 'Here, that's a great idea, hen. It'll give me somethin' tae dae an' ah'll no' be much o' an engineer if ah cannae manage tae fix a wee sewin' machine.'

'It'd be a real help, Daddy. We'd be able to make more money.'

'Right, hen. You give me the exact address an ah'll be off. Ah'd better look nippy or the bin men might get there before me.'

Charlotte scribbled the address on to a piece of paper and Erchie hurried to snatch his jacket from the peg in the lobby. Within seconds the outside door banged shut and he was away. He could be heard whistling as he clattered down the stairs.

Teresa's tired eyes glowed with enthusiasm and gratitude towards Charlotte. 'You're a clever girl, Charlotte. That'll give your dad a job—just what he needed.'

'Huh, some job,' Granny grunted. 'What good's a job wi' nae wages?'

'Once the four of us really get going, we could earn enough to give Dad something,' Charlotte said. Wincey, now settled in and feeling like one of the family—indeed more so than she'd ever done in her own family, spoke up with enthusiasm.

'Yes, and maybe we could even find more machines and have more people work on them. That's how big businesses are built up.'

Granny scoffed. 'What would the likes o' you know about big businesses, or any kin' o' business, ye cheeky wee tramp!'

'Now Granny,' Teresa said, 'there's no need to talk like that. Wincey's a good girl and she's been a great help to us.'

It had always been Bridget and Euphemia's job to go on errands to the shops. They had become quite expert at tracking down bones for soup, or stale cookies or bread that a baker in town was going to throw in the bin at the end of the day. Local bakers were more likely to ask for a penny or two for their stale bread and scones. While her mother was taking her turn at the sewing machine, Florence helped with the cooking—at least Florence would peel the potatoes and scrape the vegetables for the soup. She boasted she once made scones, but mostly she was out wandering about, asking for trouble as Granny said. Wincey opted for the scrubbing and cleaning of the house. Teresa said she didn't need to do that because the three girls, Florence, Euphemia and Bridget, usually took turns doing the cleaning. Instead, Charlotte said Wincey could accompany her on her rounds, collecting or delivering clothes for different customers. 'That way,' Charlotte said kindly, 'you'd be able to get away from here for a wee while and see all the lovely houses the gentry live in.'

But Wincey insisted she'd rather stay in and clean and scrub. It wasn't just her fear of being seen and recognised in one of the more prosperous areas that made her want to stay indoors. She had discovered she preferred to do things on her own. Not only that, there was an obsessive streak about her at times. Concentrating completely, silently, going to extremes, scrubbing the floors, the sink, the outside of the coal bunker, the fire, polishing the black grate, washing the windows—it somehow made her feel safe in herself. It also gave her a deep sense of achievement. This total obsessiveness even overcame her revulsion at cleaning the outside toilet.

'Never,' Teresa told her, 'since this building was built, has that toilet been kept so spotless.'

It was a tiny cubicle situated downstairs on the half landing and shared by two other families, next door neighbours of the Gourlays on the top floor. It had a cracked wooden seat and a cistern mounted over six feet up the wall, and it was flushed by pulling a hanging chain. It had been a dark, putrid smelling place before Wincey attacked it. She had even scrubbed the walls and the cistern, climbing on to the toilet seat to reach it.

'Ye must be mad,' Florence said. 'It's no' as if we're the only wans makin' a mess o' it. It's that McGregor bunch. There's sixteen o' them. Filthy wee middens o' weans!'

Teresa tutted. 'Och, poor Mrs McGregor has her hands full trying to cope with so many, and her always pregnant with the next. I am sorry for her, right enough.'

'I don't mind keeping the toilet clean,' Wincey assured everybody. 'Honestly, I enjoy working away by myself.'

Florence laughed. 'Enjoy, did ye say? Enjoy cleaning filthy toilets. You definitely are mad!'

'You can cut up Erchie's old *Daily Workers* for toilet paper, if you like,' Teresa suggested helpfully. The *Daily Worker* was Erchie's only luxury in life, except the odd Woodbine cigarette, but that was only an occasional treat.

'Oh, thanks Teresa,' Wincey said. 'I could put holes in each bit and thread string through them and hang them all onto a nail on the wall.'

'Och, we aye take a bit o' our Daddy's old paper down wi' us anyway,' Florence reminded her.

'I know, but this is more efficient. I mean it's tidier, and it helps everyone.'

Eventually Teresa said, 'That toilet's like a wee palace.'

And everyone—including the McGregors and the other family on the landing, the Donaldsons—wholeheartedly agreed. Both families began boxing their children's ears or slapping their legs if it was discovered they had made a mess in the toilet, or the lavvy as it was more commonly known. Teresa and family were more polite and proper than most of their neighbours. Granny was a trial, however. She couldn't get down to the toilet since her arthritis was so bad and she'd gained so much weight.

'Ma hips are murder,' she kept informing everyone, 'an' it's even gone intae ma gums. That's why ah cannae wear ma teeth.'

'Och well,' Teresa said with a look of wide eyed innocence, 'it hasn't affected your jaws, Granny. You're still able to talk, dear. Your jaws never stop moving.'

'What dae ye mean by that?' Granny demanded angrily.

'Now, now, Granny, you know fine we're all concerned about you and do our best for you.'

They certainly did do their best for Granny, as Wincey soon discovered. When Granny needed 'to go', as she called it, it was a real challenge of strength and endurance for everyone who happened to be in the house. The challenge arose again now. Erchie was out collecting the sewing machine. Euphemia and Bridget were out looking for any vegetables that had been thrown out by the fruit shops in town. Their bins at the back of the shops could prove a treasure trove of food. Other grocery stores in the centre of the city could delight the sisters with tasty morsels, often in packets or tins, which had just been burst or bashed and didn't have the perfect appearance that fussy people with too much money always insisted on.

Florence was out trying to scrounge some bits of coal lying about in one of the coal yards.

'Ah need tae go,' Granny announced, her small rheumy eyes betraying some anxiety.

Teresa said, 'Can't you wait a wee while until someone else comes in, Granny. There's only Wincey just now.'

'What's up wi' her then? Is she paralysed, or what?'

Teresa rolled her eyes. 'You know fine she's only a wee slip of a thing, and there's not much more of me. I don't think we'd be able to lift you. The girls won't be long. Just try to hang on a wee while longer.'

'Ah cannae.' Granny's voice rose to a wail. She was obviously in genuine distress.

'All right, all right, we'll do our best,' Teresa said hastily. 'I'll fetch the chamber pot,' she said, giving it its proper name. It was a chanty to everyone else. Once the chamber pot was ready at Granny's feet, Teresa told Wincey, 'Now you get a grip of her at one side and I'll hang on at the other and we'll both try and heave her up.'

In a matter of seconds both Teresa and Wincey were scarlet faced and panting with their exertions. Granny felt like a solid and immovable mountain. But eventually they did manage to prise her out of the rocking chair and stagger forward with her.

'Wait a minute,' Teresa gasped, 'till I pull her knickers down. Hang on.'

Like grim death, Wincey hung on.

'Right, lower her down now.'

The lowering down proved to be worse than the raising up. Wincey felt her legs and her back would never be the same again. Once safely deposited onto the chamber pot, Granny's face acquired an expression of deep concentration and Teresa cried out, 'Och, not number two, Granny!'

Granny grunted, 'Ye'll be auld yersel' wan day.' This was an expression Granny often used in self defence.

'Never mind,' Teresa said to Wincey. 'I'll empty it, dear.'

Afterwards Wincey swung the outside door to and fro to allow comparatively fresh air to waft in. She also opened the kitchen window while Teresa masked a pot of tea 'to help us get our strength back'.

'Are you two tryin' tae freeze me tae death noo?' Granny wailed.

'Now, now, Granny,' Teresa said, 'a nice cup of tea will soon heat you up.'

'There's never any biscuits these days,' Granny complained. 'I used tae enjoy a nice digestive tae dip intae ma tea.'

'Never mind. Once we get another machine, we'll be able to make more money, as Charlotte says. Then you can have your digestives.'

'Ah'll believe that when ah see it.'

'Are you all right, dear?' Teresa gazed anxiously at Wincey.

'Yes, fine, thank you.'

'Here, drink up your tea.'

'Thank you.'

'You're such a polite wee girl. Where did you learn such nice manners?'

Wincey shrugged. 'My mother, I think. She was . . .' An idea occurred to her. 'She was from the Highlands, like you.'

'Ah, that explains a lot dear. As well as your nice voice. You don't sound a bit Glaswegian. Your parents died in an accident, did you say? Or was that Florence? I get mixed up with all her stories.'

'I'd rather not talk about it. It upsets me even to think about. Please don't ask me.'

'Oh, I'm so sorry, dear,' Teresa interrupted hastily. 'it's not like me to be nosy.'

'Ha,' Granny snorted. 'That's a laugh!'

'Now, now. I've never asked Wincey anything about her background before, have I, Wincey?'

'No, everyone's been very good. I'm so grateful.' And she was. She didn't feel that she'd ever been accepted just as herself before. To her grandfather she had been nothing more than a sex object. To her grandmother she had been a younger edition of her mother, and it was only too obvious that her grandmother hated her mother. To her mother and father, she barely existed at all. They were so caught up with all their clever, articulate friends. She was a joke. They often laughed at her shyness and the way she could get tongue-tied. Sometimes she even stuttered. She never stuttered here, no longer even felt shy. She was as happy as could be, as long as she was able to blot out the past and keep her guilty secret locked safely away in a dark recess of her mind.

5

'What does Nicholas think of Galsworthy getting the Nobel prize for literature?' Mathieson asked once he'd led Virginia into the kitchen. 'I've just made a pot of tea—do you want a cup?'

'Yes, all right.'

She sat down on one of the wooden chairs at the table and watched her ex-husband limp towards the press at the side of the grate and fetch a cup and saucer. The kitchen was almost identical to the one they'd had when they lived together in the Calton. It even had the same furniture. Yet Virginia experienced no feelings of nostalgia. In those days Mathieson had been as totally immersed in politics as Nicholas was now totally taken up with writing. She suspected that this obsessive devotion was one of the things that both men knew right from the start they had in common.

Nicholas had been good to Mathieson while he had been lying in his hospital bed, unable to move or talk. Nicholas had kept him in touch with everything by reading the newspapers to him every day. She suspected that, with such a silent listener, Nicholas had also poured out his heart to Mathieson. He'd certainly told him all about his passion for writing, even reading out chapters of his new novel to him.

At first, when she'd discovered that Nicholas had gone to see Mathieson, she was both horrified and afraid. After all, she had been having an affair with Nicholas and had had his child. That was before she had met Mathieson. She was married to him by the time it was discovered that Nicholas had not been killed in the trenches. And when she'd married Mathieson, he knew nothing about either the affair or the baby.

After Nicholas had returned, they had restarted their affair and eventually she confessed everything to her husband. She told him she was leaving him. As a committed socialist, Mathieson had always hated the rich and powerful—men like Nicholas's father. As well as the munitions factory in which Virginia's brother had been killed, George Cartwright had owned property in many of Glasgow's most notorious slums. At that point, however, Mathieson had not met Nicholas. She tried to tell him how different Nicholas was from his father, but he had refused to listen and became more and more enraged. That was when he had taken his stroke. For a long time she had blamed herself. She had been so distressed that she had stopped going to see him in hospital. She couldn't bear to look at his grotesquely distorted face. She had believed that he was not aware that she was even there, that he was not aware of anything.

Nicholas had been appalled when he heard this. 'I know what it's like to lie alone and confused in a hospital bed.' And that was when he took over the visits. It must have been during this time that Mathieson had come to accept that Nicholas was indeed different from his father. Nicholas had learned to embrace socialism himself since his experiences in the war. He wasn't as radical as Mathieson, but a socialist nevertheless.

'I express my beliefs in action,' Mathieson once told him. 'I spread the word by teaching and I take an active part in protests and the like. You express your beliefs in your writing. Who's to say which of us is more effective, Nicholas?'

The divorce had been traumatic for all of them, even though they'd all agreed that for Mathieson to divorce Virginia on the grounds of adultery was the best and quickest solution. Long before Mathieson had got out of the hospital, she had already set up house with Nicholas.

If anyone had told Virginia before Mathieson had taken ill that one day he and Nicholas Cartwright would become firm friends, she would never have believed them. But friends they had become. She often thought that they got on better together than she'd ever got on with either of them. They seemed at times to have far more in common.

'We've been thinking, and talking about, nothing else but Wincey,' she told Mathieson now.

'Oh yes, of course,' Mathieson said. 'It's awful for you both, and I suppose it hasn't got any easier as time has passed.'

'It's got worse, if anything. It's beginning to affect our relationship.'

'How do you mean?' He poured out two cups of tea.

She shrugged. 'Oh, I don't know. All the tension and worry, and not being able to do anything, I suppose.' She took a few sips of tea. 'I as much as told him this morning that he was totally selfish and didn't care about Wincey. He'd just announced, you see, that he was going back to work in his room.'

'He does care, Virginia.'

Miserably, she nodded.

'It's just not being able to do anything, not knowing.'

'We've all done everything we can, especially Nicholas. What more do you expect him to do?'

'I know. I know.' After a few minutes she added, 'I'm dreading Christmas.'

'There's a few weeks to go yet. You could still hear good news.'

'Do you really believe she could still be alive, James?'

'People go missing all the time and many of them do turn up again, often in another big city, like London.'

'London?' Virginia echoed incredulously. 'How on earth could the child get to London?'

Mathieson shrugged. 'It has been known. I've read about cases like that, haven't you?'

'I suppose so, but I can't imagine Wincey being so resourceful. She's always been such a quiet, slow kind of child. She never did very well at school, you know. Not compared with Richard. Richard has always been so clever, and self-confident, and outgoing.'

'And everybody's favourite,' Mathieson said.

Virginia paled. 'You don't think . . . I mean, have we been unfair or unkind to her? Did we neglect her? Oh James! Whatever she might have believed anyone else thought of her, she definitely knew her grandfather thought the world of her. We used to smile when he called her his clever girl. Poor Wincey. She was probably so grief stricken, she couldn't cope, didn't know what to do except run away from the awful truth of her grandfather's death.'

'Maybe she imagined she'd have nobody to care about her after he'd gone.'

'But we did care about her, James. Maybe we've been thought-less. Maybe we didn't spend enough time with her, pay her enough attention. But we did care. We still do.'

'Of course you do,' he soothed. 'Children are always getting strange ideas into their heads. I haven't worked for a lifetime as a teacher not to know that, and especially young people of her age. Once they get into their teens, life can be terribly difficult for them—and for their parents.'

'I'm sorry to keep bothering you like this, James. You've been very supportive.'

'You're not bothering me. I only wish I could be of more help.'

'Were you not at the College today?'

'It's Saturday.'

She rolled her eyes. 'I really have lost track of things, haven't I?'

'It's time you showed some common sense like Nicholas. Get on with your life. You're not going to do yourself or anybody else any good by cracking up.'

'It just shows you, though. Saturday, Sunday, come hell or high water, it doesn't matter, it doesn't make any difference to Nicholas as far as his writing is concerned.'

'It's the nature of his work, Virginia. You always knew that.'

She sighed. 'I suppose so.' Then after a minute, 'Would you like to come to lunch tomorrow. Maybe you'll be able to drag him away from his desk.'

It was Mathieson's turn to sigh. 'You just can't accept it, can you?'

She thought he was going to add, 'Just as you could never accept the time and commitment I gave to politics.' She almost dared him to say it, so that she could argue with him, take her frustration out on him. After all, she'd helped him as much as she could and in every way she could. She even spoke at political meetings. But in the end she'd seen that all of Mathieson's passion was for politics. His political work and the time he spent on it took precedence over everything else.

It seemed to her now that, although Mathieson's work and Nicholas's were very different, they had much the same attitude to it. But Mathieson added nothing to his statement and so she repeated, 'Will you come?'

'Yes, all right. But don't expect me to go into Nicholas's room and drag him out.'

'Maybe if I ask George or Jimmy as well?'

George Buchanan was Labour MP for the Gorbals. James Maxton was MP for Bridgeton.

'Maxton's too busy fighting Ramsay Macdonald and opposing rearmament just now to be socialising with us. Buchanan's been having a go at Macdonald as well. I'm hard put to it to decide which of them is the more brilliant speaker. I think George is the more fiery one— him and his red hair, but they're both equally charismatic as far as I'm concerned.'

'So they're in London just now?'

'As far as I know.'

'Oh well, make it about one o'clock, James. That'll give him a morning on his own. He surely can't complain about that.'

'One o'clock it is. And try to discipline your mind to concentrate on something else. Invite some of Nicholas's friends for supper. He won't mind that and you enjoy listening to them.'

'I suppose I could. You know them only too well, don't you. None of them would leave their desks early enough to come for lunch. Writers!'

'Well, you know what Nicholas always says. He'd never have continued with his writing in the first place if it hadn't been for you.'

'I sometimes wonder now if I did the right thing.'

'I've never been more certain about anything, Virginia. You did the right thing. One day, it might be Nicholas receiving that Nobel prize. In my opinion, Nicholas is a far better writer than Galsworthy, and his work shows him to be far more committed to social reform.'

'You think so?'

'I always say what I think.' At least this was true.

'All right, I believe you. But living with a writer is not easy.' She wanted to say, 'any more than it was easy living with a politician.' But she didn't. And she left Mathieson's house feeling even more frustrated than when she'd arrived.

6

'You're really a very smart girl,' Teresa said. 'You've picked up sewing so quickly.'

'I'd like to learn the cutting too,' Wincey said eagerly.

Teresa looked doubtful. 'Oh, that's a bit more tricky, dear. Maybe you'd better leave that to Charlotte and me for a wee while yet.'

'Yes,' Charlotte agreed. 'But you're doing very well, Wincey. I will let you do some cutting eventually, but it's so important—it's not a thing you can rush. I could start taking you out with me and show you the measuring and fitting. That's very important too.'

Wincey shook her head. 'No, I'd rather stay here and work.'

'You are a funny child,' Teresa said. 'Any of the other girls would jump at the chance to see into some of the houses that Charlotte goes to. You can't be that shy. You're not shy with us.'

'It's different here. I feel at home. I'm not frightened any more.'

'What on earth is there to be frightened of?'

Wincey shrugged. 'I don't like posh places or posh people.'

Granny, who had been dozing by the fire, spoke up with a splutter, 'Bloody parasites, the lot o' them. Ah'd put them up against a wall an' shoot them.'

'Now, now, Granny,' Teresa said. 'You know fine well you would never do any such thing.'

'They've done it tae oor kind though.' Granny raised her voice. 'Shot decent pacifist lads an' poor fellas who were aw tae bits wi' shell shock. Called them cowards an' shot them in cold blood.'

'Yes, all right, Granny. Just try and calm down now. You know what getting too excited does to you.'

Getting excited caused Granny to lose control of her bladder. Sometimes, a whole row of Granny's knickers festooned the pulley above the kitchen table.

'They as good as killed poor Johnny, the way they tormented him in prison. Did ye know that?'

'Yes, Granny, we know how poor Johnny Maclean was treated in prison. You've told us before.'

'Aye, but no' often enough, it seems. They'll be doin' the same tae Jimmy Maxton if we let them get away wi' it. He's a pacifist as well, don't forget.'

Wincey imagined how amazed and fascinated Granny and all the Gourlays would be if she told them that she had met Maxton—first of all when she'd gone with her mother and father to hear him speak, and later when he had been invited to Kirklee Terrace. Like Mathieson, he had been a school teacher and she'd heard him say that he had been converted to socialism by speakers such as Keir Hardy, Philip Snowdon and Ramsay Macdonald. But none of these men, Wincey felt sure, could match James Maxton as a dramatic and witty speaker. During the war, he was dismissed as a teacher, charged with sedition, found guilty and imprisoned for a year. Her father said that his suffering in prison was still etched on his lantern-jawed face. His long hair was, her father suspected, one of the ways Maxton had of cocking a snook at the establishment and its conventions. In appearance at least, he was very unlike his fellow socialist MP, John Wheatley—a short, serious man with a chubby, bespectacled face. Wheatley had been both her father and mother's favourite. They admired his courage and intelligence and supported his campaign for better housing in Glasgow. Wheatley had proposed a scheme for the building of municipal cottages instead of tenements in Glasgow, and he'd succeeded in getting his Housing Act passed successfully. His plan was to create a partnership between political parties, local authorities and building employees and build as many new council houses at modest rents as possible.

Wincey had been brought up on stories about socialist politicians like Maclean, Maxton and Wheatley, but these stories had seldom, if ever, been told directly to her. She had heard them discussed between her parents and their friends. Her parents had seldom even noticed that she had been there. How Granny Gourlay would have loved to hear some of those stories about her socialist heroes—but Wincey couldn't risk breathing a word of any of this.

Instead she said, 'I've read all about them. The socialists, I mean. And seen pictures of them.'

'Where did you get the books and pictures?' Teresa wanted to know.

'The library,' Wincey said hastily, wishing that she had just kept her mouth shut as she usually did about anything outside of the house and the immediate concerns in it.

'I'm surprised you had the time, dear. But I'm glad you did. I know how happy I am if I can find a few minutes to get to the library and pick up a nice romance. But as you can imagine, it's not so easy getting the time to read it. Now with Christmas and the New Year coming near, all our clients will want party dresses made.'

'Aye, they'll aw be lookin' forward tae toastin' anither happy Hogmanay,' Granny growled, 'while aw we huv is the clankin' away o' these sewin' machines.'

'That reminds me,' Charlotte said. 'It's time I was getting back to the room and getting on with it.'

'Och, have another wee cup of tea. You've been at it since the break of dawn, Charlotte,' her mother said worriedly.

'It's just we're doing so well now,' Charlotte said. 'It's word of mouth, you see. One satisfied customer tells another. We're even getting a pound or two in the bank. Come on, Wincey, it's time you relieved Florence. She's been through there on her own for long enough.'

'If you're hinting at me,' Teresa said, 'I had to see to Granny as well as make a bit to eat for everybody.'

'I know, I know. I'm sorry. It's just that we're really beginning to get somewhere, so it's important to keep going.'

'I know, dear, but what's the use of having money in the bank when we're still having to scavenge for food.'

'Capital, Mammy. We need capital for a successful business.'

Erchie arrived in the kitchen then, rubbing his hands and going over to try and heat them at the fire. 'Whit's this, hen?' He peered up at Charlotte from underneath the skip of his bonnet. 'Are ye turning intae a capitalist or somethin'?'

'I'm only trying to make a decent living for us all, Daddy. Have you seen any more machines yet?'

'What on earth do you need any more machines for,' Teresa said.

'Where would we put them. The room's packed as it is, and all that cloth lying about—we've hardly an inch to put our feet.'

'I know!' Wincey suddenly exclaimed. 'How about asking around to see if anyone else has a machine and asking them if they would do some work for us, but in their own houses.'

Teresa was silent for a moment, and then Charlotte said, 'You might have something there, Wincey.'

'Aye, she's a clever wee lassie, right enough,' Erchie said in admiration. 'How aboot Mrs MacIntyre? She used tae huv a machine, didn't she. Ah wonder if she's still got it.'

'She used to make lovely wee things for her children when they were small,' Teresa said. 'But that was when her man was alive and making some money. I don't know how the poor soul survives nowadays, since wee Betty and Andy died of the cholera. And then losing her man in that pit accident. I often wonder why God gives some folk such a heavy burden. I thought she looked thinner the last time I saw her. Her shawl was awfy frayed and worn.'

'I'll speak to her,' Charlotte said. 'I'll go right now.'

'Och, it's pouring doon and pitch dark outside, Charlotte. It's terrible the way they don't mend these lamps. Wait until tomorrow, dear.'

'I'll come with you,' Wincey said eagerly. She hardly ever set foot out of the house but was beginning to feel hemmed in. In a way, it was as if she was in prison, albeit a self-imposed imprisonment.

'You are a funny child,' Teresa repeated. 'You can't face visiting posh houses but you're perfectly happy to go out on a dark, wintry night to visit Mrs MacIntyre in her wee single end.'

'All right,' said Charlotte. 'Come on, Wincey. Can she borrow your shawl, Mammy?'

'Yes of course, dear.' Teresa fetched the faded tartan shawl, draped it over Wincey's head and tucked it around her shoulders.

7

For Richard's sake, they felt they had to do something about Christmas and the New Year. Nicholas was not all that enthusiastic about Christmas. But then he never had been.

'It's a holiday in England, not here,' he always insisted. Which was true, but she knew that Nicholas just grudged taking time off from his writing on Christmas Day. He hated holidays at the best of times.

'Everyone else works on Christmas Day,' he said in self defence when Virginia accused him of this. 'Why shouldn't I?'

'Not everybody,' Virginia insisted. 'And anyway, you're different. You don't need to work.'

Nicholas raised a sarcastic brow. 'Really?'

Virginia felt irritated. He knew perfectly well what she meant. His books had already made enough money to keep them in comfort for years. There was no excuse for him not taking a whole week off over Christmas and New Year, never mind one day. Eventually he agreed. Virginia could see, however, that he was restless and resentful. Nowadays, out of his writing room, he was like a lost soul. It made her so angry—it was all very well for him to escape into his fictional world, but what about her? Didn't she deserve something more from him, some support in the real world that she was having such a struggle to survive in? He might as well have deserted her, walked completely out of her life. She knew that even outside of his room, he was not really with her. His mind was still far away.

'Why don't you switch off when you come out of that room? Is that too much to ask?'

'You don't understand,' he protested. 'It's not as easy as that. Not when I'm in the middle of a book. The characters are still speaking and living their lives in my head. It's not like being a shopkeeper and just shutting up shop and walking away from it. Creating a book isn't like that.'

The conversation ended abruptly as they had to go out, but the bad feeling between them remained in the room, like an enemy lying in wait until they returned. They had booked seats for the Alhambra theatre for Mrs Cartwright, Richard and themselves. Mrs Cartwright was still in mourning for her husband and wore a heavy, ankle-length black dress and a silver fox stole. Her black hat was festooned with a veil shaped to fit under her chin. Virginia wore one of the new style three-quarter length astrakhan coats, with leg of mutton sleeves and a perky little hat balanced on one side of her head. But she didn't feel perky, although she did manage to smile at Will Fyfe's antics on the stage. Nicholas laughed uproariously, as if he hadn't a care in the world.

They had Mrs Cartwright to Christmas lunch with turkey and all the trimmings, followed by the traditional exchange of expensive gifts. Virginia couldn't help remembering her childhood Christmases. There were no turkeys then, and they were lucky if their mother could find scraps with which to make a pie. She remembered the excitement of hanging up her stocking on Christmas Eve and praying for a doll. On Christmas Day she'd find her stocking three quarters filled with ashes, with just an orange or an apple on top, and, if she was lucky, there would be a bar of Fry's Cream chocolate. Her brothers usually got the same and, if they were lucky, a torch or even a mouth organ. The Co-op always had a Santa and if her mother and father could scrape up a few extra pennies, they'd take her to the Co-operative Hall where Santa sat at the bottom of a big chute. After you paid your sixpence, Santa pulled a lever and your present came down the chute.

Richard had been brought up in the lap of luxury by the Cartwrights for his first five years or so, and had never known poverty—or any deprivation whatsoever. Nor had Wincey. Virginia kept telling herself that she had done her very best in every way for Wincey. She kept going over everything that had happened with Wincey since the year of her birth. She had loved the child from the first moment she had seen her little red wrinkled face, and the downy crop of ginger hair. Nicholas had laughed at the first sight of her.

'Where on earth did she get that ginger mop?'

The bright ginger mop had darkened as Wincey got older until it was a rich auburn. She was a lovely girl—despite her freckles. Nicholas and Virginia had given her everything—there had never been any stockings filled with ashes for her. Each Christmas, she had been given whatever she asked for, although she never asked for very much. She was a quiet, introverted child, but nobody could be blamed for that. She just had a different nature, a different personality, from Richard. They hadn't sent her to a boarding school like Richard, but that was for her own good, and anyway, she didn't want to go. Nicholas didn't want to send Richard either, as he had unhappy memories of his own time at boarding school. Eventually he had been persuaded by Mr and Mrs Cartwright, who had insisted Richard should have the best education in the country. And after all, Edinburgh wasn't far away and he could come home for weekends and holidays.

Nicholas had agreed on condition that, if Richard was not happy there, he had only to say and they'd immediately take him out of the school. As it turned out, Richard was always perfectly happy, but then Richard had never been a problem.

Wincey, however, had always been shy and awkward. They had many clever and talented friends. They had lots of lovely parties but the child had always hung back when anyone tried to include her in the company. Both Richard and Wincey had been given piano lessons, and even when he was quite small Richard would often entertain everyone with a tune. He was naturally talented and everyone went into raptures of praise. Then when Wincey was also asked to perform, it was a terrible carry-on to persuade her. Once or twice, she did play and made a quite unnecessary and stumbling mess of the piece which she could play perfectly well when she wanted to. She only seemed to want to play when she was alone.

Eventually they gave up asking her to do anything. She was such a difficult child. Immediately the thought made Virginia feel guilty. No, she was not difficult. She was just a very shy wee girl. No two children were the same in any family. Why should they be? No doubt Wincey was relieved when everyone stopped asking her to do things she didn't want to and just left her alone.

Mrs Cartwright thought Wincey was like Virginia, but Virginia believed that was quite wrong. Wincey had not her mother's light golden hair, for a start, and as far as her nature was concerned she was more like Nicholas if she was like anyone. Not in looks, but in some aspects of her nature. Nicholas could be quite a loner, and was not afraid to disagree with everyone else. Virginia could go out and speak at political meetings to support the socialist cause, especially to support Mathieson in his arguments for Home Rule for Scotland. Nicholas would not entertain any ideas about Home Rule, despite the fact that it had been seriously debated in the House of Commons.

'It'll come eventually,' Mathieson insisted.

'That may be so,' Nicholas said, 'but I believe we should be trying to get on better with each other, not splitting up. I'm surprised at you, James, for advocating such an aggressive policy.'

'It's not an aggressive policy,' Mathieson insisted, and so the argument went on—but they never fell out over politics, or anything else. They just agreed to differ. Nicholas would never agree to speak about politics in public, although he was a socialist—much to his parents' fury and disgust. They had always been true-blue Conservatives, and they blamed Nicholas's political conversion on Virginia, just as they blamed her for everything else. They had certainly always held her responsible for encouraging Nicholas to take up writing, and they were not at all proud of his success.

As well as being a loner, Nicholas used people. He did what he called 'research'. He went to Salvation Army hostels and mission halls and spoke not only to the inmates, but to the people who were in charge. He gathered and used everyone's experiences, including his own. Virginia did not know what he was writing at the moment— since Wincey's disappearance he had stopped talking to her about his work—but she was sure he would be using Wincey's disappearance as the basis of a plot, and exploring how such an occurrence could affect everyone. He had probably even used his father's death in a dramatic scene. He was quite ruthless when it came to his work.

Virginia could see that now. It had never occurred to her before— she had always believed he was a very sensitive man. But now, looking back, she could see that he'd always been using people and experiences, especially emotional experiences, for his own purposes. Even—come to think of it—in his poetry. Once, her favourite had been 'Shy Love'. She had read it so often in the past, she had the words off by heart. Now she realised that, even so many years ago, he'd been using their private sexual experience.

Passion eased
Wearing the same skin
Your breath flows
Like slowing winds in my ear
Afloat on a pontoon of tenderness
Fleetingly, we forget
The flinty landscape
That encircles us.

Ardent for expression
I want to honour your kisses
Sing of your soothing skin
Celebrate your languid smile.

Instead I stutter raw whispers
Into the pliant flesh of your neck
Pray you unravel
The braille from my lips
And read those three little words.

It had just been another opportunity for him to put words together. She had begun to feel cynical about everything, even about the favourite songs that everyone else loved. 'Love is the Sweetest Thing' and 'Love's Last Word is Spoken' and 'Night and Day' were continuously on the wireless. More and more now, she could not bear to hear them and switched off. When Nicholas did take the occasional hour or two away from his work, it was to take his mother out to lunch. The old woman didn't want to come to visit them at Kirklee Terrace for lunch or anything else, if she could avoid it, unless Richard was there. Mrs Cartwright had always disliked and disapproved of Virginia, and that animosity had grown over the years.

'She's lonely without Father,' Nicholas explained. 'She misses him more than she will admit.'

'She has Richard often enough,' Virginia said. 'And you.'

'Do you really begrudge an old woman the occasional company of her son and grandson, Virginia?'

She hated Nicholas for making her feel guilty and ashamed. 'No, of course not,' she protested. 'It's just that you never seem able to take any time off to be with me.'

'What nonsense! We have every evening together.'

'Most evenings I have to share you with friends, and even when there's no-one else here, you're not really with me. Your mind's on your writing.'

'When I'm with you now, you seem to do nothing but nag. It's enough to drive me back to my room, mentally and physically.'

Virginia didn't think she nagged. He was only using that as an excuse. She could complain a lot more about his mother but didn't. The visit to the theatre and the Christmas lunch had been more of an ordeal than a pleasure, thanks to Mrs Cartwright and the way she had of looking down her long nose at Virginia, especially when she used her lorgnette. Hopefully New Year would be better. At least Mrs Cartwright would not be at Kirklee Terrace on Hogmanay. James Mathieson and their other friends would be coming to bring in 1933 with them.

The company would perhaps help her to keep her mind off Wincey, at least for an hour or two. She doubted if Nicholas gave the child much serious thought now. Poor Wincey would now be little more to him than a character in his book. She had asked Nicholas what the name of his main female character was in his current book and he'd reluctantly muttered, 'Cathy.'

'Young?' she'd queried.

'Yes, but I don't like having to put up with pointless questions about my work while I'm in the middle of it, Virginia. So just leave it, will you.'

Oh yes, Cathy was Wincey all right. And he was feeling furtive and guilty about it. Virginia was sure of it. She didn't say any more. She just walked away from him thinking,

'How could you? How *could* you?'

8

The Gourlays had been very busy with all the extra work that was now coming in. Mrs MacIntyre proved a fast, willing and efficient machinist. Wincey usually collected work from her which was not only beautifully sewn but carefully pressed and folded. On one occasion, Wincey asked her if she knew of anyone else who owned a machine.

'It doesn't matter how old or broken down it is. Erchie's great at fixing anything.'

Mrs MacIntyre looked worried.

'If you get someone else, would it mean I'd get less work?'

'No, no,' Wincey assured her. 'The more people we have working for us, the more customers we can take on.'

'Well, there's Mrs Friel up the stairs. She has one. And maybe Mrs Andrews in the next close. I know she used to have one, but that was years ago.'

'Great!' Wincey said. 'I'll go and check on them right now. And don't you worry, Mrs MacIntyre. This way things can only get better.'

Both machines were in a pretty bad state, but Erchie lost no time in repairing them and getting them into good working order. He was a happy man now, revelling in his new job—especially as he was being paid a wage, albeit a small one. Charlotte had suggested to Wincey that she could take charge of organising the wages for each member of the family who helped in what was known now as 'the business'. It was recognised that Wincey was old for her years, and more serious than other girls of her age. She was more intelligent too.

'How did you learn so much?' Charlotte asked. 'You even seem to

271

know all about politics.'

'Not really,' Wincey laughed, secretly regretting offering an opinion when Erchie had been pontificating on the subject. So often, when she opened her mouth, she had given something away about herself. 'I used to hear my father talking about what was going on in Parliament and he used to let me read his newspaper as well. I'm just good at remembering things, that's all.'

The truth was she had heard her mother and her mother's friends talk more about politics than her father ever did. Also, she'd had a very good education, including a private tutor one evening a week after school hours, and twice a week during school holidays.

Between them, she and Charlotte worked out a system of payment for everybody, including themselves. They kept proper books listing all income and expenses. Wincey had saved most of her money and was now able to start a Post Office savings book. Charlotte had opened a bank account for the business. Having a bank account had been unheard of in the family before.

'You've brought us luck, dear,' Teresa told Wincey. 'Everything's gone that well ever since you arrived. It's a good job,' Teresa cast a sly, triumphant look in Granny's direction, 'I didn't listen to Granny. If she'd had her way, you would have been back out in the street.'

Granny gave a loud snore that didn't fool anyone. She was obviously just pretending to be asleep.

One day the local Co-op couldn't supply them with the particular shades of thread they needed and Charlotte asked Wincey to go into Copeland and Lye's in Sauchiehall Street to buy a stock of the necessary colours. Copeland and Lye was one of her grandmother's favourite stores. She often shopped there and had morning coffee or afternoon tea in their restaurant. Wincey refused to go for the threads, and Charlotte became annoyed. She was a mild natured girl, rather like Teresa, but on this occasion—partly, no doubt, because of the stress of the heavy workload she had taken on—she lost her temper with Wincey.

'This is getting ridiculous, Wincey. You're like a hermit. Why won't you set foot anywhere out of Springburn? It's not as if you even belong to the place. Where exactly was it you lived before?'

This frightened Wincey. Nobody had quizzed her in detail about her origins. They'd taken it for granted, helped by the hints she'd given them, that she did indeed belong somewhere in the Springburn area. After all, it was in Springburn that Florence had found her. Charlotte though was smarter than the rest, despite her quiet and modest manner. It had obviously not escaped her that Wincey spoke with a different accent—the others had thought that she must have taken after the Highland mother she had told them about, but Charlotte, judging by other questions she'd asked, had also been wondering about her standard of education.

To avoid answering any more questions Wincey said, 'Oh, all right. I'll go into town.'

As she set out, she felt so tense and nervous that pains stiffened up the back of her neck and gripped her head like a vice. The town was busy with pre-Christmas shoppers, despite the wind and rain. Women were protected from the weather with long fur coats and little head-hugging hats. Brollies were being blown inside out by the wind. Wincey was wearing a raincoat she'd picked up at Paddy's Market on her first journey outside of Springburn—she'd had no fear of meeting anyone from her other world among the 'shawlies' at the Market. Business men, lawyers, accountants, insurance brokers and bankers all wearing bowler hats were thronging into Langs Restaurants in Queen Street and St Vincent Street. Langs had been a favourite place of her grandfather's, where self-service was *de rigueur*, the price of every item was clearly marked, and each customer simply announced his total to the cashier when leaving. Her grandfather said that this self-regulating system was rarely, if ever, abused. If anyone was spotted trying to abuse it, the regulars would be quick to point them out to the management. This would result in the offender being called into the manageress's office, only to be freed after a generous contribution was made to a favourite charity.

Wincey reached Sauchiehall Street, keeping her head down and her eyes furtively glued to the pavement. The worst ordeal was entering the old established and highly thought of Copeland and Lye's. She made straight for the haberdashery department and the thread counter. Rows and rows of trays packed with reels of every shade of every colour were stacked against a wall behind the counter. Wincey showed the assistant the bundle of small fragments of cloth she carried. The assistant went to the trays and, with amazing speed and accuracy, picked from each an exactly matching shade for each cloth sample. Then she packed the whole order into a bag and Wincey handed over the correct money.

Trying not to look around, she hastened out again by the side door, but she didn't feel in the least relaxed until she had boarded the red tram car bound for Springburn and it was swaying and clanging its way back along Springburn Road. Only in the jungle of towering black tenements could she feel safe.

'There you are,' Charlotte greeted her. 'I knew you could do it if you wanted to.' She examined Wincey's purchases. 'We should really get all our threads from them. They have such a good selection.'

Granny piped up then, Wid ye listen tae her! She's really gettin' above hersel' noo. What about the Co-op divvy? Many's the time ye've been glad o' that, the lot o' you. The Co-op's been good an' loyal tae the workin' man. The least we can dae is be loyal back.'

'Och Granny,' Teresa said, 'we get everything else in the Co-op. You know fine we do. We've been loyal members all our days.'

'Aye, well, ye'd better watch her. It's that Wincey's fault, if ye ask me. She's too hoity-toity for ma likin'. It's no' natural.'

'Nobody's asking you Granny.'

The twins came trailing through from the room.

'Can we knock off now, Mammy? We're tired.'

'Me too.' Florence followed them and slumped down onto a chair. 'You're gettin' to be right slave drivers, so you are.'

'Now, now, Florence. You're glad enough of your wee wage at the end of the week. You can't get out quick enough to spend it.'

There was no hope of either Florence or the twins saving, it seemed, but they did work hard and still managed to do most of the scaven ging for cheap food. Wincey thought they looked too thin and were probably anaemic, or worse. There were a great many people in the area going down with tuberculosis. Or consumption, as it was called. One of the women down the stairs had lost a son to the disease only a few weeks ago.

'Yes,' Teresa agreed, 'you do look tired, right enough. Sit down and I'll make us all a nice cup of tea. I've no milk though.'

The girls groaned. 'Och Mammy, we cannae go for any noo. We huvnae any energy left.'

'I'll go,' Wincey offered. 'I'm the one with the waterproof coat and it's pouring with rain.'

'Thanks, dear.'

Teresa carefully examined what she had in her purse before handing over some coppers to Wincey. 'See if the Co-op has any rolls left as well. That would be a nice treat for us. Either that or a wee pot of jam, I've still got half a loaf here.'

Wincey nodded and struggled back into her coat. She liked to get out on her own to roam around the Springburn streets. The crowded room and kitchen could get so claustrophobic at times. Sometimes it felt as if it was suffocating her. However, on this occasion, she knew that she mustn't waste time roaming about. They would all be waiting eagerly for the rolls or the pot of jam to enjoy with their tea.

When she was on her way back, she met Erchie trundling the battered old pram he used to transport sewing machines. He had his latest find balanced on top of the pram.

'Gosh, another one,' Wincey gasped. 'That's great, Erchie. But where will we put it.'

'Och, there's surely a wee bit space left in the room. Ah picked it up in a rubbish dump. It must've come from a big house somewhere. It's in quite good nick. Believe me, it'll be perfect after ah've had a go at it, hen.'

'You're soaked.' Wincey stared worriedly at him as they passed under one of the street lamps. Rain was dripping off the skip of his flat bonnet and darkening his thin jacket.

'Och, never mind, hen. Ah'll soon dry off.'

Once in their close, Erchie heaved and bumped the pram up the stairs while Wincey balanced it and tried to help lift it at the other end. They were both panting and out of breath by the time they reached the top landing. Wincey pulled the bell and the door was opened by Teresa.

'My, my, another one, Erchie. I expect Charlotte will be pleased.' She sighed. 'But soon the place'll be that full of sewing machines, there'll be no room for any of us.'

'Och well, never mind. We'll manage somehow.'

Erchie lifted the machine off the pram and staggered into the house with it.

'My God,' Granny howled. 'No' another yin. The noise o' them's sendin' me aff ma heid. Ah'll be endin' up in Lennox Castle next.'

Lennox Castle was the local mental asylum.

'Now, now, Granny,' Teresa winked at the others, 'Lennox Castle isn't such a bad place.'

9

Wincey enjoyed her late night walks. She was no longer afraid of the dark. In a way, it had become like a friend. It was good to escape from the cramped conditions of the Gourlays' house and the constant whirr and clatter of sewing machines. Not that Springburn Road was quiet. There was the clanging of tram cars, and the hustle and bustle of people streaming out of the Prince's Picture House, the Wellfield, and the Kinema. The latter was nicknamed 'the Coffin' because of its shape and its proximity to Sighthill Cemetery. This did not put anyone off visiting the Kinema, and Wincey had recently gone with Florence for a special treat after they'd finished an important order sooner than they had expected.

On that occasion, they received praise as well as payment from their satisfied customer. It had been a Saturday afternoon and Florence had thoroughly enjoyed herself at the Kinema. Wincey had found the Flash Gordon serial more ridiculous than exciting. In one scene Flash had been blown up but, she was quick to notice, he came down with his hat still on. There were equally ridiculous cliff-hangers with heroines tied to railway tracks who somehow never got run over. Tom Mix was another hugely popular hero who failed to excite Wincey.

Florence complained, 'Och, ye take everythin' far too serious, so ye do.'

But life had become a serious business. Wincey did not want to lose the new home she had found, and felt anxiety whenever Charlotte asked her to run errands far from Springburn. Once, Charlotte had insisted she accompany her to deliver wedding outfits to customers over the other side of town. Each of the customers had two outfits made—bride and mother of the bride.

'I'm not going to have any more of your nonsense,' Charlotte said. 'I can't carry all this. You'll just have to come with me, whether you like it or not!'

Wincey had been terrified but after racking her brain, she couldn't think of anyone who knew her, or her family, in the area where these particular customers lived. All the same, she felt sick at taking such a risk. Fortunately all had gone well, and she had remained in the kitchen while Charlotte and one of the maids carried the garments upstairs to the lady of the house.

Coming back through the town to Springburn on the tram car, a drunk had got on. Like many Glasgow drunks in this situation, he had a burning desire to communicate and it was only a matter of time before the dreaded 'Hey youse' broke the silence. Then came the problem of deciding if he was the type who, if ignored, would keep demanding attention with self-fuelling indignation. Or would he take the opportunity to lapse into lengthy and maudlin reminiscences about his time serving in the HLI.

Now, as Wincey and Florence made their way back, it was closing time and drunks were spilling out onto the pavement, many of their voices raised in song. Sometimes a prancing, staggering attempt at a dance accompanied their words.

> *Just a wee doch an dorris,*
> *Just a wee yin that's aw,*
> *Just a wee doch an dorris,*
> *Afore ye gang awa'.*

One man coming out of Quinn's pub at the bottom of the Balgray-hill accosted Wincey, clutching at her arm and staggering against her.

'Hello, hen. My, ye're a bonny wee lassie, eh?'

She flung his arm off and began to run, the man's indignant words ringing in her ears, 'Och, ah wis only tryin' tae be friendly.'

Probably he was, she thought, once she had reached a safe distance and had slowed down. But she still had an underlying fear and distrust of men. She managed to hide it, or to control it, most of the time. Sometimes she even convinced herself that she had lost it, that she had cured herself. Then, unexpectedly, it would return in a rush of panic. In her distress, she suddenly found that she had run off the main road and was in a dark cul-de-sac, at the end of which was a derelict looking warehouse. Propped in front of it was a sign which read *To Let. Apply Belling & MacKay*, followed by an address and telephone number.

Wincey felt excited. It suddenly occurred to her that the next step in the business had to be getting premises in which all the sewing machines could be kept and worked. The women with machines of their own could continue working in their own houses if they wanted to. But the machines in the Gourlays' house and any other machines Erchie or anyone else could find could be put in a place like this, and other women in dire need of a job could be engaged. There would be no shortage of willing workers, Wincey felt sure.

She began to run again, this time happily, eagerly. She could hardly wait to tell Charlotte. Along the gas-lit road she flew, in the close and up the stairs two at a time. The older girl was collapsed into the hole-in-the-wall room bed and half asleep when Wincey reached the top floor house.

'Charlotte, Charlotte,' Wincey cried out. 'I've just had a wonderful idea.'

The twins stirred beside Charlotte.

'For pity's sake, shut up, Wincey,' one of them groaned.

'Aye,' Florence agreed from her hurly bed on the floor, 'we've aw had a hell o' a hard day an' need our sleep.'

But Charlotte was too good a business woman to miss any opportunity, no matter how exhausted she felt. She propped herself up on one elbow. 'Never mind them. What is it, Wincey?'

Wincey told her about the warehouse to let and what she thought could be done with it.

'Yes, yes, you're right. But it would depend on the rent, wouldn't it? And then we'd need more machines and more work to keep us going.'

'It looks pretty run down. I shouldn't think the rent would be too much, and maybe we wouldn't need to stick to just private customers. Maybe we could ask about supplying shops, or wholesalers, or something. I mean, who makes all the shirts for men's shops and departments? They've got to be made somewhere. They must come from somewhere.'

'It's worth a try,' Charlotte said. 'We could inquire about the rent first and if that was something we could afford, then we could try and find out about other kinds of work. Oh, Wincey, I'm so excited now. I'll never be able to sleep a wink.'

Teresa had appeared at the room door, her shawl wrapped over her nightie, her thin hair loosened from its bun and straggling down to her shoulders. 'What's going on. Granny's complaining like mad through there. She's cursing me for giving you a door key, Wincey. This is a bit late to be coming in. You know we're all up early for work in the morning.'

'I'm sorry,' Wincey said. 'I'll be as quiet as a mouse after this if I come in late. But something exciting has just happened and I had to tell Charlotte.'

'What's that, dear?'

Charlotte answered her mother before Wincey had the chance. Teresa was impressed but worried. 'Do you think you can do it, dear? It's all right Wincey coming out with these grand ideas but it's not so easy to put them into practice. A lot could go wrong, couldn't it.'

Wincey said, 'We'd never get anywhere if we didn't take any risks. What's the good of just staying as we are. I suppose we could stay as we are for the rest of our lives. Is that what we want? Is that what you want for the family?'

'Well, dear, we've got a lot better life now than we had. I mind the days when we couldn't even afford a loaf of bread.'

'You see, we can afford lots more now. That's because we moved on. We took a risk with the extra machines, and we took another by starting to employ more people.'

'Yes, Mammy,' Charlotte agreed. 'Wincey's right. We've at least got to try to do this. We might not even manage to get the warehouse in the first place but we've got to try.'

Teresa sighed. 'I expect you're right, dear, but right now we all need our rest.'

'Tomorrow's Saturday,' Wincey suddenly remembered. 'Maybe the office will be shut. The one on the To Let notice.'

'No, no,' Teresa said. 'They'll be working, same as us. Everybody's got to make a living.'

Charlotte lay back on her pillow. 'I'll go round there first thing in the morning, Wincey. I can hardly wait.'

Teresa sighed again as she turned away. 'Try and get some sleep.'

Wincey couldn't go out with Charlotte next morning because it was her turn at the machine. She didn't stop working but her mind was waiting in an agony of suspense for Charlotte to return. Right away, she knew that it was all right. She had only to look at Charlotte's bright eyes and flushed face.

'It's a giveaway price,' Charlotte sang out. 'It's been lying empty for so long, apparently. It's an awful big place. They sent someone from the office to show me over it. Far more space than we'll need. But we can just shut some bits off. They offered to sell it to me but that would be stretching things a bit far just now. I said I'd consider that in due course, though. Meantime I've to go back tomorrow to confirm everything.'

'Great, great!' Wincey caught Charlotte's outstretched hands and they hugged one another in triumph and delight.

'She'll huv ye goin' too far, that yin,' Granny said, meaning Wincey. 'She'll mean trouble tae us aw yet, you mark ma words. She's gettin' beyond hersel' wi' aw them grand ideas.'

'Och, never mind Granny,' Charlotte told Wincey. 'If this succeeds and we get it going, I'll make you my partner, Wincey. Would you like that?'

'Thank you, Charlotte. That would be wonderful, and I just know we can make it succeed. I'll work my fingers to the bone to make it succeed.'

Charlotte hastily washed her face and hands and brushed her hair. Wincey polished Charlotte's shoes. She also loaned her her waterproof coat. Granny was persuaded to part with a pair of gloves she'd worn in better days when she was able to get out to attend the church and the Orange walks.

'You mind them good gloves noo,' Granny warned Charlotte. 'If ye lose them good gloves, ye neednae show yer face back here again.'

'Don't worry, Granny. I'll take good care of them, I promise.'

'Aye well,' Granny muttered. 'Ye'd better.'

'Do ye want yer daddy tae go wi' ye, hen,' Erchie asked. He was rubbing his hands together and almost dancing with excitement. More than any other member of the family, Erchie was full to overflowing with enthusiasm for every aspect of the business.

'No thanks, Daddy. I'll be fine. As well as working on the machines, me and Wincey are going to be in charge of organising and planning everything. You have to be in charge of the machines.'

'Aye, right ye are, hen.' Erchie gave her an exaggerated salute. 'Ye're the boss. You an' wee Wincey. Ye're a couple o' wee stoaters.'

Soon Charlotte had returned from town and everything was signed, sealed and delivered.

'I've just thought of something else,' she told Wincey. 'I wouldn't be able to do all the cutting if we're going to expand. Even both you and I couldn't manage it, could we?'

'It depends on what orders we get, and the size of them, I suppose,' Wincey replied. 'Anyway, no doubt we'll be able to find unemployed cutters if we try.'

They had already found that married women who had been experienced workers in the clothing trade before their marriage and whose children were now more or less off their hands were the best bet. But they soon discovered a pool of younger women too. Mrs McGregor's eldest was a trained cutter. 'Wan o' the very best,' Mrs McGregor assured Charlotte and Wincey. 'Cuts like a flash. Naebody tae beat her.'

They were all set—at least they'd scrubbed out the part of the warehouse they planned to use. The place now awaited more machines before they could go any further and recruit any more women workers. Erchie set to like a greyhound after a hare. He shot about everywhere— back courts, back gardens, the Corporation rubbish tip, the Barras market and Paddy's market. He knocked at doors, asking for old machines. 'Ah'll take it oot yer road, hen,' he'd say.

Eventually he had found and repaired seven machines and he'd picked up a couple of tables suitable for the cutting. And so, counting the ones from the house, they had eleven machines ready to start in what was now called the factory. While he'd been doing his bit, Charlotte and Wincey had been out searching for orders. To their delight, they had found a big one for shirts and it looked as if it would be a regular order.

'They said if we made a good job of the first order, we're in,' Charlotte announced joyously. 'And of course we will.'

They did, and they were.

But not without difficulties, setbacks and worries. One worry in particular Wincey had not foreseen and—much as she tried—could do nothing about.

1936

IO

'Noo ah'm no complainin', hen,' Erchie told Charlotte. 'Ah'm just sayin' that if ye could let me fix masel' up wi' a tradesman, or some sort o' strong young fella, it wid be an awfae help tae me. Ah'm no' as nippy as ah used tae be an' these past couple of years, ah've been a jack o' aw trades. It's no' just been the machines. It's been mendin' the lights, an' the plumbin', an' God knows what else. But ah'm no' complainin', hen. Ye understand me.'

'Of course, Daddy,' Charlotte said. 'I'm so sorry. I've been treating you like a slave, expecting you to do so much. You're right, we definitely need another man to take over some of the workload. Will I advertise, or do you know somebody?'

'Aye, ah know a few good lads who served their apprenticeships an' now cannae find work. Just leave it tae me, hen. Ah'll send a fella tae ye, an' ye can tell him what ye'll pay him. Ye're the boss.'

'Fine. Do it right away, Daddy. I feel terrible about this. I've been so caught up with the women's work. You look dead beat—I'm so sorry.'

'Och, be quiet. Ah'm aw right. Just a bit tired.'

'Come to think of it, Daddy. Now that we've got over twenty machines and opened up another couple of areas, we could do with two extra men. There's the new office to paint and fit out—it's a right dump at the moment.'

'Well, we'll see how it goes, hen. Ah'll talk tae wan or two fellas first.'

The first result of Erchie's intervention was the appearance at the factory of Malcy McArthur. Wincey suspected right away that he could

284

mean trouble. But she was suspicious of all men. That was just how she was. Unlike most local unemployed men, Malcy was not thin and pale and emaciated. He boasted a hard muscular body, a head of fair curly hair and light blue eyes. He had done some boxing, kept himself fit by regularly working out at the boxing club, and often went running or hill climbing out at Campsie Glen. He was a Glaswegian born and bred, but had the cheek of the Irish and sounded at times as if he'd kissed the Blarney Stone. He had tried his best to charm Wincey, without success. She ignored his compliments and returned them with cold stares.

Once, in the course of trying to tease her, he put his arm around her. She had furiously shaken him off and ordered him to go about his business and not waste time. If he continued to waste time, he'd end up without a job. She'd see to it. And she could, now she was a legal partner in the business.

The trouble was that it wasn't long before Malcy had turned his full attention on Charlotte, and he was far more successful in charming her. More than a few times Wincey had seen Charlotte go all giggly and blush when Malcy was speaking to her in the factory. Wincey tried to warn Charlotte against him.

'Charlotte, he's a right rascal and out for all he can get.'

'Nonsense,' Charlotte laughed. Wincey had never seen her look so happy. 'He's a marvellous worker. We couldn't do without him now. He can turn his hand to anything, and he's always so cheerful and willing.'

'Oh, he's willing, all right,' Wincey said sarcastically.

Charlotte shook her head. 'What on earth has made you such a man-hater, Wincey? Other girls of your age are courting. You've never even looked kindly at a boy. I appreciate all the time and dedication you give to the business, but now it's so established, Wincey, there's no need to devote every hour of the day and night to it.'

'I enjoy the work.'

'But it doesn't seem natural, all work and no play—you know the saying. You need some fun in your life.'

'It's natural for me, Charlotte. There's no need to worry about me. It's you I'm worried about.'

'Why, for pity's sake? I'm perfectly fit and happy. I've never felt so happy in my life.'

Wincey groaned to herself. Charlotte had obviously fallen in love with Malcy.

'For one thing, he's too old for you.'

'Who?'

'Charlotte, don't act daft. You know perfectly well who.'

Charlotte giggled. 'For goodness' sake, Wincey. He's only been joking and having a bit of a laugh with me. He's good fun. And anyway, what's a few years between friends.'

'Ten years to be exact. And he's not your friend, he's your employee.'

'Oh, don't be such a snob. And a man should be older and more mature than a woman. My daddy's a few years older than my mammy, and it's never bothered them.'

Wincey felt a real stab of fear. Surely Charlotte had not already got marriage on her mind? But if she was really honest with herself, Wincey knew that it was the business more than Charlotte she was worried about. If Charlotte loved the man—mistaken though it was in her opinion—that love would probably keep Charlotte happy enough. Wincey was concerned that it was much more likely to be the business that was in danger. Malcy McArthur was on the make, she felt sure of it.

Seeing him more than once in a nearby close making bets with the local bookmaker did nothing to help her peace of mind. A gambler was an untrustworthy person to have near money, and Wincey began to keep a closer eye on Malcy's activities. She discovered he was not just an occasional, but a frequent visitor to whatever close the bookie was using for business. She'd pass along the street and see the crowd of men making their bets, and the runner hovering about outside, watching for the police and ready to shout the warning cry of 'Edge up'. Hearing it, everyone would scatter. Malcy was a gambler all right.

One day she caught sight of Erchie handing over money to Malcy. Later she questioned Erchie about this.

'Och, it's all right, hen. Ah was just givin' Malcy a wee loan until pay day. He had a wee bit o' bad luck on the horses.'

'Gambling, you mean?'

'Och, now, there's nae harm in a fella havin' a wee flutter now an' again. He deserves a wee bit pleasure. He's a hard workin' fella, ye can't deny that.'

She couldn't say any more on the subject, either to Erchie or Charlotte, or even to Malcy. The retort would be that what Malcy did in his own time, or how he spent his hard earned wages, was Malcy's business. She tried to tell herself that this was true and there was nothing more to it, but in her heart of hearts, she knew perfectly well that there was much more to it. Or at least there would be in the future, if something wasn't done to stop him. She believed he was taking advantage of Charlotte's love and trust, and she couldn't help being reminded of how a man had once taken advantage of her. It was a very different situation, but nevertheless Malcy McArthur *was* taking advantage of Charlotte. Wincey had seen him flirt with other women. Not in the factory—oh no, he was too clever for that. She had seen him, however, at street corners laughing and carrying on with girls.

Even Charlotte had caught him on one occasion. It had been at a hen party at Green's Playhouse. A neighbour's daughter, Mary Purdie, was getting married. Mrs Purdie had been a good friend and neighbour to Teresa for years and all the Gourlay girls and Wincey had been invited to a fish and chip tea in a local chippie and then a noisy ride in a tram into town to the famous Green's Playhouse.

Green's Playhouse had the reputation of being the largest picture house in Europe, and high up at the top of the building was a dance hall that always had the best bands.

Wincey hadn't wanted to go but both Charlotte and Teresa more or less bullied her into it—or as near to bullying as their natures allowed. Charlotte especially was a gentle soul.

Teresa said, 'Now, now, Wincey, Mrs Purdie has been good to me and it'll really upset me if you insult her daughter by refusing this invitation.'

'Yes, you've no reason not to go,' Charlotte said. 'You're just being difficult for no reason at all, Wincey.'

And so she'd gone.

Once safely inside the building, Wincey began to relax. Out on the streets in the centre of the city, there was always the chance of someone recognising her. Her mother, or grandmother, or some of their friends, might well be out shopping. But no-one had recognised her, and certainly there would be no danger of anyone of her mother and grandmother's generations cavorting about up in the dance hall in the skies.

The ladies' room was like a bird sanctuary. It was crammed with loudly chattering girls. There was a crush at the mirror, as a whole crowd of them strained to check their hair or rub powder puffs over shiny noses. Dresses rustled and made a rainbow of bright colours.

Charlotte was wearing a short-sleeved plum-coloured silk dress with a demure little collar and a flared skirt. Wincey favoured a long-sleeved dress in dark green wool with a spotted bow tie under a flat collar.

The crowd of Gourlay girls and their pals and Wincey burst from the ladies' room on a wave of giggles. Wincey had been joining in the banter and laughter. Until, that is, she saw all the couples locked in each other's arms on the dance floor. She hadn't realised how most of the dances meant full frontal contact. Waltzes, foxtrots, quicksteps, tangos—it was all the same, it seemed. Along one wall stood a row of girls and across the moving throng of dancers, a line of young men stood nonchalantly smoking cigarettes.

Occasionally one of them would nip the lighted end of his cigarette and tuck it into his pocket. Then he'd swagger across to the line of girls and put out an inviting hand. In a second, he'd be clutching her against him and they'd be circling the floor.

The last thing Wincey wanted was to be clutched in any man's arms for any reason. However, she didn't want to appear a spoilsport and so she joined the line of girls along with Charlotte and the others.

As luck would have it—bad luck as far as she was concerned—she was the first to be lifted. He was a tall thin man wearing horn-rimmed spectacles. His body was hot against hers.

'What's your name,' he asked, his feet making fast, complicated movements that Wincey was having to concentrate on in an effort to keep up with him.

'Wincey.'

'That's a funny name. What's it mean?'

'Short for Winsome. I was christened Winsome. Don't ask me why.'

'I love your red hair.' Next he'd be telling her he loved her freckles. 'My name's Ian, by the way.'

She made no comment.

'Is anybody seein' you home?'

'I've only just got here.'

'Later on, I mean.'

'I'm with friends. I'll be going home with them.'

'Oh.' He sounded disappointed. 'Couldn't you—'

'No,' she interrupted.

'Oh well, if that's how you feel,' he said huffily.

Before the music had finished, he'd begun leading her back to where they'd started. Fortunately, the music had stopped by the time they'd reached the others and so Wincey was saved from making any explanations.

It was then that she noticed Malcy leading a girl back just a few yards from where they were standing. He had his arm around the girl's waist and was laughing down at her. He kept his arm around her as they stood for a few minutes and then, as soon as the band struck up again, he began a smoochy dance with her.

'Look at that,' Wincey said. 'What did I tell you, Charlotte.'

Charlotte looked upset but she tried to put a brave face on by saying lightly, 'For goodness' sake, Wincey. He's not married to me or anything. We haven't even been walking out together.'

'But he has asked you, hasn't he?'

'The fact remains, we still haven't been out together. Between you and me, I was a bit worried about what would happen. I mean, about discipline in the factory, if the girls found out. You might think I don't care as much as you do about the success of the business, Wincey, but I do.'

'Of course you do. I know that. I just worry about you sometimes, Charlotte.'

Charlotte gave an unhappy smile. 'There's no need. Oh dear, I think he's seen us.'

Malcy, dancing cheek to cheek with his partner, was passing quite near to them now. As soon as he saw them, he immediately held his partner at arm's length. Then after the dance, he made his way over to Charlotte.

'Charlotte! Now the whole evening's turned to magic because I've the chance to dance with you.' He held out his arms invitingly, his eyes soft and loving. Wincey had to admit to herself that he did have a most attractive smile, and who could resist that look? She could, but she feared that Charlotte could not.

II

During the Glasgow Fair holiday in July, the Gourlays and Wincey decided to go 'doon the watter'. They planned to stay for a whole week in Dunoon. It was the first holiday the family had had in years and everybody was looking forward to it. They had booked a two-room and kitchen. They were used to a two-room and kitchen house now since some of the profits from the business had gone into the removal and renting of a bottom flat in the same close in Springburn Road. Money had also been spent on a wheelchair for Granny which meant that she could now get out and about, and even come on holiday with them. Although it was hard work pushing the chair, especially up the gangplank of the ship.

The factory had closed for the fair fortnight but after the week's holiday, all the family—and the family now included Wincey—were going back to the factory to catch up with some odd jobs that needed to be done. Somehow there wasn't usually much time for any extra jobs, especially if they'd a big order in. Joe, the odd job man, couldn't be at the factory during the holiday week because he was going to Rothesay with his family for the whole fair fortnight.

Teresa had her hands full all the time attending to the domestic chores, the shopping, and looking after Granny. She had had plenty of practice pushing the wheelchair to the shops for the 'messages', which she piled onto Granny's lap—not without some complaints from the older woman.

Malcy had volunteered to help out in the factory during the second week of the holiday. Another volunteer was the latest cutter they'd got, a man called Bert Brownlee. He was in charge of the new electric cutting machine. A woman would spread out the pattern on top of layers of cloth. Then Bert used the huge upright thin blade attached to an electric belt from above. Twisting and turning the blade, he could slice through over twenty layers of material without any difficulty.

Then another woman collected all the cut material into a basket and hauled it through to the machinists. The machinists sat in rows now at their machines in the biggest area of the factory, a vast high-roofed hall of dark brown wood. It had rows of pegs along part of one wall on which the machinists could hang their coats. A lavatory out in the back yard served their other needs. Disappearing out to the back yard too often, or for too long, was disapproved of, however, and a sharp eye was kept on any movement away from the machines. Even the twins and Florence came under the same scrutiny as all the others.

At first they'd complained bitterly about this. 'We're the boss's sisters, for goodness' sake,' the girls protested to Charlotte.

'All the more reason,' Charlotte said, 'for you to show a good example to the others.'

Charlotte had a quiet authority that was respected by all of her employees. Wincey was respected too, but regarded as more of an unknown quantity. Most of the time she was shut away in the office doing the books. Also she was the one who every now and again disappeared from the premises to go and negotiate or seek out new orders. Charlotte could on occasion have a pleasant chat or even a laugh with the girls, when they had a brief break to eat their sandwiches. Wincey was more reserved. They called her Miss Wincey to distinguish her from Miss Charlotte, because as far as everyone at work and most other people knew, they were both Gourlays.

The twins and Florence had been instructed—indeed, were made to swear—that they would never divulge the way in which Wincey became part of the family. This was really unnecessary because they had long since accepted Wincey, and more or less forgotten that she wasn't originally part of the family.

Because Malcy and Bert had been 'good enough'—to use Charlotte's words—to volunteer to work a week of the holidays, they were allowed to accompany the family on their sail 'doon the watter'. Their fares were paid, also their wages, but not their holiday accommodation in Dunoon. The two men were going to share a single end in one of the side streets near the pier. Not far either from the two-room and kitchen that was to house the family.

First there was the exciting and wildly enjoyable sail in the packed paddle steamer. Even before the paddles were thumping and the boat had started waddling away from Bridge Wharf across from the Broomielaw, a band had started playing cheery tunes and people were singing. Women were chattering and laughing. Children were racing about getting lost.

The band consisted of four men in navy blue suits and caps. One man, with great concentration, strummed the banjo. Another had a white hanky spread over his shoulder on which rested his fiddle. Another energetically squeezed a concertina and a fourth, with concentration equal to that of the banjo player, thumped on an ancient piano.

The gangplanks were lifted, ropes flung aboard, the steamer gave a warning hoot and then, with much creaking and groaning and splashing, the ship's paddles were set in motion. Slowly at first, the water foaming and frothing, then gradually, as it pulled away from Bridge Wharf—just by the George V Bridge—the paddles quickened and found their joyous rhythm. The steam drifted away, past giant cranes jagging the sky and over the silent shipyards which, like everything else, were closed for the fair.

Normally the shipbuilders—swarms of men high up like ants on the sides of hulls, noisily banging and clanging, or leaning over, or up in the clouds working cranes—would stop and wave hands or caps and bawl friendly greetings at any passing ships. Today, however, there was nothing to compete with the noisy paddle steamer except the hoots of other ships and the raucous screeching of gulls. The white breasted birds swooped and dived alongside, and followed the holiday cruises from Glasgow, knowing that there would be plenty of eagerly proferred handfuls of food.

All the old Scots songs were being bawled out now—'Roamin' in the Gloamin' ', 'Road to the Isles', 'Stop your Ticklin', Jock', 'Ah'm the Saftest in the Faimily' and 'I belong to Glasgow'.

Wincey enjoyed the sail and breathed deeply of the tangy fresh air. The journey was only spoiled for her by the sight of Malcy following Charlotte around. Eventually he managed to detach her from the rest of the family and walk with her on his own. Wincey kept getting glimpses of the pair of them on deck, with him gazing fondly down at Charlotte, and Charlotte looking up at him with an even stronger emotion.

Everyone wanted to visit the engine room and Wincey was no exception. Every steamer had a vantage point from which passengers could watch the enormous drive shafts, pistons and valve gear, and experience the thunderous, deafening noise. Through the latticed paddle boxes could also be seen revolving wheels with torrents of water gushing from the blades.

It was while Wincey was watching this scene that she noticed Malcy and Charlotte again. Now he had his arm around her waist. Feeling suddenly depressed, Wincey turned away and climbed back up to the deck. She loved Charlotte like a sister and she had become more and more concerned about her involvement with Malcy. What depressed Wincey was the knowledge that there was nothing she could do. Charlotte was twenty now and free to do as she pleased. She could of course marry if she wanted. And in marriage it was going to end—that much was perfectly obvious. They had now started walking out.

All during the holiday, Malcy stuck by Charlotte's side. Bert, an older man than Malcy, spent most of his time in one or other of the local pubs. The twins and Florence disappeared every morning and only reappeared at mealtimes. During the day, Erchie took his turn with Teresa at pushing Granny's wheelchair along the front. Often they met their neighbours from Glasgow and it seemed like the whole close—indeed the whole street—had come on holiday because it was the fair.

Wincey was quite happy to be left to her own devices, walking for miles to reach lonely and deserted places. She enjoyed climbing the Castle Hill, then sitting on the grass hugging her knees, gazing down at the pier, and listening to the kilted piper playing one of the steamers away to the haunting lament of *Will ye no come back again*.

'Oh, we're no awa' tae bide awa' ', the ship's passengers lustily sang. 'We're no awa' tae leave ye. We're no awa' tae bide awa', We'll aye come back an' see ye.'

It was agreed at the end of the holiday week that it had done everybody good. Even Granny's sallow complexion had acquired some colour, so had Erchie's, and even Teresa's thin face had a bit of a glow about it. But no-one was more glowing than Charlotte. Wincey had worn a wide brimmed straw hat most of the time to protect her skin because she burned so easily.

293

'Red haired folk are aye like that. Right nuisances,' Granny said. 'Ye cannae take them anywhere.'

Then of course there was the struggle to heave Granny's wheelchair up the gangplank again and squeeze a place for her among the throng.

'Oot o' ma road,' she kept bawling and jabbing mercilessly at all and sundry with her umbrella.

Back in the house in Springburn Road at last, Teresa said, 'I'll put the kettle on.' In this house, they had the luxury of not just one gas ring on which to boil the kettle, but two gas rings on the range. Nowadays, Teresa didn't even have to balance her soup pot on the fire.

The kitchen was much bigger too than the one they'd had in the house upstairs. There was the usual hole-in-the-wall bed but now in each of the two rooms at the front, there were two recessed beds. As a result, Charlotte and Wincey had a bed each in one room, Florence and the twins occupied the beds in the other, Florence having one of the beds to herself. Granny still had to have the hurly bed in the kitchen. Teresa and Erchie attempted to relegate her to one of the rooms but she was having none of it.

'Ah've slept in ma hurly bed in front o' the kitchen fire for years,' she insisted, 'an' ah'm no gonnae change noo.'

She'd also accused Teresa and Erchie of wanting to get rid of her.

Teresa said, 'Now, now, Granny. You know that's not true. It's just that Erchie and I would like a wee bit privacy.'

'Whit fur?' Granny wanted to know.

Neither Erchie nor Teresa had the nerve to tell her.

On the whole, the quality of Granny's life was much better since they'd moved downstairs and had the extra accommodation and the wheelchair. Now she could be wheeled into one of the front rooms and parked at the window so that she could watch the world go by on Springburn Road. This at least gave Teresa some peace to do the cooking, baking or cleaning without sarcastic comments or a string of instructions, or stories of how Granny used to do everything so much better in her day. From the front room, Granny kept roaring things out like, 'There's that Mrs Fisher wi' her fancy man, brazen as ye like. A right disgrace.' Or 'There's her frae up the stairs wi' anither mucky wee wean. How many's that she's got noo? Must be surely a hundred or mair. It's absolutely terrible!'

Teresa was in a state of constant anxiety in case anyone outside could hear Granny's comments. Probably they did but were just suffering in silence because Granny was an old woman. Teresa, Erchie and the whole family agreed that Granny was a terrible trial of an old woman, although sometimes they couldn't help laughing.

It was no joke, however, trying to get her to take a bath. They could now hurl the wheelchair to the steamie. As well as a big area for washing clothes, the steamie had cubicles, and in each cubicle there was a bath. As a result, Teresa insisted that they no longer used the zinc bath in the kitchen. It had always been a terrible struggle to get Granny in and out of the bath. For one thing, it was too tight a fit. Every time she plumped down in it, a surge of water flooded out, soaking everyone around her.

'You're going to the steamie, Granny, whether you like it or not. You've got far too fat for that wee zinc bath,' Teresa told her, but she also told the girls, 'You'll all have to come and help me. I can't manage to bath Granny on my own at the steamie, any more than I ever could here in the kitchen.'

'You know fine Wincey and I couldn't be of much help, Mammy,' Charlotte said. 'Just take Florence and the twins. They're heftier and stronger than us.'

While this was an exaggeration, they were certainly growing into big healthy girls, helped no doubt by their improved diet.

After some discussion, it was agreed that Florence and the twins would accompany Teresa to the steamie and do battle with Granny.

'The real reason I couldn't go,' Charlotte confided in Wincey after the family disappeared up Springburn Road, 'is because I'm meeting Malcy. Oh Wincey, try to be happy for me. Malcy and I are so much in love.'

Wincey tried to smile reassuringly but her heart was not in it.

12

It was on the front page of the *Daily Record* —'A Scots Queen. King George VI and Queen Elizabeth to be proclaimed. Coronation next May.'

Erchie read the headlines out to Granny and continued with, 'Future plans of Edward VIII. As the unparalleled drama of the abdication King Edward VIII unfolded itself yesterday, a wave of relief swept over the country, spreading right throughout the Empire. The succession of the Duke and Duchess of York to the throne is being hailed as not only the best, but the only solution to the crisis.'

'Aye, a great relief tae us aw, ah don't think!' Granny said. 'It disnae matter wan jot tae us whit that crowd dae. If that whole crowd o' royals went up in a puff o' smoke, it wouldnae matter wan jot tae a soul in Springburn.'

'The King's going to broadcast tonight.'

'Which wan? As if ah cared!'

'Edward.'

'Him an' his fancy woman. They don't know they're born, that lot. They'd know aw aboot it if they had tae try an' survive on a few bob in a single end in Springburn. That's how me an' ma man started our married life.'

Erchie laughed. 'It'd be the death o' them, Ma.'

'An' brought up five weans there as well. Four o' them carted off on the fever van, wan by wan, an' ah never saw any o' them alive again.'

Teresa joined in the conversation. 'Aye, they were hard times in those days, Granny.'

'Whit dae ye know? Ye were enjoyin' yersel' up among the hills an' glens. Whit dae ye know about life in Glasgow?'

'Now, now, Granny. You know fine I've lived here most of my life. But I remember when I was a child, what a hard life my mother and father had, trying to make a living on a wee croft. I'm sure they were glad to come to Glasgow. I know I was.'

'Aye,' Erchie said. 'It's no' such a bad place.'

'It's aw right fur you noo,' Granny scowled at him. 'Ye're a bloody capitalist!'

Both Teresa and Erchie laughed and Erchie said, 'Ye're bletherin' now, Ma. Ah'm still as much of a socialist as ah ever was.'

'Ye cannae say your Charlotte's no' a capitalist,' Granny insisted. 'An' she's tight-fisted as well. She must be makin' a fortune in that place, an' we're aw still livin' up a close in Springburn Road. No' that ah'd want tae be livin' any place else,' she hastily added.

'There's a lot more room, Granny, without the machines cluttering up the place. You were always complaining about the noise of the machines.'

'Aye, it's a funny old world,' Erchie said, and went back to reading his *Daily Record*. It wasn't long before he was interrupted by the jangle of the doorbell.

'That'll be Charlotte now,' Teresa told Erchie as he went to open the door. 'She said she and Malcy would be going to the first house of the pictures and she'd be bringing him home for a cup of tea. I've made some nice salmon sandwiches.'

'Any digestives,' Granny asked hopefully.

'Yes, Granny, there's plain and chocolate.'

Erchie was now returning along the lobby with Charlotte and Malcy.

'You two look happy,' Teresa greeted them. 'Was it a good picture?'

'Mammy,' Charlotte cried out excitedly, 'Malcy and I are engaged. We're going to be married in the spring.'

'Oh, congratulations to the both of you.'

'Here,' Erchie said, rubbing his hands, 'this deserves a wee celebration. Never mind the tea, Teresa. I've got a bottle of whisky in the press.'

He went over to the cupboard and produced a bottle of Johnny Walker.

'Nothing but the best for Charlotte an' Malcy. Come on, Teresa. Get some glasses oot, hen.'

They were toasting the happy couple and Erchie was refilling the glasses when Wincey arrived back from one of her solitary walks.

'What's going on?' she asked, but with a sinking heart, she knew.

'Charlotte and Malcy are engaged, dear. They're going to have a spring wedding. Isn't that lovely? It'll give us all something to look forward to.'

'Congratulations,' Wincey muttered, but she could have cheerfully killed the grinning Malcy. 'Smug bastard,' she thought.

'Well?' Malcy came swaggering towards her. 'Am I not going to get a kiss from my future sister-in-law?'

Wincey turned her cheek just in time as his lips were about to meet hers. She hated the proximity of his face and the mocking, triumphant look in his eyes. It occurred to her that he'd never forgotten or forgiven the way she'd spurned his original advances. It took an almost superhuman effort on her part to raise the glass Erchie gave her and wish the engaged pair every happiness. She sincerely wished Charlotte every happiness. The trouble was she now very much doubted if Charlotte would get anything but worry and grief from Malcy.

Florence and the twins arrived and they all had another few whiskies. Then they had a sing-song. Even Granny joined in. Eyes closed with emotion, she gave a gumsy rendering of

> *'If I can help somebody as I go along,*
> *If I can help somebody with a word or song,*
> *If I can help somebody as I go along,*
> *Then my living has been worthwhile.'*

Everybody gave her an enthusiastic clap and cheer. Erchie sang, or rather droned, 'The Bonny Wells o' Weary' and Malcy sang to Charlotte, 'Just the Way You Look Tonight'. The romance of this rendering was somewhat spoiled by Granny dropping off to sleep and loudly snoring.

'Oh here,' Teresa said, 'we'd better get Granny to bed while the rest of us are sober enough. It's such an awful struggle.'

'I'd better go,' Malcy said.

Charlotte gazed up at him, her soft brown eyes adoring. 'I'll see you to the door.'

It was quite a long time before she reappeared. Erchie had climbed into bed with all his clothes on and Wincey was closing the bed curtains. The twins and Florence were helping Teresa to get Granny's clothes off. Wincey pulled out the hurly bed.

Wincey turned to Charlotte, 'It's time we moved again. We still could do with more space, and we could afford a bigger place now. Even one of these nice red sandstone tenements up the Balgrayhill. That would be nearer the park. Then we could take Granny there without having to struggle all the way up the hill every time.'

Granny liked to watch the crowds in the park and listen to the brass band. She especially enjoyed the Salvation Army band, and she could often hear them and watch them from her window when they played in Springburn and marched along Springburn Road. Like the Pied Piper, the Sally Army band attracted all the children in the neighbourhood to follow it.

Teresa shook her head. 'When Charlotte gets married, you'll have the room to yourself, dear.'

'I wasn't thinking of myself. I was thinking of Granny. And it can't be a perfect situation for you and Erchie having Granny sleep in the same room as you like this.'

'That's true, dear, but you know how she likes to be near the fire. She likes to be cosy.'

'But she could go on sleeping in the kitchen, but by herself. There could be another room for you and Erchie. We could get a three-room and kitchen.'

Charlotte spoke up then. 'If that's what you wanted, and Wincey agreed, it would be all right with me. Wincey got a great order the other day. But don't tell Granny, for goodness' sake. It's for shirts for the Army. Wincey has been marvellous. I don't know how she does it. We're having to take on more girls, men as well.'

'It's not so much me,' Wincey said. 'It's the quality of the work. Our reliability in getting orders done on time, and our prices. But mainly I think it's the high standard of work.'

'That's good, dear, but I can see what you mean about Granny, with her being a pacifist, and having all these pacifist folks as her idols.'

'She'll be telling us that her Johnny Maclean would birl in his grave at you helping the armed forces.'

'We're not going to war, Mammy. We're just sewing clothes.'

'Does your Daddy know yet?'

Charlotte shook her head and Wincey said, 'I don't suppose he's going to like it either. But we can't help it, Teresa. It's going to be the making of us. If we do well with this first small order, we could end up supplying the whole of the Army, and maybe the Air Force as well. We're in line to make a fortune.'

Charlotte laughed then. 'You're about as bad as Florence with your imagination, Wincey.'

'It's not imagination. It's hard facts. Why shouldn't they give us bigger orders if we show we can do a good job with this one. And we can. You know we can.'

'All right, dear, but it's time we all went to bed. Och now, look what's happened. The girls have fallen asleep and we haven't got Granny sorted yet.'

Florence and the twins were slumped over the table, head down on the crook of arms, eyes shut, mouths hanging open.

'We'll try and help,' Wincey said. 'Come on, Charlotte.'

Before long, they were scarlet-faced with their exertions at trying to get Granny to bed. Then they had to half drag, half carry Florence and the twins through to their beds.

'Don't bother lighting the gas,' Charlotte said, once she and Wincey were in their own room. 'If we don't pull the blinds, there'll be enough light from the moon and the streetlamps.'

'That's another thing,' Wincey said. 'It's time we had a place with electric light. Or at least had electricity put in here.'

'Well,' Charlotte sighed, 'it's up to you, Wincey. Malcy and I are going to start looking around for a place of our own. You mentioned up the Balgrayhill and the park. I was thinking of buying one of these nice villas in Broomfield Road, opposite the park.'

'Buying? A villa?' Wincey echoed incredulously. The villas in Broomfield Road opposite the park housed lawyers and doctors and ministers.

'Yes. Fancy me buying a house—and a villa of all things! Actually, Wincey, we've already been looking at one. It was Malcy's idea.'

'I'll bet,' Wincey thought.

'He just loves Springburn Park,' Charlotte went on. 'It's always been his dream to live in one of those houses looking onto the park. It would be a dream come true for him, he said.'

'I'll bet,' Wincey thought again.

13

An unshaven, shabbily dressed man was crouched on the bottom step of the stairs outside the Gourlays' door. He was greedily supping a bowl of soup and tearing at a hunk of bread with his teeth. As Wincey was putting her key in the door, he jerked his head towards it and said, 'She's an awfae kind wuman, that, for a teuchter.' Wincey couldn't help smiling at the Glasgow word for a Highlander. Teresa often gave soup or bread to beggars who asked for it. So did many folk up other closes.

For years now there had been quite an army of beggars, the plight of many, Wincey suspected, caused by the Depression. They were unemployed men who, through no fault of their own, were reduced to either begging or starving.

'That man out there is fairly enjoying your soup, Teresa.'

'Oh, there you are, dear. You look tired. Sit down and relax and I'll dish your soup. Have you had a busy day?'

Wincey flopped into a chair. 'Yes, but it's better to be busy than idle, like some of these poor men.'

'That's true, dear, and I know you've done your best in giving jobs to as many as possible.'

'There's only so many we can take on, unfortunately.'

'You do your best, dear. Would you like a wee nip of whisky to help you get your strength back?'

'No thanks, Teresa. I'd rather wait for your soup.'

'I'll go and get my plate back from that poor soul out there before I start setting the table.'

'Is Granny at the front room window?'

'Yes, I'm going to bring her through in a minute.'

'I'll fetch her.'

'No, you sit where you are, dear, and rest yourself.'

'Have the girls been home yet?' Florence and the twins had recently escaped from the factory. Florence was working in the millinery department of Copeland & Lye's and had become quite toffee-nosed, or so her father said.

'I have to speak proper in the millinery department of Copeland's, Daddy,' Florence had explained. 'It's all posh customers that go there.'

The twins had found jobs in the Co-op. Euphemia was in ladies' underwear, and Bridget in hosiery. They too had polished up their accents.

'Yes, the girls have been in and away again. Since they've all started courting, they're hardly ever in. I'm looking forward to Charlotte's wedding, though. Aren't you? Just three months to go now.'

Wincey nodded but looked away.

'You never seem all that enthusiastic about it, Wincey. Aren't you pleased that she's happy.'

'Of course I want Charlotte to be happy. It's just . . .'

'What, dear?'

'I'm not all that keen on Malcy. I just hope she's not making a mistake, that's all.'

'Och, Malcy's a good lad. What on earth can you have against Malcy? Erchie says he's a hard worker, and he's been that nice and polite to me, and to Granny. He brought us a box of chocolates last week, and look at the nice presents he gave us all at Christmas. Erchie got that box of Woodbines and that was a lovely scarf he gave me. And—'

'I know, I know,' Wincey cut in. 'Just forget I said anything. Have you made up your mind what you want to wear at the wedding yet? You just need to tell us what you want, you know, and we'll make it up for you.'

'No, dear. Thanks all the same, but I know how busy all of you are at the factory, and Florence was telling me of the lovely dresses there are in Copeland's. Lots to choose from, she said, and I could try hats on while I'm there. Match colours and everything. So that's what I plan to do. Malcy was saying that Charlotte should get her wedding dress there. Nothing but the best, Malcy says. Charlotte's started an account there. Fancy!'

'And I expect Malcy will be getting everything he needs there too.'

'I don't know, dear. Why?'

'Well, nothing but the best, as he says.'

'You sound—'

A roar from the front room cut Teresa short.

'Are you gonnae let me sit through here till ah die o' starvation or whit?'

Teresa tutted. 'I was forgetting about poor Granny. She has been sitting through there for quite a while.'

She hurried from the kitchen and in a few minutes returned pushing Granny's wheelchair.

'Ah wis frozen stiff as well.' Granny stared at Wincey. 'Whit's up wi' your face?'

'Hello, Granny. Nothing.'

'I'll dish the soup. That'll soon heat you up, Granny.'

Teresa hustled over to the range. These days she had her hair professionally conditioned, cut and finger waved. She wore a pretty floral pinny over her navy skirt and frilly lavender blouse. Wincey thought how different and how much better she looked now than when she'd first set eyes on her. That seemed a lifetime ago now.

'Wincey and I were talking about the wedding, Granny. May's usually a good month for weather. It makes such a difference to photographs if the sun shines.'

Wincey said, 'You'll have to get a new dress as well, Granny. We're all going to be dressed up to the nines.'

'Ah've already got a good dress. The one ah used tae wear tae church.'

'Granny, it's reeking of mothballs,' Teresa said, 'and it's an old thing.'

'Ah'm an auld thing.'

Wincey and Teresa laughed. 'Yes, and a right awkward torment of an old thing. Here, eat up your soup. There's nice lamb chops as well.'

'Any puddin'?' Granny had a sweet tooth.

'Of course. Guess what it is. Can you not smell it?'

Granny's nose twitched at the spicy air. 'No' a clooty dumplin'?'

'The very same.'

Sheer joy flashed into Granny's eyes but hastily she lowered her head and began slurping at her soup, muttering in between slurps,

'Aye, well, it's taken ye long enough. Ah've been askin' for years aboot a clooty dumplin'.'

Teresa winked at Wincey. 'Now, now, Granny. You're getting worse than Florence for exaggerating.'

Soon Erchie had arrived to join them at the table. At least he—like his mother—had never changed, Wincey thought. He still wore his skipped bunnet all the time and a comfortable old jacket and trousers.

'Huv ye seen the papers yet, Ma?'

'Ye know fine ah cannae read noo wi' ma eyes. How? Whit's been goin' on?'

'Lots of men are goin' over tae Spain tae fight in the Civil War. Mind the other day I read tae you about whit's happened there.'

'Naebody'll thank them for it,' Granny said.

'It's a good cause, right enough,' Erchie conceded. 'It's against Fascism. It says in the *Record* crowds o' intellectuals are goin', even fellas from Cambridge. An' fancy! The British government has warned Britons who enlist on either side that they're liable to two years in prison.'

'Och, it's gettin' beyond me,' Granny complained. 'Wan minute they're jailin' men for no' goin' tae fight—good men like our Johnny Maclean. Noo they're jailin' men who *are* goin' tae fight. Whit dae they think they're playin' at?'

'Never mind, dear,' Teresa said. 'Here's a nice pork chop.'

'Ah know whit their game is,' Erchie said. 'It says in the *Record* here they're goin' tae spend one thousand five hundred million— fancy!' His voice rose to a screech. 'One thousand five hundred million—to build up arms stocks. They're plannin' another bloody war, that's whit they're playin' at.'

'Now, now, Erchie, watch your language.'

'Well, it's enough tae make anybody swear. They told us the last war was tae be the war tae end all wars.'

'Ah never believed a word o' it at the time,' Granny growled.

'No, Ma, an' neither did ah. Ye cannae believe a word they say.'

'Remember how Johnny prophesied another war wis on the cards?'

'Aye, we could always believe whit Johnny said. He wis an honest man. An' his prophesy'll come true. You mark ma words. It says in the *Record*—'

'Och, Erchie,' Teresa protested. 'Will you put that paper away and let us have some peace to enjoy our food.'

'All right, all right, hen. It's just that Ma likes tae be kept up tae date wi' whit's in the paper.'

'Well, dear, you can read every page of the *Record* to Granny later. Through in the front room.'

'She's aye shovin' me through there oot the road. Ah've been sittin' through there frozen stiff aw day.'

Teresa sighed. 'I'll light a fire for you, Granny. Then you and Erchie'll be nice and cosy while he reads you the paper.'

'Aye, well . . .' Granny said grudgingly, but with one eye on the clooty dumpling now drying out at the fire. A fine sight it was—fat, dark brown, fruity and spicy and with a beautiful shiny skin.

'I've cream as well, Granny.'

'Cream? Cream?' Granny echoed incredulously. 'By Jove, it's well seen we're well off nooadays.'

'I was just thinking,' Teresa said, 'what with Charlotte getting married, and no doubt Florence and the twins won't be long behind her, and there's you as well, Wincey . . .'

'Oh no,' Wincey said, 'I'll never get married.'

'Nonsense, dear. Of course you will. One day. But you're still young, so don't worry.'

'I'm not worried. It's not that.'

'I was just thinking, you see,' Teresa interrupted, 'there would be no point in us going through all the upheaval of moving again. This'll do fine for us, won't it, Erchie? It's such a nice close and we've such good neighbours.'

'Aye, ye're quite right, hen. This is where we belong, no' among the toffs up the Balgrayhill.'

Wincey shrugged. 'Well, if you're happy here, it's all right by me.' And yet she felt a pang of sadness. She didn't know where it came from.

1937

14

'Don't be ridiculous, Nicholas,' Mathieson said. 'You're forty-two.'

'So? What does age matter?'

'I would have thought you'd have had more than enough of fighting. I thought you'd become a pacifist.'

'This is different, James. It's against the growth of Fascism. I think it should be nipped in the bud before it spreads any further. Derek and Nigel and Peter have already gone.'

Mathieson sadly shook his head. 'Good men, and we'll never see them again. Good, intelligent men who could have been an asset to Scotland.'

'What a pessimist you are, James. Of course we'll see them again.'

'Have you forgotten all you told me about what it was like in the trenches? And how many good friends you lost there? The flower of British manhood was sacrificed in that war.'

'This is different.'

'Not as far as suffering and killing are concerned. We must find other ways, Nicholas. Socialists all over the world must use every means at their disposal to stop every country building up arms. A lot of good Stanley Baldwin was. It was him who started it all again here. Remember George Lansbury's last speech? He quoted Jesus. "Those who take the sword will perish by the sword." But it's the arms dealers and the men who make fortunes out of munitions factories who are at the root cause of war. They encourage war because it feeds their greed.'

Virginia had come into the sitting room then and said, 'Well, that was a bit tactless of you, James.'

'Oh sorry, Nicholas. I'd forgotten about your father.'

Nicholas smiled. 'It's all right.' He turned to Virginia. 'James has been trying to talk me out of my idea of going over to Spain.'

'I should think so too,' Virginia said with feeling.

'Think of Virginia,' Mathieson said. 'She still hasn't completely recovered from losing Wincey.'

'I doubt if I ever will. But there's no point using me in trying to persuade him, James. You're far more likely to succeed if you use his precious writing.'

'She hates my work,' Nicholas told Mathieson sadly.

'No I don't,' Virginia protested. 'It's just the way you always put it first—before me, before everything.'

Nicholas shook his dark head and said nothing.

It was Mathieson who spoke up. 'Don't be so selfish, Virginia.'

'Selfish! Me?' She flushed with anger. 'You've got a nerve!' She glared at his twisted face, his shaggy mop of prematurely grey hair and bent shoulders, and suddenly her anger seeped away. She thought—what was the use.

Mathieson spoke again. 'Nicholas has been a good husband and provider for you, Virginia. Not only that, he has given pleasure to thousands with his books. But as well as all that, he has conveyed the socialist message more effectively and reached more ordinary people than you or I or any of our friends have done in all the years of our work in politics. You should be proud of him.'

'I am, I am.' Tears filled her eyes. 'It's just . . . I can't bear the thought of him going away again.'

'All right, darling.' Nicholas hastened to put his arms around her shoulders. 'I won't go. I promise.'

'I still think of Wincey,' Virginia said.

'So do I, darling, and I worry.' He gazed over at Mathieson. 'Do you think she felt neglected, James?'

'Why should she? She had a good home here. She had everything any child could have wished for.'

'Every material thing, yes,' Nicholas said. 'That's not what I meant. Remember our get-togethers with all our friends when she was here, James. You think of it. Where was she? Who spoke to her? Did I speak to her? My God, James, I can hardly remember seeing her. I've got now so that the more I try to remember what she was like, the less I can remember. Sometimes I think I've never known her at all.'

'Now you're being ridiculous again, Nicholas. She was a shy girl, that's all. She kept herself in the background. She didn't want to mix with everybody. And why should she, when you think of it? It was always adult company. She was just a child.'

Virginia spoke up then, her tone as worried as Nicholas's. 'We should have invited more children to the house for her. We should have encouraged her to bring her friends home.'

'But as far as I could see,' Mathieson said, 'she didn't have any friends. It wasn't your fault. There are people like that—loners. It's just their natures.'

Virginia chewed at her lip. 'She was far too much in her grandfather's company. I used to say to her, Be a good girl and keep your grandfather company. When I think of it now, I shouldn't have said that. I shouldn't have done that.'

Nicholas gave her a little shake. 'You must stop tormenting yourself like this, Virginia. You're only harming yourself.'

'Yes,' Mathieson agreed. 'It's time you faced facts, Virginia. And you too, Nicholas. Because if you ask me, you're just as bad. Wincey is long dead and it was nobody's fault. She loved her grandfather. She liked him and wanted to be with him. Her death was a tragedy but nobody's fault. You've got to accept that—both of you. It's the only way. Your child wouldn't have wanted you to be so unhappy and tormented like this. She loved you too, you know.'

'Do you really think so, James?' Virginia gazed anxiously over at him.

'Of course she loved the pair of you. How can you doubt it? It was perfectly obvious to everyone else.'

'Was it, James?' Nicholas asked with an anxiety that matched that of his wife.

Mathieson rolled his eyes. 'For God's sake, you're both being ridiculous now. I've never been more certain of anything in my life. Of course Wincey loved you. And she was proud of you both. I used to see it in her eyes every time she looked up at either of you.'

'Thank you, James,' Virginia said quietly.

'Yes,' Nicholas echoed. 'Thank you.'

'Nothing to thank me for. I'm just stating facts. Now, you've had your grieving time, so put it behind you. Get on with your lives. And try to be happy, for God's sake.'

'All right. All right.' Nicholas smiled. 'We take your point. Now let's have a drink. Let's drink to the future.'

'That's more like it.' Mathieson gave one of his grotesque twisted grins. 'How's Richard these days?'

'Better you didn't know,' Nicholas said.

'Don't tell me he's taken after your father and gone into munitions?'

'No, but my father would have been pleased, I suppose. He's joined the Air Force. He's training as a pilot and loving it.'

'So he's going to be cannon fodder this time around.'

Virginia cried out in horror, 'James, don't say that. I can't bear it.'

'I'm sorry, Virginia. But it does look as if there's another war brewing.'

'You're such a pessimist, James. You always have been.'

'Well, I only hope I'm wrong.'

Suddenly Nicholas said, 'There's still that money, you know.'

'What money?' Mathieson asked.

'In my father's will. He left Wincey a large sum in trust until her twenty-first birthday. It gave my mother quite a shock when she found out about it. I'll never forget her face at the reading of the will.'

Virginia said, 'She never really liked Wincey. She thought she was too much like me—which was utter nonsense, of course. Poor Wincey wasn't a bit like me, either in looks or in any other way.'

'What are you going to do about the money?'

'She would have been seventeen now. We can't bear to touch the money yet. After her twenty-first, we'll see. But at the moment, both Virginia and I feel we'd rather give the whole lot to charity. It's not as if we need it.'

Virginia said, 'You'll stay for dinner, I hope, James.'

'Thanks. If you're sure it's all right.'

'When has it not been all right, James?' Nicholas laughed. 'You're one of the family, and always welcome. You know that.'

'I'll go through and see to it.' Virginia went through to the kitchen. She had a daily cook and a cleaner—Mrs Rogers and Jessie Conway. Mrs Rogers was just taking off her apron when Virginia arrived in the well-equipped, spacious kitchen.

'I've left the potatoes peeled and ready salted in the pot,' Mrs Rogers said. She was an efficient cook and enjoyed the job, but she was glad to be heading home regularly every afternoon. She was a widow with two children at school. 'And the pie's all ready there just to pop in the oven. There's fruit salad in the fridge and a jug of custard. Or you could heat up an apple pie. I made two yesterday.'

'That's fine. Thanks, Mrs Rogers. Now off you go. Jessie got away on time, did she?'

The cleaner just came in for four hours.

'Yes, she did the stairs and the bathroom and cleaned up here.'

'Fine. See you tomorrow then.'

After Mrs Rogers had gone, Virginia switched on the kitchen wireless. It was a request programme and George Formby was twanging away at his ukulele and cheerily singing 'Leaning on a Lamppost'. Then came a woman vocalist who began the sad refrain, 'Can I Forget You'. Virginia rushed over and switched the wireless off.

15

Wincey knew it was only a matter of time. She knew it would come, and it did.

Charlotte said, 'It's only right that we should make Malcy a partner, Wincey. He can't just go on working in the factory as an ordinary employee.' Her eyes shone. 'I thought I could make a partnership my wedding gift to him.'

Wincey took a deep breath. She must try to keep calm and not criticise Malcy. She knew it would only make matters worse. Charlotte would never listen to a word against him.

'I'm sorry, Charlotte. I can't agree to that.'

'Why not? What have you got against Malcy?'

'It's just that I believe the secret of our success is *our* partnership— just the two of us. I don't want to spoil it by changing anything. We could give Malcy another job. He'd make a good salesman. He could travel about as—'

'I don't want Malcy to travel about, as a salesman or anything else. I want him here beside me. No, it has to be a partnership, Wincey. I can't disappoint him.'

'So you told him.'

'Well, just hinted a bit when he was so worried about how awkward it was going to be at work once we were married.'

'I see.'

Charlotte brightened again. 'So it's all right with you?'

'No. I'm sorry, Charlotte. It isn't, and it never will be.'

'So Malcy was right.' Charlotte sounded bitter now. 'He said you would try to spoil everything for us. He said he didn't know what he's ever done to you to make you dislike him so. And neither do I, Wincey.'

'Can we just leave it now, Charlotte?'

'No, we can't. I'll go to a lawyer. I'll get Malcy a partnership one way or another.'

'Well, you'll no longer have me as a partner. Or anything else. I'll wash my hands of the business altogether.'

'You can't do that.'

'Just watch me.'

'You know I can't do without you. Especially now. You're the only one who knows—'

'That's right, Charlotte. And what does Malcy know?'

Charlotte's cheeks were crimson. Wincey had never seen her look so angry. 'I'd give up the factory and sell everything and be content to be Malcy's wife, rather than hurt or insult him.'

'I don't want to hurt or insult him, Charlotte. And you can give up the factory if you like. I've no doubt that I can find other work if I have to. I have plenty of contacts now.'

Charlotte left in high dudgeon. She was off to meet Malcy—their last meeting before the wedding, in fact. Wincey was confident that Malcy would not welcome the idea of Charlotte killing the goose that laid so many golden eggs. Charlotte returned late that night and Wincey pretended to be asleep. She knew, however, by the way Charlotte was banging about the room that she was angry—and it was with her.

Next morning at breakfast, Charlotte addressed Wincey with bitterness. 'Well, it's only too obvious that my Malcy is a lot more reasonable and generous-hearted than you.'

Before Wincey had time to say anything, Teresa asked, 'What's wrong? What do you mean, dear?'

'I wanted to give Malcy a partnership in the firm as a wedding present. As I told *her*, it would be awkward for us both if he continued as an ordinary employee after we were married. But oh no, she wouldn't have it. She threatened to ditch the business altogether rather than have my Malcy as a partner.'

'It has never worried you,' Wincey struggled to control her temper, 'to have your father working as an ordinary employee.'

'That's different.'

'Yes. Erchie is a much more experienced and more senior member of the staff, as well as being the head of the family.'

Erchie said, 'Ah appreciate what you're saying, hen, but ah've always been quite happy to leave the runnin' o' things to you an' Charlotte.'

'I know, Erchie. But what do you bet Malcy wouldn't be. That's what I'm afraid of. I don't blame Charlotte for not understanding and being angry with me. She loves Malcy and good luck to her. I sincerely wish her and Malcy every happiness as man and wife.'

'Och aye, hen, ah'm sure ye do. Come on, Charlotte. Ah don't like tae see you an' Wincey fallin' out. Ye've been like sisters tae each other for years. Closer than the twins.'

'That's right, dear. We don't want either of you to be upset so near to the wedding. What did Malcy say? Is he angry as well?'

'No, he is not.' Charlotte assumed a quiet dignity. 'That's what I was trying to say. He simply told me that he would be the last one to come between me and Wincey, or have us give up the factory, even though he'd have loved to have me just stay at home and look after him all the time. I tried to insist that he was the only one who mattered to me, and I'd gladly give everything up for him. But he wouldn't hear of me giving up the factory.'

'I'll bet,' Wincey thought, but she said nothing.

'How about making Malcy the manager, hen? That would be something, would it no'?' Erchie turned to Wincey. 'How about that, hen?'

Wincey shrugged. 'Yes, that's all right with me.'

'Charlotte, hen?'

'I suppose it's the next best thing. I'll mention it to Malcy and see what he says.'

'Good, good.' Erchie rubbed his hands. 'An' whit are ye aw goin' tae dae wi' yersels the day?'

Florence and the twins had already left for work but Wincey and Charlotte were not going in to the factory. It was the day before the wedding and there was still quite a lot to do.

Teresa said, 'We're having our hair done for a start. And there are dresses to collect. Away you go out the road, Erchie. And remember, keep in the pub with your pals tonight. We're having Charlotte's hen party.'

'What? In here?'

'Yes. Charlotte doesn't want to be traipsing away into town and coming in late at night. She wants to get her beauty sleep tonight. We're just going to have a few of the neighbours in for an hour or two and a bite of supper. But no men allowed. Do you hear?'

'Poor old Erchie,' Wincey thought. 'He's not even been invited to Malcy's stag party.' No doubt Malcy would be living it up in town, treating all his gambling pals, lording it, showing off. She prayed that he would be kind to Charlotte. Charlotte had always been such a loving and generous-hearted person. She deserved someone who would love and cherish her.

Gradually, during the rest of the day, Charlotte's coolness towards Wincey was melted away by the happy preparations for the wedding. By the time the neighbours started to arrive, it was as if there had never been any bad feeling between them. Charlotte was not a person to harbour ill-feeling for long.

Mrs McGregor arrived with her three eldest girls, Lexie, Minnie and Jeannie. Each one of them brought a bottle.

'Oh here,' Teresa laughed. 'Do you want us all to get drunk?'

Then came Mrs Donaldson and her two girls, Mary and Joan. Then a couple of Charlotte's friends from the church, Sarah and Betty. By this time the kitchen was packed and so they all moved through to the front room. There Wincey started the gramophone going with a cheery record of 'Seventy-Six Trombones', which could hardly be heard above the excited chatter. They were all coming to the wedding and were eagerly looking forward to it.

By the time they'd had a few drinks, Mary and Joan Donaldson were well away. They got up to sing a duet—first of all 'Some Day My Prince will Come' and then, for an encore, 'I'm Wishing'. Both efforts sent everyone into a splutter of giggles because unfortunately neither Mary nor Joan had the slightest chance of a prince or any other man coming, no matter how much wishing they did. For one thing, they'd inherited their mother's ample girth, chubby faces and short-sightedness, which required very thick pebble glasses. Blissfully unaware of the cause of everyone's mirth, however, the girls continued to put heart and soul into their performance, even going on to their tiptoes and doing a little dance for good measure.

The party, including the supper that Teresa had prepared, was a huge success and everyone agreed that it was much better 'havin' a pairty in yer ain hoose—ye can let yer hair doon'. Even Granny agreed that it had been 'a rerr night'. She had also treated the company to a couple of songs, first of all 'The Bonny Wells o' Weary', then, after another few drinks, a rousing rendition of 'The Red Flag'.

The next day everyone had a long lie in bed. Teresa as usual was up first and making a pot of tea. Soon everyone was milling about trying to get ready.

'This is ridiculous, Mother,' Florence complained. She'd recently changed from addressing Teresa as Mammy to Mother. Copeland & Lye's was having a terrible influence on Florence, Granny said. Who would have thought it, her of all folk.

'She's been totally corrupted by the bourgeoisie, She'll be callin' me Grandmother next!'

'What's ridiculous, dear?' Teresa asked.

'This awful dump of a house. I mean, that black hole of Calcutta of a toilet for a start. And out on the stairs, Mother! It's just not hygienic. And not being able to have a bath without traipsing about a mile up the road. It's high time we moved to a decent place with a room for each of us, and a bathroom.'

'Now, now, dear. It's just a wee bit of a crush today because of the wedding. Give yourself a wash at the sink.'

'That's another thing. It's not hygienic to sleep, eat, cook and wash in the one place. And Granny's chanty is absolutely disgusting. We'll have to move, Mother.'

'Ye'll be auld yersel' wan day,' Granny wailed.

'Now, now, Granny,' Teresa soothed. 'She didn't mean that you're disgusting, dear. Just your chamber pot.'

Charlotte said, 'We've offered to pay the rent of a bigger place with a bathroom, haven't we Wincey?'

'Yes. And it's an awful nuisance having to go out to the close for the toilet, right enough, Teresa. Especially in the winter. And the girls should have a room of their own, and not a room that has to double as a sitting room either. And now that Granny has her wheelchair, we could hurl her into the bathroom no bother.'

Teresa sighed. 'Right enough. A bathroom would be a great help.'

Florence, forgetting her poshness for a minute, shouted out, 'Oh Mammy, does that mean we can move to a better place?'

The twins joined in. 'Please Mammy. Please.'

'Och well, as long as it's still in Springburn.'

'Hurray!' Florence and the twins joined hands in a circle and danced around.

Charlotte said, 'I'm going through to the room to get ready.'

'All right, dear. I'll just see to Granny. I've just her hair to give a wee tidy.'

Granny's hair had once been long and jet black. Erchie always cut it for her, making it neat and short. She wore it sleeked down with a side parting and fixed on one side by a large brown kirby-grip. Teresa gave the dark grey head a gentle brushing and then replaced the kirby-grip.

'There you are, Granny. All smartened up.'

'Them shoes are killin' me. Ye know how bad ma feet are.'

'You can't wear your old slippers to a wedding, Granny. Try and suffer them till after the service. At the reception I'll slip them off under the table. Will that do?'

'Ah suppose it'll huv tae.'

Soon the packed kitchen was rustling with taffeta dresses in pale blue and lavender. Then the kitchen door opened and Charlotte came in looking like an angel in her white dress and veil. Tears came into Erchie's eyes.

'Oh hen, ah'm that proud o' you. Ye look that nice.'

Wincey embraced her. 'You look lovely, Charlotte. I'm so proud to be your bridesmaid. We all are, aren't we girls?'

There was an enthusiastic yell of agreement. Once more, Wincey made a secret prayer.

16

Virginia left the house and entered the Botanic Gardens by the side gate. With its famous Kibble Palace and pleasant grounds, it was a popular park for residents of the West End of the city. It was after lunchtime. She'd eaten the meal alone, as usual. Nicholas was shut away in his writing room with his flask of coffee and sandwiches to have if and when he remembered.

Walking in the park in the warm May sunshine was better than sitting at home doing nothing. May Day was past, with its exciting marches and colourful banners carried aloft. Then all the rousing speeches. Nicholas hadn't even taken a day off for that. She had gone with Mathieson and a crowd of other socialist activists. Afterwards they'd enjoyed a meal and lots of heated talk in Miss Cranston's famous Willow Tearoom in Sauchiehall Street. It was designed by Charles Rennie Mackintosh and much admired for its unusual furniture and decor. The talk as usual had been wide ranging and not solely about politics. It had been an exhilarating day altogether. In the days since then, quietness and loneliness had crept up on her once more.

Nicholas was not enthusiastic about having friends round very often while he was working on a book. Nor did they go out as much as they used to. At least not to the jazz evenings which had been so lively and such fun. They had got to know quite a few musicians. They had met them through Andy Daisley and his Balmoral Enterprises. Andy represented many of the best musicians and organised festivals and concerts in Glasgow. Through him, famous musicians from all over the world came to perform in the city. All she and Nicholas seemed to do together nowadays was visit his mother, even though, she suspected, this was more of a duty than a pleasure for Nicholas.

The park was quite busy with strollers like herself. Some wore nanny's uniforms and pushed prams. Virginia entered the heat of the Kibble Palace and wandered among the tropical plants, trees and statues. Virginia killed a half hour or so admiring the plants and passing the time of day with one of the workmen. He told her that they made up a yearly seed list which went out to all the botanic gardens in the world. Requests came back for seeds from countries as far away as Czechoslovakia and Australia.

The heat made her feel thirsty and so she left the Kibble Palace and walked towards the main gate, beside which Gizzi's Cafe was situated. Or the Silver Slipper Cafe, to give it its proper name. It was the usual thing after a stroll around the gardens for people to go and have an ice cream in the cafe.

Afterwards Virginia went down Byres Road to do a bit of shopping. She passed the subway with its special smell—a mix of archangel tar and water. Virginia had often seen women with children suffering with their chest standing at the side and letting the children breathe in the subway air. It was supposed to be good for them. She bought a paper on the way back and once home, made a cup of tea and sat down at the kitchen table to read the paper. There were pictures of the King's gilded carriage drawn by eight white horses passing through Trafalgar Square in London. It was on the way to the Abbey for the coronation. There was a big picture of the newly crowned King on the balcony of Buckingham Palace. The King, Virginia thought, appeared a serious but sensitive man. His Queen looked pleasant and smiling, and the two children, Elizabeth and Margaret, were also smiling happily. They looked quite ordinary little girls. Behind the royal family, though, were other royal ladies and peeresses wearing elbow length gloves and coronets on their heads. Their supercilious stares and primped mouths were all too familiar to Virginia. They were the type of employers she and countless other poor girls had suffered under. Women who thought they were far superior to the 'servant class' and treated them like dirt. Women who lived in pampered luxury, enjoying one round of pleasure after another, while their servants slaved for a pittance from the crack of dawn until they dropped exhausted on to their attic beds. 'Useless, upper-class twits!' Virginia thought, as she turned the page.

Inside there was a picture of the wedding of Charlotte Gourlay, owner of the prosperous Gourlay factory which made clothing for the armed forces. Her bridegroom apparently had been one of her employees. 'Well, well,' Virginia thought, 'things were surely looking up and getting more democratic.' She looked a nice gentle girl, and no doubt she was a good and a kindly employer. It said that that four Gourlay sisters had all been bridesmaids. They weren't in the picture though, only the bride and the groom. It was obvious what the gentle looking factory owner saw in him. The paper described him as 'the handsome groom', although he wasn't the type that Virginia thought attractive, with his creamy fair hair, brows and lashes, and pale blue eyes. 'Oh well, good luck to her,' Virginia thought, turning another page.

Florence's boyfriend lived at the St George's Cross end of Great Western Road and he and Florence did quite a lot of their courting in the Botanic Gardens. During the summer at least. One day, not long after Charlotte's wedding, Florence invited Wincey to come on a picnic with them to the Botanic Gardens. Part of Wincey longed to see the place again—the beautiful gardens, the elegant Grosvenor Hotel and terraced houses opposite, and further along, Great Western Terrace. Then on the opposite side of the road from that, rearing up from the grassy bank, Kirklee Terrace and her original home. At times she longed to see her mother and father again, but sadly the longer time passed, the more certain she was of how impossible that was.

'No, Florence. It's very kind of you and Eddie but I'd rather not play gooseberry. You ought to know me by now. I prefer to be on my own. I'm just funny that way.'

'You certainly are,' Florence said. 'But are you sure?'

'Yes, honestly. I thought seeing it's such a nice day I'd either go up to Springburn Park or even to Glasgow Green. I'd like to visit the People's Palace again.'

Glasgow Green was an important historic site and one of the great battlefields of Scotland. In many ways, the history of the Green was the history of Glasgow itself. A thousand battles had been fought there. Meetings and demonstrations had been held on the Green in the struggle for a living wage. The fight for political freedom—first one man, one vote, and then one woman, one vote—had taken place there. Different wars against all sorts of social injustices had been conducted on the Green. It was also the place where not only did women do their washing, but everyone enjoyed their leisure time. At school, Wincey had learned that it was here that the idea came to James Watt that changed the entire course of industrial and human history—the steam engine.

Wincey enjoyed her walk on the Green, watching all the people, and at the same time immersing herself in the colourful history of the place. She made straight for the People's Palace. It was different from other museums inasmuch as its collections all related to the history and the industry of the city and the life of the ordinary working people. It also housed a heated winter garden which was designed and arranged to serve as a hall where musical performances were given to large audiences. So it was a unique municipal enterprise, with the combination practically under one room of a museum, picture gallery, winter garden and music hall.

Wincey had barely stepped inside the entrance when she had an unexpected shock. She saw a familiar face. She had felt sure that neither her parents nor her grandmother would ever come here, unless there was some sort of political rally going on. Then her mother and some of her mother's political friends might turn up. Wincey had made sure before she'd ventured out that no such rally or meeting was taking place. She had not, however, considered the possibility of meeting one of her mother's or her grandmother's servants. But here, only a few feet from her, was Mrs Rogers and her two children.

Wincey quickly turned away and retraced her steps through the doorway and out onto the Green again. Her heart was thumping in her chest, making her feel as if she was in danger of fainting. She tried to calm herself with the thought that Mrs Rogers had not seen her. She was almost certain the older woman had not seen her. Nevertheless, as she hurried away, she wished she'd had a scarf with her to tie over her head. Her red hair was the thing that might draw attention to her. She couldn't get back to Springburn quick enough. Never had a tram car seemed so slow.

Only once she was in Springburn, hastening into the close and then safely into the house, did she feel secure. It had been as if she had relived the horror of her grandfather's death again and her dreadful part in it. Her panic had been exactly the same.

'What's wrong, dear?' Teresa asked. 'You look as white as a sheet.'

'I don't know. I just felt a bit faint.'

'Och, you've been working too hard, Wincey. Sit down, dear. Try to relax now and I'll make you a cup of tea.'

Granny wailed, 'Ah'm needin' ma medicine. If she had tae suffer aw the bloomin' agonies that ah huv tae, she'd know aw aboot it.'

'Now, now, Granny. You'll get your medicine with your cup of tea. The kettle doesn't take a minute on the gas. These gas rings are marvellous. They're so much quicker than the fire. Are you all right, Wincey?'

'Yes, I feel much better now that I'm home.' She must always remember that this was her home. There was no use allowing memories of her childhood home in Kirklee Terrace to creep into her mind. How could she explain to anyone why she'd run away and why for so long she'd stayed away? There could be only one explanation and that was guilt. Everyone would know that without her attempting to explain. She could offer no excuse for what she'd done. Even now, as an adult, she knew that by refusing to give her grandfather his medication, she had caused his death. She couldn't make the excuse that she hadn't known what to do to help him. Everyone was well aware that she knew perfectly well. How could she bring herself to say, 'He was a pervert. He was abusing me. That's why I let him die.' No-one would believe her. Her grandfather had appeared such a pleasant, loving, generous old man. Her grandfather, of all people! Anyway, such a thing had never been heard of. Everyone would revile her and despise her for even thinking of such disgusting behaviour. They would believe it was nothing more than an example of her dirty mind and they would be a hundred times more horrified at her callous treatment of her own grandfather. As far as everyone else was concerned, the old man had been nothing but good and kind to her from the moment she was born.

Wincey gratefully accepted the cup of tea from Teresa who said in surprise, 'Wincey, you're trembling. What on earth's the matter? Has something happened to upset you? Is that what it is?'

'I nearly got run over by a motor car. That's all.'

'That's all?' Teresa cried out. 'Oh my, you might have been killed. Oh Wincey, now I feel all shaky. You know you're as dear and as precious to me as my own flesh and blood.'

Wincey felt guilty about lying to Teresa and tears of shame welled up in her eyes. 'Thank you, Teresa.'

'Nothing to thank me for.'

'Where's ma medicine. It's well seen naebody cares about me. Ye'll be auld yersel' wan day, the pair o' ye.'

I7

At last they made the move to a handsome red sandstone tenement near the top of the Balgrayhill. For Granny's sake they had waited until a bottom flat had become available. It was a spacious, high ceilinged four-room and kitchen and bathroom. It also had quite a large square hall. Granny said, 'Ye'll huv us aw votin' Tory next.'

The twins shared a room. Wincey had a room to herself, and so had Florence. The other room was to be the 'best room', used only for entertaining visitors. Granny had refused to move from the kitchen, nor would she countenance being left to sleep alone.

'Ah cannae get up on the bed in the kitchen or anywhere else. Ah'll aye huv tae use the hurly. So there's nae reason fur you an' Erchie no' tae stay in the kitchen bed. Anyway, what if ah needed tae "go" in the middle o' the night? Ye'll be auld yersel' wan day.'

They had to buy more furniture. For the sitting room, as Florence called it, they bought a three piece suite—a settee and two easy chairs, so cushioned that you sank deep into their comfort. But as Erchie said, 'We'll need a crane tae lift Ma oot o' them chairs.' A walnut china cabinet was also purchased. It was filled with a coffee set with a cream coffee pot in a fashionable angular shape, with a geometric pattern of orange, yellow and black. A milk jug and sugar bowl and matching cups and saucers were proudly arranged alongside it. On the shelf underneath, there was a matching biscuit barrel. On the remaining shelves, there were crystal glasses. On a table beside the tiled fireplace sat a lamp in the form of a bronze lady holding a beach ball aloft. Another larger walnut table over against the opposite wall had a folding leaf to save space. On it were photographs of

Charlotte's wedding.

Above the mantelpiece hung a large mirror and along the mantle shelf were two bronze figures of dancing ladies and a stylised black panther. On either side were low book shelves. The floor was of highly polished linoleum, covered with a large carpet. The carpet had a striking design of figures entitled 'The Workers'. It was a purchase insisted on by Erchie and Granny. They both said, 'Ye've aw had a say in everythin' else and we're no' that keen on any o' it. But we like this rug. That's the rug for us.'

'Carpet, Daddy,' Florence corrected.

Eventually everyone capitulated. Admittedly the carpet was a very modern design and it did fit in with the overall style of the room. But no sooner had they all settled into the new house when Florence announced that she was going to get married. She and Eddie had found a place in Clydebank, near Eddie's work. She refused a big wedding like the one Charlotte had. All she wanted was a quiet registry affair and then to a restaurant afterwards with the twins and their boyfriends. Granny loudly proclaimed, much to Florence's affront and embarrassment, 'Aye, it's well seen it's a shotgun affair.'

Teresa sighed. 'It'll be the twins next. I just hope they don't follow Florence and Eddie away to Clydebank. What's wrong with old Springburn?'

'Ah telt ye,' Granny said, 'they're aw gettin' above theirsels. Springburn's no' good enough for them noo. Even the Co-op. *The Co-op.*' Granny repeated the word with high pitched incredulity. The twins had followed Florence into Copeland & Lye's. Both were in 'Mantles'.

'You mean frocks,' Granny had said, but the twins just rolled their eyes.

'What worries me, Granny, is that they've always been so close. The girls, I mean. And even their boyfriends are brothers. It's good that they're close, of course,' Teresa added hastily. 'It's just I hope they won't follow Florence away to Clydebank. I'll miss them.'

'Aye,' Erchie said, 'the house'd be awfae quiet without the girls.'

'Quiet as a grave,' Granny wailed. 'We'll aw rummel aroon' this big, empty hoose like peas in a drum.'

'Now, now. It's not empty, Granny. The twins won't be getting married for ages yet.'

As it turned out, Teresa was wrong in this pronouncement. No sooner had Florence and Eddie tied the knot than the twins announced that they too planned to marry. Florence's wedding went smoothly. She was a June bride and looked very pretty and smart in a white embroidered linen dress with short puff sleeves and a wide brimmed navy hat trimmed with white flowers. The twins wore navy jackets and skirts and white satin blouses. Wincey looked unusual in a dark green dress, matching cape, and a brimmed hat pulled down over her eyes. But then, as Teresa said proudly, 'Our Wincey always looks that wee bit different and mysterious.' Wincey smiled wrily at the word mysterious. If only Teresa knew.

It had been a quiet afternoon affair, just as Florence wanted. Nevertheless, Teresa insisted on giving her, as she said, a decent send-off. 'Just a wee family party, dear.'

And so that is what they had in their new sitting room on the evening of Florence's wedding. Although Teresa cheated a little and had the neighbours in as well. Their old neighbours, as Teresa called them, from their last close. They hadn't got to know the new neighbours yet. They seemed to like to keep themselves more to themselves. A good time, including a few energetic reels and a hokey kokey, was had by one and all. Granny, in her best black dress and her hair slicked to one side with water, sang loud and long with the rest of them.

The twins had a winter wedding. Fifth of November to be exact. Granny said, 'They'll huv fireworks soon enough after they're married, an' no' just the kind they're buyin' in that fancy shop in the town.'

'Och, Granny, it'll be good fun. It'll be a laugh. I'll hurl you round to the park.' We're going to have quite a crowd. All our old neighbours are coming, and Mrs Chalmers from upstairs.' Mrs Chalmers was the only neighbour up the new close that Teresa had really got to know and become friends with. Although young Mrs Beresford, also on the top flat, usually smiled and said good morning or good evening. But she always seemed to be in such a hurry. The next-door neighbour on the bottom flat, Miss McClusky, was even worse. She was always rushing about like a ferret with a duster in her hand.

Granny said, 'A right house-proud horror, that one! She's aye beatin' carpets an' cleanin' windows an' even sweepin' oot the bins. An' ah'm sorry for the poor auld faither o' hers. Fancy her no' lettin' him huv his pipe in the house!' A chair was always placed in the draughty close and the old man had to sit there to have his pipe. And his daughter, a spinster who obviously wasn't used to men or pipes, always came out afterwards and wafted a tea towel about like mad to rid the close of any smell of smoke. 'Whit she's needin',' Granny said, 'is a big man an' a crowd o' weans.'

The neighbours one up the stairs were Davy, an old bachelor, and next door to him was Jock. Jock was a widower. Granny said, 'Here, Wincey, ye should set yer cap at him. Ye could walk right intae a ready made house.'

Wincey laughed. 'Are you wanting rid of me or something? He's far too old for me, Granny.'

'It's no' good for a woman tae be left on her own. Or a fella for that matter. Jock cannae be more than forty. An' he's got a good job on the railway.'

'You *are* wanting rid of me.'

'No, ah'm no'. But the likes o' you cannae be too fussy, hen. Ye're nae oil paintin' wi' all them freckles. An' no' everybody goes for a ginger heid.'

'Now, now, Granny. Wincey's got very nice hair and it's not ginger. It's a lovely warm auburn shade. And he *is* too old. Wincey's not yet eighteen.'

'Och, she's near enough. An' anyroads, she's auld fur her age, an' looks it.'

Teresa rolled her eyes but Wincey just laughed again. She was well used to Granny by now and had grown to be very fond of her.

The twins' wedding was a great success and a great crowd of people, many of whom they didn't know, joined in the fireworks party in the park—until the 'parky' came and put them out because he was going to lock the gates. After they'd all said their goodbyes at the park gate, Wincey was still waving enthusiastically to the twins and their new husbands in their retreating car, and without realising, she stepped out into the road. There was an immediate screech of brakes, and screams from Teresa and Granny, who had already crossed to the other side. A man leapt from a car and glared furiously at Wincey.

'What do you think you're doing, you idiot?'

The car's front bumper had barely touched Wincey but she felt terribly shaken and angry.

'How dare you call me an idiot?'

'You ran right out in front of me. It's a bloody good job there's nothing wrong with my brakes.'

Erchie came hurrying over. 'Come on, hen. Say ye're sorry tae the man an' we'll be on our way.'

'I'll not do any such thing. I wasn't running anywhere. If anyone's the idiot, it's him.'

'A right little charmer,' the man remarked, turning away and getting back into his car.

'Come on, hen,' Erchie repeated, putting an arm around her. 'Ye're jist upset.'

'I'm not upset,' Wincey said, shaking Erchie's arm off and glaring at the driver, who cast her a look of disgust before driving away.

'What an insufferable man,' Wincey said as she walked across the road with Erchie to join Teresa and Granny. Charlotte and Malcy had gone into their house but had rushed out again to see what the screaming was about.

Granny said, 'Dae ye no' think ah've enough wi' ma arthritis, without givin' me a heart attack as well?'

'It wasn't my fault. He must have been driving too fast.'

'If he'd been drivin' too fast, he'd huv splattered ye aw over the road. Ye wernae lookin' where ye were goin'.'

'Och well,' Teresa said. 'You're all right, dear. That's the main thing.'

'Oh look,' Charlotte said. 'He's stopped at that big house at the end of the road. He's turned into that garage.'

'Well, thank you, Wincey,' Malcy said. 'That's all we needed to help us get on with our neighbours.'

Wincey felt like bursting into tears. She was still shaken and now angry with herself. More than anything she regretted giving Malcy a chance to score a point over her.

'Come on, Wincey.' Teresa began pushing Granny's wheelchair. 'We're all dead beat. It's time we were home. Good night, Malcy. Good night, Charlotte.'

Wincey gratefully followed Teresa away along Broomfield Road, and then round onto the Balgrayhill, where Erchie took over the chair. Granny said, 'Ma tongue's hangin' oot fur the want o' a cup o' tea.'

'All right, Granny. I'll put the kettle on as soon as we get in.'

Teresa hurried on in front and up the close to unlock the door. Wincey took off her coat and hat and scarf and in the privacy of her room, breathed deeply a few times before she could get control of her emotions. A cup of tea was a comfort and she was able to say, 'I'm sorry for giving everybody a fright. It was my fault, right enough. I was so taken up with waving the twins off.'

'Och, just forget about it, dear. You're all right. That's all that matters.'

Wincey drank another cup of tea before going to bed. Then she lay for a long time feeling strangely uneasy and apprehensive.

18

'I don't know what the world's coming to,' Virginia said. 'You would have thought that some kind of lesson would have been learned from the last war. But no. Did you see that terrible picture in the papers of that Chinese baby sitting among the debris of Shanghai's railway station, screaming for its dead mother? Poor wee thing.'

'I know.' Mathieson shook his head. 'The Japanese air force were responsible for that. But what about when the Chinese were supposed to be bombing Japanese warships on the river, and the bombs fell on an amusement park. Over a thousand civilians were killed that time. They reckon over two thousand civilians have been killed so far. That's the insanity of war. Life's short enough as it is, but instead of making the best of it, and learning how to live in peace with each other, the whole human race is hell bent on exterminating each other.'

Nicholas sighed. 'Burns knew what he was talking about. "Man's inhumanity to man", and it's not just the Japanese and the Chinese, by the look of it. The Germans and the Italian Fascists are just as crazy.'

'Yes,' Mathieson said, 'I don't like the sound of what's going on over there. Have you heard about the new 'concentration camp' the Nazis have built? Buchenwald, I think it's called. For years they've been these camps to imprison Jews, communists and trade unionists. But what signals have our government and our leaders been sending out? The Duke and Duchess of Windsor said they were charmed with Hitler and delighted by the Nazis. And look at the reception they got when they visited Germany. They certainly didn't give a damn about shaking hands with murderers.' Mathieson's face contorted with disgust. 'The aristocracy and all the religious leaders, including the Pope, have been doing the same old pals act. Have any of them condemned fascism or supported the Jewish people? Or the communists? Or the trade unionists? Not on your life! I'm sick to my soul of their hypocrisy.'

'I'm with you on that, James,' Nicholas said. 'Remember what the priest Camara said. "When I gave food to the poor, they called me a saint. When I asked why the poor were hungry, they called me a communist." '

'Yes,' Mathieson agreed, 'and it could apply to quite a few good socialists I've known.'

'If only someone like Maxton could stir things up and open people's eyes to what's really going on,' Nicholas said, 'But then again, I don't think he's been the same since Wheatley died. Wheatley had the long term vision.'

'The sad thing is' Nicholas continued, 'I don't think even Maxton could do much to influence the way things are going. It's just like last time—war's on its way and there seems to be no way of avoiding it. . . .'

Virginia had been making a pot of coffee. Now she filled the cups that were set out on the coffee table. Mathieson shook his head, then after a few sips of coffee, he said, 'How's the book going, Nicholas?'

'I've hit a tricky bit. I'm not sure where it should go from here.'

'What they call a writer's block, is it?'

'Not exactly. I've several choices and I'm just not sure which ones to take.'

'Would it help to talk about it?'

'Huh!' Virginia gave a sarcastic laugh. 'That'll be the day. Nicholas guards his writing as if he's got state secrets locked away in that room.'

'I used to talk to you about my writing,' he reminded her.

'That was a long time ago.'

'Yes.' Nicholas looked away. 'A lifetime, it seems now.'

'Well, it's not my fault you've changed,' Virginia snapped.

'For goodness' sake,' Mathieson said, 'nobody's said anything was your fault, Virginia. What's up with you these days? You're so touchy. I don't know how Nicholas puts up with you. No wonder he shuts himself away so much.'

'That's right.' Nothing made Virginia more furious than when Mathieson defended Nicholas. 'Gang up against me as usual. I'm getting sick of this.'

Putting down her coffee cup, she left the room.

'She's never been the same,' Nicholas told Mathieson, 'since Wincey disappeared. I don't know what to do. At the moment I couldn't share my writing with her, even if I wanted to. I'm in too much difficulty with it. I need all my concentration, but I keep getting distracted . . . I'm worried about Virginia.'

'She used to help you sort out difficulties.'

'Yes. But that was mostly with my poetry. Novels are different, and she wouldn't understand this one. I got the idea from Wincey's disappearance, you see. It's not Wincey but it is about a young girl who suddenly disappears.'

'I see.'

'I keep wondering what Virginia will think. It's death to the writing of a book if you feel someone's breathing down your neck all the time.'

'But she isn't. Time enough to worry about what anyone thinks once the book's in print.'

'That's normally my attitude. But this feels different.'

'It's only fiction. You're a novelist. Everyone knows that.'

'Yes, but . . . the girl in my book is still alive. I worry in case this could awaken the hope in Virginia that Wincey might still be alive. She's liable to grasp at any straws and I don't believe for one moment that my daughter is alive, James. I only wish the story I've worked out *could* be true. But it's only a story. And I'm just a storyteller.'

'A very good one, and much more, Nicholas.'

'Can you understand my dilemma, James? With Virginia, I mean.'

After a moment's silence, Mathieson nodded. 'Poor Virginia. You're right, of course. She hasn't been the same. Over the years, she has changed. But then I suppose we all have. She should realise that you loved Wincey as much as she did and you've suffered too. But life has to go on. It's over five years now, she can't go on grieving for ever. No-one would expect either of you to forget Wincey but life has to go on and there's your son to think of.'

Nicholas smiled. 'It's fortunate I suppose that Richard is so self-sufficient. I'm sure he felt as devastated as any of us about what happened five years ago but he's been getting on with his life. Doing very well in the RAF, by all accounts. Virginia thinks he looks very handsome in his uniform. She's very proud of him. So is my mother—she dotes on the lad, always has done. He's coming home this weekend.'

'That should cheer Virginia up.'

'I'm hoping so.'

'Can I give you a word of advice?'

'Fire away.'

'For God's sake, Nicholas, take the weekend off work. It might even help you. Maybe then you'd go back to it with a fresh mind and a new perspective.'

Nicholas looked worried again. 'I'll see.'

'Nicholas, you're not helping anyone by shutting yourself away so much.'

'It's the nature of this job. You've often said so yourself, James.'

'I know. But there's surely a limit. Anyway, I suspect that it's more than that. It's your method of escape. You've not properly accepted or faced the loss of your daughter, any more than Virginia has. Only she has no escape. And not much support from you either, by the look of it.'

Nicholas flushed with annoyance. 'Now that's not fair, and you know it, James. I don't work twenty-four hours a day. I do spend time with Virginia. But you see what happens when I do. It's like walking on eggshells.'

'Nicholas, just take the weekend off and be with your wife and son.'

For a few seconds, Nicholas looked like a trapped animal, then he suddenly capitulated. But not with good grace. 'Oh, all right, if it'll stop the pair of you nagging at me.'

'Cheers.' Mathieson lifted his coffee cup and took a careful sip. His twisted mouth made drinking and eating difficult but with careful concentration, he usually managed. Only rarely did he have a spill and he liked to have a napkin handy just in case.

'Is Richard going to get home for Christmas as well?'

'We're hoping so, but we're spending Christmas at my mother's this year. She insisted. She's still very strong willed, my mother.'

'Yes, I have noticed,' Mathieson said wrily.

'I'm sorry she's never very pleasant to you, James.'

'Oh, it doesn't bother me. We don't meet very often, after all.'

'We'll have the usual party here at Hogmanay though. You'll come to that, I hope.'

'Yes, I'll look forward to it.'

'What'll you do for Christmas? I hope you're not going to be on your own.'

'No, one of the other teachers at the college has invited me to his place on Christmas Day.'

'Good.'

Just then Virginia re-entered the room. 'What's good?'

'James has been invited to spend Christmas with one of his colleagues.'

'Did Nicholas tell you of the jolly Christmas we've to look forward to? Or at least, I have to look forward to. It'll be all right for him.'

'Here we go again,' Nicholas groaned. 'I don't know how much longer I'm going to be able to stand this.'

'How much *you'll* be able to stand this?'

Virginia's voice rose and suddenly Mathieson snapped, 'Oh, shut it, the pair of you. I'm off.'

'Oh, you're all right,' Virginia said bitterly. 'You can just walk away.'

'Virginia,' Mathieson said, his voice quiet again, 'look at me. And you say I'm all right.' With the help of his stick, he managed—but not without a struggle—to get up out of his chair.

'James, I'm sorry. Half the time I hardly know what I'm saying these days.'

'That's only too obvious, Virginia. And if you don't pull yourself together, you're not going to be all right. And that's putting it mildly.'

19

Wincey had been doing some shopping in the Co-op in Springburn Road when she heard the commotion. On approaching to investigate she discovered what was a fairly common occurrence in the winter. The cobbles were icy, causing a horse to slip and clatter down. On this occasion it was the coalman's horse.

'Come on, Mac,' the coalman was encouraging the terrified animal. 'Up ye come. Come on now, son.'

A crowd had gathered around watching in anxious sympathy as the beast struggled, with rolling eyes, to rear up and try to get hooves on the ground. Neighing loudly and struggling valiantly, it fought to reach a standing position. Then failing and crashing down again, it lay, eyes bulging, in helpless terror. Eventually the coalman was forced to loosen it out of its shafts. This took a bit of time and effort. Every strap and buckle had to be loosened until the animal lay free and had only itself to raise, with no shackling cart to make its task more difficult. Sparks flew from its hooves as, with a tremendous effort, it heaved itself up and found its balance.

As soon as this happened, a cheer went up from the crowd. Wincey shared their relief. She was fond of horses. She remembered holidaying in the Highlands and being taught to ride a pony. It was one of the few really happy memories of her childhood.

She crossed the road, a shopping basket slung over her arm, and quickened her pace along Springburn Road. She had come out to do the shopping in her dinner break from the factory. Granny was suffering one of her bad turns and Teresa didn't like leaving her to go out to the shops. Wincey was very conscientious about taking time off work and never took advantage of her senior position in the firm. She expected her employees to be conscientious workers and time keepers, and believed that bosses should show a good example. The employees knew, of course, that there were occasions when she had to be away from the factory on business, and that was different.

Unfortunately, Malcy was neither as conscientious nor as good a worker as he used to be. He often disappeared from the factory floor and on more than one such occasion, Wincey had seen him with the local bookie. She tried to keep her mouth shut and not say anything, either to Malcy or to Charlotte. She felt it was Charlotte's responsibility to speak to Malcy and had no doubt that if she did complain to either of them, she would only be met by indignation and anger. In the first place, Malcy would deny his gambling and Charlotte would be only too eager to believe him. She'd heard him tell Charlotte when he'd returned to the factory after over three hours' absence that he'd been helping someone who had been involved in an accident. He described how he had administered first aid and then gone with the man to the hospital. It has been one of the occasions when Wincey had been out negotiating a new order. Returning along Springburn Road, she'd seen Malcy so she knew that he was lying.

And what a liar he was. He had looked genuinely offended and hurt at Charlotte, when she had asked him in her usual gentle way where he'd been.

'It's too bad if the husband of the owner can't take a few hours off for whatever reason, and not be quizzed like a common criminal when he returns.'

Charlotte had been upset and effusive in her apologies. He had taken his time in grudgingly forgiving her. Wincey felt like killing him and it was only with great difficulty that she managed to control her feelings.

By the time she reached the close, she was quite out of breath with hurrying the Balgrayhill, carrying the heavy shopping basket. She had forgotten her key and had to pull the door bell. A harassed Teresa opened the door and immediately turned back along the hall and into the kitchen.

'Granny's not been at all well. I was just saying that I think we should send for the doctor.'

'Och,' Granny said, 'fur aw the good he is, we might as well save oor money.'

'Now, now, Granny. Surely he can do something for you.'

'The same as he aye does. Gives me more painkillers an' if ah get any stronger wans, they'll be knockin' me unconscious. Ah'm half asleep aw the time as it is.'

'Well, at least we could get a prescription for more, so that we have plenty in reserve for you, Granny. I wouldn't like you to go short, and maybe run out on a Sunday when all the chemists are shut.'

'Och, please yersel'. Ye'll dae that anyway.'

'I could go to the surgery for the prescription, Teresa,' Wincey said. 'I could run along for it now.'

'You've had nothing to eat yet, dear.'

'It doesn't matter.'

'Yes it does. You can go for it after work, on your way home maybe. There's enough to keep Granny going just now. Just you sit down and have some stovies. And there's apple and custard for pudding. Erchie's been and away.'

'The coalman's horse fell down the road,' Wincey said as she took off her coat and draped it across the back of the chair. She kept her hat on. 'The poor beast was terrified but the coalman loosened it from its shafts and it managed to get up. It was still trembling though.'

Teresa dished a steaming hot plate of the potato, onion and sausage mixture.

'Och, the poor beast,' Teresa sympathised.

Granny said, in between groans of pain, 'Ah once saw wan gettin' shot. It broke its legs goin' doon.'

'Oh dear. Could you manage a wee spoonful or two of stovies, Granny?'

'Well, starvin' me's no' goin' tae be likely tae cure ma pain, is it?

Teresa settled herself on a chair beside Granny and began feeding her with careful spoonfuls. Granny usually managed to feed herself but today her hands had swollen up.

'I hope Charlotte's taking her share of the work nowadays, Wincey,' Teresa said unexpectedly.

'Oh yes, I've no complaints about Charlotte.'

'It's just I get the feeling you're getting the heavy end of the stick these days, dear.'

It was true that Charlotte was taking time off but that was as a result of Malcy persuading her to have occasional days in Edinburgh.

Actually, they'd had quite a few days in Edinburgh now. He'd also taken her—for a special treat, he said—to the races at Ayr and they planned to go there again. Perhaps Charlotte had mentioned this to Teresa, but Wincey would never be disloyal to Charlotte, even to her mother. Charlotte genuinely loved Malcy and he could twist her round his little finger. That was Charlotte's trouble.

Wincey wondered how much money Malcy had bet at the races. No doubt a great deal. Surely Charlotte must realise now that Malcy was a compulsive gambler. At least Wincey hoped Charlotte wasn't still fooling herself. For the sake of the business, Charlotte must see the danger that might lie ahead if she didn't do something about Malcy.

Wincey tried to reason with herself that Charlotte would continue to think of the interests of the business, as she'd always done in the past. But at the back of her mind, there was a feeling of apprehension and worry. All she said to Teresa, however, was 'Honestly, I'm fine. Everything's fine.' The last thing she wanted to do was to add to Teresa's worries. Teresa had enough to do caring for Granny.

'Do you think we'll be able to visit Florence next week, Granny,' she asked the old woman. 'She's looking forward to showing us all around her new house.'

Granny nodded. 'Ah hope so, hen. Ah cannae thole tae be as bad as this for much longer.' The only consolation Granny had was that when really bad attacks flared up, they usually only lasted for a few days before calming down again.

Florence and Eddie had managed to get a two-room and kitchen bottom flat in Second Avenue, Radnor Park, and they had been doing it up. No-one was allowed to visit until the house was looking the very best they could make it. They were terribly proud of it. The family had been invited for lunch the following Sunday. Up till now, it had always been 'dinner' in the middle of the day in working-class homes. But for some time now, Florence had—as Wincey could imagine Mrs Cartwright saying—'ideas above her station'. The twins had become much the same. They both lived in Dumbarton Road now. They hadn't managed to get houses up the same close, although they had tried hard enough, but their houses were only a few closes away from each other. Euphemia, now Mrs Grant, had a top flat. Bridget, now Mrs Ferguson, lived one up. Both had one-room and kitchen houses.

'It'll give you something to look forward to, Granny,' Teresa comforted.

Wincey finished her stovies and began tucking in to her pudding. Immediately afterwards, she struggled into her coat again. 'I'm away. See you later on.'

'All right, dear.'

Hurrying towards the factory, Wincey wondered if she could discuss the problem about Malcy with Erchie. She decided against it. Erchie was friendly with Malcy, always had been, and Erchie himself enjoyed what he called 'a wee flutter'. To criticise Malcy's gambling could risk Erchie becoming defensive and thinking that she was also casting aspersions at his gambling. In truth, she didn't mind in the least Erchie having his wee flutter, because that was all it was. He worked hard, earned his wages, and was entitled to spend them in whatever way he wished. They all contributed a share of their wages to the house-keeping, and what Erchie did with the rest of his own money was a matter for him and Teresa. Wincey had long ago insisted that she paid the biggest share because, after all, as a partner she had more money than him. She was too fond of Erchie now to risk offending him or making him feel guilty.

She was no sooner back at the factory office when a crisis erupted beside one of the machines. One of the women had tripped on something, and as she fell, her head banged against the corner of one of the tables. Her forehead was bleeding from a cut. It didn't look very deep and the girl said she would be all right, although she looked very shaken. Wincey said, 'It might need a few stitches. I'll take you to the doctor.'

The girl protested that she didn't want to go to the doctor's, or to bother anyone, but Wincey insisted. 'I've a prescription to pick up anyway.' She fetched a towel from the office and told the girl to hold it against her forehead. Then she led the white-faced girl out to Springburn Road. The doctor's surgery was only a few blocks away. Wincey had never had occasion to visit the surgery before but she had met the old doctor when he had visited Granny. Granny complained that all he ever did when anybody went to the surgery was asked them if their bowels had moved that day, then stuck a thermometer in their mouth. A receptionist led the girl into the doctor's room. Eventually she re-emerged to join Wincey.

'Gosh,' she whispered. 'You should see the handsome doctor. He gave me three stitches and I didn't feel a thing. I was so excited.'

'Handsome?' Wincey echoed in surprise, remembering the white haired Doctor Houston.

Just then, the doctor emerged from the room, but it wasn't the Doctor Houston she'd seen before. Wincey immediately recognised him, however, as the driver of the car which had nearly run her down. He was looking across at her, and she suddenly made up her mind. She went over to him.

'I believe I owe you an apology. I was upset the other evening, and I behaved badly. I am sorry.'

He smiled with his eyes as well as his mouth. 'Apology accepted, Miss—?'

'Gourlay.'

'Not one of the Gourlays of Gourlays' factory?'

'Yes, one of the Gourlays of Gourlays' factory.'

'How interesting. My father has quite a few patients from there. He tells me it has a very good reputation.'

'Thank you. Are you Doctor Houston's son then?'

'Yes, I am.'

'Well, perhaps you could give me Mrs Gourlay senior's prescription for painkillers, please. I promised I'd collect it.'

'I'll go and look it up.'

In a minute or two he'd returned with the prescription, but he said, 'You can take this just now, but I think I ought to pay Mrs Gourlay a visit. She may need a change of medication.'

'Oh?' Wincey was taken aback. 'She didn't really ask for a visit.'

'Nevertheless, I'll call to see her this evening. I noticed by her record she lives quite near me. I'm round in Broomfield Road. I'll call on my way home.'

'All right,' Wincey said uncertainly. 'I'll tell her to expect you.'

He stood watching her as she led the girl away. She could feel his eyes burning into her back. Suddenly she felt nervous and upset, but she didn't know why.

20

'It wasn't the old doctor,' Wincey explained to Granny and Teresa. 'It was his son.'

'Ye knew fine ah didnae want a visit.'

'I told him, but he insisted. What could I do? He passes here on his way home, he said.'

'Ah dinnae like the sound o' him.'

'He's good looking, Granny. Strong chin and very dark eyes.'

'Oh yes?' Teresa laughed. 'Are you sure it's Granny he's coming to see?'

Wincey's heart began to thump but it wasn't with pleasure. She didn't want any man to be interested in her. She didn't want anything to do with men. She could cope with them in the line of business, but that was all.

'Here, Granny, would you look at her blushing,' Teresa said. 'Maybe she's found a sweetheart at last.'

'Teresa, don't be ridiculous,' Wincey snapped. 'I've only seen the man once and he's a doctor.'

'A doctor's still a man, dear, and you know you can call me a hopeless romantic if you like, but I do believe in love at first sight.'

'For goodness' sake,' Wincey groaned, and left the kitchen.

In the privacy of her room, she took deep, calming breaths. There was absolutely no need for her to feel threatened, she kept telling herself. She had just managed to calm herself, and was on her way back to the kitchen, when the doorbell jangled. As she was nearest to the door, she was forced to go and open it. Doctor Houston towered in the doorway.

'Good evening, Doctor,' Wincey said stiffly. 'Do come in.'

He followed her into the kitchen. 'Mrs Gourlay senior and Mrs Teresa Gourlay,' she introduced. 'Granny, this is the doctor I was telling you about.'

Doctor Houston nodded a greeting to Teresa, then he went over to crouch down beside Granny and gently took one of her swollen hands in his. Then he looked down at her feet.

'Your ankles and feet look awfully painful too, Mrs Gourlay.'

'Och, ah'm sore aw over, Doctor. Even ma jaws. Ah cannae even eat wi' ma teeth in nowadays. Ah cannae walk or do nothin'. An' tae think ah wis aye that active. If ye'd seen me a few years ago, ye wouldnae huv recognised me.'

'Yes,' Teresa agreed, 'Granny was out there marching behind Johnny Maclean. She was in the middle of the riot in George Square as well. You wouldn't be born then, Doctor, but maybe you'd have heard of it.'

The doctor smiled. 'Oh, I was born then, all right. And I remember it very well.'

Granny said, 'It wis the polis that started the riot. They charged at a crowd of unarmed men, women an' weans. But ah got a hold o' wan o' the polis an' me an' some other women stripped him naked. Mair than wan o' the polis, in fact, by the end o' it. By Jove, that done for them. They didnae know where tae put themselves.'

Doctor Houston laughed. 'Good for you, Mrs Gourlay. I like a woman of spirit. Now, I'll tell you what I'd like to do to help you.'

'Och, ah've got a big enough stock o' painkillers as it is.'

'No, I didn't mean that. There are other drugs. I'd like to try dealing with that inflammation in another way. There's quite a variety of new treatments. I believe some of them would help you, including diets and special baths. But for that you really need to be in hospital and have full time supervision and nursing.'

Granny looked startled and frightened. 'Ye're no' puttin' me away intae any hospital. Ah'm stayin' here in ma ain hame.'

Wincey said, 'It wouldn't be forever, Granny, and if it would really help you—'

'You shut yer mooth. Ye've nae right. Ye're no' even a Gourlay.'

The doctor flicked a curious look at Wincey before saying, 'Only for a few weeks. Think of the relief of pain. You'd be made so much more comfortable. I promise you, you'd be well looked after.'

'Ma Teresa looks aifter me well enough. Ye wouldnae want tae get rid o' me, would ye, hen?'

'No, of course not, Granny. Nobody wants to get rid of you, dear.' Teresa turned to the doctor. 'I'll do my best. She would be so unhappy away from the family.'

'Well,' Doctor Houston said reluctantly, 'I still think she would be better in hospital. But if that's how you both feel, I'll write a prescription for the new treatment and I'll pop in as often as I can to keep a check on her.'

'Thank you, Doctor,' Teresa said.

But Wincey detected a note of fatigue in Teresa's voice and couldn't help thinking that Granny was being selfish, expecting Teresa to cope with so much. It was bad enough with two of them—and often Erchie as well—struggling to lift and lay the old woman. Wincey made a decision.

'Doctor, would it be possible for a nurse to come in, say a couple of hours—perhaps twice every day—to help Teresa. I could afford to pay for a nurse so there wouldn't be a financial problem.'

Doctor Houston nodded. 'Yes, that would be better. Leave it to me. I'll arrange it as soon as possible.'

'Dinnae bother askin' me of course,' Granny said. 'Ah'm just a poor auld woman.'

'It's more for Teresa's sake,' Wincey said firmly. 'She'll be having to go to hospital soon if we go on much longer as we have been. She needs help.'

'Aye, well . . .' Granny said, slightly mollified. 'For aw the help she gets frae you!'

'Now, now, Granny. That's not fair. You know fine Wincey does her best to help whenever she's at home. She's working all day, don't forget.'

'Aye, well . . .' Granny muttered.

'Two nurses would really be needed,' the doctor said. 'I was thinking especially of getting you in and out of the bath.'

'Two nurses!' Granny echoed incredulously. 'Huv they nothin' better tae dae?'

The doctor laughed. Then to Wincey he said, 'Will that be all right with you?'

'Yes, of course.'

At the outside door, he turned to Wincey and asked, 'May I ask what relation you are to the Gourlays?'

'I'm sorry. I'd rather not answer that question.'

The doctor shrugged. 'Very well.' But his eyes betrayed his interest. Wincey closed the door after he'd gone and leaned against it for a minute. Curiosity about her real identity was the last thing she wanted. She wished she'd thought of some imaginary explanation that he could have accepted, and then forgotten about. He looked a man who would not rest until he got to the bottom of any mystery, medical or otherwise. She felt annoyed, as well as afraid.

As if she hadn't enough to worry her at the moment with Charlotte and Malcy. In the first place, Charlotte had taken a very large sum of money from the business in order to buy the villa in Broomfield Road. Renting a house wasn't good enough for Malcy. Wincey hadn't said anything at the time, for Charlotte's sake. Charlotte had been so happy in her lovely home with her loving husband, and still was. But expenses of one kind or another were piling up, just as Wincey had always feared. A time would come when she'd have to say something, for the sake of the business if nothing else.

'Well,' said Granny, when Wincey returned to the kitchen, 'ye've opened a right can o' worms.'

Wincey secretly agreed with her but she was thinking of a different can of worms from Granny.

'It's a miracle ah'm no' gettin' pit away. If it had been up tae you, ah wid. Bad enough strangers invadin' the house. God knows whit they'll dae tae me.'

'They'll make you feel better and more comfortable, Granny,' Wincey said. 'And you'll soon get to know them and look forward to their daily visits. Try to think of Teresa, Granny. If she loses any more weight, there'll be nothing left of her.'

'Aye, well . . .'

While Teresa was filling the kettle at the sink and Wincey was getting cups and saucers out of the press, Teresa whispered, 'Thank you, dear.'

Wincey felt a wave of gladness then. She had done something that would, she felt sure, be of real help to Teresa. To herself too, of course. They both missed the assistance of Florence and the twins. Now, to come home from a hard day's work every day to face the struggle of looking after all the old woman's needs was proving to be extremely exhausting. It was far worse for Teresa, who was tied to

345

Granny the whole day.

'I see what you mean,' Teresa said, as she poured the tea. 'About him being good looking. If I was a bit younger I'd fall for him myself.'

'I haven't fallen for him,' Wincey protested. 'Will you get that idea out of your head. I'm perfectly satisfied and happy with my life as it is now. I like to be independent, and you've said yourself often enough in the past, I'm a loner. That's exactly what I'd like to remain, Teresa.'

'Yes, dear, you may believe that now. But one day you're bound to—'

'No, I'm not,' Wincey interrupted. 'Now, can we please change the subject.'

Teresa helplessly shook her head. 'You're a funny girl at times. Most girls would jump at the chance of a good looking doctor. He finds you attractive, dear. I could see.'

'Teresa!' Wincey groaned.

'All right, all right,' Teresa capitulated. 'Not another word.'

They sat in silence for a minute or two, sipping their tea and gathering strength for the back-breaking task of getting Granny undressed, wheeled to the bathroom, lifted in and out of the bath, then lowered at last on to her hurly bed.

21

There could be no hiding from the fact that the doctor was going above and beyond the call of duty. He was visiting the Gourlay house practically every day on his way home. Erchie had eventually remarked, 'Ah think he's adopted this place as his second home.' The doctor now regularly stayed to enjoy the cups of tea and home-baked scones that Teresa offered him. He now called everyone by their first names, except Granny, who was just Granny to everyone.

Teresa widened her eyes in mock innocence at Erchie's remark. 'I wonder why, Erchie. Is it my scones, do you think?'

'Aye, well,' Granny said, 'it's no' me. Ah hardly get a second glance noo. It's time that you'—she glanced across at Wincey—'woke up an' put the poor fella oot o' his misery.'

'His misery?' Wincey said. ' He looks happy enough to me. And I never asked him to keep coming here. It's ridiculous.'

'Now, now, Wincey. Do you not think it could be you being ridiculous, dear? What can you possibly have against that nice, kindly, good looking man?'

'Nothing. Nothing.' Wincey cried out in desperation. 'I just . . . I just can't be doing with it.'

Seeing Wincey's genuine distress, Teresa asked worriedly, 'With what, dear?'

'I can't talk about it. I'm going out before he comes.' She got up and went for her coat.

'Wincey,' Teresa called. 'It's blowing a blizzard. You can't go out.'

But the front door had banged shut and Wincey was away.

Granny said, 'There's something far wrong wi' that girl.'

'I think you might be right, Granny. I'm really worried about her.'

Erchie said, 'Aye, it's no' natural, the way she works aw the time an' never goes oot tae enjoy hersel' like other lassies. An' ah'll tell ye another thing—she cannae thole bein' touched.'

'How do you mean?' Teresa asked in surprise. 'I've never noticed anything different about her there. She's always been very demonstrative with me. More so often than Florence or the twins. You've surely seen her giving me a hug often enough.'

'Aye,' Erchie said, 'but no' me. Huv ye ever seen her gie *me* a hug? An' ah've long since learned no' tae touch her. Even if ah put ma hand on her shoulder, she shrinks away as if ah'm gonnae attack her or somethin'. Even after aw this time an' her knowin' fine ah widnae hurt a hair on her heid, any mair than ah wid ma ain flesh an' blood.'

'I wonder,' Teresa said thoughtfully, 'if you've maybe solved the mystery there, Erchie.'

'How dae ye mean, hen?'

'I wonder if poor Wincey was attacked before she came here. Remember how Florence found her crying in the street, poor wee soul. Maybe that's why she was crying.'

'Aye, right enough, hen. That'd explain a lot o' things about oor Wincey, right enough. It must have been some swine o' a man as well. She's fine wi' everybody else, but see if any man even looks at her in what she thinks is the wrong way, she either explodes wi' anger at him, or gets off her mark, just like she's done the night.'

'Oh dear, poor Wincey. I wonder what we should do, Erchie.'

Granny was quick to answer. 'Keep yer neb oot o' other folks' business.'

'How can you say that, Granny? Don't you care about Wincey?'

'Ah'm sayin' that because ah know the chances are ye'll just make things worse for Wincey. Ye're mair likely tae frighten the life oot o' her than be any help tae her.'

'You don't know that at all, Granny.'

'Ah know,' Erchie said. 'How about askin' the doctor for advice? That's his job, helping folk.'

'Huh,' Granny snorted. 'Wincey's gonnae love the pair o' ye fur that!'

'Now, now, Granny. She doesn't need to know. This would be a good chance tonight while she's not here. I'll have a quiet word with Doctor Houston. It can't do any harm.'

348

'Huh! Did ye come up the Clyde in a banana boat?'

'Come on, Ma. Teresa's just trying her best tae help Wincey.'

It was then the door bell rang.

'That'll be him.' Teresa rose in some agitation. 'Should I take him through to the room, do you think? Have a private word there?'

'Aye, you dae that, hen. Then Granny'll no' get the chance tae poke her nose in.'

'Me! Poke ma nose in?' Granny howled. 'Whit dae ye think she's doin'?'

Teresa hurried from the kitchen.

'Oh, come in, Doctor. Eh, would you mind coming through to the sitting room first? I'd like a wee word in private.'

He made a gesture with one hand to indicate that Teresa should lead the way. Once in the room, Teresa sat down and asked him to do the same. For a moment, there was silence and then Doctor Houston said gently, 'Would you like to tell me what's worrying you, Teresa?'

Teresa nodded. 'It's about Wincey.'

'Oh?' His expression, his whole body, tensed with interest. 'What about Wincey?'

'Well, it's difficult to explain, and of course we could be wrong . . .'

'About what, Teresa?' he prompted.

'Well, we've come to notice over the years that she keeps clear of men. Won't have anything to do with them. She even dislikes my son-in-law, and a nicer man and a better husband to my daughter you couldn't meet. The only man she gets on with is Erchie, but even he tells me he daren't touch her, take her arm or anything. It seems to make her frightened.' Teresa hesitated. 'We've been wondering . . . We've wondered if she had a bad experience at some time in her young life.'

Another silence followed. Then Doctor Houston said, 'First of all, Teresa, can I ask how you came to know Wincey? She's not a relation, is she?'

Teresa shook her head. 'Will you promise to keep this strictly between you and me, Doctor. She'd never forgive me otherwise, and maybe we'd lose her forever. I couldn't bear that—she's like a daughter to me.'

'What passes between doctor and patient is always strictly confidential, Teresa. You have my word on that.'

'Well,' Teresa began unhappily, 'years ago, Florence found her sitting in the street crying and brought her home with her. She said that Wincey's mother and father had been killed in an accident and she'd nobody. So the authorities were going to put her in an orphanage—or the workhouse, Florence said. But I have to confess, Doctor, that Florence used to be troubled with a terrible imagination. She's mostly grown out of it now but at the time—'

'What did Wincey say?' the doctor interrupted. 'Did she do along with this story?'

'The poor wee thing was in such a state, I think she would have agreed with anything as long as we didn't put her out in the street again.'

'And she's never spoken about her background since?'

'Not a word. She immediately clams up if we mention it, or ask her any questions. We've given up trying. We're just glad to accept her as one of the family. But now we're getting really worried about her.' Teresa avoided his eyes for a moment. 'If you'll forgive me, Doctor, she seems to have got worse since you've been calling so often. Tonight she ran out in all this weather, just so that she wouldn't be here when you arrived.'

The doctor stared at Teresa in silence for what seemed a very long time. Then he said, 'Leave this with me just now, Teresa. I'll have to give this matter some serious thought, and also make a few discreet enquiries.'

'Oh, Doctor, please don't let Wincey or anybody . . . *anybody*,' she repeated, 'know anything about this.'

'I assure you, you've no need to worry. I'll be very discreet, very discreet indeed. Rest assured, Teresa, this is strictly between you and me.'

Teresa sighed. 'Erchie and Granny know I was going to talk to you. Erchie won't say anything, but I'd better warn Granny.'

Doctor Houston smiled. 'Tell her I'll pack her off to the hospital if she says one word. That'll do the trick.'

Teresa rose. 'Thank you so much, Doctor. I feel a bit better now that I've confided in you.'

He rose too. 'I'd better say good evening to Granny. And I'd especially appreciate my usual cup of tea tonight.'

'Come on through, then, and I'll put the kettle on.'

Granny greeted him with, 'Aye, well, huv ye had a good gossip then? Are ye gonnae interfere in Wincey's life as well?'

'I don't gossip, Granny,' the doctor said with the patient good humour he always showed the old woman, 'and my concern is for the happiness and well-being of my patients, especially you.'

'Aye, well, you watch ye dinnae open a can o' worms that'll destroy oor Wincey.'

Doctor Houston gazed at her very seriously. 'Granny, listen to me now. I'll do nothing, nothing, do you hear, that would ever hurt Wincey in any way. Trust me. And I want to be able to trust you. I want you to promise me that you won't mention to Wincey anything that's been done or said in her absence this evening. It's especially important that Wincey does not know that Teresa has spoken to me about her. Do you promise me?'

'Aye, well, ah suppose so.'

'Right.' He smiled again. 'Now, where's my tea?'

22

Time passed and they heard nothing from Doctor Houston. Christmas came and went, then Hogmanay was nearly upon them and still he hadn't made an appearance. There were no more visits, either to see Granny or for any other reason. They all wondered about this. Wincey thought, with a mixture of sadness and relief, that he had given up on her at last. Teresa, Erchie and Granny wondered if he was busy finding out about Wincey's past.

Eventually Teresa asked the nurses when Doctor Houston was coming back to see Granny. The nurses said that they were to report regularly on Granny's condition and if the improvements she was now enjoying ceased, or if in their judgement she needed a visit, they were to contact the surgery.

'We haven't of course, because Granny is so much better. All she needs is her present treatment to continue. Anyway, involving him would be a last resort as far as we are concerned. Doctor Houston has enough on his plate.'

'How do you mean?' Teresa asked.

'He's had a very heavy workload because Doctor Houston senior became ill a while ago, and then started getting worse and worse. And well, I'm sorry to say he died yesterday morning.'

'Oh dear, I'm so sorry to hear that. We knew the old man was semi-retired but just thought it was his age. We've known him for years. Oh, I am sorry.'

'He wisnae a bad soul,' Granny conceded, 'but aw he ever asked wis . . .'

'Yes, all right, Granny. We know all about that,' Teresa hastily interrupted. 'It's a bad time of year to suffer a bereavement too. It won't be a happy New Year for Doctor Houston.'

As soon as Wincey came in from work, Teresa told her the news. 'Such a nice old man too,' she added.

'Aye,' Granny said, 'but aw he ever did was ask if yer bowels had moved an' stuck a—'

'Yes, all right, Granny, you've told us that before.'

Granny's memory was beginning to fail her and she often forgot she'd already said something. Or she couldn't remember what she wanted to say. But physically she was a good deal better. The swelling of her hands and feet had gone down and as a result she wasn't in nearly so much pain.

'Ah just wish ah'd got the son earlier. If ah had, ah might no' huv been stuck in this chair the day.'

One of the nurses said, 'I believe Doctor Houston junior worked in the Royal before. He came into the practice to help his father once the old man began to go downhill.'

'Actually,' Wincey said, 'I found out earlier on today. The obituary was in today's *Glasgow Herald*. I was going to tell you.'

The nurses were ready to leave. They had settled Granny in her hurly bed although it was, as usual, far too early for bed time. Granny had indignantly—and loudly—objected at first.

'Ah'm no' a wee wean that has tae be in bed the back o' six o'clock.'

'You can sit up in bed for as long as you like,' the nurse told her, 'but at least you're in bed. This way it'll save Teresa and Wincey struggling to undress you and get you down.'

Granny grumbled and muttered, but eventually accepted defeat. The nurses had become too valuable and important in Granny's life for her to want to cross them. Often she looked quite anxious if they were late in arriving. They came every morning to get her up and bathe her, and then every evening to settle her down. She even had once admitted to Teresa, 'You aye did yer best, hen. Ah know that. But by Jove, them nurses really help me. They make me feel that much better. Ah don't know what ah'd do without them now.'

Tonight, however, she had been—as she told the nurses—'black affronted'. 'It's Hogmanay. Ah cannae be sittin' here in bed an' aw ma clothes off when the first foots arrive.'

'All the more need that we get you settled,' the nurse said. 'Nobody would be able to do anything for you by the time they have a few drinks. You're wearing your nice shawl—you look fine.'

And so Granny accepted defeat again.

Teresa sighed. 'It'll kind of dampen any enjoyment of our Hogmanay thinking of the sad time it is for poor Doctor Houston.'

'Och, he'll huv his family around him for support,' Granny told her. 'An' ah'm sure he widnae want us tae be down in the dumps. Our time'll come soon enough.'

'I don't think he has any family. He was an only child, as far as I know. And his mother's long dead.'

'Och, there'll be aunties an' uncles an' cousins. They aw come oot the woodwork at funerals. It wis the only time ah used tae see aw ma relations.'

'I suppose you're right, Granny. I wonder if I should ask Mr McCluskey to come in for a wee while. I feel sorry for him in this freezing weather. He has to sit out in that draughty close to have his smoke. I've asked him more than once to come in here to enjoy his pipe but I think he was frightened he'd get a row from her.'

'Mind he did come in once,' Granny said.

'Yes, but she was away in town that day.'

'Here,' Granny suddenly chortled. 'Ah could solve his problem. Aw he needs tae dae is get merrit tae me. Ah'd soon sort that wan oot.'

Wincey laughed. 'I believe you'd do it if you were given half a chance, Granny.'

'Her trouble,' Granny said, 'is she cares more about her bloomin' hoose than her auld father. Aye scrubbin' an' polishin'.'

'I know,' Teresa agreed. 'I even saw her out the back sweeping the middens. And dusting the railings. Dusting the railings! Would you credit it?'

Granny rolled her eyes.

Teresa said, 'Mrs Chalmers is coming and Davy and Jock from up the stairs. I asked young Mrs Beresford but she said she was going to stay with her folks over New Year. They come from somewhere over in the West End.'

The mention of the West End startled Wincey but she managed to calm herself, Hundreds, if not thousands of people lived in the West End. Mrs Beresford's parents would no doubt live in the tenements, not in one of the big villas. Also, Mrs Beresford hardly ever saw anyone in the Gourlay house, far less spoke to them, so how could she know about anybody's background?

'I think she must be a young widow,' Teresa said, 'and she's had to go back out to work. She's always dashing away, isn't she? Never has time to talk.'

'Or disnae want tae,' Granny said. 'Stuck up, probably.'

'No, dear. I don't think so. She's got quite a nice smile. Just a bit harassed. I wonder what it is she does. Anyway, she'll not be here for Hogmanay.'

'Did ye warn Malcy nae tae first foot us, him wi' his fair heid?'

'Yes, don't worry, Granny. He knows it's bad luck. No, Davy from up the stairs is dark enough. I've told him to knock the door first.'

Wincey was thinking that Malcy could bring them enough bad luck without being their first foot.

'Well,' Teresa said to Wincey. 'We've had our tea, dear. Yours is in the oven. This is my day for acting house proud. That's why Erchie is away out the road. It's bad luck not to have everything spotless to greet the new year.'

Wincey used a tea towel to lift her plate of stew and dumplings from the oven. Then she settled at the table to enjoy the meal.

'Wait till I've finished this,' she told Teresa, 'and I'll give you a hand. Although the place looks spotless already.'

'Yes, well, I've cleaned and dusted the rooms and the lobby. But I've still this floor to scrub. I'll leave emptying the ash pan to the last minute. Maybe you could do the brasses, dear.'

'I could scrub the floor as well.'

'No, no, dear. I'll manage the floor. It won't take a minute. But I must change that bed first. Could you go through and change yours?'

'As soon as I finish my tea.'

By eleven o'clock the house was sparkling and Teresa and Wincey had spread a crisp white tablecloth over the table and were now setting it with plates of fruitcake, cherry cake, Madeira cake, black bun and shortbread. Erchie was laying out the bottles and glasses.

'Whisky for the men,' he said, 'an' plenty beer. Sherry an' gin for the women.'

'I hope you've got soft drinks as well, dear.'

'Soft drinks?' Erchie cried out in disbelief. 'Who's goin' tae want soft drinks?'

'I mean to put in the gin, Erchie, like tonic water.'

'Oh aye, ah've got some o' that.' He rubbed his hands in glee as he surveyed the table. 'A good spread, eh?' He turned to Granny. 'You look grand as well, hen.'

Granny's hair was well slicked down and held in place not by her usual brown kirby-grip, but a fancy one with a sprinkle of tiny diamante. The new grip had been one of her Christmas presents from Wincey, who had also given her the beautiful crocheted shawl that was now draped around her plump shoulders.

She looked pleased at Erchie's compliment but she said, 'But son, dae ah no' look daft sittin' here in ma bed? What'll folk think?'

'Och Ma, ye're an auld woman, an' ye're no' well. Everybody'll just admire ye for bein' sae spunky. Relax an' enjoy yersel'.'

'Aye, well, put another cushion at ma back, would ye?'

'Sure, Ma.'

The fire crackled brightly as they settled around it, all gazing up at the alarm clock on the mantelpiece as it ticked away the last few seconds of 1937. Then suddenly Erchie got up and rushed over to tug the kitchen window open. Everybody for miles around was doing the same thing, allowing the old year out and the new year in, and hopefully with it, good fortune. There were shouts of 'A Guid New Year' all around, both outside and inside the kitchen.

The new year greetings inside the kitchen, however, could hardly be heard for the riotous sounds from the river of the ships' hooters. Then there was a loud battering at the door. Teresa ran to open it wide and welcome in their first foot.

'Davy, Happy New Year.' She gave him a hug and a kiss. Davy grinned and blushed and handed over the lucky piece of coal, the packet of shortbread and his bottle of whisky.

'No dear, you keep a hold of your bottle so that you can offer Erchie and the other men a drink from it.'

'Oh, aye, right.' Davy was obviously not very used to socialising. Either that or he was a bit shy. Or both.

Behind him crowded Jock and Mrs Chalmers and, coming up noisily behind, Mrs McGregor from the old close, and Mrs Donaldson and her two plump bespectacled daughters, Mary and Joan, who were famous locally for their romantic but unintentionally hilarious duets. The merry crowd made for the kitchen where they knew the table would be loaded with the usual festive fare. Everyone made a great fuss of Granny and plied her with drink from each of their bottles. Soon Granny was insisting on treating the company to a song.

As Erchie said next day, she was giving it such big licks, she nearly fell out of the bed. Even Wincey had become a little tipsy but, although she laughed with the rest and joined in the community singing, she felt secretly weighed down by sadness. She wondered how her mother and father would be bringing in the New Year and her brother and her grandmother. Normally she never allowed herself to think about them. Now she realised that although she had adopted a new family and loved them dearly, her feelings for her original family were still there, buried deep in her heart. She could have wept, yet no-one noticed that anything was wrong.

Afterwards, Wincey blamed the drink and vowed to avoid alcohol in future. She had been reminded of what Granny had once said when talking of how she'd felt when she'd lost her other children with the fever. 'Ma hairt wis sair.' Wincey's heart had felt sore too.

1938

23

Wincey was about to enter the office when she heard something most unusual. It was Charlotte's voice raised in—perhaps not anger exactly—but certainly acute exasperation. She was saying, 'I couldn't give you a week's wages in advance, even if I wanted to. Wincey keeps the books and sees to the wages. Anyway, Malcy, what have you done with all your money? You get paid enough, and it's not as if you put any of it into the housekeeping. I'm paying for everything now. No, I'm not going to be soft-soaped any more, Malcy. We're already taking more money than we should out of the business. No, Malcy, please . . .'

Wincey felt self-conscious standing outside the office door. Everybody at the machines behind her could see her. It might look odd if she suddenly walked away. She turned the door handle and went in. Malcy had his arms around Charlotte and was trying to kiss her.

'Oh, sorry,' Wincey said and made to leave again, but Charlotte called out, 'No, it's all right, Wincey. Come in. Malcy was just leaving. I'll see you when I get home, Malcy.'

His pale eyes were cold with annoyance as they met Wincey's for a brief second, but he smiled back at Charlotte before leaving.

'See you later then.'

'Trouble?' Wincey asked after he'd gone.

'You'd like that, wouldn't you?' Charlotte said with some bitterness. 'You've always had it in for Malcy.'

'No!' Wincey protested. 'I've never wanted trouble for you, Charlotte. I swear it. Or for Malcy. But it's his gambling, Charlotte. That's what's always worried me. And it's got worse, we both know it has.'

Charlotte avoided Wincey's eyes and her voice was barely audible. 'I'll speak to him.'

For all the good that'll do, Wincey thought, but decided it would be wiser to let the subject drop—for the moment, at least.

Later, Charlotte said she was going out to the shops for something for Malcy's dinner. Wincey always went home in the middle of the day for a bite to eat. She had been out in Springburn Road when she remembered the pair of shoes to be mended that she'd left in the office. She wanted to hand them in to the cobbler on the way to the Balgray. She hurried back into the factory.

The girls were all huddled at one corner of the machine hall—chatting, drinking tea and eating sandwiches. They didn't notice her reappearance. She went through to the office and, on opening the door, nearly bumped into Malcy who was coming out. Before she could say anything, he said, 'Just looking for Charlotte.' And he was off.

Wincey picked up the shopping bag that contained her shoes and then hesitated. A thought had struck her. At first she dismissed it with the unsaid words, 'Surely not.' But then she opened her desk drawer and saw right away that the petty cash box was empty. There had been quite a few pounds in it that morning. Wincey stood looking at the empty box, inwardly groaning and wondering what she should do now. It was one thing Malcy trying to wheedle extra money out of Charlotte. But this was different. This was thieving. She thought of confronting Malcy—privately and discreetly perhaps. She suspected though that Malcy would immediately act the injured victim and go straight to Charlotte. He would complain that Wincey was always trying to get at him.

He was a master at appearing the hurt innocent. Wincey often thought he should have been in the acting profession—he even had the looks for it, with his curly blond hair and even features. She tried to imagine ways she could frighten him, warn him, but couldn't think of anything that would work. In the end she decided that, for now at least, she'd just have to depend on Charlotte's business sense. Surely Charlotte would call a halt if things began to get too serious. Hadn't she been trying to do that when she had been interrupted in the office? Wincey felt less anxious when she remembered what Charlotte had been saying to Malcy. She had used such an unusually strong tone of voice. Yes, Wincey assured herself, Charlotte was too good a business woman to allow anyone—even Malcy—to ruin what she'd worked so hard to build up.

So Wincey said nothing to Malcy about the stolen money. But she couldn't resist giving him some cold and knowing looks. Even when he and Charlotte came visiting, she never addressed a word to him if she could avoid it. When Charlotte invited the family to Sunday lunch in the villa, it was as much as Wincey could do to be civil to Malcy. She hated him for what he was doing to Charlotte, as well as what he might do to the business.

Charlotte's normally sweet, open face had developed a strained and worried look. Even Erchie had begun to notice it.

'Are ye aw right, hen?' he asked on one occasion. 'Ye're no' lookin' so well.'

'I'm fine, Daddy. I just get a headache now and again. Maybe I need my eyes tested.'

'Maybe ye should get Doctor Houston tae gie ye a wee check over, hen. Jist in case yer sair heid's caused by somethin' else.'

'Yes, all right, Daddy. Maybe I'll do that.'

Wincey kept quiet, but not without some difficulty. She was thinking—what use was a doctor? It was a good divorce lawyer that Charlotte needed.

Then for a time, all seemed well. Charlotte looked more relaxed and happy. On catching Wincey staring at her one day, she laughed and said, 'No need to look so perplexed, Wincey. I told you I'd speak to Malcy, and it worked, bless him. He's been as good as gold. I'm so happy, Wincey. I'm as much in love with him now as I've always been, and he with me. Aren't we lucky?'

Wincey smiled and nodded, and Charlotte went on, 'So many couples get into a bad patch in their marriage and instead of discussing the problem with each other and trying to sort it out, they just allow things to go from bad to worse. I always think it's so sad when that happens. Love's such a precious thing. I only hope one day you'll find the same happiness as I have, Wincey.'

God forbid, Wincey thought, but she tried to feel glad for Charlotte. She tried to believe that Malcy had changed. But somehow she couldn't convince herself of his sudden conversion.

Then one day, after Teresa had hurled Granny down to the Co-op to do some shopping, Granny burst out, 'Here, Wincey. Ye'll never guess whit we saw the day!'

'Now, now, Granny.' Teresa appeared very anxious to stop Granny in mid flow. 'We could have been mistaken. Drink up your tea, dear.'

Granny was not so easily put off her stroke, however. 'Malcy, comin' oot o' Mrs O'Donnell's place.'

'Who's Mrs O'Donnell?' Wincey asked.

'Och, it's well seen ye hide yersel' away in that factory too much. Everybody knows Mrs O'Donnell.'

'Granny, dear. I've got nice chocolate digestives. Would you like one to dip in your tea?'

Granny cocked her head in Teresa's direction. 'She's black affronted, an' nae wonder. Naebody in oor family his ever gone tae a moneylender before. Never in oor lives! We'd rather starve first. Right capitalist rascals. Ah remember an auld neighbour o' mine was ruined by the wicked interest they charged her. She ended up committin' suicide ower the heid o' it.'

Wincey looked over at Teresa and Teresa said, 'It might have been somebody else.'

'It was Malcy!' Granny insisted. 'Ye know fine it was Malcy.'

'I mean, he could have been seeing somebody else. He could have been visiting a friend up that close.'

'Pull the other wan,' Granny said. 'Ah'm no as daft as ah look!'

Teresa gazed worriedly over at Wincey. 'Is the business in any difficulty, dear?'

'No, the business is fine.'

'Well, I don't understand.'

'I do,' Wincey said. 'He's a gambler. He always has been.'

'Oh, but . . . Erchie likes a wee flutter as well, but I don't think he would ever . . . I mean, I don't understand.'

'There's a big difference, Teresa, between the odd wee flutter, or even a regular wee flutter, and a compulsive gambler.'

'Aye,' Granny said, 'Wincey's right. It's like an alkie. An' an alkie never can jist take wan wee drink. He's aye tae scoff the bottle.'

'Oh dear. Do you think Charlotte knows?'

'She knows he's that kind of gambler but she thinks he's cured. I don't think she knows about the moneylender.'

'Oh dear. And Malcy's such a nice man. And I'm sure he loves Charlotte. She certainly loves him. I hope this isn't going to cause any trouble between them.'

She turned to Granny. 'Now you listen to me, Granny. Don't you dare upset Charlotte by letting on about this. Do you hear me?'

'Oh aye,' Granny said. 'There'll be nae need for any o' us tae put oor oar in. She'll find out soon enough for hersel'.'

'Maybe he'll have a big win soon,' Teresa said without much conviction, 'and be able to sort himself out.'

'Huh!' Granny gave Teresa a sarcastic look. 'Mair like some o' Mrs O'Donnell's hard men'll sort him out, if ye ask me.'

'We're not asking you, Granny,' Teresa said with unusual sharpness, 'so just keep quiet.'

Granny lapsed into a huff. 'Ye'll be auld yersel' some day.'

Again Wincey was in a quandary. She asked Teresa for advice.

'No, dear,' Teresa said firmly. 'I don't think any of us should interfere. It's between Malcy and Charlotte. They should be left to sort it out themselves and in their own way.'

All very well, thought Wincey, but it could involve the business. It was already doing so. However, she took Teresa's advice and just hoped that Malcy and Charlotte would be able to sort themselves out.

Anyway, just shortly after that, she had something more to worry her—even closer to home. Doctor Houston turned up again. Teresa and Erchie had gone to the Princes Cinema and she had been in the middle of reading to Granny from Granny's favourite paper, *The People's Friend*. Although Granny always insisted it was a lot of sentimental rubbish, and it was really Teresa who liked it.

After Doctor Houston's usual chat with Granny, Wincey saw him to the door. There he said, 'Could you come to the surgery tomorrow on your way home from work, Wincey?'

'Why?' Wincey said abruptly.

He smiled. 'There's no need to look so scared. I just want a little chat about Granny and the family. There's just one or two problems needing to be discussed.'

'Oh, all right,' Wincey said. She thought it might be about Charlotte and Malcy. Maybe Charlotte had been seeking the doctor's advice.

The next evening, when she arrived at the surgery, she was the last patient to be seen. Even the receptionist had left by the time Doctor Houston ushered her into his consulting room. Wincey suddenly felt nervous. More than that. As she passed close to the doctor in the doorway, she felt sick with apprehension. Especially when he took her by the arm and led her across to a mirror hanging on one of the walls.

'Look into that, Wincey. What do you see?'

She saw, standing behind her, a tall, broad shouldered frame, a handsome face, straight black hair and very dark eyes.

'I don't need to look in a mirror to see you,' she said. 'What's the idea?'

'The idea wasn't to look at me, but at yourself.'

'Why?'

'To see for yourself your white, frightened face. And I can feel you trembling. As a doctor, I have to ask myself why.'

She shrugged. 'I didn't come here to talk about myself.'

'Don't you think it's time you did?'

'I don't know what you mean.'

'Wincey, part of my training was to observe people, and I've been observing *you*. I wanted to help you, and so I've been trying to think, first of all, of why you are like this. I have, as a result, been making a few discreet enquiries.'

Wincey felt faint. 'My God,' she thought, 'my God.' She had to sit down. The nearest chair was one in front of Doctor Houston's desk. He went round and sat behind the desk. She felt trapped, like a wild animal . . . too afraid to move. She looked over the desk at the man sitting there . . . he was wearing a white coat and he had a stethoscope hanging around his neck . . . she fixed her eyes on the stethoscope, trying desperately not to faint.

24

Virginia sat in silence, staring dully at Nicholas and Mathieson. They were talking about Sigmund Freud, the founder of psycho-analysis. The Nazis had been persecuting Freud for some time.

'It's a disgrace,' Mathieson said. 'A frail old man like that being hounded from pillar to post. A man of ideas. The Nazis couldn't put up with that, of course. Not in a Jew anyway.'

'But at least he's had permission to come to Britain to live,' Nicholas said. 'And his family and some of his students as well. He'll be all right here. Thank God for Roosevelt's intervention, he'd never have got an exit visa otherwise.'

'Yes, but what about all the other Jews who haven't been able to get special permission, Nicholas? America and Britain have known all about them for years, but what have we done about it? Even the Pope hasn't raised his voice in protest or tried to defend the Jews or anyone else in Nazi Germany. On the contrary, the only people who ever raise their voices against fascists are the ordinary working folk. Look how they saw Mosley off—and not only in London. They chased him off Glasgow Green.'

Nicholas grinned, remembering. 'Yes, good old Glaswegians. That was a sight worth seeing.'

Virginia thought, 'I might as well not be here.' They were two of a kind, Nicholas and Mathieson. Oh, they looked very different but they were both men of words, and both were equally obsessive. How ironic that she had chosen to marry each of them. Talk about out of the frying pan into the fire! At least Nicholas had been a better lover than Mathieson—much more romantic. Her eyes glazed, remembering how they'd danced naked in the woods and made passionate love on the mossy, fragrant ground. She remembered the beautiful love poetry he'd written and read to her.

Tears began to well up in her eyes and she hastily blinked them away. They hardly ever made love now. The romance had gone. How often did they even speak to one another? Nicholas spoke far more to Mathieson. She and Nicholas had drifted far, far apart. Yet he seemed perfectly happy, sitting there relaxed and enjoying his glass of malt whisky and his conversation with Mathieson.

She was beginning to come round to Mrs Cartwright's way of thinking, or at least some way towards it. Mrs Cartwright claimed that it wasn't decent for her ex-husband to be so friendly with her husband. Certainly Virginia had begun to resent the friendship. Although she suspected that even if Mathieson never came near Kirklee Terrace again, it wouldn't make the slightest difference to her relationship with Nicholas. More than likely it would only make matters worse. Nicholas would sink into one of his silent moods, or he'd emerge from his writing room less and less.

She took a deep shuddering breath. Maybe it would be best if she just disappeared into thin air, like Wincey, never to be seen or heard of again. The thought settled like a stone in her mind, weighing her down, draining away her energy.

Nicholas was saying, 'I fancy a bite of supper, James. How about you?'

'I wouldn't mind.'

'Right. Virginia . . . Virginia,' he repeated.

'What?'

'Supper?'

She rose automatically and without saying anything, walked from the sitting room. While she did so, she had the distinct feeling that Nicholas was shaking his head. She had caught him doing it before, after she'd said or done something. He'd shake his head at Mathieson as if to say, 'See what I've to put up with?' Or 'See what I mean?' Or 'What can I do with her?'

She banged shut the sitting room door—anger and resentment had brought energy rushing back. Who did he think he was? What did they both think they bloody were? How dare they treat her like this? Let them make their own bloody supper. From the hall, she shouted back towards the sitting room, 'Make your own bloody supper.'

She went through to the spare bedroom and locked herself in. It seemed safest to be alone. Rage was building inside her, and she could not face the idea of sleeping in the same bed as Nicholas tonight. She punched the door, then leaned against it and wept. She didn't know what was happening to her life.

Next morning, Mathieson arrived on the doorstep. Nicholas was shut away in his room. Virginia turned away from the door and went through to the kitchen. Mathieson hirpled after her, his stick thumping on the hall floor. She put the kettle on and placed a couple of cups and saucers on the table.

'I hope you haven't come to give me one of your lectures, James. I'm not in the mood.'

'I have, as a matter of fact.'

'Well, you might as well leave right now. I'm sorry but—'

'You're not sorry at all,' Mathieson interrupted. 'You're wallowing in self pity. You've often used the word *obsession* about me and now Nicholas, but at least we're obsessed with something outside of ourselves. You're just self-obsessed. You can't see past yourself and your problem.'

'Is that it?'

'No, it's time you did something for others less fortunate than yourself. All right, you lost a daughter. But here you are in a comfortable—no, luxurious—home with a talented husband, a handsome son and a wealthy mother-in-law. Has it ever occurred to you that there are people out there who have lost children, but have no comfort and are struggling with a thousand other worries? Or drunken husbands who abuse them, and no money for food. Need I go on?'

'I'm sorry, but there's nothing I can do about other people.'

'Yes, you can. There are innumerable societies and charitable organisations who work to help the poor, the ill and the desolate. They're all desperate for volunteers. Seek them out. Offer your help. Do something really practical for a change. And do it now, Virginia. For your own sake, as much as anyone else's.'

'I've done my share of all that in the past. I've lived in the world of tenements and suffered poverty myself.'

'All the more reason to help now. You know what it's like. You more than most will understand. I appreciate the work you've done for me, Virginia, but by doing something like this, you'll be putting your politics into practice. You'll not only be arguing that the poor should have a better deal, you'll be at the grass roots helping them to have it. I'm sure you'd feel you were doing a worthwhile job. People like Maclean and Maxton always believed that the workers and the poor should be educated, so that they can help themselves in the fight for equality and a decent life. Both of them used their teaching skills at a practical level, and so have I. It's time now for you to do something practical, Virginia.'

She made the tea and sat down at the table. 'I'll think about it.'

'You're thinking too much, that's your trouble.'

'Oh, all right. Anything to get you off my back.'

He gave her one of his grotesque twisted smiles. 'That's my girl.'

'Shouldn't you be teaching this morning?'

'I haven't a class until eleven. I'd better be off as soon as I've finished my tea.'

After he'd gone, Mrs Rogers arrived after having packed her children off to school. She helped herself to a cup of tea and Virginia went through to the sitting room, out of her way. The sitting room was heavy with silence. Virginia went over and gazed from the window, down over Kirklee Terrace and the grassy bank onto Great Western Road.

Mathieson was right, she supposed. She was lucky in many ways. She remembered the tenement close in the Gorbals where she'd once lived with her mother and father and brothers, and her sister Rose. Poor Rose had died of tuberculosis. One brother had been killed while working in the munitions factory, the other killed in the war. When she thought of all that her poor mother had had to suffer, and yet she had kept going with such courage and unselfishness, she felt ashamed. Not only had her mother coped with all the family tragedies, but she had had to struggle with life in a terrible slum. She had to fight to rid the place of bed bugs and to slave endlessly for some level of cleanliness, not only in the room and kitchen house, but in the overflowing lavatory out on the landing.

Virginia leaned her forehead against the window. Oh, her poor mother! No doubt there had been many other working-class women like her. No doubt there still were—the unsung, unknown heroines, often with a wonderful sense of humour despite the tragedies in their lives.

Mathieson was right. For far too long, she had been blinded by self pity. She had been wallowing in it. But not any more. She was shaken by what he had said. Yes, Mathieson *was* right—she must do something.

She was suddenly impatient. Where to start though? Should she ask at the nearest church? She wasn't a churchgoer, however, and still had no inclination to become one. Nor was she a member of the Salvation Army, who did so much good work in the city. They had always been more practical and certainly more visible in the poorer districts, doing their best to help people, and *they* were courageous. Their female members with their bonnets tied under their chins did not shrink from going into the rough male bastions of pubs to collect money for good causes. Virginia, however, couldn't imagine herself either wearing the uniform, or going into the pubs. Again she felt ashamed. Where had all her courage gone? She used to have a reputation of being a really spirited young woman. Spunky was the word often used to describe her. She wasn't young any more, of course. She wasn't all that far off forty. 'Forty!' she thought incredulously. Where had all her life gone?

She forced her mind back to the problem at hand. There must be lots of charitable organisations that she could help, even if it simply meant dishing out hot soup at street corners to the unemployed and homeless. She'd seen them queuing up in the streets of poor districts and she'd heard about soup kitchens. She would phone around. She would speak to one of her Labour councillor friends. She would ask a doctor. Not her local West End doctor but a doctor from one of the poorer districts. She would talk to people at the next political meeting Mathieson organised. She had long since given up going to most of these meetings, but just this once, she would go to seek advice. There must be something worthwhile she could do, especially—as Mathieson said—with her life experience. She would not be just another middle-class do-gooder, she would know from first hand experience what it was all about.

For the first time in years, she felt drawn to go back to her roots, even just for a brief visit. On an impulse, she went for her coat and hat. It was a fur hat and the coat she put on was a rust coloured wool with a huge fur collar. She immediately took them both off again and found instead a Burberry tweed travel coat and a plain, soft brimmed hat. She decided she wouldn't take her motor car. Instead she went in search of a tram that would take her to the Gorbals.

25

He knew her real name. He'd consulted not only the police missing persons files, but those of the Salvation Army. She felt angry, as well as afraid. How dare he interfere in her life!

'You had no right!' she told him.

'I keep telling you, Wincey, I just want to help you.'

'I don't need your help.'

'I think you do.'

'I don't care what you think. I'm living a new life and I was perfectly happy until you started interfering. The last thing I want to do is go back to my old life. You say I look frightened. Nothing fills me with more fear than the thought of that.'

'Why? What happened, Wincey? It might help you to talk about it.'

'You've done enough harm as it is.'

'I've done nothing to harm you, and I've no intention of ever doing so. If you want to go on living as you are—as Wincey Gourlay—I'll respect that. And I'll also respect and keep confidential anything you tell me about yourself, or anything I already know about you.'

'What *do* you know about me, apart from my name?' She couldn't keep herself from asking the question. Nor could she control the anxiety in her voice.

'I know that your previous address was Kirklee Terrace in the West End. And your mother and father are Virginia and Nicholas Cartwright. Your grandmother and grandfather lived in Great Western Road and it was in their villa that you were last seen. It is believed that you found your grandfather dead—or the heart attack that killed him was witnessed by you—and you ran from the house in grief and panic.'

And so he knew everything—or nearly everything.

'Promise me, please, that you'll never tell anyone—*anyone*—that you know who I am, or where I am.'

'Wincey, I thought I'd already made that clear. You have my word. I swear to you that no-one, either in your past or your present life, will know one thing about you from me.'

She tried to relax. 'I need to believe you.'

'I know. And you can.'

She nodded, still wide eyed and anxious. She felt weak and trembling, as if she'd been through a terrible ordeal. Or as if she'd experienced a nightmare that she still wasn't quite able to shake off.

'I think,' the doctor said gently, 'we've talked enough for today. I'm going to drive you home now.'

'No, I'm all right.'

He smiled. 'I'm the doctor, remember, and you my dear girl are proving even more perverse and difficult than Granny.'

She couldn't help smiling herself then, despite her inward trembling. She allowed herself to be led from the room and the surgery, and helped into the doctor's car. He drove the short distance in silence. Then when they arrived at her close, he smiled at her as she was getting out of the car and said, 'Don't worry. You're perfectly safe, and you *are* going to be all right.' She nodded and hurried away into the close.

Granny had been sitting in her wheelchair at the front room window, gazing avidly at what was going on outside. 'Wis that the doctor's car ah saw you gettin' oot o'?' she bawled from the room.

Wincey called back, 'Yes, he kindly offered to drop me off on his way home.'

'Wid wan o' ye hurl me back tae the kitchen. Ah'll be losin' ma voice next. As if the power o' ma legs wisnae enough.'

Wincey answered her call and pushed the wheelchair through to the kitchen.

'You can't say you're frozen any more, Granny. That's a grand big fire in the room.'

'Aye, aboot time tae. Whit wis the doctor sayin' aboot me that he couldnae say tae ma face?'

'Nothing. He was just summing up your progress. He's really very pleased with you.'

'Seems funny he couldnae sum it up tae me.'

'He's a busy man, Granny. He can't keep coming in here to visit you now that he's running the practice single-handed.'

'His auld faither did that for years.'

'Yes, but you know what he was like.'

'Aye, well, whit's for ma tea?'

Teresa said, 'A nice wee bit of cod, Granny, and stewed apples and custard.'

Granny's eyes lit up and her jaws began chomping at the mere idea. She liked a nice bit of fish softened with one of the tasty sauces that Teresa made. Granny admitted that Teresa was 'a dab hand at comin' up wi' tasty sauces'. And stewed apples and custard slipped down without any bother.

'How did you get on at the doctor's?' Teresa asked. 'Granny said he'd asked you to go to the surgery tonight.'

'Yes, I was just saying—he's too busy to keep spending so much time in here. He was just explaining about Granny's progress and how we'd no need to worry. But if we do need him to make a visit, we've only to let him know.'

'Oh, isn't that kind of him. He's a nice man. Clever as well.'

'Yes, he is very clever,' Wincey agreed.

'Are you all right, dear?'

'We've been awfully busy. I'm exhausted but I'll be fine after I've had my tea.'

In the homes of Florence and the twins, the evening meal was now referred to as dinner. Lunch was in the middle of the day, dinner was in the evening and tea was only something one took mid-afternoon. In the Gourlay home, however, it was still dinner in the middle of the day and tea in the evening.

Erchie arrived then with the paper, after having enjoyed a couple of pints in Quinn's with his mates on the way home. Quinn's at the bottom of the Balgrayhill had one entrance on the Balgray and another on Springburn Road. The place was a landmark in Springburn with its tower on which there was a large clock. Erchie flung the paper down and rubbed his hands.

'By Jove, ah've a horse's appetite on me the night. How long's tea gonnae be, hen?' he asked.

'Just about fifteen minutes.'

Granny said, 'Tell me whit's in the paper while we're waiting'. I don't suppose there's anythin' cheery?'

'Naw. It gets worse every day. Noo there's whit they're callin' spring cleanin' of thae Austrian Jews.'

Teresa, busy over at the range, shook her head. 'Spring cleaning? Is that not awful? Poor souls!'

'Aye,' Granny said. 'Thank God we wernae born Jews, that's aw ah can say.'

Erchie lifted the paper. 'An' it's been carried oot at great speed, it says. Jews huv been dismissed from their professions, Jewish judges huv been dismissed, shops huv been forced tae put up placards saying "Jewish concern". It says as well that theatre an' music halls huv been already "spring cleaned" an' among the artists that Vienna will know no more are Richard Tauber an' Max Reinhardt.'

'Is that no' awfae?' Granny said. 'Whit's the world comin' tae, him such a good singer as well?'

'An' here's a bit about a church leader—Pastor Niemoeller. He's been detained in Sachsenhausen concentration camp where he's tae join three thousand inmates under the "Death's Head" Battalion o' the SS.'

'The poor soul,' Teresa said. 'A man of God. How wicked can anyone get?'

'Here,' Granny said. 'Ah mind in the war, the British an' the Germans were slaughterin' each other by the million. Half the time just for a few yards o' muddy ground, as well. An' good men like oor Johnny bein' tormented in jail because he stood up against it.'

Teresa sighed. 'Must you tell us all this before we eat our tea, Erchie? It's enough to put us off.'

'Sorry, hen, but Granny—'

'I know, I know, but as I've said before, you can read to Granny through in the room after we have our tea.'

Granny snorted. 'Hiding' yer heid in the sand never does anybody any good, or solves anythin'. That's the trouble wi' a lot o' folk.'

'You were hoping for something cheery yourself earlier on,' Teresa reminded her.

'Aw ah said wis, ah didnae suppose there was anythin' cheery in the paper. An' aw wis right!'

'I used to think Erchie's *Daily Worker* was awfully serious, but this paper's just as bad.'

'It's no' the *Record*'s fault, hen. It's what's goin' on in the world. The *Record* jist lets us know.'

'Yes, yes, but just do me a favour, Erchie, and keep it until after tea.'

'Anythin' you say, hen.'

'You're awful quiet, Wincey,' Teresa said.

'When's she ever been a blether,' Granny wanted to know.

Wincey tried to pull herself together and pay attention to her immediate surroundings. She had been far away in Kirklee Terrace, remembering her home there and the way her mother sang as she moved about. She remembered the loving looks that passed between her mother and father. How happy and so much in love they'd been. She'd never seen—before or since—such a happy, loving couple.

'I'm sorry, I was dreaming,' Wincey said.

'Nothing to be sorry about, dear. As long as you're feeling all right.'

Wincey smiled. 'I'm fine. Can I help you dish the tea?'

'No, no, sit where you are. Everything's under control. Granny, can you manage on your own?'

'Aye, now the swellin's down in ma hands, ah'm no' that bad at aw. Ah wish ah could say the same for ma hips an' ma knees.'

Teresa put a tray on Granny's knee. Then she tucked one of Erchie's big hankies into the top of the old woman's dress.

'I've mashed it up nice to make it easier for you.'

'Ah'm no' a wee wean. Ye didnae need tae dae that!'

Teresa rolled her eyes and served Erchie, Wincey and herself with plates of fish in a cheese sauce. Then she put a dish of boiled potatoes on the table. 'Wire in now.'

'Ah saw Malcy earlier the day,' Erchie said. 'Ah forgot tae tell ye at dinner time.'

'What do you mean, Erchie?' Teresa said in a puzzled voice. 'Surely you see him every day in the factory?'

'Aye, ah know, but this was dinner time. He wis comin' oot o' O'Donnell's close. Ah didnae think he knew anybody up there.'

Teresa and Wincey exchanged glances and Erchie caught their look. 'My God, dinnae tell me it was O'Donnell's he wis at!'

'Now, don't you say anything, Erchie,' Teresa warned. 'We're best not to interfere. Leave it to Charlotte. Any problem they have is between them. They've worked things out all right before. Charlotte can be quite firm when she wants. And she loves him that much. I'm sure he loves her as well, so they'll come through this.'

'Ye're probably right, hen. Ah like a wee flutter masel' as you know, but ah've been thinkin' for a while now that Malcy seems tae have been goin' over the score. Ah widnae like tae get on the wrong side o' Mrs O'Donnell though. She's got quite a few hard men at her biddin'. But och, if Malcy's got in too deep wi' Mrs O'Donnell, Charlotte'll bail him out an' save his bacon. He'll be OK.'

26

'I was thinking it might be a good idea,' Doctor Houston said, 'if we met for a quiet meal and a talk in a more relaxed atmosphere. Somewhere away from the surgery.'

His car had drawn up beside Wincey as she was walking home.

'I'm your patient.' Wincey felt a bit shocked, as well as frightened. 'You're not supposed to take your patients out.'

He laughed. 'If we're going into the ethical and legal niceties, you're not actually registered with me, are you, so you're not officially my patient.'

'Well no, but you said—'

'I'm a doctor, yes. And yes, I want to help you. And it's true that I respect anyone's confidence. Would it make you feel better if I said I just want to help you as a friend. Forget I'm a doctor if you like.'

'I'm on my way home. Teresa will be expecting me for my tea.'

'We'll make it tomorrow then. I'll pick you up at seven thirty.'

'Wait a minute—'

But he'd wound up the window and the car had slid away.

What a terrible cheek! He'd struck her as the kind of person who always had to get his own way. She felt harassed, as well as everything else. Her emotions were in turmoil. She couldn't eat her tea.

Teresa looked worried. 'Are you sickening for something, dear?'

'Ah'll eat hers,' Granny eagerly volunteered.

'Granny,' Teresa chided, 'you'll do no such thing.'

Wincey hesitated, then thought she may as well tell the truth. They would be sure to find out, or one of the neighbours would probably see her getting into the doctor's car.

'I'm a bit taken aback, that's all.'

'What about, dear?'

'Doctor Houston has asked me out for a meal. He says he's calling for me tomorrow at seven thirty.'

Teresa's face lit up with delight. 'I knew it! Didn't I tell you? I knew he liked you, Wincey. Oh, I'm so pleased for you, dear.'

'Aye,' Granny said, 'it's high time she had a man.'

'I don't want to go out with him, but he didn't give me a chance to say no.'

'Good for him,' Granny said. 'He's the fella for you. It's a strong fella you need tae sort ye out.'

'Now you must wear something really nice,' Teresa said excitedly. 'And take time off tomorrow to get your hair done, dear. Get a bit cut off that fringe. You always look as though you're trying to hide underneath it.'

'You're making me feel nervous with all this fuss. I told you, I don't want to go.'

'Oh, don't be silly, dear, of course you'll go. And you'll have a lovely time.'

'Ah'll gie ye a loan o' ma good kirby-grip wi' the diamonds on it,' Granny offered.

In a sudden impulse, Wincey rushed over and gave the old woman a hug and a kiss. 'Thanks, Granny, you're very kind.'

'Away ye go an' don't be daft.' Granny looked embarrassed but pleased at the same time. Teresa looked pleased as well, and Wincey thought there was nothing for it but to keep the appointment with Doctor Houston, if for no other reason than to avoid disappointing Teresa and Granny.

The next day, she couldn't concentrate on her work. Charlotte noticed, and even Malcy's eyes kept wandering curiously towards her. Charlotte said, 'Has something happened, Wincey? You look all flushed and sparkly-eyed.'

'Not really. I'm going out for a meal tonight, that's all.'

Charlotte clapped her hands in delight. 'Oh, at last, Wincey. I was getting worried about you. It's not natural never to go out and enjoy yourself. It's a boyfriend, isn't it? You wouldn't be all aglow like this if you were going out with a girl.'

Wincey fussed and tutted and protested she was nothing of the kind, but Charlotte just laughed at her. The truth was of course that she *was* excited. But it was an excitement tinged with apprehension. She tried to be sensible. Doctor Houston was a perfectly respectable, kindly man who just wanted to help her. Why on earth should she feel so nervous of him? She felt angry with herself. She told herself not to be so stupid—all to no avail. The more she thought about it, the more she began to convince herself that nothing she could ever do or say would cure what was wrong with her. It had nothing to do with Doctor Houston. It was an irrational fear that was always there, deep inside her. No doctor had any pills or potions or could give any advice that would ever help her.

'For goodness sake, dear,' Teresa said, as seven thirty was drawing near, 'try to look a bit cheerful. You'd think you were going to a funeral, not out for a meal with a handsome man.'

'Aye,' Granny said, 'she's never been wan tae talk much, but noo she's gone completely dumb. Ah sometimes think she's aff her heid, that yin.'

Still Wincey didn't say anything. Even when they heard the car hooter, she just left the house with only a wave and a faint smile to the two women.

'Quick,' Granny shouted at Teresa, 'hurl me through tae the room windae.'

Doctor Houston got out of the car and opened the door for Wincey. The faint nervous smile stuck to her face as Wincey climbed into the front seat. He slid in beside her and the car moved off. They didn't talk much until Doctor Houston said, 'You're looking very nice.'

'Doctor—' Wincey began.

But he immediately corrected her, 'Robert. Friends, remember?'

'Robert,' she said, although it felt very odd to be saying it, 'I'm nervous of sitting in a restaurant in town in case one of my family or their friends might see me.'

'Don't worry, I've thought of that. I'm taking you to a little hotel I know out near the Campsie Hills.'

'Oh.'

'So relax.'

She nodded, and they lapsed into silence again. The hotel was an old coaching house and the restaurant had once been the stables. It still had the original flagstones under foot, whitewashed stone walls and dark oak beams. A huge log fire crackled cheerily in the ancient hearth.

'This is lovely,' Wincey said.

'I thought you'd like it. I'll go over to the bar and fetch some drinks. What'll you have?'

'A gin and tonic, please.'

'Right.'

She watched him stride over to the bar and smile and chat to the barmaid. She noticed that above the bar there hung horse brasses and horse shoes. Her attention kept being drawn, however, to Houston's muscular back and his head of blue black hair. Even from this distance, she could sense the strong aura of masculinity and self-confidence emanating from him. He returned and sat down opposite her. He raised his tankard of beer.

'Health and happiness.'

'Health and happiness,' she echoed, raising her glass.

After a moment, he said, 'Wincey, your grandfather was an old man and there's no doubt he died of natural causes. You do know that, don't you?'

She stared down at her drink and said nothing.

'I just wondered if you felt guilty in some way about his death, and that's what made you run away—and stay away,' he added. 'But believe me, you had nothing to do with his death. I've looked into this and he died of a heart attack. He had a heart condition. There's absolutely no doubt about that.'

Just then a waitress came to take their order for the meal and Houston said, 'Let's concentrate on enjoying the meal. We can talk about that afterwards.' And he turned the conversation round to Granny, reminding Wincey of some of Granny's hilarious pronouncements. Soon Wincey was laughing and adding some anecdotes of her own that he had not heard. She enjoyed the meal and afterwards they took their glass of wine over to one of the more private areas that had wooden partitions on each side. Wincey guessed that perhaps they had been where the horses would have been stabled.

'So,' Houston said, 'was I right about the guilt?'

She hesitated, her heart thumping. 'In a way,' she managed at last.

'In what way?' he asked gently.

She shook her head. 'You won't understand. You'll just hate me. Everybody would if they knew.'

'Try me.'

Wincey didn't answer.

'Wincey, try to let it out. You've obviously been harbouring some secret that you believe is terrible. And for so many years. It's time you got rid of the burden of it and got on with your life. As a doctor, I've seen and heard some terrible things. I've long since stopped being shocked at anything. If I ever was shocked at all. I've always been able to take things in my stride—you have to be like that working in the Royal in Glasgow. That's where I was before.'

Wincey took a deep breath. 'I killed him.'

Houston shook his head. 'No, no, Wincey. I've just told you—'

'I watched him.' In anguish Wincey closed her eyes. 'I can still see him gasping for breath. I'll never forget it. And how I let him die.'

'My dear girl, you were only a child. You couldn't have done anything.'

'Yes, I could have run upstairs as I'd done before, and fetched his tablets. But I didn't. I just stood there and watched him die.'

'Wincey, you were a child. You were in the house alone with him. You were in shock. It stands to reason, especially when it was someone you loved. Anyone would have understood that. My dear, believe me. You weren't able to do anything but just stand there like that.'

Wincey looked down at her hands. She was twisting them tightly together. 'Perhaps.'

'No perhaps about it. I've seen too many people in shock to have any doubt whatsoever. You were in shock,' he repeated firmly. 'You must rid yourself of all these guilty feelings.'

Wincey kept twisting at her hands. 'You don't understand. I wanted him to die. I hated him. He had . . . he had . . .' her hands now moved, instinctively, down between her legs, in an unconscious attempt to cover and protect, even from the memory . . . 'he had been touching me, doing things . . . for years. It was wrong, horrible . . . but what could I do? He was my grandfather . . .'

'Oh my dear!' Houston's big hand covered hers. 'My poor Wincey. Now I really do understand.'

Tears began gushing down Wincey's cheeks. He moved closer to her and put his other arm around her shoulders.

'It's all right. You're going to be all right, do you hear?'

She tried to nod and after a minute or two, he said,

'It's one of the terrible things about this kind of abuse. The victim gets the idea that it's their fault. This is totally wrong. It's always the fault of the abuser. But I've known this to happen over and over again. Whether the victim is a child or an adult, they feel dirty and they feel guilty. And these feelings can ruin their whole lives. I've known elderly women who were abused as children, and were still suffering deep inside as a result. They've never got over it. It's tragic. You mustn't go on suffering like that, Wincey. I won't let you.'

She raised a tear-stained, anxious face. 'You don't hate me?'

'Wincey!' He drew her head down against his chest. 'Of course I don't hate you. Quite the contrary. Now, in a minute or two, I'm going to go and fetch you a glass of brandy. That'll steady you up a bit. Then I'm going to drive you home. You'll have a good night's sleep and I'll see you again tomorrow. All right?'

'All right,' she murmured into the hard warmth of his body.

27

As Virginia walked about in the Gorbals, memories of her past life came flooding back. It was almost as if she was back in the teeming tenements of her youth, with their cavernous closes—man-made tunnels between the bottom of stairs and the streets. They were dark, cold and draughty places which the sunlight could never penetrate. She knew the worn stairs, and the flickering shadows of the gas light, and the stench of the overflowing lavatories. She heard the children crying, the racket of husbands and wives arguing, the drunk men, some aggressive and some maudlin. She returned to the close where she had been born. Seeing it, Virginia wondered how she'd ever survived in the place. Many others had not.

She heard again the deep melancholy booming of a foghorn from the river. The Gorbals had been the subject of a great many stories in newspapers and books in the past few years and had acquired a terrible reputation for violence. Reading these stories led outsiders to think that it was an area of constant violence and one pitched battle after another. But this had never been Virginia's experience. The main problem as far as violence was concerned was wife beating. And it took place on Friday or Saturday nights, after the husbands came home from the pub. She'd often seen women with black eyes and bruises at weekends. It was quite common to see or hear a child rushing along the street to the Southern Division police station shouting, 'Ma faither's killin' ma mither.'

There were two other types of violence Virginia had witnessed. One was caused by men coming out of a pub where they'd been talking and arguing, and continuing the argument in the vicinity of the public lavatories at Gorbals Cross. Another was at the intersection of Gorbals Street and Cumberland Street, near where she'd lived. Again it usually happened on a Friday or a Saturday night. An argument would become heated and lead to a street fight. This was always conducted with fists, and as a rule by no more than two men. A crowd of spectators would gather around though, and fair play was always insisted on. If the police saw the crowd and heard the disturbance, they would come along and order the fight to stop. It usually did. The policemen were often big Highlanders, well known and respected by most of the locals. If the police order was ignored, or if one of the fighters abused or attacked the police, there would be an arrest, with the policemen grabbing the offenders by the scruff of the neck and marching them off to the local police station.

The only other form of violence Virginia knew of was street fighting—but between youths of seventeen and under. They named themselves 'Cumbies' from Cumberland Street and 'Billy Boys' from Bridgeton. There was another gang of older men, she remembered, called the 'Beehives', after a shop at the corner of Cumberland Street and Thistle Street. They were unemployed men who used to hang about nearby and air their grievances. Sometimes their bitterness and resentment would boil over and once or twice a year, they'd gather together on a Saturday evening and march along a few streets, shouting and waving sticks. Sometimes groups of youths formed themselves into gangs and had tussles with the Beehives, but again only fists and sticks were used.

Virginia often wondered why this myth about the Gorbals as a hotbed of vice and violence had arisen. Mathieson said it was government-inspired—all part of an attempt to discredit men like Maclean and the other Red Clydesiders. In his view, this was why every minor incident that occurred in the Gorbals was blown up out of all proportion in the press and made to sound like a civil war was going on.

Virginia had a heavy heart as she wandered through the familiar streets. She remembered her mother and father and brothers, and many kindly neighbours and friends of long ago. She hardly knew anyone in Kirklee Terrace. It suddenly occurred to her that she missed the teeming life of the tenements, the closeness of neighbours and the involvement in each other's lives. Had she still lived in the Gorbals when Wincey disappeared, she would no doubt have had much sympathy, compassion, support and practical help from everyone around her.

Nevertheless, she could still imagine her mother and other working-class women, even without any help, soldiering on with courage and tenacity. It made Virginia feel ashamed of her own weakness and dependency. She made her way through the Gorbals streets with their crowds of ragged, barefoot children at play and women, some wrapped in plaid shawls, standing in groups at close-mouths or leaning on folded arms on windowsills, having what they called 'a hing'.

By the time she'd boarded a tram car and was on her way home, she had made a vow to be stronger from now on. To look forward with courage and optimism, not backward with sadness and regret. On the main street, she saw a placard outside a stationer's advertising the Empire Exhibition in Bellahouston Park and, feeling more cheerful already, she suddenly took the notion to sample the wonders of this new Glasgow venture.

As soon as she got home, she prepared a special evening meal for herself and Nicholas and while they were eating it, she suggested that they should visit the Exhibition together.

'I don't think as a writer you should miss this experience, Nicholas.'

His eyes brightened with interest. 'Yes, you could be right.' And so it was arranged—their first outing together for longer than she cared to remember.

On the way to Bellahouston Park in the car with Nicholas at the wheel, she made a point of showing interest in his writing. She'd shown nothing but bitterness and resentment towards it for too long.

'How is your work progressing, Nicholas? I hope it's going well.'

He glanced round at her in surprise but he also looked pleased. 'I've been having a bit of a struggle for a while,' he admitted.

'I'm sorry,' she said, 'if I've been less than helpful or encouraging recently. I know I've been far too self-obsessed.'

'Darling, if anyone's been self-obsessed, it's been me. I should be the one apologising. Come to think of it, I haven't been of much help or support to you. I've withdrawn so much into myself as well as into my room. I'm sorry.'

'Never mind. Let's both try again, shall we? Let's make a go of our marriage, I mean. It's been drifting dangerously near the rocks, don't you think?'

He nodded, his eyes still on the road ahead. 'Yes, we've been needing to talk for a while.'

'And we will,' Virginia said, 'but let's relax and enjoy our visit to the Exhibition. Let's pretend we're a young courting couple again and we're out on an exciting date.'

He grinned. 'Well, if we're going to act as we used to, you're not going to have much chance to talk, Virginia.'

'We can't behave exactly as we used to. There are no woods around here for a start.'

'There's the trees in the park, and lots of nice springy grass.'

She laughed and playfully smacked his hand. 'Do you want to get us arrested?'

'It would be worth it. I'm game if you are.'

She tutted and shook her head, but she was light-hearted with happiness.

After Nicholas parked the car and they entered the park, Virginia linked arms with him. He looked down at her with surprise and pleasure lighting his eyes again. Soon their whole attention was riveted by the fantastic sights all around them. There was the Highland clachan built beside a loch among a grove of trees. It consisted of thatched roofed cottages clustered around an old castle. At one of the cottages, wool was being spun. In the castle, ceilidhs were being held, songs were sung, and stories told that had been handed down from father to son for centuries in the Highlands.

There were the noisy thrills and spills and looping the loop of the amusement park, including a scenic railway, and the Rocket ride. Virginia and Nicholas stood for a time admiring the lake with its beautiful fountains and cascades. Everywhere there were magnificent pavilions, each representing a different part of the Empire—Australia, Canada, and Africa—all illustrating the Exhibition's theme of modernity.

Eventually Virginia said, 'We'll never be able to see it all in one afternoon. I'm exhausted already, aren't you?'

'Yes, let's have a leisurely meal and then make for home. We can come back again another day. In fact, I think we'll have to come back several times, Virginia, if we're to see everything. Next time, let's come in the evening, so that we can see the illuminations. I've heard they're really special.'

'Right.' Virginia was studying her map. 'Let's go to this treetop restaurant. It's on the first storey of the great Tower of Empire. It says the tower is a three-hundred-foot-high triumph of engineering. It certainly looks impressive, doesn't it?'

They strolled towards the tower and were soon settled at a table in the unusual restaurant where trees were growing up through the floor and enormously high windows sparkled all around. They had champagne with the meal and Virginia became quite giggly.

'If I don't get you home right now,' Nicholas told her with mock seriousness, 'you're going to give me a showing up. Come on.'

Arms encircling each other's waists, they made their way back to the car. On the way home, Virginia leaned her head against his shoulder.

'Oh, Nicholas, I'm so thankful we've still got each other.'

'Don't go all maudlin on me now.'

'No, I'm not. I mean it.'

'I know, darling. I feel the same. I love you. I've never stopped loving you.'

As they drove along, she said, 'I want you to make love to me.'

He glanced round at her with laughing eyes. 'I know I'm a genius but my talents don't include making love and driving at the same time.'

She punched his arm. 'You know what I mean.'

'Yes, as soon as I get you into the park . . .'

'Don't you dare.'

They were the young couple again that they once had been, laughing and teasing, loving and passionate. Back at home, he carried her to the bedroom and they undressed one another and caressed one another, as if for the first time. They made deep, passionate love, and afterwards she lay in his arms and he said, 'I thought I'd lost you, Virginia, and it was my own fault.'

'No, it wasn't, Nicholas,' she told him firmly. 'It wasn't anybody's fault. We were both just struggling to cope with the loss of our child. And we were both feeling guilty. But I've come to see that people always feel guilty to some degree after a loved one's death. I remember my mother saying things like "If only I'd said this", "If only I'd done that" after my brothers died. And my father was the same after my mother's death.'

It was the first time Virginia had accepted, and openly admitted, that Wincey was dead. She knew Nicholas had never truly accepted the truth either.

'Oh, Virginia.'

'Shh . . . Shh . . . '

She put her arm around his neck and pulled his head down and nursed it against her breast.

28

The next time they had a drive out to the Campsies, Wincey took a picnic basket. They spread a travelling rug on the grass and Wincey poured homemade soup from a flask into cups. There was a plate of salmon sandwiches and a crisp apple tart baked by Teresa. A flask of coffee finished the meal.

Houston said, 'That was a feast. I really enjoyed it. And look at that view. That's a feast for the eyes.'

Wincey gazed into the distance, where Glasgow was out in the valley below. She remembered a short poem called 'Glasgow'. It must have been the same view, only in the evening, that had inspired the poet,

> *A huge town*
> *Lying in a plain*
> *With a valley*
> *Atwinkle with lights*
> *Defies time*
> *And radiates warmth from a million hearts*
> *Back to the skies.*

'I wouldn't want to live anywhere else, would you?'

Houston shook his head. 'And I've been around and seen a few places. The thing that annoys me, though, is what a bad reputation Glasgow seems to have, especially down in London.'

'I know. I could hardly credit it recently when I invited one of our English customers to visit us in Glasgow. He seemed quite shocked.

"Oh no," he said, "I'd be too frightened to go up there." ' Wincey laughed, remembering. Houston laughed too.

'A Glasgow accent stands you in good stead in an English pub, though. As soon as any thug looking for a fight hears it, they give you a wide berth.'

After they finished their coffee and Wincey had packed everything back in the basket, Houston said, 'Wincey, have you given any thought to what I said the other day?'

'About contacting my family?'

'Yes.'

'It hasn't made any difference, Robert. They would be liable to die of shock if I suddenly appeared. You told me I'd been given up for dead.'

'I wasn't suggesting you suddenly turn up on their doorstep. You could write them a letter.'

'But what would I say? After all this time. It would seem wicked of me to have let them suffer for so long. It *was* wicked.'

'No, it was not,' Houston said firmly. 'How often have I to spell it out to you? Your grandfather had been abusing you for years, and you'd only begun to realise what he'd been doing to you. You felt confused and betrayed. But you also thought it was somehow your fault. You didn't know what to do. When he had his heart attack, you were still confused, Wincey, and you were in shock. Then you felt horrified and guilty, and afraid, and you ran away. The longer you stayed away, the more afraid you became, especially to go back and face your family. Now that's the truth, Wincey, and that is exactly what you must write and tell your mother and father.'

'What if they don't believe me about what he did to me? What if they think I'm just making up lies to try to excuse my behaviour?'

'What behaviour?'

Her expression strained with anxiety. 'He was such a successful and respectable business man, Robert. I suppose you could call him a pillar of the church, and the community. He was an elder in the church, and he donated a lot of money to the restoration of the building. Oh Robert, who would believe me? It makes me sick to my soul just to think of how people would revile me.'

'Darling!' He gathered her into his arms. 'Did I revile you when you told me?'

'You're a doctor. That makes you different. And . . .' She flushed

389

and gazed up at his face, her expression still uncertain. 'You love me.'

'Yes, I love you. I love you very much. And I'm sure your parents love you as well, in a different way, of course. I want to make love to you, and don't look so anxious, darling. I've every intention of waiting until you want it too. Although . . .' His tone became teasing. 'You're really testing my curative skills as a doctor, as well as my will-power, to the limits. I hope you realise that.'

'I do love you, Robert, and I do want to make love to you, but it's just . . . it's just . . . this awful feeling comes over me. It's disgust as well as fear. Not disgust at you,' she hastily added. 'Oh, I know I'm being stupid.'

'No, you're not, Wincey. You just need time, darling. And you need to get all this out in the open. You must get all aspects of your life, and your guilty feelings, sorted out. I know you think you love me but—'

'Oh, I do, Robert, I do,' she cried out in distress.

'Wincey,' he continued firmly, 'you've got to learn to love yourself before you can really love someone else.'

'Love myself?'

'Yes, and accept yourself. Now, to get back to what I was saying— are you going to write that letter?'

Worriedly, she hesitated. 'It's the terrible shock it would give them. I've left it too long, Robert.'

'It might have given them a shock if you suddenly appeared before them without any warning, but if you wrote them a letter, Wincey . . . You're just making excuses. It's far more likely they'd be absolutely overjoyed.'

'I'll . . . I'll think about it.'

'What good will it do to allow more time to pass?'

'I need more time to adjust to the idea, and to pluck up enough courage, I suppose.'

'You've got me now, remember.'

She smiled at him. 'Yes, you're my rock.'

'Well, I've been called many a thing, but never a rock. Is that meant to be a compliment?'

'Of course.' She thought he was going to kiss her but it was as if he suddenly changed his mind. He turned away and got to his feet.

'Do you fancy a walk, or are you ready to go back home?'

She rose too. 'It's getting a bit late, and we've both early starts in the morning.'

'Right.' He lifted up the picnic basket. 'Let's walk back to the car. Then we'll be on our way.'

The closeness that had existed between them earlier was now gone. On the way home they still spoke pleasantly to each other, but there was an edge of politeness that made Wincey feel sad. She suspected that if she didn't pull herself together soon, she was going to lose him. She couldn't expect him to be patient for ever. He would have no difficulty in getting any woman—for sex, or whatever he wanted. He didn't need to put up with a guilt-ridden neurotic.

He didn't come into the house with her but just carried the picnic basket into the close and deposited it on the Gourlays' doormat.

'See you again soon.' A brief wave and he was gone.

Wincey stood listening to the car start up and then the sound of it fade away. Then she put her key in the door.

'Ah'm tellin' ye,' Granny was bawling at Teresa, 'there's gonnae be another war. Ah huvnae lived aw this time no' tae know aw the signs.'

Teresa didn't seem in the least perturbed. 'Och, you're always such a pessimist, Granny.'

'Whit dae ye think they're conscriptin' fellas o' twenty for? Tae send them tae Rothesay for their holidays?'

'Oh, there you are, Wincey.' Teresa greeted Wincey with some relief. 'Did you have a lovely time, dear?'

'Yes. That's the rain coming on now, but we got it dry for the picnic. Robert thought your soup was delicious, by the way. And your apple tart. He sends his compliments.'

Teresa flushed with pleasure. 'Such a nice man. And he'll make you a wonderful husband.'

Wincey forced a laugh. 'He hasn't even asked me yet.'

'He will, dear. He will.'

Wincey wished she could feel half as confident as Teresa sounded. Suddenly Erchie said, 'Ma's right, ye know, hen.' He had been sitting reading his *Daily Record*. 'First there's the conscription plans. An' now they're even havin' wee weans practice wearin' gas masks.'

'There was gas in the last war, wasn't there, Erchie?' Granny said. 'It did terrible things tae poor fellas in the trenches. See if they gas us over here, we're aw done for, gas masks or no. Anyway, where's oor gas masks?'

'Will you be quiet, the pair of you!' Teresa said.

'Aye,' said Erchie, ignoring Teresa's command, 'an' it'll no' stop in this war. There's aye another generation comin' up, aye ready tae be fooled an' indoctrinated an' encouraged tae hate their fellow men. Now German weans have been recruited by thae Nazis. Could ye beat it? Wee fellas o' thirteen, an' even younger, are marchin' intae a Jewish neighbourhood wi' brushes an' buckets o' white paint. They're daubin' the star o' David on Jewish premises pointed out tae them by the grown-ups.'

'Is that no' wicked? Wee weans,' Granny said.

'Aye,' Erchie agreed, 'an' it's forbidden tae play wi' or even speak tae Jewish weans.'

Teresa sighed and shook her head. 'I don't know what it's all coming to.'

'Ah telt ye,' Granny raised her voice again, 'it's comin' tae another war, that's what it's comin' tae.'

Wincey had been emptying the picnic basket and washing the cups and plates and she spoke up in an effort to change the subject. 'Does anyone fancy going to the Empire Exhibition. Some of the machinists have been and they were raving about it. Some of them have been two or three times.'

'Yes.' Teresa brightened. 'I was talking to Mrs McDougall just this morning, and she was telling me she had gone with her man and the family and she thought it was marvellous. And it was packed, she said. She'd never seen so many folk packed together before.'

'Whit? An' her wi' such a mob packed intae her room an' kitchen. She must have aboot a hunner by noo.'

'Now, now, Granny, don't exaggerate. Yes, I'd love to go, Wincey. How about you, Erchie? And do you think we could manage Granny's wheelchair if there's such a crowd?'

'Whit?' Granny said. 'Ah'll soon clear a path wi' ma brolly. Don't you worry.'

Wincey laughed. 'We'll probably all need umbrellas. I don't remember such a wet summer before, do you?'

'Maybe Robert will want to take you on his own. I think you should go with him, dear. We'll be fine with Erchie.'

'Yes, I am going with him, but I could go with you as well. We could go in the morning. That way Granny wouldn't get too tired. It's easier for Robert to get off at night after his surgery, and he was saying that in the evenings, everything's illuminated and looks extra beautiful.'

'Ah widnae get too tired. Ah'd just be sittin' in ma chair.'

'Now, now, dear. You know fine you fall asleep in your chair if we don't get you to bed before nine. And you need your wee nap in the afternoon as well.'

'Dae you want tae deafen everybody in the exhibition wi' yer snores, Ma?' Erchie said.

Granny drew down her brows and sucked in her gums. 'Ye'll be auld yerself wan day.'

'Right,' Wincey said. 'I'll organise it, shall I? And we'll have a nice meal in one of the restaurants. My treat.'

'That's very kind of you, dear. I'll really look forward to that.'

Wincey looked forward to it as well, especially the evening when she was going with Robert. For one thing, she felt safer in the darkness. And for another, maybe that would be the moment that Robert would propose. As his wife, surely she would feel more secure, more safe, less frigid and neurotic. She would gladly give up the factory to concentrate on being a good wife to him, assisting him in his work, making him happy. Although in fact Robert wasn't in favour of women just staying at home. He said, 'Outpatient Departments are full of what you might call suburban neurosis—lonely women who are left at home all day with not enough to do and too much time on their hands, which they spend worrying about their troubles.' There had been several suicides and attempted suicides brought in when he had worked in the Royal.

'Even in this area,' he said, 'I have my share. It's become a grave social problem.'

Was she what he regarded as a suburban neurotic? Even though she had plenty to do. And she'd plenty to worry about. Charlotte was looking thin and pale and anxious. She had confessed to Wincey that Malcy was getting in deeper and deeper with the moneylender. Charlotte had paid Mrs O'Donnell off more than once and pleaded with Malcy to stop gambling. Often he did for a few days or weeks, and then he'd start again, worse than ever. He always believed that the next bet would be his lucky one and he'd be able to pay off everything he owed. Although it never worked out that way, he never lost his optimism and hope.

It made Wincey so angry. 'For goodness' sake, why don't you leave him, Charlotte?'

'I don't leave him, Wincey, and I'll never leave him, because I love him. He's not a bad man. He's been nothing but kind and gentle and loving to me. He can't help the gambling. It's an illness. We'd be perfectly happy together if only he could be cured of that.'

Wincey didn't believe he'd ever be any different. Even Erchie had become disenchanted with Malcy and had stopped helping him out with money. Everybody had now stopped giving Malcy any cash, except Mrs O'Donnell, and Wincey feared a time of reckoning was likely to come with the moneylender. Charlotte had recently, in desperation, told Malcy that she was no longer going to bail him out with what he owed Mrs O'Donnell.

'I had to tell him that I just couldn't afford it any more, and it's the truth,' she admitted to Wincey. 'I'm hoping that if he knows I'm definitely not paying off Mrs O'Donnell any more, he'll realise he'll just have to stop going to her. It just can't go on, Wincey. I feel I'm only encouraging him. The interest that that woman charges is wicked, really criminal.'

Wincey agreed and hoped and prayed that Charlotte's new strategy would succeed. But when Erchie heard, he groaned. 'If Malcy disnae pay up soon, O'Donnell's men will put the frighteners on him. Ah hate tae say this, but maybe a right doin' is the only thing that'll bring Malcy tae his senses.'

'Oh dear,' Teresa said. 'I hate violence.'

'It's Charlotte I'm worried about,' Wincey said. 'I don't care what happens to him.' And the flame of hatred she had felt for her grandfather now encompassed Malcy and burned stronger than ever.

Virginia spent the morning doing some shopping. Time hung heavy on her hands until Nicholas stopped work half way through the afternoon. After making a few purchases, she wandered along Sauchiehall Street, and then down West Nile Street. Trace horses were plodding up the cobbled road on their way to Buchanan Street Station and the factories in the north of the city. The carts' wheels trundled along the two broad stone lines, especially formed to make the journey smoother for the carts. In each case, the huge Clydesdale horse in front was yoked to the horse at the back, helping one another to haul the heavy load up the steep hill. A carter sat on the cart, a clay pipe stuck in his mouth, his sleeves rolled up. Walking along side the front horse was a trace boy, leading and urging the beast on with a rope attached to it. Then once the destination at the north of the city was reached, and the load delivered, the horses would be unyoked and the trace boy would mount astride the lead horse's back. With a whoop and a clatter, he'd joyously make a headlong dash down the hill towards the River Clyde again, sparks spraying in all directions from the horse's hooves. That is, if he was lucky and a policeman didn't catch him.

Virginia couldn't help wondering if the police, for the most part, turned a blind eye, because she'd so often seen the wild descent of trace boys with their horses, manes and tails flying. It was one of the most familiar sights in Glasgow. So too was the sight of young lads with home-made barrows and shovels, with which to scoop up all the horses' dung to sell to people with gardens or allotments.

She glanced at her watch. Hours to go yet. She thought of visiting

Mathieson and then remembered that he'd be at the college. Anyway, she had made up her mind not to see so much of Mathieson, at least not without Nicholas. It was one thing Nicholas being such close friends with Mathieson, but it had begun to occur to her that it wasn't just Mrs Cartwright who thought her close association with Mathieson odd, to say the least. She had been helping Mathieson not long ago at one of his political meetings, and at one point another woman helper had said, 'Your husband is such a courageous man. What a wonderful spirit he has. Despite his disabilities he teaches others and works tirelessly for the cause in so many ways.'

'Oh, you mean James?' Virginia said. 'He's my ex-husband. I'm married now to Nicholas Cartwright, the novelist.'

The woman had given her such a strange look and later that day, she'd seen her in a huddle with some other women, talking together in lowered voices. They'd immediately stopped when she appeared. Virginia had no doubt they'd been gossiping about her. At first she'd thought, To hell with them. Why should she care what anyone thought? It wasn't as if she was being unfaithful to Nicholas. She wondered what the women would say if they knew it had been Mathieson she had been unfaithful to. But that was so long ago.

However, the more she thought about it, the more she realised that perhaps she had been visiting Mathieson too much on her own. Perhaps it wasn't fair to Mathieson, or to Nicholas. She should try to be more self-reliant. Her efforts to find charity work had so far not been very successful. It would have been easier if she'd been a member of one of the local churches, or the Salvation Army. Recently, however, she'd remembered from her youth the Model lodging house, a kind of poor man's hotel known simply as the Model. Why the word 'model' was applied to such a place, Virginia never knew—the dilapidated building had always looked ready to collapse. It housed weary-looking, unshaven, unemployed men, eyes deadened with hopelessness. They shuffled about in tattered clothing and boots with soles flapping off. She wondered if the place needed a voluntary worker, perhaps to dish out food. One morning she'd gone along to the Drygate, plucked up courage and walked straight into the Model. The first thing that hit her was the stench of frying fat and sweaty feet. A doddery man in a long army greatcoat flopping at his bare ankles shuffled past her. She called to him, 'Where can I see the manager?'

The man jerked his head towards a door. 'The kitchen maybe.'

Virginia opened the door and found herself in a large kitchen and dining area which had a broad, flat hotplate stretching the full length of the place. The fumes from greasy frying pans mixed with the stench of dozens of unwashed bodies. It all but overcame Virginia—she felt sick. One man who looked comparatively clean and was dressed in a blue shirt and grey flannels came hurrying towards her.

'Good morning, madam,' he said. 'What can I do for you?'

He indicated that she precede him back out of the door. Then he hastily led her across to another room which was obviously his office. 'I'm Mr Scott, the manager.'

'How do you do.' Virginia suddenly felt foolish. There wasn't another woman in sight. It looked as if no woman had ever stayed here, or worked here. 'I think I've possibly made a mistake. I was wanting to do some voluntary work and just wondered, in passing, if there was anything I could do here.'

Mr Scott looked shocked. 'Oh, I couldn't allow a lady like yourself to have anything to do with a place like this. What would your husband say?'

What indeed? In fact when she got home Nicholas thought it hilarious. 'Darling, it's an old doss house. It'll be moving with fleas for a start. I bet you had to have a bath the moment you came home.' She had, in fact—after being horrified to see several fleas jumping about her person. She'd also had to wash her underwear and stockings and stuff her outside clothing into a bag ready to take to the cleaner's.

'I suppose it was a bit daft to try a place like that,' she conceded, 'but I was getting desperate. Surely there's some kind of voluntary work I could do.'

'Have you thought of the Red Cross?'

'Nicholas,' she cried out in delight, 'you're a genius.'

He grinned. 'I know.'

'I'll go to their office first thing tomorrow.'

'Good idea.'

'The Red Cross does a lot of good work.'

'Yes, all over the world. But,' he came over and gathered her into his arms, 'don't you dare go stravaiging all over the world, doing your good works. I want you here with me. I'm totally selfish, like all true geniuses.'

She flung her arms around his neck, a great wave of love for him engulfing her. She kissed him with all the passion that was in her. In a matter of seconds they were on the floor, tearing at one another's clothing, rubbing, licking, biting each other, making love over and over again. At last, exhausted, they rolled apart.

Virginia managed, 'Mrs Rogers'll want to know about dinner in a minute. I'd better go through to the kitchen.'

'Now that you've had your wicked way with me.'

Virginia gave him a quick kiss and scrambled up to fix her clothing back in place and tidy her hair.

'You'd better get up and make yourself respectable as well. Mrs Rogers could suddenly come in here.'

He propped himself up on one elbow. 'So what? It would liven up her day. She needs a bit of spice in her life, by the look of her.'

Virginia shook her head. 'You're incorrigible. By the way,' she asked at the doorway, 'do you fancy going to the Exhibition later on? You promised we'd go and see the illuminations one night.'

'Yes, fine.'

Happily she went through to the kitchen for her usual talk with Mrs Rogers about menus and also to make out the weekly shopping list. Mrs Rogers had cooked a delicious roast of prime beef, surrounded by roast potatoes. In a separate dish were golden brown, light as a feather Yorkshire puddings. For sweet there was a fruit salad and cream. Because Mrs Rogers always left early, Virginia dished the meal, and afterwards Nicholas helped her to clear the table. In the kitchen, Virginia washed the dishes and Nicholas dried them. Eventually, arm in arm, they left the house, and soon were on their way to the Empire Exhibition in Bellahouston Park.

Granny's gums were chomping with excitement as she related to Mr McCluskey what a great show good old Glasgow had put on. Mr McCluskey was sitting in the close having his smoke, his thick straggly moustache wet at the ends with sucking on his pipe. Erchie and Teresa had brought Granny home just after lunch time. Then Erchie had gone off to the factory. Wincey was already at work. Granny had insisted on her chair being parked beside Mr McCluskey's so that she could tell him all about her adventures. She quite often parked in the close beside Mr McCluskey now.

'Ah'm the only wan the poor auld soul can enjoy a good blether wi',' Granny insisted.

Before she got started, Teresa had run into the house and fetched Granny's shawl and also a blanket to tuck around her waist and legs.

'Now, will I get you a scarf to tie round your head?' she asked the old woman.

'Stop yer fussin',' Granny said. 'Can ye no' see ah've got ma hat on. Away ye go an' make Mr McCluskey an' me a wee cup o' tea.'

'Can I fetch you a blanket, Mr McCluskey?' Teresa said.

'No thanks, hen. Ma long johns keep the cauld aff ma legs.'

He was also wearing a tweed bonnet with the skip pulled well down over his brow, and a big woolly scarf knotted high under his chin, and hanging down over his chest.

'A wee cup o' tea would be very welcome though, hen,' he said, and settled back in his chair to enjoy another few puffs at his pipe. 'And,' as he'd said many times before, 'a guid crack wi' Granny.'

Granny described in glowing detail everything from the hurly burly of the amusement park to the British Government pavilion with its steel and glass globe of the world, apparently unsupported in space. She took Mr McCluskey through the Scottish Pavilion South, with its hall of youth, and the Scottish Pavilion North, with its striking twenty-five-foot statue called The Spirit of Modern Scotland. Each Scottish Pavilion was coloured blue and each had a tower.

'Ma favourite though wis the Peace Pavilion. It wis tellin' ye about aw the things folk dae tae try to live in peace thegither. Well, no everythin', mind ye. Ah could huv telt them a thing or two tae put in there if they'd asked me. Still, it wis better than nothin'. Somebody or somethin's got tae speak up for peace at a time like this. Dae ye no' think so, Mr McCluskey?'

Mr McCluskey removed the pipe from his mouth. 'Aye, ye're quite right, Granny. Aw the generals an' high heid yins telt us the last war wis tae be the war tae end aw wars, an' we wis comin' home tae a land fit for heroes. Bloody lies, if ye'll excuse the French. Ye'll no' get me rushin' aff like an idiot tae jine up this time.'

Teresa, returning with a tray of tea and digestive biscuits, couldn't help smiling at the idea of poor Mr McCluskey rushing off anywhere.

'Here, Mr McCluskey, can you hold the tray on your knees?' Teresa said.

'Aye, fine, hen.'

Teresa took one of the cups and placed it between Granny's hands. 'Will I dip a biscuit for you, Granny?'

'Ma hands are fine. Gie me ower a digestive an' away ye go an' leave us in peace.'

After a while, Mr McCluskey's daughter came bustling into the close and started tutting the moment she saw her father's pipe.

'That woman jist hates that poor fella's pipe,' Granny had said. 'He's tae hang on tae it like grim death—even sleeps wi' it under his pillow, he telt me, in case she takes it aff him an' throws it in the midden. She's tried aw sorts o' tricks tae get her hands on it. He's that feart he loses it, the poor auld soul. Ah telt him no' tae worry— if the worst came tae the worst, ah'd get him anither yin.'

'Come on now, Father,' Miss McCluskey said, 'it's time you came in and washed your hands, ready for your dinner.'

Obediently the old man got up, still clutching at his pipe.

'Put that disgusting thing out,' Miss McCluskey yelped as if the pipe was going to leap up at her and bite her. 'I will not have its dirty fumes contaminating my house. It's bad enough out here in the close.'

'*Your* house?' Granny said in wide eyed innocence. 'An' here wis me thinkin' that the hoose wis in Mr McCluskey's name.'

Miss McCluskey flushed and pushed past them to unlock the front door.

'Ye're an awfae woman, Granny,' Mr McCluskey said, but gave her a wink.

After Granny had settled back in the kitchen, Wincey arrived and Granny said, 'That wis awfae good o' ye, hen, tae take us tae the Exhibition an' pay for everythin' like ye did. Ah really enjoyed masel'. Glasgow's put on a rare show, eh? Good old Glasgow.'

Wincey gave Granny a kiss. 'Yes, but there's nothing old looking about the exhibition, is there? Everything's ultra modern.'

'You're not rushing out again, are you, dear? You must be exhausted.'

'No, I'm fine, Teresa. I'm just going to get changed.'

'Sit down and have a bite to eat first.'

'No thanks. Robert and I are going to have a meal at the Atlantic Restaurant at the exhibition. Remember that one that's been built exactly like the bow of a ship? And all the waitresses are dressed as stewards. I'm really looking forward to it. So is Robert.'

'A cup of tea then?'

'No, honestly, Teresa. I'll away through to put on my new dress.'

'The long black velvet one? Oh, wait until Robert sees you in that.

You could pass for a film star.'

Wincey laughed, and once she was through in her room, they could hear her singing.

Teresa smiled and shook her head. 'What a girl! What would we do without her?'

30

It was raining yet again when they left the Atlantic restaurant. Wincey had just tied her headsquare over her hair when suddenly Robert grabbed her, pushed her against the hull, or wall outside, and started passionately kissing her. Wincey was too astonished to struggle. Robert was not a man who believed in indulging in uninhibited public displays of emotion. On the contrary, as a doctor, he always showed a quiet self-confidence and calm authority.

Eventually he let her go and she gasped breathlessly, 'What on earth was that all about?'

'Your mother passed within yards of us.'

Wincey paled. She was glad now of the wall at her back to steady her. At last she managed, 'How did you know? I mean, you've never seen her before, have you?'

'No, but I've seen plenty of photographs of Nicholas Cartwright, and she was hanging onto his arm.'

Wincey looked fearfully, wistfully, around. 'Where are they now?'

'They were going in the direction of the exit, I think. Anyway, the opposite direction from us, so don't worry. But you know, Wincey, it's bound to happen sooner or later. Glasgow's not all that big a place. One day you're going to give her a terrible shock. You've got to write that letter.'

Wincey nodded. She was still shaken. 'Yes, you're right. I'll do it this weekend.' Her heart was pounding at the thought, but as they moved away, she couldn't help being diverted and uplifted by the breathtakingly beautiful scenes all around them.

Earlier she'd read Robert's copy of *The Times* and could now agree with what its arts critic had said.

> 'The best effect of the exhibition is at night, when to the
> straight lines and delicate colours of the pavilions is
> added floodlighting and the changing effects of
> illuminated water in movement. The lake, lit by
> submarine floodlights of changing colours, presents a
> magnificent spectacle. High up over all shines the fixed
> red, yellow and green of the Tower of Empire
> observation balconies. From the foot of the tower
> cascades descend, lit from below with changing colours,
> the water being made semi-opaque by aeration to give
> value to the colours.'

'This is like a dream world,' Wincey said. 'It's all so beautiful,
isn't it.'

Robert agreed and, arm in arm, they wandered around speechless
now with admiration. Although Wincey couldn't relax completely.
Every now and again she'd gaze uneasily at people in the crowd.
Eventually, Robert said, 'Relax, will you.'

'I am.'

'I can feel your tension. I told you, they went away in the opposite
direction.'

She clung tightly to his arm, glad of the strong, hard feel of it. 'It's
just been a bit of a shock, but I'm fine really. I'm glad we came. I am
enjoying it. It's wonderful. Thank you for bringing me, Robert.'

He smiled down at her. 'Maybe I've been going about this in the
wrong way.'

'Going about what?'

'Courting you. Do you realise that's the first time you haven't
trembled or shrunk away from me when I've kissed you?'

'Oh Robert, I don't shrink away from you. I never—'

'Imperceptibly perhaps, but I'm not a doctor for nothing. You can't
fool me.'

'Oh Robert, I'm sorry. It's not you . . .'

'Don't get all agitated. I know what it is. I also know that you'll
never be free of the past, Wincey, and all the negative emotions that
are still twisted up inside you, if you go on like this.'

'Like what? I've been trying to free myself of the past for years,

Robert. I thought I had.'

Robert stopped walking and turned her towards him. 'Have you forgiven your grandfather?'

'What?' All the hatred she'd felt for the old man came careering back, making her tremble violently. 'Never!'

Robert said, 'You see. You haven't even begun to free yourself, Wincey. And this hatred only harms you, it doesn't do anything to your grandfather. He's long gone.'

'Change the subject, for goodness' sake,' she suddenly snapped at him. 'You're spoiling the evening.'

He shrugged and they began walking again, but this time not arm in arm. Eventually Wincey couldn't bear it any more and she said, 'Robert, I'm sorry. I'm over-tired, that's all. It's been a long day. Do you mind if we go home now?'

Later, alone in the silence of her room, she wept. A horrible certainty was creeping over her. She was going to lose him. That night she dreamt she was sinking deep into a quagmire and couldn't get a foothold, couldn't struggle up. She woke sweating and exhausted.

It wasn't a good start to what turned out to be a dreadful day—one of the worst days of her life. A day that banished everything else from her mind.

She could see right away that Charlotte was tense and upset and eventually she asked her, 'Charlotte, what's wrong? Please tell me. Maybe I can help.'

She knew of course it would be something to do with Malcy. Only he could make Charlotte look so desperately worried and unhappy. Charlotte shook her head. 'I'm trying hard to stick it out and not give Malcy any more money, Wincey, but it's been terrible these last few days. He's begged and pleaded and says Mrs O'Donnell's men have threatened to kill him if he doesn't pay up by today. Today's his last chance, he says. But he's lied to me so often before, Wincey. I don't believe him now. And I do so much want him cured of his gambling. I feel I really must hold out this time and not give him any more money. He always just goes and gambles it away, you see. But at the same time, I'm so afraid. I mean, what if he *is* telling the truth this time? I'll never forgive myself if anything happens to Malcy. It'll be my fault if anything does.'

'Of course it won't be your fault,' Wincey said. 'This is all Malcy's doing, not yours.' Wincey took Charlotte's arm and held her and Charlotte wept broken-heartedly on Wincey's shoulder.

After a minute or two, Wincey said, 'The only thing I can think of is if I go and speak to Mrs O'Donnell. Find out exactly what the true situation is.'

'Oh, could you, Wincey? Maybe if we went together. I probably should have confronted Mrs O'Donnell before, but to be honest with you, I never thought of it. I've just kept trying to talk to Malcy and sort things out between ourselves.'

'I don't mind going on my own,' Wincey said. 'You're upset enough.'

'But could you do it discreetly, Wincey? Without Malcy knowing. He'd never forgive me if he thought I'd allowed you to interfere. I'm sorry, Wincey, but you're not his favourite person at the best of times.'

'I know, but don't worry. I'll say nothing to Malcy about this. And I'll slip away just now while he's with Erchie through in the back workshop. I won't be long and I'll be able to tell you exactly what he owes Mrs O'Donnell, or if he owes anything at all. If necessary, I'll warn Mrs O'Donnell that her men had better not lay a finger on Malcy or I'll go to the police.'

'Oh, thank you, Wincey, and tell her if he does owe her something, I'll pay it. Oh hurry, Wincey, in case he comes back to the machine room and sees you.'

'It's all right even if he does see me, Charlotte. He knows I often go out on business.'

'But the sooner we know about what's going on, the better.' Charlotte was getting more and more agitated. 'I mean, what if we're too late and something happens to Malcy. Oh please hurry, Wincey.'

Wincey struggled into her coat, eyes averted from Charlotte in case Charlotte might detect the dark hatred she was nursing. It would be the best thing if, on this occasion, Malcy was telling the truth and he did get set upon by Mrs O'Donnell's hard men. However, for Charlotte's sake, she vowed to do her best to get things safely sorted out.

The moneylender's close was only minutes away from the factory and Wincey ran inside the close and up the stairs. At the door with the brass name plate which said 'Mrs Frances O'Donnell' she both pulled the bell and rattled the letterbox. There was no reply. Wincey tried again, this time battering at the door with her fists. Still nothing happened. She peered through the letterbox, she shouted through it.

'Mrs O'Donnell.' She knocked on the other door on the landing and after a few minutes, she heard the shuffling of slippers along the lobby. The door opened to reveal a frowsy looking woman with uncombed hair and a sallow, unhealthy looking face. She seemed to be having difficulty in breathing.

'Whit dae ye want?'

'I've been trying to get hold of Mrs O'Donnell. It's urgent. Have you any idea when she'll be back?'

'There's aye folk comin' an' goin' there. Her as well. Ah couldnae keep track o' them aw, even if ah wanted tae.'

'You've no idea where she could be?'

'Naw.' And she shut the door.

Wincey decided to try the other neighbours, just on the off chance Mrs O'Donnell might be visiting any of them. Again she drew a blank. Eventually she stood at the close-mouth wondering if she should look in at the local shops. Mrs O'Donnell might be out for her messages. But then she happened to glance at her watch. 'Oh God,' she thought, suddenly agitated and apprehensive. Soon it would be closing time at the factory. She could well believe on this occasion that Malcy might be telling the truth. He might well be in immediate danger. Not that she cared what happened to him but she cared terribly, urgently, about Charlotte. She began to run back along the road.

Nicholas circled Virginia in admiration. 'Yes, very smart. Sexy as well.'

She rolled her eyes at him. 'Don't be daft. How can a Red Cross uniform be sexy? But it is smart, right enough.' She went over to the full length wardrobe mirror and, hands on hips, surveyed herself this way and that. She liked the well-cut navy-blue costume and crisp white shirt, dark tie and navy cap with white bands and Red Cross badge and stiff peak. The cap had also a thin leather chinstrap. Navy stockings and shoes completed the outfit.

'The first aid course was interesting,' Virginia said. 'I quite enjoyed it. They had actors and actresses made up to look like injured people—blood and everything. It was very realistic. We learned how to do dressings and how to put on splints and all sorts of things.'

'Come away from that mirror. You'll be getting so big-headed your cap won't fit you.'

'I volunteered to do some nursing training in one of the hospitals. You don't mind, do you, darling?'

'Mind? Why should I mind? I have a job that I enjoy and find fulfilling. Why shouldn't you, Virginia?'

Virginia smiled lovingly at him. 'Not every Scotsman is as liberal as you, Nicholas. I remember so many husbands where I lived who regarded their wives as part of their goods and chattels. All the poor women did was bear children and slave in houses that weren't fit places for animals. They struggled endlessly to keep their homes clean and respectable and to feed and clothe their families. The husbands—even the best of them—would never dream of washing a dish or doing anything to help in the house. It would have been considered unmanly.

Maybe that's still the attitude, for all I know.'

'I wonder why that's so much the case in Scotland,' Nicholas said thoughtfully. 'I don't think it's like that in England. I must remember and do some research on that.'

Virginia laughed. 'You never stop being a writer, do you? Always curious about what makes people tick.'

'I know what makes you tick.' He made a lunge at her and, squealing with laughter and protesting, she struggled out of the room.

'Get your hands off my good uniform, you sex maniac. I've a Red Cross meeting to go to.'

In the hall, they bumped into Mrs Rogers and nearly upset a tray of dishes she was carrying.

'Sorry, Mrs Rogers,' Nicholas said. 'I didn't see you. I was too busy trying to ravish this woman.'

Mrs Rogers flushed, hurried past and disappeared into the dining room, dishes loudly clinking.

'Get back to your book,' Virginia said, 'and behave yourself.'

'I've done my stint for today.'

'Well, go to the Mitchell and do some research or something. Visit your mother. Or go and have a drink with James. I won't be more than a couple of hours at most.'

She blew him a kiss before leaving. Outside she got into her car and drove away down the terrace and onto Great Western Road. Her thoughts now took a serious turn. Despite their happy banter, both she and Nicholas had been concerned for some time about the way things were going in the country and in the world. So was Mathieson. They all agreed that it looked as if there was going to be another war. Above all, she was worried about what might happen to Richard. Losing one child was bad enough. To lose both children would be far, far too much to bear. She had told Nicholas, 'If anything happened to Richard, I'd die. I mean it, Nicholas. I know I just wouldn't be able to bear it.'

He'd tried to soothe away her fears. 'Nothing's going to happen to Richard, darling. If there was a war, it wouldn't be like the last one. There wouldn't be fighting in the trenches. There wouldn't be hand to hand fighting or anything like that. And Richard is a pilot, remember.'

She didn't see how that could make him any safer, and she was sure Nicholas didn't either. They tried not to talk about it but the subject of war was inescapable. Germany and Italy had made their pact of steel. Germany and the Soviet Union had signed a non-aggression pact. Two thousand Nazi guards had arrived in Danzig. Attacks on Poles had become a regular occurrence. Virginia felt as if she was living on the edge of a nightmare that was gathering in horror as each day passed. There could be no ignoring it, even at Red Cross meetings where they discussed every eventuality and what their role might be if the worst came to the worst. These days Virginia was often reminded of the well-known verse Robert Burns had written after witnessing a thanksgiving service after a victory in battle:

> *Ye hypocrites, are these your pranks?*
> *Tae murder men an' gie God thanks.*
> *For shame, gie ower, proceed nae further,*
> *God won't accept your thanks for murder.*
>
> *Then let us pray that come it may,*
> *As come it will for a' that,*
> *That Sense and Worth, o'er a' the earth*
> *Shall bear the gree, and a' that.*
> *For a' that, and a' that,*
> *It's comin' yet for a' that,*
> *That Man to Man, the warld o'er,*
> *Shall brothers be for a' that.'*

*   *   *

At the Red Cross meeting, Virginia was given a list of things she would need for her nursing duties. It consisted of a light blue dress, a white bibbed apron (to be kept crisply starched at all times), a white 'butterfly' cap (also to be kept starched) and a broad navy belt and white cotton elasticated cuffs. The cuffs were to be worn over sleeves if and when the sleeves were rolled up.

After the meeting, she went straight into town and bought the lot. She had to report for duty in a couple of days' time at the Royal Infirmary, so instead of going home with her parcels, Virginia decided to go and have a look at the Infirmary. She'd seen it many times before, but just in passing, and had never paid it much attention.

When the huge new building had been opened in July 1914 by King George V, it was the largest public building in the United Kingdom. It probably still was, Virginia thought, as she viewed its enormous bulk, blackened by the smoke that had belched out over the years from Glasgow's tenement chimneys.

Virginia parked the car, and in a few minutes found herself in the emergency outpatient department, where a disturbing number of real-life patients—no actors these—sat around or milled about in various degrees of bloody injury and obvious suffering. Virginia beat a hasty retreat, somewhat less confident in her ability to cope with the duties that awaited her. She had enjoyed the make-believe of the Red Cross classes where she'd ministered with such ease and success to the actor patients. Now she could see that enjoyment would definitely not come into it. However, she was undeterred. She had never shirked hard work, even dangerous hard work, and she remembered only too well her time working in the munitions factory in her youth. If she could survive that, she could certainly survive Glasgow's Royal Infirmary.

Thinking of the munitions factory reminded her of her poor brother. Ian had been killed in one of the many explosions in that death-trap of a place. Losing him, and then her other brother Duncan, had broken her mother's heart. And to think that munitions factory had been owned by George Cartwright, Nicholas's father. Who would have thought that the charming, smiling old gentleman of his later years was that same ruthless capitalist? Indeed, he'd always appeared to be the more kindly and reasonable half in his marriage. Mrs Cartwright was the one feared and hated in the Cartwright household, by all the staff at least.

As Virginia drove back to Kirklee Terrace, her mind kept slipping into the past. Her mother, her father, her brothers returned to her like ghosts. And Wincey. Poor shy Wincey, with her straight red hair and fringe, and her dear freckled little face. Had she lived, she would have been a young lady now, married probably. Virginia sighed and tried to banish all such gloomy thoughts from her mind. She drew up in front of her house, then gathered her parcels together.

Once inside, she greeted Nicholas cheerfully. 'That's me all organised. I'm starting at the Royal on Saturday.'

'In at the deep end, then,' Nicholas said.

'How do you mean?'

Nicholas shook his head. 'Darling, you are so innocent sometimes, despite your tough upbringing. Saturday night in Glasgow?'

'Oh, you mean the drunks. I know, but don't worry, I can cope with all that. Drunks don't worry me. It's the poor women who'll come in after being battered by their drunken husbands. That'll upset me, but I suppose I'll just have to get hardened to it all.'

He gathered her into his arms. 'I can't imagine you ever being hard, darling. You're the sweetest, softest, most sensitive and caring person I've ever known.'

'Ah,' she smiled up at him, 'but you're prejudiced. You love me.'

'Yes, I do. More than anybody or anything in the world.' He held her close. 'God knows what's going to happen to the world. It seems to have gone crazy. Again,' he added.

'You really do believe there's going to a war, then?'

'Oh, there's going to be a war, all right, Virginia. The whole of Europe's mobilised. Children are already being evacuated from the cities.'

'Oh God!'

'By the way,' Nicholas said, 'James was on the phone. I've invited him to join us for dinner. Is that all right?'

'Yes, of course. He'll be upset about all this.'

'Yes, he's worried about what's going to happen to all the young men he's been teaching. War's such a waste.'

'I hate violence,' Virginia shuddered. 'I always have.'

32

'She wasn't in,' Wincey told Charlotte breathlessly. 'Where's Malcy?'

'Did you not see him? He left a few minutes ago. I wanted to lock up early and walk back with him but he said he didn't want to put me at risk. And anyway, he thought if he left early, he'd be all right. He said he'd be able to run home in a matter of minutes. He said no-one could catch up with him, even if they came early and saw him.' She took a bundle of keys from the desk drawer. 'But I'm still going to lock up early. I've already told the girls and the other men to go.'

'I saw them leaving right enough. I wondered what was going on.'

'I told Malcy I'd pay what he owed but that I'd go and see Mrs O'Donnell personally tomorrow. I was hoping you'd be able to tell me if he did owe her anything. But when he left early just now, I saw him racing away down the street. I knew then he must have been telling me the truth. She really must have threatened him. Quick, Wincey, I must go after him and make sure he's all right. I'm in such a state now.'

Wincey followed Charlotte out of the building and they'd barely turned the corner onto Springburn Road, when they heard the commotion. Women were screaming. Someone shouted, 'Ye never see the polis when they're needed. There's a man bein' murdered along there.'

'Oh dear Jesus,' Charlotte cried out and began to run.

Wincey ran too, heart pounding. They could see ahead on the other side of the road three men kicking the figure of Malcy who was curled up on the ground in the fetal position, arms trying to protect his head.

'Malcy!'

Before Wincey could stop her, Charlotte had suddenly shot out into the road. It happened so quickly. One minute Charlotte was by her side, the next she had darted away. A car was coming along, and didn't have time to stop, or even swerve to miss her. Rigid with horror, Wincey saw Charlotte's body hit the car, fly into the air and land with a sickening thud on the cobbles. Wincey couldn't move. People were milling about . . . somebody had run to the doctor's surgery, the driver of the car was being sick, then the police arrived. The next thing she remembered was Robert kneeling down beside Charlotte. He was gently closing her eyes.

Wincey remembered no more until she came to in Houston's surgery. 'Oh Robert,' she wept, 'tell me it was only a dream. It was only one of my nightmares.'

'No Wincey,' he said, 'it wasn't a dream. Charlotte was killed instantly. Malcy's in the hospital but he'll survive.'

'Do Teresa and Erchie and Granny know yet?'

Houston shook his head. 'There hasn't been time. I'll drive you home now. I'll probably have to give them a sedative. You too. It'll at least help you all to get some sleep tonight.'

'Oh Robert, I can't bear it. It's not fair. It would have been far better if it had been me, not Charlotte. She's never hurt a fly, or said an unkind word to anybody in her life. Could *you* tell the family?'

'No, this is something you must face, Wincey. They regard you as part of the family. It would be better coming from you.'

Normally Wincey would have walked the short distance home but now she was glad of being able to sit in Houston's car. On the way up the Balgrayhill, she dried her tears and struggled to find the strength to face the ordeal that awaited her.

With a trembling hand she opened the front door with her key and, followed by Houston, she went through to the kitchen. Erchie was sitting at the table reading his *Daily Record*. Granny was in her usual place beside the fire and Teresa was stirring a pot on the gas ring over at the range. She looked round, smiling.

'Oh hello, dear. You're early. And Robert . . .'

Her smile faded at the sight of the tragic expression in Wincey's eyes and the doctor's sad, sympathetic look.

'What's wrong? What's happened?'

'You'd better sit down, Teresa,' Houston said.

Teresa did as she was told, her face as pale as Wincey's now.

'It's Charlotte,' Wincey said. 'She's been killed in an accident.'

'Naw!' Erchie shouted. 'Ah said cheerio tae the lassie jist a wee while back. She let us away early the night. She wis fine.'

'She saw men beating up Malcy and she ran across the road to try and help him. She didn't see the car and the driver didn't have time to do anything.'

Wincey went over to Teresa and put her arms around her shoulders.

'She didn't suffer,' Houston said quietly. 'She died instantly.'

Suddenly, they became aware of a whimpering noise that turned into a terrible wailing. 'Oh Granny.' Both Teresa and Wincey ran over to try to comfort the old woman.

'She wis such a good wee lassie,' Granny sobbed, 'an' aye that nice tae me.'

'I know.' Wincey hugged and kissed her, while Teresa held and patted the gnarled, misshapen hands. 'And she wouldn't have wanted you to get all upset, Granny.'

'How can ah no'? She had aw her life before her, an' you say there's a God.' She turned a tragic gaze at Teresa. 'What kind o' a God's that.'

'God works in mysterious ways, dear.'

'Don't ye gie me any o' that claptrap. There's nae mystery aboot a lassie bein' run doon by a car.'

Erchie blew his nose. 'Teresa's only tryin' tae comfort ye, Ma.'

'Well, she's no' daein' a very good job o' it.'

Houston had opened his black medical bag. 'I'm going to give you all something that'll calm you and help you to sleep tonight.'

'Aye,' Granny said, 'they'll maybe knock me oot the night but ah'll still have tae face the morrow.' She wiped away her tears with the back of her sleeve. 'But ah'll face it, don't you worry. An' better than any o' them. Ah've had tae face the loss o' weans before.'

It was much later, after Houston had gone, that Teresa suddenly said, 'What about Malcy? Is he all right?'

'Oh yes,' Wincey said bitterly. 'He's all right. They're keeping him in hospital for a couple of days but he'll survive all right. His kind always do.'

'Wincey,' Teresa said gently, 'Charlotte loved him so much and he loved her. He'll be broken-hearted. We'll have to go and see him, give him a bit of support.'

'What? Oh no, Teresa, you can count me out of that.'

'Now, now, it's what Charlotte would have wanted.'

'I'm sorry, Teresa, I couldn't. It'll be as much as I can manage to be civil to him at the funeral.'

Erchie sighed. 'We know he had his weaknesses, hen, but he's no' a bad man. He was good tae Charlotte in his own way. He made her happy.'

'Oh really?' Wincey queried sarcastically. 'You think so?'

'Ye're an awful bitter wee lassie.' Erchie shook his head. 'Ye've aye felt the same about Malcy, an' he never did ye wan bit o' harm.' He hesitated. 'Have ye no' been mixin' him up wi' somebody else, hen? Are ye still daein' that? Maybe that's yer problem.'

'I have no idea what you're talking about, Erchie.' Wincey rose. 'All right, I'm off to bed. I feel the tablets beginning to work, don't you?'

'Thank goodness they've worked for Granny anyway.' Teresa gazed over at the hurly bed where Granny was lying, toothless mouth hanging helplessly open. 'Goodnight, Wincey,' Teresa added, 'although it's been anything but a good night, hasn't it?'

Wincey kissed Teresa, said goodnight to Erchie in passing and went through to her own room. There she quietly wept.

Next morning she got up very early and went to the factory to pin a notice on the door saying what had happened and that the factory would be closed for the rest of the week as a mark of respect. All the employees would be shocked, she knew. Charlotte was very well thought of by everyone. Then Wincey saw the undertaker about a date for the funeral before putting a notice in the local paper, as well as in the *Glasgow Herald*. Teresa had sent telegrams to Florence and the twins, and was now awaiting their arrival.

Wincey booked the Co-op for the funeral tea. They had all agreed that it was best to keep busy, and they were soon dealing with a steady stream of friends and neighbours coming to the house to express sympathy and to grieve with them. Teresa kept making pots of tea and putting plates of sandwiches and cakes and biscuits on the table. The blinds were kept pulled down, and during the day the kitchen and all the rooms were in a ghostly twilight.

'It doesn't seem right that Charlotte's lying in the Co-op under-taker's parlour,' Teresa said. 'She should have been here in our front room.'

415

'Naw, naw, hen,' Erchie said, 'her place wis in her own front room, up in Broomfield Street. But ye can understand Malcy jist lettin' her go to the Co-op. He's no' gettin' oot till the funeral day, so he couldnae be wi' her in their hoose.'

'I suppose so,' Teresa said, 'but it doesn't seem right, not having a wake for Charlotte.'

'A wake?' Granny bawled. 'There'll be nae Popish carry-on while ah'm here. An' when ah go, don't ye dare hae one for me, Teresa Gourlay, or ah'll come back an' haunt ye. Ah'd birl in ma grave if ye did that.'

'Oh, all right, Granny. I won't have a wake for you. But it's not just folk of my persuasion who have wakes, you know. It used to be—'

'Never mind what it used tae be. It's no' gonnae be. Can you no' take a bloody tellin'?'

'Now, now, Granny. It's not like you to swear.'

'It's no' like me tae have a wake either.'

Teresa rolled her eyes and gave up.

Wincey sat quietly for much of the time. She was dreading the day of the funeral, not only because of her grief at Charlotte's untimely death, but also at the prospect of facing Malcy. As far as Wincey was concerned, Malcy—and Malcy alone—had been the cause of Charlotte's death. Never before had she hated him so much.

At the funeral, he looked a pathetic figure, with his bruised and swollen face, his head in bandages and his arm in a sling. He sobbed through the service. Everyone felt acutely sorry for him and Wincey hated him all the more.

'Look at the two-faced hypocrite,' she said to Houston at the funeral tea.

Houston stared at her in silence for a moment. 'He's genuinely upset, Wincey. I've spoken to him more than once in the hospital. He's more than upset. He's broken-hearted and he blames himself.'

'And so he should. He was to blame. I'll never forgive him. Never.'

'Just as you'll never forgive your grandfather? Do you think you'll ever change, Wincey? Do you think you'll ever forgive yourself? I'm beginning to wonder.'

She had begun to recognise the warning signals in his expression, in his voice. She was going to lose him all right.

After the funeral tea, he said he had to go. He had a patient to visit and so Wincey returned to the Balgrayhill with Erchie and Teresa. Erchie pushed Granny's wheelchair. Florence and the twins returned to Clydebank.

Eventually the time came to reopen the factory. Life had to go on. Wincey was sitting at her desk in the office when Malcy knocked at the door and came in.

'What do you want?' Wincey asked him coldly.

'I feel terrible about this, but I don't know what to do.'

'Do about what?'

He hesitated. 'They're still after me for the money. Charlotte said she was going to pay Mrs O'Donnell.'

'I'm not Charlotte.'

'Look, Wincey, I'll never gamble again. I swear. This has finished me.'

'I'm glad to hear it.'

'But if you don't come up with the money in the next few days . . . They've given me a week's grace because of what happened to Charlotte. But they're going to kill me. They've told me, Wincey. They said they'd finish the job this time. And I believe them.'

'All right. I've got a week to let you know. Now, if you don't mind, Malcy, I'm busy.'

'Wincey, don't do this to me, please. I feel bad enough as it is. I loved Charlotte. Maybe I didn't as much as I should have at the beginning, but who couldn't grow to love her once they knew her? She was such a sweet and loving person, Wincey.'

'She was indeed, Malcy. Now I really am very busy.'

After he'd gone she thought she'd feel some sort of satisfaction. But she didn't. She knew he was a weak man and she didn't believe his vow about never gambling again. She did believe, however, that Mrs O'Donnell's men meant what they said.

'Here,' Wincey thought, 'is revenge being handed to me on a plate.'

Yet it didn't feel sweet. She kept remembering Charlotte saying, 'I love him, Wincey. He's not a bad man. He's been nothing but kind and gentle and loving to me. He can't help the gambling. It's an illness. We'd be perfectly happy together if only he could get cured of that.'

'Oh Charlotte,' Wincey thought, 'if only I could be like you.'

She still felt Charlotte was near to her. There were two desks in the office, her own desk, and Charlotte's directly opposite. How often had they sat like this working quietly across from one another, every now and again glancing up and smiling at each other. If Charlotte had been here and heard how she'd just spoken to Malcy, how would she have felt?

'Oh Charlotte,' Wincey said to the empty desk, 'I'm so sorry.'

She sat for a long time struggling with herself. Then she went out to the machine room and said to one of the girls, 'Tell Malcy to come to the office.'

In a few moments, he had returned to stand in front of her desk like an errant schoolboy. She suddenly felt tired of hating him, tired of hating.

'This is what Charlotte wanted, Malcy.' She handed him the cheque. 'She also wanted to go to Mrs O'Donnell to talk to her and make it perfectly plain that there would be no point in lending you any more money. I'll do that now, shall I?'

'Thank you, Wincey.' He accepted the cheque. 'You can talk to her if you want, but there's no need. I won't be here to borrow money from her again. I'm joining the Army. There's nothing to keep me here now.'

'I see.'

Again she struggled with herself. 'Take care then, Malcy.'

He nodded and turned to go. Just before he left, Wincey said, 'I'm sorry we haven't always seen eye to eye, but rest assured, for all your faults and no matter what you did, Charlotte always loved you.'

He nodded and quickly closed the door.

A few minutes later Erchie came in, and without his usual knock at the door.

'What huv ye been sayin' tae Malcy?'

'Why?'

'The poor fella came oot o' this office an' across the machine room like a bat oot o' hell wi' tears streamin' doon his face.'

'Poor Malcy,' Wincey said. 'I just told him that, for all his faults, Charlotte always loved him.'

'Oh?' Erchie looked taken aback. 'That wis nice o' ye, hen. He did love her, ye know.'

'Yes,' Wincey said. 'I know.'

'Well,' Erchie said, 'ah'll see ye later, hen. Ah can see ye're busy the now.'

She managed to smile. 'Yes, I've an important letter to write.'

Then after she was alone again, she took up her pen and began.

'My dear mother and father . . .'

VOLUME THREE

CLYDESIDERS
AT WAR

1939

I

The only thing that hinted at what an ordeal it must be for Wincey was the way she kept nervously tucking her hair behind one ear. Dark, ruby red hair, it was. Her fringe seemed longer too, as if she was trying to hide behind it, yet her steady, determined stare was still the same.

She was sitting in the Gourlay kitchen. The table was pale and grooved by the many scrubbings Teresa Gourlay had given it over the years. Around it sat Teresa and Erchie, and their daughters, Florence—a slim girl with large dark eyes and a proud tilt to her head, and the plump, round faced twins, Euphemia and Bridget. Granny sat in her wheelchair at one side of the fire, her short grey hair fastened with a large kirby grip, her fawn crocheted shawl clutched round her shoulders. Doctor Robert Houston sat at the other side of the fire.

The oppressive silence was only broken by the sparking of the fire in the old fashioned, black grate.

Then Florence said, 'You're kidding! You must be.'

Wincey shook her head.

'But you said . . . I mean, that first time when I found you, you said you were an orphan. Your mother and father had been killed and you had nobody else and you were going to be shut away in an institution.'

'No, Florence, *you* said that. You always had a very dramatic imagination.'

Wincey remembered every detail of the night Florence had found her and every word that had been said. 'So you're an orphan?' Florence had said.

Wincey had nodded.

'So you've run away so they won't put you into an orphanage, or into the workhouse?'

Forgetting her tears, Wincey had stared curiously at the girl. She managed to nod again.

'Och, never mind,' Florence had said. 'My Mammy'll take you in. She's always taking folk in.'

'Is she?' Wincey said in surprise.

'Och, aye, our place is like a doss house sometimes. Girls come down from the Highlands and stay at our place for a few days until they get fixed up with a nurse's job at one of the hospitals. My Mammy used to come from the Highlands. Come on.'

'Well, you didn't contradict me,' Florence said now. 'Did you?'

'I was just a wee girl and I was frightened. I thought I'd murdered my grandfather and everybody would be after me, including the police. I just wanted to hide away somewhere where I could feel safe. And you were so kind to me. I know this must be a shock for all of you, and I'm sorry, but I just couldn't tell you before.'

'Why couldn't you?' one of the twins asked. 'You've had plenty of time. You've lived with us for donkey's years. You owed it to us. You've taken our name. Our Mammy and Daddy have been your mammy and daddy. We've been like sisters.'

'I know, I'm sorry.'

Granny piped up then, 'Ah always knew she wis different frae us. A bloody capitalist. We were quite content wi' oursels wi' oor Charlotte an' Teresa workin' one sewin' machine in that wee hoose in Springburn Road. Then, before we know whit had happened, she had Erchie fixin' up machines frae aw ower the place. Then it was that auld warehouse made into a factory—an' then we'd moved hoose a couple o' times.'

'Now, now, Granny. You know fine it wasn't just Wincey, it was Charlotte as well.' Teresa's eyes darkened with sadness at the thought of her eldest daughter, who'd died so tragically in a road accident. 'And this is a much better place than the wee house in Springburn Road. Think of our nice bathroom now, instead of the lavatory out on the landing. And it's been Wincey who's been paying for these two nurses to come in every day to see you.'

'Aye, well,' Granny muttered.

'I wanted to tell you,' Wincey said. 'I longed to tell somebody, but I felt so guilty and frightened. If it hadn't been for Robert, I expect I'd have taken the secret to my grave.' She glanced at Robert Houston who had taken over as family doctor after his father had died. He smiled his encouragement. But Wincey noticed that, as usual, his smile was not reflected in his eyes. He had very serious eyes.

'Robert persuaded me to write to my real parents and tell them everything, and also to confess to you. He gave me the courage. But please don't think I'm not grateful to all of you. I have felt that you, Teresa, have been more of a mother to me all these years than my real mother. And Erchie, you've been more of a father than my real father. And Florence and Bridget and Euphemia have been my only sisters.'

Erchie jerked the peak of his cap, or 'bunnet' as he called it, further down over his brow. He always wore a bunnet outdoors and indoors because he was bald and said he felt the cold in his head something terrible. He always wore his boots indoors too. Teresa, who had given him a nice pair of checked slippers for his birthday, had been forced to wear them herself.

'Well, hen, as ah've often said, ye've aye been like ma ain flesh an' blood. Ah knew somethin' was worryin' ye, right enough. That was why me an' Teresa decided eventually to ask Doctor Houston's advice.'

'I'm glad you did now, though God knows what'll happen next. They'll get the letter tomorrow. It took me weeks to get it right but in the end, I just told the truth. I put it in the post earlier today.'

'It'll be a terrible shock to them after thinking you've been dead all these years.' Teresa's gentle face creased with worry.

'They'll probably wish I was after reading my letter. They'll maybe want nothing to do with me. They never actually had much to do with me when I lived with them.'

'You were only—what—twelve or thirteen when you came here,' Teresa continued, 'Now I can understand why you never told us your full name, and would hardly ever put your foot outside the close. But your parents must have been distracted with worry and grief, thinking their wee girl had been drowned in the Clyde. They'll surely be overjoyed to have you back.'

'That's what I keep telling her,' said Houston. 'I've had one hell of a job trying to make her see sense. She's about as difficult and thrawn as Granny here.'

'Well, wan thing's for sure—that auld rascal deserved tae die,' Granny said. 'An' if ah had the chance, ah'd huv murdered him masel. Him an' his munitions factory. He wisnae content in causin' the death o' folk in his slums, he had tae find a way tae kill a lot mair.'

Houston groaned. 'Wincey did *not* murder her grandfather.'

'She's just telt us she did. She's just telt us that wis the reason she was feart tae go back tae her real mammy an' daddy.'

'He died of a heart attack. He had a heart condition. He had been abusing her for years and she was in a state of shock. That was why she didn't run and get his heart tablets. I keep telling her. But it's quite common, unfortunately, for the victim in this sort of case to feel everything's their fault. It never is, but it's always a devil of a job to get them to believe that.'

Wincey detected the glint of impatience in his eyes. She had seen it before and knew that it wasn't caused only by her guilt. The hatred of her grandfather and the bitterness she felt towards her family were going to cause her to lose him.

Theirs was a strange, uneasy sort of relationship. She knew she loved him, but he insisted that she could not truly love anyone else until she could love herself. And also forgive her family, including her grandfather.

She'd been trying to follow his advice. According to Houston, writing the letter to her parents had been an enormous step in the right direction. But she felt far from sure, remembering how isolated she had always been as a child.

Her father was Nicholas Cartwright, the famous poet and novelist. Wincey remembered how he was usually shut away in his paper cluttered, book lined, writing room. And when he wasn't immersed in his writing, he was either in the downstairs sitting room or the upstairs drawing room talking with friends. Her mother, Virginia's interests were political. Her first husband, James Matheson, had been a disciple of the celebrated Red Clydesider and pacifist, John Maclean. Matheson had long since been crippled by a stroke and hirpled about with the help of sticks. He had a grotesquely twisted face and, as a young child, Wincey had been rather afraid of him. He had also become friends with her father, and he and his political friends regularly filled the tall, terraced house, with lively discussion and heated debate.

Her older brother, Richard, sometimes took part in these verbal confrontations but as often as not, he was out playing cricket or rugby, or getting into some sort of mischief. However, in the eyes of the family, he could do no wrong. Tall, dark and handsome like his father, he had, as Matheson said, 'the gift of the gab'. He could have been a politician but they all knew that if he had gone into politics, it would have been as a true blue Conservative, like his grandparents. He never made any secret of the fact that he had no truck with his parents' radical views, or with Matheson's fervent socialism.

Wincey had always felt like she was the cuckoo in the nest. She hadn't her father's glossy black hair and dark eyes, nor had she her mother's long golden hair. A shy child with red hair and freckles, she couldn't match her brother Richard's extrovert and daring personality. Always hovering on the fringes of life in Kirklee Terrace, she felt ignored and neglected. More often than not, she was sent out with a dismissive, 'Go and keep your grandfather company, there's a good girl.'

Her grandparents lived in a big grey villa on Great Western Road, not far from Kirklee Terrace. Her grandmother regularly went out to her bridge club and also the church Women's Guild. Her grandfather couldn't get out and about because of his heart condition and so she was often left alone with him to 'keep him company'. Much too often, she realised now.

Richard was her grandmother's favourite—he was everyone's favourite really. She was supposed to be her grandfather's. She didn't realise the truth at first. She felt confused and sick and miserable. She didn't understand what was going on, or why.

A wave of rage swept over her as she sat at the table in the tenement kitchen, with its recessed, cream curtained bed. Opposite was the window with the sink underneath, or jaw box as it was called. The view outside was of the back yard, with its midden and wash house. This kitchen, this house, was the only real home she had ever known. The Gourlays had come to mean so much more to her than her 'real' family. How much better they had treated her than the wealthy Cartwrights ever had! For years she had been known as one of the Gourlay girls, and that's how she wanted it to stay.

'What saddens me,' Teresa's voice broke into Wincey's thoughts, 'is the idea of us losing you.'

'You won't be losing me,' Wincey protested. 'Nothing will change as far as I'm concerned. I've been a Gourlay for years, and I'll always be a Gourlay.'

'Wincey,' Houston groaned, 'you'll have to accept that your whole life will change. For a start your parents will want you to go and live with them.'

'My home is here with Teresa and Erchie and Granny.'

Florence rolled her eyes. 'I don't get this. Why would you want to go on living in a tenement flat in Springburn when you could live in a big posh house in the West End?' Florence, like the twins, had not long been married and she was especially proud of her new flat in Clydebank. She had acquired airs and graces since working in Copeland & Lye's in Sauchiehall Street.

Wincey knew that snobbish Grandmother Cartwright would have described Florence as having 'ideas above her station'. Grandmother Cartwright had never forgiven Wincey's mother—her former scullery maid—for having such ideas, and—much worse—for eventually marrying her son. Or, as she put it, 'trapping him into marriage'. Virginia had been pregnant with Richard, but in 1914, war had intervened and it wasn't until Richard was six that the marriage finally took place. Mrs Cartwright had taken the child away from Virginia at birth because she had been wrongly informed that her son had been killed in action in the trenches. She believed that the baby was all she had left of him. She hated Virginia for taking her grandson back after Nicholas had been found in a military hospital, and reunited with Virginia.

To keep in touch with young Richard was the main reason she visited the house in Kirklee Terrace, and was at least frostily polite to her daughter in law.

'I've been happy here,' Wincey insisted. 'I was never happy in Kirklee Terrace.'

'Things will be different now,' Houston said.

'Yes, worse!'

Houston rolled his eyes. 'Will you stop being so pessimistic.'

'Well,' Erchie said, 'at least you didnae turn up on her doorstep without a word o' warnin'. Yer mammy would probably huv died o' shock.'

'Of aw the families in Glasgow,' Granny shook her head, 'she had tae come frae that bloody lot.'

'Granny,' Teresa said, 'watch your language. Wincey didn't choose her family.' With a meaningful look at the old woman, she added, 'Whether we like it or not, we've all to make do with what we've got.'

Wincey smiled. 'I didn't choose the Cartwrights, right enough, but I did choose the Gourlays, and I still do.'

'Well, that's nice o' ye, hen,' Erchie gave her hand a pat, 'but ye cannae ignore yer ain flesh an' blood. An' after aw, it wisnae yer mammy an' daddy that hurt ye. It was yer auld villain o' a grandfather. Everybody hated him. Good riddance tae him, that's what ah say, but yer mammy an' daddy huvnae done anybody any harm. Quite the opposite, hen. Ah've read some o' yer daddy's books. An' yer mammy's been active at many a socialist meetin'. Ah've even been tae a meetin' that she spoke at, along wi' that friend o' Johnny Maclean, James Matheson.'

'Yes, he was my mother's first husband. My mother knew Maclean as well. I vaguely remember him. I was very young, but I even have a memory of being at his funeral. I remember my father carrying me on his shoulders. I was a bit frightened to see such a big crowd.'

'Fancy! Ah wis there as well,' Erchie cried out. 'Whit a turn out, wisn't it. Over ten thousand crowdin' the streets. Aye, James Matheson, that wis his pal's name. He went tae jail along wi' oor Johnny. Mair than once. It wis what Johnny suffered in jail that killed him in the end. Ah bet it wis the same thing that nearly killed Matheson. It wis a miracle he survived that stroke.'

Granny spoke up then. 'An' a man like him friendly wi' yer daddy? Whit's the world comin' tae?'

'Now, now, Granny,' Teresa said. 'It's a very civilised way to behave. What good would it do him to be bitter against his ex-wife's new husband?'

'Naebody got divorced an' had auld an' new husbands in ma day. They've nae sense o' shame nowadays.'

'Anyway,' Teresa smiled at Wincey, but her eyes remained dark pools of anxiety, 'if your mother and father arrive here tomorrow, or any day, they'll be made welcome. And . . . ' she hesitated, then continued with some difficulty, 'and if you leave with them, we'll understand.'

Houston said, 'You'd better stay off work tomorrow, Wincey, to be here when they arrive. As I'm sure they will.'

Wincey nodded, tucking her hair behind her ear and seeming to shrink beneath her fringe. She wanted to say that she wished she had never agreed to write that damned letter. No good would come of it, she was sure of that.

2

Virginia was on her way to do early shift in the Royal Infirmary, dressed in her Red Cross uniform of navy blue skirt and jacket, white shirt and peaked cap. She'd managed to get her Red Cross certificate, but was finding the experience in the Royal like being thrown to the sharks. The Outpatients Emergency department was especially fraught. At weekends it was like a battlefield, peopled mostly by wounded drunks with a lot of aggression to get rid of. There were other, more distressing cases of women who had been beaten by drunken husbands. Some of them were half dead, with broken bones and unrecognisable, bloody faces. It made Virginia sick, but at the same time she counted herself lucky that neither of her two husbands had ever physically abused her.

Her first husband, James Matheson, had been—and still was—obsessed with politics. His obsession had developed to such a degree that, although she'd tried her best to help him, most of the time he was hardly aware of her existence. They got on a lot better now as friends than they'd ever done as man and wife.

She'd repeated the pattern by marrying Nicholas Cartwright. Writing was his obsession. There had been a time when she'd hated Nicholas for isolating her, shutting her off from his life, leaving her to grieve alone for Wincey and to face the terrible trauma of not knowing what had happened to her. There was the awful guilt too. Round and round in her mind went the terrible question: had she and Nicholas neglected the child? They hadn't meant to, but the house had always been filled with either her friends or Nicholas's friends. Perhaps they had not always been as attentive to Wincey as they might have been.

But she'd always been a difficult child, so quiet and shy. Richard had been a complete contrast to his sister—outgoing, full of energy, always wanting to join in with everything. Secretly, Virginia knew that all their love and attention had been lavished on Richard—and what had that done to Wincey?

Virginia's heart contracted in pain. How could they have been so thoughtless and insensitive? She had asked herself and Nicholas that question a thousand or more times over the years. It was easier for him. He could—and always did— escape into the seclusion of his writing room.

She'd challenged him about this eventually and they'd talked things out as much as they were able. Life had become more bearable after that, although secret little pinpricks of resentment still bothered her. Making love had helped. Nicholas had always been a very passionate man. All right, a great deal of his passion went into his writing, but he could still make love with great enthusiasm and virility.

Virginia also tried to get on with her life by joining the Red Cross and becoming a VAD nurse. To some degree she had Matheson to thank for that. He had lectured her on how she was allowing guilt, bitterness and hatred to ruin her life. He said taking her feelings out on Nicholas was helping nobody. Nicholas had suffered and grieved over Wincey's disappearance too. He'd done all he could. What more did she expect him to do? Matheson always seemed to be making allowances for Nicholas. But perhaps that was only natural—they'd been friends ever since he'd been in hospital unable to talk, and hardly able to move after his stroke. When Nicholas returned to Glasgow, he had gone to visit Matheson every day. He read the newspapers to him, and spoke to him about how he too had been hospitalised, with his memory gone, after being blown up in the trenches during the war.

Virginia had been shocked at Nicholas visiting Matheson. She had lied to Nicholas, who was her lover then, about her marriage to Matheson being over. She feared what would happen if and when Matheson recovered, imagining him trying to kill Nicholas. But instead the two men had become firm friends in that hospital. She supposed that Matheson had been grateful for Nicholas's conscientious attempts to help him. Admittedly, she'd not been much use. She'd even stopped going to the hospital, unable to look at Matheson in the dreadful state he was in, believing that he wasn't able to even recognise her, far less understand anything she said to him. Obviously she'd been wrong in this.

It turned out Matheson was perfectly able to understand every word, and he'd got to know Nicholas, it seemed, far better than she'd ever known him.

Matheson told her it was time she stopped feeling sorry for herself and started thinking of someone else for a change. And the best way to do that was to help other people with their problems. So she'd turned to nursing in the huge, soot blackened Royal Infirmary.

Now, despite the difficulties of the blackout, she was managing to make her way to the bus stop. The blackout order had gone out earlier that summer, before war had even been declared. As the threat posed by enemy bombers became a reality, all external lights and street lighting had to be totally extinguished. No lighting in houses was to be visible from the outside. Advice had been given about using close fitting blinds and curtains of dark cloth. Skylights, glass doors and fan lights had to have sufficient coats of dark distemper or paint. Roads were completely unlit and private vehicles had no lights. Travelling by public transport meant moving about in your own dimly lit world. Train compartments were now filled with the ghostly glow of a single blue bulb. Windows were painted out, except for a small circle. Even if you raised the blind and peered out through this circle, you couldn't read the station's name because it had been painted over.

Already, only weeks into the war, there had been a three hundred percent increase in fatalities in Glasgow due to road accidents. Virginia felt safer walking and then catching a bus. At least pedestrians were now allowed to carry torches, providing they were covered with a double layer of tissue paper. But it was becoming increasingly difficult to get hold of number eight batteries.

She was kept busy in the Royal every day of the week with casualties who'd fallen down steps, off railway platforms, had bumped into lamp posts and walls, or stepped into canals or rivers. It was even more dangerous trying to drive a vehicle in the pitch blackness.

Virginia certainly hadn't the nerve to drive her car. Now, as she slowly shuffled forward, she felt alone in the darkness that mirrored the black hopelessness inside her. Her hand edged along walls and railings, and slid across the icy glass of shop windows. Once at the bus stop, despite the regulation that told civilians not to wave torches at the bus driver, she felt it necessary to make the driver see her and stop. On the bus, she sat lost in thought as the vehicle crawled along through the gloom.

Matheson had been very supportive about her nursing. As long as she had nothing to do with the war effort, he was satisfied. He was a pacifist, as well as a socialist—her mother in law insisted that he was 'an out and out communist'. Maybe she was right. He had certainly remained steadfast in his beliefs, like his mentor, John Maclean, before him.

'I'd rather die in prison than have anything to do with this war,' he insisted.

She knew this to be true. He had nearly died in prison during the 1914-18 war, but her feelings on the subject had never been as extreme as his. Her position was between that of Matheson and Nicholas. Although she regarded herself as a pacifist, she saw no reason for refusing to take a nurse's post—in the forces, if necessary. She had also volunteered to be an ambulance driver, and Matheson had no objections to her becoming involved in a humanitarian service that was now more vital than ever. It was something that many Quakers did. They were well known as pacifists, but that didn't stop them organising a 'Friends Ambulance Service'.

Nicholas, however, was all things to all men. She blamed his writing for this. He was always so obsessed with understanding other people's point of view and motivation, 'what makes them tick,' as he said. He was proud of the fact that their son Richard had become a fighter pilot in the RAF. On his desk there was a photograph of Richard standing proudly beside his gleaming new Spitfire. Her own heart melted every time she looked at the photograph. He was very like his father—tall and handsome with his black hair ruffled in the breeze and the sheepskin collar of his leather flying jacket turned up. He had his father's dark eyes and winning smile. No doubt he'd already broken a few hearts.

She loved her son as much—perhaps more—than his father did. For that reason alone, she wished he'd never joined the RAF. She lived in constant fear now of him being shot down and killed. She couldn't understand Nicholas's attitude. He seemed so proud and happy when he spoke of Richard in the RAF. She had always hated war, and she hated it all the more now. The last war had robbed so many mothers of their sons. The flower of British manhood had been thrown away in a brutal, pointless struggle over a few pitiful miles of French and Flemish wasteland. A land fit for heroes was what they had been promised, but many of the survivors who had returned were nervous wrecks, suffering from shell shock. Thousands of others came back badly wounded, mutilated or enduring the terrible after effects of poison gas. And all they got in the land they'd fought for and returned to were homelessness and unemployment.

Now, hardly twenty years later, there was another war to suffer. A war that would no doubt consume another generation of young men. Men like Richard.

'But this time it's different,' Nicholas insisted.

'Why is it different?' she'd wanted to know.

His tall, regal looking and infuriatingly snobbish mother had been there at the time. Mrs Cartwright had always been a regular and very active churchgoer, sailing to the church every Sunday morning in her musquash coat, or fox furs and an old fashioned cloche type hat. She had been president of the Women's Guild and God knows what all else in the church. It was enough to make anyone an atheist, Virginia thought bitterly.

'Do you not even know what that dreadful little house painter once said?' Mrs Cartwright peered through her lorgnettes at her daughter in law in disgust. ' "One is either a German or a Christian. You cannot be both." That is all he was, you know. An ordinary house painter.' She repeated the words in disgust. 'A house painter'. 'This has always been the danger. My late husband always maintained— give the workers an inch and they'll take a mile. Oh, how right he was!'

She glared at Virginia as if accusing her of proving the point. Virginia did not rise to the bait although she fumed in secret. She could remember a time when she would have argued with Mrs Cartwright. Now she didn't see the point. Her mother in law was too old and too set in her ways. No good would come of arguing with her. All it did was to turn Nicholas against her.

'She's an elderly lady and she's grieving for her husband. For goodness sake, Virginia, try to have a bit of patience and under-standing.'

So now, for the most part, Virginia kept silent or tried to avoid Mrs Cartwright altogether. But it was very difficult trying to maintain this pretence of civility. The woman was such a snob, and she never missed a chance of running down the working class, or of reminding her daughter in law of her lowly origins and how she could never be 'one of them', meaning the upper class. All of which infuriated Virginia, who remembered only too vividly the suffering endured by her hard working mother, father, and brothers. Her mother and father were worth ten of Mr and Mrs Cartwright, and there was no comparison between her brothers and some of the wealthy chinless wonders who used to visit the Cartwright house.

Nicholas said, 'We tried our best for peace. We had to do something about Poland.'

'We?'

'Don't quibble, Virginia. You know perfectly well what I mean.'

Mrs Cartwright drew herself up, back stiff, bosom held high. 'Nicholas and I are proud of Richard fighting for his country, even if you are not.'

As far as Virginia knew, Richard had not as yet been involved in any fighting. She prayed every night that this situation would continue. It seemed as if nothing much had happened since war had been declared. To many people it had been a bit of an anti-climax, and some people were beginning to call it the 'phoney war'. Anxiety and expectation of the worst had been at fever pitch at first. Everyone had been issued with gas masks, Anderson shelters had been dug in almost every back garden, and brick shelters had sprung up in tenement back yards. New walls—known as baffle walls—had been erected in front of the shelter entrances and on pavements in front of closes. These brick walls were supposed to save lives by lessening the effects of blast, but already hospital emergency departments were inundated with cases of people having run or walked into them in the blackout. Virginia had seen some horrific facial injuries that had been caused in this way.

At least Mrs Cartwright was against Hitler, although for the wrong reasons in Virginia's opinion. However, at least up until the declaration of war, many aristocrats had been openly sympathetic to the Nazis. She remembered not so long ago at a dinner party she had been to with Nicholas, a woman at the table had said, 'Personally I like the Germans and I admire their leader. They are the best organised people in Europe.'

Nicholas ignored the remark but Virginia had said icily, 'Well, I certainly don't admire Hitler.'

Sir Oswald Mosley and his blackshirts were still marching in the streets of Britain, although not in Glasgow. He'd visited Glasgow Green and had to make a quick exit in his van with a howling mob of Glaswegians chasing him. Mosley's Fascists preached simplistic philosophies and easy answers. They just blamed the Jews for everything—from mass poverty to the war itself, but according to Matheson, there were other people in Britain who were far more helpful to Hitler than Mosley. There were at least nine other organisations supporting Hitler, Matheson said. One of these organisations had over four thousand members. They included two dukes and the chairman of Morris Motors. Another of the organisations, the Anglo-German Fellowship, boasted that its membership included sixteen peers, the governor and a director of the Bank of England, the chairman of ICI and the chief political advisor to the Foreign Office.

'They're all hoping Hitler's Storm-troopers will be a buffer between them and a communist revolution. Their greatest fear is something like the Russian Revolution happening here, and they'll do anything to avoid losing their privileges and their wealth.' It was the sort of thing that made Matheson so furious that Virginia feared he would have another stroke. 'These people don't care about the ordinary working man,' he told her bitterly, 'or woman. Remember how you were treated when you were in service, slaving in some of their houses. And in the munitions work that killed your brother. They know, as well as I do, that trade unionists are being arrested and jailed by Hitler and his henchmen and they're all for it. They don't care about anything or anybody but their own selfish, greedy . . . '

'I know, I know,' Virginia soothed, 'but you're not going to change anything by making yourself ill. Calm down, for pity's sake.'

He always did calm down but his anger left him trembling. She felt sorry for him. She despaired of the whole complicated mess. But most of all, she worried about her son and the fact that, whatever happened, he and his fellow pilots would soon be in the front line.

3

Florence still couldn't quite take it in. Nor could the twins. While Wincey was saying goodnight to Dr Houston at the front door, they whispered together in the kitchen. 'There she was,' Florence hissed as if she was an actress in a melodrama, 'admiring my new house as if it was a palace. She even said it was like a palace, and all the time she knew her place in the posh West End was ten times the size of my wee house in Clydebank.'

'Now, now,' Teresa said, 'her place was here in Springburn. She still thinks it is. You heard her just now.'

'There was me so proud because my new house had a bathroom,' Florence continued. 'Not like most of my friends who start off with a toilet out on the landing. But I bet she was used to bathrooms en suite. Here,' her eyes became enormous, 'remember how she used to clean that outside toilet when we lived in the room and kitchen. She must be mad. I even thought so at the time.'

'Stop that, Florence. She was always a good, hard working wee girl. I won't have you, or anyone else, saying a word against her.'

Just then Wincey returned to the room. She was clutching her bottle green cardigan around her as if she was freezing. 'I didn't say to Robert, but I honestly wish I'd never sent that letter now. I feel terrible. I won't be able to get a wink of sleep tonight. We were perfectly all right the way we were. I was perfectly all right.'

Erchie shook his head. 'Naw, ye wernae, hen. Ye were awfae awkward wi' men, for a start. Even wi' Robert, an' ye couldnae meet a nicer fella.'

'Well, I suppose . . . But writing that letter isn't going to help that.'

She sank onto a chair at the table. 'It's only going to make everything worse. What's my father going to think about what I've said about his father? It doesn't bear thinking about.'

'The chances are he'll wish his father wis still alive so as he could tell him whit an auld bastard he wis. Ah mean, ye were only a wee lassie, hen. It wis terrible whit he did tae ye.'

'The thing that worries me,' Teresa nursed her cup between her hands, 'is you letting your parents think you were dead all this time. I can understand how you felt, of course,' she added hastily. 'You were frightened, dear. Your grandfather dying like that and everything.'

'Well, I just hope they'll understand, but I doubt it.'

'Well never mind, it's not as if you'll have to face them on your own. Granny and Erchie and I will be right there beside you.'

Wincey went over to Teresa and hugged her. 'Oh thank you, Teresa.'

'Goodness me, you're an awful wee girl.' Teresa patted her straight, grey speckled hair and smoothed down her floral apron. 'I'll pour you a fresh cup of tea.'

Florence and the twins cried out, 'Can we stay overnight, Mammy? Then we can be here too.'

Wincey felt a bit overwhelmed but grateful at the same time. She knew she'd feel safer with all the family around her. She still felt the Gourlays to be her family—far more so than the Cartwrights.

'But what about your man, Florence?' Teresa asked.

'Eddie's coming here after his work.' Eddie worked in Singer's factory and had escaped conscription because of mild epilepsy. Nobody outside of the family knew he had it, and at first the mere idea had frightened Florence, but she'd discovered that he only very occasionally took a 'wee turn' in which he just seemed to lose the place for a few minutes. Then he 'came back' and was all right again. Anyway he was a lovely man with brown curly hair and laughing eyes, and she loved him. They just didn't mention the epilepsy to anyone and he took his pills on the quiet.

The twins' husbands, Joe and Pete, had been conscripted but both had ended up in the Highland Light Infantry in Maryhill Barracks, which they regarded as a right bit of luck. Maryhill wasn't all that far from their homes in Dumbarton Road in Clydebank. Apart from bayonet practice, which meant them charging about thirty yards to plunge fixed bayonets at four foot sacks hanging on a line, they had never been involved in any action. Some men talked about the 'phoney war' and the 'bore war' and were restless for a fight, but Joe and Pete were very content with the way things were. They could see their wives regularly and Euphemia and Bridget were proud to walk along Dumbarton Road arm in arm with their men in their smart new HLI uniforms.

'Oh well, if Eddie's all right about staying . . . ' Teresa turned to the twins. 'What about Joe and Pete?'

Euphemia helped herself to another biscuit. Both she and Bridget enjoyed eating and didn't care how fat they got. The twins never used the word 'fat', they always proudly maintained that they were 'generously moulded'. Florence, on the other hand, was very careful of her figure.

Euphemia said, 'Joe isn't off until the weekend.'

'Pete's the same,' Bridget added, 'so I can stay the night as well.'

Teresa made a fresh pot of tea and put some more digestive biscuits onto a plate

Granny said, 'This is gonnae be a right circus, if ye ask me.'

'Now, now, Granny, nobody's asking you. Have another digestive and drink your tea.'

Granny's gums chomped over the biscuit. Her arthritis was so bad that these days she couldn't even cope with wearing her teeth. 'Aye well, ah'll soon tell them whit ah think o' the Cartwrights.'

'You'll do no such thing, Granny. You'll be nice and polite to them.'

'Or jist keep yer gob shut, Ma,' Erchie said. 'It's gonnae be hard enough without you stirrin' things up.'

'Nice an' polite tae the Cartwrights?' Granny spluttered biscuit crumbs onto her shawl. 'Johnny Maclean'll be birlin' in his grave at the very idea!'

Florence lit up a cigarette, her eyes dreamy. 'Maybe they'll invite us over to their place. Fancy visiting in the West End! Wait till I tell the other girls about this.' Florence was now in the glove department of Copeland & Lye's. Ladies came in and, with hands stuck up, rested an elbow on the velvet cushion Florence placed on the counter. Then Florence would gently, expertly, smooth down over the hand a beautiful and very expensive leather glove. Maybe Mrs Cartwright senior and junior had been among her ladies.

'Aren't you girls supposed to be at work tomorrow?' Teresa asked

438

as she went over to dust the crumbs off Granny and tidy her kirby grip further into her hair.

'For pity's sake, Mammy,' Florence said, 'I wouldn't be able to do a stroke. I'll get Eddie to phone in and say I'm sick or something.'

'And I'll phone Pettigrews,' Euphemia added. Both she and Bridget worked in the millinery department of Pettigrew & Stephen's in Sauchiehall Street, just along from the equally high class Copeland & Lye's. Florence always insisted that Copeland's was *the* place, far more high class than Pettigrews, or anywhere else.

'Don't be silly, dear. They won't believe both you and Bridget are sick at the same time.'

Euphemia giggled. 'Yes they will. We're twins. We're supposed to do everything together.'

'That's right,' Bridget agreed. She looked exactly like her sister, they both had the same chubby faces, brown hair tucked behind their ears in a bunch of curls held firmly in place with kirby grips. A smaller, shorter but equally tight bunch of curls decorated each forehead, and they both had mouths slashed with the same scarlet lipstick.

'A right circus,' Granny repeated, stretching a shaky hand out for another biscuit.

'Well now,' Teresa said, 'if you're staying, you can make yourselves useful. This place will have to have a good clean. And that rug will have to have a good shake out in the back yard.'

Granny had made the multi-coloured rag rug many years ago, before her arthritis was so bad.

'For pity's sake, Mammy!' Florence cast her eyes upwards. 'Haven't you any modern equipment?'

'What do you mean, modern equipment?'

'I have a special mop for my kitchen floor. Nobody goes down on their knees with a scrubbing brush nowadays.'

'What nonsense. You're getting too stuck up for your own good, Florence. Ever since you've been in that Copeland & Lye's.'

'The kitchen's fine the way it is,' Wincey interrupted.

'Anyway,' Euphemia said, 'you should show them into the front room, not the kitchen.'

Bridget eagerly nodded her agreement. 'Yes, that's definitely the done thing,'

'A right bloody circus. Ye're no' gonnae wheel me through tae that cold room. Ah'm stayin' here by the fire. Far better tae bring them in here anyway. More natural in the kitchen. They won't thank ye for puttin' on airs an' graces, an' tryin' tae impress them. They'll no' be comin' here tae admire oor front room. They'll no' be seein' anythin' or anybody but Wincey.'

'Yes,' Teresa nodded. 'You're quite right, Granny. It's best if we all just try to relax and be natural. After all, when anyone else drops in, especially in the morning, it's the kitchen we welcome them into. The kitchen's the heart of the house, I always say.'

Florence heaved a sigh. Her mother had no idea. She had never mixed with ladies. And she was so old fashioned. She had too many grey hairs for a woman not yet fifty. She refused to get it coloured and just had it cut short and held on one side by a large kirby grip, just like Granny's. Florence's own hair was long and glossy and smoothly curled in behind her ears and down onto her shoulders. Outside she always wore a smart brimmed hat, tipped well forward over her brow. Fancy entertaining the gentry in the kitchen!

'Yes, I'll feel much better if there isn't any fuss,' Wincey said.

'For pity's sake, Mammy! You've a four room and kitchen house here. Anybody would think you'd never moved up the Balgrayhill and were still in that horrible wee room and kitchen in Springburn Road. What's the point in having four rooms if you're always stuck in this wee kitchen?'

'It's not a wee kitchen, Florence. It's a lovely big kitchen.'

'She's worse than Wincey,' Granny said. 'Stuck up wee madam. Ah'll say that fur Wincey—she wis never stuck up. She wis different frae us—ah always knew that. There was aye a bit o' capitalist aboot her, wi' aw her money makin' ploys, but she wis never stuck up.'

'Thank you, Granny.' Wincey laughed and went over to plant a kiss on the old woman's loose skinned cheek.

'Get aff!' Granny roughly shoved her away. 'Ah cannae stand folk droolin' ower me.'

'That's settled then,' Wincey said. 'We're all just going to be ourselves. I still wish I'd never sent the letter though. It's all very well for Robert. He's not going to be here.'

'He has his patients to see to, dear,' Teresa reminded her. 'He's a very hard working doctor. You can't expect him to be always at your beck and call.'

'I know, I know, it's just . . . I'll be so glad once tomorrow's over. Of course,' she suddenly added, 'they might not come. That'll be worse in a way—the suspense!'

'Oh, they'll come all right, hen,' Erchie assured her. 'Ah'd bet ma life on it. As soon as their postie's been, they'll be over here like a shot.'

'We'd better all be up really early then,' Florence said. 'By the time I have a bath and do my hair and make up . . . '

'Ye selfish wee madam!' Granny shouted. 'Ye're no' gonnae keep us aw oot that bathroom. Forget yer bloody bath. It's no' you the Cartwrights are comin' tae see.'

'For pity's sake, Mammy, can you not do something about her language? What if she swears tomorrow. She's liable to give us all a right showing up.'

'Who's *her*?' Granny bawled. 'Ah'll *her* ye. An' ye dinnae need me tae gie ye a showin' up. Ye can dae that yersel'— ye're aye daein' it.'

'Have your bath tonight, dear,' Teresa soothed. 'That'll give you more time for your hair and make up tomorrow.'

'Oh, all right.'

'Now on you go through—the pair of you as well,' she added to the twins, 'and make up a couple of beds for yourselves. There's plenty clean sheets in the room press.'

'Oh very well.' The girls bounced up. Florence rose with more dignity and, despite her bored tone of voice, there was an air of eagerness and excitement clinging to the three of them. They were in fact dying to get on their own to discuss all that Wincey had told them, not to mention the potential drama of the next day.

4

It was lunchtime before Virginia returned from her shift. Usually she just relaxed with a sandwich and a cup of tea beside the Aga in the kitchen with the fragrant herbs hanging down from one of the oak beams. Gone were the days when her housekeeper, Mrs Rogers, would prepare a big pot of soup and perhaps a steak pie and vegetables and leave them just to be heated up. Mrs Rogers had been evacuated with her children to some safe haven in the country. Thousands of children, some accompanied by mothers, teachers and helpers, had already been evacuated. Walter Elliott, the Minister of Health, had described it as an exodus bigger than that of Moses. 'It's the movement of ten armies,' he'd said, 'each of which is as big as the whole expeditionary force.'

At least Mrs Rogers would be with her children to make sure that all was well with them. Virginia had heard that not every child had been welcomed or was having a happy time. She knew of one country host who'd written to a friend saying that there were six evacuated children in their house and he and his wife hated them so much, they'd decided to take away something from them at Christmas.

There hadn't been any evacuees during the First World War. Even the songs were different in this war. There were no rousing marching songs as there had been in August 1914. Instead there were now songs of longing for wives and sweethearts. And there was no talk of heroism or glory or adventure. Just a dull sense of foreboding and uncertainty about what the future might hold.

As often as not, while Virginia was eating her sandwich and drinking her cup of tea, she listened to the wireless. She always seemed to be on her own. Now, as her heels clacked across the marble floor of the hall, she remembered how, when she'd first heard about this house and been told about the marble floor, she'd imagined a huge palatial building. In fact it was quite a modest sized hall.

She pushed open the kitchen door and was suddenly taken aback to find Nicholas sitting waiting for her in the kitchen. He looked very strange—white faced, agitated, yet eager and shining eyed.

'What on earth's wrong?' Virginia asked. It had to be something really cataclysmic to bring him out of his room at such an early hour.

'Virginia, you'll never guess—never in a million years.'

'Guess what?'

'Sit down.'

Obediently she sank onto a chair.

'A letter came this morning.'

'Good news about your book?'

'No. Even better.'

What could be better than that to Nicholas? For a moment she thought he must have gone mad. She'd often wondered if his intense concentration on so many fictitious people and situations might one day tip him over the edge.

'You'd never guess,' he repeated. 'Never in a million years.'

'For goodness sake, Nicholas.'

'A letter came this morning from Wincey.'

Virginia stared at him. Now she *knew* he had gone mad. He repeated the words, 'From Wincey. She's alive and well, Virginia.'

'Wincey?' Virginia felt faint.

'Yes, Wincey. Read the letter. It's beside you on the table.'

She stared at it. Then, at last, with a trembling hand, she picked it up and began to read. As she did so, tears welled up and trickled down her cheeks. 'Forgive me,' the letter said.

'Forgive me?' Virginia said out loud. 'Oh Nicholas, it's us who need to be forgiven. If only we'd known.'

Nicholas dazedly shook his head, making a lock of black hair flop down. 'When I think of us—time after time—sending her over there and all the time, her being so frightened and not able to tell us. And for all these years, she's felt—she obviously still feels—guilty and afraid. Oh Virginia! We must go to her right away.'

'Yes, right now. It's an address in Springburn—the Balgrayhill. That's up near Springburn Park. We've been there. To think we went there once to hear that brass band recital. Remember? In the park.

She might have been in the crowd.'

'I know. Are you ready?'

'I'm not sure if I can even stand up, Nicholas. I feel shattered, don't you?'

'Yes, but I've had a little more time to recover. Come on, I'll help you out to the car.'

'I'm still in my uniform.'

'Does that matter?'

'I suppose not.' It still hadn't sunk in. Virginia felt utterly drained. She wanted to believe that Wincey was alive and well and that they were about to be reunited, but she wasn't able to get used to the idea. She didn't believe it. Perhaps it was some sort of cruel joke that somebody was playing on her and Nicholas. It was too cruel. She couldn't bear it. She allowed Nicholas to support her, half carry her, outside. She sat very still beside him in the car.

'I wonder what she'll look like,' Nicholas was saying. 'She'll be what, twenty, now. Remember her red hair with the fringe and her freckles and her lovely long lashes? I expect she'll still look the same. I wonder if she'll be as quiet and shy.' His voice tightened. 'Maybe she was so quiet because she was afraid. That never occurred to us, did it? But then how could it?'

A silence held between them until Nicholas began speaking again.

'I wonder what this Gourlay family are like. They've obviously been good to her. Thank God they took her in and looked after her. God knows what might have happened to the child if she'd been left to wander the streets in the dark.'

'I think I must be in shock, Nicholas. I can't believe this is happening.' Virginia stared at his long-fingered hands clutching at the steering wheel and shook her head. 'I just can't.'

He laughed. 'It's happening all right, darling. And isn't it wonderful? A miracle. She's come back from the dead. That's what it feels like. We've believed for so long that she was dead.'

The car was slowed down by tram cars trundling along the dusty Springburn Road with its lines of shops at either side and the windows of tenement flats glimmering above them. Virginia noticed a long queue of women outside the Co-op grocers. Food rationing had just started, with butter, sugar, bacon and ham the first to be rationed. Rationing had been introduced partly because, in the first few weeks of the war, people in poorer districts were infuriated by the sight of well heeled middle-class matrons motoring into working class areas, stopping at one grocer's shop after another, and buying up large amounts of essential foods like sugar. Obviously to hoard. Now when something extra would arrive in a shop, the word would spread like a hallelujah and bring local women running to the shop to form a queue. Virginia had done it herself for a packet of raisins. Bananas were one of the things that had completely disappeared.

Virginia couldn't stop her mind from wandering. She realised this was partly due to fatigue. Never in all her life had she worked so hard—or felt so tired. On top of her work for the Ambulance Service, she had just finished a long and harrowing shift at the Royal Infirmary. She hadn't even had time for a cup of tea before receiving the shock of the letter. Not only her mind, but every nerve and sinew in her body, was absolutely exhausted.

She could see the Balgrayhill now, along at the far end of Springburn Road. Balgrayhill looked much wider and airier. She could see a church steeple at one side and at the top, a block of respectable looking red sandstone tenements. Her heart pounded and she felt faint again. One of these houses, in that block of red sandstone tenements, was where Wincey lived.

The tram rails stopped at the foot of the steep hill and the car was able to increase its speed until it reached the top.

'There's the number,' Nicholas said, stopping the car outside a close. 'The bottom flat, the letter said. Look, that must be it. There's somebody at the window.'

Virginia couldn't look.

'Is it . . . ?'

'No, an older woman. She's gone now, probably to open the door. Come on, Virginia. Don't just sit there, darling.'

Somehow her legs carried her across the pavement and into the close. The door of the house on the left was open and a woman with a slight stoop and speckled grey hair held neatly on one side by a kirby grip stood waiting. Beside her was a small, skinny, beaky-nosed man wearing a peaked cap pulled well down over his forehead. Both the man and the woman put out a welcoming hand.

'I'm Teresa Gourlay, and this is my husband, Erchie.'

They shook hands and followed the couple into a windowless lobby.

'Wincey's waiting in the kitchen with Granny and our other girls, Florence, Euphemia and Bridget. Poor Wincey is so nervous, she

445

couldn't come to the door. She's in a right state, poor soul. We've all been up and waiting since early morning.'

'I've only just seen the letter,' Virginia managed. 'We came right away.'

And there she was. Just the same as ever. The same dark red hair fringed over her forehead, the same rich, dark sweep of lashes, the same sprinkle of freckles, the same tense, apprehensive looking Wincey.

Virginia and Nicholas rushed towards her with arms outstretched. The three of them locked together in a wild embrace.

'Oh, Wincey. Oh, darling, we can't believe it. It's so wonderful, wonderful . . . '

Eventually Virginia had to sit down.

'Are you all right,' Teresa asked. 'You've gone awfully pale, dear. Would you like a nice cup of tea? The kettle's on the boil.'

'Oh yes please. I've just come off duty at the Royal and we dashed straight over.'

Nicholas kept a grip of Wincey's hand as they too sat down, but he had to release it as introductions were made and he politely shook hands with Granny and the three Gourlay sisters who kept staring at him in obvious admiration. He wasn't young like them but nevertheless they thought him breathtakingly handsome.

'First of all, my wife and I must express our deep appreciation to you for taking Wincey in and for looking after her so well for all this time. It was truly wonderful of you and we cannot thank you enough.'

'Och,' Erchie grinned, 'she's a grand wee worker. She's been the makin' o' this family. She an' my eldest daughter Charlotte, God rest her soul, built up a great business. Now Wincey runs it on her own.'

'Not on my own, Erchie. I couldn't do it without you, and such a good team of managers, and a marvellous workforce.'

'What line of business is it?' Nicholas asked, not taking his eyes off Wincey's face.

Erchie said, 'We started in the dressmakin' but now we've a great contract for shirts for the forces.'

'Whit?' Granny suddenly roared. 'Ah never knew that. Ye sly, traitorous devils.'

Erchie laughed. 'Granny wis a disciple o' John Maclean an' she's against aw wars, includin' this one.' He turned to the outraged old woman. 'It's no' as if we're makin' guns an' bullets, Ma. Just shirts for the boys.'

'It's helpin' the bloody war effort.'

'Have a biscuit, do.' Florence leapt up from the table which was, as a concession to the momentous significance of the day, covered with a pristine cream lace table cloth. She offered the plate of biscuits first to Virginia and then to Nicholas.

Teresa passed around the teacups. 'You'll have to forgive Granny. She's . . . '

'Ah'm no' wantin' or needin' anybody's forgiveness. It's them two faced, lying warmongering villains that need forgiveness—an' that's somethin' they'll no' be gettin' frae me.'

'We never lied to you, Granny,' Wincey protested. 'When did I ever lie to you?'

'You let me think ye were still sewin' clothes.'

'Well, so we are.'

'Ye've jumped on the bandwagon tae make yer fortune durin' this war.'

'No, no, we were making the shirts before the war.'

'See her,' Granny addressed Nicholas, 'she's a Cartwright, right enough. A bloody capitalist. But,' she added with a grudging mutter, 'no' a bad wee lassie for aw that. Ah huv tae admit she's been a good wee lassie tae me. But ah want none o' yer stupid carry on,' she suddenly bawled at Wincey, stopping her en route to deliver a kiss. 'Ah've telt you before, ah cannae dae wi' folk droolin' ower me.' She turned to Nicholas and Virginia. 'Are you two dumb or whit? Dinnae think we're gonnae let that lassie go away wi' you until we know somethin' about ye. So ye'd better tell us what the pair o' you huv been up tae.'

5

It was agreed eventually that Wincey would continue to live with the Gourlays in Springburn during the week. At weekends she would stay with Nicholas and Virginia in the West End.

'It's so handy for the factory here, you see,' Wincey explained. 'I can walk to work and all my friends are here.'

Erchie laughed. 'She means her fella, Dr Houston. He's got a local practice. Ye'll like him. He's been a good friend tae all o' us, especially tae Granny. Isn't that right, Ma?'

'Aye, well, at least he's a bit better than his auld man wis. Aw he ever did was stick a thermometer in yer mooth an' ask if ye were constipated.'

'He was the one who persuaded you to write to us, wasn't he?' Nicholas said to Wincey.

'Yes.'

'Well, God bless the man. I can't wait to meet him and thank him.'

'You'll stay for a bite to eat?' Teresa said. 'It's just stovies but there's plenty. I always make a big potful.'

'Gosh,' Virginia sighed, 'that brings back memories. My mother used to make stovies. I don't think I've ever tasted them since she died.'

'Where did your folks live, dear? Were they from the West End too?'

'Oh no, I was brought up in Cumberland Street in the Gorbals.'

Florence gasped. 'Cumberland Street? The Gorbals? Then how did you . . . ? I mean . . . '

'I originally worked as a scullery maid for Nicholas's mother.'

'A scullery maid?' Florence echoed, making Granny bawl, 'Dae you think ye're a bloody budgie? Stop repeatin' everythin' the woman says.'

'Then Nicholas and I fell in love and eventually got married and moved to Kirklee Terrace.'

Teresa sighed with pleasure. 'That's so romantic. Just like in a book.'

'That's what I do,' Nicholas said, 'write books.'

'Aye, ah know, son,' Erchie said. 'Ah've read a few o' them. Good stuff. Ah like yer style an' the way ye work yer poems in.'

'That's how I began—by writing poetry. Virginia was the only one who encouraged me in my writing. I didn't dare confess to my parents that I wanted to be writer.'

'De ye no' make a livin' at it, son? Is that why yer wife has tae go out tae work?'

Nicholas laughed. 'Oh, I make a living at it all right.'

'I joined the Red Cross because . . . well, because I was bored at home,' Virginia said. 'I suppose. I'm glad I did now because I believe nursing is a worthwhile job.'

'Aye, well,' Granny nodded her agreement, 'ah suppose ah cannae say anythin' against the Red Cross. They help everybody an' anybody. It disnae matter whit side ye're on.'

Florence and the twins had set the table with all the best rose patterned china from the display cabinet in the front room. Teresa began dishing the stovies.

'Come on now, pull in your chairs. Make yourselves at home. It's a wee bit of a crush but never mind. I'll sit over beside Granny and help her. Usually she feeds herself but her hands are swollen today so she needs a wee bit help, don't you, Granny.'

'Aw, get on wi' it. They're no' wantin' tae hear about ma problems.'

As they were enjoying their steaming plates of stovies, Virginia said to Wincey, 'Are you sure you can't come home with us today, darling?' It was Thursday, and Friday evening seemed a lifetime away.

Wincey shook her head. 'I've already taken today off work. I must go in tomorrow to make up for it and get a few things organised. I've also an important meeting tomorrow afternoon but I'll come over on Friday straight from work and stay until I leave for work on Monday morning. I'll do that every weekend, I promise.'

Virginia tried to feel content with this arrangement but she hoped that soon, she'd be able to persuade Wincey to come back home to Kirklee Terrace for good, to live there all the time—weekdays and weekends. She felt sure that this is what would happen sooner or later. Hopefully it would be sooner.

Eventually Teresa said, 'You're welcome to stay as long as you like, Mrs Cartwright.'

'Virginia.'

'You're welcome to stay as long as you like, Virginia. But you look so tired, dear. I think you should go home and have a rest.'

'Yes, Mother,' Wincey said. 'You'll be collapsing if you don't. I'll see you tomorrow night.'

'You'll come home in time to have dinner with us?'

'Yes, I promise.'

Reluctantly Virginia and Nicholas rose and took their leave of the cosy crowded kitchen, but not before they'd shaken hands with everyone again and thanked them again and warmly embraced Wincey.

'Oh Wincey,' Virginia said, 'we're so glad we found you.'

Nicholas kissed Wincey and said, 'Let's make this day a new start in all of our lives. Let's put the past behind us and make the most of our second chance. All right?'

Wincey smiled and nodded. 'Yes, all right.'

In the car on the way home, Nicholas was almost bouncing with happiness and delight. Virginia could hardly keep her eyes open. She managed to say though, 'We must get word to Richard. He'll be so pleased.'

'I'll send a telegram the moment I get home. I'll try to phone as well. In the circumstances, I'm sure his C.O. will give him compassionate leave, even if it's only for this weekend.'

'He's already been off quite a few weekends visiting your mother. I shouldn't think there'll be much difficulty.'

Richard and Mrs Cartwright were very close. The old woman adored her grandson and, Virginia suspected, she was far too generous with financial gifts to the boy. She'd even arranged for a regular allowance to be paid to his bank account. Nicholas had told his mother, 'You're spoiling him, Mother. He gets paid by the RAF. He doesn't need all that extra money.' But Mrs Cartwright had always been a strong minded woman and would not be diverted from 'helping the dear boy'.

At that moment, her 'dear boy' was in a local pub not far from the airfield. He needed to talk. So did the others. There had been a scramble earlier in the day. He remembered first of all the feeling of relief. The suspense of waiting for something to happen had ended at last, and he was on his way, running, with his parachute bumping awkwardly against his legs. He felt keyed up, trigger happy, ready for anything, as he jumped on to the wing of his Spitfire and clambered in. The engine started up and the whole airframe seemed to come to life, roaring and shaking. Never before had he felt so fully alive. He was strapped in. The trolley accumulator was pulled away, he was given the thumbs up, the chocks were pulled away. Then it was tail up, ease back the stick, and he was off.

The ground dropped away beneath him, until it was just a vague patchwork of greens and greys. Breaking through the clouds and emerging into the searing brilliance of the sunlight above, he suddenly found himself directly above a formation of Heinkel bombers. Without hesitation, Richard threw the Spitfire into a shallow dive, switched on his gunsight and opened fire on the leading bomber. A moment later the Heinkel burst into flame and spiralled out of sight. Now his own aircraft was rattling, shaking, and screaming as his dive took him back down through the clouds. Just as he levelled out, he checked his rear view mirror. His heart raced as he saw a German fighter—probably an Me 109, he thought—appear right on his tail. Throwing the Spit into a violent climbing turn, he prayed that the German pilot's reactions weren't as swift as his own. As he scanned the sky all around, he breathed a sigh of relief. The 109 was nowhere to be seen. He decided to get out while the going was good.

'All our chaps OK?' He asked the airframe mechanic as soon as he landed.

'Yes, they're all back.'

It was a relief. He felt good as he sauntered away from his Spitfire, dangling his flying helmet in one hand. The next stop, as ever, was the local pub. Somebody said they'd downed a few 'kites'. The squadron had been lucky today. Nobody had been killed—although the word 'killed' was never used. 'Bought it' was a much better phrase. The RAF had a slang language all of its own. It was known for its understatement, its throwaway lines. Pilots flew a 'kite', and put it away in a 'shed'. They often slept in an 'iron lung' (a Nissen hut), bombing was referred to as 'leaving visiting cards' or 'laying eggs'.

When they talked about going on operations 'over the ditch', they hoped they would not 'go for a burton', 'write themselves off' or 'have had it'.

That night, he'd had something to eat and was relaxed and laughing at one of Knocker White's jokes when a WAAF rushed in in great excitement. They all knew this girl. She was always getting into a flap about something. They couldn't see her lasting long in the service. Most of the WAAFs were pretty cool and capable types.

'A telegram.' She was almost shouting at him. 'And a phone call. She's been found alive.'

'Silly bitch,' he thought.

'Who's been found alive?'

'Here, read it.' She pushed the buff coloured piece of paper at him.

'Well, what do you know?' he said eventually. 'That's a turn up for the book. What the hell has she been up to all these years?'

The others were intrigued and wanted to know what it was all about.

'My young sister, Wincey. She disappeared donkey's years ago. We all thought she was dead. Now, apparently, she's turned up out of the blue. I'd better have a word with the C.O.'

And so he found himself next day on a train bound for Glasgow. First he called on his grandmother at her great hulking villa crammed with Victoriana. He loved his grandmother, but could not honestly say he even liked her house. He said that he wanted to accompany her over to Kirklee Terrace. He knew it would please the old girl.

'Can't have my favourite person wandering about on her own?' he joked with her. She was so happy and proud, as he knew she would be, to hang on to his arm as they walked along Great Western Road. She had been invited to join the family for a special celebratory dinner to welcome Wincey back into the fold. He knew of course that Wincey had never counted for much with his grandmother and so he wasn't surprised at the lack of enthusiasm the old woman had for the event.

'Wicked, selfish girl,' she said. 'Disappearing for so long, and then just turning up as if nothing was amiss. Nicholas is delighted. She's his daughter after all, and so I suppose it's understandable. But nothing that girl could do would surprise me. She takes after her mother, you see.'

Richard felt amused. It was as if he had had a different mother from Wincey. He knew he could do no wrong in his grandmother's eyes. He had come to the conclusion that she saw him as a reincarnation of her son as a young man, and somehow she'd completely shut her mind to any blood connection he had to his mother. True, he had never felt he had much in common with his mother—or his father for that matter. They could be such bores, his father with his constant talk of books and writers and his mother with all her Commy friends. Her first husband, for instance, was the absolute dregs, and a pacifist to boot. He hoped to God Matheson hadn't been invited to the dinner. He found himself saying the words out loud to his grandmother as they made their way along Kirklee Terrace.

'Oh, I do hope not, Richard. What a dreadful man he is, and it's just not decent that he should keep visiting Nicholas's house. Apart from being a Communist, he is her ex-husband.' She gave shocked emphasis to the words 'ex-husband'.

'I know,' Richard agreed. 'I can't imagine what Mother's thinking of, allowing him to hang around. I think he's mad. He certainly looks mad.'

'If he's there, I'm just going to ignore him. You should do the same, Richard. Oh, I couldn't have faced this ghastly dinner party on my own.'

He patted her hand. 'I'll hope I'll always be here when you need me, Grandmother.' He smiled down at her and she thought what a handsome boy he was and how good to her he'd always been. She was glad she had made a new will, cutting everyone out—even Nicholas. Everything, everything down to the last halfpenny and the last teaspoon, was to go to Richard. Her 'dear boy'.

6

Wincey went home for lunch, and also to collect an overnight bag. She could have had a sandwich and coffee in the factory, as she often did. She could have taken an overnight bag with her when she left the house in the morning, but she had developed a sudden need to spend as much time as possible with Granny and Teresa and Erchie. Erchie worked in the factory, but he was usually so busy that they seldom saw each other during the day, and he never went home for lunch. Every day, regular as clockwork, he and a couple of the other men went to a local pub and had a pint or two. She at least could sit down with Granny and Teresa, enjoy a bowl of Teresa's home made soup and just appreciate being with them.

The reunion of the day before with her mother and father had been heart warming, and such a relief, that she was glad she had written the letter. The burden of worry and guilt had been lifted from her shoulders. At the same time, she felt a need to cling to the Gourlays. No way could she risk losing them.

'I'll feed Granny,' she told Teresa.

'You've your work to get back to, dear. I've plenty of time to see to Granny.'

'I've plenty of time as well. I don't mind.'

'Will the pair o' ye stop talkin' about me as if ah'm no' here,' Granny said irritably. 'Whit's got intae you?' she asked Wincey. 'Away ye go out the road an' no' annoy us.'

'Granny. Wincey's just trying to be kind.'

'I'm not looking forward to this dinner tonight. Mrs Cartwright's going to be there. I wish I could keep out of *her* road. She never liked me.'

'I'm sure she'll be so relieved to know you're all right, dear, she'll welcome you with open arms.'

'I can't imagine it. I *will* be glad to see my brother, though. I always secretly admired him. He was so handsome and clever and daring. I'm not surprised he's a fighter pilot now. I can just imagine him being wonderfully brave in the face of danger.'

'A fighter pilot?' Granny said in disgust. 'Whit next? Whit a family! Ah'm no' surprised ye're no' lookin' forward tae goin' there the night.'

'I'll wash up the dishes,' Wincey said in desperation, but Granny raised her voice,

'Will you get away tae yer work. We're no' wantin' ye here.'

'Granny,' Teresa gasped, shocked.

'Ah just mean the now,' Granny muttered. 'We want ye tae come back on Monday. Ye ken fine whit ah mean.'

Wincey nodded and reached for her camelhair coat, belted it, then pulled on her fawn beret. 'Yes, I know. It's all right, Granny. I'll see you on Monday. I'm meeting Robert for lunch but I'll be home at tea time. OK?'

The evening meal was still known to the Gourlays as tea.

'Aye, OK.'

'I'm going to kiss you now whether you like it or not.' She kissed the old woman's hollow cheek. 'You behave yourself while I'm away, do you hear me, Granny.'

'There's nothin' wrong wi' ma ears.'

Wincey kissed Teresa before picking up her overnight bag and leaving the house. All afternoon she struggled to concentrate on business but at the back of her mind, the return to Kirklee Terrace hovered like a sword of Damocles. She tried to tell herself that she was being foolish. After all, meeting her mother and father had been a happy occasion. She should be looking forward to her visit to her old home, seeing her grandmother Cartwright again, and her brother Richard. She should be remembering with pleasure sitting in the elegant dining room, sleeping in her old bed. Yet all she felt about the visit was apprehension.

The first person she saw after her mother embraced her and ushered her across the hall and into the sitting room was Richard. He looked taller and even more handsome than she remembered. He suited his moustache. He suited his RAF officer's uniform too. Its tailored lines accentuated his broad shoulders and the way his body tapered to a slim waist and hips. The grey blue colour of the uniform matched his eyes.

'Wincey!' He came towards her with outstretched arms. 'You little devil. Why on earth did you disappear like that? Where have you been all this time and what have you been up to?'

Nicholas cut in before she could say anything. 'We've agreed to put the past behind us, Richard. We don't want any third degrees. We're just glad she's back and it's a happy future together now that matters.'

Wincey returned Richard's hug. 'I've been living in Springburn and running a small factory. I was in partnership with one of the Gourlay sisters that I lived with—Charlotte, her name was. Then when she was killed in an accident, I took over the factory. We probably made that shirt you're wearing.'

'Good for you,' Richard said.

All the time Wincey had been trying to suppress feelings of panic at seeing her grandmother Cartwright again. Not that she was afraid of her. But somehow the old woman catapulted her back into her grandfather's presence. She felt afraid of him again, and guilty again, and dirty.

Mrs Cartwright sat on a silk covered chair, shoulders back, spine stiff and straight. 'I fail to see,' she said coldly, 'what is good about disappearing without one word of warning or explanation. Apart from anything else, you cost the tax payer a great deal of money. The police search was very extensive, I remember. There were even divers.'

'Yes, we know all that, Mother, but as I said, it's in the past. Wincey has explained everything to her mother and myself and we understand, and totally accept the reason for her action. We just think it's best if we don't say any more about it. What happened, happened. There's nothing anybody can do now except look to the future and build a new life together.'

He poured champagne into glasses and passed them around. 'Let's drink to that.'

They all raised their glasses high, except Mrs Cartwright, who only raised hers as far as her thin lips. The champagne helped Wincey to suppress her panic, or at least to hide it. She concentrated on talking to Richard and listening to his stories about his 'Spit', as he called his Spitfire, and how he loved flying.

'It's the feeling of power and exaltation it gives you,' he said, his eyes glowing. 'It's being up there above the world, alone, and entirely responsible for one's own return to earth. Marvellously exciting. We haven't seen much real action yet, but it'll come and we'll be ready.'

Wincey spoke about Charlotte and what a marvellous person she'd been and how she'd been killed in a road accident. She'd dashed across a road in an effort to save someone she saw being attacked and hadn't seen the car speeding towards her. What Wincey didn't say was that the person being attacked was Charlotte's husband, big Malcy McArthur. He was a reckless gambler who owed a huge amount of cash to a local money lender. It had been the money lender's hard men who had been attacking Malcy. Charlotte's tragic death seemed at least to have cured Malcy of his gambling, or so he said. Shortly after the funeral he had joined the Army. The last she'd heard he was somewhere in France.

She still missed Charlotte. Charlotte had always been closer to her and felt more like a sister than Florence or the twins ever had. Charlotte had been kind and loving, but clever too, with a really good business head on her shoulders. Right from the beginning, she'd recognised Wincey's business capabilities, despite her youth. She'd coached her and encouraged her. The only thing that ever come between them or caused any friction was Charlotte's love for Malcy.

Everybody except Charlotte, it seemed, knew exactly what Malcy was like. He had been well on his way to ruining the business, in Wincey's opinion. Not content with wheedling money out of Charlotte, he'd even resorted to stealing the petty cash from the office. Charlotte's death, however, had shaken him badly. Even Wincey had to come to the conclusion that his tears of grief were genuine.

Richard announced that he would be spending the night at his grandmother's house. 'I'm walking Grandmother home so I might as well stay. I'll see you again tomorrow, Wincey, and we can talk some more. We could have a walk through the Botanic Gardens and then go for a coffee down Byres Road.'

'Yes, fine,' Wincey agreed.

'Well, you see that she's back in time for lunch,' Virginia said. 'You mustn't keep her all to yourself all weekend, Richard.'

Wincey kissed her brother goodnight, then she forced herself to kiss Grandmother Cartwright, but only when she was free of the old woman's presence could she completely relax. Indeed it surprised her how peaceful she felt as she stood at the tall windows of the sitting room and looked out towards the quiet terrace and the elegant Great Western Road beyond, faintly lit by the moon. She watched her brother and grandmother leave arm in arm from the front door. Their torches casting faint grey fingers of light.

'Would you like another glass of champagne?' Nicholas asked behind her.

'Or a milky drink?' Virginia suggested.

'Champagne'll be lovely, thanks,' Wincey said, despite knowing she'd already drunk too much.

'You'd better come away from the window, dear, and shut the curtains,' Virginia said, 'or we'll be having an ARP man shouting, "Put that light out!".'

'Oh, sorry, I was forgetting.' Wincey tidied the heavy curtains shut. 'I bet the ARP men would turn the moon off if they could, but I'm always glad of it. Aren't you?'

'Yes, but even so, I never drive now. Except during daylight hours.' Virginia passed Wincey a glass of champagne. 'Nicholas manages somehow though.'

Nicholas shrugged. 'Not that either of us venture out much at night. There's nowhere to go, now that they've closed all the cinemas and theatres.'

'That won't last, surely. People are already getting far too bored and depressed.'

The three of them settled round the fire and Nicholas added another piece of coal and used the poker to bring the flames warming out.

'I've put a hot water bottle in your bed,' Virginia said. 'It's such a cold night. Perhaps we should have lit a fire in the bedroom, Nicholas.'

'I could do it now. I could take a shovelful from here . . . '

'No, no,' Wincey protested. 'Please, I'll be fine. I've never had a fire at home—I mean, in Springburn. You mustn't spoil me.' Although in fact it felt very nice to be spoiled.

'Why not?' Nicholas said. 'We ought to have paid so much more attention to you when you lived here before.'

'The past has gone. Remember what we agreed—the future is all that matters now.'

'I must remember that myself,' Wincey thought. 'The past has gone,' she told herself. 'I'm all right now. Everything's all right.'

Nicholas nodded, then said, 'I'm looking forward to meeting your

Dr Houston. When can we see him? How about bringing him for dinner next Friday?'

'He usually has a surgery on a Friday evening but he's got a partner now. I'm sure he'll be able to arrange something.'

'Good.'

Virginia said, 'I would suggest this Sunday but we just want to keep you to ourselves this weekend. We can still hardly believe it, you see. That you're actually here, beside us. It's so wonderful.'

The champagne was swimming around in Wincey's head, making her feel warm and relaxed. Later she lay in her old bedroom, with its blue and silver wallpaper and its looped blue curtains and silver blinds. How beautiful it was. She could hardly believe that nothing had changed. Even her old teddy was still there. She took it into bed with her and cuddled it close, just as she used to. She became aware of her mother tip-toeing in and heard her whispered 'Goodnight, darling'.

She heard her father's whisper too. She knew now that they loved her. Now she realised they always had, and felt hugely grateful and relieved. Snuggling down under the crisp sheets, warm blankets and satin quilt, she drifted happily into peaceful sleep.

1940

7

At the end of January 1940, Malcy McArthur was stationed in France in a village called Bondue. On pay day, which was usually on a Friday, he and some of his mates would take a bus into Lille where they had a few drinks and a meal. In a street there they called ABC Street, every house was a brothel and at each one, there were long queues of soldiers waiting their turn. Malcy stood in one of the queues. Sex had become almost as strong an addiction as gambling had once been. He'd conquered the latter urge, even though he now had money in the bank. He resisted the temptation because his weakness had led to Charlotte's death and he'd never forgiven himself for that.

The best he could do now was to avoid any form of gambling. It could be said though that the sex with prostitutes was taking a chance. He was well aware of the risk of venereal disease, but like everyone else he took precautions and hoped that he would be all right. He missed Charlotte for sex as well as for everything else. Not that they had had a very active sex life. For most of the time she was too exhausted with working so hard in factory. But she did love him. She was always telling him she loved everything about him.

'I especially love your laughing eyes and your dimpled chin,' she said. Sex wasn't the only way to be close to someone and to show them that you cared about them. Tired or not, he bet her fiery haired partner wouldn't say no to sex.

Even before he'd started going out with Charlotte, he'd had his eye on Wincey. She'd been a bit young then, nevertheless he'd seen that quiet, smouldering quality about her that spelled sex to him. Unfortunately she'd also been greedy and suspicious. Making money and the factory had been everything to her.

Charlotte would have given it all up for him if he'd let her. But not Wincey. She'd hang on in there come what may. He was sure of it. The factory and making money was her life. He'd one thing to thank Wincey for though—or two, to be exact. She'd paid off his last debt to the money lender. It was what Charlotte would have wanted, she'd told him.

Then she'd said, 'Rest assured, for all your faults, Malcy, and no matter what you did, Charlotte always loved you.'

He would be forever grateful to Wincey for that. He had been feeling so grief stricken after Charlotte's death, and so guilty. Wincey's words had comforted and reassured him, although at the same time they had made him weep. One thing he could say in his favour—he had never been unfaithful to his wife. Despite often feeling sexually frustrated, he never turned to anyone else for sex.

It was different now. He had no one to consider but himself. No one to be faithful to.

As he was shuffling forward in the brothel queue, his mind strayed back to Wincey. He wondered if she'd made any time yet for a man in her life. He doubted it. Unless just for sex. She wouldn't want any serious distraction from her journey to the top. She'd get another, bigger factory, or she'd extend the one she had. She'd buy up half Springburn if necessary, if she decided on the latter course. You had to admire her in a way. She was a right little devil. Looked it too, with her red hair and eyes like grey-green glass. He'd had a few spats with her, and even though he had never done her a moment's harm she obviously hated his guts. He'd come to the conclusion eventually that money was behind it—her fear of losing it. She had found out about Charlotte keeping him going with cash handouts.

Now, without poor, generous hearted, loving Charlotte and without him, Wincey would be coining it. The factory was already going full blast making clothes for the forces before he'd left to join the army. Probably the shirt on his back at this very moment had been made at Wincey's factory.

His part of the queue moved into the first brothel. Down the stairs came a young girl wearing only a pair of knickers. She looked no more than sixteen and her face was completely blank. It made him feel sad. A huge wave of depression engulfed him. What was he doing here in this god-forsaken country? He could see no point in the whole business. He had been perfectly willing to fight the Germans in order to defend Britain but since joining up, the worst thing they'd had to fight was boredom. The 'Bore War', they called it. Sex with prostitutes depressed him even further, yet the next week he was back, hopefully trying a more expensive, supposedly higher class brothel.

He spent some time in a room lined all round with red plush seats. On one side of the room, on some of the seats, sat five girls in underwear. They were quite attractive and he tried to believe that they wanted him and enjoyed having intimacy with him. But all the time he knew he was conning himself.

He had acquired what could only be described as an ache to be back in Glasgow. He'd been born and brought up in the city but he'd never bothered or thought much about it while he lived there. Now he thought about little else. He remembered with real longing the ornate Victorian buildings. It was always said that to appreciate Glasgow, you had to go about looking up all the time and that was certainly true if it was architecture you were interested in. And what other city had so many parks? The dear green place was supposed to be what the word Glasgow meant. And it certainly could boast many green places. Even the East End had its Glasgow Green and the People's Palace. Many a time he and Charlotte had enjoyed walking arm in arm on the Green and then exploring the history of the city in the People's Palace.

Glasgow was a hilly place. Streets reared up everywhere until, within half an hour's journey from the centre of the city, you were among the green hills of the Campsies. Or you were away in the glorious scenery of Loch Lomond.

But it was the heart of the city that he loved and longed for most. The tenements, warm and welcoming—especially at night—with the street lamps and the close lights beckoning. And busy family life lighting up every window.

He had never had a family. Often he made one up. Sometimes he almost believed his stories to be true. The truth was he'd been an orphan and the only home he'd known was a children's home. He seldom allowed himself to think about his life there. He had certainly never experienced any love as a child. Plenty of punishments, though. He had been branded a liar because of the stories he used to tell about imaginary parents. He had a card hung round his neck with LIAR written on it in big capital letters. On other occasions he'd been forced into cold baths.

He'd wanted so much to prove himself worthy of Charlotte. He told himself that's why he gambled. He had this dream of winning a fortune and spending it all on her. Impressing her with expensive presents. Showing her what a big man he was.

Sometimes his horse, or dog, or whatever he'd bet on, did win. Then he would give Charlotte a great time. He'd take her to the best restaurant in Glasgow and order champagne. They had lots of laughs, despite her protests. He'd enjoyed being good to her, although he could see now he had been showing off as well, acting the big man, showing her—and Wincey—that he could be just as clever as them, or even more so, at making money.

Then of course he began losing and in trying to rectify the situation, he'd made it worse by getting into the money lender's crooked hands. He kept believing that he'd win again. Next time he'd win and he'd be able to pay everything back. But the interest the money lender heaped on made paying back impossible.

What a bloody fool he'd been! He realised that now. He'd no Charlotte to go back to but still he longed for their native city. The bustle and noise of the Barras and Paddy's Market, the discussions and arguments in pubs about everything from football to politics and the state of the world. He thought about Springburn with its proud history of engineering. He remembered seeing steam locomotives being towed through the streets en route to the River Clyde. There they were hauled aboard a ship destined for India or some other far off land.

He remembered the concerts in Springburn public park. All the works had their own band and took turns playing in the bandstand in the park. The best known and loved, by all the children at least, was the Salvation Army Silver Band. They marched from Flemington Street to the Citadel in Wellfield Street every Sunday with a whole ragged army of children dancing after them. He remembered the noisy shuffling of hobnail boots of the workmen on their way to clock on at the various workshops. Then the housewives trailing zinc baths, or pushing prams laden with clothes to catch their turn at the steamie.

After five o'clock, the place would be black with workers dashing home for their tea. Later, young folk would be turning out for entertainment at the pictures, or the theatres, or the dancing.

Oh, how he longed for it all. Even just to hear a Glasgow voice on the street. He hated the yattering sound of the French. He couldn't understand a word of it and felt completely alienated. Again and again he asked himself, 'What the hell am I doing here?'

He remembered the Gourlays. Good old Erchie. And Granny—what a character! And Teresa who reminded him so much of gentle Charlotte. Snobby Florence and the fat twins, who thought they were a cut above everybody else. The last he'd heard, they'd all got their own houses. Florence was as proud as punch of her place in Clydebank in the area known as the Holy City because, from a distance, the flat roofed houses looked so much like Jerusalem. The twins were living just a few closes apart from each other in Dumbarton Road and were equally carried away with themselves—even though they had only one room and kitchens. He could imagine Florence believing she had really made it to the big time with her two room and kitchen and bathroom flat.

He had once been as proud as punch himself of the house he shared with Charlotte in Broomfield Road, facing the park. Now that *had* been a house to be proud of. But it was gone now and meant nothing. Nothing was of any value, or had any meaning, without Charlotte. Still, he would dearly love to be back in Glasgow and in Springburn and walk again where they had once walked together.

He'd even begun to think nostalgically about Wincey. He wished he could see her again and talk to her. There had been a lot of bad feeling between them, but before he'd left, that had evaporated. They had their grief at losing Charlotte in common and for once Wincey had been sympathetic to him. And Wincey had loved Charlotte like a sister.

To everyone else they were sisters. Wincey was just Wincey Gourlay—one of the Gourlay girls. Charlotte had confided in him, however, that in fact there was a mystery surrounding Wincey. Years before, they had found her in the street and taken her in and she'd become one of the family. He wondered who she really was. Even Charlotte hadn't known. As soon as he got back to Glasgow, he'd make a point of finding out.

Oh, it would be so good to see them all again. The thought kept him going through the weeks and months of the Phoney War. But it wasn't long before everything changed for Malcy, and pleasant thoughts of the Gourlay girls and the dear green place were the last thing on his mind.

8

'But you're needed here,' Wincey protested to Robert Houston. 'What about all your patients in Springburn?'

Houston's eyes narrowed and hardened with impatience. 'They'll still have Doctor McLeod. It's my duty to do something for the war effort, Wincey. After all, you're doing your bit by keeping our forces supplied with uniforms.'

'But you might be sent overseas.'

Houston shrugged. 'I might be at some point, I suppose.'

She could hardly believe the coolness of him. Had he never loved her after all?

'I don't suppose you've ever given me a thought,' she said bitterly.

'Now don't be like that, Wincey.'

'Like what?'

'All twisted and bitter. I thought you were beginning to come to terms with that.'

'Don't you dare accuse me of being bitter and twisted. How am I supposed to feel? I thought we cared about one another. Yet you suddenly announce, cool as a cucumber and without any previous discussion, that you've joined the Navy.'

'When do you take enough time to discuss anything, Wincey? You're a workaholic. I see less and less of you these days, especially since you've been spending every weekend over at Kirklee Terrace.'

'You've been there too—for lunch, every Sunday.'

'I hardly get to speak to you, Wincey. They do all the talking. The three of you talk together. I don't blame them, or you. They've a lot to catch up with. So have you.'

'We usually manage to go for a walk together.'

'Yes, for a few minutes in the Botanic Gardens, with your parents waving and eagerly watching our every move from their side windows.'

'Well, Robert, it was you who started all this,' she reminded him. 'I was perfectly all right before—just being a Gourlay girl.'

'No, you weren't.'

She shrugged. 'I thought I was. Now I don't know what to think.'

'I'll probably still be able to see you most weekends. I've been posted to the hospital at Port Edgar. That's at South Queensferry. I'll let you know when I can get off duty.'

They were having a drink in the bar of a small country hotel near the Campsie hills. They'd been here before—on their very first date, in fact. The hotel was an old coaching house and the restaurant and bar had once been the stables. It still had the original flagstones under foot, whitewashed stone walls and dark oak beams. It had been a beautiful spring day but now in the evening, it had turned cold. Icy winds were whipping the trees outside, but inside there was a huge log fire crackling cheerily in the ancient hearth. It was cosy where they were sitting. It was only when the door opened and someone came in that an icy blast flurried about their ankles, chilling them for a second or two.

'It's not just at weekends,' she said. 'We see each other during the week—like now.'

'Only occasionally, when you're not working late at some urgent order, or when I haven't got an evening surgery.'

'What are you trying to tell me, Robert?'

'What do you mean?'

'Are you trying to tell me that you don't want to see me again?'

'Wincey, for goodness sake.' He put his hand over hers. 'Of course I want to see you again, darling. I love you. I'm just telling you that I feel my duty lies as a medical officer in the Navy at the moment. They're crying out for doctors. There's a war on, remember, and it's not a phoney war any more. Fighting has started in earnest.'

She tried to be reasonable. After all, he'd always been a man who'd been in charge of himself and didn't give way to any display of strong emotion. He wouldn't have been as good and as reassuring as a doctor if he'd been any other way.

'How about . . . ' he said quietly and still holding her hand, 'if we book in here for the night and I show you how much I love you.'

She was about to say that she couldn't possibly do that because she had a thousand and one urgent things to attend to at the factory first thing in the morning. She had planned to go into work an hour early.

Just in time she controlled her tongue. She smiled and nodded her agreement. They'd never made love before. He knew how she shrank with distaste at any thought of sex. Not because of him. It was something inside herself. He knew it and she knew it. It didn't matter how often he explained that she was not to blame for what her grandfather had done to her. She ought *not* to feel guilty or dirty. But she did.

As an adult, she knew perfectly well that she was being illogical and unfair to Robert Houston. She admitted to him that she knew he was right. What she did not admit to him was that deep inside her, she remained that frightened, sickened, guilty child.

Tonight, however, she was determined to ignore her foolish, infantile emotions. Robert was going away and this was her chance—maybe her last chance—to show him not only that she loved him, but that she trusted him and because of that, she could express her love in the most intimate, physical way.

Upstairs in the low ceilinged bedroom, however, she began to feel claustrophobic. Panic skittered about in her stomach. Determinedly she fought to quell it.

'Darling,' Robert sighed, 'you look as if you're about to face your execution. I thought that maybe tonight . . . But I see I was wrong.' His face drained of expression. Suddenly he was the polite doctor that his patients saw sitting behind a desk in his surgery.

'Don't worry,' he said. 'I'm not going to force myself on you. So just relax. We'll have another drink and then I'll take you home.'

'No, Robert, I'll be all right. I'll have to get over this. I must.'

He shook his head. 'Not this way. Not when you're so tense and anguished. It's as bad—if not worse—than it would be for me to force you. Come on,' he said brusquely, 'get your coat on. I'm taking you home right now.'

She could have wept. Instead she sat beside him in the car, silent and white faced. She felt suicidal. She hated herself. She despaired of herself. What a fool she was, what an idiot. No sane woman could treat the man she loved like this. The awful thing was she wanted him, she wanted to belong to him, she desperately wanted to. The car stopped outside the close in Balgrayhill and she managed to say, 'Oh Robert, I'm so sorry.'

He put an arm around her shoulders. 'It's all right, I understand. I'm sorry for rushing you tonight. Originally I'd planned to give you much more time to get over this—for both of us to work through the problem—but because I'm leaving, I'm afraid I allowed my feelings to get the better of me.'

'Robert, I love you. You do know that, don't you?'

'Yes.' He dropped a gentle kiss on her lips. 'And I love you, Wincey. Don't worry, darling.' He grinned at her. 'I'll cure you if it's the last thing I do. I wouldn't be worth my salt as a doctor if I don't.'

She clung round his neck. 'You'll write to me?'

'Yes, of course. You look after yourself now. Don't be working too hard and getting even more anxious than you are at the moment.'

'It's just . . . I never dreamt the factory would be so successful. We can hardly keep up with all the huge orders. I'm trying to buy up some adjoining property . . .'

'Never mind all that now. Just let me know how you get on.'

'Yes, I will.'

They kissed again and he opened the car door. 'On you go before my feelings get the better of me again.'

Her smile hid a secret twitch of fear, followed by relief once she was safely out of the car.

Later she lay in the blackness of the recessed bed listening to the occasional bout of coughing from Teresa through in the kitchen. She felt deeply worried and depressed. She wondered if she ought to see a psychiatrist. It was so illogical to keep the man she loved at arm's length the way she did. Of all men, he was the one she should be able to trust and feel at ease with. He was a highly thought of and respectable doctor. She'd even known his father, who had been equally loved and respected by the people of Springburn. If she couldn't trust Robert Houston, she'd never be able to trust anyone. But it had really nothing to do with him, she reminded herself. Something had gone wrong deep inside her. Maybe only a psychiatrist could root it out, heal the sickness in her mind.

In an effort to make up for the night before, she took time off work, despite the urgency of the workload, and she went to see Robert off at the railway station. His face lit up with surprise and pleasure when he saw her.

'Darling, I never expected . . . '

'I know, but believe it or not, Robert, you're more important to me than my work. How handsome you look in your uniform. You know what they say—all the nice girls love a sailor. I'm jealous already of all the nice girls who'll fall for you.'

She'd bought some newspapers and magazines for him to read on the train.

'Here, just concentrate on these for a start.'

He laughed as he accepted the reading material. 'I promise I'll not look at any other woman. Well, maybe a nurse or two . . . '

She gave him a playful punch on the arm. 'Don't you dare!'

The guard was blowing his whistle and Robert had to board the train. Wincey blew him a kiss and he waved to her as the train steamed away. It disappeared from view, leaving her drained and empty. If she'd never felt lonely before, she felt it now. She forced herself to walk from the station and into her car. Work was what she needed now. She mustn't give herself time to think about anything else.

She had a meeting with a government official in the afternoon and she was wearing a chic spring dress and jacket in soft green boucle wool with a cinnamon coloured belt for the occasion. A brimmed cinnamon coloured hat pulled down over her brow topped the outfit, and she wore good brown leather gloves, especially fitted by Florence in Copeland & Lye. It was there she'd also purchased her matching and very expensive leather handbag. She could see the government official was impressed by her and the hard working girls in the factory, all beavering away at line after line of sewing machines.

He did however express some doubt at her capacity to take on another, bigger order. She assured him that she was extending her premises and installing more modern machinery. He had no need to worry about her capabilities to deal with any size of order, she assured him. Her self confidence was infectious. She had no problem in business—never had.

There had been the problem of Malcy McArthur, but there was nothing she could do about that. Big Malcy, as he was known, had been Charlotte's responsibility. Poor Charlotte. It had been under-standable how she'd adored Malcy, despite his obvious weaknesses. He was an attractive devil, with his laughing eyes and his swaggering, muscly body. She wondered how he was getting on in the army. Erchie said Malcy would be in the thick of the fighting now.

'Poor auld Malcy,' Erchie had said. 'He hasnae had much luck in his life, wi' one thing an' another. Now he'll be lucky if he gets out o' this lot in one piece.'

Teresa sighed. 'Such a nice big man. He was always good and kind to Charlotte. She always said so. I hope he'll be all right.'

'Aye, but ye can never trust a gambler,' Granny said.

'Now, now, Granny. He's given up gambling. It was a wee weakness he had for a time. None of us are perfect.' She turned to Wincey. 'I know you never liked him, dear, but I always had a soft spot for him. He wasn't a bad man.'

Wincey shrugged. 'I got over that in the end. I could see he really did love Charlotte. I don't feel any dislike for him now.'

'Oh, I'm so glad, dear. We can all welcome him back when the time comes, God willing.'

9

'Believe you me,' Mrs McGregor said with grim satisfaction, 'ah gave her what for.'

Mrs McGregor was one of the Gourlays' old neighbours from Springburn Road. She had fourteen children, the youngest of whom had been evacuated to a supposedly safe haven in the country. 'She'll no' torment another wean. The police are gonnae keep an eye on her, for a start. I telt them, an' ah showed them ma weans, aw bleedin'. Aw bleedin', they were. Their clothes were soaked wi' blood. That monster had been beatin' them wi' a horse whip. Put her in jail, ah telt them. Lock her up an' throw away the key. Fancy doin' that tae weans.'

'Is that not terrible!' Teresa's eyes widened. 'And her supposed to be a respectable farmer's wife. Isn't it a mercy, Mrs McGregor, that you decided to pay a surprise visit?'

'Aye,' Granny said, 'an' good for you, givin' her a good punchin'. Ah jist wish ah'd been there as well, tae get ma fists in along wi' ye.'

'Thank goodness they're not all like that, Mrs McGregor. The Donaldsons are being very well treated, I've heard.'

'Ah widnae trust anybody wi' helpless wee weans,' Granny said. 'There's far too many bad bastards goin' about. Rich or poor, it's aw the same wi' bastards like that. They're no' right in the heid.'

'Granny, watch your language.'

'Granny's quite right, Teresa. That's what they are. Do you know, ah'm that upset. It's gonnae take me ages tae get over seein' ma weans aw bleedin' like that.'

'Have another cup of tea, dear. The children are all right now. It's amazing how resilient children can be.'

'Aye, the doctor sorted them an' they're out playin' as happy as larry now.'

'No' always, they're no',' Granny said, chomping her gums on a piece of Teresa's home made shortbread. It was a special wartime butterless recipe but quite tasty all the same.

'What do you mean, dear?'

'Weans. They're no' aye able tae bounce back as right as rain. Look at oor Wincey. Ah always knew there was somethin' far wrong wi' her.'

Mrs McGregor perked up with interest. 'Was Wincey beaten when she was wee?'

'Granny, you know what we promised.' Teresa turned to Mrs McGregor. 'It happened a long time ago, before she came to us. We promised—swore on the Bible—we'd never talk about it to a living soul. All I can say is that poor Wincey has never quite got over what she suffered as a child. Now please, dear, promise me you'll never mention a word of this to anybody. Wincey would never forgive us. She's really a very private kind of person.'

'Ma lips are sealed, hen. Ah'm no' a stair heid gossip, Teresa. Never have been. But is that no' terrible. Poor wee Wincey. Ah'm glad she's got pally wi' Doctor Houston. A nice man, that.'

'Yes, I know. I was hoping for wedding bells but nothing's happened so far. An' now he's away to the Navy.'

'Aye, so ah heard. They were needin' doctors. Now they're cryin' out for women tae join up. My eldest's goin' tae the WAAFs and she's goin' tae work on somethin' awfy secret. She's aw excited. "It's a lovely uniform, Mammy," she says, as if that was aw there was tae it. It's the same wi' ma next one. It's the WRENs wi' her. "The WRENs have the smartest uniform, Mammy," she said. See weans!'

Just then the front door bell rang.

'That'll be Florence.' Teresa got up to answer it. 'This is her half day off. She usually does a bit of shopping and then pops in for a cup of tea.'

In a minute Florence was in the kitchen looking very smart in a Dorita wool coat, topped with the fox fur her husband Eddie had bought her for Christmas. Her hat was from Pettigrews, a fashionable little number decorated with two bird's wings and some veiling draped around the brim and down the back. She peeled off her gloves, finger by finger.

'Hello, everybody. Oh, tea, good. I find shopping so exhausting.'

'What are ye bletherin' about,' Granny wanted to know. 'You work in a shop. Ye spend aw yer days in a shop.'

Florence rolled her eyes. 'It's different trailing about, Granny. Anyway, in Copeland & Lye's, we're treated as ladies. That's what we're known as.'

She took off her coat and draped it carefully over the back of the chair, before checking that her hat was perched at the right angle. Then she sat down.

'Sales ladies. The ladies from the glove department, or the millinery, or whatever. It's all very high class.'

'High class?' Granny snorted. 'We're aw workin' class here, an' don't you forget it. Ah'm proud o' that fact. Always have been. Ah remember . . . '

'Have another piece of shortbread, Granny,' Teresa interrupted. Then to Florence, 'What have you been buying today, dear? Anything nice? Help yourself to shortbread.'

'Oh, just a half dozen table napkins, but they're very good quality linen.'

'Table napkins?' Granny hooted. 'What next? Here, Mrs McGregor, ah hope ye've stocked up wi' enough table napkins for your crowd.'

Mrs McGregor's chest bounced up and down with laughter. 'Ah dinnae think ma crowd would know what a table napkin was, tae be honest.'

Florence nibbled daintily at a piece of shortbread. 'Yes, I could believe that, Mrs McGregor.'

'Florence, there's no call to be cheeky to Mrs McGregor.'

'I wasn't being cheeky. I was just agreeing with her.'

'It's OK, hen. Ah'm no' that thin skinned,' she assured Teresa. Then to Florence, 'How's yer hoose daein', hen. Ah hear it's like a wee palace.'

Florence preened with pleasure. 'Well, it is rather nice, though I say it myself. You must come for afternoon tea one Sunday with Mother.' She was calling Teresa Mother instead of Mammy as often as she could remember.

'Well thanks, hen, ah'd love tae come. Just you say the word.'

'I'll study my diary and let you and Mother know what Sunday.'

Granny spluttered out some tea and crumbs. 'Study her diary?

Could ye beat it? Honest tae god, our Florence is a better turn than anythin' in the Pavilion.'

'Granny, everybody has diaries nowadays,' Teresa said.

'Ah huvnae, an' neither huv you. Ah bet Mrs McGregor hasnae such a thing either, huv ye, hen?'

'No' me, but ma eldest has, right enough. Her that's goin' tae be in the WAAFs.'

Florence held up a pinky as she sipped from her tea cup. 'Joe and Pete have been posted to France, Mother. Did you know?'

'Yes, dear, the twins told me.'

'Of course my Eddie wanted to volunteer but I said, "No Eddie, you're doing important war work at Singer's. That's where you're most needed." ' Everybody knew the secret of Eddie's epilepsy but out of consideration for Florence, as well as for Eddie, no one referred to it.

Mrs McGregor nodded wisely. 'Aye, ye're quite right, hen.'

'Poor Euphemia and Bridget are really worried now,' Teresa said. 'They were quite happy while the boys were at Maryhill but now, when they're so far away in a foreign country . . . Oh, I do hope they'll be all right. They're good boys, both of them.'

'Well,' Granny said, 'that's war for ye. The chances are they'll be blown tae smithereens.'

'Granny!' Florence and Teresa cried out in unison.

'Ah always said . . . '

'We know what you always said, Granny.'

'Aye, but naebody wid listen tae me, wid they? Or tae yer daddy. Ah've been a Socialist and a pacifist aw ma life, an' so has ma Erchie. Ah mind the first war. The war tae end aw wars, they said, an' look at us now. Ah always said . . . '

'Yes, all right, all right, Granny,' Teresa interrupted desperately. 'Mrs McGregor, can I pour you another cup of tea.'

'No thanks, hen, it's time ah wis back down the road. They'll aw be in soon wantin' their tea. Ah've still the tatties tae peel.' She rose. 'Nice tae see ye, Florence. Ye look lovely, hen, but ye'd better watch that hat disnae fly off yer heid.' She left the kitchen with a howl of laughter, followed by a smiling Teresa.

When Teresa returned to the room, she said, 'Fancy! Mr McGregor's been called up.'

'He'll be glad to escape that mob of his,' Florence sniffed. 'I mean, fourteen, Mother. It's not decent.'

'Oh well, at least it'll give Mrs McGregor a rest. She's the one I'm sorry for. Poor soul. She's been pregnant nearly every year since I've known her.'

'It's sheer ignorance, Mother. There's ways and means after all.'

'Oh aye!' Granny cast a sarcastic look in Florence's direction. 'Miss know all. See if your man wisnae . . . '

'Granny,' Teresa almost shouted, 'have another piece of shortbread. I made it specially for you.'

'First ah heard o' it.'

Nevertheless Granny couldn't resist another piece and chomped away quite happily for a few minutes while Teresa admired Florence's purchase of linen napkins.

'Are you going to keep them for special occasions, dear?'

'No, no, Eddie and I like to do everything properly. We'll use them all the time. He's the same as me. He likes to see a nice table, so I always set it nice. We always use fish knives and forks.'

'All the time?'

Florence rolled her eyes. 'No, of course not, Mother. When we have fish for dinner, I meant. By the way, has there been no invitation to the West End yet?'

'To the Cartwrights'?'

'Can't you at least drop a hint to Wincey, Mother? After all, they've been here and they know how good we've all been to Wincey. One would think the least they could do . . . '

'Doctor Houston has been for lunch a few Sundays but that's different. I don't see the need for all of us to go over there, Florence.'

'Well, I do, Mother. Does Wincey suddenly think she's better than us, or what?'

Teresa sighed. 'Don't be silly, dear. Wincey's still the same as she's always been. She only goes over there to the West End at weekends anyway.'

'Well, I think we're entitled to an invitation. And if you don't say anything to Wincey, I will. If you and Father don't want to go, that's fine. And of course Granny wouldn't be able. But I think me and the twins are entitled. After all, we've been like sisters to Wincey all these years.'

'Oh, all right, Florence. I'll have a word with Wincey.'

Florence brightened. 'Thank you, Mother. I'll get a new dress. I saw a really smart one in Pettigrews today. A ginger crepe trimmed with black cord and a gorgeous hat that was really a huge bow attached to a tiny cap.'

'Sounds ridiculous,' Granny said. 'Ah can see you makin' an ass o' yersel, as usual. She enjoyed a good laugh that revealed her pink gums. 'Aye, as ah said before, hen, ye're a better turn than anythin' in the Pavilion.'

10

'That awful old man,' Florence said, 'was sitting in the close smoking a pipe when I came in.'

'Oh here, Teresa.' Granny became anxious. 'Get me oot there, hen. Mr McCluskey likes me keep him company. Poor auld soul. That daughter o' his should be shot for the way she treats him! What harm would he dae havin' his pipe in the house?'

'He'd make it all stinky and horrible,' Florence said. 'I perfectly understand why Miss McCluskey won't allow that filthy old pipe in her house.'

'*His* house,' Granny corrected. 'Come on, Teresa, hurl me oot.'

'All right, I was just getting your tartan rug and your hat. There's a cold draught whistling through that close.' Granny was already clutching a shawl around her shoulders. Now Teresa tucked the tartan rug over the old woman's waist and legs and pulled a felt hat over her wiry grey hair. Then she pushed the wheelchair from the kitchen, along the lobby and out to the close. Mr McCluskey's wrinkled face, with its bushy moustache and eyebrows, lit up with pleasure.

'There you are, hen.'

Granny pushed Teresa's hands off her shawl. 'Stop fussin' about me. Away ye go an' listen tae Florence talkin' a whole lot o' rubbish.'

After Teresa had retreated back into the house, she added to her companion, who was well wrapped up in jacket, muffler and bunnet, 'See oor Florence! She's a younger version o' your lassie. Mad about her house! She wid shoot ye rather than let ye smoke in her place. Ma Erchie—that's her daddy —wisnae allowed tae enjoy a Woodbine when we visited her. We were frightened tae move. Ah've never gone back.

Ah dropped a scone on her front room floor. Ye know how ah suffer wi' ma hands. My God, ye widnae believe what a carry on Florence had. She was runnin' about like a headless chicken. Ah telt her, "See you an' yer stupid house, it'll no' see me again." An' ah've kept ma word. Ah've never gone back there.'

Mr McCluskey sucked at his pipe. 'Awfu' hard tae thole lassies like that.'

'At least ah'm no' stuck wi' oor Florence aw the time. Or the twins. They're about as bad. Ah don't know what's got intae the three o' them. Wincey's no' like that. Ah telt ye about oor Wincey, didn't ah?'

'Aye, fancy the Cartwrights, of aw folks! Ah mind him. Bad auld bastard!'

'The son—that's Wincey's daddy—isnae like his auld man. Ma Erchie says as far as he can judge by his books, he's maybe no' a pacifist but he does seem tae be a bit o' a Socialist.'

'Auld Cartwright'll be birlin' in his grave if that's true.'

Granny nodded. 'Aye, mind that munitions factory he had? He made a fortune out the last war. He'd be doin' that same wi' this one, if he wis alive.'

'An awfu' business. Ah saw ye had Mrs McGregor in. She said her man had been called up.'

'Aye, they're aw gettin' shoved over tae France, ready tae stop the Germans in case they turn up there. But it's no' now that Adolf Hitler should have been stopped, it's at the time o' the Spanish Civil War when he was flexin' his muscles that he should've been told tae get off. But did ye hear a peep out o' the high heid yins then? Naw. They were aw for him. So of course he thought he wis ontae a good thing.'

'Aye, an' now it's ordinary lads like your grandweans' men and Mrs McGregor's man left tae clean up the mess. An' if they dinnae manage it, he'll be over here.'

'Hitler, ye mean?'

'Aye, wait till you see. If he gets intae France, it's only a hop, skip and a jump from there tae here.'

'What a carry on, eh?'

'Aye,' Mr McCluskey sucked contentedly at his pipe. 'Ah mind Johnny Maclean prophesyin' that there would be another war.'

Granny sighed. 'We'll no' see the likes o' him again. Our Johnny had the courage o' his convictions an' he suffered an' died for them.'

It was Mr McCluskey's turn to sigh. 'He wis a good man, our Johnny.'

Suddenly Miss McCluskey's lean, aproned frame appeared in the doorway of the house. As usual, she was gripping a duster in one hand.

'You're tea's ready, Father,' she announced. 'Put that filthy thing out.'

She began flapping her duster around in an effort to dispel the sight and smell of tobacco smoke. 'That filthy thing will be the death of you yet.'

Granny let out a sarcastic 'Mair like *you* will! Always naggin' at the poor auld soul. Ye'll be auld yersel wan day.'

Miss McCluskey's face tightened with anger but she turned back into the house without another word.

'Ah'm sorry, Mr McCluskey,' Granny said. 'Ah should have kept ma mouth shut. But she makes that angry, the way she treats you.'

'Och, she's no' a bad lassie. It's just she's that house proud. She'll have a nice tea waitin' for me an' she aye puts a hot water bottle in ma bed at night. She knows ah feel the cold somethin' terrible.'

In that case, Granny felt like saying, she shouldn't force you to sit in this cold draughty close every day. However, for once, she controlled her tongue.

'Ah'd better away in,' Mr McCluskey said, extinguishing his pipe and fixing a wee metal lid on it before stuffing it into his pocket.

'Nice talkin' tae ye, Granny.'

'See ye tomorrow, Mr McCluskey.'

'Aye, fine.' He staggered up and struggled to lift his chair.

'Leave that. Ye'll do yersel a mischief. Teresa,' she suddenly bawled.

Slippers scuffing on the linoleum, Teresa came hurrying along the lobby, shouting, 'What's the matter, Granny?'

'Help Mr McCluskey in wi' that chair, will ye, hen. He's no' very steady on his feet.'

'Yes, of course.'

Teresa took the chair from the old man. 'On you go, Mr McCluskey. I'll follow you in.'

In a couple of minutes, Teresa had returned and was pushing Granny's wheelchair back into her house.

'You gave me a fright there, Granny,' she said, shutting the door behind her. 'I thought you'd taken a wee turn.'

'When have ah ever taken wee turns? Ah'm no' like Florence's man. It's arthritis ah've got, no' . . . '

'Yes, all right, Granny.' Teresa raised her voice as they entered the kitchen. 'Oh, is that you ready to go, Florence? Are you not waiting until your daddy comes home. He'll be sorry to have missed you.'

'I know,' Florence said, smoothing on her gloves, 'but I like to be home in time to set the table properly for Eddie's dinner and have a nice meal ready to dish up.'

'Wi' yer fish knives an' forks?' Granny said.

'No, it's not fish this evening, Granny. It's spaghetti bolognaise.'

'Oh!' Granny pretended to sound impressed. 'Isn't Eddie the lucky one.'

'Yes, but he's very appreciative,' Florence said. 'I believe this Sunday would be all right for afternoon tea, Mother. You can bring Mrs McGregor and I'll invite the twins as well.'

'Oh that'll be nice, dear.'

'About two thirty, then?'

'Yes, I'll look forward to it. Maybe Granny will be able to come this time.'

'Naw.' Granny sadly shook her head. 'It's funny but ma arthritis is aye worse on Sunday afternoons. But maybe ye can keep a wee bit cake for me, Florence hen.'

'Yes, of course, Granny. I'll give Mother something nice for you. Now I'd better go.'

'Cheerio, hen.' One of Granny's arthritic hands raised in a feeble effort to wave.

'You could have gone. You know fine,' Teresa said, after she'd returned from seeing Florence to the door. 'It would have been a nice wee outing for you.'

'A nice wee outin', ma erse!'

'Granny!' Teresa scolded as she removed Granny's hat and eased a comb through her hair to neaten it again and secure it with the oversized kirby grip.

Granny said, 'Well, ah cannae be doin' wi' aw this fuss she makes an' that house o' hers. An' dinnae kid yersel'. She disnae want me clutterin' up the place.'

'She doesn't mean any harm, Granny. She's really very fond of you.'

'Och, ah know. What's for oor tea the night?'

'Shepherd's pie. And there's some apples and custard for pudding.'

'Great.' Granny's eyes brightened. 'That's Erchie's favourite as well. Is Wincey goin' tae be here.'

'Yes, it's just Tuesday, Granny. You know fine well she doesn't go to the West End until Fridays.'

'Aye, but she sometimes goes out wi' Doctor Houston straight from her work.'

'He's gone away to the Navy, Granny.'

'Och aye, ah forgot. Ah hope that's no' the end o' it.'

'Oh, I don't think so. I certainly hope not—for Wincey's sake. He's just going to be in the naval hospital at Port Edgar. He says he'll probably get home for the occasional weekend.'

'What dae ye bet he'll end up in France wi' the rest o' them.'

'Oh, I don't think so, Granny. It's just the army that goes over there. Anyway, don't say anything like that to Wincey. You'll just upset her.'

'Maybe. Maybe no'.'

'What do you mean?'

'She's a funny lassie. Ye widnae know how she's feelin' about him goin' away. She could be feelin' relief for aw we know.'

'Now, now, don't be silly, Granny. She loves the man. That's always been obvious enough to me.'

'Aye well,' Granny muttered. 'Aw ah say is, she's a funny wee lassie. No' that ah blame her, mind, after aw that she's been though. It's no' surprisin' that she's no' normal.'

'For goodness sake, Granny, don't exaggerate, and don't you dare let Wincey hear you saying anything like that.'

'She'll work night an' day until she forgets aw aboot him, if ye ask me.'

'Nobody's asking you, Granny, so just hold your tongue.'

'Aye, well,' Granny humphed, 'ye'll be auld yersel' one day.'

II

'Have you read this?' Virginia asked, showing Nicholas the newspaper. He nodded gravely. The doom-laden message confirmed that this was no longer a 'phoney war':

LOCAL INVASION COMMITTEE

A local invasion committee has been set up in order to deal with invasion conditions. During the present period, the committee is engaged in making preparations to deal with the local problems which will arise in invasion, such as:

1 *Organisation of civilian labour to assist the military in preparing defence works, digging trenches, clearing roads etc.*
2 *Care of wounded.*
3 *Housing and sheltering the homeless.*
4 *Emergency cooking and feeding.*
5 *Emergency water supplies.*
6 *Messenger service.*

If invasion comes, the committee will direct its action:

a) To meet the requirements of the military.
b) To attend to the needs of the civilian population.

'It'll never come to invasion, surely?' Virginia said.

'Didn't you hear what's just been announced?'

They had finished supper and Virginia had read the newspaper while Nicholas listened to the wireless. The announcer had said, 'Here is the BBC Home Service. The German Army invaded Holland and Belgium early this morning, by land and by landing from parachutes. The BEF are fighting a desperate battle in the northern zone of the Western Front . . . '

'But never here, surely, Nicholas?'

'Why not? If the BEF can't hold them back, they'll be into France. Then what's to stop them crossing the Channel? Except . . . ' A look of pride registered on his face. 'the RAF. Boys like our Richard.'

'You really think it'll come to that?'

'I hope not, but it doesn't look too promising at the moment. I was thinking of joining the local defence volunteers. Anthony Eden was on the radio earlier appealing for volunteers.'

'Local defence volunteers?' Virginia echoed—so he couldn't take time off from his writing to have lunch with her or to go for a walk in the gardens in the afternoons but he could join the army without a second thought. 'Aren't you too old?'

'No, it's men aged sixteen to sixty five, and I'm sure my experience in the last war will come in handy,' he said. 'It's an important job—guarding railways, factories and canals and opposing enemy paratroops.'

'What about your writing?'

'The LDVs will only be part time. I'll still be able to write.'

'Oh great,' she thought, 'you'll write every morning and most of the afternoon, as usual. Then for the rest of the day and evening you'll be playing at soldiers.' But she managed to control her feelings. She had come to face the fact that she had a deep seated jealousy of his writing—or at least the time and priority he gave to it. She was ashamed of these feelings and, as often as possible, affected an interest in Nicholas's work. But secretly she wished she had never encouraged him to develop his talent in the first place. It seemed so long ago now that he'd needed her praise and encouragement to boost his self confidence. Now he didn't need her for anything. As far as she could see he was perfectly content. And why not? He was a fine poet and novelist, respected by critics and admired by his many loyal readers.

She loved him and was proud of him. If only he was not so obsessive about his work. He never seemed to be free of it. If only he would just work in the mornings, and then switch off at lunchtime as soon as he left his desk. According to Nicholas, however, it was impossible for writers to switch off like that. She tried to be fair. After all, she had her nursing duties now. One week she worked mornings and another week she was on late shift. He could complain about how often she was immersed in her work. But he never did.

She suspected he was quite glad of the opportunity to put in extra hours at this writing when she was out of the house. For the first few weekends that Wincey had been staying, he had not worked his usual Saturday and Sunday morning stints. He had devoted all his attention to his daughter.

Last weekend, however, he'd explained to Wincey that he needed continuity at his writing and had to work Saturday and Sunday mornings. But, he assured her, he'd finish in time to have lunch with her, which he did. Nevertheless, Virginia thought it was terrible of him—in the circumstances—to shut himself away even for half an hour while Wincey was in the house.

Wincey assured both her parents that she didn't mind. 'After all,' she said to Virginia, 'it gives *us* a chance to do lots of things together and to talk on our own.'

Wincey appeared perfectly content with the arrangement. But Virginia was secretly furious. It was so typical of him. After all, she'd got herself into trouble by refusing to work in the Royal at weekends. Her work was surely every bit as important as Nicholas's work. After all, she was dealing with real people.

Now Wincey was talking about just coming on Saturdays in time for lunch, instead of on Friday evenings in time for dinner.

'That gives you the chance to work Friday evenings and Saturday mornings, if need be, Mother,' Wincey said. 'We shouldn't forget there's a war on. We've all got a duty to give our best for the war effort. I often have to work late on Fridays as well.'

It had been Nicholas's fault that they were going to see less of Wincey. He had started the rot with his selfishness. She hadn't minded the time he'd spent digging the hole in which he'd built the Anderson shelter in the back garden. She'd even helped him fill the sandbags. She'd carried chairs and cushions and blankets down to try to make the awful damp, fousty smelling place with its ugly corrugated steel roof as comfortable as possible. She hadn't minded that they'd got sweaty and dirty, and she'd had to pin her long hair up because it had worked loose from her normally tidy chignon. None of this mattered to her—because they were doing something together. And all the time she prayed that they'd never need to use the Anderson shelter.

But she'd enjoyed working with him. It was different when he chose to shut himself away from her—even from Wincey now—to concentrate on his precious writing. Sometimes she longed to burst into his room and tear up every piece of paper in sight. Tear up and destroy whole manuscripts. Yet she managed to remain in control and act in a civilised, even caring manner. She'd put on kindly enquiring looks and ask how his current book was progressing.

He was so pleased when she did that. His face would light up with eagerness and gratitude and he'd launch into a news bulletin of what stage he was at and what problems he was having. She strained every nerve in her body to appear interested and she believed she succeeded, when in actual fact his writing bored her. He was dealing with a make-believe world and make-believe people. She had to live in the real world and nowhere was more real than Glasgow Royal Infirmary. Recently she'd driven an ambulance ferrying servicemen with venereal disease to the military hospital in Cowglen. Most of them had been over in France. As far as she could see, the disease was reaching epidemic proportions over there.

Had the men over there nothing better to do? She was perfectly aware at the same time that the soldiers abroad had been having plenty to do. It was just that her frustration and irritation with Nicholas was spilling over into the other areas of her life. She was having a continuous struggle with herself to be fair and reasonable.

She could hardly contain her anger at him, however, when Wincey began coming half way through Saturdays, instead of on Fridays when they'd enjoyed dinner together and a pleasant evening of talking and relaxing over a glass or two of wine. As for Sunday mornings, surely no one in their right mind would work on Sunday mornings unless they had to. But now he was joining the Local Defence Volunteers. He would work all day Saturday and Sunday if they asked him.

That didn't happen, but he did work as an LDV weekdays and Saturday afternoons, digging secret bunkers, helping remove all sign posts which might help enemy invaders, manning roadblocks and practising fighting.

James Matheson shook his head when she told him. 'I'm

disappointed in Nicholas. If he'd done something like you, Virginia—medical work, driving ambulances or whatever—I could have understood it. But he has in effect joined the army.'

'I know, and the other day he had bayonet practice, he told me. Can you imagine it? He insists that it's a case of defending one's country. That's what it comes down to now, he says. He feels he has no choice.'

Matheson sighed. 'He showed me a pamphlet he was issued with. It's called *Shooting to Kill*. Real gung-ho stuff written by an army colonel. I took a copy of it and used it as a subject for discussion in one of my classes. Have you seen it?'

'No.'

'Here, read it.'

She took the piece of paper and allowed her eyes to skim over it.

'In the invasion of Britain, there will be no quarter given. It will be you or the other fellow. The taking of prisoners will probably be out of the question for both sides . . . Make sure that everyone hides his week's supply of food. Burying it in the vegetable garden is probably the safest place until the enemy has passed . . . A service rifle will kill anything from a Nazi to an elephant . . . The experienced and practised shot should have no difficulty in bagging five Nazis, in a charge as short as fifty yards. Pick out your enemy and shoot him . . . '

Matheson said, 'They're in their element now, these army men. I bet that colonel really enjoyed writing that.'

'I keep having difficulty in believing all this is happening, James. Despite the blackout, the rationing and these monstrous barrage balloons hanging above us, it all seems like a dream somehow.'

'Oh, it's no dream, Virginia. I only wish it was. Although I can't see it coming to invasion, but that's just my opinion —or gut feeling, if you like.'

'Everything seems to be happening so quickly now.'

It was always a comfort to speak to Matheson. She had more in common with him now, it seemed, than with Nicholas, or even with Richard. Richard was so naively enthusiastic about the war and the part the RAF were going to play in it.

'One minute you're nipping along the deck,' he had told her excitedly, 'and then with just a gentle pull on the stick, you're soaring up and up. What power you feel at your fingertips. The Spitfire was designed by a genius, Mother. It's too beautiful to be a fighting machine, yet what better weapon of war could anyone want.'

The way he talked and his obvious eagerness for the fight made her tremble with anxiety and fear. It made her hate war all the more. Oh, how desperately she prayed for his safety and how she hated Nicholas for apparently encouraging his son to talk so proudly about his life as a fighter pilot. Nicholas loved to listen to Richard and lit up with pride every time he set eyes on the boy.

It would all be grist to his novelist's mill. That was all that mattered to him. Him and his stupid, unreal world in which, no doubt, everything would end happily. 'Oh, wake up,' she wanted to shout at him. 'Can't you see what terrible danger our son is in?'

It was getting more and more difficult to put on a show of sweet reasonableness in the face of everything Nicholas said and did. Emotion kept building up inside her, ticking away remorselessly like an unexploded bomb.

12

They could see by Florence's flushed face and shining eyes that she was excited. She had obviously gone to a great deal of trouble preparing for the visit. As she showed them around, the pungent smell of Mansion polish was heavy in the air in every room.

'This is our bedroom,' she announced, her chin tipped up with pride as she led Teresa and Mrs McGregor into the room. 'Just put your coats on the bed. I bought that gold satin bedspread in Daly's.'

'It's lovely, dear,' Teresa said.

'Aye, just lovely, so it is, hen,' Mrs McGregor agreed.

'This other room we use as both sitting room and dining room. See, we've made a dining alcove where the set-in bed used to be.'

'Oh, here, is that no' a great idea, Teresa?'

'Yes, it must be really handy, dear.'

'Do you like the HMV portable gramophone. It's got a rather unusual leather cover, don't you think?'

'It's lovely, so it is, hen.'

'We've done the same with the set-in bed in the kitchen.'

'Fancy!'

'Our kitchen is so big and roomy that we eat there most of the time. That's where we'll have our afternoon tea, if you don't mind.'

'That'll do us fine, hen.' Mrs McGregor looked relieved. She'd heard the story of Granny's scone. It had been spread liberally with jam and it had stuck to Florence's carpet. The linoleum in the kitchen was highly polished, the range sparkled. Even the swan-necked tap at the sink under the window glistened with cleanliness. As Mrs McGregor said afterwards, 'Ah could see ma face in that tap.'

'We're going to get the range taken out soon,' Florence announced. 'I've got my eye on a modern gas cooker.'

'Fancy!'

The table in what had been a bed recess was a picture with its crisp white table cover and napkins held by chrome napkin rings. A three tier cake stand graced the middle of the table, surrounded by plates of sandwiches without crusts, scones and pancakes. Florence's finest china tea cups, saucers, plates and little white handled tea knives completed the meticulous arrangement.

'Oh here!' Mrs McGregor was quite overcome. 'Isn't that just lovely.'

Florence could hardly contain her joy and delight. 'The tea service is genuine art deco.'

'Fancy!' Then after a pause, 'Whit's art deco when it's at home?'

Florence gave a long suffering sigh. 'Just sit in at the table, Mrs McGregor. And you too, Mother. Do you recognise this apron, Mother?' Florence patted the little frilled apron tied in a large bow at her waist.

'Isn't that the one I gave you for Christmas, dear?'

'It is.'

'I thought you'd like it.'

'I knew you got it in Copeland's, Mother. They have such high quality goods. Nothing but the best, I always say.'

'Yes, I know you always say that, dear.'

Florence perched herself on a chair at the head of the table and with great dignity lifted the tea pot.

'Where's yer man, hen? He disnae work on a Sunday, dis he?' Mrs McGregor scratched one side of her loose, sagging breasts.

'He does now, Mrs McGregor. The war effort, you know. Everyone must do their bit.'

'Aye, right enough. Ma man's away doin' his bit for the army. The HLI. The same as Joe an' Pete. Ah'm that worried about him. They aye shove oor boys in first in any fight. Scots soldiers are aye on the front line, so they are. He'll go an' get himself killed, so he will.'

'Let's hope not,' Florence said kindly. 'Have a sandwich, Mrs McGregor. Egg or meat paste?'

'Thanks, hen. Egg. What a treat.'

'I made the scones and pancakes myself, by the way.'

'Did ye, hen. My word, Teresa, ye've got a clever wee lassie here, so ye have.'

'I know, and I'm very proud of her.'

'Eddie's a lucky boy, so he is.'

Florence smiled and said modestly, 'I'm lucky to have such a good husband, Mrs McGregor. Every penny Eddie earns goes into his home. Not like some men who spend all their earnings on gambling and cigarettes and drink.'

Teresa said, 'Joe and Pete are good boys. I hope they don't get shoved to the front of any fight. The twins are missing them terribly.'

'Mind for a time they used to go wi' brothers,' Mrs McGregor said, treating herself to another scratch.

'Yes, that seems ages ago now, doesn't it?'

'I invited the twins round today,' Florence said, 'but they'd already promised to visit one of the ladies they work with in Pettigrew's.'

'Ah'll see them some other time then,' Mrs McGregor said, in between enjoying her sandwich. 'Yer mammy says they've got real nice houses as well.'

'They only have one room and kitchens, but they certainly have made them very nice,' Florence conceded. 'They copied my idea of making a dining alcove in their kitchen. They've had their range taken out and got a modern gas cooker instead, as I think I mentioned Eddie and I are going to do. By the way, Mother, did you have a word with Wincey. I can't wait to see her mother's posh house in Kirklee Terrace. Fancy, a big house in Kirklee Terrace!'

'Fancy!' Mrs McGregor echoed.

'Yes, dear, and she's promised to arrange something very soon.'

'Thank you, Mother. I can't wait. I'm so excited.'

'Nae wonder, hen,' Mrs McGregor said, helping herself to another sandwich. 'Whit did ye dae wi' all the crusts? Did ye feed them tae the birds?'

'Oh no, I made breadcrumbs. Breadcrumbs are very handy. Will the twins be included in the invitation, Mother? You know what they're like. They'll go into such a huff if it's just me.'

'No, the twins as well.'

Florence clapped her hands in excitement. 'I can't wait, and of course I'll return their hospitality. This house won't be as big as theirs and Clydebank isn't exactly Glasgow's West End, but I'm not ashamed of my home. Quite the reverse.'

'Quite right, hen. It's lovely. A credit tae you an' Eddie, so it is.'

After the visit was over and Teresa and Mrs McGregor were on their way to Springburn, Mrs McGregor said, 'Ah enjoyed masel', an' tae be honest wi' you, Teresa, ah didnae expect tae. Florence isnae a bad wee lassie . . . '

'I know, she just gets a bit carried away at times.'

'Och well, good luck tae her. She might as well enjoy her house the now. Once she has a few weans, she'll have more tae bother her.'

'Strictly between you and me, Mrs McGregor, I think Florence is frightened to have any children.' Teresa lowered her voice and moved her pale face quickly from side to side as if to make sure Florence wasn't anywhere near. 'You know, it's Eddie's problem. It could be passed on.'

'Och, the poor wee soul.'

'And poor Eddie. I'm sure he feels guilty but he tries to make it up to her. He's done a lot to that house. All the decorating and improvements and everything—he's done it all himself.'

'Fancy! It's no' the same as havin' weans though. Ah don't know what ah'd do without ma crowd. It disnae bear thinkin' about.'

'I know. I miss Wincey when she goes away at weekends. And she's not even my own flesh and blood. But somehow I've always felt she was a Gourlay. Right from the start she fitted in so well with us— I couldn't bear the thought of losing her.'

'Well, ye're no' goin' tae lose her, are ye, hen?'

'No, and it's such a relief, especially now that Florence and the twins have left. It's only natural. I know that. They've their own lives to lead.'

'Aye, so has Wincey.'

'It would be different if she'd been getting married. Doctor Houston lives just round the corner from us in Broomfield Road. She wouldn't have been as far away as Clydebank or even the West End.'

'They were like two peas in a pod, the doctor an' her. What's wrong they're no' married yet?'

Teresa fixed her friend with an anxious stare. 'I don't know. But strictly between you and me, Mrs McGregor, I've a feeling it's Wincey to blame. She's funny about men.' Hastily she added, 'It's not her fault she's like that, you understand. It's because of what she suffered in the past.'

'Is that no' terrible. The poor wee soul.'

'I just hope and pray that Doctor Houston can help her and

493

everything will work out eventually.'

'Aye, well, he's a good doctor. If anybody can sort that lassie out, it's him.'

They parted in Springburn Road and Teresa plodded on to the Balgray and then up the hill to her house.

Granny was sitting at the front room window. She shouted at Teresa as soon as the front door opened, 'Hurl me through, hen. Ma tongue's hangin' out for a cup o' tea.'

'Where's Erchie? He shouldn't have left you on your own, Granny.'

Shoulders hunched forward, Teresa pushed the wheelchair through and parked it in its usual place beside the kitchen fire. Then she tucked the crocheted shawl tighter around Granny's shoulders and up under her chin.

'Ah wis cravin' for a wafer,' Granny said, 'an' he said he'd try an' get one for me. But he hasnae much hope, noo that they've taken the Talies away an' locked them up. What harm did they Talies ever do anybody? All they ever did was sell us ice cream. Nice folk like that, it's a bloody disgrace.'

'Yes, I know. I'm sure everybody in Springburn felt terrible about that.'

'No' everybody, hen. Erchie telt me some ignorant rascals had broke their shop windows.'

'That's awful. As if the poor souls haven't enough to worry them.'

'Aye, ah know. An' them wi' a son in the army. Ah wonder how he'll feel when he finds out his mammy an' daddy have been interned.'

Teresa filled the kettle and put it on the fire. 'You'd think the authorities would have better things to do than arrest a decent Italian couple like that.'

'Aye, it's a bloody disgrace. Dear knows when ah'll get a decent ice cream wafer again.'

13

Belgium had been overrun. Now France was being battered into submission. The British army was retreating, trying to make for the sea, and it had been like walking through hell. Villages and towns were bombed. The terrible stench of death and smoke from burning lorries hung over everything. Injured horses struggling to stand up had to be finished off with rifles. For a time, in order to get past the slow moving civilians, soldiers took to the fields and so when the German aircraft attacked, it was mostly the refugees they hit. Horses, carts, and people were being blown to bits, pieces flying everywhere.

Now the army was trapped in a narrow strip of land that was choked with refugees. Malcy and many of his fellow soldiers, including Joe and Pete, kept taking cover in the nearest ditch but there was always somebody shouting, 'Get a move on. Get a move on. That way. Keep moving.'

German aircraft swooped and dived from the brilliant blue of the French sky. Machine guns chattered and plumes of earth made their deadly progress along the road until they met the churning mass of humanity. Men, women and children huddled together, while at the same time desperately trying to keep moving along. Some were pushing bicycles heaped with belongings, some shuffled along carrying loads on their backs, others were pushing hand carts. There were innumerable horses and carts all piled high with family possessions. Children plodded along at the side of the road, old people collapsed with exhaustion and others struggled to lift them on top of a cart.

Malcy felt sick as he watched machine gun bullets rake over the lines of helpless, terrified people. He didn't know where the refugees were going. He doubted if they knew themselves, but they were moving in the opposite direction from the army who were retreating to Dunkirk. Already Malcy, Joe, Pete and the others had trudged for miles across country until they were in a kind of trance, dazed with fatigue caused by lack of sleep. Their faces were taut with exhaustion and fear, the soles of their boots had completely worn through and their feet were bleeding. They could only hobble very slowly and painfully. The broken flesh absorbed the dust of the road, forming a skin that cracked and recracked as they trudged on, leaving tiny crimson flowers on the grey dust as they passed.

While they were in the ditch, Malcy said, 'By God, if I ever get back home to Glasgow, I'll count my blessings. Just to be back in that place'll be enough for me. I won't care about bloody money, or anything else. Just to get back to Glasgow in one piece, that's all I ask.'

'Me too,' Pete agreed, 'and see if Bridget starts wittering on about her precious china tea cups or stupid ornaments, I'll break them over her empty head.'

'Fuckin' right,' Joe fervently agreed. 'See Euphemia and her fuckin' floor polish! I'll tell her where to shove it.'

Malcy wanted to laugh but hadn't the energy. He kept fading into a hazy dream world. The only thing that saved him from floating into complete unconsciousness was the agonising pain in his feet. Once again, during a lull in the bombing and shooting, they struggled from the ditch onto the road and followed other ragged soldiers. As they got nearer to Dunkirk, they saw more and more discarded equipment cluttering either side of the road.

Eventually they were forced to walk in single file. They shambled painfully across two canal bridges and at last came out on the dunes.

'Christ!' Malcy said. 'What chance to you think we've got here?'

All the sea front buildings had been bombed and miles of white sand in both directions were littered with abandoned vehicles like huge, dead insects. The bodies of soldiers lay scattered around and vast numbers of troops were huddled in the dunes, while queues snaked over the sand. German fighters were strafing the beaches, seemingly unmolested by the RAF, and every now and again the queues of soldiers scattered as the Messerschmitts flew low over the top of them.

Malcy and the others joined the nearest queue. Despite British and French ships being sunk, the evacuation went on. The next day, more small boats appeared manned by fishermen, lifeboatmen and almost anybody else with any experience of handling boats. There were pleasure craft that without doubt had never ventured anywhere near as far from home. They had certainly never crossed the Channel before. Nor had many of the civilian volunteers who were manning them.

The next day the sea was flat calm with a dense sea fog and the bigger ships were hardly troubled by the Luftwaffe, while the smaller craft were busy trying to lift men off the beaches.

Malcy and the others were still in a long queue that stretched across the beach and into the sea. They had waited for endless hours, trying to ignore the floating corpses that gently nudged the waiting boats as if, even in death, they were trying to escape the beaches of Dunkirk. Ahead of him, Malcy saw a small boat coming in. A crowd of men all tried to clamber aboard on one side and tipped the boat over. It was a scene that Malcy had already witnessed many times that day. As these desperate, overladen soldiers sank beneath the waves, other small boats, all with soldiers cramming the decks, headed out to sea. After their terrible experiences on the beaches, the exhausted survivors were just glad to be moving out into deeper water and the relative safety of the bigger ships

Malcy, Joe and Pete eventually found themselves wading out neck deep into the sea, before being pulled on board one of the smaller craft. In no time they were being transferred onto a British destroyer and were on their way across the Channel.

As soon as they were safely on board, most of the men collapsed. Malcy lay on the deck, unable to cope with the enormous relief he felt. He was ashamed of the tears flooding down over his face and salting his lips, but he couldn't stop them.

He knew the ship could be bombed. Messerschmitt 110 fighter bombers and the dreaded Stuka dive bombers were still flashing about in the sky. Joe crawled alongside him. 'It's OK, mate. We're going to make it. Glasgow here we come.'

Malcy heard himself give a feeble laugh. 'Aye, right.' He could barely make out Joe's rugged, dirt streaked face topped with lank, black hair. A vague recollection came to him of Joe helping him, half dragging him, along the road towards Dunkirk. He remembered too a man lying by the side of the road. Both of his legs had been blown off. He had been blinded in one eye and he was slowly dying in agony.

497

Joe had killed him—shot him through the back of the head. Nobody else could bring themselves to do it.

Pete joined them. He was dragging himself along the deck on his hands and knees. 'See when I get back. The first thing I'll have is a double Johnny Walker.'

'They'll maybe no' have any, Pete. It's England, no' Scotland, we're goin' to.'

'Och, every civilised country has Johnny Walker.'

'That's right, but as I said, it's England they're takin' us to.'

Malcy managed a weak laugh. 'Watch what you're saying, Joe. Some of these English sailors might chuck us overboard.'

'We'll surely get some leave after this,' Joe said. 'Then it's Glasgow here we come, eh?'

'Aye.' Malcy took a deep determined breath in an effort to stop another gush of tears. He had no one to go back to. Still, as long as he got back. There was always the Gourlays. They had never blamed him for Charlotte's death. On the contrary, they had shown him nothing but sympathy. Even Wincey had been all right in the end. He clung to the thought of Springburn and the Gourlays' house on the Balgrayhill.

'I'll get in touch with the Gourlays,' he said out loud.

Joe said, 'The very thing. And if you can't go there, Malcy, you can always come to my place.'

Pete joined in. 'You'll be welcome to stay with me and Bridget.'

'Great, thanks. But I expect the Gourlays will want to put me up for a wee while anyway.'

It was then that Joe shouted, 'My God, look at that.' The air to the east was seething with German aircraft—bombers, with their fighter escort high above them. They watched as dive bombers peeled off towards the evacuation fleet and the hundreds of smaller civilian boats. The destroyer they were on tore through the water at full speed, trying to evade the Stukas attacking it from different directions.

'Oh no,' Malcy thought, 'please God, no.'

The ear-splitting shriek of the Stuka filled their world. Then they saw the dark cruciform shape of the plane flash past the bridge. Everything now seemed to be happening in slow motion. A huge yellow bomb tumbled from its rack under the fuselage of the bomber. Another bomb scored a direct hit on the side of the ship. Water cascaded over the deck, the ship shuddered and slowly started to lean

498

further and further, the deck canting over at a steep angle. Yet another bomb exploded with shattering force deep within the ship. On the signal deck, the coxswain bellowed, 'Abandon ship!'

Pete said, 'Oh Christ. Jesus Christ.'

Malcy tried to struggle up.

Joe said, 'There's a ship coming alongside. Come on, boys, we've still got a chance.'

Ships were sinking all around. They could see other destroyers going down. But they weren't quick enough to get onto the ship that had come alongside. Anyway, one of the sailors shouted that they were only taking wounded on board. As they watched the ship move away, they saw a bomb go straight down its funnel and blow the whole vessel sky high. When the smoke cleared, they saw the crew of that ship were now in the water, along with survivors from several other ships—men who only moments earlier they had been trying to save.

Everywhere, men were floundering around in the oil-covered water, screaming and yelling. A couple of sailors cut a life raft clear and Joe, Malcy and Pete were lowered into it. The sailors—who were wearing cork life jackets—jumped into the water, hung onto the sides of the raft and paddled slowly away from the sinking destroyer. Only a few minutes later, two Messerschmitts swooped down straight at them. Bullets and cannon shells tore through the water, killing the two sailors in an instant. As their bodies floated aimlessly away, the three soldiers huddled together in the bottom of the raft.

Malcy opened his eyes for a second, only to see the fighters turning once more, closing in for the kill. 'Oh no,' he thought. 'Oh please, God, no.'

14

Virginia had invited the Gourlays, more to please Wincey than anything else. She didn't mind Teresa, or Erchie, or Granny. But the
girls were a bit tiresome. It was arranged they would come for afternoon tea on Sunday. As it turned out, Granny couldn't come and
Erchie had to stay and look after her, so it was just Teresa, the Gourlay
girls, and Wincey.

Florence and the twins looked as if they were wearing brand new
outfits. Wincey looked very smart too, but business-like in her black
suit and crisp white blouse. Florence's tip-tilted face was framed by
an off-the-face halo hat. Her dark blue coat and paler blue dress had
square padded shoulders. The twins each wore an ensemble of skirt,
jacket and coat.

They were shown into the sitting room. It was a comfortable room
with an Axminster carpet and gold covered chairs and sofas. Tasselled
curtains draped the tall windows.

Florence and the twins gasped in undisguised admiration.

'Do sit down and make yourselves at home,' Virginia told everyone.

Nicholas appeared for a few minutes to say hello, then excused
himself. He had to go out to tend his vegetable garden. The back
garden at Kirklee Terrace had become a blessing. Vegetables, like
everything else, were scarce, some were unobtainable, and the government were telling people to grow their own wherever possible.

A tea trolley was set ready and Virginia began pouring the tea. 'It
gets so irritating, doesn't it?' she said to Teresa. 'So many government
posters and pamphlets telling us what we must or must not do. The
other day, on my way to the hospital, I spotted forty eight posters

telling people things like "Eat wholemeal bread", "Don't waste food", "Keep your children in the country".

'Well, I'd have second thoughts about that after what happened to Mrs McGregor's youngest. Thank you, dear,' Teresa said.

'Oh, I know. Wincey told me. Wasn't that awful?'

Florence said, neatly crossing her legs, 'I saw one poster which told you how to help build a plane and to fall in with the fire bomb fighters, whatever that meant.'

'And of course,' Virginia sighed, 'newspapers, magazines and the wireless are endless founts of wi'dom. I keep thinking, when will it ever end? I sometimes feel quite worn out with it all—so many regulations and instructions.'

Wincey helped Virginia by passing round a plate of sandwiches.

'How do you manage this big house, dear,' Teresa asked, 'and you out working?'

'I miss my housekeeper but I'm lucky. At least I've got a cleaning lady. She's elderly and only comes in for two hours a week but she does manage to do the washing and ironing. And she runs the carpet sweeper over the carpets.'

'Your hall, of course, doesn't need a carpet. Marble,' Florence's voice dropped with awe, 'like a palace. I do admire this carpet, Mrs Cartwright. What a beautiful rich colour! And so soft under foot. I have a very nice carpet in my front room. Not as expensive as this one, no doubt, but very nice all the same. You must come and visit Eddie and me. Come one evening for supper so that Eddie would be in.'

'That would be very nice. Thank you, Florence, and please, just call me Virginia.'

'Virginia.' Florence put her cup and saucer back on the trolley and immediately fumbled in her handbag. 'Let's consult our diaries and make a date.'

Teresa looked embarrassed. 'For goodness sake, Florence,'

Wincey said. 'At least give Mother time to finish her tea.'

'Oh.' Florence looked disappointed. 'Oh, all right then.'

Euphemia said, 'Bridget and I live in Dumbarton Road. Just room and kitchens, but I believe you once lived in a room and kitchen, so you'll know it's nothing to be ashamed of. We've got ours very nice. Our front room has a carpet as well.'

'That's right.' Bridget earnestly nodded. 'Hers is more reddish and mine is more bluey, although it does have some red in it.'

Virginia tried to look interested.

'And,' Bridget went on proudly, 'I've got a lovely china tea set.'

Florence said, 'I think you'll like my art deco table wear. Genuine art deco,' she repeated the phrase in order to make absolutely sure that Virginia understood the importance of it.

Virginia managed to appear suitably impressed.

'Have a fruit scone,' Wincey urged, knowing that Florence would be too lady-like to speak with her mouth full.

Teresa said, 'Did you bake the scones yourself, Virginia?'

'Oh no, I've barely enough time these days to cook dinner, far less bake anything. Especially after having to wait in endless queues. You know what it's like.'

'Oh, I do, I do, dear, but it's the shortage of cigarettes that's upsetting Erchie. He always enjoyed his Woodbine so much. I feel really sorry for him. He get so nervy without his smoke.'

'I'm quite friendly with our local newsagent. I'll try to get an occasional packet from him, and Erchie will be welcome to it.'

'Oh, that's awfully kind of you, Virginia, and I know it'll cheer Erchie up.'

Wincey said, 'Robert has started to smoke. He gets them issued from the Navy. He'll probably get rum as well—but I think that's only when they're at sea.'

'Does he like it?' Euphemia asked.

'What? The rum?'

'No, silly, the Navy.'

'I think so, but he doesn't talk much about it and we haven't been seeing so much of each other lately. He's been posted down south somewhere. Robert says things are going from bad to worse in France, and as many ships as possible are needed to go across the Channel. But he's not supposed to talk about it, or even say where he's going, so I don't know exactly what's happening.'

Virginia sighed. 'Nicholas says our troops are retreating and trying to make for the coast. It's turning into a very dangerous situation. If the Germans reach the coast, what's to prevent them coming over here?'

'Oh!' Bridget's plump face tightened with anxiety. 'I hope Pete's all right.'

'And my Joe,' Euphemia said.

'Oh, I'm sure they will be, dear,' Teresa comforted. 'As far as I understand it, the battle's over. Our lads can't hold the Germans back any longer—they're just trying to get away now. They'll be home soon. That's why extra ships are needed—to bring our boys safely back home.'

'Do you really think so, Mammy?' In her anxiety Euphemia forgot to use the more polite 'Mother'. 'They'll come back safe?'

'Of course, dear. Don't worry. Everything's going to be all right.'

Virginia felt guilty at upsetting the girls. At the same time, it seemed a bit foolish of them to be hiding their heads in the sand, or in their precious houses. The war news was not good. It didn't look as if everything was going to be all right at all. Richard had recently been moved to an RAF station down south, and she felt increasingly anxious about him. In a way, she was glad that she had such a lot to do. It kept her from thinking too much about Richard and the danger he was in. Eventually Teresa said, 'Let me help you with the washing up, Virginia.'

'No, I'll do it.' Wincey started gathering up the dishes and putting them onto the tea trolley.

Florence sprang to her feet. 'No, please. The twins and I will do it. We insist, don't we girls?'

'Oh yes, please. Let us do the dishes.' The twins bounced up like two rubber balls.

It was obvious to Virginia that they just wanted to see her kitchen and probably have a sneaky look into the other rooms of the house, but what did that matter? Thoughts of Richard had brought more important concerns to her mind. She nodded. 'Yes, if you want.' And she told them where to find the kitchen.

Off they hurried with the loaded trolley, their faces alert with excitement and expectancy. Wincey sat down, rolling her eyes in exasperation.

Teresa shook her head at the three retreating backs. 'They're not bad girls, you know. They just get a wee bit carried away at times.'

'That's all right. How's Granny?'

'Her arthritis comes and goes, and she's got one of her flare ups just now. When that happens, she suffers awful pain, poor soul. We're very grateful to Wincey for getting these two nurses. I don't know what Granny would do without them. Or me. I was beginning to get awful puffed trying to move her. The nurses are big strong girls, they get her up every morning, give her a bath and dress her, then every night they settle her down.'

'I could afford to have got Granny into a private nursing home, but she doesn't want to leave the family. I can understand how she feels.'

Virginia's heart missed a beat. Was that a hint that Wincey didn't want, and would never leave the Gourlays? If only Wincey would settle properly in Kirklee Terrace, where she belonged. Not that Virginia felt any ill will towards the Gourlays. Far from it. She liked them, but her daughter belonged with her. She would have to have another talk with her, be firm with her.

Just then, Nicholas appeared, slim and tanned in rolled up shirt sleeves, his black hair rumpled. He was carrying a basket in which nestled a cabbage, some carrots, potatoes and a leek.

'I thought you might like these,' he said, handing the basket over to Teresa. 'They're jolly good, though I say it myself.'

'Oh, thank you, Nicholas. I'll be able to make a lovely pot of soup. What a treat!'

'You're welcome. I'd better go and have a wash. I've a meeting of the LDVs tonight.' He grinned. 'It's all go these days.'

Virginia immediately felt depressed. Another long night on her own. Wincey had an urgent order to fulfil, which meant she had to spend this Sunday evening in her factory office. Virginia tried to convince herself that Wincey couldn't help that. Both Wincey and Nicholas were doing their best in every way for the war effort.

'Don't forget there's a war on' had become the most used phrase in the country and after all, there were lots of things she could do. There were potatoes to peel for the next day's dinner. She also had to make a pot of soup. Although she tried to organise her time as efficiently as possible, being on day shift tomorrow meant she wouldn't have enough time to do the cooking . It would have to be done tonight. She could even set the table in readiness for the next day.

'Are you feeling all right, Mother?' Wincey asked.

'What, darling?'

'You look a bit pale and tired.'

'Oh, I'm fine. Don't worry.'

'I'm sorry I have to go to the factory tonight, but it is so important. There's so much paperwork to do these days.'

'Yes, yes, darling. I understand. Of course you must go.'

And it meant Wincey would go 'home' afterwards. She still referred to the Gourlays' place as home, which hurt Virginia more than she ever cared to admit. 'I'm fine,' she repeated.

When Florence and the twins returned, Florence immediately burst out, 'Gosh, what a lovely big kitchen. I love your Aga. And I hope you don't mind, but we popped into your bathroom. It was lovely too. Your whole house is lovely.'

'Just lovely,' the twins echoed.

Virginia felt like saying, 'Oh shut up, you silly, empty headed girls.' But instead she gave them a smile and said, 'Thank you.'

As if sensing her irritation, Teresa struggled to her feet and said firmly, 'Come on, girls. It's time we were away. Virginia has had us long enough.'

'Oh no,' Virginia said, feeling guilty now. 'You're all very welcome to stay as long as you like.'

'I know, Mother,' Wincey said, 'but I must get back to my office as soon as possible. And I'm giving everyone a lift home.'

The word 'home' wounded Virginia again.

And later, sitting at her dressing table gazing bleakly at herself as she undid her loop of long hair, she allowed tears to spill from her eyes and trickle helplessly down her face.

15

Richard was proud of the luxuriousness of his moustache. He combed it regularly, put on a discreet spot of wax and tweaked it up at each end. The local girls certainly seemed to like it. The uniform too. RAF pilots were very popular with the ladies. They weren't so popular with the local men. In the pub, after a few pints, angry words were often exchanged, along the lines of 'Why are you lads loafing down here drinking, instead of up there shooting the bastards down?'

The last time somebody said that to Richard, he'd been with a buxom upper class girl called Davina. She'd had to hold him back and hustle him out of the place. He was so angry and humiliated that he'd wanted to punch the ignorant fellow. Once outside with Davina, he'd gazed up at the searchlights criss-crossing in the dark sky and said, 'I would be up there now if it had been left to me. Even though our Spits aren't really any good as night fighters.'

'They were only teasing you,' Davina soothed. 'I expect they're jealous. They're just old men who aren't able to do anything to help with the war effort.'

Davina, he discovered, was a member of the Women's Land Army. A land girl, of all things. She explained that she had been used to horses and was familiar with everything that went on in 'Daddy's estate'. As a result, she thought working on the land would be her most suitable contribution to the war effort. Davina, just like most of Richard's fellow officers, had a very upper class English accent. But this didn't worry Richard. He hadn't gone to a private school for nothing, and no one could guess from his own accent that he came from Scotland, far less Glasgow. Glasgow had a very bad image down south. It was enough to put anyone off. Edinburgh, being the capital and known as a beautiful, historic city, was different.

Nowadays, if asked, he just said he had been brought up first of all in the country and then in Edinburgh. To an extent, this was true. He had lived with his grandmother and grandfather in their country house for the first few years of his life. Then he'd been sent to a boarding school in Edinburgh. That had been paid for by his grandparents. No doubt the idea had been to prevent him living under the same roof as his mother. His grandmother hated his mother. He didn't. Not at all. He got on well with her, and with his father. All the same, both his parents were a bit Bolshie.

His father had begun to see sense now that there was a war on, but his mother was still influenced by her first husband, the ghastly James Matheson. The man was not patriotic. But he'd always been the same, apparently. He'd been a damned conscientious objector in the last war. Richard could never understand his mother having anything to do with a chap like that. At least she was doing her bit as a VAD. He'd told Davina about that and she had been impressed.

'They work jolly hard. Good luck to her.'

'And my father's doing his bit in the LDVs. He served with distinction as an officer in the last war.'

'You must be very proud of them both.'

'Yes, I am.'

'I'd like to meet them some day.'

He smiled down at her tanned, unmade-up face. 'Remind me to arrange that. There doesn't seem to be much possibility of leave at the moment, though.'

'No, things don't look good, do they?'

'Don't worry, the Jerries won't set foot on British soil. Not once we get a real crack at them.'

Davina linked arms with him. She had a good firm grip. 'When I see any Spitfires going up now, I wonder if it's you and I hold my breath and keep my fingers crossed that you'll be all right.'

He felt touched. She really cared about him. Gently he turned her towards him and kissed her on the mouth. She responded warmly and he tightened his grip. They both opened their mouths, their tongues exploring. Eventually they were startled by the sound of a crowd of men approaching through the darkness, bawling and singing. The pub had shut and the drinkers were making for home. He and

Davina drew apart and began walking along side by side. Too soon, they reached Davina's billet and she bade him a quick goodnight.

'Wait,' he called after her retreating back. 'When can I see you again?'

'Next Tuesday. Same time, same place.'

'Jolly good.'

He turned away quite happily then. It was something to look forward to, something to dream about. Life was suddenly even better than it had been before. He loved his Spitfire. He loved flying. He loved his life in the RAF. Now, this was a different kind of love. He savoured the experience. Yes, he was in love with the girl. All right, he hadn't known her for very long, but she was the girl for him. He was sure of it. He swaggered whistling cheerily all the way to the camp.

The only thing that would have increased his happiness at the moment was if he could be sure of being involved in more action. Almost every other fighter squadron had done a stint covering Dunkirk, but the evacuation had ended just before he'd got a turn. He had acted as 'Arse-End Charlie' a few times recently, weaving backwards and forwards above and behind the squadron, to protect them from attack from the rear. On the last occasion, he'd had reason to remember the truth of the warning, 'Beware of the Hun in the sun'. He had been peering into his mirror when out of the sun, and dead astern, he saw bullets peppering his port wing. It was a miracle he got home that day—but then, he'd always been lucky.

Once up in the air, they all believed they were immortal. No one accepted that they could be killed. And Richard was a born optimist. Even this business in France didn't depress him. He knew they'd sort it all out eventually. The only thing that really got to him these days was the growing chorus of undeserved criticism that the RAF was subjected to.

One evening, in the local pub, the regulars were treating a group of Dunkirk evacuees to round after round of free drinks. Before long, Richard and his RAF companions were involved in heated arguments with some of the soldiers.

'Where were the RAF when they were needed? They certainly weren't over Dunkirk,' someone said.

Richard found it very hard to keep his temper. He had known several pilots who had been killed over France, even before Dunkirk. Lysanders, for instance, had been flying across the Channel two or three times a day in an effort to drop supplies to the besieged garrison in Calais. Sometimes they had only a solitary fighter for support. And there had been British planes over Dunkirk.

Fortunately, a Frenchman spoke up to remind the others that there had been times when there was a heavy fog over the beaches and the planes were high above it. He also told of one fight he had seen between a lone Spitfire and four Junkers. He had watched it shoot down two Germans and cripple a third. The fourth made off.

Now the invasion scare was on. No one was allowed more than half an hour's call from the airfield. All leave had been cancelled, and all officers had been ordered to carry side arms. Richard was issued with an antiquated, short nosed .45 and six soft lead bullets. But he'd managed to get himself another twelve bullets. Now every newspaper had as its front page an appeal to every citizen to stay put. And people had come to believe that it could actually happen—that England's peaceful, pleasant land could at any moment be filled with the thundering noise of German tanks. At any moment, an army could drop from the skies.

But they were reckoning without the RAF, Richard told himself. He and his fellow pilots were ready for anything the Luftwaffe could throw at them. Far from being apprehensive or afraid, Richard was keyed up, and raring to go. They had learned a lot about the Germans, and their aircraft. The Germans had a mass psychology that they applied even to their planes, which were so constructed that their crews were always bunched together. This gave them confidence and a false sense of security. And the RAF had soon learned how to shatter that. The crews of the Heinkel bombers soon came to feel intensely vulnerable, hunched inside their greenhouse-like, perspex cockpits, with precious little protection against the white-hot tracer from the Spitfires eight machine guns.

Richard and the other fighter pilots could almost sense the bomber crews wincing as the Spits dived in for the kill. But some of the German gunners stuck to their task to the bitter end, and there were always one or two of Richard's squadron who didn't get back. But that was how it was. Kill or be killed. And he was always lucky.

16

'It's called the Home Guard now,' Erchie told Wincey. 'The LDVs that yer father's in.'

Granny glared suspiciously over at her son. 'Whit are ye suddenly so interested in them for? Ye're no' thinkin' o' joinin' them, ah hope.'

'Och, don't worry, Ma. Ah'm quite happy doin' ma bit keepin' a shirt on their backs. That's essential enough work for me. Anyway, wi' ma flat feet, they wouldnae huv me, especially now ah've caught yer ruddy arthritis.'

'It's no' infectious, so don't you go blamin' me. Anyway, aw ye've got is a few twinges in yer knees. Think yersel' lucky ye've no' got ma arthritis. Ye'd know aw about it if ye had.'

'Aye, OK, OK, Ma.' He turned his thin face towards Wincey. 'How's yer father doin', hen? Does he still get enough time tae write his books. Ah suppose he'll have tae make the time. It's his livin', isn't it?'

'Yes. I don't think he gets paid for being in the Home Guard and I shouldn't think Mother'll make much in the VADs. I offered to pay for my keep at weekends but they wouldn't hear of it.'

Teresa was busy at the kitchen table, her hands and arms floury with making a batch of scones. 'I'm sure they appreciated the offer though, dear. You're a very generous girl.'

'I can well afford to be generous, Teresa. The factory's making a lot of money.'

Erchie laughed. 'She's made me take another raise, wid ye believe.'

Teresa stopped kneading the scones for a few seconds. 'Oh, now Erchie, do you think you should?'

'He works for everything he gets, Teresa. I don't know what I'd do without Erchie. He's worth his weight in gold to me.'

'Oh well, dear, if you're sure . . . Have you heard any more from Doctor Houston, by the way?'

Wincey tucked her hair behind her ear. 'No, not since that last letter and a quick phone call to the office. To be honest with you, Teresa, I'm very worried about him. There were so many ships lost at Dunkirk.'

'They would have let you know, dear. No, I'm sure he'll be all right. He'll turn up unexpectedly at that door any day now.'

'If we'd been married, they would have let me know as next of kin, but he has nobody.' Much to her own embarrassment, and to everyone else's surprise and distress, she suddenly burst in to tears. It wasn't like Wincey to indulge in any outward displays of emotion.

Teresa rushed over and despite her floury hands, pulled Wincey close to her. 'Och now, now, don't be upsetting yourself. We'll hear these wedding bells yet. He'll be back safe and sound—just you wait and see.'

Desperately, Wincey took deep calming breaths and rubbed at her eyes with the sleeve of her cardigan. 'I held him at arm's length, Teresa. He said he understood but oh, I wish I could have been different.'

Erchie said, 'Of course he understood, hen. Anybody would, once they knew what ye'd been through as a wean. It's no' so easy to get over things like that, but ye will. Just give yersel' time.'

She gazed at him with tragic eyes. 'Oh but Erchie, have I got time? I'm so worried about Robert.'

'He'll be back, hen, an' ye'll be all right.'

Granny said, 'There's surely ways tae find things out. Just sittin' bubbling' isnae any use. Write or phone to the Navy. Somebody's bound to be able to tell ye whit's happened.'

'I never thought of that.' Wincey fished for her hankie and rubbed it over her face. 'I know the name of his ship. He couldn't tell me in his letters because they were censored, but that last time he phoned, he let it slip.'

'Well then . . . '

'Thanks, Granny.'

Wincey lost no time in taking Granny's advice. As soon as she was back in her office, she wrote to the Admiralty. Several days passed before she received a reply. It was to inform her that Robert's ship had gone down during the evacuation of Dunkirk. There were no survivors.

The letter had arrived by the second post and Wincey had been sitting at lunch in the Gourlays' kitchen when she opened it. It was strange, she thought, that now no tears would come. She just sat, staring at the letter.

'Whit's up?' Granny hunched forward, pushing her spectacles closer to her eyes.

'The ship was bombed. There were no survivors.'

'See bloody war!' Granny bawled. 'What a bloody waste! Rabbie Burns was right aw these years ago, an' he's still right —Man's inhumanity to man makes thousands mourn.'

'Oh dear,' Teresa said, not knowing what to do or say for the best.

'A decent fella like that,' Granny raged on. 'Aw he ever did —or wanted to do—was tae help folk. See these bloody high heid yins an' politicians, ah know whit ah wid do wi' them. Ah'd . . . '

All right, all right,' Teresa interrupted. 'Oh Wincey, I'm so sorry. If there's anything we can do to help, you know you've only to ask.'

'I know. Thanks, Teresa. I think I'd better get off to work now.'

'Oh no,' Teresa protested. 'I don't think you should, Wincey. You've had a terrible shock. Why don't you take at least the rest of today and tomorrow off.'

'I'm always better if I keep busy. I must keep busy.' She rose, automatically collected her bottle green coat and matching hat, and called back from the front door, in a parody of her normal cheerful sing-song, 'Bye, see you later.'

Just before she left the door to go through the close, she heard Granny's outraged bawl, 'See bloody war!'

Wincey escaped out to the street and began walking smartly down the Balgrayhill. She was concentrating on what she had to do in the factory that afternoon. She had to keep her mind safely on ordinary, routine problems. Such a lot of paperwork nowadays, it was getting worse all the time. Inside the office there was one kind, and outside there was another. Everywhere paper was stuck up on walls. Everybody was being bombarded with it. Even cigarette packets contained cards which gave instructions for everything, including air raid precautions, how to deal with incendiary bombs, how to use a stirrup pump, how to protect your house from the danger of flying glass.

There were instructions on how to black out your home. They were contained in *Public Information Leaflet Number 2*. There were other instructions on how to make your home safe against gas and anti-bomb blast measures. 'Women of Britain,' yet another urged, 'give us your aluminium. We want it and we want it now. We will turn your pots and pans into Spitfires . . . '

'Women of Britain,' was the rallying cry on some posters, 'come into the factories.' So many posters, leaflets, pamphlets, forms to fill in. She had so much to do in the office. Her feet quickened towards it. She wanted to run but instinctively knew running would let loose the panic that she was desperately trying to control.

Another poster caught her eye. 'Be like Dad—keep mum. Careless talk costs lives.' And yet another: 'Your courage, your cheerfulness, your resolution WILL BRING US VICTORY'.

Victory? What did victory mean to her? What did anything mean any more? So many so-called helpful instructions but who could instruct her? Who could help her now?

Suddenly she was at the factory door. She went inside to her office. Her secretary, Mrs Allan, who should have retired long ago but refused to give up, appeared in the doorway. 'Are you all right, Miss Gourlay? Would you like me to fetch you a cup of tea?'

A cup of tea—the panacea for all ills. What a bloody joke!

'Yes thank you, Mrs Allan,' she said, picking up the nearest pen and beginning to write.

17

In July Adolf Hitler ordered preparations to be made for the invasion of Britain. Previously however, in a speech to the Reichstag, he had made it clear that he hoped for peace with Britain. It was, he said in his speech, his 'Final Appeal to Reason.'

> '*A great empire will be destroyed, an empire which it was never my intention to destroy or even to harm . . . I consider myself in a position to make this appeal since I am not the vanquished begging favours but the victor speaking in the name of reason.*'

A *Daily Express* journalist was quick to respond on BBC Radio. The tone was suitably uncompromising and full of defiance,

> '*Let me tell you what we here in Britain think of this appeal of yours to what you are pleased to call our reason and common sense. Herr Fuhrer, and Reichskanzler, we hurl it right back at you, right in your evil smelling teeth . . .*'

The German High Command made no secret of how they felt after hearing their Fuhrer's words being ridiculed on the BBC. They thought the British were crazy, and after the rejection of the Fuhrer's terms, the Luftwaffe began to attack in force. They planned to wipe out RAF Fighter Command and so clear the way for the invasion. But their first targets were the slow-moving convoys. The RAF tried to defend the convoys, and for the first time, radar equipment was used. But often things didn't work out. Sometimes radar contacts proved to be friendly aircraft, sometimes delicate equipment malfunctioned in wet weather.

But the main problem was timing. Often by the time the Spitfires and Hurricanes were scrambled, the convoys had already been attacked and the German planes were returning home. Coastal convoy losses became alarming, and as a result squadrons had to be sent further south to smaller stations much nearer the coast. There, in small tents, pilots slept, or wrote letters, or played cards—ready to scramble at a moments notice.

Richard's squadron was not among those that had been moved and he was disappointed. However, he made the most of his time by getting to know Davina better. They met at every opportunity now and more than once, they'd spent some memorable hours in a room at a local hotel. He'd asked her to marry him and she'd said yes. She'd phoned her parents and they lost no time in motoring down to meet him, knowing that he couldn't get any leave at present, or travel any distance from the airfield.

They had turned out to be a charming upper-class couple. Lord Clayton-Smythe was tall and lean, with slightly protruding eyes. His wife was almost as tall as him, with grey hair and an aura of dignity and elegance. They knew the estate his grandparents had once had in the Highlands. They had been guests on a neighbouring estate before the war. Lady Clayton-Smythe knew of his father's reputation as a talented writer. Both Lord and Lady Clayton-Smythe were impressed when Richard told them of his father's distinguished record in the last war. They were extremely patriotic, and great admirers of the RAF. They also understood that nothing was normal during wartime, and that long courtships were out of the question. They believed, although Richard certainly did not, that he could be killed at any moment while defending his country. He basked in their warmth and admiration.

Recklessly he suggested a wedding while they were there so that Lord Clayton-Smythe could give his daughter away. It was a registry office affair with only Lord and Lady Clayton-Smythe present. But they had a good meal afterwards and it had all been very jolly. He had phoned his parents but neither his father nor his mother could get away at such short notice. But they spoke to Davina and her parents on the phone and sent their best wishes. His grandmother was too old to make the long journey from Scotland but when he phoned her with the news, she said she was immensely proud of him and it was so typical of him to make such a good match. They all looked forward to meeting his new wife, and her family, as soon as possible.

He was in seventh heaven. Davina was a super girl—well bred, courageous, generous hearted, beautiful and she loved him. How lucky he was. On their honeymoon night, he watched as she sat at the dressing table in her white satin nightdress brushing her short brown hair, and he experienced a wave of deep tenderness. She had full breasts, a flat stomach and rounded hips. Her face had a glow of health about it. So had her shining grey-green eyes. He imagined the beautiful, sturdy children they would have. His love and happiness encompassed everyone, including his parents and his sister, Wincey. His parents weren't so bad. Very decent, actually. He didn't quite know what to make of Wincey choosing to live for years in a slum in Springburn, instead of with her family. Still, she was his sister and he couldn't think badly of her.

After the war was over and done with, and the Germans sent packing, he must make a point of seeing more of his parents and his sister. He felt a pang of guilt when he thought of how much more of his time and attention he had devoted to his grandmother.

Davina smiled at him in the mirror and he went over and gathered her gratefully into his arms. Later in bed, he made love to her with a hungry passion that was almost a desperation. It was as if he was suddenly afraid it might be his last chance of loving her—the very last time.

The next day he saw her back to her billet and stayed with her until she changed out of her moss green wedding dress with its fashionable padded shoulders and into her Land Army Uniform. It consisted of a wide brimmed, khaki coloured felt hat, a green pullover over a shirt and tie, belted breeches with thick wool socks that reached to below her knees and sensible laced up shoes. Around her upper arm was a band showing the letters WLA. Even in this somewhat masculine and unflattering uniform, Davina looked lovely. He was so proud of her.

They kissed goodbye and he made his way back to his airfield. He had only been back for a few minutes when he heard the controller's voice: 'Large enemy bombing formation approaching . . . Take cover immediately.'

At first Richard didn't see anything. Then he saw them—about a dozen Heinkel bombers, their wings glinting in the sun. He heard the rising scream of the first bomb. Then his feet shot from under him and his mouth filled with dirt. He scrambled up and sped like a rocket for the shelter. He shot through the entrance before falling on his face again in its gloomy interior. One of his ground crew spoke to him. He could discern the man's mouth moving but the scream and crump of falling bombs made it impossible to hear him. The shelter filled with dust and shuddered with every explosion. Bedlam reigned outside for about four minutes, and then ceased.

The sudden silence was as much of a shock as the noise at first. For a long minute, neither Richard nor his companions moved. Then they all rushed outside to view the damage. The Germans were clearly attempting to destroy the RAF on the ground. The runways had been left in a real mess. Deep, smoking, craters were everywhere. A bomb had landed near Richard's own Spitfire and covered it with earth and rubble.

The first thing he did was have it cleaned up and checked over. All the other machines, he knew, would be landing at the reserve landing field. The station commander immediately ordered every man and woman onto the job of repairing the runways and in a few hours, they were back in service. Casualties had been relatively light—there had been four men killed in a lorry, another got a bullet through his foot and three pilots had suffered a few scratches. It had been a lucky escape because, apart from the bombing, the entire station had been repeatedly strafed.

Before long the pilots were back in the mess, relaxing, or playing poker, until the voice of the controller ordered them to scramble. They raced for their Spits. Soon they were getting instructions to intercept about twenty enemy fighters. They climbed until they reached twenty eight thousand feet. Then with a yell of 'Tally ho', Richard led his section in a shallow dive to intercept the approaching German planes.

They were about two thousand feet below him. The Germans had spotted them, however, and began to take evasive action. One after the other, the Spitfires peeled off in a power dive. Richard picked out one of the enemy aircraft and switched his gun button to 'Fire'. Immediately he got the leading enemy plane in his sights, he opened up in sharp, four-second bursts. Then he pulled up so hard, it felt as if his eyes were dropping down through his neck. The sky had become a mass of individual dogfights. Then, in an instant it seemed, the sky changed from a bedlam of machines to a silent emptiness with not a plane to be seen.

Back at the airfield, Richard discovered that a couple of his fellow pilots had not returned. All he could hope was that things wouldn't get any worse. As things stood, he reckoned they'd just about have enough pilots and aircraft to stop the German onslaught.

Morale was high, despite the loss of friends, and all the pilots shared a burning desire to live life to the full. For Richard, there was the unique excitement of combat flying, and the joy of seeing Davina at every possible moment. Even though he was often shattered by the lack of sleep, in the air he could still maintain the intense concentration every fighter pilot needed simply to stay alive. He still felt a wild, leaping of his heart when he saw the enemy. Switch on sights, range and wingspan indicators checked, gun button on 'Fire', then into action—his body stiff against the straps, his teeth clenched, thumb ready on the gun button, his eyes narrowed intent on getting the enemy in his sights, and holding him there. Then the kill, the moment of victory, and the savage, primitive exaltation.

He hadn't told Davina about how he felt when flying. Only another fighter pilot would understand. Nevertheless, he and Davina talked a lot together. They planned what they would do after the war, where they would live, how many children they would have, whether they would have sons or daughters. Two of each sex, they eventually decided, would be perfect. They even thought of suitable names. She told him of her happy childhood roaming around her father's estate.

She had been a difficult child, she said, but he refused to believe it. 'Darling, of course I was,' she laughed. 'I nearly drove my nanny to despair. Then after I was packed off to boarding school, I hated being cooped up and having so many rules and regulations to conform to, so I rebelled and failed everything. Eventually I was expelled and sent home in disgrace. At least that's what the school thought. I was overjoyed at living at home again. Oh, the glorious freedom of it.'

He could understand what she meant. Often now he felt that

glorious surge of freedom. But boarding school had never bothered him. There were all sorts of sports on the curriculum and he'd been good at that sort of thing. He'd also enjoyed the company of his fellow pupils and indeed, practically everything else at the school. He'd never felt he'd been denied any freedom.

'Maybe it's different with boys,' Davina said. 'With so many rough games like rugby. Hill climbing and rock climbing sounded super as well. We were mainly taught to be sedate and ladylike.' She made a face. 'What a bore it was.'

He had to laugh at her. They laughed a lot together. He thought of her a lot too. But never while flying. Especially when things began to hot up.

18

'Talk about lucky?' one of the sailors told them. Malcy and the others had been rescued a second time, hauled once more onto the heaving deck of a destroyer. But this time they were wounded. Malcy had copped it down one side—his face, his shoulder and his arm. Joe and Pete had taken some shrapnel in the legs. Now they were in Dover, all bandaged up and grateful to be alive. Women were handing out sandwiches and big mugs of steaming hot tea. They'd never tasted tea or sandwiches like it.

Afterwards, they were led onto a train, with no idea where they were going. All was confusion, around them a teeming mass of unshaven, oil-streaked, filthy, humanity. The news that greeted them was worse than they had expected. Hitler was winning the war. Most of western Europe had fallen to his storm-troopers. Churchill's marvellous rhetoric didn't change the fact that they were getting beaten.

Now Churchill was saying that the RAF was going to blow the Luftwaffe out of the sky and save Britain. Knights of the air, he'd called the pilots. Well, Malcy and his pals agreed, they hadn't seen much of them so far. Certainly not at Dunkirk.

Malcy, Joe and Pete found themselves delivered to a hospital. There they had various pieces of metal cut out of shoulders, face and legs. Malcy had trouble sleeping—he suspected it was much the same for Joe and Pete and the rest of the survivors, although none of them admitted it. When he did eventually fall asleep, Malcy had nightmares. He was always back in the life raft with Joe and Pete, with the fighters diving down on them and the bullets tearing across the water towards them. He remembered becoming sleepy then as he bled into the sea. In his mind, everything became mixed up. Planes shooting at ships, ships shooting at planes, the endless queues of men on the beaches, dead bodies floating, machine gun bullets spluttering and boiling the water. He couldn't clear his head of it all. He suspected that he'd never again enjoy a peaceful, dream-free sleep. Not like he used to— it seemed so long ago now. In another life. And what a fool he'd been in that life, how he'd wasted it.

Malcy, Pete and Joe were eventually transferred to the nearest barracks, en route to a short survival leave. It wasn't even long enough for them to make the journey home to Scotland and back. Nor did they feel fit enough. They wrote home, however, and told their families that they were all right. Malcy wrote to Erchie and Teresa Gourlay. In the local pub where they spent most of their few days of freedom, they found LDVs masterminding the defence of the country. They seemed to have a wonderful faith in the Navy. The Navy and Winston Churchill.

The three survivors weren't all that sure of either, but they kept their thoughts to themselves. During the day, they often lay on the grass outside the pub and watched the vapour trails criss-crossing the sky, as RAF fighters struggled to defend their airfields.

'Right enough,' Malcy said, 'if the Germans knock out the RAF, what's left to stop them landing here and taking over the whole place. I mean, I'm more than willing to make a stand. I'm sure we all are. But look at us. What good would we be against thousands of Hitler's bloody storm-troopers?'

'Aye, ye're right,' Joe agreed. 'The battle's up there, and no mistake.'

It made them feel even more depressed. They had fought the best they could and been defeated. What did these LDVs know about it? Damn all. They didn't enjoy their leave. They felt distanced from the local population. Oh, they were kind enough—plying them with drinks and talking as if Dunkirk had been some sort of wonderful victory. It was well seen they hadn't been there.

'Victory my arse,' Joe said, but only once they were out of the pub and walking together through the solid blackness of the night outside. There was no point in getting into arguments or fights with the locals. Some of them were often drunk enough to be blind to the state the soldiers were in, and start a fight. Joe for one was still unsteady on his feet and unable to venture far without the help of his crutches, but he had great spunk and determination.

'Fuck them.' He was meaning the crutches. 'I'm going to get rid of them any day now if it's the last thing I do.'

'That's the spirit, Joe,' Malcy laughed. 'You've got to be a hundred per cent by the time Jerries arrive. Britain's depending on you.'

'You can laugh if you like,' Pete said, 'but soon enough we'll all have to be fit and ready to have another go at them.'

'Aye,' a more serious Malcy agreed, 'and this time we'll have to make a better job of it.' Secretly Malcy thought it would be stretching their luck too far to believe that they'd survive another onslaught.

Then one night, as Joe and Pete were writing to their wives, he began to think of Wincey, and to remember her red hair, her pale, freckled face and unblinking stare. He felt curious about her more than anything. She'd always been a bit of an enigma. He had already written to Teresa and Erchie to let them know that he was all right. Now he wondered if he should write to Wincey. At least it was something to do. He never took part in any of the card games that went on because they played for money. Not that it amounted to much—just coppers mostly. Even so, he rigidly avoided anything that involved gambling.

So he settled down and began writing a letter to Wincey. He told her about Dunkirk, going into more graphic detail than he'd been able to do in his hasty note to Teresa and Erchie. He poured out his thoughts on the course of the war, and the bravado of the locals. Then he asked about life in Glasgow, and if the factory was still doing well. It was a long letter—so long that he wondered if he should send it at all. In the end it went off to the post with the other envelope that contained Joe and Pete's letters home.

Immediately afterwards, he felt strangely anxious and agitated. He put it down to the state of his health. Very few of the survivors had fully recovered from the trauma they had suffered. Malcy had come to believe that most of them never would. His own experiences continued to haunt him, although on the surface he appeared quite normal. Or at least he thought he did. He never cried out in his sleep like some, or gave in to the humiliation of weeping. Nor did Joe or Pete. But a few others he knew had been reduced to pitiful wrecks of humanity.

He wished he was back home in Glasgow. He talked about Glasgow a lot with Joe and Pete—the football matches they'd gone to and the teams they'd cheered on, their favourite pubs. Joe had been born and brought up in the East End and Pete had come from Springburn. Both Joe and Pete confessed that they'd rather have stayed in the East End and Springburn than move to their new homes in Clydebank. But at least the twins were happy, that was the main thing.

'So once I'm home in the dear green place,' Joe said, 'I'll never step out of it again. At least never out of Scotland. You can keep your foreign countries. You can stuff England as well.'

'Me too,' Pete fervently agreed.

'The dear green place,' Malcy echoed dreamily.

Pete shook his head. 'The English seem to think we all go about with razors up our sleeves and do nothing but fight each other. I was talking to one of the locals and when I mentioned I came from Glasgow and asked if he'd ever visited the place, he actually said, "Oh, I'd be too frightened to go up there." '

Joe laughed. 'Never mind, it's bad enough worrying about being invaded by Jerries, without having to think about hordes of Englishmen coming up north.'

'I mean . . . ' Pete was still feeling insulted, 'it's such a good place to live, and damn it, it's a friendly place as well. It's a damned sight friendlier than London.'

'Aye, well,' Joe said, 'they're no' so bad around here. They've treated us to a few good drinks, you have to admit.'

Pete shrugged then said, 'I still wish I was in Glasgow. I'd give anything to be enjoying a drink in the Boundary Bar right now.'

Malcy nodded in agreement and his mind wandered far away.

19

It was strange how Malcy, who had once come between Wincey and the rest of the Gourlays, now had the opposite effect. They had all liked and defended Big Malcy while she had despised him. She would have got rid of him from the factory if she had her way. But it was always Charlotte who had the last say, and he had been Charlotte's husband.

Now, however, Wincey was glad to share Malcy's letter with the family and Teresa and Erchie and Granny were glad and grateful.

After poring over the first long letter that Wincey received, Granny said, 'Och, it's just wicked what that poor fella had to suffer.'

Teresa sighed. 'I remember him in my prayers every night. I pray that one day soon he'll be back safe and sound.'

'He's no' out o' the woods yet, hen,' Erchie said.' Aw the soldiers down there'll have to pitch in an' fight the Germans if they start invadin'.'

'But,' Wincey looked worried, 'Churchill said the RAF would . . . '

'See him,' Granny interrupted, 'he's got the gift o' the gab, I'll gie him that, but aw this grand talk is no' goin' to be any comfort to aw the mothers that's lost their sons. An' aw the mothers that's gonnae lose theirs. An' he'll no' be any help to oor Malcy, will he? Just the opposite, if ye ask me. See him an' his finest hour—ah'd finest hour him if ah got ma hands on him.'

Teresa's voice came out sharper than she intended. 'I wish you'd just keep your opinions to yourself, Granny. You're always such a pessimist. We're all worried enough without you making us feel worse.'

It was true that they were all worried and depressed. Life in general had become more and more difficult. It was a struggle now even just to get a few lumps of coal for the fire. Teresa had to trundle a home-made barrow to the nearest coal yard and stand for ages in a queue—even though she wasn't really fit enough for such heavy and exhausting tasks. As she said herself, she was 'a wee bit chesty'. More often than not, a few coal briquettes made with dross was all she got after her long wait in the pouring rain. Now in August coal wasn't so urgently needed as it had been in the winter months, but Granny still felt the cold and with her arthritis, she had to be kept warm. Teresa couldn't even find the wool now to darn Granny's stockings.

Autumn would soon be here, and winter creeping in, and food getting scarcer. Teresa had always believed it was important to eat plenty of good nourishing food to generate heat inside you, and energy. Food—or rather the lack of it—was now a real worry. A lot of folk had to have their pets put down because they weren't able to feed them. Only warehouse cats were entitled to a dried milk ration. Queues, queues—there were queues everywhere for everything. It was beginning to get them all down, although everyone tried their best to keep their spirits up. Or at least to make an outward show of doing so.

There was the black market, of course, but on principle (and for fear of Granny taking a heart attack if she found out), they never had anything to do with it. Dealing on the black market was a criminal offence, although everyone knew people who were getting away with it.

It was difficult too to keep cheery when there was so much bad news around. Closest to home had been the loss of Doctor Houston. None of them had quite got over that tragedy yet. Then poor Mrs McGregor's man had been killed. And as if that wasn't bad enough, Jimmy, one of her sons—a mere lad not long out of school—had been killed in a bombing attack on an airfield. He hadn't been a pilot or anything glamorous like that. All he'd ever wanted was to be a mechanic. Mrs McGregor said he'd just been happily working on the ground when a whole lot of bombs had rained down on the airfield. That's what she'd been told.

'Poor wee Jimmy,' Teresa said. 'It's just terrible. What can I say to poor Mrs McGregor? Her heart's broken.'

'I'm glad Malcy survived Dunkirk,' Wincey said, and meant it. 'It's a miracle anyone did, when you think of it.'

'Aye,' Erchie said, 'poor fella. His face got it, he said in the letter, an' him such a nice lookin' fella. Always so cheery.'

'Yes,' Teresa agreed, 'and with such bright twinkling eyes. I never could get angry with him, even when I knew about his gambling.'

'He told me before he left,' Wincey said, 'and I believe him, that he'd never gamble again.'

'It was a weakness he had,' Teresa said, 'but he was never a bad man. Charlotte always said he was good to her.'

Erchie examined the letter again. 'Maybe he'll no' be scarred. He seems to go on more about his shoulder an' his arm, but he makes it all sound as if it's more of a nuisance than anythin' else.'

'Have you replied to his letter yet?' Teresa asked Wincey.

'Yes, I wrote quite a long letter back giving him the news about Glasgow, as well as the family. I tried my best to keep it as cheerful as possible.'

'Good for you, dear. You'll let us know when you get any more word from him?'

'Yes, of course.'

It had not been as difficult a letter to write as Wincey had thought it might be. Once she'd got started, there seemed to be no stopping her. She'd described all the places in Springburn he knew, and told him everything that was going on. She gave him all the news about the factory—how they'd to work with the lights on day and night because they'd had to paint all the windows black, how Erchie was one of the few men left in the place. The others had either been called up or volunteered. It wasn't so easy nowadays to get or keep women workers either. Quite a few of the girls he would remember had joined the WRENS or the ATS or the WAAFs. Nevertheless the factory was still managing to keep going. She told him how she'd shared his letter with the Gourlays and that they sent him their love and best wishes, and how Teresa was remembering him in her prayers. She hoped she managed to make him smile or laugh at the some of the things Granny had said or done and finished her letter by urging him to take good care of himself and to write again if he could.

For a few seconds she hesitated about how she should sign the letter. She couldn't quite bring herself to write 'Love', so eventually she settled 'Kind regards, Wincey.'

His next letter caused some dismay among the Gourlays and with Wincey. It spoke about the increasing number and ferocity of aerial dogfights. He was obviously too near an airfield for comfort.

'It's all right,' he assured them. 'The RAF is knocking out dozens of Messerschmitts every day. I've lost count of the ones I've seen going down in flames. I can't see the Germans being able to mount an invasion now.'

It was good news in a way, but they still worried about Malcy's safety.

'Tell him in your next letter to go on bein' careful an' to look after himself, hen,' Erchie urged. Wincey, they all knew, had been better educated than them and could write a better letter. As a result, they'd elected her to write on behalf of them all. She spent quite a few evenings now bent over the kitchen table, her auburn hair flopping forward, a writing pad in front of her, chewing at her pen and thinking of what to write. Erchie and Teresa and Granny kept chipping in with 'Tell him this', or 'Remember to tell him that', and she did. It was the personal bits from herself that always proved difficult. She had always found it difficult to speak about her feelings, in fact, she seldom spoke about herself. Oh, it was all right to go into great detail about how she was running the factory, how she now visited her mother and father every weekend. She had not been able to tell Malcy about the reunion with her mother and father, but Teresa and Erchie had in the first letter that had been written. Now she could describe what they were like, but not her feelings towards them. She'd mentioned Robert Houston's death but nothing about how devastated she'd been, what regrets she'd had. She tried to shut it all out of her mind now. Life had to go on. Malcy was a survivor, but she was a survivor too.

She worked hard. That helped. She was lucky in having the love and support of the Gourlays, and her mother and father. She was glad that her mother and father had met Robert and liked him. Although she was a bit worried about her parents at the moment. Her mother was working longer and longer shifts as a VAD. Her father had more and more to do with the Home Guard. What spare time he had he was using to try to catch up with his writing. Recently, when she'd been having tea with a client in Copeland & Lye's restaurant, she'd seen her mother sitting at another table with a man with silvery grey hair. They were chatting and laughing together, oblivious of anyone else. Wincey decided not to approach her.

She'd told herself later that it could have been a perfectly innocent meeting. The man could have been an ex-patient or someone connected with her work. It made her feel uneasy all the same. She didn't like the thought of any trouble between her mother and father, especially if it meant her father getting hurt. She wondered if she should mention seeing her in Copeland's. That would give her mother a chance to explain, to say who the man was. She kept wondering, and doing nothing about it, until she saw her mother with the same man again. This time she was getting into his car.

Wincey decided to speak up then. It turned out the man was a doctor from the Royal. Her mother had laughed and said, 'Don't worry. It wasn't a clandestine meeting. We just happened to bump into one another and we were talking shop.'

Maybe it was just her suspicious nature, Wincey tried to tell herself. All the same, she couldn't help thinking that her mother had acquired a guarded look and she'd spoken too cheerily. Instinct told Wincey that something was wrong.

20

Just for the first second or two, Richard was stunned at the sight of well over a hundred planes with black crosses on their wings. Then he became very still and cool. He banked his Spitfire hard around until he was behind a twin-engined Messerschmitt 110. With the throttle fully open, he closed in and opened fire. The 110 flopped onto its back and went hurtling down, trailing smoke. Richard pulled up just in the nick of time as another ME 110 latched onto him. Flinging his plane around the sky in a series of desperate evasive manoeuvres, Richard suddenly saw the silhouette of another 110 filling his gunsight. He fired a long, withering burst that raked the German fighter from end to end. Smoke poured out of one engine, then flames. As it fell away and plunged down, a parachute blossomed and drifted out of sight.

A moment later the sky was empty and so were his magazines. He turned back towards the airfield, landed on the grass and parked his Spitfire away from the hangars. This was just as well because within twenty minutes, the hangars were bombed. He only stayed long enough for his ground crew to refuel his aircraft, put in a new oxygen bottle and more ammunition before he took off again. As the day wore on, Richard lost count of how many dogfights he had been involved in, how many of the squadron had 'gone west', and how many times he himself had cheated death.

By the end of the day, the runways and a couple of hangars had been damaged again, but it was nothing compared to what had happened at other airfields. One had recently been hit by a hundred bombers. The station HQ, the sick bay and three of the four hangars had been destroyed. A lot of people had been killed and many fighters destroyed on the ground.

Whenever they weren't in the air, Richard and the rest of the squadron tried to snatch some sleep, still wearing their clothes, including their flying jackets. They had to be ready to scramble at any minute, and ready to do it again, and again, and again. Despite his exhaustion, once Richard was up in the air he was completely alert. The exaltation rushed back as he wheeled and dived and fired. There was terror too, but it was all part of the excitement. He loved it. Sometimes, lying half asleep in his bunk, Richard would wonder if there was something wrong with him. Maybe he had already been at it for too long. Death and killing excited him. Even when he was with Davina now, he was restless to be back in the mess with the other pilots with their silly jokes and edgy remarks, and the way his stomach jumped when the tannoy clicked.

The other young pilots, mostly from public schools like himself, were even more reckless than him. They got their excitement on the ground as well as in the air. Any time off was spent driving their Jags or Bentleys into London at breakneck speeds, bumping into obstacles, bouncing off and careering wildly onwards. Once in London, they had one hell of a time with women and booze before rampaging back to base again.

Any time off Richard had was spent with Davina. It was good to be with her, to hold her strong body and to make love to her. Afterwards, she would stroke his black hair and brows and trace her finger gently over his features. She'd say, 'How handsome you are, Richard.'

Jokingly he'd reply, 'I know,' and they'd both laugh.

He had less and less time off now, but he'd managed at least one letter to his mother and father, and one to his grandmother. He'd apologised for not writing more often, but said he was being kept rather busy at the moment. Understatement was becoming more and more the done thing. The last ten days of August had been very difficult. There just weren't enough fighters or pilots. Richard wondered whether they had enough left to last more than a few days. The Germans, on the other hand, seemed to have an unlimited supply of men and aircraft. Hundreds of bombers overwhelmed the Fleet Air Arm, damaged Coastal Command and the radar stations. Raid after huge raid swept over a wider and wider area. Fighters kept being diverted all over the place to meet the bombers and try to stop them. And as the battle intensified, men and machines were being lost at an unprecedented rate. It became so bad that even the WAAFs at the control centres started to be affected. They often had to listen to pilots crying out over the radio when they were hit. Men who, only hours before, had been chatting and joking with them, and who were now trapped in burning cockpits of doomed aircraft.

From September onwards, things began to change. London was now the bombers primary target. Richard had heard all about it from the American journalists who had been staying at one of the local pubs. Up till then, they had been fully occupied watching the spiralling vapour trails above the airfields, reporting on the dog fights, and predicting the outcome of the 'Battle of Britain'.

Now, the journalists returned to the pub only to collect their belongings and to have a last few drinks. The next big story was in London. All was in chaos, they'd told Richard. The bombers were wreaking havoc throughout the city, causing large numbers of civilian casualties. Later he'd learned that many of the dead in London had to be buried in mass graves. In one of the worst incidents, more than two hundred people died as the result of a direct hit on a school in Agate Street.

Richard prayed that the bombing wouldn't escalate and extend to Scotland. He began to worry about his parents, his grandmother and his sister. He tried to banish any idea of Scotland getting hit. He had more than enough on his plate at the moment.

Night after night, the bombers returned in force, each time widening their target area. On the ground, there was a shortage of anti-aircraft guns, and in the air the Blenheim and Beaufighter night-fighters were blundering around in the darkness with precious little success. Guns were hastily pulled out of the ports, factories and RAF bases they'd been protecting and rushed into London—but to little effect. From the top of hills miles outside the city, German planes could be seen each night dropping their marker flares, while tracers arced back up towards them, and searchlights lit up the sky in a last-ditch attempt to pick up the bombers.

And every night, the bombs fell and the fires raged.

As London burned, Richard thought with a sinking heart of Glasgow's East End and all the tenements along the River Clyde.

But there was nothing he could do about any of it. All he could do now was to get on with the job.

21

At first it had been perfectly innocent. She'd met him while working in the Royal. She was still frightened to drive her car in the dark and so he had begun giving her a lift. He lived in the south side of Glasgow but insisted he didn't mind going out of his way to drop her off in the West End. His name was Donald Hamilton and he was a doctor at the Royal Infirmary. He was older than her—quite fatherly she'd thought at first, with his silver-grey hair and moustache.

She'd met him in one of the corridors. She'd been leaning up against a wall, clutching at her white-aproned waist, grey-faced and feeling sick. He'd stopped to ask if she was all right. She'd blurted out, 'That poor man. There was surely no need to be so rough.' She'd realised almost immediately that she should have kept her mouth shut. She would not say another word.

Doctor Hamilton, however, was determined to find out exactly what she was talking about. Then, even though she knew that it would mean she'd suffer hell from the nursing sister involved when she found out, Virginia told him what had upset her. She'd been holding the kidney dish for Sister by the bedside of a man suffering from VD. It had been a shock in the first place when the sister pulled the bedclothes away to reveal the man's enormous, grotesquely swollen testicles. Then with one vicious movement, the sister jerked the sticking plaster from the testicles. The man had cried out in pain. Virginia almost fainted. She was relieved when the ordeal of renewing the dressing was over and she could escape into the corridor.

Doctor Hamilton said gently, 'She wasn't really being cruel. She did the right thing. It would have been much worse, and only prolonged the agony if she'd tried to remove the plaster slowly.'

After a moment, Virginia said, 'Oh, I see.' She felt a bit of a fool. 'I'm sorry. I think tiredness must be affecting my judgement, or something. I've been up since the crack of dawn. I'm not usually as feeble as this.'

'You're not feeble, you're caring. A caring nurse is a good nurse. When are you off duty?'

'Now, actually.'

'So am I. Let me take you somewhere nice for a cup of tea—far away from the smell of illness and death and disinfectant.'

She had changed out of her blue cotton uniform dress, white apron and starched cap into her outdoor uniform, and had met him outside the Royal Infirmary. They had gone to Copeland & Lye's and drank tea and ate delicious cakes while listening to Copeland's orchestra playing. It was very soothing and relaxing and just what she needed. They talked easily and happily together. He told her of his home in Clarkston where he'd lived for many years with his late wife, Mary. She'd gone down south to visit an elderly relative to try to persuade her to move to Glasgow. There was so much danger in the coastal towns and villages now. This had been tragically proved when Mary and the old lady had both been killed in an air raid. He and Mary had no children, nor had either of them any living relatives left. That elderly aunt of Mary's had been the last.

'You live alone then?' Virginia said.

'Yes, I'm glad of my work. If I didn't have that, I think it might be a very lonely life.'

She knew what loneliness was and she too was glad of having her work to go to. She confided in him about Wincey and he was intrigued.

'Talk about truth being stranger than fiction?'

'Yes, I don't think I've really come to terms with it yet. So many years of worry and fear and uncertainty. Eventually the terrible grieving. Then the shock of her letter.'

'But it must be wonderful to have her back.'

Virginia sighed. 'The only thing is, she isn't properly back with me. I mean, she's living most of the time with the Gourlays. I only see her briefly at weekends. Any time she refers to the Gourlays' place, she calls it home.'

His hand covered hers. 'Well, it was her home for so many years. It will have become a habit to call it home. It's perfectly understandable. I'm sure she doesn't mean it as slight on you.'

'I suppose not. That's what I keep trying to tell myself.'

He was so kind and sympathetic and she needed somebody to talk to. They went on talking in the car and it was agreed that whenever possible, he would give her a lift home. They'd also have tea in Copeland's again, he promised. Their hours on duty did not always coincide, and there were times when he could not meet her, or take her home. More and more however, she looked forward to and enjoyed the times when he could. He was such a nice man—kind and attentive to his patients, and to her. Only when they were alone, of course. Hospital protocol frowned on the most innocent of familiarity between doctors and nurses, even in wartime. A nurse spoke when necessary to the staff nurse. The staff nurse communicated with the ward sister. The sister could speak to the matron or the doctor. The matron was top of the nursing pile and greatly feared by one and all, even by some of the doctors.

So every time Virginia met Doctor Hamilton outside the hospital, she'd hop into his car and they'd speed away like two naughty children. The idea made them laugh. She hadn't laughed for ages. After all, there was very little to laugh about these days.

Even listening to the wireless only added to the general feeling of doom and gloom. The latest news was that night after night, London was being bombed. There weren't enough public air-raid shelters and people fought to get into underground stations. At first the gates had been locked against them but eventually the authorities and the government were forced to give in after a large crowd of angry East Enders burst into the Savoy hotel demanding shelter. Now thousands of people trooped down into the bowels of the earth to sleep on draughty platforms.

Those who emerged from the shelters, or did not go down in the first place, stood and cheered on the Hurricanes and Spitfires as they tore into the German bombers. The onlookers cheered themselves hoarse as bomber after bomber plunged to the ground. One Spitfire pilot who had run out of ammunition deliberately crashed his plane into a German Dornier. As the two aircraft were sent spiralling to the ground, both pilots bailed out. The German pilot landed in the middle of an area that had recently suffered many casualties in the bombing. As he did so, a crowd of civilians came running from their houses with pokers and kitchen knives to attack him, forming a screaming melee around the dying man.

The bombers still came back every night, and not only to London. Now they were bombing Liverpool, Swansea, Hull, Southport, Bristol, Birmingham and many other cities, including Glasgow, although so far the raids on Glasgow had caused little damage and only a few casualties.

A tenement in the Scotstoun district had been hit. A bomb had dropped on Killermont golf course. Another bomb fell in George Square in the centre of Glasgow, and one hit HMS Sussex, moored in Yorkhill Basin. Virginia had been more aware of the noise of the anti-aircraft guns than of the bombs at the time, and her life continued more or less as normal. Well, as normal as it could be in wartime.

She saw so little of Nicholas, and when she did see him, he was mostly in uniform, forever caught up with his Home Guard duties. Then there was the vegetable garden to attend to. He also took his turn fire watching. Nowadays, he hardly had any time even for his writing. Virginia herself was mostly in uniform and hardly ever in the house either, what with long working hours and queuing for food, and God knows what else. And now there was her relationship with Donald Hamilton. It had grown into a relationship. She hadn't meant it to happen. She didn't think he had either, but it had. He knew about Nicholas, and admired his writing. He'd remarked that he hadn't seen a new book of his in the shops for a while and she'd explained about all his other commitments.

'He still keeps his hand in, but he only manages a couple of hours in his writing room every now and then. There will be a new book coming out, but not for a few months yet. He had to get an extension of his deadline.'

Gradually it had come out that they had drifted apart.

'I'm not blaming Nicholas,' she said, not wanting to sound disloyal. 'It's my fault as much as his.'

'It's the war,' Donald said. 'It's affecting everyone's life in all sorts of ways.'

One evening, Donald phoned and invited her to dinner at his house in Clarkston. Nicholas was going to be out on Home Guard duty that evening. She said goodbye to him and he left dressed in his khaki uniform and tin helmet, and armed with his rifle. She hadn't been looking forward to spending the evening on her own so she gladly accepted Donald's dinner invitation.

'I'll take a taxi over,' she said.

'That would be best,' he agreed. 'I daren't leave the cooker. I'm not a very confident cook. You don't know what you're letting yourself in for.'

She wore a sheath dress in a soft blue material and little diamond earrings. Her hair was still an attractive golden brown, with very little grey. It was long and, for the evening, she wore it swept up. She began to feel flushed and as excited as a young girl as she set off for Clarkston. The taxi dropped her off at a villa on the main road. It was fronted by a rather unkempt looking garden. At the back of the house there was a much larger, secluded but equally wild and neglected garden lined with trees.

'I never get time to attend to the garden,' Donald explained, 'and it's impossible to find any gardeners nowadays.'

Virginia was surprised at how old-fashioned everything was inside. The walls were covered with dark brown embossed paper, up to a dado, with floral printed paper above. The patterned carpet looked faded and dusty. The furniture was heavy and of a Victorian or even earlier period. All of it was made of dark mahogany with a reddish tinge. There were button-backed chairs and an intricate floral arrangement displayed under a glass dome. The curtains were of brown chenille. A matching cover edged with long fringes was draped over the table in the dining room. Unfortunately, it reminded her of Mrs Cartwright's house.

'I'm sorry,' Donald said. 'I've been so long in the kitchen, I haven't had time to set the table through here.'

'Why don't we just eat in the kitchen,' Virginia suggested. 'It's so much homelier.'

'Well, if you're sure you don't mind.'

'Of course not.'

She followed him through to the kitchen which, to her relief, turned out to be brighter and more attractive than the rest of the house. It had cream walls and blue and cream linoleum tiles on the floor. She soon found out where dishes and cutlery and glasses were kept, and she set the table while he stirred a pot with great concentration. He had made liver savoury.

'Sorry it couldn't be fillet steak,' he said.

'Lucky you to find some liver,' Virginia told him. 'I haven't seen any in the shops for ages.'

537

'I've to thank my cleaning lady for queuing for it. The soup is made from vegetables out of her garden, but I did all the cooking myself.'

'It looks wonderful.'

He turned round for a second. 'And you look wonderful.'

After the meal they took their coffee through to the sitting room and settled next to each other on an uncomfortable horsehair sofa. By that time, she'd had quite a few glasses of wine. She blamed the wine for what happened afterwards but knew it was a weak excuse.

They had made love upstairs in the brass bedstead with its flounced valance. Across the foot of the bed was a chaise longue and the fireplace had polished copper scuttle and tongs, and a poker set on show within the fender.

Virginia felt as if she'd stepped back into another age. It was a peaceful feeling. In a way, her lovemaking with Donald was also peaceful. Certainly it wasn't a mad passionate encounter, as lovemaking with Nicholas had been at the beginning. Once she'd danced naked with Nicholas in the woods and they'd made passionate love on the soft mossy earth. Now Nicholas usually fell sound asleep as soon as he collapsed into bed each night. If she was on late shift, she did much the same thing once she arrived home.

This evening, with Donald, at least she was relaxed and happy.

22

'If Grandmother Cartwright knew what my mother's up to, all hell would be let loose.'

'You're not going to tell her, are you? Teresa's gentle face creased with worry.

'A doctor too!'

'How do you know that, dear?'

'Well, I told you I saw her with him a couple of times. Then on Saturday, I decided I'd meet her as she came off early shift, and take her out to lunch. I went into the Royal and there they were in reception, talking together. He was in his white coat, and with his stethoscope hanging round his neck. I recognised him right away.'

'But it needn't mean she's having an affair with him, Wincey. They could be just colleagues and friends. That's what she said when you spoke to her before, wasn't it?'

'Oh yes, that's what she said, all right.'

'Well then, dear.'

'But I saw how they were looking at each other, Teresa. They're having an affair, believe me.'

Teresa hesitated. 'It's really none of your business, Wincey. Although,' she added hastily, 'I know how you feel, dear.'

'It's my poor father I'm thinking about.' Wincey replied, 'He works very hard but Mother always seems so resentful, instead of having any sympathy or understanding.'

'That may be so, but all the same, you don't want to cause any trouble.' The words 'You've caused them enough trouble already' hung in the air, unsaid.

'Oh, I suppose you're right, Teresa, but I can't understand her doing this—after all they've been through, all that they've managed to overcome. Not to mention the opposition from the Cartwrights. And Father's so handsome and talented, isn't he? Whereas this man is just old. I can't understand it,' she repeated.

'But you won't say anything, will you, dear?'

'I suppose not. But Father's such a nice man. It makes me so angry. Guilty as well, because I have to watch Father innocently trusting Mother, never questioning her, while all the time I know what she's up to.'

'These things happen a lot nowadays. Everybody's life is upside down because of the war, and couples separated for ages, and all the temptations . . . '

'Mother and Father are not separated, but they will be—and for good—if she continues like this. I'd hate to see that happen. I want us to stay as a family now that we've found each other again.'

'I know, I know. Just try to be patient, dear. It'll probably all work out in the end. But it's for your mother to sort things out. Or your mother and father. Not you.'

'Oh, all right.'

Just then, Granny bawled from the front room. 'Are you two tryin' to send me to ma grave before ma time. It's like the bloody North Pole through here.'

'I'll get her,' Wincey said, and went through to fetch the old woman and her wheelchair.

'I thought you were enjoying yourself, Granny, watching the world go by.'

'Feel they hands.' Granny lifted a couple of gnarled, shaky hands. Wincey took them in hers, gently rubbed them, and Granny said, 'Aye, it's well seen ye've been heatin' yersel'. Yer hands are like hot water bottles.'

Laughing, Wincey began pushing the wheelchair through to the kitchen and manoeuvred it as near to the fire as possible.

'There you are. You'll be as warm as toast in a minute or two.'

'Ah'm starvin' as well. An' ah see the table's no' even set. What have you two been bletherin' about aw this time?'

'I've just made a pot of tea,' Teresa soothed. 'That'll keep you going until Erchie gets in. There's a nice Skirly-Mirly.'

'No' that again. Tatties an' turnip wi' nae meat. What good is that to a workin' man, or to anybody for that matter.'

'We've used up all our meat ration, Granny. I'm not a magician, you know.'

'Ah suppose ma sweety coupons are aw done as well.'

'Yes, but I'll get your peppermints with mine. I haven't such a sweet tooth as you.'

Erchie had breezed into the room. 'Ma hasnae any teeth at aw, have ye, auld yin. But ye're a great souker, eh?'

'Aye, well, ye'll be auld yersel' wan day.'

Erchie laughed and rubbed his hands. 'Is that tea on the go, hen?'

'Yes dear.' Teresa poured him a cup and passed it over to him.'

'Here's the paper, Ma.' He tugged a rolled up newspaper from his jacket pocket.

'Ye know ah cannae see right to read. Just tell me what's in it.'

Teresa groaned. 'Here we go again.'

'Ah dinnae make aw the bad news happen,' Granny protested. 'Ye cannae blame me for that.'

'I know, but I wish you didn't need to hear it every night. It puts me off my tea—all these poor folk getting bombed. It's getting worse instead of better.'

'Aye, that's war for ye. Oor Malcy coppin' it'll be the next bit o' bad news.'

Teresa rolled her eyes and Wincey said, 'Malcy has suffered enough. They'll surely not put him into any more fighting.'

'Would ye listen to her,' Granny howled sarcastically. 'She's one that did come up the Clyde in a banana boat.'

Erchie lit up a half-smoked Woodbine. He inhaled with rare appreciation. He had to ration his smokes to a half at a time, they were so scarce now. 'Are ye gonnae write to him again tonight, hen?'

'Well, I hadn't planned on it, Erchie. I wrote a few days ago, remember.'

'Och, but the poor laddie's got nobody else, an' he's far from home. Ah'm sure it cheers him up to get aw the news from auld Glasgow.'

Wincey shrugged. 'I don't mind.'

And so after their meal, they all settled round the table again, Wincey with the notepad and pen.

Erchie said, 'Tell him no' to worry about the bombs up here. We're aw fine. It was nothin' like as bad as London. Mind an' tell him that.'

'Uh-huh.' Wincey tucked her hair behind her ears and began to write, reading out loud every now and again.

'Dear Malcy,

you remember the kitchen? Well, it's still the same. The fire's crackling and sparkling in the grate. There's the brass candlesticks and the black tea caddy with the Japanese picture on it. Tea's rationed now, of course, so the caddy's never as full as it used to be. But there's still the same cream curtains over the hole in the wall bed, and the matching valance hiding Granny's hurly bed underneath it. And there's the same green linoleum on the floor, and the rug in front of the fire that Granny had made with lots of bits of coloured rags. At the moment we're all sitting round Teresa's scrubbed wooden table. Erchie is wearing his bunnet as usual, Teresa is in her floral, wrap-around pinny and checked slippers, and Granny is keeping cosy in her fawn crocheted shawl. We've tucked a tartan blanket around her knees because she got a bit chilled sitting through at the front room window. Erchie says not to worry about Glasgow being bombed. We've got the Home Guard very active here. There's even machine gun posts around the city. My father helps to man one. He does all sorts of things to help. He's making a great job of growing vegetables too and he often gives some to Teresa so that she can make her soup. He hasn't a very big garden so he even grows things on the earth covering the Anderson shelter. It's a great help getting the vegetables. Teresa says she'd never manage any soup without them. She sends you her love. Erchie says to tell you that Willie Henderson's joined the Navy and Benny McKay was turned down for the RAF and was terribly disappointed. His eyesight let him down so it's still the factory for him. He and Erchie are about the only men left there. Granny says she hopes you're behaving yourself. You'll have her to answer to when you come back if you're not. She still has her blether with old Mr McCluskey out in the close every day and she still gives his daughter cheek, which never fails to infuriate Miss McCluskey. Teresa says she'll give you a

*welcome home party when you come back, and she'll use up
everyone's rations in one go, but nobody will mind. We'll all
be so glad to see you come home safe and sound. We hope
your injuries have healed all right. We're all well except for
Granny's arthritis, which flares up worse every now and
again, but as Erchie says, she's a tough old bird and she'll
be belting out a song at your welcome home party, don't you
worry. Florence and the twins send their love as well. The
twins hope you'll always keep an eye out for Joe and Pete,
and see that they're OK. They were so glad that you
managed to keep together the way you did. They're looking
forward to their own welcome home party for Joe and Pete.
They're keeping their houses lovely for the boys coming
home. They're sure Joe and Pete will be prouder than ever of
their nice homes. They say they can't wait to hear what Joe
and Pete think of some of the improvements they've made
and the lovely velvet curtains they've hung in their front
rooms—blue velvet in Joe's house and gold in Pete's. The
twins say Joe and Pete'll just love these curtains when they
see them.'*

'I think that should do,' Wincey said to the others.

'Ye huvnae said much about yersel', hen.'

'Nothing much to tell, Erchie.'

Wincey signed the letter, folded it and put it into an envelope.

'At least it'll keep him in touch,' Teresa said. 'I'm sure Malcy will
be glad of that. It's very good of you, dear.'

'Ye could have said more about Springburn,' Granny complained.
'Ye never even mentioned the Sally Army band, an' ye never telt
him about Mrs McGregor's man, and wee Jimmy McGregor getting
killed.'

'For goodness sake, Granny, have a wee bit of sense,' Teresa
snapped.

'Ah cannae open ma mouth these days.' Granny chomped her gums
in agitation.

'Never mind, Granny,' Wincey said. 'I'll make you a cup of tea.'

'Thanks, hen. Ah miss ye when ye go away at weekends. Ye're the
only one that's nice to me these days.'

Teresa rolled her eyes and Erchie said, 'Ye're a right auld blether, Ma.'

Granny ignored him and asked Wincey, 'How's yer mammy and daddy gettin' on, hen?'

'Fine, thanks, Granny.' Turning away, Wincey thought sarcastically, 'Oh just fine.'

1941

23

'Is that another letter from Wincey?' Pete asked.

He passed it over for Pete to read. After a minute or two Pete groaned. 'Listen to this, Joe.' And he read out the bit about Euphemia and Bridget.

It was Joe's turn to groan. 'Fuckin' curtains. Can you beat it? What do I care about fuckin' curtains?'

Pete nodded in agreement. 'I don't know what to write to Bridget. I feel as if I haven't much in common with her any more.'

'I know what you mean,' Pete said gloomily.

Malcy replaced the letter in its envelope. 'Och, the girls don't mean any harm. They just don't know how things have changed for us. You'll be able to explain to them once you get back home.'

'The trouble is,' Joe said, 'I still love the silly wee midden.'

'How about you, Malcy?' Pete asked.

'What do you mean?'

'You and Wincey?'

Malcy looked astonished. 'Me and Wincey?' he echoed. 'That would be a turn up for the book. She always hated the sight of me.'

'Doesn't sound as if she hates you now. She's going to a lot more trouble keeping in touch with you than the twins are doing with us.'

'Well, I know, but . . . '

'But what?'

Malcy tried to laugh. 'You don't really think she might be interested? I mean, in *me*?'

'Are you daft, or something,' Joe said. 'Of course she's bloody interested. She's writing to you every other day, isn't she?'

'I know but . . . '

'Never mind your stupid buts, Malcy. Get in there man. She's one hell of a good catch.'

Such a thought had never occurred to Malcy before. Wincey of all people. He'd thought of her before right enough, and he remembered lots about her. He'd never imagined, however, anything like what he was trying to imagine now. He could accept that she had changed towards him. Even before he'd left Glasgow, she hadn't seemed too bitter. Hadn't seemed bitter at all, in fact. He reread all her letters and began to detect an increasing warmth in them. They certainly gave no indication of either bitterness or hatred.

Then he had an attack of anxiety and lack of self confidence. His face and scalp were scarred. He studied his reflection in the mirror. The doctor had assured him that it would heal in time and if he was lucky, it would only leave a faint mark. If he was lucky. Had he ever been that lucky? He tried to put Wincey out of his mind, but it wasn't easy because her letters kept on coming. In one of his letters he'd half jokingly referred to his scars and said that he now had a face that only a mother could love—and he hadn't even a mother. In her next letter, she said what did looks matter. It was the person that was inside that was important.

For the first time she signed her letter 'Love, Wincey'. Previously she'd signed 'Sincerely, Wincey' or 'Kind Regards, Wincey'. He read the ending of her last letter over and over again. 'Love, Wincey'. 'Love, Wincey'. 'Love, Wincey' until it turned into 'Wincey love, Wincey love, oh Wincey love'.

The next time he wrote to her, he spoke of his longing to get back to Glasgow. But there was so much he wanted to tell her that he couldn't put in a letter. He tried to give her some hints about recent events in the south and why leave had been cancelled, but he learned from a subsequent letter from her that almost everything he wrote had been censored. Malcy reckoned such strict censorship wasn't really necessary. He no longer believed there was going to be an invasion, and by the look of things, Hitler had changed his tactics and was now trying to bomb the civilian population into submission. Even Glasgow was beginning to get it, albeit not as badly as London and elsewhere in England.

Malcy was becoming heartily sick of the whole business. He'd just missed being sent abroad again to fight. His shoulder and arm had not improved enough and he still had to wear a sling. He'd also caught a dose of flu. Poor old Joe and Pete had not been so lucky and were gone. He couldn't help wondering if he'd ever see them again. He hadn't relished the job of telling Wincey about that. The boys had been packed off so suddenly that they hadn't had the chance to write to the twins before they left.

Wincey had written back saying it hadn't been much of a Christmas and New Year for any of them. Teresa had made an eggless Christmas cake with carrots, of all things. He couldn't imagine it. She said shops were hiring out cardboard cakes, especially for weddings. They were decorated with chalk icing sugar and a real, much smaller cake was underneath the cardboard cover.

The twins were very worried about Joe and Pete and hadn't felt very festive. Granny had talked wistfully and in some detail about the family she'd lost, and about her dead husband. It was something she'd never done before and it worried them all. Wincey's letters were vivid and she portrayed Springburn Road and the Avenue and Wellfield Street and the 'Wellie' cinema so clearly that it brought a lump to his throat. Many's the time he'd sat in that flea pit of a picture house. There was sometimes an amateur variety show in the interval, and he and some of his pals used to boo and throw orange peel at the performers. Then there were the public baths in Kay Street and the Balgrayhill, leading to Springburn Park. He'd often fished for minnows in the pond there and collected them in a glass jam jar filled with water.

Now there was the Gourlays' house near the top of the Balgray. If he walked up there now, no doubt he'd see Granny wrapped in her fawn crocheted shawl, hunched forward, glasses balanced on the edge of her nose, peering out of the front room window. Or her wheelchair would be parked in the close beside her old pal, Mr McCluskey. He would gladly give a year's pay and more to be able to walk up that hill and into that close right now.

Malcy tried not to get depressed but the physical pain he was in didn't help. Still, he was lucky to have survived. He kept telling himself that. He managed to get a bit of time off and took the train into London. The journey seemed to take forever, as the train crawled cautiously along. In London, the devastation was terrible to witness and among the bombed buildings, notices had been stuck up reminding people that looting was punishable by death.

St Paul's Cathedral had miraculously survived undamaged amidst a sea of fire. Everything around it was bombed. The fires had been so bad that they were very close to becoming fire storms—raging infernos so strong that people could be sucked into them. Malcy tightened his stomach against flutters of panic at the thought of that ever happening in Glasgow.

He was tempted to tell Wincey about what he had seen in his next letter, but didn't want to frighten her. Although he couldn't help thinking she was not a lady who would be easily frightened. Not with that steady stare. He began to realise just how much he admired her. Again he felt lucky. Without Wincey and the rest of the Gourlays, he would have had nothing, and no one, to go back to.

He'd thought he'd got used to that long ago. He was illegitimate, didn't know to this day who his father was, and when he'd been very young, his alcoholic mother had abandoned him. He'd been discovered stealing food from a grocer's shop and handed over to the police. They had taken him home only to find there was no one there. He'd been trying to survive on his own. From there he was taken to an orphanage. He ran away from there more times than he could remember. Eventually he'd got a job. He'd got digs. He was determined to make it, and dreamed of being wealthy. He was going to make something of his life, to show everyone who ever doubted him.

Now, showing them didn't matter any more. Everything had become very simple. He lived for the moment. Survival was the only thing that mattered. He needed to survive to get back to Glasgow. He needed to get back to Granny and Erchie and Teresa and Florence and the twins.

And Wincey.

24

The routine was now so familiar to Granny that she could have done it herself. She had come to enjoy it almost as much as the bewhiskered and bescarfed Mr McCluskey. First the old man got his pipe and his knife ready. He cleaned out the dead tobacco from the pipe and gave it a knock to loosen any remnants at the bottom. After that he took the plug of tobacco from the pouch and cut a slice off it. He rubbed the slice between his hands until it was all loose and small. Then he filled it very carefully into the pipe, making sure it was not too tight. After that he put the pipe in his mouth and gave it a suck to make sure air was coming through. Next he took a box of matches, sparked a match, applied it to the pipe and sucked contentedly. It made Granny feel contented too.

'Aye, ye like yer smoke, auld yin,' she said.

'Aye,' Mr McCluskey agreed.

After a while Granny said, 'See war, ah mind seein' at the pictures the Germans dive bombin' an' machine gunnin' folk in Spain. Do you?'

'Ah do. Ah mind the Daily Worker said it wis a rehearsal for the bigger war tae come.'

'Aye,' Granny said, 'an' the Daily Worker wis right, wisn't it?'

Aye,' agreed Mr McCluskey.

Granny said, 'See if that siren goes again the night, come into oor lobby, Mr McCluskey. There wis about a dozen o' us the last time. Them frae upstairs came as well. We shut aw the lobby doors, ye see, so that nae glass or any o' that shrapnel stuff could come flyin' in. Tell yer lassie she'd be welcome as well. It's no' good to be on yer own at a time like that.'

'Ah'll tell her, but whether she'll come in or no' is another story. An' ah widnae like tae leave her.'

'Ah'll get Teresa to speak to her.'

'She's a nice lassie, your Teresa.'

'Aye.' Granny would like to have said—but didn't, 'No' like your lassie. That bitch wouldn't even let you into our house to enjoy yer smoke.'

'Don't you dare go into anyone's house and fill it with your filthy smoke, and give me a showing up,' she'd warned.

Granny was well wrapped up with a muffler wound round her neck and hanging down the front of her shawl. Although it had been a lovely spring day, a March wind was blowing through the close. Earlier Florence said the river was all shiny and beautiful when she'd looked out her window in Clydebank. Now the wind tugged at the rug protecting Granny's legs and ankles.

Mr McCluskey, despite his bunnet and muffler, must be feeling the chill because he had no rug or shawl wrapped around him. His jacket and trousers had worn pretty thin too, Granny noticed. It worried her. She knew only too well how your blood got thin when you were old and you were easily chilled. Poor old Mr McCluskey could catch his death of cold. The selfish bitch of a daughter of his never even got him to the barber's often enough—certainly not recently. His white hair was straggling down from his bunnet and his moustache looked neglected as well. He wasn't in a wheelchair but he was a bit shaky on his feet and would need a helping hand or an arm to hang on to to get him down the road to the barber's.

'A bloody disgrace,' Granny had told Teresa. And Teresa had promised to ask the barber if he'd call up to see Mr McCluskey.

'Although,' Teresa added, 'dear knows what Miss McCluskey will say about me interfering, Granny.'

'Och, tell the barber to kid on that he just happened to be passin' the close. Warn him no' to let on that it was us that put him up to it.'

'Oh, all right. I'll try.'

She was a good lassie, right enough. She never thought twice about inviting everybody to shelter in their lobby if there was an air raid. There was a brick shelter in the back yard but it had no lights, no seats, no heating—nothing. It was a damp, dark horror of a place and nobody wanted to set foot in it. Especially Teresa, because dampness tended to go for her chest. Granny sat up all night in her wheelchair and tried to get a few minutes sleep when there was a raid on. Everyone else sat either on one of the chairs Teresa had brought from the kitchen, or they crouched on cushions on the floor. At first they had a bit of a blether—caught up with everyone's news. Then they had a singsong, more in an effort to drown the noise from outside than anything else. Eventually, fatigue overcame them and they just sat dozing, and listening to the racket, and trying not to feel afraid. Teresa always wanted to go through to the kitchen and make everyone a cup of tea but no one would let her in case a piece of shrapnel or a bullet got her. They'd heard of that happening to other folk. None of them were sure what was going on outside and causing the bedlam of noise.

In the morning when they emerged, there never seemed to be any bomb damage. At least not as far as they could see in Springburn. Erchie said it was the noise of anti-aircraft guns trying to shoot the bombers down. There were bombers right enough because the drone of them could be heard as loud and heavy as if they were only inches above the roof.

Next day, Granny would doze in her wheelchair by the fire, her head falling heavily down on her chest, her toothless mouth hanging open. Sometimes Teresa would say, 'You look awful uncomfortable like that, Granny. I'll bring out your hurly bed and you can have a proper sleep, even if it's just for a couple of hours.'

Granny hoped the siren wouldn't go again tonight. Mrs Faulds, a new neighbour in the top flat, was a terrible pessimist and last time she had maintained that tonight the sirens would go and it would be the worst raid ever.

'Oh,' Granny had said, 'has Hitler been in touch wi' ye then, hen?'

'It's the thirteenth,' Mrs Faulds said with a knowing look.

'Even if ye believe in that rubbish,' Granny said, 'it's supposed to be Friday the thirteenth that's unlucky. This is Thursday.'

'I've always believed that thirteen is an unlucky number.'

'Oh aye, an' what else do ye believe that could cheer us aw up?'

It was a mistake to have asked that, because Mrs Faulds launched into such a long list that Granny had eventually to interrupt.

'Aye, aye, we've got the message, hen. Now just gie yer tongue a rest.'

The siren did go however. Its eerie wail made all of their hearts sink in despair. It meant another apprehensive, sleepless night trying to be cheerful, trying to hide the fact that everyone felt worried.

To the surprise of all the Gourlays, old Mr McCluskey and Miss McCluskey returned with Teresa. Teresa had gone next door after the raid started to repeat her previous invitation to join the rest of the neighbours in the Gourlay lobby.

'It does sound rather worse tonight,' said Miss McCluskey, keeping her head held high and her back stiff. Teresa offered two chairs for the McCluskeys to sit on. This meant Teresa had to make do with the floor.

'I told you,' Mrs Faulds cried out triumphantly. 'Didn't I tell you?'

'Aye, aw right,' Granny said, 'ye don't need to tell us again.'

It certainly did sound much worse.

'What a shame,' Teresa said, wrapping her woolly cardigan closer around her thin chest. 'After us having such a lovely time visiting the twins.'

It had been the turn of Euphemia to entertain her mother and sisters to a late afternoon tea. The twins and Florence had managed to get away early from work. This time Granny had gone with the twins because Erchie was busy in the factory and couldn't take any time off to look after her. Wincey had been working too. A factory was regarded as essential work, not like a department store, but Granny had been warned not to say this to the girls. Wincey had treated them to a taxi that took them all the way to Clydebank. It was even booked to call for them later to return them to Springburn. Teresa had been horrified at such expense and Granny had said, 'Folk'll be thinkin we're aw turned into bloody Tories an' capitalists noo!'

Nevertheless she allowed herself to be helped into the taxi and her wheelchair folded up to travel along with her. The journey was actually a real treat for Granny, although she'd never admit it.

Euphemia had a lovely spread waiting for them in her kitchen and Granny was duly impressed. She also greatly pleased the happy, sparkling eyed Euphemia by admiring the cream and brown kitchen with its splendid new gas cooker.

Bridget said, 'Mine is lovely as well, Granny. We could take you along after tea to see it. Both our toilets are out in the close, but there's a big cupboard in the hall and I'm saving up to get my cupboard turned into a toilet. Amn't I, Euphemia?'

Euphemia nodded enthusiastically, making her fat cheeks quiver and her curls bounce. An inside toilet converted from a cupboard was very impressive indeed.

'Fancy!' Granny said, not really believing it was possible but not wanting to burst her grand-daughter's bubble of happiness.

'I'm going to have it done too,' Euphemia informed them, her face even ruddier than usual with excitement.

'Are ye, hen? Good for you.'

Bridget said, 'We can't wait to hear what Joe and Pete will say when they see what we've done to make our houses so nice. They'll be over the moon, don't you think.'

'Oh aye,' Granny said, struggling to keep the sarcasm from her voice. 'They will that, hen.'

It had been a good outing all the same, Granny had to admit. The sandwiches, scones and cakes had been delicious. Indeed, they'd enjoyed the meal so much that they weren't able to eat their evening meal with Erchie and Wincey when they returned home. Teresa had written down Euphemia's recipe for carrot cake and eggless sponge and was planning to make them the next morning. Now she wondered if she'd have enough energy. Poor Erchie and Wincey were worse off though. At least she and Granny could have a rest the next day, but Erchie and Wincey had their work to go to.

'Maybe it won't last so long tonight,' she said to the crowd now crushed into the lobby, shoulder squeezed against shoulder and hip against hip.

'I told you.' Mrs Faulds sorrowfully shook her head. 'It'll be worse—much worse. It's a bright moonlight night. They'll see their way here no bother.'

Erchie said he was going to have a quick look outside and despite both Granny and Teresa's efforts in trying to dissuade him, he slipped out to the close. He seemed a long time in returning and Teresa was getting quite breathless with agitation. She had struggled to her feet and was about to leave the safety of the lobby as well. As she said, 'Erchie might be lying outside in the street injured and helpless.'

But just then he suddenly appeared again. His thin, beaky face had turned a sickly grey and his eyes, staring from under the peak of his bunnet, were wide and anxious.

'Whit's up, son?' Granny asked before Teresa could say anything.

'There's awfae big fires. The sky's red wi' them.'

'In Springburn?' Teresa cried out in alarm.

Erchie hesitated. He shook his head. 'One o' the wardens told me it's Clydebank.'

'Oh Erchie, the girls!'

25

Florence washed up and dried Euphemia's tea dishes and tidied them away in the kitchen press. Bridget carefully wiped around the sink and draining board. Euphemia brushed under the table. Granny was such a messy eater. Finally, Bridget packed away what food there was left into tins.

As soon as the kitchen was spick and span once more, Florence asked, 'What's on at the pictures?'

Euphemia picked up the paper and read out loud, 'Shirley Temple and Jack Oakey in *Young People* at the La Scala and the Regal. Gene Hersholt starring as the "pocket Ginger Rogers" at the Pavilion. *Maryland* is at the Bank cinema and *Daughter of the Tong* at the Palace. Anything there you fancy?'

Bridget made a face. 'I don't fancy *Daughter of the Tong*.'

'*Young People*, I think,' Euphemia said. She took a mirror out of her handbag and tweaked at the bunch of curls on her forehead. 'Shirley Temple has lovely curly hair. I wonder if it's natural.'

Florence said, 'Do we really want to go?'

'It's all right for you,' Euphemia said. 'You've got Eddie to go home to. We're on our own. It's boring as well as lonely.'

'Well, there's nothing to stop you and Bridget going. I'd like to come but it's not fair on Eddie. We hardly see each other as it is, with us both working and him having to do such long hours. These days, the union has to go along with these awful hours, Eddie says. They need all the guns they can get, you see. Fancy Eddie making Sten guns. Him that used to make sewing machine cabinets!'

'Doesn't he usually work a few extra hours on a Thursday night?'

Bridget asked.

'Dash, I forgot it was Thursday. I tell you what, I'll go home and see to his dinner. He nips across for something to eat to keep him going. After that, I'll go to the second house with you.'

'Fine, see you later then.'

Florence took out her compact, powdered her nose, smoothed a hand over her hair and then pulled on her new navy velour hat. Outside it had got a bit colder and she turned up the collar of her coat and quickened her step towards the Holy City. She always experienced a little thrill of pride and pleasure when she thought of the name—Holy City. Every time she saw the flat roofs too. Her colleagues had expressed surprise and curiosity when they came to visit her and saw the flat roofs and heard the name. She enjoyed explaining to them how the flat roofs were like those in Jerusalem. It was so unusual, so different. Not at all like your common or garden Glasgow tenements. Some people tried to tell her that apart from the flat roofs, the area was nothing like the real Holy City but she never paid any attention to them. They were just jealous.

She made a nice quick meal for Eddie because he hadn't much time. Then she cleared the table and washed up and swept the floor. She always swept the floor after every meal, although there was no need. Neither she nor Eddie were messy eaters, not like Granny.

Eddie said, 'Poor old Granny. You can't blame her, with her arthritis. She can't get a right grip of anything.' Eddie was such a thoughtful and understanding man, even about the house. He always wiped his feet on the doormat before coming in.

'I'm not angry with her or anything like that, dear,' Florence assured him. 'I'm terribly fond of Granny. I always have been, you know that.'

She told Eddie she was going to the pictures with the twins, in case he got back before her. After kissing him goodbye, she went to the window to give him a wave. She always did that, and he always turned and smiled. She sang under her breath as she went to meet her sisters, and then the three of them set off, arm in arm and giggling. It wasn't like Florence to be so unladylike but she felt quite reckless with happiness.

The picture house was packed and they settled down to enjoy the movie. After a while they heard the wail of the siren and the usual notice went up on the screen. 'There is an air raid in progress. Anyone wishing to leave the cinema should do so now.' No one moved. They were getting accustomed to the siren going and nothing happening. The picture continued but soon they began to hear alarming noises from outside. The noises became thunderous, then the screen went blank. A ripple of panic went through the audience. People got up and made for the exit.

Outside, white faced and trembling usherettes told everyone that bombs were dropping all over Clydebank and they would be taking their lives in their hands if they went outside. Some people retreated back into the hall to huddle under the balcony for safety.

Florence said, 'I've got to get home to Eddie.'

But neither she nor the twins moved when they saw and heard bombs screaming down. For a minute or two they were immobilised with shock and disbelief. It was such a terrifying and incredible scene. All around the sky was lit up by incendiaries, and raging fires quickly took hold, turning the blackness of the night into bright orange and scarlet.

'Oh my God,' Florence whispered. 'That must be Singer's timber yard. All that wood! I've got to go and make sure Eddie's safe at home.'

They all began to run, oblivious now of each other, just desperate to get back to what they believed was the safety of their homes. It was like running through a nightmare. After a few horrific minutes, Florence hardly knew where she was going any more. Every street was impassable at some point or another. It was difficult even to cross a road because tram lines had been torn up, and reared to the sky— distorted, grotesque iron sculptures.

On the ground rubble lay in heaps around deep bomb craters. Houses had been sliced in two and revealed—like open doll's houses— shelves with ornaments and books undisturbed, clocks and candlesticks on mantelpieces, and pictures hanging on walls. Other tenements had sunk into chaotic piles of concrete and rubble, from which muffled screams and faint cries for help could sometimes be heard. From the top flat of one blazing building came the eerie sounds of a piano. Florence thought it was somebody playing who had gone completely mad. Until a policeman said that it was the intense heat bursting the piano strings.

The policeman tried to stop Florence. He had a soot blackened face and his uniform jacket and trousers were grey with dust. A dense cloud of dust was billowing about the whole street.

'You can't go any further,' he said. 'There's unexploded bombs down there.'

'My husband,' Florence insisted. 'I have to get back to my husband.' And before the policeman had a chance to say or do anything else, she had sped away. She passed rescue workers struggling to extricate the living and the dead. There was the incessant drone of low flying aircraft, and she even saw one plane actually below the level of the flames machine gunning a number nine bus. She was forced to slow down because the ground beneath her feet was covered in a sea broken glass. There was an explosion some way in front of her and before her horrified eyes, she saw—by the light of the flames—dismembered bodies flying through the air. She had to stop to vomit.

Somehow, eventually, she found her way to Second Avenue in the Holy City. There she stopped, shock immobilising her for a few minutes. The buildings had been turned into gaunt, smoking skeletons. Windows were now black gaping holes. A few tattered curtains flapped from the holes. The flat concrete roofs had collapsed down through the houses. Only the tall rows of chimneys had mysteriously survived.

Florence began to stumble towards what had been her home. 'Eddie! Eddie!'

Wardens and rescue squad men caught her and held her back. One of them said, 'If he's in there, hen, we'll get him out. Don't worry. Just try and keep calm and stay out of our way.'

A tired looking nurse in a filthy and blood stained apron took hold of Florence's arm.

'I have to find Eddie,' Florence told her dazedly.

'They'll do their best. Just leave them be.'

'I want to help find him.'

'You're in no fit state,' the nurse said wearily. 'You're the one that's needing help.'

It was only then that Florence realised there was blood running down her face and staining her coat. She felt a sudden stabbing pain in her skull. She put a hand to her head.

'I've lost my new hat,' she wailed and began to weep broken-heartedly.

★   ★   ★

Euphemia and Bridget's plumpness prevented them from running for very long. They became so out of breath that they had to stop. They stood scarlet-faced, gasping and choking.

'Euphemia,' Bridget shouted, suddenly too terrified to be without her.

'Over here,' Euphemia called and, sobbing with relief, Bridget picked her way across the road, skirting pockets of fire and twisted metal. Nearby, a tram car stood with its top deck half ripped off. Euphemia was crying too and the sisters clung together in distress. They didn't know whether to try to go on or stay where they were. The options were equally terrifying. Everywhere there were crowds of ARP men, policemen, rescue squads—all scrabbling about in the ruins of buildings, desperately searching for survivors. Some survivors were rescuing what they could of their belongings. Euphemia saw one woman handing out a tea trolley and chairs from a window to a man standing outside. Another man had a pillow and rose pink, gold and green satin quilts tied on his back. In the darkness he looked like the hunchback of Notre Dame.

Firemen were working in terrible conditions. The fire engines couldn't get near enough because of craters and debris, and fire hoses were damaged by being hauled over sharp glass and stones.

It had been discovered that there was no uniformity in hoses and hydrant couplings, and many of the fire brigades who had been brought in from outside Glasgow could not use their own hoses. Or they were unable to fix them to the fire hydrants. However, the Forth and Clyde canal was close to Singer's timber yard and to the sites of some of the other fires, so it was used a water supply instead.

The twins asked one of the firemen if there was a shelter nearby and the harassed and exhausted man said there was, but it had taken a direct hit and everybody inside had been killed.

'I want to go home, Euphemia,' Bridget wept.

'All right. Come on, we'll try.'

Hand in hand, they gingerly stepped forward. The ground shook under their feet as another bomb exploded. It quickened their pace until they were running, then gasping and choking, and having to stop again.

'We're nearly there,' Euphemia breathlessly tried to comfort a distraught Bridget. 'We're going to be all right. Don't worry.'

Starting and stopping, starting and stopping again, somehow they eventually reached home. They ran into the close, fumbled the key into the lock and got into safety. They wept with thankfulness.

'Thank God.' Bridget sank into a chair in the kitchen. 'What a ghastly nightmare. Just ghastly.'

'I know, but never in my worst nightmares . . . ' Words failed Euphemia. Eventually she managed, 'I'll make a cup of tea. I've never needed a cup more.'

'Me too,' Bridget said. 'I wish we'd never gone out in the first place. All these poor people. Did you see some of the ones they were bringing out? I'm sure most of them were dead.' She shuddered. 'And it's still going on out there— listen to it. Oh Euphemia, I'm frightened.'

'First thing tomorrow,' Euphemia said, 'we'll go to Mammy's. There's all this bombing here because of the shipyards and Singer's. We'll be safe at Mammy's, don't you worry.'

'I wish we could go now.'

'So do I, but I think we'll be safer to stay here for a wee while.'

Then, before they could even drink a comforting cup of tea, they discovered they were not safe at all.

1942-43

26

It had been a close-run thing, but the RAF had managed to stop the German campaign of bombing British cities. Now Germany had turned on the Soviet Union. They had invaded Russia along a one thousand eight hundred mile front. Italy and Romania had also declared war on the Soviet Union. With the entry of the Russians into the war, Britain had gained a powerful ally, and housewives now handed over their pots and pans to help build tanks for the Red Army. While the Russians stood firm against the might of Hitler's Panzers, the British navy escorted arctic convoys carrying vital supplies to Russia. Defying both the U-Boat wolf packs and the perils of the arctic ocean, the Merchant Navy performed feats of heroism that ensured Hitler would never win the war on the Eastern Front.

At long last, Richard began to get some leave. On his first leave since God knows when, he set off with Davina to visit his family. He made a point of going to his mother and father's first and they stayed at Kirklee Terrace for the first few days. For the next few days, they went to his grandmother's villa in Great Western Road. He was shocked to find that the villa had been damaged during one of the recent bombing raids on Glasgow. The top storey had been sliced off and workmen were repairing and reroofing the place. The rooms downstairs had been made habitable but the building now looked very odd and out of proportion. He was glad, although not surprised, that the old lady seemed untroubled by the whole thing. She had always been a strong character.

Apparently his father had wanted her to go and stay at Kirklee Terrace but she had refused. She wasn't at all pleased when Richard went to Kirklee Terrace to stay there for part of his leave, but for some time now he had been feeling guilty that in the past he had spent far too much time with his grandmother, and not nearly enough time with his parents.

It had been a pleasant and happy time as Davina got on so well with his parents and they obviously liked her. On the other hand, it was pretty awful to learn how badly Glasgow and Clydebank had suffered during the bombing raids. Wincey said that two of the Gourlay girls had been killed. Their homes in Dumbarton Road had suffered a direct hit. Another had survived but had lost her home and her husband.

He could see that Wincey had been deeply affected by the loss of the twins. She obviously thought of them as her sisters. But that was war. He had lost more than a few fellow pilots and friends. He had nearly had it himself when, after running out of ammunition, he had tried to ram a German bomber. It had been a mad thing to do but he would never forget that wild, reckless moment. It was the thrill of a lifetime.

A few months after that leave, he'd managed to get another break during which he'd gone with Davina to visit her parents. He was delighted and very impressed when he caught his first glimpse of her parents' house. It was called Castle Hill and he could see why. It wasn't so much a house as a castle—with towers and turrets, set high above a many tiered garden lined with birch and silver birch. There was a dignified silence about both the house and the garden. The green hills beyond were turning purple in the dying light, giving the whole area a ghostly glow. The interior of the house was equally impressive, as he said to Davina, 'Crikey, you could get lost in here. So many corridors, stairways and rooms.'

'Oh, half the place is now taken over by the military. They're using it as a hospital. If you look out of the back windows, you'll see some of the men who are convalescing, sitting on the garden seats or walking about the grounds.' She laughed. 'You could easily get lost in the part we still have though. Or in the grounds, for that matter.'

Richard found the visit fascinating. It was like stepping back into a far distant past. Despite the fire crackling and sparking in the enormous stone fireplace in the hall, the place had a gloomy chill about it. Richard wasn't surprised that the heat didn't reach every corner when he saw the size of the hall and the wide dark stairway that led to innumerable corridors and other smaller stairways.

Davina enjoyed showing him around. 'The hospital part is completely cut off,' she explained, 'so feel free to just wander about.' He had no intentions of wandering about after the tour that Davina gave him. She obviously loved the house despite the shadowy gloom and the icy cold. It was beginning to send shivers creeping up his back. She'd been used to it all her life, he supposed, and she no longer noticed. But then she was used to working outside in all sorts of weather. He was proud of her and loved her, from her cheerful tanned face down to her sensible laced up shoes. Running around like a child again, she pulled him by the hand up many turreted stairs into tiny secret rooms where she'd hidden from her nanny if she'd been naughty. There she could peek out at what was going on in the garden below and on the private winding road beyond. Sometimes she'd watched the gardeners at work, or watched her mother sunning herself and enjoying tea brought out by one of the maids. Sometimes no one would be there and she would just sit with her chin resting on the window sill and admire the beautiful scenery.

'It is a wonderful place, isn't it, Richard? You love it too, don't you, darling?'

He assured her he did. It was certainly true to say that he was fascinated and impressed. What he refrained from saying was that he didn't much care for the dead animals' heads cluttering the walls in the hall. Nor did he greatly admire all the solemn paintings of ancestors in their heavy gilt frames crowding together and glowering down onto all the rooms in what he felt was a horribly intimidating and depressing manner. There was even one whole room devoted to stuffed animals, mostly birds, all covered in glass domes. He knew what he'd do if he ever got the run of the place—as no doubt he would one day. Davina was an only child and would eventually inherit everything. He would get rid of all the stuffed birds.

They had dinner by candlelight in the huge dining room at a long, heavily carved table. Three candelabra cast flickering light over the table. Another two sat on the sideboard. Even with all those candles, the room still seemed gloomy and oppressive. The meal was served very slowly by an ancient butler, who shuffled about as if he was half asleep.

The food turned out to be excellent. They either had a wizard of a cook, or somebody was taking advantage of the black market. The meals at his parents' house had been much more frugal. His mother had apologised for them, and spoken at length about rationing and how she was working such long hours, she hadn't time to stand in many queues. He assured her it was fine and so it was really, although he and Davina had fared better at his grandmother's. His grandmother had been saving up her sugar and tea ration and standing in queues all over the place so that she could do her best for him and Davina.

'Fancy the old girl standing in queues at her age,' he'd said to Davina. He'd felt guilty about it, but touched as well. He was fond of his grandmother; she'd always been good to him, although when he'd been younger and more selfish, he hadn't really appreciated how good she'd been.

That Glasgow visit had been a great success, and now the visit to Castle Hill was proving to be equally successful.

'Mother says you're extremely handsome, darling,' Davina told him. 'Tall, dark and handsome, that's you. I'm so glad they like you. And of course they're so full of admiration for how you won the Battle of Britain.'

Richard laughed at this. 'Me and quite a few others, Davina.'

After dinner, over port and cigars, he and Lord Clayton Smythe discussed the state of the war. The Pearl Harbour attack had brought America in. It meant that both Britain and America had now declared war on Japan. Japan had invaded Siam, Malaya and Singapore. Germany and Italy had declared war on America. Then the Americans declared war on them. Now Japan had attacked Burma. Total war had engulfed the world and there seemed no end in sight.

Lady Clayton Smythe, in conversation with her daughter, bemoaned the acute shortage of staff and the rationing of clothes. 'Silk stockings, as you know, are a thing of the past,' Lady Clayton Smythe told Davina. 'But what I feel the greatest blow to so many women— including myself—is the rationing of corsets and bras. They are essential to every woman, but especially as one gets older.' She sighed. 'Gravity sets in, my dear. One needs a little support.'

Davina wholeheartedly agreed. Her figure was far from sylph-like and she worried about not being able to replace the underclothes she had. She wouldn't have cared so much had it not been so important to remain attractive to Richard. A handsome RAF pilot could get any woman he wanted.

'Don't you know any place we could get any foundation garments,' she asked her mother hopefully.

Lady Clayton Smythe looked sadly apologetic. 'Darling, if I did, I'd be only too glad to tell you. But in any case, we probably don't have enough coupons. Oh, isn't this war such a nuisance at times!'

Richard said, 'What are you ladies looking so serious about?'

'Nothing, darling.' Davina managed a smile. 'Isn't it time for the news?'

Her father leaned over and switched on the wireless. 'Although,' he said, 'that's not likely to cheer us up.'

'Oh, come now, sir,' Richard said. 'The Allies are doing very well, surely. All right, we lost Tobruk and Dieppe was an absolute shambles—I lost one or two very good friends there, and I had a few close calls myself. But we certainly gave the Jerries a hell of a beating at El Alamein.'

His father in law chuckled. 'Yes, good old Monty. I'll never forget what he said about Lord Mountbatten—a very gallant sailor, had three ships sunk under him . . . ' Then he paused. '*Three* ships! Doesn't know how to fight a battle.' Lord Clayton Smythe gave a hearty laugh. 'Obviously Montgomery does.'

'Yes indeed.'

Davina and her mother both smiled, but their thoughts were still on corsets and bras, and the difficulties caused by the lack of them.

But later that night when Davina and Richard were lying together in the four poster bed, Davina said, 'I hope you won't be involved in any more battles, darling. You've done more than your bit.'

'None of us are out of danger yet. There's still a lot to be done, Davina.'

His wife sighed and rolled over to entwine her arms around him. 'I wish I could keep you here for ever. This is where you belong— here with me in Castle Hill.'

He kissed her and held her close in a loving embrace, but he was thinking of friends who at this very moment would be soaring up into the clouds, far above the world, in a wonderful, lonely euphoria. That's where he belonged—with the lords of the sky.

27

'She was a fine woman,' Donald Hamilton said. 'Since the war started, she began doing a great deal of charity work—too much, I used to tell her. She was in the WVS, you know.' His gaze dimmed, remembering. 'She looked very smart in her uniform. I was so proud of her.'

Virginia tried to look interested and sympathetic, but she felt cut off and isolated. Donald's heart and mind were obviously still with his late wife. He frequently talked about her. Her name was Mary and they'd known each other since childhood. Virginia had heard so much about Mary that she felt she knew her. Mary had been very house-proud and had spent a great deal of time before the war lovingly polishing the furniture and all the valuable ornaments. She'd had a cleaning woman who came in two or three times a week, but Mary would never allow the woman to touch either the furniture or the ornaments.

Virginia secretly thought that nearly everything in the house was old fashioned and ugly. She visited Donald regularly now and the place had begun to depress her. Donald's talk of his dead wife was beginning to have much the same effect. He hadn't been like this at the beginning of their relationship. He had been very thoughtful, and loving, and gentle. He still was loving and gentle, and she appreciated that. At the same time, however, she hungered for the passion she had revelled in so often with Nicholas in the part. Thoughtfulness and gentleness were all right in a friend, but not enough in a lover. At least not for her.

She was also beginning to feel that he was becoming thoughtless in imposing so many memories of Mary on her. In a way, she could understand how it had happened. He now felt comfortable with her, and he trusted her. It was no doubt a relief to open his heart and to talk about his life with Mary and the happiness they had shared. Mary had been his friend, his dear and sympathetic lifelong companion.

His grief at his loss was now being released. Virginia could see all this and she tried to be a silent and patient listener, but she was feeling sad and isolated. She began to wonder if it was her fate to feel like this. Was it something in herself? Did she create situations in which she always ended up with this sense of isolation? Yet still the hunger was there, burning forever inside her.

It occurred to her that the isolation is what Wincey might have felt when she was a child and living at Kirklee Terrace. The crowded Gourlay house and the close knit Gourlay family and their total acceptance of her must have been a welcome—indeed wonderful—change for the child.

Virginia suddenly felt truly grateful to the Gourlays. The seeds of jealousy that had begun to take root were firmly dug out and destroyed. Now, she asked herself, was she beginning to feel jealous of the dead Mary? She didn't think so. She felt sorry for Donald. It was terrible to have lost such a loving companion, and such a wonderful relationship. She felt sorry for the poor woman, having her life suddenly cut off in such dreadful circumstances. But things like that happened all too often nowadays. And as the war dragged on, each new tragedy somehow seemed less shocking than the last, just part of the routine of everyday life.

The war was to blame for breaking apart so many things, and so many people's lives. She had such a longing for peace—perhaps that was part of the attraction Donald had for her at the beginning. She had felt some sort of peace with him. Even now, when he spoke about his wife, she would relax and her mind would lazily wander. She resolved to see more of the Gourlays and try to be more supportive to them, especially as they had suffered such a grievous loss. She was so lucky, when she thought of it. She was alive and well, thank God, and so were her husband, her son and her daughter.

There was hardly a family in the land that hadn't been affected by the war. Wincey had lost Robert Houston. It struck Virginia how strange it was that both she and Wincey had taken a doctor as a lover. Being a passionate woman herself, she took it for granted that Wincey and Robert must have been lovers.

She had always hated war, and now her hatred hardened to bitterness inside her. Recently a WVS woman had come to the door at Kirklee Terrace wanting her to agree to donate the iron railings at the end of the back garden to the war effort. Angrily she'd told the woman, 'I won't give as much as one nail to help kill another human being. There's been enough killing already.'

She felt sick of it all, so helpless and hopeless. She longed for the time before the war but it was like another world now. She wondered if that world would ever come again. Often now, her mind would wander far back to the days of her youth when she lived with her mother and father in their cramped tenement house. No hot water, no inside toilet (far less bathroom), no washing facilities except the communal wash house down in the back yard, where everybody had to wait for their turn to do their washing. Teresa Gourlay probably still had to do that even now.

Sometimes her mother had to take her turn at night, and she didn't like to do her washing at night. There was no chance then of hanging it outside to be dried in the sun and wind. Virginia vividly remembered those nights in the wash house—guttering candles stuck in the neck of bottles along the window ledge casting mysterious shadows that flickered eerily in corners. Her mother would lift the lid of the brick boiler to check how the whites were doing, and steam would immediately fill the wash house. She remembered her mother's brightly flushed face shining with the sweat of heat and work. Her beautiful mother.

'I'm sorry,' Donald said, 'if I'm making you feel sad talking about Mary.'

'Oh no,' she assured him. 'I'm just tired, that's all.'

'I'm not surprised,' Donald said. 'We're so short staffed these days, it's not just ridiculous, it's downright dangerous.'

'I know.' Virginia shrugged. 'But what can we do, with everybody away at the war? And the air raids.' One way or another, it was always the war, the war, the bloody war.

'Another year gone, and it still doesn't look as if there's an end in sight,' Donald said.

She gazed at his familiar face. He looked exhausted. She realised with some shock that he was old. He was a tired old man. Unexpectedly, she experienced a flutter of panic. She felt guilty too. For some time now, she had realised that she did not love Donald. At least, not in the same way as she had loved Nicholas—and, she realised, still loved him. There was a passion and an intensity about Nicholas that was different from anyone else she had ever known. They still made love, although not nearly as often, and his passion never failed to awaken her. Thinking about it, she realised that the times in between making love with Nicholas had lengthened. It had now been a very long time since he had turned to her in bed and taken her in his arms.

Again she felt panic. This time it was more acute. She should have tried harder to talk to him, to confess how she felt. She should have made more of an effort to work out the problems between them.

'It's time I went home,' she suddenly announced to Donald. 'I've so much to do before tomorrow's shift.'

'Yes, of course. I'll go and get the car out.'

'No, please, Donald. You look so tired. Just phone a taxi for me.'

'Are you sure?'

'Yes, definitely.'

He went out to the hall and she could hear him speaking to the taxi company. He returned to the room with her coat and hat. She pulled on her Red Cross cap and he helped her on with her navy uniform coat. Supposedly being at work was a useful cover for these clandestine meetings. So much deceit. They kissed goodnight and she thankfully left the gloomy old house and returned to Kirklee Terrace with its wide bright hall, cream speckled marble floor and the polished woodwork of the stairway. The kitchen was at the back of the hall and she was surprised when she entered it that Nicholas was lounging on one of the chairs by the kitchen table, nursing a glass of whisky. His long legs were stretched out in front of him. His dark eyes when he glanced up at her were slightly quizzical, slightly sarcastic. He didn't say anything and she felt frightened. He knows, she thought.

She forced herself to act calmly. She went over to the Aga and set a pot of potatoes to boil. 'Dinner won't be long. I've everything more or less prepared. What kind of day have you had? Did you get any writing done?'

'Not much. Richard phoned. He's been awarded a DFC.'

Her eyes brightened with astonishment and pride. 'A Distinguished Flying Cross! How wonderful! That'll make him so happy.'

'He deserves it too. He's a very brave young man.'

'Oh, I'm so happy for him, Nicholas.'

'I tried to reach you at the hospital.'

'Oh, when?'

'Hours ago. They said you'd left.'

'Oh, oh yes. I was going round the shops to see if there was anything. I stood in a couple of queues but no luck. Nothing left when it came to my turn. Have you told your mother about Richard yet?'

'Yes, she's immensely proud of him, but then of course she always has been.'

Maybe the whisky was just by way of celebration and that look in his eyes had simply been irritation at not having been able to share his news with her right away.

'I'm so sorry I wasn't in when he phoned. Was he speaking from Castle Hill? Can I reach him there if I phone just now?'

'No, it was just a quick call from his airfield, I think. He's off on some hush-hush operation. Something big is in the offing, I suspect. You'll just have to wait.'

She felt frightened again. This time it was about Richard. He had always been such a daring, adventurous boy, even at school. It was one thing, however, being reckless or daring on the rugby field or on a rock climbing expedition. She had worried about him then but he wasn't playing games any more. Now she felt ill with apprehension.

'I hope he'll be all right,' she managed. 'Oh, I wish I had been in when he phoned.' She'd never forgive herself if anything happened to Richard and she had missed the chance to speak to him one last time. And especially because she had been with a lover. It was too awful to think about.

'Well,' Nicholas said, 'you weren't.'

Again the suspicion that he knew returned. Oh God, she silently prayed as she blindly fussed about with more pots and pans, please keep my son safe. Please, oh please. She felt Nicholas's dark eyes boring into her back. She felt distracted. Forgive me, forgive me, she kept thinking.

28

Nicholas had been watching her, or having her watched. She knew, because he had caught her out again. This time, as it happened, she had gone to Donald's home to tell him as gently as she could that their affair was over. He had pleaded with her to think about it, not to make any hasty decisions.

'Take some time on your own,' he advised. 'Give yourself time away from me to think about it. Make sure it's the right decision, that it's what you really want, Virginia.'

Feeling sorry for him and not wanting to hurt him, she'd allowed him to hold her in his arms and tenderly kiss her. She really was very fond of him, but more as a kind of father figure. She had promised that she would at least give herself more time to think things through.

She'd arrived home to find Nicholas sitting waiting for her. She was struck more forcibly than ever by the difference in appearance between the two men. Donald's skin was paler, and his hair, eyebrows and moustache were silver. His muscles had begun to sag. Nicholas, on the other hand, still had a full head of black hair. His skin was tanned and his body was lean and fit.

This time she recognised the look in his eyes. She'd seen it directed at other people. It wasn't the same quizzical, sarcastic look as the last time. It was the concentrated, unblinking stare of the writer—darkly, deeply probing into a person's character and motivation. She resented such a look being directed at her.

'What's wrong with you?' she asked defensively. 'Why are you staring at me like that?'

'There's nothing wrong with me, Virginia.'

'Yes, there is, and I've known it for a while now. You've changed out of all recognition.' She felt angry and reckless. What had happened was as much his fault as hers. 'You're not the same person I used to know at all.' She struggled to calm down and be more reasonable. 'It's the war, I suppose,' she continued, echoing something that Donald had once said. 'It's changed everything and everybody.'

'I'm the same person that I always was, Virginia. There's never been anyone in my life but you. I have never been unfaithful to you.'

She felt sick with regret. Miserably she searched for words of explanation, justification, excuse or even denial, but before she could think of any words, he rose and said, 'I don't suppose you've noticed, far less cared, but my mother has been far from well. She's never been right since the bombing. I'm going to stay with her for a while so that I can keep an eye on her and try to arrange for some professional care. We'll talk later.'

She watched him go and, determined to retain some dignity and self respect, as well as show proper concern, she said, 'I hope your mother's health will improve and if there's anything I can do, just let me know.'

He didn't answer and left her feeling angry again. He knew perfectly well that she'd tried long ago to get on better terms with his mother. Originally she'd even tried to get close to her. It was his mother who had created the distance between them. All she'd ever had from his mother was hatred. Yet despite that, she'd continued to be pleasant and civilised to the old woman. She'd continued to welcome her at Kirklee Terrace. She was made far from welcome, however, at the ugly villa on Great Western Road. What did Nicholas imagine she could do in the circumstances? He must know perfectly well that his mother would never allow her to do anything.

At the same time she knew that she was dodging the real issue. She continued however to clutch at any straws of justification. Nicholas had been neglecting her and their marriage for years. Not in any material sense. He had always been a good and conscientious provider. It was his time and personal attention he had always been mean with. Well, not quite always. When she'd first known him, he'd been only too glad of her company and he'd treasured every moment of it. That's what he'd told her.

It was perfectly true what she'd said. He had changed. All right, it could be argued that everyone changes as they get older and have to cope with life's problems. Surely though they should have spent more time coping with them together. She'd been more than willing to do that but he had shut himself away in his writing room at every opportunity. Now it was the Home Guard and God knows what else.

The house acquired an oppressive silence after he'd gone. She roamed restlessly about, unable to settle. Eventually she forced herself to prepare some food for the next day's meals. Normally she was very well organised and planned most things in advance. Suddenly she thought, what was the point now? It seemed such a waste of time and effort to prepare meals just for herself.

Damn him, she thought, and wept with anger as much as grief. She'd never allowed any man—or woman for that matter—to get the better of her. Her father, she remembered, always said that she had a lot of spunk. He was right. She wasn't going to sit around feeling sorry for herself. She dried her eyes, put on her hat and coat and went out. Immediately, she was engulfed in the blackout and it was with some difficulty that she made her way to Springburn and the Gourlays' house on the Balgrayhill.

Teresa and Erchie and Granny were delighted to see her. Wincey said, 'Is there something wrong, Mother?'

'No, no, darling. I'm off duty tonight and I just thought I'd pay you all a visit.'

'Sit down, Virginia,' Teresa said. 'Make yourself at home. The kettle's already on the boil.'

It was then that Virginia noticed the soldier sitting opposite. He was a big, tough looking man with cropped hair and a scar down one side of his scalp and face. Wincey introduced him as Malcy McArthur, Charlotte's husband. Charlotte, Virginia remembered, was the Gourlay girl who'd died—not in the Blitz but long before that. Poor Teresa, losing three children. Granny was frail looking and bent and her fingers twitched constantly on her knees.

'He's on leave frae doon in England somewhere. That right, son?'

'Yes, Granny. I wish I didn't need to go back down there, I can tell you.'

Teresa said, 'Never mind, Malcy, the war won't last forever and then you'll be able to come back for good.'

'Aye,' Granny said, 'if he's still aw in one piece.'

'Ma!' 'Granny!' Erchie and Teresa cried out in unison.

The old woman paid not the slightest attention to either of them.

'He's had a few close shaves already, haven't ye, son?'

Malcy laughed. 'You could say that, Granny.'

Malcy had brought Erchie some Woodbines and Erchie gratefully lit one up and enjoyed a few puffs. 'By God, it's a wee while since ah've had a decent smoke. Ah'm fair enjoyin' these, son.'

Teresa made the tea. 'I'm so sorry I haven't a biscuit or a bit cake left in the house.'

'My fault,' Malcy said. 'There was a bit of a welcome do for me here last night and all the rations were used up. It's a wonder there's any tea left.'

'Oh, that reminds me.' Virginia delved into her handbag and brought out a packet of digestives. She handed them over to Teresa. 'I get most of my food at the hospital so I've always something extra.'

'Oh thank you, dear.'

'Ma favourites.' Granny's face brightened with pleasure and anticipation. 'Ah love a digestive tae dip into ma tea.'

'How long are you here for, Malcy,' Virginia asked, as Teresa opened the packet of biscuits and put them onto a plate.

'They gave me a couple of weeks and it's been great to be back in Glasgow. I'd hoped to have been here before but I was in hospital for a while and what with one thing and another, I don't know what I would have done without Wincey's letters. They kept me going.'

He smiled so warmly over at Wincey that Virginia wondered if there was more than just letter writing going on between them. Wincey hadn't said anything and it was difficult to tell by looking at her. Virginia made a mental note to ask her the first chance she got.

'You'll have to forgive Florence for not coming through.' Teresa lowered her voice to a whisper. 'She's been staying here since . . . you know . . . '

'Yes.' Virginia's face screwed up with sympathy. 'Wincey told me. Poor Florence. It's just terrible.'

Teresa said. 'She goes to her bed awful early. She's not been well for a while. The doctor can't find anything wrong but she's got no energy. We don't know what to do for the best.'

'Poor Florence,' Virginia repeated helplessly. 'Tell her I asking for her, won't you.'

'I will, dear. How's your husband? Could he not come with you tonight?'

'No. Busy as usual with all his war efforts.'

'Bloody war,' the old woman growled.

'Granny!' Teresa cast an harassed, apologetic look in Virginia's direction. 'Sorry about Granny.'

'Don't you dare apologise for me, Teresa Gourlay. Ah'll curse this bloody war as much as ah like. It costs us dear enough.'

'Quite right, Granny,' Virginia agreed. 'I'm so sick of the whole business. I just hate it.'

'Are ye still workin' hard at the hospital, hen,' Erchie asked.

They chatted for a while and Virginia felt relaxed and was glad of their company. If it had been possible, she would have stayed all night. She dreaded going back to her empty house. However, the time came when she had to make a move and on finding that she hadn't brought her car, Wincey said, 'I'll drive you back, Mother. We can't have you hanging about waiting for trams at this time of night.'

In the car, Virginia said, 'Malcy seems a nice man.'

Wincey was concentrating on her driving and didn't respond. Virginia tried again.

'Are you . . . I mean, are you and Malcy . . . '

'We're just friends, Mother,' Wincey said.

'I'll see you at the weekend, as usual, I hope?' Virginia asked.

'Yes, of course.'

Wincey didn't come in with her but just waited and watched from the car until she got safely inside. Virginia stood motionless, her back to the door, listening to the car drive away, dreading moving further into loneliness. Eventually, her heels clicked across the hall as she went into the sitting room. There she drew the blackout curtain shut and switched on the light. She did the same in all the rooms, upstairs and downstairs, except the writing room. She didn't dare go in there. How still and silent the house was. Even when Nicholas had been shut away in his writing room, the house had never felt like this.

She was devastated to realise how much she missed him—and he'd only been away for a few hours. They'd occasionally been apart before, but this was very different. This time he might not come back.

29

Teresa was keeping going for Florence's sake. They all were. Even Granny, who was up at Springburn Park at the moment. Erchie had volunteered to take her to hear the Sally Band, her favourite. Florence sat at the room window most of every day, gazing out with blank eyes. Or she lay in bed all day. She couldn't work, couldn't do anything. Hardly ever even spoke.

'It would be so much better if she could get out to work,' Teresa whispered to Wincey in the kitchen. 'Being with all the other sales ladies in Copeland's would bring her out of herself, take her mind off things.'

'I would be perfectly willing to give her a job in the factory if necessary, Teresa, but . . . '

'I know. Poor Florence, you know what she's like. Yes, the factory would probably just make her feel worse. She was always so proud of being in Copeland's. Not that I think there's anything wrong with working in the factory, dear,' Teresa said hastily. 'And it's not that Florence ever meant any harm.'

'I know. I was only saying I'd do anything I could to help her. But it's so difficult, isn't it?'

'I keep asking the doctor but all he seems to give her is pills and potions that make her more lethargic and sleepy than ever. She seems to have lost all hope, as well as energy.'

'I really do wish there was something I could do to help her. And you too, Teresa. You've had a worse loss than Florence. You've lost three children. Florence should try to think of you instead of thinking of herself so much. That would probably do her more good than anything.'

'If she would just get better, I'd be all right.'

'Time is supposed to heal but it's been over two years now, Teresa. There have been so many people who have suffered much worse than her. Look at that family who lost fourteen—or was it fifteen—from a baby of five months to a boy of nineteen years of age. Compared with them, Florence should think herself lucky.'

They hadn't noticed Florence come shuffling into the kitchen like an old woman. Her once glossy, well dressed hair was now straggling down over her face. Her eyes were dull and dark shadowed.

'I try to,' she said tearfully. 'I really do. It's just that I feel so tired all the time.'

'I know, dear.' Teresa ran to put an arm around her. 'We all understand that you're ill and we just wish we could help you get better. Isn't that right, Wincey?'

'Of course it is, Florence. I'm sorry if I sounded unsympathetic or unkind. I didn't mean to.'

Florence nodded. 'If I could just get back my energy, Wincey. I want to get back to work. I long to get back to work. But I'm so tired all the time. What's wrong with me, Mammy? Why can't the doctor help me?'

Teresa bit at her lip. 'Maybe if we tried to get another doctor. Asked for a second opinion, or something.'

'I could pay for private treatment,' Wincey said. 'And how about if you and Florence have a wee holiday somewhere, Teresa. Some sea air might help. How about somewhere up north? Money's no problem.'

'Well, it's very kind of you, dear, but there's so many other problems just now about travelling. There's these posters all over the place—Is your journey really necessary?—and all that.'

'Even if it meant going by taxi, Teresa, that would be all right by me. I could arrange it.'

'Oh, I don't know. Such an expense, dear,' Teresa said worriedly.

Florence widened her eyes. 'Maybe a holiday, right enough. Maybe that would make me better. If I could just get enough energy.'

Wincey said, 'Erchie and I could carry you out into the taxi if necessary, Florence. Or if I could arrange some time off, I'd drive you there myself. You don't need to worry about anything. All you need to do is leave everything to me.'

Tears blurred Florence's eyes. 'Thanks, Wincey. I'm so sorry for being such a nuisance.'

Wincey rushed over to give her a hug and a kiss. 'Don't be daft. You're not a nuisance. You're my dear sister.'

Florence clung to her. 'Am I?' she asked tremulously.

'Of course. Always have been. Now you sit over there beside the fire and have a nice cup of tea with me and your Mammy and we'll talk about where you'll go on your holiday. I've another idea as well. I've heard about a thing called homeopathic treatment. I think that'd be worth trying, if I can find a suitable doctor.'

'I've never heard of that, dear,' Teresa said, as she helped Florence over to a chair, then put the kettle on to boil. 'What kind of thing is it?'

'It was my mother that mentioned something about it. She'd read an article somewhere. I'll ask her if she knows any more when I see her this weekend.'

True to her word, that weekend Wincey asked her mother about homeopathy, and her mother showed her the article, and a pamphlet she'd found on the subject.

One of the principles of homeopathy, it said, was that because people varied in their response to an illness, the homeopath does not automatically present a specific remedy for a specific illness. He tries instead to determine the patient's temperament and so prescribe on an individual basis. Homeopathy provides remedies to assist the body's natural healing process, it said. It treats the patient, rather than the disease, and it treats like with like—the law of similars. It also acted on the belief that there were 'emotional diseases originating in the mind' which could be 'transferred in health of both mind and body by physical means'.

'I'm not sure what to make of it,' Virginia said, 'but it does sound interesting, doesn't it?'

'Yes, especially that bit about the emotional as well as the physical aspects of the person being used as a basis for diagnosis,' Wincey said. 'That's what Florence needs, I think. She's been emotionally shattered.'

Wincey watched her mother as she poured out a cup of tea and handed it to her. She looked tired and worried, instead of excited and happy as Wincey had expected her to be after getting the news of Richard's DFC.

'Are you all right, Mother?'

'Yes, of course, darling. A bit tired, that's all.'

'I thought you'd still be over the moon about Richard's DFC.'

'I'm so proud of him, of course. I told you, it's just that I can't stop worrying about him.'

Wincey smiled and tried to sound reassuring. 'Mother, he's got a special angel looking after him. Either that or he's got the luck of the devil. Look at all he's come through with hardly a scratch. He'll be all right. I'm sure of it.' And she was.

Her mother smiled in return. 'All right, I'll try not to worry.'

'Promise?'

'I promise.'

'Where's Father?'

'He's staying with Mrs Cartwright for a while. She's not been well. All that trouble with the house. She could have come here, but you know what she's like. Your father wants to make sure that she's being properly looked after. He's gone to keep an eye on her.'

Was it her imagination, Wincey thought, or had her mother's eyes become evasive. She was reminded about her mother's secret affair with the silver haired doctor and was for a moment tempted to confront her with the knowledge. She decided against it. What good would it do if she interfered?

'How is Teresa?' her mother asked. 'She doesn't look a physically strong woman but I do admire her spirit, after all she's been through. And Granny's.'

'Granny's looking awfully frail, don't you think? But as Erchie says, she's a tough old bird.'

'I must try to visit them more often, and they're always welcome to come here.'

Suddenly Virginia had an idea. 'Wincey, do you think it would help Florence to come and stay with me for a time? I could easily take a few weeks off. I've never had any proper leave since I started at the Royal.'

'Oh Mother!' Wincey was both astonished and touched. 'How good of you to even think of such a thing!'

'I mean it, darling. I think she'd enjoy it here. I could take her out to the Botanic Gardens and she could rest in the Kibble Palace. It's so lovely in there, and so warm.'

'Oh Mother!' Wincey repeated, this time in delight. 'She'd love it, I'm sure. I bet it would be just what she needs to perk her up. And I'll see about getting her some homeopathic treatment while she's here.'

'Well, if you're really serious about that, there was a hospital listed in that pamphlet I showed you. It's a big villa along Great Western Road. You could enquire about doctors there.'

'Wonderful!' Wincey felt really hopeful and excited now. 'I wonder if I should phone right away and tell Florence.' She forced herself to think calmly. 'No,' she said out loud to herself. 'Better to wait and tell her to her face. Anyway, you'll need time to arrange things at the Royal.'

'Of course, she might not want to come, Wincey. We shouldn't take anything for granted.'

'Oh, I'm sure she'll want to come, Mother. Trust me. I just know we'll be able to help her this way.'

'Well, I'll certainly do my best, darling, for your sake as much as for anyone else's.'

Wincey went over to her mother and hugged her. She wanted to say the words 'I love you' but no words would come.

But her mother seemed to understand. She nodded and smiled and said, 'Drink up your tea, darling. Everything's going to be all right.'

1944-45

30

Malcy was disappointed that he'd never had a minute with Wincey on her own. In the house there was always Florence or Teresa or Granny or Erchie, and all the neighbours coming in to say good luck. Then Wincey took Florence over to her mother's and stayed overnight with her to help get her settled in.

He'd called in to the factory, but even there in the short time he'd had, he'd been surrounded by people wanting to talk to him and wish him well. Even in Wincey's office he had no luck. She was with some man, talking business.

He gave up in the end. Anyway, he didn't just want a few minutes alone with her. He needed time to explain his feelings for her, and to try to find out exactly what she felt for him. He knew now without a doubt that he loved her.

Not in the same way that he had loved Charlotte. That would not have been possible. Wincey and Charlotte were two completely different people.

As the end of his leave drew near, he experienced a feeling of urgency that was almost panic. God knows when he'd see her again. He might never see her again. There were all sorts of rumours flying about amongst the men. It looked as if the final preparations were being made for an invasion. Not a German invasion this time, but an Allied one. He doubted if his luck would hold out through that.

On the last night of his leave, there was a crowd of well-wishers in the house and the next morning, the family all came to see him off at Central Station. They even managed to pack Granny into the taxi.

He shook Erchie's hand, he hugged and kissed Granny and Teresa.

Then when he took Wincey into his arms, he just had time for an urgent, desperate, 'Oh Wincey, I'd so much I wanted to say to you.'

'Write to me,' she said.

The guard blew his whistle and they hustled him onto the train. He didn't want to go. If he'd been a child, he would have wept. He was weeping inside as he leaned from the window of the train and watched Wincey and the Gourlays gradually disappear.

He sank back into his seat and struggled to put them out of his mind. It was too painful to think of them. Instead he visualised what might lie ahead in the next few days and weeks.

All sorts of preparations were being made. Concrete blocks of various sizes had been transported to Selsey in Sussex, where they were fitted together. Nobody knew for certain what they were for. The rumour was that they were going to be towed across the Channel, where they would be used as piers, causeways and breakwaters. Other mysterious new devices were constantly appearing—like Flail tanks, fitted with rotating chains to destroy landmines. A vast armada of warships, aircraft, landing craft and transport ships was being assembled. There was going to be an invasion all right.

Finally, at 4am on the fifth of June, American and British soldiers, sailors and airmen got the command to go.

Malcy only just managed to appear calm on the outside. Inside, fear was rampaging through him. He remembered only too well the terrifying journey back from Dunkirk when he had waded up to his neck in the same water. Now here he was listening to the order, 'Lower the boats'. With a heavy splash, the door went down and seconds later he was in the water again.

Another soldier began to cry, and plead and cling to the deck. He was screaming that he couldn't move. Malcy and the others left him behind, the whine of bullets speeding them on. Suddenly there was a terrible explosion and Malcy felt himself losing consciousness. 'This is it,' he thought. But the next thing he knew, he had come to in the water. He could feel another soldier kicking and clutching at his legs, trying to make it to the surface but only succeeding in dragging Malcy down. Frantically Malcy kicked and struggled until he was free of the man. He shot to the surface and soon the body of the soldier who had been clutching at him floated by, its limbs still twitching.

Malcy sobbed at the horror unfolding all around him, but he had no choice—he had to move on if he was going to survive. Somehow, he struggled out of the water and joined the thousands of other men landing on the beaches. Now he could hear the incessant rattle of enemy machine guns, and his blood froze at the ghastly sight of countless bullets cutting a swathe through the men in front of him.

Mortar rounds were landing close by, exploding in a cacophony of ear-splitting noise. Landing craft were being sunk yards from the shore, and tanks were being hit by incoming shells almost as soon as they trundled onto the sand. Malcy could hear their crews screaming, trapped inside the burning vehicles. Men were being killed all around him, while in the water and on the beach the wounded were shouting for help. Malcy turned back to try and pull a soldier out of the shallows, but an officer bawled at him to leave the man and push on. They had no time. And so, without a backward glance, Malcy turned once more to face the storm of steel.

Wincey knew the sort of thing that Malcy had been wanting to say. She wasn't sure if she was ready to cope with that sort of intimacy, but she couldn't help herself from softening inside and thinking, 'Poor Malcy'. She didn't want anything bad to happen to him, of that she was certain. She wanted him to come back to Glasgow, safe and sound. In bed at night, she would think about him before drifting off to sleep. 'Poor Malcy,' she thought.

She kept seeing his gaunt, scarred face and close-cropped skull. His eyes now had a strangely haunted look. He had always had such a sturdy muscular body, but now it was painful to see the amount of weight he'd lost. 'Poor Malcy'. Thoughts of him and how he had suffered just wouldn't go away—no matter how hard she tried to banish them from her mind. Fortunately, her work helped to occupy her and tire her out, so that each night she could escape quickly and mercifully into sleep. She dreaded being vulnerable. She couldn't bear to suffer loss again, and be hurt again.

Wincey also occupied herself at weekends, helping her mother to attend to Florence. Whether it was the homeopathic medicine, or living at Kirklee Terrace, or perhaps a combination of both, Wincey didn't know. The happy fact was that Florence was getting better. There could be no doubt about that. They were at the stage now of taking her to the theatre or the cinema on Saturday nights. Her mother insisted that she could stay on at Kirklee Terrace as long as she liked.

She was only too glad of the company, as Nicholas was still with Grandmother Cartwright in the house in Great Western Road. Wincey knew now that there was something seriously wrong between her mother and father. After all, Grandmother Cartwright's house wasn't all that far away. He could have seen the old woman every day but still slept at Kirklee Terrace.

Wincey guessed he must have found out about the affair. Once, he had popped into Kirklee Terrace to see her and to say hello to Florence. He hadn't stayed long, however, and he had been noticeably cool to her mother. It was so sad, and she longed to say or do something that would bring them together again. But in this day and age, when so many dreadful things were happening, did an illicit love affair really matter all that much? Especially now, in the aftermath of D-Day, as Britain faced the new terror of Hitler's 'revenge weapons'.

These were the dreaded flying bombs—the V1 or 'Doodlebug', and the even more deadly rocket powered V2. The V1s could be heard coming, but then their engines cut out and there was fifteen seconds of ominous silence while they fell to the earth, where they exploded. They were very difficult to intercept—although a few brave fighter pilots did manage to shoot one or two down before they reached their targets. The V2s were much worse. These giant rockets flew much faster than the V1s. Travelling at supersonic speed they arrived without warning, causing so many casualties that people feared them more than anything.

Wincey hadn't heard from Malcy for months, which wasn't surprising. No doubt he'd taken part in the D-Day landings and would be fighting his way through France by now. Newspapers reported that the Allies had secured the beaches and were pushing ahead. Granny, Erchie, Teresa, Florence, Wincey and even her mother were all worried about Malcy.

Her mother said on one of her visits to Springburn, 'He didn't look fit enough to be going through all that again.'

'I know,' Teresa said. 'I'm really worried about him.'

'See war,' Granny muttered. 'It's bloody wicked. Ah'd put all them generals an' politicians in a field an' tell them to fight it out between themsel's an' leave ordinary lads like Malcy in peace.'

'If only,' Wincey said.

'Well, dear,' Teresa said, 'all we can do at the moment is to pray for all the lads to come home soon.'

'A Protestant or a Catholic prayer?' Granny asked sarcastically. Fond as she was of Teresa, she had never quite got over the fact that her Protestant son had married a 'Pape'. The house was full of 'Papish' ornaments and trinkets, and a picture of a mournful-looking Jesus hung above the kitchen bed.

'What difference does it make?' Teresa said. 'Every and any kind of prayer you like, as long as it helps.'

'Aye, well,' Granny grudgingly conceded.

By now Florence looked well enough to return to Springburn for good but she made it clear that she preferred to remain where she was.

'I hope you don't mind, Mother,' she said to Teresa. 'There's too many memories of Eddie here. It's been so good for me being in the West End. Virginia takes me to all sorts of interesting places, including the Art Galleries. And we had lunch in Copeland's. It takes my mind off everything. I can't bear to think about the past. I'd go mad if I was on my own, just thinking about it.'

'You'd never be on your own, dear,' Teresa said. 'There's always Granny and me here.'

'Please don't be angry with me, Mother. Please try to understand.'

Granny cast a sarcastic glance in Florence's direction. 'It's well seen ye're on the mend. Ye're gettin' more like yersel' every day. Whit happens, ah'd like tae know, when Virginia's oot workin'.'

'I have quite a lot of leave due to me,' Virginia explained before Florence could reply. 'In all the time I've been at the Royal, I've never taken one holiday. I've just taken it all at once now.'

'My word, ye must be well in.'

'Well, VAD is a voluntary service.'

'Whit dis yer man say about you keepin' a lodger?'

'Granny,' Teresa cried out. 'Mind your own business and don't be so cheeky. Have a piece of sponge cake. It'll be nice and soft for your gums.'

'Whit's in it?' Granny eyed the sponge suspiciously. 'No' any eggs, ah bet.'

'Dried eggs, Granny.'

'Dried eggs,' Granny howled in disbelief. 'What's up wi' the bloody hens now?'

'Nothing. They're from America.'

'America? They're no' bloody fresh then.'

'Do you mind if we say goodnight now, Virginia,' Florence suddenly announced. 'I get so quickly fatigued.'

'I should have noticed.' Virginia rose. 'Wincey, darling, could you drive us home?'

'Yes, of course.'

'Aye,' Granny said, 'oor Florence is on the mend, right enough.'

31

At first Virginia didn't mind Florence staying with her. She was glad her invitation had helped the girl. Florence's energy had returned and she was now trying to make herself useful, keeping busy, washing not just the breakfast, lunch, tea and dinner dishes every day, but dusting every ornament she could lay her hands on. She polished everything in sight as well, ignoring Virginia's pleas that she didn't need to do so much. She even polished the marble floor in the hall. Eventually, Virginia just let her get on with it, accepting that Florence was at her happiest being house-proud. There she was every day, glossy brown hair held firmly back in a bandeau, a crisp apron tied round her waist, searching out every speck of dirt or dust.

It was a bit pathetic in a way. It was also becoming very irritating. Virginia had never put much value on material things, nor did she like showing off. Florence was quite the opposite. On one occasion—admittedly with Virginia's permission—she had invited some of her former colleagues from Copeland's to afternoon tea. What a carry on that had been. It had taken every ounce of Virginia's patience to refrain from telling Florence not to be so ridiculous. How Florence had revelled in showing the girls around the house!

'This is the drawing room. Look at these pelmets and the way the curtains are draped. Satin, I think, or maybe heavy silk. The drawing room is where we always entertain guests. The sitting room downstairs is more for private family use. Isn't this a gorgeous bathroom? These bedrooms are so bright and modern, yet so cosy and comfy too. Feel the deep pile of that carpet. This staircase is so elegant, isn't it. And here's the sitting room I mentioned. Look at all the bookshelves. Of course, Nicholas is a writer, don't you know? These are some of his books. The kitchen is so well equipped too. One could eat here all the time if one wanted to, but there's also that elegant dining room. And here is Nicholas's writing room.'

Virginia had just caught her in time. 'No, we never go in there. That's Nicholas's private place.'

'Oh yes, of course, I forgot,' Florence said, leading her little group away across the hall again. 'Look at that marble floor. Isn't it so elegant?'

Virginia was embarrassed beyond words.

And Florence's company in no way made up for the lack of Nicholas's presence. On the contrary, once Florence no longer needed to be looked after, time hung heavy on Virginia's hands. She was glad to get back to work.

By that time, Florence was even cooking the meals. Virginia began to feel as if she had moved into another life. A life that was gradually becoming a waking nightmare. Every day her true life, the only life she wanted—her life with Nicholas—was disappearing further and further into the past. She longed for him, ached for him, made love to him in her dreams over and over and over again.

To make the nightmare worse, the situation between Florence and herself was becoming more and more of a problem. Their roles had been reversed—Florence was trying to look after her now. 'Just you sit down and relax, Virginia,' she kept saying. 'Enjoy this drink while I put the finishing touches to dinner.'

Normally Virginia and Nicholas ate in the kitchen, but Florence now insisted on doing everything 'properly'. They sat at opposite ends of the long dining room table. Florence always wearing her best dress for dinner along with her pearl earrings and necklace.

'Isn't this lovely,' she would coo, 'just like in a film.' Everything had to be done properly. And while every day Florence grew stronger and happier, Virginia became more and more depressed.

'Virginia, you're looking tired, and no wonder. You're on your feet all day. Just you sit back and listen to the wireless now while I clear up.'

Eventually, in desperation, Virginia spoke to Matheson about the situation. And not just about the situation with Florence. She got everything off her chest. He knew that Nicholas was staying at his mother's place, but she'd originally told Matheson it was because Nicholas's mother was ill and needed him there.

'You what?' Matheson's voice raised incredulously.

'I had an affair with a doctor at the hospital and Nicholas found out.'

'Well,' Matheson said, 'I can only say I know just how Nicholas feels. You once did the same to me, remember.'

'Oh, James, that was different. I thought Nicholas was dead when I married you, and I'd been his lover long before I met you.'

'Are you still seeing this man?'

'Since I've been back at work, I've seen him, but not on his own. The affair's finished. It was a terrible mistake, James. I was just feeling so lonely and neglected.'

'I told you before what I think of that attitude. It's Nicholas I feel sorry for.'

She felt an unexpected surge of her old fighting spirit. 'Oh, that's right. Stick up for him as usual. I know I have my faults, James, but I can assure you Nicholas isn't as blameless as you always make him out to be. He's as much responsible for our break-up as I am.'

After a brief silence, Matheson said, 'Do you want him back?'

'Of course I want him back.'

'Well, don't just sit there talking to me about it. Go and talk to him. Get him back. And do something about that girl. I'm surprised at you letting her take you over so much. Why don't you tell her it's time she was back in Copeland & Lye's.'

'I'm exhausted most days when I get home from the Royal, and I'm glad of her help in the house. But she can be so irritating sometimes.'

She watched Matheson limping about the kitchen and putting two cups and saucers on the table. Recently he'd grown a moustache and beard, and it helped to disguise his twisted face. His hair was white, but thick and glossy, and he looked fitter than he'd done since he'd had his stroke. The fact that he was still teaching, she felt sure, had helped take his mind off his disability and keep him going.

He was right about what she should do about her marriage. After all, she'd fought for Nicholas before and won. If she was worth her salt, she should at least make an attempt to fight for him again. She determined to call at the Cartwright villa right away.

As soon as she'd had a cup of tea with Matheson, she set out to do just that. The builders had made a good job of reroofing the house; nevertheless it now had an odd, stunted, look. Virginia wondered if it would be Mrs Cartwright who came to the door. If so, she knew she would be lucky if the old woman allowed her in. She would have been milking the situation for all she was worth. Getting her son away from her former scullery maid was, after all, what Mrs Cartwright had always wanted.

Virginia realised that she could have waited until the weekend, when Nicholas usually called in to see Wincey, but it was difficult trying to speak to him at any length, on his own, in those circumstances. Far better to face him and have it out with him right now.

She gave the bell a strong pull. It made an eerie jangle that seemed to echo all through the house.

Mrs Cartwright's house had always been gloomy, filled as it was with dark, Victorian furniture. An elderly woman in an apron made of coarse sacking material and carrying a pail of water in one hand opened the door.

'Oh,' she said. 'I was just coming out to scrub the front steps.'

'I'm Mrs Cartwright's daughter in law.'

'Oh, right. You'd better come in then. But she's having a wee rest just now.'

'Is Mr Nicholas Cartwright in?'

'Aye, I think so.'

Once inside the hall, Virginia caught sight of Nicholas emerging from the room she remembered as the Cartwright library. No doubt he was now using it as his writing room.

'Has something happened to Richard?' he asked anxiously.

'No, no, he's fine.'

'Or Wincey?'

'No, she's fine too. I just came to talk to you, Nicholas. We need to talk.'

'Come through to the drawing room.'

Following him through to a room across the other side of the hall, she couldn't help thinking, 'Oh, nothing's changed then. I mustn't interfere with your precious writing.'

With some difficulty, she controlled her feelings. This attitude had become at least part of the problem in their marriage. For years now, she had been jealous of Nicholas's writing. Or at least the time and priority he gave to it.

It had become a downward spiral. And her resentful attitude had only made him withdraw more and more into his work.

'Drink?' He raised a questioning brow.

She nodded and sat down on one of the uncomfortable horse-hair chairs beside the fireplace. The empty grate was fronted by an ornate folding screen. The room had a fousty smell and felt as if neither a fire nor the sun had ever penetrated its chilly atmosphere.

'Thank you.'

She accepted the gin and tonic and took a few sips before breaking the silence. 'Nicholas, I don't want to excuse my behaviour. I'm sorry I was unfaithful to you. It was a terrible mistake. Rightly or wrongly— probably wrongly—I was feeling lonely and neglected. We hardly ever saw each other. You were always either shut away in your writing room, or out doing some sort of war work.'

'You were out working too.'

'I know. Most of the fault is mine. I admit that for years I've been jealous and resentful of the time you've spent at your writing. But I felt I didn't matter to you any more.'

'That's nonsense, Virginia.'

'Maybe, but that's what I felt. Think about it, Nicholas. Try to think honestly about the priority you gave to your work, and the time you shut yourself away from me.'

He hesitated. 'Maybe latterly.'

'Yes, and I was thinking that's probably been my fault too. The more angry and resentful I became, the more you shut yourself away. I'm so sorry, Nicholas. I'm so sorry for how everything's gone wrong between us and I bitterly regret my part in what's happened.' She struggled for calmness and composure. 'I keep remembering how happy we used to be at the beginning. Surely that makes it worth trying again.'

Suddenly, remembering it again, she burst into a flood of tears. 'Oh, Nicholas, please forgive me. I'm so miserable without you.'

He sighed, then came towards her, arms outstretched. 'What a couple of fools we've been. I'm as much at fault as you for everything that's happened.'

'Have you thought about me at all since you've been here?'

'Thought about you? Of course I've thought about you. I've thought about you all the time. I've just been too proud and stubborn, I suppose, to do what you've just done.'

He drew her towards the door. 'Come on, I want to show you something.'

To her surprise, he led her towards the library and then inside the room. A desk was scattered with books and papers. He picked up a sheet of paper and handed it to her. 'How do you think I got the inspiration for that? As you know, I haven't written poetry for years, but I wrote this after visiting Kirklee Terrace one weekend.'

It was a poem, headed *Creator* and she read:

> *I lived here, I had been in here.*
> *And if my intuition is right,*
> *I loved you long ago,*
> *I had bought this book in the tiny antique shop*
> *In the old town,*
> *I was touching those yellow pages,*
> *I was sensing fragrant flowers of wisdom.*
> *I was drinking wine and water together with you,*
> *I was watching the twilight,*
> *I was sitting in a straw chair,*
> *I was cradled on the waves in the ocean,*
> *Somebody wanted me to miss this rough water for the rest of my life . . .*
>
> *I had felt this bitterness of wind in April,*
> *I lived here, I had been in here.*
> *And if I had been here,*
> *One rainy day,*
> *When everybody had forgotten I was here,*
> *I will come again,*
> *It would be the wonderful act of the Creator,*
> *To repeat everything once more*
> *Saying that nothing is wasted in this world,*
> *And you will love me again,*
> *And I would not complain about my destiny.*
> *It brought home to her so vividly what a uniquely talented man he was.*

'It's beautiful, Nicholas. Thank you for sharing it with me.'

Nicholas said, 'This is what we always used to do, remember? Share everything.'

She sighed. 'Yes, if only we could get back to the way we were in those days.'

'We could try,' he said. 'Maybe this is the first step.'

She gazed hopefully up at him. 'Does that mean you'll come back?'

'Yes, if you still want me.'

'More than anything else in the world, Nicholas. I'll give up my work if you like.'

'Not at all. Not unless you want to. But maybe it would help if we could both cut down on the hours we spend at work. And I include my writing in that. Now you get back home and leave me to break the news to Mother. It won't be easy. You know what she's like. I'll have to be very firm.'

He kissed her lightly on the cheek, grinned and said, 'I'm not going to kiss you properly just now, because I know within a few seconds we'd be rolling on the carpet. But look out lady, I've got a lot of passionate love making time to make up for.'

Virginia hadn't felt so happy and excited for years. She could have danced her way back to Kirklee Terrace. She almost had an orgasm at the thought of living with Nicholas again. But as soon as she stepped inside into the now immaculate hall, heavy with the pungent odour of Mansion polish, she remembered the other problem she had to tackle. This one might prove more difficult—in the sense that Florence's stay at Kirklee had become her buffer against her terrible loss. Maybe it was her only lifeline now. How can I take it away from her, Virginia thought. Yet they couldn't go on as they were, especially with Nicholas returning.

As soon as Florence saw her, she rushed to put on the kettle. The kitchen used to have a homely feel about it, with herbs hanging from a beam on the ceiling, old cushions softening the seats of the wooden chairs, newspapers lying about, shopping lists pinned to the wall, and pictures of Wincey and Richard propped up in front of a cocoa tin. Now everything was bare and sterile. Even the photographs had been tucked neatly away in an album in the sitting room.

'You must be tired out, Virginia. Dinner won't be long but you can relax with a cup of tea now. On you go through to the sitting room. I'll bring it to you.'

'I'm fine,' Virginia assured her. 'I went to see my husband and I'm happy to say his mother is all right now and he's returning home this evening.'

'Oh, I'll set another place for dinner, then,' Florence said happily.

'I must give that table an extra polish to have everything nice for him.'

Virginia groaned inside. Florence meant well, but she was such a silly girl. Couldn't she even see that she and Nicholas needed to be alone together? What did either of them care about a table, polished or otherwise.

'I tell you what,' Virginia said. 'How about if you went to visit your mother and father this evening? You haven't seen them for a while, Florence. You mustn't neglect your own folks.'

'But your dinner,' Florence protested.

'I'll see to the dinner, Florence. I'd really like to do everything for Nicholas tonight. It's been such a long time since I've had the chance.'

'Oh well, if you're sure.' Florence sounded far from sure.

'Yes, definitely, Florence. Stay overnight. There's no need to struggle back through the blackout. Now please,' she raised a hand, 'do as I say, Florence. I'm not going to take no for answer.'

Reluctantly, Florence agreed, and after she was gone, Virginia danced around the house forgetting, in her new found joy, that Florence would soon be back.

32

'Oh, I'm so glad,' Wincey told her mother and father. 'It's just so wonderful to see you both together and happy again.' It was also disturbing. There was such a strong sexual chemistry sparking between them. It was in the way they looked at one another and in the way they touched, and they were always touching. Wincey was genuinely glad that they were happy together but the strong sexual element forever sizzling in the air made her shrink into herself. One day she'd been coming into the sitting room and had seen her mother sitting loose limbed on a chair. Her father was leaning over the back of it and sliding his hand down the inside of her mother's blouse to cup her breast. Her mother's eyes were closed, her face uptilted in ecstasy. Wincey had drawn back unseen and stood in the hall for a few minutes in something akin to distress and fear. She was reminded how she had only loved Robert Houston with words, never with actions. She felt like weeping, desperately wanting to love and be loved, but unable and afraid to break through the protective barrier she'd built around herself.

Later Virginia managed a whispered few words with Wincey while Florence was through in the kitchen fetching the tea trolley.

'Darling, what am I going to do about Florence? I don't want to hurt her or anything, and I appreciate what a wonderful help she is in the house, but she has got rather carried away, don't you think?'

'It's your own fault, you should never have allowed her to go this far, Mother.'

Virginia sighed. 'I know. I know.'

'Your mother was only trying to help the girl,' Nicholas said. 'I've offered to have a word with her, but she won't hear of it.'

'Let me handle it then,' Wincey said. 'Florence and I are like sisters. I know her better than anybody.'

Just then Florence came bright eyed and smiling into the room, the trolley bumping and chinkling before her. She had discarded her bandeau and apron and changed into her best afternoon dress of cinnamon coloured wool. She was wearing a little string of pearls and her hair was brushed smooth and curled neatly in at the ends. She looked flushed and extremely pretty.

'Tea everyone?'

'I'll pour.' Virginia moved forward.

'No, no, I can manage,' Florence said. 'Sit down and relax, Virginia.'

Wincey felt the air immediately become tense, but obviously Florence was unaware of it. She was very ladylike in the way she poured out the tea and handed china teacups and tiny cakes around.

'A new recipe,' she informed everyone as she settled down with her teacup and raised pinky. 'Dried eggs, of course, but I find it very good. And some porridge oats, would you believe. Do have another one, Nicholas. They're very small, I know, but they look so dainty, don't they. Appearance is important, I always think. In food as well as in everything else. I just refuse to do as everyone else is doing now and make a coat out of army blankets or a dress out of curtain material. I'd rather go on wearing my old, good quality garments. Purchased in Copeland's, you know.'

'I was just saying to Mother,' Wincey told Florence, 'that she and Father should treat themselves to an evening out tonight to celebrate. They could have a meal somewhere and then go to the pictures.'

'But I've got dinner all planned. It's vegetable soup, spam and salad and uncooked chocolate cake,' Florence protested.

'Sounds great. I'll stay and have dinner with you and we can have a long talk like old times.'

'Good idea,' Nicholas said, lifting his newspaper. 'Let's see what's on.'

Virginia smiled over at Florence. 'Your mother would be pleased to see you the other night. And Erchie and Granny.'

'Yes, although poor Granny is getting very frail.'

'Wonderful spirit though.'

'Oh yes. I have to laugh at her at times.'

'I must pay her a visit soon, Florence. Next week I'm on late shift but I could drop in one afternoon, perhaps.'

'No, no, Virginia. That would be too tiring for you. Better they come here for morning coffee, or lunch perhaps. That way I could organise everything and save you any bother.'

'It's no bother going to visit friends, Florence. I enjoy it.'

Wincey could see that her mother was struggling to be patient. 'Why don't you go and get ready, Mother?'

'Yes.'

Nicholas rose too. 'And I'll see about booking a table.'

'We should do this more often,' Nicholas told Virginia, taking her into his arms the moment they reached the bedroom.

Virginia smiled. 'We do it all the time.'

Nicholas tutted at her in mock reproof. 'Treat ourselves to a meal out and a show at least once a week, I mean.'

'Don't tell me it's because I need a rest or it's too tiring for me to make a meal here or I'll scream.'

Nicholas laughed and rubbed his face into the curve of her neck. 'You're very patient with her, darling. I just hope Wincey can get through to her and she gets the message.'

'It's not that I don't appreciate her help, especially now when there's no Mrs Rogers.'

'Forget about Florence. Get yourself out of that uniform and into something really glamorous. We're going to forget about everything except enjoying ourselves—and each other—tonight.'

She clung to him and as they kissed, he danced her slowly round the room, as they'd once danced naked in the woods when they were young.

'That was a lovely meal, Florence. I really enjoyed it. You must give Teresa the recipe for that chocolate cake. I bet Granny would appreciate it.'

'I'll write it down for you and you can give it to Mother.'

'I don't think you realise, Florence, how much they're missing you. It was so terrible for Teresa losing the twins, and then you.'

'She hasn't lost me.'

'It feels like that. They hardly ever see you. I wouldn't see you either if I wasn't coming here every weekend.'

Florence looked uneasy. 'Well, I'll try to get over to Springburn more often.'

'I think the best idea would be if you shared yourself between here and the family. After all, that's what I do.'

'What do you mean?'

'I think you should help your mother and father by living there with them, but every morning come over here to help my mother and father from Monday to Friday, say from ten o'clock until two. Then I'd take over here as usual at weekends. It would make Teresa and Erchie and Granny so happy, Florence, and you know my mother feels terribly guilty about taking you away from them for so long. It's your own family who really need you now, Florence.'

An anxious, unhappy look appeared in Florence's eyes. 'Am I really making Virginia unhappy? She's been so good to me and I was just . . . I was just trying . . . '

'I know, Florence.' Wincey hastened to put a comforting arm around Florence's shoulders. 'And she's so grateful for all the help you've given her. And she wouldn't want to lose you. But she wouldn't have to if you agree to what I've suggested. That way everyone would be happy.'

After a few seconds, Florence nodded to herself. Then she gazed round at Wincey and said, 'Do you think I'll be all right?'

In her eyes, Wincey could see the shadow of grief—or the fear of grief—that had never after all gone away. Florence, it occurred to Wincey, had been frantically busying herself in order to avoid thinking about the loss of her home, and her Eddie. Wincey suddenly realised that she had been doing the same to cope with the grief of losing Robert Houston.

'Of course you will. You'll have the family, and me, to look after, as well as everybody here, every day. But it won't be all work and no play.' Wincey smiled and gave Florence's shoulders a squeeze. 'We can go out for a meal and to the pictures as well, you know.'

Florence managed a smile in return. 'I was missing Mammy and Daddy right enough. And awful old Granny.'

'You don't mind if she's cheeky to you then?' Wincey said.

'She is awful cheeky to me but I'm used to it. No, I'm very fond of her really.'

'That's settled then. Will you tell my mother, or shall I?'

'No, I'll tell her, Wincey. Or we both can when she comes back this evening. I always have a hot drink ready for her if she's been out at night.'

'Right, that's what we'll do then.'

After a moment, Florence said, 'I was just thinking. Something ought to be done to that house in Springburn. It needs a proper clean out for a start. And I don't suppose anything in the house has ever been polished.'

Wincey had a sudden terrible vision of Florence struggling to polish Granny's wheelchair.

'Well, you'll have your own room, Florence, and I'm sure you'll have it looking a picture in no time.'

By Sunday evening, everything had been arranged and agreed to and Florence returned to Springburn and the Balgrayhill with Wincey.

'I'll see you tomorrow at ten,' Florence assured Virginia and Nicholas.

'I'll look forward to that,' Virginia said. 'Although you won't see much of Nicholas. We mustn't disturb him at his work.'

'Except when I clean out his room. Or take him his morning coffee.'

'No!' both Nicholas and Virginia cried out in unison, and Virginia added, 'Nicholas has so many papers and books lying around and only he knows where to lay his hands on them. He sees to his own room, Florence. It only gets a good clean out when he's safely finished writing his novel. No one must interrupt him, not even with a cup of coffee. It's a strict rule. He takes a flask and sandwiches in with him. The same applies to lunchtime.'

'Well,' Nicholas said, 'I think I could relax the lunchtime rule if I started a bit earlier in the morning.' He winked in Virginia's direction. 'I'd hate to miss Florence's cooking.'

Once they were out on the Terrace, Wincey and Florence turned and waved. Virginia and Nicholas waved back. Wincey had never seen them look so happy. She linked arms with Florence as they walked towards her car.

'It's going to be all right,' she said. 'Everything's going to be all right.'

She tried to believe it, but the war still cast its shadow over them all. The whole country was war weary. They continued to put on a show of keeping their spirits up but the pretence was wearing a bit thin. It was all very well for the government to plaster pictures all over the place of happy smiling mothers sealing vegetables and fruit in jars, and a happy smiling child saying, 'We'll have lots to eat this winter, won't we, Mother?' And big letters underneath the picture saying' Grow your own, can your own.'

But as Erchie said, 'Most folk here live in tenements with no gardens. So where are we supposed to get the vegetables an' fruit? Where do we even get the bloody cans?'

There was a big pig bin out in the back yard beside the brick shelter, into which they were supposed to put all their so-called waste food for the pigs to eat.

'What waste?' Granny asked. 'We eat it aw oorsels.'

'Aye,' Erchie agreed. 'Anythin' out there'd just give the rats a treat.'

They couldn't even get away for a wee holiday any more. 'Is your journey really necessary?' the posters kept demanding. Petrol rationing, even if you could get your ration, made holiday travel impossible. Trains were so uncomfortable and slow that no one travelled on them unless they had to. 'Go by Shank's pony,' another poster urged.

'When's it aw gonnae end?' Granny asked. 'Ah'm fed up. Ah cannae even get a decent bit o' sponge cake any mair.'

Christmas and New Year and other times that they had once celebrated came and went. They were not worth celebrating any more. But the worst thing about the war, and the thing that was seldom spoken of—in the Gourlay house at least—was the terrible loss of life. The loss of their friends and neighbours was bad enough. The spectres of first Doctor Houston, then poor Eddie and young Bridget and Euphemia continued to haunt them.

Now they were anxious about Joe and Pete and Malcy. 'Write to Malcy again hen,' Erchie said to Wincey, 'an' ask him if he's heard anythin' about Joe an' Pete.'

She had written several letters recently and received no reply. She was secretly beginning to feel panicky. She kept remembering Malcy when he'd had his last leave. He wasn't at all like the jack-the-lad character he'd once been. No longer was he the laughing, twinkling eyed man who had the gift of the gab and a great way with the girls. His gaze was serious. He was a tough and seasoned army man who'd seen too much death and suffering, and who'd been longing to reach out for some love and happiness again.

In her heart she had known that—and she'd denied him it. Just as she'd denied loving Robert as she should have, and as he deserved to be loved. Poor Malcy, she thought, and prayed that wherever he was, he was safe and well. She got out her pen and notepad and began another letter.

This time, instead of beginning 'Dear Malcy', she wrote 'My dear Malcy' and she ended the letter with 'All my love'. She doubted if she could ever address him in person in such affectionate terms but it might be a step in the right direction. She hoped so.

33

Now Malcy really knew what heart sick meant. He was sick to his very heart at what he'd seen in Buchenwald and Belsen. It was completely beyond him to understand how human beings could do to fellow human beings what the Germans had done to the inmates of these camps. Were the Germans human, he began to wonder. It was difficult to believe after the terrible scenes he had witnessed. It was equally difficult to comprehend that the crowds of ghostly, skeletal figures he had seen wandering around the camps were the lucky ones. At least they'd survived. Unlike so many others, who had died horrible deaths at the hands of Nazi doctors who had performed hideous experiments on them. Malcy could only guess at how many people had been tortured or starved to death, or met their terrible end in the gas chambers. Perhaps no one would ever really know.

For the rest of his life, he would never forget these sad remnants of humanity. Never, never, would he forget what the Germans were capable of. Or indeed any nationality. The Americans had dropped an atom bomb on Hiroshima and the pilot, looking down from a height of thirty three thousand feet, said afterwards that in two minutes, the surface was nothing but blackness, boiling like a barrel of tar. Where before there had been a city with distinctive houses, buildings, now you couldn't see anything.

And what was the target? Ordinary men, women and children. Young typists in offices, old people sitting at home, nurses in hospitals, mothers out shopping, babies in prams—everybody going about their ordinary, everyday business. All in the boiling tar barrel. And the Americans are on our side for God sake, Malcy thought.

Then three days later, they dropped another bomb on Nagasaki. Why? Nobody could yet figure it out. Malcy was unable to figure it out. How could human beings be like this to one another? War brought out so much cruelty and evil in so many people, of all sides and all nationalities. He had killed, hadn't he? And he'd seen a decent young man—Andy, his name was—who normally would never have hurt a fly, machine gun a dozen German soldiers in one go. And these Germans had been giving themselves up, walking towards Andy with their hands above their heads. But Andy had seen some of his best mates blown sky high in a boat bombed by a German Stuka.

And so it went on. The whole sickening business. What could be normal any more? Even knowing the war was over didn't help much. He'd known it was the beginning of the end when Berlin had fallen to the Red Army. Then in May the war in Europe finally came to an end. Now, the war with Japan was over. It was all over, so they said. But it wasn't all over in his head. Or, he suspected, in the minds of many other servicemen. He'd learned Joe and Pete had been prisoners of war. The Red Cross had passed on postcards from them. They'd been captured by the Japanese and used as slave labour, building a railway where men had died like flies—one for every sleeper that was laid. He didn't think he could bear it if Joe and Pete had died after all they'd come through together. But he knew he'd have to bear it, just as he'd had to bear everything else.

Then he'd been shipped back to England and he heard that Joe and Pete were back in Britain as well. He found out that they were in hospital in the south of England. His relief was enormous and the hospital was the first place he made for when he landed. He'd spend all his leave with them, if need be.

And there they were—nearly as emaciated as the people he'd seen in the German concentration camps. But at least they were alive. That was the main thing. They were even up and about, although still wearing pyjamas and dressing gowns. There they were, grinning all over their gaunt faces.

'Well,' Joe cried out, 'you're a fuckin' sight for sore eyes!' They shook hands and then Malcy thought, To hell, and hugged the pair of them. He didn't say anything about them losing their wives. The Red Cross had already been in touch with them and let them know what had happened. They'd realise that he felt for them, and one day perhaps they would talk about it. At the moment, they were just grateful for being reunited.

They told Malcy they weren't allowed out yet, and were only allowed out of bed for a few hours every day. 'They're trying to build our strength up, so they say,' Pete explained.

'I'll find a place to stay locally,' Malcy told them, 'and come in and keep you company every day.'

'Don't be bloody daft,' Joe said. 'Away you go home and enjoy your leave. We'll have a right get together when we get back.'

'I don't mind waiting here for you,' Malcy said.

'Go home now, Malcy. The Gourlays, especially Wincey, will be desperate to see you.'

'They'll want to see you as well, don't forget. They want you both to stay with them, at least until you get fixed up.'

'We know that. But you get up there as quick as you can, mate, and best of luck to you.'

'All right, I'll go, but not right this minute.' He settled down on a bedside chair and they slumped onto the beds. Malcy offered them a cigarette and after lighting up, he said, 'How did you hear the war had ended?'

Joe said, 'We'd been working as usual. Then the guard told us to rest before we began the march back to the camp. On the march, we passed another crowd of men and this big, bearded guy with a shovel over his shoulder shouted out to us, "They've had it".'

'Then,' Pete said, 'when we got back to the camp, the commandant told us that the war was over. We heard later that he'd been hanged.'

Joe took up the story again. 'But the next thing that happened was a great bulky guy in a fancy American uniform arrived. He must have thought he was a bit of a comic. Everyone crowded around him and asked him to tell us all the news. He said Charlie Chaplin was the father of Joan Barry's kid. It wasn't until much later that we found out about the atomic bombs.'

They talked until a nurse came and told Malcy that his time was up.

'See you in the Boundary Bar,' Malcy said as he left.

Joe and Pete gave him a thumbs up sign and another big grin and Joe shouted out, 'You get stuck in there with Wincey.'

Malcy had sometimes thought of Wincey but not often now. He had to cope with so many other more vivid and more immediate images filling his mind. He supposed that what he still wanted was to get home to Glasgow to try to pick up some of the threads of normal, ordinary life. Although he wasn't sure what that was any more.

He wasn't even sure if he wanted to make his home with the Gourlays. They had insisted, via Wincey's letters, that that was what he must do. He didn't know what to do about anything any more, except perhaps to be on his own to try to sort himself out.

Maybe he could rent or buy a place of his own. However, he wrote to Wincey and told her when he would be arriving in Glasgow. He almost dreaded the reunion in his home city—and to think he'd once longed to be back among all the people he knew there.

Now, they seemed as if they were from a different world. Only fellow servicemen like Pete and Joe belonged to his world. Only they knew what it was like. He had moments of near panic when he decided not to go back at all. He'd stay in London. There were plenty of clubs and places for servicemen there. He tried to pull himself together. To chicken out of this last ordeal would do no one any good, especially himself. He'd faced the war. Now he'd have to face the peace.

He bought his ticket to Glasgow and boarded the train. That wasn't easy for different reasons, but mainly because he was so loaded down by his kit bag that he could hardly manoeuvre himself through the door. Finally, he had to sling it onto the train before clambering on himself.

He sat in a corner by the window, smoking and trying to prepare himself for what was to come. They'd probably meet him at the Central Station. Teresa and Erchie and Wincey. Or maybe Wincey would decide she couldn't take time away from her factory.

Thinking of the factory made him remember Charlotte. Yet even she had become not only a ghost from the past, but someone from another world. Had he ever belonged to that world?

He felt as if he was on his way to meet a crowd of strangers. He kept trying to brace himself. He wished he could have stayed in the hospital, been allocated a bed next to Joe and Pete. Maybe he didn't look as ill as they did and in need of rest and treatment, but he felt as if he did. That's what he secretly longed for. He was so tired. Perhaps it was his exhaustion that was distancing him from everything. He just sat there, hunched in the corner smoking one cigarette after another and listening to the rhythm of the train and allowing it to rock him into a mindless trance.

For a while at least, it gave him a blessed respite from waking dreams of men being blown to bits; drowning men clutching at his legs; men screaming for help; men, women and children crawling towards him from the concentration camps; men, women and children burning.

He became conscious eventually of the train's rhythm slowing down. Opening his eyes he saw the first sign of Glasgow—the shining silver of the River Clyde. Frantically he struggled not to weep.

34

They all waited excitedly on the platform—Teresa, Erchie, Florence, Wincey and Granny. Granny's specs had slid to the end of her nose and she was wearing a bashed black felt hat, a long coat of the same colour and a tartan blanket tucked round her legs.

Wincey stood on tiptoe and cried out, 'There he is,' and waved. Then she said, 'Go and help him, Erchie. Look, he's loaded down.'

Erchie was already running towards the carriage door. The rest of the family hurried as quickly as they could behind, bumping Granny's wheelchair and jostling her about in the process. She clung grimly on, but didn't complain.

'Welcome home, son,' Erchie took hold of Malcy's kitbag after giving him an awkward hug. They all hugged him and echoed that cry of 'Welcome home, Malcy'.

Malcy gave a half smile. He looked confused. He allowed himself to be led away, his gear stuffed into the boot of Wincey's car and himself pushed into the front seat beside Wincey. She drove very confidently, laughing and chatting with Teresa and Florence who were in the back seat. Erchie and Granny were following on in a taxi. Malcy tried to respond to some of the questions that were fired at him until Wincey said, 'Give him a break. He's tired. He's probably been travelling for days.'

He gazed out of the window at places he'd come to believe he'd never see again. His eyes strayed up to the ornate facade of the Central Hotel. They didn't build them like that nowadays. There was Hope Street with its equally beautiful Victorian architecture. And St Vincent Street and Renfield Street. Street after beautiful street, everything seemed intact and just the same as it had always been. It was as if the war had never happened.

Then there were the high black tenements of Springburn Road. There was the Avenue on the right with Wellfield Street branching off it. The Wellie picture house would probably still be there. Further along Springburn Road now, there was the Balgrayhill rearing up in front of them. He cringed as he saw the banner stretching across the top of the street with huge letters emblazoned on it, 'Welcome home, Malcy.' There was another one draped across the close, and flags and balloons floated at windows.

He managed a smile and a wave to the neighbours standing around the close and greeting him with shouts of 'Glad to see you, son' and 'Have a great party'.

Oh God, he thought, a party! The smile stuck to his face and he waved back as if he hadn't a care in the world. Inside the house was all decorated with paper chains and balloons. Somebody helped him off with his heavy khaki greatcoat and shoved a drink into his hand.

Soon Erchie and Granny joined them, followed by a crowd of neighbours, until the kitchen was packed and the rag rug became rumpled against the fender. The table was cluttered with glasses and bottles. People were perched on the draining board at the side of the sink and on the high bed in the recess. Teresa had a struggle to get the press door open to fetch out more glasses. The noise of chattering voices and laughter bounced off walls and ceiling.

The only thing for it, Malcy supposed, was to get drunk. Even getting drunk, however, proved difficult but at least it helped him to loosen up a bit and become more talkative. He assured everyone that Pete and Joe were all right, and would soon be home too. He warned however that they had suffered a lot and were very thin and under-nourished. They needed to stay in hospital and have their strength built up before they'd be fit enough to travel.

'Ye've lost a pound or two o' flesh yersel, Malcy,' somebody said.

'Poor laddies,' Granny kept muttering. 'Poor laddies.'

Florence told him that there had been lots of marvellous cele-brations on VE Day and VJ Day and all the neighbours agreed. There were shouts of 'Marvellous', 'Smashing', 'Magic'. Florence assured Malcy it was especially good fun on VE Day. Her eyes rolled with pleasure, remembering.

'You should have seen the mass of people crushing into George

Square, Malcy. Chock a block, it was.'

There were cries of 'Like sardines we were'. Then one woman added, 'Ah said tae wan man, if we get any closer, we'll huv tae get married.'

'It's a wonder no one was seriously hurt in the crush,' Florence said. 'But we managed to dance all the same, didn't we, Wincey? Everyone was dancing like mad. What a laugh it was.' Florence giggled. 'Men we'd never set eyes on in our lives kissing and hugging us. What a scream it was, wasn't it, Wincey? A real scream.'

'Ah bet them wernae the kind o' screams Malcy's been used to,' Granny muttered. She was very bent and shaky nowadays, and spoke as much to herself as to anyone else.

'Granny, for goodness sake, this is supposed to be a happy occasion. Don't you go spoiling it.'

'Ah cannae open ma mooth these days,' Granny muttered into her chest. 'Ye'll be auld yersel' wan day.'

Malcy went over and took the old woman's hands in his. 'You're quite right, Granny. But I suppose I've got to try and forget all that now.'

'Aye, well, ah just hope ye'll be able to, son.' After a minute's thoughtful silence, she added, 'But maybe it's no' good to forget aw thegither.'

'I know what you mean, Granny.'

'Ah'm no' talkin' about bloody useless stone monuments an' paper poppies, mind.'

'I know.'

'Aw these names frae the First War on aw them stone monuments. Every town an' village has them. Now they'll be carvin' other ones for another million or mair poor laddies. What good is that tae their wives an' mothers? Folk like Mrs McGregor doon Springburn Road. Her man an' her poor wee Jimmy.'

'For God sake, Ma!' It was Erchie's turn to protest. 'This isnae the time or the place. We're tryin' tae gie Malcy a cheery homecomin'.'

'Aye, well, ah'm glad tae see ye're back aw in wan piece, son. Ah am that.'

'Thanks, Granny.'

They put records on the gramophone. *It's a grand night for singing*, and *I've got a lovely bunch of coconuts* and *Don't fence me in*. They belted them all out until Granny complained, 'Where's aw the good auld Scots songs.'

So they launched into Scots songs, including the favourite, *I belong to Glasgow, dear old Glasgow town.*

Everyone joined in, including old Mr McCluskey and his daughter, Miss McCluskey. She, by force of circumstances including war work, had mellowed somewhat. It turned out that she had quite a sweet singing voice. The house was packed and the party went on well into the early hours. Granny fell asleep in her chair despite the racket. Her head sunk forward into her chest, her mouth puttering with snores. There was a lot of talk about rationing, which was still going on, and the difficulty folk coming back from the war were having in getting a place to live. But mostly the talk was about scarcity of food and other items. Theirs had been a different war from Malcy's.

At last people began to say goodnight. They shook hands with Malcy again, and told him again how glad they were to see him. Before they left, of course, they all joined hands to sing *Auld Lang Syne.* He appreciated their warmth and friendliness, although he was so exhausted that he was glad to see them go. Refusing a cup of tea from Teresa, he collapsed into bed and oblivion. He hadn't even the energy to get undressed.

Next morning, he was thankful that, unlike most of the tenements in Springburn, this house had a bathroom. He couldn't remember the last time he was able to relax in a warm bath. Through in the kitchen, Granny, Erchie, Florence and Teresa were at breakfast. Wincey was nowhere to be seen.

Teresa said, 'I was going to give you your breakfast in bed, Malcy. I thought you needed a long lie.'

'This is late for me.'

Florence said, 'Did you know I'm housekeeper for the Cartwrights of Kirklee Terrace now, Malcy?'

Granny said, 'She means she dusts an' polishes an' makes whit she calls their lunch.'

'I start at ten,' Florence pressed on with determined cheerfulness. 'And it's time I was away. Wincey says she's taking the afternoon off, so she'll be seeing you then too. She'll be back earlier than me though, in time for lunch. Then this evening, we've all to visit Kirklee Terrace as guests of the Cartwrights. We can call them Virginia and Nicholas, of course, because we're family in a way. Wait until you see that lovely house, Malcy. You'll be so impressed.'

Malcy tried to look impressed.

Erchie rose. 'Wincey wanted me to stay off as well today but somebody needs to be there to keep an eye on things. Ah'll see you the night, Malcy. OK?'

'Right, fine,' Malcy said.

After Erchie and Florence left, and Teresa was washing up the breakfast dishes, and Granny had nodded off, Malcy announced that he was going out for a walk.

'A good idea, Malcy. You relax and enjoy yourself, son.'

He needed to be alone to think. It was as if he was convalescing from an illness. He felt not only that everyone around him was a stranger, but he was a stranger to himself. He clumped along Springburn Road in his big army boots, occasionally catching a glimpse of his reflection in a shop window. He saw a big, rough looking man with a scarred face and shaved head showing under his khaki bonnet. That wasn't the man who used to swagger whistling along Springburn Road, winking at all the pretty girls. So many years ago.

He wandered away up to the park and sat on a bench, staring ahead at nothing in particular. It was only when the cold began to seep into his bones that he made a move. As soon as he entered the close, Teresa had the door open and was rushing out to meet him.

'Malcy, I was worried sick about you and Granny's been watching for you at the window for ages.'

'Sorry, I seem to have lost track of the time. I was just wandering about.'

'Come on through, son. You need to get yourself in front of the fire. You look blue with the cold.'

'Where's Granny now?'

'Here she comes. Wincey's pushing her through.'

'Whit dae ye think ye're playin' at. Ye nearly had me freezin' tae death.'

'Sorry, Granny. I don't know where the time went.'

'Whit a bloody daft thing tae say. Get oot o' ma road. Ah'll have tae get a cup o' tea tae thaw me oot.'

Teresa had already started to pour out tea for everybody. 'I've only made scrambled eggs on toast tonight, Malcy, because I'm sure we'll get lots to eat at Virginia's later on.'

'Oh yes,' Florence said. 'I offered to prepare supper in advance but Virginia wouldn't hear of it. But rest assured she'll do us proud.

And wait till you see the house, Malcy. You'll be . . . '

'Yes, yes, dear, we know,' Teresa interrupted. 'Now all sit round the table and have your tea. I'll help Granny.'

'Did Virginia tell you that Richard is coming home soon,' Wincey asked.

Florence ate a dainty mouthful of scrambled eggs before replying. 'I believe she did mention it.'

'And his wife of course. I thought he'd end up living in Castle Hill, but apparently it has been taken over by the National Trust,' Wincey said. 'His mother and father in law are now living in a cottage in the grounds. Castle Hill got to be too much for them to cope with in their old age. I'm not surprised. What a size of a place it was.'

'Will Richard and his wife be living at Kirklee Terrace, do you think?' Florence asked.

'No. With old Mrs Cartwright.'

Florence said, 'I think she must have spent all her money making that place of hers habitable again, but it still looks awful. And it must be terribly cramped inside. The bedrooms were upstairs and they're all gone now. I don't think Richard and his wife will stay there for long.'

Wincey shrugged. 'I suppose he'll have to find a job and a place of his own eventually. It'll be changed days for Richard, I'm afraid.'

'Especially,' Florence went on, 'when she's not a pleasant character. The old woman, I mean. I know she's your grandmother, Wincey, but I'm sorry, I just don't like her.'

Wincey shrugged again. 'I can't say I'm all that keen on her myself.'

'Now, now, girls,' Teresa said. 'She's an old woman and she's had to suffer being bombed.'

'Well, actually Mother, she was a couple of miles away at her bridge club meeting when the bomb dropped.'

Teresa wasn't listening. She was gazing worriedly at Malcy, her fingers tucking and twisting at her floral, wraparound apron. 'Eat up, son. You've hardly touched your eggs. Oh, there's Erchie. I was so worried about you that he went out to look . . . Well, not especially to look for you,' she hastily corrected herself. 'He had to go out for his paper, you see.'

Erchie's small, skinny figure breezed into the kitchen and waved his paper at Granny. 'Plenty tae read tae ye the night, Ma. Hello there, Malcy. Had a nice day, son?'

'Yes, fine thanks, Erchie.'

'Do you not like scrambled eggs?' Teresa said worriedly. 'I can easily make you something else. Just say the word, son.'

'No, it's great, Teresa. I just don't seem to have much of an appetite these days.'

'No wonder you've lost so much weight, Malcy. You're a big man. You need to eat. Now how about some baked beans. I could quite easily . . . '

Suddenly Granny bawled, 'For God sake, Teresa, will ye shut up an' leave the man in peace.'

Teresa's pale face acquired two pink blotches. 'I was just trying to help.'

'And I appreciate it, Teresa,' Malcy assured her. 'I really do. I feel so lucky you've all accepted me as family like this. Where would I be, what would I do without all of you.'

'Och!' Teresa went over to give him a hug, her old slippers scuffing across the linoleum. 'You'll always have a home here, Malcy. You'll always be one of the family.'

Granny had nearly dropped off again but she suddenly roused herself. 'Aye, that's right, son. Now forget about the bloody eggs. It's jist that dried stuff anyway. Jist think yersel' lucky it wisnae spam. See aw that Yankee junk.'

'Granny, it's wicked, talking like that,' Teresa scolded. 'It was very kind of the Americans to help us out with all that food, and spam's really tasty. So is dried egg. Everybody thinks so.'

'Ye cannae have it poached or boiled, and spam cannae hold a candle tae a pork chop or a plate o' good steak mince.'

'But if we hadn't had things like spam and dried egg, we'd have had next to nothing, Granny. I know because I'm the one who's had to trail around all the shops looking for a bite to eat. I'm the one who's had to wait in mile long queues for hours on end.'

They were at it again. Food and rationing and shortages. It was all they seemed to talk about. Malcy sat staring at his plate, allowing the conversation to wash over him, as he drifted further and further away.

35

Kirklee Terrace was an elegant cul de sac separated from Great Western Road by a sloping green bank that in spring was covered in crocuses, then daffodils. It had been designed by the architect C. Wilson in 1845. Overlooking Great Western Road at the front, the Cartwright house also had excellent views of the Botanic Gardens.

Florence gave Malcy a running commentary on the house as they travelled in Wincey's car. 'There's a gorgeous entrance hall,' Florence enthused, 'with a marble floor—a marble floor, would you believe. Downstairs there's the kitchen and the dining room and sitting room and a study that Nicholas calls his writing room. A grand staircase leads up to the bedrooms and the bathroom. There's a drawing room upstairs as well. Wait till you see that drawing room, Malcy.'

'All right, Florence,' Wincey said. 'Just let him wait, will you.'

She swung the car off Great Western Road at the junction of Kirklee Road, then sharp right onto Kirklee Terrace. A golden carpet of autumn leaves crackled under their feet as they walked from the car towards the front door.

'Of course, in the old days,' Florence said, 'there would have been a maid to open the door. But it's impossible to get staff since the war. Everyone has to do more or less everything themselves.'

'Aboot time tae,' Granny said. Erchie had helped her from the taxi which had followed Wincey's car. 'Spoiled, lazy sods! They lived the life o' Riley an' tried tae make oot they were superior tae the likes o' us. They gave folks like us absolute hell an' we were supposed tae believe we were the inferior ones. Well, no' me. Ah believe it's the other way roon.'

Teresa rolled her eyes. 'Well, not any more, Granny. At least the war has evened all that out.'

'Ah aye said you came up the Clyde in a banana boat.'

Just then the door opened and Virginia welcomed them in.

'An' dinnae think they're aw like her,' Granny persisted. 'She came frae a Gorbals slum, an' used tae work as a scullery maid.'

'Granny!' Teresa looked distraught. 'I'm black affronted, Virginia. She was going on about class, you see, but I'm sure she didn't mean any offence.'

Virginia laughed. 'Don't worry. I'm not ashamed of my background.'

'Ah should think no',' Granny said, ignoring Teresa's furious glare. 'Come away in.'

'See what I mean about the hall, Malcy.' Florence, head tipped proudly back, gazed around in a kind of ecstasy. She was dressed for the part in her best hat with its winged birds and draped veil.

'Will somebody shut her up?' Granny said. 'Ah'm fed up wi' her witterin' on aboot this bloody hoose.'

Virginia laughed and led them into the sitting room.

'We could carry Granny up to the drawing room,' Florence said, easing off her hat. 'We could all go up there.'

Wincey said, 'Florence, will you never learn. We've come to visit my mother and father.'

Florence withdrew into a silent huff. They all knew however that this would not last. One of the unfortunate things about Florence was she never remained offended or silent for long.

Nicholas rose to greet them and, as Florence had told Malcy more than once, he was a very handsome man indeed. 'And a genius as well, Malcy. An absolute genius.' Florence had always had a dramatic imagination and a talent for exaggeration.

'No, Florence,' Wincey said. 'Not a genius.'

'But he's won literary awards, and he's made a fortune.'

'He's a good writer, and he makes a good living, but he's not a genius and he doesn't make a fortune.'

'Fancy you denigrating your own father!'

'I'm not denigrating him. I'm only telling the truth. He'd say exactly what I've said about himself.'

'He's so modest too, Malcy. Just wait till you meet him.'

The two men shook hands and after warmly welcoming Malcy,

Nicholas turned to Granny. 'And how are you, Granny?'

'Fine, son. An' how's yersel?'

'Well, I'm glad to say I've a lot more time now. I'm no longer with the Home Guard. I've still to see to my strip of back garden though.'

Teresa nodded. 'Yes, it looks as if food's going to be scarce for a long time yet. Only the other day I waited for hours in the biggest queue I've ever seen. I stood there . . . ' Teresa was off on her favourite theme.

Malcy allowed his mind to drift. He wondered how Joe and Pete were. He now hoped that they would be kept down south for as long as possible. He couldn't see them fitting very easily into civilian life here. If he felt a stranger in Glasgow, how much worse would Joe and Pete feel after all they'd been through. He suspected that it would take them years to get over their experiences, no matter where they were. Maybe they never would.

It suddenly occurred to Malcy that maybe he wouldn't either. But he knew he had to make the effort. He took a deep breath and attempted to join in the conversation, or at least to look interested. A couple of times he caught Wincey's eye. He remembered that straight, deep, determined look. His heart became heavy again. He didn't know what to think about Wincey any more. He was fond of her, had been for some time now. How could he not be when she'd been so kind and loyal and supportive in writing to him so often?

She still looked the same, with her fringed red hair and delicate sprinkling of freckles. That strong steady gaze was certainly the same as he remembered it. She was some girl. He'd always thought so. Later she came over and sat beside him. The others were through in the kitchen sampling the food and drink that Virginia had set out ready.

'A buffet supper,' Florence had explained. 'One just helps oneself.'

He had just put a spoonful or two of potato salad on his plate, lifted a glass of wine and returned to the sitting room. Wincey had been the first to follow him through.

'We never get a chance to talk on our own,' Wincey said. 'How about me taking you out tomorrow to, say, the Central Hotel for supper. They have a nice lounge there where we can relax with a drink after the meal and talk as long as we like.'

After a second or two's hesitation, Malcy said, 'Yes, all right.' The truth was he just wanted to be on his own. He needed time to at least try to free his mind from the horrors still milling around in it. Dead men on land and sea still returned in his nightmares to haunt him, along with the living dead of the concentration camps. It was too soon to get back to normal. He didn't know how to do it. The next day, however, there was no getting out of the date with Wincey. Everyone colluded with it.

'Come on now, son.' Teresa encouraged. 'It's what you need, to get out more. Wincey'll take you a wee drive around Glasgow and it'll make you feel really at home again.'

'Aye,' Erchie said. 'Ah bet many a time ye've dreamt about the dear green place.'

He supposed he had.

'Away ye go, the pair o' ye,' Granny said. 'Enjoy yersels.'

They didn't speak in the car and Malcy was grateful for the silence. She drove round George Square and he was as impressed as he always had been with the magnificent architecture of the City Chambers. They passed Hutcheson Hall with its clock and steeple and the City and Courts building, with its twenty nine bays along one side. The Robert Adam Trade House he knew well. All the buildings in Virginia Street too. Malcy remembered the tales he had heard as a schoolboy— of how this part of the city had been developed as a result of the tobacco trade with America. In Royal Exchange Square there was a magnificent building that had once been a mansion of one of the tobacco lords.

Familiarity brought a trickle of pleasure moving slowly through his veins, relaxing him. Everything he saw reminded him of some distant memory, some bit of folklore about his beloved city. They passed the point where Argyle Street was bridged by the Central Station. With a smile of recognition on his face, he recalled how that part of the street was known as the 'Heilanman's Umbrella'—because at one time it had been a meeting place for Highlanders on wet days.

The elaborate Victorian ironwork of the entrance to the Central Station signalled the end of their journey. They parked the car and went up the steps into the Central Hotel.

Malcy and Wincey strolled in together, still in complete silence. Eventually she said, 'Do you fancy a drink before dinner?'

'Fine by me.'

They went upstairs to a lounge with a bar and settled in a quiet corner with their drinks.

Another silence, then she said, 'Are you glad I wrote to you while you were away?'

He stared at her in surprise. 'Of course. Your letters meant a lot to me.'

'Did they?'

'Yes, they did.'

'I'm glad,' she said. 'I think we got to know each other a lot better through them, don't you?'

'Yes,' he said, remembering the letters now, and how their tone and contents gradually grew warmer, more intimate.

'For me it was a release, in a way,' she said. 'It's funny how much easier it is to express yourself in writing than it is face to face.'

'You're doing all right,' he said with a smile.

To her it was only the ghost of the cheeky grin she remembered from so long ago but she said, 'You're still the same.'

'No,' he said. 'I'm not the same person I was, Wincey.'

She nodded, then fixed him with one of her serious, concentrated stares.

'And I'm not the same woman that I was.' She tucked a stray lock of her auburn hair behind an ear. 'I've been thinking . . . ' Her stare clung earnestly to him as she went on. 'How about if you booked us a room here for tonight. That way we could have a chance to find out more about the new Malcy and the new Wincey.'

He studied her in silence for a minute or two. Then he half laughed and shook his head at her.

'Wincey!'

'Don't you dare turn such a good offer down,' she said.

His smile returned again, still faint and ghostly, but a smile all the same. 'I know the war has had an effect on me, Wincey, but it's not made me that daft.'

'Fine then.' She raised her glass. 'Cheers!'

He shook his head again and helplessly repeated, 'Wincey!'

But as he raised his glass to hers, he began to feel better.